PASSIONATE CHARLOTTE MOREL

As Napoleon is desperately trying to save Paris from destruction by the Germans, beautiful Charlotte Morel is just as desperately fighting to hold on to Thomas Becque, her brilliant journalist lover. And as Paris society becomes more decadent under siege, Charlotte finds her own morals crumbling as Thomas moves farther and farther away from her grasp.

Charlotte Morel had defied every convention to go after the man she loved. Now she was willing to risk everything—even her life—to win him back!

The CHARLOTTE MOREL novels
of Maria Lodi

CHARLOTTE MOREL
CHARLOTTE MOREL: THE DREAM

Charlotte Morel
The Siege

Maria Lodi

Translated by Anne Carter

AVON
PUBLISHERS OF BARD, CAMELOT, DISCUS, EQUINOX AND FLARE BOOKS

AVON BOOKS
A division of
The Hearst Corporation
959 Eighth Avenue
New York, New York 10019

First Avon Printing, October, 1972.

AVON TRADEMARK REG. U.S. PAT. OFF. AND
FOREIGN COUNTRIES, REGISTERED TRADEMARK—
MARCA REGISTRADA, HECHO EN CHICAGO, U.S.A.

Printed in the U.S.A.

1

IT WAS the beginning of the terrible year of 1870. As early as January France was shaken by the first of several waves of crime, violence and unrest. The great Empire was at its last gasp. The Emperor's advisors could no longer ignore the deep anger of his subjects. Napoleon III, ill and tired, still tried to delude himself into a belief in his own popularity, but most of his followers were more clear-sighted and knew how precarious every government success would be from now on. The régime was crumbling like a badly cracked house; but the Empire might still be shored up by a foreign war to whip up patriotic feeling. The Empress Eugènie, who was determined to see her son on the throne, looked to a war to bring about a renewal of prestige. Indeed, the likelihood of war with Prussia was viewed with increasing satisfaction in her circle and by certain extremist financial and industrial interests.

The possibility of a French defeat occurred to no one. There was no doubt as to the strength of the French military forces. The public still basked in the memory of former trials, in which the national genius for improvisation as well as the heroism of the revolutionary and Napoleonic armies figured largely. But the men and those who led them were no longer the same and the touch of greatness which had inspired them at the time of their great conquests was gone.

On 15 January a small girl arrived in the rue Monsieur-le-Prince where Charlotte lived. Her neighbor Valerie had finally decided to bring her daughter back from the nurse in Auvergne who had been looking after her. She was not a pretty child. She wore black pinafores and wooden shoes, she had red hair and more freckles than her mother, her body was skinny, her complexion pasty and her nose too pronounced for her age. Her pale eyes with their almost colorless lashes seemed to shun the light.

She hung about the house, mute and resentful, refusing to go out and spending her time biting her nails and staring at the courtyard and the gray rooftops of Paris. She was small and pathetic like a frightened animal, an impression added to by her uncared-for appearance and the faint rank smell which hung about her. City life obviously did not suit her.

"She'll get used to it," Valerie would say, observing her with loving anxiety.

"It will be the death of the child," was her neighbor's comment. "If you love children you don't use them for your own selfish ends."

They were quick to condemn Valerie and to add that in any case it would probably have had a bad effect on her business. There was a good deal of ill-humored gossip, but ill-humor came regularly to people's tongues in those days of high prices and increased rents. The men talked politics in the cafés, arguing endlessly over the news. Prince Napoleon had killed Victor Noir, and when charges were brought against him after the funeral, he received little open support.

Life went on. Valerie's daughter, the next quarter's rent, unpaid taxes. Léon Ferrat fell in the street and broke a leg and his cousin who looked after him had rheumatism. There was a rumor that Delphine Delobelle was ill and her parents were concealing the fact from everyone. She was never seen out of the house, and there were no more parties. The suitors had all disappeared. Madame Delobelle hurried out like a whirlwind to do her shopping, avoiding all conversation.

In the main body of the house life seemed to go on secretly, like the subterranean stirrings of an ant heap. The life of those who lived off the courtyard was more public and exposed. No faintly interested observer could help seeing the students descend the winding staircase at the back of the court. All the inhabitants of the fifth floor used it, Charlotte's brother Gabin coming down to fetch kindling wood for the fire, Illa his wife, muffled up like a Bretonne fisher-girl, to do her shopping. Millau would appear dressed to kill in a second-hand suit purchased from a certain Monsieur Royal of the Cirque Imperial. He had become one of the pillars of the cabaret where he was in love with a singer. He had pawned everything disposable in the room to provide himself with two shirts and enough money for tips. He was content to let his beloved pay the bill, saying that tipping was what marked the true man of the world.

For Charlotte, it was a difficult time and one in which she needed all the courage which she had told Worski was above heroism. She had always feared the monotony of everyday life. Now her fear verged on panic.

She tried to pull herself together, busy herself with new plans, but it seemed as though all hope had died within her. She felt as if she had lost some important part of herself; a light which had once given her a sense of pride and superiority had gone out, and she was cut off from the living.

It came to her that it was her youth which had died, and she had known that melancholy night in the Pole, Worski's room that she had lost it forever. The thought was almost more than she could bear. She was no longer royal. From now on she would simply be part of the anonymous mass. She discovered that even pain and disappointment had tasted different in the days when her youth and beauty had set her apart from other people. Then she had been everybody's darling, surrounded with sympathy and admiration on all sides.

She indulged in a bitter fit of crying before her mirror. She had always believed herself superior, unique. But it had all been a cruel delusion. Her reign was over and other girls of sixteen had succeeded her. She was alone. Soon she would be short of money. The thought made her want to die.

That day she tried on all her dresses and decided they were out of fashion. She would have liked to buy a new one but knew she could not afford it. She kept on the maid for the sake of appearances and there were expenses for

7

Elise, for the house at Juvisy, the taxes, the rent. She dare not do her accounts for fear of finding that they would not stretch. The longing for a new dress tormented her. She wanted to be beautiful, as always when she was hurt or unhappy.

The memory of Worski had curiously left her. It was Thomas Becque she thought of now and the thought was no longer painful but tender and insistent. She forgot their rupture and imagined them meeting again and gliding effortlessly into a deep and total intimacy. It was as if the passing of time had smoothed out all rancor and bitterness, leaving only the light froth of their love.

Like many another woman haunted by the image of a man, she found her dream becoming confused with her everyday life. Their imaginary life together became so real to her that even memory was changed by it.

She had to have money. She took the manuscript of a short novel to Delbrèze and he succeeded in placing it in a provincial newspaper under the name of Charles Toll, the masculine pen-name she had chosen for herself as a kind of anagram of her own Christian name. But the sale of the novel did not bring in a great deal. In addition, Charlotte was writing two regular columns, one in Delbrèze's own paper and the other in a woman's magazine. This brought her in a small regular sum, though not enough to live on, pay Annick's wages and provide for everything else. She was beginning to feel real anxiety. Delbrèze offered to help her but she felt regretfully obliged to refuse an offer of money which would have put her under too much of an obligation, although by now she knew the journalist well enough to realize that he was not inclined to owe his conquests to this kind of blackmail. He preferred favors freely given.

She had in fact been more than a little surprised that Delbrèze had been willing to help her so readily after the trick that she had played on him, leaving him in the dance hall at la Courtille when she went off with Worski. He had teased her somewhat acidly about it but without appearing to bear her any real ill will. Yet even this might have been affectation. He seemed to have an immense capacity for malice. Charlotte could not remember meeting anyone with a more venomous tongue than Delbrèze when he had a mind to it. It was hard to believe that such a man could be really disinterested. He was probably an expert at concealing his wounds.

She nearly asked him, but then thought better of it. In any case, Delbrèze's motives were a mystery to her. She was too straightforward herself to understand a man of his cynical, depraved temperament, as incapable of real anger or indignation as he was of real affection.

Because she was lonely and disorientated, Charlotte found herself drifting back into the old group of ne'er-do-wells and unsuccessful artists who made up Aurore Dumoulin's circle.

She no longer felt any particular fondness for Aurore or her friends but she went to her house for the fickle comfort and reassurance they had to offer. She found their frivolous and amusing company could be a greater consolation for a broken heart than the well-meant efforts of a more solid and lasting friendship. She even found herself avoiding Valerie's kindness because the mere thought of it depressed her.

So she went back to Aurore and was influenced despite herself by Aurore's circle. She took to dressing a little more flamboyantly, indulging in tiny eccentricities such as a new dashing hair style *à la Grecque* which attracted a good deal of attention. All the same, her critical faculties had not so far deserted her that she could not judge Aurore's friends with the crisp, realistic eye of her Poitevin upbringing. She saw them for what they were: decadent, lazy and useless. Aurore's big green and maroon salon was always full of them.

Even so, with the chairs pushed back, there was always room for dancing near the grand piano with its clutter of ornaments. Charlotte drank a good deal and laughed uproariously. The other women were inclined to be jealous of her energy and enthusiasm. Most of Aurore's friends were older. Aurore herself was constantly attending to her face, putting on layer upon layer of powder until in the end her tiny features were plastered into a solid pink mask which made her look like an effigy in terracotta.

They all regarded Charlotte with a mixture of contempt

and admiration. A good many young men also frequented the house. They came from all levels of society but most of them were unsuccessful artists of one kind or another. On arrival they would invariably stand stock-still on the red carpet, transfixed by Charlotte's gaiety and exuberance. It was always she who led the dancing, until the crystal chandeliers overhead tinkled wildly in accompaniment.

The young men could not help themselves. They crowded round her, eager to burn their ragged young wings, oblivious of the refreshments for which they had come. They were bewitched, with eyes for nothing but Charlotte, pouring out their misunderstood genius at her feet like a roll of drums.

She was indifferent to them all but she flirted madly. A most insignificant admirer, the most banal compliment, received the full measure of charming attention. She was determined to prove to herself that she could have anything she wanted. Worski's rejection had cut deep. Now she would go to any lengths for the sake of reassurance.

One evening she allowed herself to be carried away by a youth whose name she could not bother to remember but whose fair, rather nondescript good looks reminded her vaguely of Worski or Alphonse.

They were in a small secluded room on the ground floor. The mistress of the house and the other guests were still in the main salon. In the absence of her husband and of Paul Boucher, Aurore was permitting an insistent painter to admire her ankles. The rest were drunk, very drunk.

It was the first time that Charlotte had been alone with a man on one of these occasions. She had allowed herself to drift into it from a kind of self-destructive urge to be like the others but she could not feel the same bored indifference. She was ready to make love to anyone to kill the emotion in herself, and to be free.

The boy was not unattractive. He had curled blond hair and a long face in the manner of el Greco, as innocent of expression as an engraving. She toyed with the mother-of-pearl buttons on his waistcoat while she allowed him to kiss her.

It was dark in the room and the dying fire in the hearth

10

threw a ruddy glow on the carpet. His lips nibbled softly and Charlotte ran her hands through his fair hair, stiff from the curling irons, trying unobtrusively to make out some vague likeness to her ideal face in the half light. She thought she had found it but the mental effort was too great and the boy an impersonal copy.

It was over very quickly. Charlotte was left wondering in astonishment how to attach any importance to an act so trivial while at the same time the brief interlude had revived all her old torments and memories.

The boy sat in embarrassed silence, disconcerted by his silent partner's sudden loss of interest. She stared into the dying fire while the young man stroked her hair and murmured softly words to which she did not answer.

The following night she went again to Aurore's and was drunk once again. She danced with a young Spaniard named José who could not have been more than eighteen but moved with the grace of a gypsy. He was scarcely taller than she was, rather horse-faced with hollow cheeks and large teeth. She was attracted by his clean-cut profile and narrow, slanting eyes, the color of spring catkins. Heavy dark eyebrows gave him a stormy, passionate look. He told her she was beautiful and she let him hold her tight, conscious of an unusual thirst for admiration.

They were dancing a shottische to a rhapsody by Liszt being murdered by the bald pianist hunched over his piano, a bottle of champagne and a glass within easy reach. The whole room seemed caught up in a frenzy of excitement. To Charlotte's drunken senses the moment seemed to last for an eternity. People had lost the art of living in the present, they were always caught up in the past or the future. Each time she passed the piano, held close in the arms of her diminutive jealous Spaniard, she caught up the glass belonging to the frantic pianist, Pierre Ortobiz, and drank from it. Then, one false start and they were off again. Time stood still as they moved to the pulse of the universe itself. Those who fall while dancing to the rhythm of the world become immortal as the stars.

Young José's arms tightened around her. Across the room Delbrèze was watching her with a set face. She thought of Thomas. Happiness was too far away. The

11

Spaniard was inexpert and intense. He got her into a corner by the window and swore to her that he would never love anyone else but her and that he was a virgin. Then they danced their way to the same small dark room where it seemed to Charlotte some ribald faun must be watching in the shadows. It seemed heavily ironic to find herself in the same room where she had been with the blond youth the night before. She felt no sense of shame, only a cold detachment which she took for liberation.

He spoke in Spanish. He was passionate and inexperienced and in the end she took control with the dedicated fury of a school mistress, yet conscious at the same time of the absurdity of this fumbling association.

Soon she made her escape, leaving him like a corpse in the salon. He reappeared but Charlotte ignored him. He stood watching her mournfully from a distance. She was drinking again heavily. She wanted to forget everything now, herself and the ridiculous degrading business of love. One day, she thought, I'll be free, and not ashamed. It is one of my last weaknesses but nothing and no one can reach me now.

She danced with Count Kazlov the Russian. He was besotted about her in a way that was both senile and childish. He had offered her a turquoise necklace worth five thousand francs which she had refused. Then Kazlov tripped over the carpet and she went on dancing alone like a will-o'-the-wisp. It seemed to her that she was alone in the room with the bald pianist who played on obstinately, deaf and blind to the general indifference. Perhaps he too was pursuing his own dreams across the starry ceiling, and in the beaded gold of the champagne in his glass, no longer clear but smudged with fingerprints and cigar smoke. The raspberry-colored carpet underfoot reminded Charlotte as in a nightmare of marauding visits to the kitchen garden as a child with their attendant ill-effects. The same color was repeated in the curtains, closed at this dead hour of night on the empty square with its shuttered mansions. Beyond lay the Seine, snaking like a dark, shiny ribbon through the length of Paris.

She danced on until the first glimmer of daylight, her mind beset by scorching memories of Thomas. When she

12

had no strength left, that alone remained like a diamond cut and polished to even greater brilliance and hardness.

She woke lying on a sofa in the salon where she had slept. Someone must have thrown a wrap over her and she was still half entwined in the fur. She saw Count Kazlov stretched out on the ground, breathing heavily, in an uneasy sleep. Charlotte was sorry for him, he looked so incredibly old and tired.

She saw another figure huddled in a foetal position in an armchair, knees drawn up to chin, and discovered that it was José. A look at the grey light filtering in through the curtains told her it was morning. She searched her mind for the date. The 18th of January. The room was a shambles. They all looked dreadful and she closed her eyes in an effort to sleep again and escape the misery of waking.

At that moment Aurore appeared followed by Delbèze. They were both fully dressed and Charlotte found herself absent-mindedly calculating the chances that they had spent the night together. Both of them looked elaborately unconcerned.

Aurore flung back the curtains noisily, announcing that they must wake up as they were all going for a ride in the carriage. They were used to her whims and no one uttered any protest. Kazlov, a sorry sight with his tousled hair, found some difficulty in standing upright. Charlotte did not bother her head about the object of their outing. She was too tired to be anything but glad to have the decisions made for her whatever they might be. She asked herself what she was doing here with these people. She knew it was absurd but she was content to let things take their course.

In the carriage, Charlotte sat in the back between Kazlov and young José, who was sulking and shivering. He stared around him moodily. Charlotte too was cold in spite of Aurore's fur.

The carriage had set off in the direction of Père la Chaise. Soon they came in sight of the prison of la Roquette.

"Come along," Aurore told them. "I am taking you to see something."

The carriage drew up and they followed her into a shabby old house and up to the third floor where a knock on the door was answered by an unshaven individual in a white shirt without a collar.

"Come in, m'sieur, dame—"

They entered a miserable room which seemed to be bedroom and kitchen in one. A woman looked up from the drab-colored garment she was washing and said a timid good morning. Three children popped their heads out of bed and stared fearfully.

"Aurore, this is ridiculous, what are we doing here?" Charlotte protested.

Aurore seized her arm. "Come along," she said. "Today is Tropmann's execution. You are going to see the guillotine."

Charlotte drew back in disgust. "You are out of your mind," she said.

"Come along, I tell you. I have rented a window from these good people. Don't be frightened, they shan't have all their trouble for nothing. Come over here."

She was clutching Charlotte's wrist in a cruel grip. There was a throaty chuckle from Delbrèze, behind her. The others, Kazlov and José, were pushing forward eager for a glimpse. Charlotte felt the cold rail of the iron balcony under her hands.

"You are too sensitive, Charlotte my dear," Aurore was saying. "This Tropmann is a dreadful man, a murderer."

"What pleasure can it give you to see a man killed?" Charlotte answered without looking at her.

"I don't know. That is precisely what I'm here to find out."

There was a crowd outside gathered in front of the scaffold where stood a small group of men dressed in black. In the early morning light the huge grim prison seemed unnaturally silent.

They waited. Aurore's face was blotched and disfigured.

"You're afraid," whispered Delbrèze's voice in Charlotte's ear.

She hit him sharply on the wrist with the edge of her hand.

"Get back—"

14

He got back. The blow had hurt. He was taken aback by her set face.

"You are cowards, all of you," she said with contempt.

"Be quiet." Aurore was almost hysterical.

Silence fell again. They saw a faint stir of movement round the door of the main prison building. A group of men came out.

"They're coming," Aurore whispered faintly. She clutched the balcony rail till her knuckles whitened.

They saw a man in a shirt and canvas trousers surrounded by prison guards, the governor, the chaplain holding a crucifix and the Chief of Police, Monsieur Claude. The man appeared to be small and slight, like one of the seedy ruffians to be seen hanging round the bistros on the outskirts of the city.

They saw the condemned man hesitate. He was seized by the armpits and dragged forward bodily, his mouth gaping open. A dreadful silence hung over the courtyard, and the group of black-clad men around the scaffold.

They had almost to carry him to the scaffold. Inarticulate sounds came from his throat. He had killed eight people, five of them children, and buried them hurriedly. And all for nothing, or almost nothing. It was the senseless crime of a madman. Tropmann was surely the very dregs of society. The horror of his crime was past imagining and this fearful punishment seemed almost too solemn for him. By now his terror had communicated itself to the onlookers. Even contempt for his cowardice was no longer possible. The presence of death was overwhelming.

"My God, why don't they get on with it?" muttered Aurore in a hoarse whisper.

Charlotte stood with a set face. She was not afraid. She remembered the big red-brown bullocks in Niort, and the grief she had felt, as a child, watching the quiet, gentle-eyed beasts being driven to their death in the slaughter-house. She had less pity for Tropmann. He had killed children. If he had killed her own little Elise, she would have released the knife with her own hand.

Even so, she felt a growing disgust, mingled with a kind of pity. Pity for a murderer whose courage was only

15

enough for the death of others. There is a depth of wickedness to which pity is the only response.

She glanced at Aurore. Her face was blotched as though with eczema, and she looked ill. She, Charlotte, was strong, and not afraid of death. She saw Aurore hide her head in her hands, but she kept her own eyes open. Down below, they had got Tropmann onto the scaffold. They forced him down, struggling, so that his head fitted neatly to the half-moon shape there to receive it. He began to scream hideously.

A man in a dark suit raised his hand. They did not see the knife fall. There was a dull thud, and the screams stopped short. The backs of the men in black hid the scaffold itself. A deep sigh from many breasts seemed to go up into the still morning air, like a flight of wild birds.

There was nothing more to see. In the street a small girl was playing hop-scotch. A woman in an overall appeared in a doorway and called, "Marinette" in a shrill anxious voice. The child stood on one foot, one skinny pigtail sticking out behind her, and her nose in the air as if she too were listening to that deep beating of wings over Paris.

Aurore uttered a choking sob. She seemed about to be sick. Flinging a purse of money on to the table, she hurried to the door followed by the others. Charlotte could not bring herself to look at the family whose poverty they had invaded. One of the children had begun to cry. Charlotte felt utterly wretched.

They descended the rickety staircase. Outside there were people everywhere. Carriages were driving off and a man with a three-wheeled cart was selling steaming hot soup. Street vendors were clutching at passers-by with offers of souvenirs, charms, trinkets, copies of Tropmann's last lament, all the popular imagery surrounding the crime of violence. Police were making some effort to keep the crowd under control.

Aurore's brougham was waiting some way off beyond the cordon of police. They had to make their way through the crowds of people who were now looking at one another with a kind of dull curiosity. Charlotte saw three men standing near a stationary carriage. One of them, wearing a tall hat and facing the other way, had only one arm.

Something seemed to catch at the back of her throat. She felt a flutter of excitement, not a pleasurable excitement, more like a panic fear of approaching danger inspired by this ominous district, and the uncertain daylight that was beginning to show whitely above the rooftops of Paris. The pavement ended suddenly and became a gutter. The street was a jumble of broken stones. Charlotte stumbled and felt the black, stinking water soak into her shoes and stockings, licking like small verminous tongues at her ankles. She found herself unable to move. It had all happened so quickly. She stood staring fixedly at the group of men standing twenty-five yards away from her, with a searching in her heart for the certainty of recognition which would tell her that this stranger's back belonged to Thomas. He was bending a little forward and the set of his broad shoulders under the smooth, dark cloth of his coat gave him the burly, stooping look of a bull. Charlotte's eyes sought the empty sleeve which hung straight down by his side.

It had to be him. But still she hesitated, afraid of being mistaken and finding herself in the absurd position of being moved almost to tears by an indifferent stranger. But she knew in her heart that it was he. There could not be another one-armed man among that clan of black-clad journalists.

She glanced at her companions who were now some way ahead. Young José had paused a yard or two farther on and was watching her anxiously. She turned back to Thomas. He still had his back to her and as he raised his hat briefly she recognized the powerful neck with its fringe of small curls lying smoothly against his head like those of a figure carved on a coin.

She stepped back involuntarily, her heels sinking into the dark ooze between the paving stones.

It was not grief for a lost love which made Thomas take possession of her again so suddenly and violently, but the desperate hunger of starvation. It was something too deep and terrible for understanding and she had no thought

17

now but to turn her back on that street, and on the carriage which Thomas had entered, now moving slowly away. She turned quickly, hoping to catch a glimpse of him as he passed, but saw only the blank square of the open window, and the profile of a man's head who was not Thomas.

She hurried to catch up with the others.

"What were you doing?" Aurore asked. She was holding one end of her stole up to her eyes to hide the sudden blotchiness of her features, the nervous reaction to her fear which made her face resemble a half-peeled transfer.

On the way home the others chatted together, but Charlotte did not hear them. She wast lost in the drumming of her own thoughts. She was tired to death, with an empty stomach and feet which ached from the previous night's dancing. She was in a state of complete blankness in which the thought of Thomas rose like the arch of a gigantic bridge.

The others had fallen silent. Kazlov cleared his throat. José looked desperate. Aurore's face was very flushed.

"You'll come in with me?" she asked Charlotte when they came to the Rond-Point.

But Charlotte could not wait to get away. Where she did not know. Home, perhaps, for the first time properly in the whole of this long week.

"Goodbye then, for the present," Aurore said sulkily. Kazlov kissed her hand and the others went on into the house. Charlotte had taken only a few steps, when José caught her up.

"Have you nothing to say to me? Would it be too much even to say goodbye?"

He glared at her, unconcealed anger bringing out the small discontented lines on his face. By daylight he looked very ordinary, too short and uncomfortably Spanish. The jealous eyebrows were drawn together in a dark line above his eyes.

"Forgive me, I was very tired. Goodbye," she said awkwardly.

"May I hope to see you again?" He was bitterly angry.

"Is this necessary—"

She could not bear to look at him, miserably conscious

18

that she could never explain her reason to this stranger, this angry child, with his wounded pride and vanity. She would have given a great deal never to have committed such a folly.

"Is that all?" he said trembling.

She was suddenly afraid, sensing him capable of making a scene. People were turning to look at them. She was weak with horror.

"Forget me," she whispered tormentedly. She tried to flee but he was gripping her arm furiously.

"Whore," he spat in her face. "Filthy French whore!"

Charlotte tore herself away and began to run. His angry shouts pursued her as she dived in among the trees.

Two hours later she learned that an epidemic of croup was rife in the neighborhood, and that Madame Arnaud's child was ill. Then, early in the afternoon she had a telegram from Juvisy to tell her that her own little Elise was seriously ill.

She was ready to leave at once. She was in a dreadful state of agitation and Frédéric, who went with her to the station, did his best to soothe her.

"Don't worry. She'll be all right. You must believe that, Charlotte. You must. You must be strong."

"I don't know if I can any more," she said, tears filling her eyes. It seemed to her that if her daughter died her own life too would be over, and she could never be happy again; even to have Thomas back would not make it better.

"You are making yourself ill. You must pull yourself together. I am sure your child will be all right. But you must take care of yourself. I know I should not say this to you—but I wish you would promise me to stop seeing these people—these friends. I do not like them and they do you no good—Charlotte, my sweet—"

Thomas, too, had called her that. His blue eyes were fixed on her with affectionate earnestness.

"Don't worry," he commanded. His hand pressed hers, full of warmth and reassurance. A gust of wind raised the dust along the *quai* and Frédéric held her close to protect her from its force. There was agony in his face as they looked at one another.

"Promise me, you will stop seeing them—"

"What does it matter?" she said hopelessly. "They are nothing, I am nothing. Only my child matters, Frédéric, do you understand that?"

"She will get better."

"Do you really believe it?"

His hold tightened gently. "Yes," he told her with conviction.

"Thank you, Frédéric, for everything—thank you for being so good to me. For loving me in spite of everything."

"Your little girl will get well," he said, "of course she will. But we may not. Perhaps the world will never get better. Charlotte, I think there will be a war. I am not saying this to frighten you or add to your worries at such a time. To warn you, perhaps—so that you can be prepared—"

"How prepared?" she said, bewildered.

"So that if it happens you will not be afraid, so that you will be brave and so that you will know. I shall help you if I can—"

"There will not be war."

"No," he said, "there will not be war and your child will get better."

He led her under an awning and sheltered her with his tall body, for she had begun to cry.

She stayed resting against the warmth of his chest, while they waited for the train. He told her he loved her, and wanted the courage to live so as to win and hold her. Slowly she relaxed.

"Promise me you will give up these people—"

"Yes," she told him quickly, "yes, I promise."

The train came in. Darkness had fallen and the massive windows of the Austerlitz station were blank and dead. The train drew in to the empty platform. There were few passengers, and Charlotte climbed into her compartment. The train moved off at last and the dreadful, interminable journey began, stopping at every station as well as a good many times in between for no apparent reason. Charlotte stared unseeingly at the villages dotted along the track. No one else had got into her compartment. The lamp went out and she sat in darkness, outwardly calm, but inwardly consumed by a growing impatience at each delay.

She ran from the station at Juvisy in an effort to save time. At last she came to the tree-lined walk where visitors strolled on Sundays, and which now rang hollowly underfoot.

She had taken the way by the river to save time, but found the wooden gate at the bottom of the garden locked. The river was dangerously high.

She had to go round by the front gate to get in. In the hall she met Lucia coming out of the kitchen with a pile of plates clutched to her chest, and she gripped her fiercely by the arm.

"Lucia, how is my little girl? Tell me, is it very serious?"

Lucia looked at her, her swollen face showed that she had been crying.

"The doctor has just left, ma'me. We have been very worried. He thinks it's the croup and says there has been a good deal of it about at Corbeil and at Ris. And the little one's in a raging fever with a nasty cough as if she were choking."

Just then Madame Morel came downstairs, and with a cry of "Maman!" Charlotte let go of Lucia and flung herself into her mother's arms. She wanted to go straight up and see her daughter, but Madame Morel restrained her.

"Wait a little—be very quiet. She is asleep now, and we should not wake her."

The look on her mother's face did not escape Charlotte. Thérèse Morel, who had always seemed to Charlotte so calm and comforting, looked drawn and defeated tonight. Her whole face seemed shrunken with the weight of fear and acceptance of the worst. In the face of such despair there seemed no possible hope of recovery. The tears were pouring down her face now.

"Here you are at last. May God help us! You have been so long!"

"I came as quickly as I could. There was no train."

"I was worried in case you had not got my message—but you did get it."

Charlotte was hurrying upstairs two at a time, leaving wet footprints on the polished wood. She went into Elise's room.

Louise was there sorting medicine bottles on the table. Charlotte started at the sight of her. She had almost forgotten her sister's existence.

"Hello," Louise said, "we have been waiting for you. Mother was in a terrible state."

"I have seen her," said Charlotte.

Louise eyed her, taking in the extravagant hairstyle and canary yellow dress with its black trimming now clinging wetly to her body.

"You are wearing yellow already!" she observed critically. "Aren't you still in mourning?"

Charlotte did not answer. She had forgotten she was wearing yellow. Somehow she controlled herself, and hurried to the child's bed, watched by her sister. Elise was sleeping under a muslin canopy which was supposed to keep dust away from her. Her face looked flushed and feverish and her sleep seemed troubled by uneasy dreams. From time to time her mouth twitched nervously and she flung her arms out from under the covers. She was coughing in her sleep, harsh, racking coughs.

"My darling," Charlotte murmured, "my sweetheart, my own little one—" She put her hand on the burning forehead. "My baby—"

She bent over the metal cot and laid her cheek against the sleeping child's, murmuring senseless loving words. All her weariness was swept away now by a boundless love which seemed to give her superhuman strength. She knew that if necessary she would be able to spend nights on end at the child's bedside, impervious to fatigue, and that her own life would hang miraculously in suspense as long as she was needed to nurse her daughter.

"You may rest now. I will take care of her," she told Louise, uncomfortably aware of the interested presence behind her. She wanted to be alone. It seemed to her that only so could she help Elise to get better.

Louise went reluctantly. The child was awake now, and

22

Charlotte pulled back the covers to take her in her arms. She wrapped her in a shawl and held her close on her knees. The little girl felt damp with perspiration. She had too many covers on. Charlotte held her in her arms until she was sleepy again, and then put her back to bed. Tears ran down her cheeks, but, for the first time in her life perhaps, she did not know that she was crying. She prayed, calling God from her sick child's room, with her hands clasped on the brass rail of the bed like a prisoner begging for freedom and hope. The tears streamed down her face, and the knuckles of her clasped hands whitened with the force of the silent prayer which burst from her heart, in a desperate appeal that Elise might get better, that Thomas would come back to her, and the war would not come, not today or tomorrow or ever.

At last, overcome by weariness, she slid slowly to the ground, and lay there without the strength to get up, her head pillowed on a dusty-smelling corner of carpet, and a piece of blanket thrown lightly over her.

2

ELISE RECOVERED, but the Arnaud child did not. Charlotte learned this from Gabin when he came to Juvisy on the Sunday, bringing his wife, who had not yet been introduced to his mother.

The doctor from Corbeil, who attended Elise, pronounced that she had had an unusually mild form of croup which would immunize her against the disease in future and keep her out of danger although it had left her with a high fever and her chest was still delicate.

The news that Madame Arnaud's child had died shook Charlotte badly, reviving all her anxieties for her own daughter. She hurried back to Elise's room where she had watched stubbornly for so many nights. The child was in a restless sleep. She had grown thinner in her week's illness and the arm that lay on the sheet and her whole childish body, stripped of its dimples looked touchingly frail, with the fragility of a plucked pigeon.

It was a fine January day of spring-like sunshine, but Charlotte's heart was heavy with mourning for another woman's child. An unspoken fear kept her from leaving the room. She sat in the warm sunshine by the window, and the afternoon was half over by the time she went down to the drawing-room again.

The family had gathered in the conservatory leading on to the veranda, which was used only in the summer. Illa was sitting close to Gabin, her hand in his. Her pregnancy was beginning to show. Madame Morel talked to her kindly and offered her cakes. Charlotte became aware of the arrival of M. Roslin, a widower since his twenty-five-year-old wife's death from consumption two months earlier.

24

What surprised Charlotte even more was the appearance of Louise. She seemed temporarily to have abandoned her mourning and was wearing an old blue dress, transformed by Lucia's efforts and a saucepan of purple dye, into an indescribable mottled shade of violet. Her hair was arranged in a series of sausage-shaped ringlets around her pinched face.

Charlotte, watching her sister, was more and more intrigued at her behavior. She was not long in discovering the reason for this transformation. It was for Roslin's benefit that Louise had gone to so much trouble.

At thirty-three, Roslin had the build of a youth of fifteen. He dressed with meticulous elegance, and the cunning of a good tailor disguised the lack of breadth to his shoulders. Like many small men, Roslin took immense pains with his clothes. His neck was compressed by a collar of extreme stiffness, and his small head emerged from his masculine finery with an air of amazing dignity. In fact, he was not unattractive if one cared for this spruce, dapper kind of man. His dark, almost blue-black hair waved from a center parting, giving him a faint resemblance to a Raphael Madonna.

It seemed that Roslin suffered continually from this Madonna-like head on his schoolboy frame. He had an excellent opinion of himself, but paid extravagant compliments to Madame Morel, who was always softened by masculine company. For the present, he was engaged with Louise, addressing her formally as Madame de Boyne, dear Madame de Boyne.

Louise played her part of the young widow of good family to perfection, wearing her weeds with a gentle grief that became almost unbearably gracious.

Charlotte followed their verbal sparring with interest. Roslin always reminded her of Étienne. He really was a pedantic ninny.

Lucia brought in little Jane in her push-chair. In the past few days Charlotte had been too taken up with Elise to see much of her. For a few months old, the baby was extraordinarily pretty, with delicate bones and unusually well-formed features in her small face. She was very like

Elise, which was scarcely surprising. She would probably be prettier but with less character.

Once again, Charlotte marvelled at her sister's acting ability in her new role of noble young widow. Roslin, she noticed, was making a great fuss over the child.

But in supposing Louise to be consciously playing a part, Charlotte was underestimating her sister's capacity for self-deception, her comedienne-like capacity for thinking herself into any situation at will. She failed to understand that Louise had become what she wished to be, she *was* Madame de Boyne, widow and mother.

Some silly feminine need for attention, to attract the notice she felt to be hers by right, made Charlotte talk with unusual animation. Roslin had politely wished her good afternoon and then hastened back to what was evidently an established pattern of 'chit chat' with Louise. But he turned around suddenly, unable to resist the rich, confident voice. He blinked at Charlotte like a man waking from sleep. She did not look at him but she could feel his eyes fixed on her, as closely as a burr stuck to her skirt.

She got up. She was wearing a canary yellow dress, trimmed with black, with a boyishly cut bodice. The wearer had to be very slim to carry it off. Little tendrils of hair strayed from her chignon making her look like a grown-up child. Exhaustion had drawn dark circles round her eyes. Louise was torn by a spasm of rage and humiliation but Charlotte was too indifferent to Roslin to feel the need for any qualms of guilt. She had too many things on her mind. But this did not prevent her indulging her power of attraction.

They took a turn outside. There was a chill in the air now and the ground was soggy underfoot. The deceptive touch of spring had gone, leaving the sun a ball of fire on the horizon while a fitful little evening breeze was blowing up from the river to stir the grasses.

Roslin attached himself to Charlotte, leaving Louise to follow. They talked lightly and at every turn in the path Charlotte managed, by a smile, a look, an unconscious swing of her skirt, to keep Louise subtly away from Roslin. In fact, her wistful expression was quite genuine.

She really wanted to go indoors and see Elise. Roslin was the least of her worries, but he stuck obstinately by her side. And Louise followed too, with her wan smile and her ringlets losing a little of their crispness in the breath of the damp night wind.

They were just going in when someone rang the bell of the little gate leading to the river. Charlotte went to answer it. To her surprise she found a strange man standing there who told her that he would like to speak to the owners of the house.

"What do you want?"

He said his name was Horace Binet. Charlotte stared at him in amazement. He was a tall, raw-boned individual, broad-shouldered and dressed in the short-coated, black-and-white dog-tooth check suit effected by the pimps of Belleville. He was clean shaven except for an impressive pair of side-whiskers, and thickly greased hair emerged from beneath a minute bowler hat, which bore an astonishing resemblance to a cheese cover.

He had in addition strongly marked features, thick, almost Negroid lips and a pair of fine black eyes with the bright, inquiring look of a fox-terrier. Charlotte saw that his trousers were fastened with elastic at the ankle and at the same time caught sight of the magnificent bicycle that was propped against the hedge.

If Charlotte hoped he would state his business at the gate, she was mistaken. Horace Binet would only unburden himself in private and she was obliged to ask him in. More than a little curious, she led him into the empty dining-room.

"As I told you, my name is Binet, Horace Binet. By profession, I am a musician. Violin and accordion. Cafés and such, you know, Sunday cafés and holidays. At your service, madame."

He removed the cheese cover and bowed. He was utterly ridiculous and yet at the same time an oddly likeable character with his flashing eyes and a demanding and overriding vitality and energy.

"Indeed, but may I ask, Monsieur Binet—"

"Madame, I am a musician. I am a responsible man. I

27

neither smoke, nor drink, nor gamble and I live with my sister, so that I have few financial commitments."

"But I do not see—"

"I am trying to explain that I have funds. There comes a day when every responsible man thinks of settling down. I'll come straight to the point; what I have in mind is a place of my own. Café and dancing. There is profit in it. See, I've got it all worked out. For weeks now I've been touring the neighborhood. Well, madame, you've got a field there running to waste. Your trees are rotting where they stand, I've seen those cherry trees of yours, you won't get a cherry off them—"

Charlotte gaped at him. "But—"

"You've neglected your pruning. And your apples, old and diseased. You won't be making anything out of your fruit. And a gardener will cost you more than he brings in. So, I'll buy the land off you. Just name your price."

Charlotte blinked at him. "You're mad!" she said, a hint of laughter in her voice.

"It's a tidy plot. Waste ground. Not earning its keep—"

"And may I ask what you intend to do with my orchard?"

"A place for refreshment and dancing."

"A *guinguette* at the bottom of my garden?"

"That's it, madame!"

"Now I really believe you are mad!"

"Not at all, you have the best site in the neighborhood. This side of the river is much more convenient. We'll be giving Père Astier some stiff competition in no time. You think about it."

"It's quite out of the question. I can't imagine why I'm even listening to you."

He sat down, uninvited, and was reclining at ease in a chair stroking back his hair. Charlotte was too entertained to be angry. She might show him the door but his enthusiasm was infectious and his smile disarming. It was an unexpectedly charming and sensitive smile for that vulgar face with a hint of a knowing, sardonic humor that reminded her of Thomas. She felt warmed by his presence and could not send him away.

He stood up. "Think it over, little lady! You're young

and pretty enough to wake the dead, but—well, I can see you're married—" He eyed her ring and Charlotte hid it clumsily in her skirt. "Money and position are not everything," Binet went on sententiously, "you think yourself safe, then bingo! All of a sudden you're a widow!"

"I am a widow," Charlotte said bleakly.

"Well, of course, when I said—" He smiled engagingly, cleared his throat and mopped his brow with a red check handkerchief.

"The whole idea is quite impossible," Charlotte told him. "There can be no question of a sale. I cannot diminish the value of the property by dividing it up and in any case a *guinguette* in this neighborhood would be most unsuitable. My dear M'sieur, surely you must see that—"

All the same she was finding it hard not to laugh and even the idea of a *guinguette* had its funny side.

"Yes, well, I see what you mean. Gentry, isn't it, round here? Of course, it needs a bit of thinking about. Name your price. And it would cheer things up a bit. When you're a widow, you need cheering up. How much do you want?"

"M'sieur Binet, pray go away and forget all about it."

"Just a minute, I'll make you an offer. I'm prepared to make a sacrifice. What do you say to a share in the profits? Fair's fair, and if I must I must. The value here's not so much in the ground itself as in the situation. We'll be partners. Three parts for me, two for you. I'll take the land at rock-bottom price. You'll make up on the lemonade and the *fol de rols*."

"This argument is leading nowhere."

"I know what I want."

She laughed, "You are a very exhausting man!"

"You think about it. It's money for jam. You're letting the place go to waste. Can you keep it up? No. I saw the grass as I came in. It takes money and staff, I tell you. And the roof on the right wing of the house is falling in. What good is property if it's going to ruin?"

She knew he was right. The Binet's lynx eyes had taken it all in, the sagging roof, the untrimmed lawn. It was true the orchard was dying. Lucia grew a few flowers around the house but the fruit trees needed expert care. There were plenty of fruit trays and cider barrels in the cellar and outhouses, but this year the apples had rotted on the grass for lack of anyone to pick them. The trees were diseased, the fences falling down.

"I've plenty of time. I'll be back," Horace Binet declared, seeing the thought had struck home and hoping events might yet turn in his favor.

"In any case," she said, tempted already, "this house is not mine, it belongs to my mother by a tacit agreement. I have no authority to deal with you."

"I've plenty of time," Binet said again. He favored her with a delightful smile, kissed her hand with ceremony and took his leave. His bicycle had been propped against a tree. He fetched it and departed under the astounded gaze of the ladies of the house and their guests.

Roslin was getting his house ready for the summer and spent several days at Juvisy, taking advantage of the fact to pay daily calls on the Morel ladies. Ostensibly, he came to see Louise, to play a game of piquet or lotto, or take a turn in the garden. But he had the expectant air of a man about to hear he has inherited a fortune. Time and again, his eyes would turn to Charlotte, including her in the conversation, and he was so reluctant to leave her side that some invisible weight might have been dragging at his heels. Louise noticed all this and suffered in silence. She could not fight against Charlotte, and although her sister now behaved towards Roslin with rigid propriety, Louise saw with dismay that the damage had already been done. She had thought to marry Roslin. He was a widower with a daughter by his first marriage to bring up. In her mind, Louise had foreseen a future of happy respectability, and now she saw her hopes dashed by Roslin's evident attraction towards Charlotte. But she could only wait. Wait for Charlotte to go away. And she longed for that moment with a fierce intensity, as if it would make everything right.

Charlotte planned to stay for another week until Elise was fully recovered. The child was already convalescent and Charlotte was growing bored with the gloomy, rain-soaked countryside. Then one evening, she and Louise quarrelled over nothing. Louise lost her temper and accused her sister of deliberately setting her cap at Roslin. She spoke from a high moral standpoint but her misery was plain to see, and her eyes were bright with unshed tears.

Charlotte retorted angrily that she had other things to worry her, and brought up the matter of Horace Binet and the orchard which she had already mentioned casually to the others. She had introduced the subject merely as a diversion, but realized as she spoke that she had given the matter a good deal of thought in the past few days. Madame Morel and Louise both cried out in horror, oblivious of the profit to be made and thinking only of the social embarrassment of having such a place on their doorstep.

Charlotte was not listening. She was busy with her own thoughts. Of course it was important to her, of course she had been thinking about it. She lived in terror of losing her irregular and somewhat unofficial work as a journalist. She was under no illusions. A share in Horace Binet's profits meant an assured income. Security. What did she care what people said. Beggars could not be choosers! How were they to mend the roof, see to the outhouses, to say nothing of the garden and general repairs—

She kept her thoughts to herself. Madame Morel and Louise were impervious to argument. Madame Morel wept. Louise called her sister a shameless hussy. Charlotte tried to make them see the facts. She explained to Louise that at their present rate their money would not last another five years. Madame Morel listened, bewildered and uncomprehending, while Louise saw with helpless horror that her sister was about to drag up the whole business of Jean de Boyne and the dowry which, as a condition of that hastily arranged marriage, had swallowed up everything. She wanted to forget, to pretend it had never happened. Her love for Jean de Boyne had become a myth by which she lived.

Charlotte saw the horror on her sister's face. She thought Louise was afraid of letting her mother know the truth. But Louise's fears were for herself, of having to face her own truths. Tired of argument, Charlotte left the

31

room. When she had gone, the two women sat dumbly, hearing her impassioned voice still ringing in their ears.

She gave them no peace until in the end they half gave way, Madame Morel from sheer passivity, Louise for fear of what she had to hide. Three days later Horace Binet reappeared. Charlotte walked up and down the field with him, making plans. Binet rubbed his hands delightedly and began marking out a ground plan with his stick in the damp earth.

"I'll do you proud, little lady. You've got a head on your shoulders, I certainly will say that. Look, here's where I'll put my caravelle! Hey, that's a good name *La Caravelle*, isn't it? See, back here will be the dance floor with the tables over there near the bar. Then a covered terrace out front and maybe a little jetty on piles built out over the river. We could have a lattice roof. Can't you just see it all with the sunshine and the parasols and the girls chattering! We could even hire out boats—"

A possessive sweep of his arm took in the familiar, sad grey landscape and the big bony hand with the fingers bent backwards at the ends like the prows of sailing ships, seemed to conjure the shapes out of thin air. Charlotte could almost see her terrace, the wooden piles standing with their feet in the river, the flickering shadows and the young girls dancing in their flowered Sunday hats.

All the rest of the week her mind seethed with plans. Binet was a fast worker and had promised to put the matter into the hands of a lawyer at once. Charlotte had taken to the idea of the *guinguette* with enthusiasm and was already counting her profits. One morning, she caught sight of Seuriot over the hedge. He had been away for a while and seeing Charlotte asked if he might come in and speak to her. She had a premonition of trouble and sure enough he began at once on the subject of her plans.

"I can't believe you really intend this, madame! My mother must have been misinformed."

"Why? Do you not like dancing?"

She had been prepared for opposition from the neighbors and was ready to face it but some slight feeling of guilt made her sound unusually aggressive.

"I dislike dancing intensely! But what is more to the
32

point I like peace and quiet. This is too precious for me to stand by and see ruined."

"Has it occurred to you," she said with dignity, "that I may have reasons—well, of a practical nature."

Seuriot laughed. He imagined them living comfortably on an income from Niort. In any case, money matters had never been his strong point.

"Seriously," he said a little huffily, "tell me it's all nonsense."

"Not in the least."

"You are going to let them put a *guinguette* here! A place that will attract all the scum of the district, right here on your own doorstep!"

"I fail to understand your attitude."

"You understand very well—" He gripped her arm, beside himself with rage. The effects of anger on his mild, ox-like countenance were disturbing and Charlotte reflected that he would not always be an easy man to deal with. He was dressed as usual in crumpled old trousers and a torn, dirty old jersey. She realized that she had intruded on his private, bachelor world and that he would not lightly forgive her.

"I tell you, I have my reasons. Perhaps your own income is sufficient to enable you to live in comfort. My own is not and moreover I have a child—"

"There were fifty other things you could have done!"

"That is scarcely your affair."

"But I'll not stand by and see this sacrilege!" he roared. "I'll guard my peace at all costs. To begin with you'll have to get a permit to open a business on this bank. I have my own contacts and I warn you I will stop it."

"What right have you?" Now it was Charlotte's turn to lose her temper and she was not sorry to have a victim for her fury.

"The right of having been happy here, once—before you came!"

Stunned by the anger and bitterness in his voice, she realized suddenly how much her presence must have galled him, and how he had come to long for them to leave. It hurt and surprised her, for she was accustomed to take the desirability of her presence for granted. On reflection the thought that Seuriot had always regarded her as an intruder seemed outrageous.

She saw that he had already turned away and without thinking, in her desire to wound him, she cried: "You have not always said so!"

He went through a small gate leading to the path between their two properties without a backward glance.

The interview left Charlotte with an uncomfortable feeling, compounded of anger, mortification and even a touch of fear, which only strengthened her determination to fight against any opposition from the Seuriots, or anyone else, to achieve her ends. She went back to Paris at the beginning of the week half out of her mind with worry. The conviction of her own importance which had filled her at Juvisy, the sense of acting constructively for the best, gave way to anxiety when she thought of the kind of life to which she was returning.

It was then that Valerie's daughter ran away from home. She was first missed at about five o'clock that afternoon, although no one had seen her go. Valerie called in the local police and well-meaning neighbors joined eagerly in the hunt, secretly delighted at this chance to interfere in the upbringing of a child they all agreed was "allowed to run shockingly wild."

"It's odd, though," Frédéric remarked to Charlotte as the two of them set out to search, "they are not really ill-natured people, and yet all this gives them a dreadful kind of thrill, as if they were hoping for a thundering good tragedy and a heart-broken mother. They'll be secretly a little disappointed if Valerie finds her daughter, and all the ones who are so sorry for her now will be the first to start blaming her again."

"They simply need a little excitement, that's all. This certainly helps them to forget their own dull lives," Charlotte answered him.

She was thinking of herself, and of the dullness of her own life. In spite of her natural self-centered indifference to other people's troubles, she had jumped eagerly at the thought of going out to look for a small girl for whom she did not in fact greatly care. The appalling thought came

34

to her that one day she might even find herself longing for some general disaster, a war for instance, to give some kind of meaning to her life.

Frédéric guessed something of her mood but he said nothing. His thoughts were all for Valerie's daughter. Some instinct told him that the small country child, feeling herself cut off from nature, might have gone to ground in the Luxembourg Garden, which must have seemed to her like a green refuge in exile.

The small gate closed early in winter but they were just in time to slip into the park before the keeper arrived. The huge deserted gardens seemed dead, as though the world had been emptied by some great cataclysm. A dusty wind was already eroding the sand castles, left by the children. In the shadows the tall trees had drawn closer together, allied against the city and its inhabitants.

Frédéric and Charlotte walked quickly between the chestnut trees, keeping an eye out for the keeper. A long way off, the horn sounded for closing time, like the knell of a make-believe Jericho. The man at a lemonade stall was putting up his shutters with an aggressive rattle, and one small, weary donkey trotted home beside its master, the day's rides done at last, with the soft tinkle of little bells.

They had to wait by the Medici fountain because a keeper was coming towards them. He had only one arm. They stood behind a large urn, with hearts and lovers' names carved deeply in the stone. A few chilly-looking sparrows hopped and fluttered round the rim of the fountain, and the water was dank and brown with last year's fallen leaves.

With the evening had come a sharp change in the weather. It was cold and a bitter wind was blowing. Frédéric drew Charlotte into the English garden where they examined every bush.

"We'll never find her here," she muttered impatiently, with a strong, female dislike of finding herself in a public place after closing time.

"Let's just go to the end of the garden," Frédéric persisted, "she often comes here for comfort. Valerie has already had to look for her several times."

They walked on as far as the greenhouses, expecting to find them locked, but one door was slightly ajar. They pushed it open cautiously. The air hit their faces like a steamy breath from Africa. Tall palms rose to press against the glass, and beneath them were the delicate tints of giant azaleas.

"*Et d'étranges fleurs . . . écloses pour nous sous des cieux plus beaux . . .*" Frédéric quoted, pushing the door wider into the straw-covered aisles. It resisted slightly.

"This is ridiculous," Charlotte said unhappily. "We can't go in." She paused in the doorway but Frédéric was already inside and after a moment she heard the muffled voice: "She's in here."

And there was Valerie's little girl, an undersized, sulky-looking little thing with her heart full of hopeless longing for her own familiar Auvergne, who hated Paris so much that she had come here to try to escape, to forget or die. She had fallen asleep on the ground beneath a potted bougainvillaea. Her pale face had lost its habitual defensive expression and looked touchingly lost and gentle.

"Poor kid," Frédéric said.

He bent over her, reluctant to snatch her unkindly from her dreams. Charlotte sat down dazedly on a cast-iron garden chair left behind by one of the gardeners and looked at the little girl. The child was wearing the pretty serge dress that Valerie had given her as a present when she first came to Paris and there was a rent in the skirt.

"Poor Valerie," thought Charlotte. "She does her best but the child hates her and won't come to her. And she's such an ugly little thing, which makes it worse. Poor child."

They watched the sleeping child in silence, busy with their own thoughts. It seemed cruel to wake her. She was so fast asleep, oblivious of the hostile world around her. Here, in the warm safety of the hothouse with its steamy smell of damp earth and tuberoses, it was possible to forget for a while the cold winds outside and be carried away by the heavy fragrance of the air into a state of mild, sleepy intoxication.

Frédéric stretched. "It's nice here, I like it," he said.

"I've always dreamed of taking you to Peru. How do you like my Peru, Charlotte?"

He waved his arms to take in the miniature virgin forest around them, dropping his voice to an intimate whisper as though inviting her to share in some mysterious private dream. Charlotte, still uncomfortably aware that they were in some sense trespassing, refused to be drawn. She was listening for a step, a whisper—

"We had better take the child home. Valerie will be worrying. And supposing the keepers come and catch us—"

"You should learn to enjoy breaking the rules now and then," Frédéric told her seriously.

He leaned against her like a child, sitting cross-legged on the ground with his back propped against her knees as she sat in the garden chair.

"Let's stay a little longer," he said. "I like the feeling of being on a journey with you. Do you remember once before we were together here in the Luxembourg. A long time ago, when we were young and eager.'"

"Yes," she said. "I remember."

"But you were a faithful wife, or at least you made me believe so and I wanted to believe it."

He was resting against her knees and she put her hand on the fair hair which felt stiff and springy under her fingers, like a horse's mane, quite different from Thomas's soft, unruly curls.

Frédéric took her hand playfully and she did not withdraw it. His hands seemed charged with a kind of electricity born of desire which she found oddly soothing.

He raised her fingers to his lips. "We must go," she told him nervously but in her heart she felt at peace with him as she would have been with no one else.

She stroked his hair and his face. The skin was young and firm to her touch. "Let us go," she said again instinctively but her hands were still on his head. He grasped her wrists, holding her prisoner.

"I like it here," he said.

He kissed her palms, first one and then the other. "Charlotte." He was not looking at her. "Charlotte . . . I could have sat here for ever with you stroking my hair. In the dark, perhaps you had forgotten who I was. And yet, I'm glad you stopped after all. I was beginning to like it too much. I was beginning to like you too much. Dear Charlotte. Dear, dear Charlotte, how I love you, don't go away. Our voyage is not over yet. Hush. We are far away. Sailing away forever with your hands in mine."

Still sitting at her feet, half turned away from her, he held her two hands on either side of his neck so that her arms were round him.

"Look at that poor child of Valerie's. Fast asleep and dreaming that she is back under a chestnut tree in Auvergne. She will never survive in Paris. She was born for country lanes. Poor little carrot. I wonder what kind of love affair brought her into the world. Why must children always pay for their parents' follies? People must be mad or very brave to have children. I should never be brave enough, Charlotte. To bring a child into the world to face this life. It's monstrous."

"It's easier than you think, Frédéric."

"I shall never dare marry and have children, heirs of my body with all my imperfections in them. You have to be either very ignorant or very strong to get children and I am neither. Oh, Charlotte—I wish I were different, I wish I had the courage for life. My instincts are not strong enough any more to fight the destructive reasoning of my mind. I am becoming a pessimist and a nihilist. I wish I had been able to face life, to do something positive, at least for my poor father's sake. So that he should not see me as a failure. As it is, I am a disappointment to everyone." He paused and went on in a low voice:

"I wish I was someone else. A man of action, someone you could have loved. Someone who could have made you love him. It is not your fault, or mine. Perhaps the blame lies in my childhood, shut up in those oppressive colleges, worse than prisons. Probably the real trouble was that I lost my mother. I could not accept it, you see, I rebelled once and for all against any kind of authority or discipline. Even my education is only skin-deep. I never studied anything properly because I am an anarchist. I began by hating school and then, as a sort of logical consequence, society. I know now that it was not even a proper hatred, the kind that builds worlds, but only a passive resentment, not even enough to make me fight for my ideals. I am not even an anarchist, I am simply apathetic and indifferent to everything." His lips brushed her hand. "To everything but you. You matter to me, much more than I ever thought. Perhaps you might have been my second chance. Loving you could have changed me. But you did not love me. And I lost it. The trouble is, I'm not even a gambler and I'm tired of losing."

"Frédéric," she begged him, "don't talk in this hopeless way." Her hand touched his hair lightly and the very thoughtlessness of the gesture stabbed him.

"Charlotte. . . ." He crushed her hand in his. "I am telling you this tonight because I am going away."

"Going away—" she echoed uncomprehendingly.

"Yes. I have come to a decision and one that surprises even myself. I am going to try and live. I shall go into exile, to Algeria perhaps, to become a settler or something. Not the army, of course, I'd still rather die in the gutter than that. But there may be a chance that a strange place will make a new man of me. It may be only an illusion. But I must do something you see, stop frittering my life away here to no purpose."

"You are going away—" she repeated.

There was a kind of finality in the words because at that very moment she had been warming herself in the comforting glow of his love for her. Frédéric's going away was like another piece of her life collapsing around her, and leaving her helpless and abandoned.

"No," she said, rejecting the thought. "You must not go, Frédéric."

"But I must."

She had freed her hands and now rose to her feet more troubled and unhappy than she would have thought possible. Frédéric too had risen and was watching her closely.

"No," she said again.

She laid her hand on his arm in an affectionate pleading gesture. She knew even as she did so that it was useless, she had nothing to give him. Frédéric was looking at her gravely, as if by doing so he could make her see the impossible gulf between her childish wish to keep him with her and his own desire for her whole and undivided love.

"Charlotte—"

She turned and made her way to the door with an aching heart. Friendship was not enough and for them there was no future, only pain. Outside, the wind caught her by surprise and she leaned against the trunk of a tree to steady herself. Frédéric was close behind her, resting his hand on the rough bark by her head. She did not move away. The hopeless, undemanding affection between them filled her with sadness. And yet he was very attractive with his grave face crowned with thick ash-blond hair looking prematurely gray in the dusk and combining with the bitter lines round his mouth to give him a curious ageing charm.

"Charlotte, my darling." His arms were round her.

"Don't go, Frédéric, don't leave me in Paris alone."

"One word from you and I'll stay. You know that. I'll go on frittering my life away. I'll stay if you want me to, Charlotte."

She hesitated, conscious that for him the decision was vital. She did not want to deceive him. But he would not be deceived. If he stayed, even for her sake, it would be in full knowledge of the cost.

But even in her dread of losing him she could not bring herself to risk pledging him her life.

"We are happy together, aren't we? Let me hear you say it. You are happy? I want to look after you. I dare say I ought not to go and if, as I expect, this war is going to come, then I shall have to stay. I know you dislike it when I talk about war. Women always do. But I want to protect you."

Yes, she was happy, even though she could feel the undercurrent of excitement in him. Now she could not resist when his lips travelled over her face and brows.

"No, let me go," she said earnestly.

His mouth covered hers with the rich, honeyed taste of ripe seed bursting against her lips. The momentary gentleness was gone, replaced by a forgotten piercing and burning. Really frightened now, she tore herself abruptly free.

They carried Valerie's little girl out of the garden without getting caught by the keeper. The child woke up as they reached the street and struggled instinctively to escape. Frédéric held her close in his arms.

"Look at me, I am your friend and this lady here is your friend too. Your name is Clarisse, isn't it? Well, Clarisse, first we are going to buy some sweets and then you shall go home and tell your mother everything is all right. She must be very worried."

"Don't want to see mother. Makes me stay in that dark courtyard. I hate Paris, m'sieur. I'll die here, really I will!"

"You'll get used to it, Clarisse. Your mother loves you."

"She doesn't! If she loved me, she'd send me back to Saint-Eudes."

Charlotte had never heard the little girl utter so many consecutive words. Then she burst into tears, asking in her thin little voice and harsh accent for her own nanny, Mère Gaspard. But Frédéric succeeded in enticing her into the nearest sweet shop from which she emerged clutching a sticky bag paid for by Charlotte.

Their arrival in the rue Monsieur-le-Prince was a sensation. They had to tell their story in detail while Valerie clasped the child to her bosom and Clarisse, softened by a delightful and unaccustomed stickiness, endured these maternal effusions without protest and eyed the assembled neighbors with an expression grown decidedly cocky.

Valerie, her eyes brimming with gratitude, thanked Charlotte and Frédéric again before sweeping the child indoors. As they went, the onlookers were suddenly struck by the resemblance between them, despite the difference in height.

Frédéric had not eaten, so Charlotte invited him to go with her. He went, seeing nothing unusual in the invitation after the previous events of the evening.

They sat rather uncomfortably in the dining-room feeling out of place together in the unfamiliar surroundings. Although this was her home, Charlotte felt strange and ill-at-ease.

Why had he come, she wondered. Was he hoping for a

41

recurrence of that moment in the Luxembourg Park? But the spell was broken now. They had nothing to say to one another, and he thought wretchedly that this had been just one more wasted effort, one more hopeless grab for happiness. And yet, she was still there close to him, all he needed was a little courage. He was not so afraid of women that he did not know how easily they could be overcome. But he hesitated, once again a prey to his eternal fear of not being loved. Yet he knew that if he failed tonight, it would be all over once and for all. There would be nothing left but flight.

He watched her, trying to gauge the strength of her affection. At the same time he was very conscious of her nearness. Charlotte said nothing, content to bask in their warm, cosy intimacy without troubling her head about how she could persuade Frédéric to go when the time came.

It was Frédéric, standing at the window, who saw the curious vehicle draw up beside the curb. Charlotte joined him to look and was surprised to recognize the antiquated carriage belonging to the Countess Lievitz with the big, Caucasian coachman, Nichka, puffing away like a volcano on the box.

"Someone you know?" Frédéric asked.

"Yes, I think so."

Her cheeks were on fire. It was certainly Worski's carriage and there was Worski himself getting out and staring up at the house front.

Worski. He must have come to find her. She had given her address to the coachman the other night, but Nichka must have forgotten the number.

That Worski should be here looking for her. He must have thought about her until the longing to see her again had grown unbearable. Charlotte herself had been too preoccupied with other troubles to think of him at all. She felt a glow of superiority, as if she had somehow triumphed. His presence was a victory, though one as unexpected and futile as their whole senseless relationship.

He was still dressed in black, looking as melodramatic as ever. The sight of him revived that mysterious attrac-

42

tion, that hint of danger and violence that had nearly been her downfall.

He was looking straight at her window, and she drew back for fear he should catch sight of her.

"Who is he, an undertaker?" Frédéric inquired unkindly. "Don't tell me that popinjay is a friend of yours. I had no idea that you frequented his kind."

"What do you mean?" she demanded.

"To be quite frank, I mean that even without his fairground costume, my dear, he is unmistakably homosexual."

"How can you tell?" she asked, flushing.

"My dear, you only have to look at him."

"You have no right to say that."

"My God, look at his hair! Like a simpering girl."

"It is beautiful," Charlotte said defiantly.

"In plaits maybe—"

"I hate you." She turned away angrily. Frédéric made a gesture of irritation.

"You are mistaken," Charlotte said after a pause, finding herself hurt and worried by Frédéric's remarks. "His appearance may be deceptive but he is not what you say."

"Indeed?"

"Do you think he would be hanging about under my window if he disliked women?"

"Let us say that his feeling for you may be—out of character."

"You are mistaken," she said again.

It was herself that she was trying to convince. The idea was painful, not only in relation to past events but to her own admiration for Worski.

She moved back to the window and watched the Pole pacing nervously along the street.

"No," she said. "No. Frank is different, you cannot classify him. Perhaps he's mad. He is beyond our reach I think, and loves no one."

"No one but you or he would not be here."

"I don't know why he is here," she said sincerely. "I had thought him too proud for that but in a way I am glad he has come. He was too inhuman."

"I dare say you are dying to go down and ask him what he wants. He seems to be waiting for you."

"Yes, it would be like Worski to expect that."

It was out of the question of course, and yet, as the sense of adventure rose in her again, it was what she longed to do.

"I could have loved him," she said dreamily.

"What happened between you?" Frédéric asked tonelessly.

She had an impulse to tell him everything, pretending to herself that Frédéric was simply a friend when she knew that he was not. It was her old trick of altering their relationship to suit herself. She described the expedition to Belleville and her own flight with Worski, and told him about the house in the Marais. When she had finished she waited for Frédéric to say: "There, he is a homosexual."

But Frédéric said nothing. He only stood looking down in silent anger at the romantic and improbable figure barely visible down below.

He hated these confidences from Charlotte. Hated the thought that she could feel attracted to that man. He sensed her impatience, the barely restrained eagerness to run downstairs to him, like a moth seeking a candle.

"You want to go, don't you?"

"No, but why shouldn't I—"

His face hardened. Gripping her arm he pulled her away from the window and drew the curtain abruptly.

Her eyes questioned him. He took her gently in his arms. Charlotte glanced back at the window with a look of mingled regret and resignation.

"What is the use?" she sighed.

"For years I have asked myself what is the use, but not tonight. I love you. I will not let you go down and meet that mountebank."

The arms round her tightened, became hard and relentless. The warmth of his lips on her neck awoke the life dormant within her. But even then she protested: "We do not love each other. I do not love you as I should—"

"What is love?"

44

"I can promise you nothing. You know I love another man."

"Becque, you mean?" His eyes bored into hers. "But do you love him? Don't you love that Pole with his long hair and don't you love others besides? Do you even know what love is?"

"Yes," she cried desperately, fired by the thought of that aching love for Thomas, still so much more real to her than Frédéric's present kisses, so that she was on the point of thrusting him away and keeping only that other love like a proud and flaming garment about her.

"You do love Becque? Have you seen him?"

"No."

"I ask no promises of you, Charlotte. Only that you should trust me and tell me the truth. I've come to the end of a road tonight. I need you. It is too late now for me to leave you and be as I was before. There is nothing more we can do. I will take such love as we have with all its risks."

He cupped her face in his two hands. "I'll make a bargain with you. You will always tell me the truth. If you want to go back to Becque, I will let you go. But in return, you will honestly try to give my love a chance."

His arms were close about her, holding her in a world of their own.

"Why must it be tonight?" she said softly.

He did not answer, knowing it was because of the man waiting below, because she would have run to that ridiculous, flamboyant Pole. It was this that had finally pierced his reserve, bringing out all his latent jealousy and possessiveness.

"I want to make you happy. Your happiness is all I want."

His words held a promise of such infinite bounty that it left her powerless to resist.

His lips were on her hair, her mouth. The two of them were alone in the flat. He drew her slowly to the bedroom, a thing he would never have dared before. At that moment his fierce determination to keep her from Worski gave to Frédéric a strength and virility he did not usually possess. He had become another man, his whole being irradiated by the urgency of his desire. In a single moment he had torn off his shirt and held Charlotte fast to his bare chest, and she felt a strange comfort steal over her at the touch of his skin. She was carried away on the torrent of his kisses while Worski and his cruel games dwindled to something vague and futile.

His passion mounting to a fury of anticipation, touched even now by the fear of losing all, his hands clawed at her dress but before he had done more than unfasten the bodice he had already abandoned himself to the promise of her half-naked body in a blind, unreasoning tempest of emotions.

The very frenzy of his onslaught defeated him. Reaching for the skies, he fell back like an exhausted bird, his beatific vision sunk to a pitiful, every-day scene which even her kisses could not survive. Now it was she who sought with the fury of desperation to capture that first, fleeting miracle of passion which had flowered between them. He offered her the gentleness that was familiar, yet even that did not displease her and she loved him in her way. Even then they might have been happy. She held him close, her eyes staring into space above the smooth curve of his shoulder. The marks of her nails left dark weals on his skin. She was crying out for love and birth and death but his arms had no power to lift her above the earth. His manhood meant nothing to her, it could bring her neither greatness nor oblivion.

For a few days Charlotte and Frédéric basked in a dream of happiness on the strength of this one night of love. Frédéric cut his hair and put on his gray serge coat and black tie and went back to his job as a schoolmaster. He seemed to have acquired a new lease of life, and his determination to break with his squalid vagabond existence made him almost a model of good behaviour. Charlotte, watching him from the dining-room window, felt a slight pang at the sight of his lanky figure, too big for its clothes. He looked like a provincial curate now and his new neatness only accentuated his poverty. She preferred the old Frédéric but she had not the heart to tell him so. She was terrified that he would start making plans for the two of them, and tried hard to convince herself that such slight love affairs were no more than a heightened form of friendship and nothing deeper was involved.

There were times when Frédéric's blue-gray eyes seemed to search her own with some urgent yet unspoken question in their cloudy, ever-changing depths. Their gentleness, which was only emphasized by the dark lashes, gave him a look of childish disappointment which went to Charlotte's heart in a way she did not understand.

She was very gentle at such times, a thing not difficult with him. It was her way of making him believe that he was happy. Tenderness became a kind of panacea and she worked hard to keep their relationship on this plane of euphoric unreality.

She succeeded by this means in deceiving Frédéric and even herself as to the real state of her feelings. He applied himself fiercely to the task of being happy, but even so he found himself uncertain how to behave to her, whether he should be discreet or demanding, outspoken or reserved.

He still shared the room on the fifth floor with Millau although the two of them no longer had anything in common. What had begun as a kind of rough comradeship continued out of habit and inertia, but they were becoming increasingly strangers and Frédéric often wished he could get away from the noisy companion who was constantly breaking in on his privacy and whose snoring disturbed his melancholy dreams.

He would have liked to go right away and take Charlotte with him, but what future could he offer her? A poor schoolmaster's wife in some provincial school! He was not foolish enough to imagine that Charlotte would ever go with him.

In any case, he was not sure of her even now. He lived in terror of putting a foot wrong, of striking a single false note. He was scared to assert himself. He came and went by the back stairs because she was afraid of the neighbors. He never even dared to tell her when he would come but relied on chance or some excuse or other. He would ring the servants' bell, pretending he had come to lend her a book or paper or to run some small errand. A more direct approach would have daunted him. They would sit chatting like old friends, but it fooled neither of them. When she said it was time to go, Frédéric, knowing quite well that he would stay, would yawn and stretch himself out on the sofa as though anchored there for the night. Looking at that lanky, recumbent form, Charlotte would succumb to the sheer force of inertia in him and to the warmth of his eyes on her.

He tried to convince himself that her feelings for Becque were only in her mind, a sort of sentimental loyalty to the past which made so many women unable to take a new lover without going into mourning for the old, as if her memories were a glittering parure of paste jewels which must be brought out and shown off on every occasion.

Of Worski on the other hand he was seriously jealous, a jealousy so sharp and tormenting that he began to look for a reason in order to be cured. It surprised him the more because he felt, or believed that he felt, nothing but contempt for men of Worski's stamp.

But he could not be free of it. It haunted him day and night until he began to search his mind for reasons why he should hate the Pole. But his intellectual training had taught him nothing of the art of self-examination. One evening, however, a chance encounter enabled him to know and understand his hatred and jealousy of Worski.

It was six o'clock and he was on his way home from the school where he taught. He paused outside a shop selling shirts to look at one he meant to buy with his first term's salary when he saw Worski jump out of a cab behind him. They were separated only by the width of the pavement. It was not the thought that Worski might have come here to see Charlotte which affected Frédéric so profoundly but the sight of their two images, his own and Worski's, reflected side by side in the shop window.

Frédéric was tall, certainly, taller than the Pole and yet he cringed involuntarily as a shameful sense of his own inferiority came home to him. His own reflection in its tight, shabby coat, seemed to fade into insignificance beside the virile figure of Worski facing him in the window.

The Pole was standing at the edge of the pavement in full sunshine and was so strikingly handsome in his eccentric black garments, his barbaric face with its high cheek-bones and splendid brown eyes framed in pale hair, that he stood out from the anonymous mass of passers-by like a figure from a girl's romantic dream.

Worski was looking at nothing in particular. Girls turned round to stare at him and leering students laughed rather too loudly as they came level with him. Their crude jokes did not hide a certain resentment but Worski seemed not to notice or to care.

Frédéric was acutely miserable but his misery was due neither to aversion to Worski nor, still less, to contempt. He was amazed that he should ever have dared to despise him. Worski was something altogether outstanding. He was beauty incarnate, living proof that the inborn gift was all, and that whoever had not received that innate, thoroughbred quality at birth could never hope to achieve it by trying. And even more than his perfection of masculine beauty, which Frédéric had no longer even the consolation of dismissing as effeminate, it was Worski's inimitable air of distinction which galled the student.

It galled him as it galled all those with whom the Pole came into contact, because men can be as easily hurt as women in the presence of an ideal of physical beauty which they have created as a dream in their own image.

Frédéric would not have believed himself capable of such frivolous feelings but he was not brave enough to laugh at himself and so he went on watching the other's reflection in the window. Men would hate Worski by instinct, like hounds sensing their quarry. Frédéric thought of Charlotte. Could she be in love with him? The other night she had been so eager, full of impatience to hurry down to the street to meet him.

Frédéric stared into the window. Laughing young men streamed by him on the boulevard.

Worski was moving away, walking with the lithe, delib-erate tread of a big cat. At that moment Frédéric did hate him with all the atavistic hatred of the ordinary man for the sensualist. To this was added his own private insecurity towards women, and towards Charlotte in particular. Was she happy with him? Frédéric could no longer be sure. He disliked this weakness in himself, like some hidden deformity invisible to others' eyes, and yet long after Worski had disappeared along the boulevard Frédéric remained staring blankly at the shop window experiencing all the pain and shock of a sudden, unwelcome self-knowledge. It came to him that man's first vision of himself, formed on the threshold of adult life, was no more than a passing phase, to be reshaped inevitably by love.

All the meticulous indoctrination in the basis of a universal culture he had undergone during the years spent in those grim, provincial colleges had deceived him as to his own nature by furnishing him with an impedimenta of erudition instead of personal values. But these notions were only acquired.

From adolescence he had adopted, like very timid or misunderstood souls, an attitude of cynical detachment as a way of protecting himself from the world around. He was tall and strong. The others were afraid of his fists and he had little trouble in making himself respected. There had been a time when he was able to believe himself strong and clear-headed.

The pain he felt in the presence of Worski brought all his doubts flooding back, shedding a cruel light on the false picture of himself he had cherished all these years. This was different from his old intellectual speculation, the doubts he felt now were those of a man knowing himself weighed for the first time at his true worth. It was the basic fear of proving unequal to the demands of happiness. And by the pain it gave him he knew that his whole life was at stake and now there could be no drawing back.

Things happened thick and fast. On 22 January Rochefort was sentenced to six months' imprisonment for his part in the events following the death of Victor Noir. Defended by his friends, including Gambetta who had put his case to the Chamber, Rochefort was able to leave the legislative assembly in the company of Gambetta himself. This was on 7 February. The same evening large numbers of police assembled in the rue de Flandres where a public meeting was due to take place. At eight o'clock, Rochefort descended from a carriage to be met by a cheering crowd. As he was about to enter the hall he was surrounded by a cordon of police. His hat was knocked off.

He was taken to the nearest police station. The crowd muttered angrily. Gustave Flourens, who was presiding over the meeting, turned pale when he heard of Rochefort's arrest.

"Citizens," he cried, "march with me against the Empire in defence of law and universal suffrage, violated by the arrest of Rochefort, our representative."

Florens was on the point of being arrested himself, but he managed to win over the commissioner of police charged with taking him in.

Flourens, a sincere, passionate and almost mystical figure, believed it his duty to rouse the people in spite of Rochefort's express instructions to avoid trouble. Some loyal supporters followed his lead. A barricade of overturned omnibuses was set up in rue Puebla running down to the canal at La Villette.

However much he might want to keep Charlotte in an ivory tower, Frédéric could not prevent her hearing the rumors of what was going on at Belleville. Her reactions frightened him. She wanted to go and see for herself. He told her she was mad and that in any case the barricade would certainly be demolished by the next day.

She said nothing, simply went out slamming the door behind her. Frédéric was left alone in her apartment, a prey to anxiety and self-disgust.

He had not dared go after her. In fact, she came back after an hour having done nothing but walk about the near-by streets. Her face was expressionless.

By the next day there were said to be eighteen barricades, at Belleville and also at Saint-Maur and in the Faubourg du Temple. Weapons had come from Lefaucheux, the armourers in the rue La Fayette.

Although it was only the beginning of February, the weather was fine with warm sunshine and a gentle breeze. The barricades were localized in the seething area of Paris

51

round Belleville at Montmartre, and it seemed as if the rest of the city was protected by invisible barriers. Everything was calm. Dances were held in private houses. But the people were not unanimous and there were nervous fears of snipers.

At dusk on the night of the 8th, the largish crowd which had been gathering round the barricades converged on the boulevard Montmartre. Another barricade was set up not far away, while the rebels were hidden from the near-by police by the complicity of the crowd, who moved to and fro watching a juggler performing on a dais. The man had an active little monkey dressed in a red coat which danced in time to a pair of cymbals. Small coins chinked in a copper bowl.

The alert and suspicious police saw through the maneuver. In no time, the juggler's platform was torn down and the man received an angry thrust in the gut with a rifle butt. The monkey screamed and clung frenziedly to the epaulettes of one of the sergeants, who yelled and stabbed at the animal with the end of his bayonet.

What followed was the inevitable uproar. The crowd panicked and the rebels, anxious to avoid unnecessary bloodshed, dared not intervene. They were relying chiefly on the moral weight of the insurrection, and hoped the movement would spread like a slow contagion throughout the city until the government would be forced to bow to the threat of popular opinion before it came to a show of strength.

But the police were in no mood to discriminate. To them the crowd and the rebels were one and the same. They were armed and fired blindly into the anonymous crowd. A number of people fell. A random selection of prisoners was rounded up and hustled into vans to be taken to Mazas and the conciergerie.

There was no knowing the number of these prisoners or of the wounded who sought refuge in near-by houses. The scene was one of utter chaos. The rebels could not fire now without endangering the lives of the people being herded by the cordon of police.

News of the riot, the shootings and the mounting unrest spread through Paris, making the other districts still watching anxiously hold their breath. People coming back from Montmarte shouted in the rue Monsieur le Prince that there was fighting and killing and the gutters were running with blood.

The voices died away. The speakers must have gone indoors. Timid householders closed their shutters and silence fell once more in the rue Monsieur le Prince.

Charlotte was at home. Frédéric had arrived at about six but they had exchanged hardly a word. Charlotte sent Annick to bed and they were left alone. Frédéric sat slumped in an armchair without speaking, his eyes on Charlotte. He was miserably conscious of her restlessness and anxiety. One word or movement could unleash a real emotional crisis.

Frédéric held his peace. He had no illusions now. He knew that there was more to Charlotte's uneasiness than simply fear of the trouble in the streets. The barricades produced a violent, physical effect on her, like something striking at her own flesh. They must be connected in her mind with the riots in the Champs-Elysées about which she had talked to him at the time in a distraught, rambling fashion. These new riots in the streets must be bound up in her mind with the rebellious image of Thomas Becque.

He understood this without her having to say it. He knew instinctively and was amazed that he could have been so jealous of Worski and suffered so much for an imaginary reason when there was a much more serious threat to his love. He looked at Charlotte's ravaged face and saw in it an intensity it had never held for him.

If he had not felt so deathly weary he could have laughed.

He had no cause for jealousy now. He had been deceiving himself. He had never possessed this woman. She had merely been living in a kind of vacuum and it was the forceful presence of Becque which really possessed her mind. This memory he could not even begin to efface and now he saw it for what it was, as inflexible, bloody and rebellious as the barricades themselves.

All his struggles to overcome his natural lethargy and give himself to life, all his earnest, laborious efforts seemed suddenly ludicrous. The waif-like tenderness he had lavished on her seemed ludicrous too, compared to the violence that was in her, a violence linked to that of the insurrection and to all the other violence of human anger and passion, the hunger or the love for which others would rise up and face even death.

Frédéric would never be capable of such strength of love or hatred. The force to cry out and take what he wanted was simply not in him. He felt very sorry for himself. Charlotte had turned her back on him. They were prisoners in this apartment, prisoners of their own deceit.

He was overcome by a maudlin sadness which threatened to obliterate his last traces of hope in the future. He rose and went to Charlotte and with the last remnant of trust in her and in the affection that lay between them put his hands round her waist.

She freed herself impulsively.

"Do I irritate you so much?" he said sadly.

"No—but go away."

"Charlotte—please—" He could not accept this dismissal. He wanted to close his ears, to bring her back to him, defenseless, and hold her fast. He had so often calmed her by holding her like this. He buried his face in her neck.

"I love you—" He strained her to him blindly. "Don't destroy us. Be merciful to us both."

Her body had gone rigid, like a block of wood. She jerked away from his arms.

"Charlotte—"

"What do you want of me?" she asked dully. "Compassion? Pity? I am in no mood for pity tonight."

She turned her back on him, her tone and the movement obliterating him from the room.

"I do not want your pity," he said in a bleak voice.

She showed no sign of turning round and he felt unbearably frustrated and shut out. His body was shaking as he gripped her arm and forced her to look at him.

"Is it only pity, Charlotte?"

She loathed that look of pained dignity. This passion for self-justification revolted her. She freed herself, her eyes unusually bright.

54

"Let me go. Don't you understand that I can't go on—waiting, hoping, living, I can't go on—"

She ran to her own room and flung herself down on the bed, like a soldier under fire, and lay there whimpering.

It occurred to him that he should hit her to bring her to her senses and force her to respect him but at the same time he knew that he would never do anything as forceful or as absurd as raising his hand to her. He was helpless and already at a vast distance, shutting himself off from the wounds she dealt him.

"Well, why don't you get out?" she shouted at him.

He came and sat beside her on the edge of the bed. For a long time he stayed there without moving. It seemed to him he was attending his own funeral.

"Go away!" she said again fiercely. She got up and dragged herself into the other room, bumping into the furniture like a woman in the last stages of pregnancy.

"I wish I could die—or kill someone—I must kill—I don't want to live—"

"Do you love him so much?" he said heavily. He meant Becque although he could not bring himself to say the name.

"Does it matter? Love, what does it mean? Who loves? You? Do you love me? How can I be sure? And he? Does he love me? Don't worry, he doesn't love me. If he were here now he would look at me just as I am looking at you, with deadly indifference."

Her eyes flashing, she bent forward suddenly and grasped Frédéric by his crisp hair, jerking back his head. His face was ashen. Charlotte thrust her own face into his, relishing his pallor, while her eyes caught and held his and her breath was on his lips.

"I hate you because you are not him."

She let him go. She thought he would leave her then. Making him suffer seemed the only way to relieve her own pain. But he did not. She began pounding on the door with her clenched fists until anyone seeing them would have thought that they had been walled up alive together in a tomb, alone with their hate and their conflicting love.

"Come here," he begged, overcome by distress and pity

55

for her. But in the end it was he who went to her and put his arms around her regardless of her fury.

"Be quiet. Why wound us both? I have never deceived myself, Charlotte. Never entirely, you understand? Trust me, tell me about Thomas—I will understand. Tell me how you love him and why."

"Not you—go away—"

"Tell me about him. Trust me. I shall not force anything on you. Just let me love you. Tell me about Becque."

"You're lying. You'll be jealous. If he came tomorrow you would try and keep me."

"I swear to you I would not. You are free. I leave you quite free. If he does come back I will not lift a finger—"

"He will not come back," she said harshly.

He held her close, wondering why he stayed with her. Probably because he knew he would suffer still more away from her. What false hopes did he still cherish? He was not of an age to play the comforter. He could have run away, saved himself. She lay against him like a block of wood.

He cursed himself for a fool. Suddenly he was tempted to leave her. Some vital spark of youth, an instinct for self-preservation came over him. Slowly he released her.

"I had better go," he said in an altered voice.

She stared at him blankly, stunned by this change of tone.

"After all, I don't think I'm old enough to be your confessor."

There was an odd look in his eyes, a dreadful longing possessed him to be dead and done with it all.

"Are you mad?"

"Probably." He was going. She was stupefied. He was mocking her.

"If you go, then never come back, never, do you understand?"

Their eyes met. He turned to go.

"You are out of your mind," she cried. "You contradict yourself every other minute. And I was on the point of believing you. Is that what you call loving kindness?"

"What is kindness between a man and a woman but a last resort?" He opened the door.

"Never come here again," she cried, her voice shaking uncontrollably. He stepped into the passage, at once she called out: "Frédéric!"

There was no answer. For a long time she thought he must be standing just the other side of the door but when she looked the landing was empty. She went up to the fifth floor and knocked on his door. He was not there.

She lingered on the back stairs, waiting for him to come home. She could not believe that he had really gone. His desertion, added to her own inner isolation, was more than she could bear. But when he still did not come she decided to go back to her own room.

The next day word went round that the barricades had been taken down and ordered restored in Paris. Appalled by the dismal prospect of a return to humdrum everyday life, Charlotte made up her mind to get Frédéric back into her life at any cost. She refused to face the fact that what she really wanted of him was an audience. Her childish egotism found more laudable reasons.

She went to meet Frédéric on his way home and found him on the boulevard. He saw her and paused as though he had half a mind to turn back. Charlotte went up to him and, trusting to the fact that they were in a public place to prevent him repulsing her, took his hand furtively and clasped it. There was an unfamiliar, brooding sadness in his eyes.

"Don't be cross with me," she whispered. "I have been so unhappy. Let's make it up."

Frédéric's fingers tightened on hers. They walked up the boulevard together. Frédéric kept his eyes on the ground. Automatically they turned towards the Luxembourg gardens. The roundabout was turning under a heavy canopy of snow and there was a smell of hot waffles in the air.

Charlotte leaned against the back of a Punch and Judy show from the other side of which gusts of childish laughter could be heard rising and falling like the sea washing against a groyne. Frédéric stood close beside her.

"You are not angry?"

He regarded her mournfully. "I thought I was being very brave. Something I had to do to keep my pride, or some idea I still had about myself. It makes no difference because I love you."

All she wanted was for him to stop being angry and talk of something else but there was still that secret grief in his manner to her. She shivered a little and snuggled into the spare, bony shoulder that was as solid and unyielding as a great ship's timber.

"Don't leave me again, Frédéric—what will become of me if you go away? I'll get older, you'll see, and more sensible. You must only give me time. I thought life would be different—but I have accepted it now for what it is, I promise you, and I know we can be happy." She gave a cracked, false little laugh.

"Don't leave me. You'll see. There is so much we can do. I feel comfortable and warm with you. I am happy. I love you very much, and that is important you know."

He stood, not daring to move, while she leaned against him, listening while she lulled herself with the timeless phrases so well worn by lovers that they seemed to have acquired some power, some special magic of their own. Charlotte uttered them like a talisman. Frédéric could feel her body trembling against him in the icy wind that whipped round the wall of the Punch and Judy stand.

"Did you hear something before you came to look for me?" he asked suddenly. He studied her closely.

"I have not read the papers, but I heard that the barricades had been taken down." She looked bewildered at the question.

"Most of the editorial staff of *La Marseillaise* were arrested last night and taken to Sainte-Pélagie," he said slowly, his eyes never leaving her face. "Thomas Becque was among them."

He went on watching her, expecting some violent reaction, prepared for her to reject him again with a look, holding him responsible, or go away all together. But she did not move, only stood there, stiff and silent.

"You are quite sure?" she asked at last in a small, pitiful voice.

"Yes."

For a fraction of a second her fingers tightened on his. Then she began to walk very quickly down one of the paths. Frédéric followed, still holding her hand. Suddenly she stopped and said in a desolate voice: "Frédéric."

He felt very sorry for her and a pang went through him to see her so pretty and so pale with her eyes full of anxiety for another man.

"There is nothing you can do," he told her and in his heart he thought: You love her and there is nothing you can do.

"Stay with me, Frédéric. Don't leave me too."

"No," he said seriously. "I won't leave you. Not now. Don't be afraid."

And yet he knew it was only the agony of her own feelings, of her love and terror for Becque, which made her beg him to stay.

"I'm not asking any sacrifice of you. You are my lover." She said it as though offering him a treat. He gave a twisted smile.

"You are happy with me? Aren't you?"

"No."

"Why not?" She was genuinely bewildered. She had wanted Frédéric to be happy while all the time she herself continued to long for Thomas with this desperate intensity, hoping and dreaming of his return.

"I shall not leave you again," Frédéric told her. He slipped his hand under her elbow and prepared to walk her home.

3

SHE WAS unfaithful to him that very night when he lay asleep beside her and she looked at him and her thoughts were for Thomas. Now her obsession had a goal to fix on. Thomas being in prison meant at once the knowledge that he could not come to her unexpectedly any day, and at the same time the chance of seeing him if she wished simply by visiting him at the prison. In the days that followed she walked past Sainte-Pélagie half a dozen times without plucking up the courage to enter.

In the end she did as she had done at Mazas, sent a parcel with a card bearing simply her name. She looked feverishly for an answer but none came.

She asked Frédéric to take her dancing and they went to the Bullier. The dances were noisier and more rumbustious than they used to be and the dancing was interrupted daily by the fierce battles which broke out between students and local youths. The lamps on the ceiling swayed furiously to the stamping feet. The alleys round the dance hall were full of courting couples, laughter and street girls. The *Closerie des Lilas* on the opposite corner sent out the strain of violins into the lamplight. Closed carriages drawn by white horses drew up outside, setting down parties of late revellers and beautiful ladies.

But Charlotte found no distraction in the excitement, the noise and the dancing. Her thoughts still turned to the prison of Sainte-Pélagie and she could do nothing to divert them.

Simply in order to get news of Thomas from Paul Boucher, she began to visit Aurore once more, though she said nothing to Frédéric.

Aurore hugged Charlotte warmly with many reproaches

for her long absence. Then, almost at once, she told her that Thomas was ill in prison. Charlotte waited with anguished impatience for Paul Boucher, who arrived after lunch.

"What is the matter with him?" she asked Boucher.

"A high fever with pulmonary symptoms. It is serious certainly, but to my mind the doctor is an ass. He diagnosed tuberculosis but a colleague who was called in says it's pneumonia. The doctor at Sainte-Pélagie sticks to his guns. He's convinced that Thomas is consumptive."

"Consumption—" Charlotte repeated with stunned disbelief. She could not credit it of a man as strong and energetic as Thomas.

"He is wrong. I am certain he is wrong. But he wants to be rid of his responsibilities. He has asked for Becque's release. Considering the appalling conditions in there it would be no bad thing."

"Let him out?" said Aurore. "But how, can they?" She paused and then went on musingly: "I know the Minister of Agriculture. You met him here, Charlotte. A little man with stomach trouble."

"He can be no use to us," Boucher snapped irritably.

"Of course not, but let me think—there is Mareuil. He is private secretary to the minister for Algeria and the colonies. I used to know him in Montmartre; he thought he had some talent as a painter and I have modelled in the nude for him too often for him to refuse me anything."

"This is ridiculous," Paul said. "What have your Mareuil and your modeling in the nude to do with anything?"

"My dear," Aurore teased him, "if you only knew as I do the effect of the nude on taxes, wars or the price of corn you would abandon politics on the spot."

"Let her be," begged Charlotte. "I'm sure she can help us."

"No," said Paul. "It's hopeless. All this string pulling can only damage Becque's reputation."

"Delbrèze has friends in the Prefecteur of Police—"

"Ask him to help us," Charlotte said. "He can do it. Ask him for my sake. Tell him I—I'll give him anything he wants—if that is the price of his assistance."

Paul made a disgusted face. "Now we're sinking into

first-rate melodrama. Good God, must you women always bring everything back to bed?"

"There is no need to be vulgar," Aurore told him cuttingly, her eyes dangerously bright. She and Paul were liable to sudden quarrels of this kind, coming without warning out of a clear sky. At such times they really seemed to hate each other, and whereas their normal conversation was conducted on a level of the most perfect formality they would descend to a tone of unctuous and offensive familiarity. At these moments Paul saw Aurore and her boon companions with morbid clarity, and in a sudden flash of insight felt nothing but contempt for her and his own degradation in loving her.

He saw himself as an intelligent, thinking man wasting his time on a cheap hussy. Now it made him furious to have to ask her help in a matter concerning Thomas Becque, to have to mix the two worlds he preferred to keep carefully apart. Charlotte's words were the final insult. He reacted by taking refuge in crude witticisms and even more vulgar abuse.

"I hate your sordid little hole-and-corner intrigues," he burst out, glaring at the two women. "The cheap romanticism which rules your lives. You're all alike, all of you, from the silliest little milliner up to the proudest lady. No amount of education or fine manners makes any difference. Even you Aurore, for all your greed and your money grubbing, you are just like all the rest. Nothing, absolutely nothing, brings out a spark of greatness or nobility in you. As far as you women are concerned, men only exist below the waist. All you think of is sleeping with him, or not sleeping with him, or who is he sleeping with at the moment or would he like to sleep with me? Permit me to tell you, the sun does not rise and set in your—"

Even Aurore blenched at this. She could listen with admirable composure to the general run of masculine conversation, indeed like many women often found it wholesomely refreshing. Moreover, her past experience as an artist's model in Montmartre had hardened her life to anything men might say or do in that line. But Paul's crude and groundless abuse struck at her very dignity as a woman. She pointed furiously at the door.

"Leave my house, Boucher. And never let me hear your filthy language here again."

"Aurore, please—do not be so hasty—" Charlotte intervened, almost beside herself with anger at this unexpected and ridiculous scene.

"Oh, very good!" cried Paul. "Now my lady gets on her high horse and throws me out. All right, my love, I'm sick of you, do you hear? Sick to death!"

He flung himself moodily into an armchair and all at once seemed calmer. He patted his forehead with his handkerchief and wiped the mist off his spectacles.

"You wretched, clumsy dwarf!" Aurore raged at him. "When I see you sitting in that chair you look like an old vicious baby. You're half blind and losing your hair. I don't know why I lose my temper with you. I only have to look at you to get my own back."

"And I only have to listen to you, my dear Aurore. Your utter stupidity, the way you prattle on with your second-hand opinions about art, never understanding a word, is balm to my spirit. If I ever had any doubts about my own intelligence I'd lose them in your company."

"Stop!" Charlotte screamed, irritated beyond bearing. "If you knew how ridiculous you are, you and your silly quarrels. You think you're important, but you're not, not you, not me, not anyone. No more than the first person who goes by in the street. You can talk as much as you like, it won't make any difference."

She really hated them. They stared at her in amazement and she turned her back on them and went out on the balcony to allow her temper to cool, biting back the cruel and irrevocable words that hovered on the tip of her tongue. She had a burning desire to go away and slam the door behind her, to show her contempt for Aurore Dumoulin and all her works. A need for something real and true. But the insidious hope that Aurore might be able to help Thomas kept her where she was, fighting to still the tumultuous beating of her heart. She stared unseeingly at the strollers in the sunlit *Place*, at the tall omnibuses and the grey horses, their hooves clattering on the cobble-stones like the short peals struck by a careless hand on the cymbals.

The scene in the Rond-Point imprinted itself on her retina without making any contact with her mind. Even so, she felt the warm touch on her arm and shoulder of the spring-like sun shining full on the balcony. It was a sensation forgotten since last summer and unconsciously associated with feelings of peace and happiness.

Charlotte did not connect the caress of the sun warming her body with the unformed belief in life and hope which sprang up suddenly within her, illogically driving out her worry and bad temper.

Unexpectedly, she heard Paul's voice through the open doorway.

"Charlotte, my dear, come in. Your exit has worked wonders."

She went back, a little shamefacedly, into the room and found Paul apparently his normal self once more. His eye had recovered its cynical gleam and the inevitable lurking self-mockery.

"I lost my temper. I said things I did not mean. My real thoughts about women are much worse. But as Aurore has pointed out, so admirably, I was merely seeking compensation for my own physical defects. In other words, I am truly sorry I lost my temper. After all, our friend Delbrèze may very likely wish to sleep with you. Who wouldn't?"

He sketched a little bow, without rising from his seat, which really did make him look like a dwarf. Charlotte was indifferent to his banter since she knew perfectly well that Paul had not the least interest in her. Gallantry from him was simply a joke.

"In any case," Paul went on, "whether Delbrèze can help us or not he will only do so if it happens to suit him and your sacrifice will be quite in vain. By the way, though, let me assure you I do admire the greatness of the sacrifice you are prepared to make in our cause."

"Stop it, Paul, we are not amused," said Aurore, who had recovered herself and now appeared perfectly self-possessed. Paul rose to his feet.

"Be that as it may, my dear," he said to Charlotte, "I am not inclined to owe my friend's liberty to the sale of your charms and Delbrèze is far too intelligent to have any truck with such a farcical arrangement."

His mobile features changed in an instant, and he was suddenly serious. Something in his voice warned Charlotte that he was no longer joking. She knew that Becque's arrest had affected him deeply. Like many men of his kind, obsessed by social problems but too weak to sacrifice pleasure for the sake of principles, Boucher had a great respect for integrity. He loved and admired Thomas, and if he sometimes laughed at what he considered the childish idealism displayed by some of his contemporaries, with their big words and noble sentiments, it was with a deep affection and a certain self-contempt.

"Can Delbrèze help us?" Charlotte asked. Unconsciously her own voice had changed, becoming crisp and business-like. Paul never ceased to be astonished at the speed with which women's moods could change.

"No," Aurore put in decisively, "let us say nothing to Delbrèze. I was quite serious in thinking of Mareuil and you may keep your sarcasm to yourself, my poor Paul. Mareuil married late, and his wife is a dreary creature who makes his life a misery. He is put upon at home and never goes out except to come here, and he has to find excuses even for that. What all this is leading up to is that in this house he met a totally unknown little actress called Fanny Molt, and he is captivated by her. He knows the child has other lovers but does not seem to mind. Now, little Fanny's principal lover, the person who really keeps her, is someone very highly placed indeed. I will not tell you his name, but I believe he would be able to do the trick if Marceuil agrees to put the matter to Fanny and ask her to mention it to the party concerned. This personage, it seems, is no longer young and so besotted about the child that he can refuse her nothing."

"Out of the question," said Paul. "Quite apart from the difficulty of making such a request, think how indiscreet it might be, the scandal if it got about."

"I see no reason why it should get about."

"No," Paul said, "we must think of something else. I will go and see a friend of mine who has certain people

65

up his sleeve, and I will pay a call on Delbrèze at the same time."

Charlotte dared not leave Aurore's house. She waited all day for news. In the evening Boucher returned, having failed to find Delbrèze or to obtain any satisfactory help from his friend.

They dined in. Aurore, highly delighted with her own plan, pressed them to call on Mareuil, but Boucher could not accept the idea.

Next day, the longing for news brought Charlotte back to her friend's house. At about four o'clock in the afternoon, Paul arrived and told them that the news of Thomas was not good. There seemed to be some difficulty in getting him moved to a hospital because he was a prisoner under close guard. The arrest of the men from *La Marseillaise* had made a considerable stir and the supporters of the régime were on the watch for any move on the part of the opposition. The number of dead in the riots in the Boulevard Montmartre had been put at one hundred and fifty. A further three hundred had been arrested, and the majority sentenced after a hasty trial to deportation or death, although most of those arrested had had nothing to do with the disturbances. This was enough to account for the difficulty of obtaining any privileges for a prisoner in Sainte-Pélagie. Anyone in an influential position daring to sign a warrant for the release of one of Rochefort's associates, even on medical grounds, ran the risk of appearing an enemy of the Empire.

It was these considerations which finally forced Paul to agree to Aurore's suggestion about Mareuil. His dislike of the plan was more on Becque's account than his own, for he himself had never made a point of looking too closely at the means if the end were desirable. Paul Boucher was a strange man, torn between conflicting motives, but in the last resort he would go to any lengths, employ the most dubious tools, if he were sure of ultimately furthering the cause he passionately believed in, the destruction of that very world of luxury and privilege which he himself could not do without.

The train of events set in motion by Aurore rolled

smoothly forward as if on well-oiled wheels. Her friends, partly from the sense of fellowship and partly from a wish not to interrupt the pleasant tenor of their relations with her, put themselves out to be useful. Little Fanny Molt who, whatever her morals, was ambitious and had a head on her shoulders, obtained Aurore's promise of an introduction to the director of the Gymnase, who was a close friend of hers. Oddly enough, in spite of her humble background—her parents kept a grocer's shop at Beaulieu—the girl had a real and rather magnificent passion for the theater as well as a good deal of talent. She was prepared to sacrifice any amount of dignity in order to get on and her one ambition was to succeed as an actress. Her friend and protector, Monsieur F., a person of some importance in the Ministry of Justice, was no longer of an age to attract women for the sake of his personal charm. He was not a particularly generous man, but one who, growing weary of celibacy when left a widower, had determined to console himself with a mistress, and make a last bid for such pleasures as life still had to offer him. Such men are more apt for betrayal than those who have spent their lives in debauchery.

In any event this was not required of him. Fanny managed the business very cleverly, swearing that the prisoner in question was a friend of her brother's—in fact she had no brother—and had never, she assured him, been her lover. She made the most of her protector's unworthy suspicions and further worked on his feelings by painting a grim picture of her own oppressed and poverty-stricken childhood. This horrifying but perfectly imaginary description of social injustice came as a revelation to Monsieur F., and it seemed to him intolerably sad. He gave Fanny a handsome present by way of amends for the regrettable comfort in which he himself had been living while she starved. More to the point, this upright gentleman who had always detested intrigue and favouritism of any kind, displayed a quite astonishing skill and consummate artfulness in obtaining the required boon.

His position was an influential one. A word here and there and the matter reached the Tuileries. The Emperor, preoccupied with other cares, granted the petition without question. Witnesses were even produced to swear that Becque had been wrongfully arrested on the night of 9 February on his way home from a journey.

Thomas Becque, pronounced tubercular by the doctor at Sainte-Pélagie and innocent by administrative degree, received the order for his release. He was being treated in the old prison hospital when he heard the news. He was very feverish and not entirely himself, but his illness had made him pugnacious. At first he refused to accept his freedom.

Rochefort came to his bedside. Political prisoners enjoyed a degree of liberty inside Sainte-Pélagie.

Thomas tried to sit up but Rochefort pushed him gently back.

"Be quiet, and be sensible. You need care and you will be better off outside this prison. Listen to me, Becque—do not reject the help of those friends who have worked to obtain your freedom and do not cavil at the means they may have employed. Just now, that is not important. What matters is for you to get better. We need you."

"I cannot stomach injustice—especially when it is all for my benefit," Thomas said furiously. His breathing was difficult and each word cost him a great effort. He was the more ill-tempered because at that moment he knew he was too weak to offer any opposition to what others might decide. He hated the thought of intrigues on his behalf.

When he was arrested on the evening of 9 February, along with most of the staff of *La Marseillaise*, whatever his anger at his arbitrary imprisonment, he had at least the consolation of knowing himself to be in the same situation as all his friends. In those days, when all freedom of thought was being tyrannically repressed, imprisonment and deportation had become almost an honour. It was even said that by the end of the Second Empire all that was best and noblest in the country was behind bars.

The prisoners were sustained by pride in the knowledge that they suffered for the cause of freedom. Becque quite naturally resented the thought of owing his freedom to a personal favor. Already it seemed to him that all his past efforts, even the collapse of his own newspaper, had been for nothing.

His illness had begun without warning on the very day after his imprisonment, with a fit of intense, uncontrollable shivering followed almost immediately by the onset of a high fever. Five minutes later he was complaining of acute pain in his chest.

His strong constitution stood up to the shock. He would not take the sudden attack of fever seriously. He refused to go to bed and dined in the communal refectory with his friends. They noticed suddenly that his face was grey and covered in beads of perspiration. They had to put him to bed by main force.

For two days he lay at the mercy of the suffocating, vice-like pain in his chest. Superstitiously, he insisted on being left in his cell rather than taken to the prison hospital. By the third day his fever had risen so alarmingly his friends called in the prison doctor. The doctor was a doddering old fellow whose face, as he examined the patient, wore the perplexed expression of a man going down into a dark cellar without a candle and wondering what he was going to find there. He had a holy terror of the human respiratory system and any suspicious noise led him to the most sinister diagnosis. His examination of Thomas convinced him that his patient was suffering from a sudden attack of tuberculosis. In his defense, it is only fair to say that in forty years as a prison doctor he had ample opportunity to observe that malignant and little-studied disease which produced a rapid decline and death within a few months. The damp, confinement and general unhealthiness of the prison were all factors which seemed to foster the disease.

Marillièr had died of a pulmonary infection in Sainte-Pélagie the previous year. Thomas had not forgotten, but he refused to accept the verdict of the fussy little doctor. Paradoxically, he felt too ill to believe that this was really his complaint. He decided that he was suffering from a form of bronchial-pneumonia, because he remembered having once seen the same symptoms in a friend's child. A second doctor was called in and confirmed Becque's intuitive diagnosis. The Sainte-Pélagie doctor shook his head sceptically.

Thomas amazed those around him by his stubborn

69

endurance. Sweat poured from his body in such quantities that he seemed to be sweating out the disease itself in an unending private struggle. The doctor observed that most men in his condition would have heard their death-knell. Through all the savage convulsions which racked him, his mind remained clear, though his body was torn by dreadful fits of coughing and retching which left him bent over the small glass vessel they had given him, shivering with anger and contempt. In fact, anger was his principle reaction to the matter thrown up by his body. They treated him as well as they could with bleeding and counter-irritants. He was put on a strict diet. But he was a difficult patient. He refused all help, demanding solid food and throwing his tisanes out of the window as soon as the sister's back was turned.

Rochefort watched Becque fighting for his life. It was, he reflected with a certain wry amusement, a magnificent spectacle. He felt a rush of affection for the angry man with his one arm, tied to his bed like a fairground strong-man in his bonds. At any moment he expected to see the sheets flung across the room. Becque refused to lie down however often he was told to, and would keep hauling himself up until his head lay propped on the bars of his bedstead, and then stiffening suddenly as the pain knifed into him and flung him back on his pillows once more.

He was very restless, constantly flinging off his covers and trying to tear open his shirt as if it stifled him. Rochefort's sharp, inquisitive eye noted with an almost morbid interest the impressive breadth of torso revealed in the sick man's wild tossings. Physical strength in others always inspired him with a mixture of awe and revulsion. His own constitution was sickly and only his immense will-power enabled him to fight his constant weariness. He hated violence and bloodshed. He was a natural pacifist, an aesthete with a sardonic vein of humour, capable of flaying an opponent verbally but apt to shrink from the use of force.

Becque was big and powerfully built, a man of the people, with muscles which stood out like the grain in seasoned wood. There were bulging sinews at the base of his neck where it joined the massive shoulders, and the muscular compactness of that right shoulder was clearly visible through his sleeve. His chest was broad and deep, the fine moulding over the rib cage overlaid by dark curly hair.

Rochefort looked away, his curiosity giving place to the embarrassment which always affected him at the sight of other men's nakedness, however much he laughed at himself for an old maid. His mouth twisted in a grin as he thought of his own boney figure and narrow chest, more like an anatomical specimen than a man.

He was amused, impressed and even a little envious. He thought that Becque was like a forge, a great furnace of formidable strength. He belonged to a race of men made strong by the constant buffeting of fate. He, Rochefort, came of a long line of aristocrats, the blood ran thin in his veins, and he possessed that civilized turn of mind, the kind of warped intelligence known as humor. It was a weapon he used to great effect but all at once it seemed to him a thing of dubious worth compared with the sheer brute strength of his companion. Becque lacked humor. Strength and simplicity made men such as he incapable of looking at life with mockery. Irony, he supposed, was the luxury of a mind which had outgrown the candor of simple faith.

Becque was a force of nature and Rochefort thought how much it took to defeat such a man. He admired him truly, not for his strength, but for his simplicity, and yet while he did so his own remorseless logic whispered to him that in the end all this honest strength would serve their cause less well than his own cruel pamphlets and ruthless cynicism, all the more effective because he no longer believed in miracles.

Becque was growing increasingly restless. It was mid-afternoon, the time when his fever mounted rapidly. His limbs began to jerk involuntarily, but despite the restlessness of his body, his mind remained clear, as if divorced from the struggle going on inside him.

One of the sisters of St. Vincent de Paul who attended to the simpler needs of the patients in the prison hospital popped her coifed head round the door.

Becque swore at her through clenched teeth. "Go to

71

vespers, sister. I'd rather have your prayers than your blisters."

The coif disappeared.

"Sadistic old hag," said Thomas. "I swore I'd strangle her with my bare hand if she came near me with her potions and her horrible little leeches." He gave a crack of harsh laughter, broken off by spasms of coughing.

"She has come back, nonetheless," Rochefort said quietly.

With an effort Thomas turned his head to look at the door. A winged, white head-dress was framed in the doorway but beneath it, instead of the elderly, cross-grained features of Sister Hortense who usually administered his needs, were the plump, innocent features of a young nun barely out of her novitiate, as fresh as a crisp lettuce heart under the starched coif.

Thomas choked back his oaths and stared. There was silence but for his hoarse breathing and a low chuckle from Rochefort.

"They have sent you an angel, my friend. I think they must mean to convert you."

The young nun busied herself tidying the bed and arranging the pillows. Thomas, very red in the face, said not a word. At last she went away.

"The nun at the bedside of the wounded hero. Very touching," Rochefort remarked sardonically, much amused by his friend's speechless rage.

"I will not be mocked. I'm no hero. My only claim to heroism was being in prison, and now they are trying to get me out." He drew a rasping breath. "I never did like to be under an obligation—"

"But you will get out of here, Becque. I am relying on you to get better quickly and continue our work. The paper has been drained of nearly all its life-blood at the moment. We shall need you. You can help me smuggle my articles out of this miserable prison and take over the editorship in the rue de Flandre."

Rochefort had already, some days earlier, succeeded in smuggling articles out of Sainte-Pélagie to appear in *La Marseillaise* under the name of Dangerville. Since newspaper articles at that time were obliged by law to carry a signature, it had been necessary to find someone to lend Rochefort his name. Dangerville was an honest plasterer who had agreed to do this in return for the sum of 10 francs a day.

"Believe me, Becque, it makes me very happy to think that you will be out of here soon."

"Who procured my release?" Thomas asked weakly.

"Your friend Boucher. He will be coming to fetch you."

"Boucher—that casanova of the demi-monde!" Thomas clenched his teeth to stop himself swearing aloud. Then he turned to Rochefort and went on with difficulty: "Who did he bribe? Or betray, in return for my freedom? Do you know, Rochefort? Tell me, what was my price?"

"My poor friend, you are too touchy. Does one ask the price of freedom?"

"Yes, if it means dishonor. Rochefort, you must understand—I have done nothing—nothing worth doing—my one pride is to be here in prison with those who fight—with you—I will not have my reputation sullied—"

He was growing increasingly feverish. His breath came in short, hurried gasps and his chest rattled like the wind in the casements of an abandoned house. His whole body was drenched with sweat.

"I want you to know—Rochefort—if I leave here—it will be against my will—and also because I hope to be useful—you may smile—but I shall work now with faith. Before—you know—I fought because I was a child of the people—I was in revolt—but revolt—is not enough—"

"Do not talk. It makes your fever worse—"

"But I want to tell you—I want you to understand—I was thinking too much of myself—" Here Thomas was once more doubled up by a painful fit of coughing, but he recovered and managed to turn back to face his companion before falling back suddenly onto the bed. His voice was much fainter as he went on: "We have done nothing—only words. We must fight—as a vocation—not—hobby—our children must not laugh us to scorn as idle poets. We—owe them—gift of liberty—equality—Rochefort, just as it says on the monuments—the right to live. If sacrifice is needed, I am ready—it must be a religion—we must change the world or what is the use—"

His voice died away and he lay very still, his eyes closed. Rochefort turned away and looked out of the window at the prisoners exercising in the yard below.

"I wonder, Becque," he said at last in a thoughtful voice, "if in the end too many sacrifices to a cause do not make us suspect in our own eyes. Complete apostolicism frightens me."

He went on musingly: "There is no such thing as the superman. True courage lies in accepting that, in accepting our own imperfection and being content with sincerity. And besides, Becque, it is reasonable to wonder what sacrifices you will feel called upon to make. I may shock you perhaps, but my answer to your profession of faith is that I believe every man's first duty is to be happy. Happiness breeds tolerance and tolerance breeds happiness. A very satisfactory chain of events."

He fumbled in his pocket for his pipe and then abandoned the idea in deference to the sick man's continued labored breathing.

"I tell you, Becque—it seems to me you are in a fair way to making service to your cause an excuse for wrecking your own life. You were made to be happy, my friend, and if you with all your strength and energy give up, the there is no reason why any man should ever succeed."

He was silent for some moments as he had the uncomfortable suspicion that Becque was no longer listening. Thomas lay on his back very still, with his eyes shut and his one hand gripping the sheet. The bedclothes rose and fell with his breathing. Was he asleep? Rochefort felt a little guilty for having talked so long. But then Thomas stirred and he realized that he was not asleep, but was slipping gently and without a struggle into a state of semi-consciousness. His fever must have been rising steadily until at last it had overwhelmed his tired brain and driven out all coherent thought.

When he touched him, Rochefort found that Thomas was burning hot. He called the attendant who came and said without interest that Monsieur Becque was delirious every afternoon and there was no cause for anxiety.

In fact Thomas remained in this state until a little after ten o'clock in the evening, when he seemed suddenly to

74

come to himself. He was bled again the next morning. He was hungry and asked for food and the doctor, who was a fatalist and tired of his complaints, finally gave in since by the end of that day Becque would have ceased to be his responsibility.

Meanwhile Boucher had been very active. It had been arranged that he should fetch Thomas at three o'clock, but for the sake of discretion he had tried to keep the hour of Becque's release a secret fearing that colleagues who were ill-disposed might turn up to spread unfriendly and damaging rumors. He was anxious to avoid the necessity of hiring a carriage and Aurore Dumoulin lent him one of her three, the largest, a big travelling barouche with nearly room enough for a man to lie down on the back seat.

Paul Boucher came from a medical family and was on friendly terms with every hospital in Paris. A doctor at Saint Louis who was a friend of his father agreed to Paul's request to attend Thomas at his own house when he was out of prison, and so save the sick man the uncomfortable crowding of the big hospital wards which, in spite of recent endeavours, still suffered from too little care and attention.

He had not been able to prevent Aurore and Charlotte from going with him and the two women followed in another carriage, also belonging to Aurore.

The light hood, designed more for shady drives in the Bois, had been put up to provide some protection from the rigours of a biting North wind.

Sitting in the pretty, beautifully appointed carriage, sheltered from the wind which drove the clouds scudding across the sky like a flock of sheep, produced a pleasant illusion of spring. Aurore, sitting beside Charlotte, had elected for some unknown reason to dress in black, for all the world as if she were attending a funeral.

Charlotte's friends had been surprised at the fury with which she worked on Paul to procure Thomas's release. She herself was only now fully conscious of the madness which had driven her. It did not seem strange to her now, since she realized that this frenzy of devotion was simply the outlet for a love which had nothing left to feed on and would endure ten times the labor to compensate for its loneliness.

The night before she had tried to explain to Frédéric why she had to be there when Thomas came out of prison. She had been seized by a perfect fury of self-justification. For hours they lost themselves in a wilderness of half-truths and private grief. He did not believe her but he had made no demands. She was free.

She would have preferred it if he had tried to rule her. By leaving the choice to her, he had only increased her feeling of guilt. Now she carried Frédéric's disappointment in her heart. By coming here she had dealt him one of those wounds which nothing in future would ever quite be able to heal. Now, whenever he thought of her, he would say to himself: She did that to me.

But she had come, obedient to the inescapable force which drove her like a basic, fundamental need.

Her coming had been a mistake, she thought now. Just one more useless gesture. When would she ever learn self-control, to be ruled by principles rather than impulse? In her mind she seemed to hear all the time-honored moral precepts by which young girls were taught: virtue, duty, conscience, rules of conduct—all the worn-out phrases which still echoed, though very faintly, from the ancient walls of convents and academies, but altered and debased by the long duration of years. In that instant the meaning came home to Charlotte again like a revelation, a nostalgic yearning for order and propriety.

Sainte-Pélagie stood silent and closed. An itinerant glazier plodded by under the walls, shouting his wailing cry.

Charlotte's nerves were on edge. There was something oppressive about this dingy neighborhood, dominated by the great, ugly prison building which had suffered so many restorations that it now looked like some dismal château with tufts of wild flowers clinging to its walls.

It was a lonely place. A feeling of desolation clutched at the heart here, as if the big familiar city had been left behind and one were plunged instead into some medieval wilderness of narrow alleys in which countless souls had lived and died.

Charlotte retraced her steps. The prison doors swung open.

She stood very still. There was a strange, sweet taste in her mouth, a sickness and heartburn, as though her stomach were being turned inside out like a pulled chicken or a gutted fish. People appeared in the open doorway. For some reason she had expected Thomas to be on a stretcher but he was on his feet, walking upright between two nuns. Their starched white head-dresses dipped and fluttered like seagulls about his shoulders. His big frame seemed to tower above them in the shapeless overcoat which hung about him.

All she could see of him was the top of his head and a mop of untidy hair. A yard or two from the carriage he freed himself irritably from the nuns' restraining hands and crossed the remaining space to the coach unaided. It gave under his weight with a soft sigh, like a woman's.

To Charlotte, it seemed as if her own body bowed in sympathy. To know that Thomas was so close—

Aurore called to her from the coupé but she did not hear her.

The wind changed suddenly, blowing from the east and bringing with it a smell of damp earth and trees from the Jardin des Plantes. Charlotte shivered at the sharp breath. The sun went in and the street looked quite different, as though some gigantic shadow were devouring the district, house by house. The gloom, together with a foretaste of rain in the wind, brought out all the hidden city smells, making everything around suddenly more solid and real.

Charlotte saw as though for the first time the blind, immemorial walls lining the street of the living, a woman walking there, the carriages drawn up at the curb and herself standing motionless on the pavement trying to seize upon this fleeting instant of her life, this moment with neither past to run from nor present hope.

But it was no good. She was utterly lost and bewildered. She was possessed by a great and growing alarm which seemed to reach every nerve in her body until she could no longer tell where it would end. Thomas penetrated her every pore like the dank, lifeless air around her. It chilled her and she shivered, a dragonfly pinned, still living, to the background of the dark street.

Everything she had thought and decided about Frédéric and herself a moment before receded into a past utterly distant, real certainly, but no longer important. She was suddenly alive. It was weeks since she had been so conscious of the weight of her body.

She shuddered as if at the first intimation of illness which heralds the remorseless progress of a disease. It was almost as if her body were experiencing a sympathetic echo of Thomas's own malady.

Aurore called again. This time Charlotte heard and looked round vacantly. The carriage was only a few yards away but Charlotte seemed to see it in another dimension of existence. She was joined to the black coach by an actual, physical bond, tied to Thomas by the mysterious thread which links two beings who have loved so closely that they retain the imprint of their union, even to the obliteration of their original form.

Nothing she had ever thought she knew about her love for Thomas seemed to have any relevance now. This tenderness for him was something she had not known was in her, something quite different from desire, with its need to attract or subdue. This was a symbiosis, a physical dependence on him like a voice in the blood—they were coupled like wild beasts and even in this great city she knew his scent.

Aurore called out and rattled angrily at the door handle which had stuck and refused to open. Still Charlotte did not move.

She was listening with pride and submission to the voice of instinctive truth inside her. She had ears for nothing else. She realized at last that by coming to this place today she had merely been following that instinct which was better and wiser than herself.

She began to run towards the black coach. Aurore saw her and got out to follow, troubled and intrigued by an overflow of feeling which she did not understand, for all the excesses of her own nature.

Paul was still standing at the curb. When he saw

Charlotte coming towards him he shut the carriage door quickly.

"Paul, let me in."

She spoke with passionate urgency. A muscle twitched in Paul's cheek and his small eyes were pale and bright behind his spectacles.

"Let me see him."

"No."

"Please, I beg of you."

Her voice was low and hard. There was a light of battle in her eyes. They confronted one another, careful to keep their voices down. Paul stood firmly blocking the doorway.

"Becque is very ill and in a dreadful mood. He will not see anyone. Do not insist. I cannot bear these hysterics. You can only do him harm."

"You will not let me?" she said, her voice shaking.

"No, I will not."

"Come along," said Aurore who was standing close behind her although Charlotte had not heard her approach. Charlotte watched the carriage move away, increasing the distance between them. She wanted to go after it but Aurore refused.

"We have done all we could to help you and your friend, my dear. What do you hope to gain by going? Be sensible—" Aurore spoke fretfully and the kid-gloved hand she laid on Charlotte's arm was soft and limp.

"Charlotte, you have nothing to hope for, you know—he is not the man for you. We have done what we could. In the end he would only make you unhappy, my dear. Do you really think it is normal the way he and his friends are always in and out of prison?"

When Charlotte made no answer she went on: "I dare say you will tell me that there is no freedom of thought these days but do not ask me to believe that all these men are disinterested! Move over and let me sit down. They are dreaming of power like all the rest. As for their theories about equality, they make me laugh. I know the poor and their troubles. None better. Nothing will ever change them. All they think about is getting drunk! Believe me, they like their dirt. If they didn't they would get out of it."

"Not everyone has charms to sell," Charlotte said.

"Do not try to vex me, my dear," Aurore said tartly. "There is nothing to prevent your doing the same."

"Where I come from we may pawn our silver if the worst comes to the worst but we don't prostitute ourselves." The words were uttered with a certain pride. Charlotte thought of her home and family. Her respect and admiration for the rather conventional standards of morality in which she had been brought up were only increased by her own failure to maintain them. She could afford to throw them in the face of this other woman just because they were not hers. She felt a rush of pride in them, saw them gleaming like hereditary honors pinned to her breast.

Without quite understanding the reason for this pride, it seemed to Aurore that Charlotte's answer was dictated by pure snobbery. She herself was painfully sensitive to anything which reminded her of her own poor and common upbringing. She gave what she hoped was a stinging laugh.

"Certainly, you are very bourgeois, my dear. Where *you* come from prostitution requires a marriage contract."

The carriage jogged on. Neither spoke. Charlotte because she felt the uselessness of argument, Aurore, to whom the thought of anyone else's contempt was almost unendurable, because she was very upset. At last it was more than she could bear. She put out her hand and touched Charlotte's with a quick careless gesture. These sudden caresses were among her most irritating traits, for she bestowed them indiscriminately on all her friends as idly as a person sprinkling holy water on the tomb of some distant forbear.

"Oh well," she said in a small voice—her little-girl voice—"let us not quarrel, my dear. It is all so silly. We women should stick together; after all we are all the same in the end, you know. And so are men. They are not worth grieving over. They do not give a fig for our virtue. Believe me, child, I have lived. You can be sure they love their horses better, if they have any, and the majority of them would rather change their mistress than their tailor." She shrugged. "Do not deceive yourself, my dear. Every one of them, from the humblest to the greatest, will admire you until they have had you and then despise you ever after. In the long run, the only women they prize are the expensive ones, because otherwise they would be obliged to despise themselves for paying and they could not bear that." She laughed unpleasantly. "Life is a jungle. We must take what we can while there is still time. Don't listen to all that idealistic nonsense. Men will never change at heart. You deserve an easy time. With your looks you could be a countess at least."

She fumbled in her reticule for her box of face powder and began studying herself critically in the tiny mirror, too small to contain all her features at once. One huge bright eye peered back at her with, below it, the stretched skin of her cheek. The keen February light showed up the web of fine lines under the heavy plastering of paint.

Aurore closed the little box with a snap, and sat with a remote, unhappy expression on her face. Absorbed in the memory of that bright eye above the faded cheek she forgot both Charlotte at her side and the streets around them.

Charlotte felt sorry for her. She could guess at the fear Aurore felt at the prospect of losing her beauty. If she had ever been tempted to fall in with her friend's reasoning, the glimpse of that anxious look in the mirror would have cured her.

Youth and beauty were Aurore Dumoulin's stock in trade. For years she had lived by drawing more heavily on that capital. Now, in spite of her marriage, in spite of Bryan's fortune, she was still haunted by the fear which beset the courtesans of old whose prosperity declined with their fading looks.

Poor Aurore. Charlotte was so far removed from her now, released from the fascination aroused by Aurore's life, which had once seemed to Charlotte the very height of civilized luxury. Vanity coupled with the desire to know had drawn her to seek Aurore's company.

No, they had nothing in common. They belonged to different worlds. Not on account of their birth. It was not birth which made people different, but the way they chose to live. Aurore had elected to turn her back on all the things which had hurt her, her humbleness and poverty. It was so much easier to pretend ignorance of things one could not see. Aurore despised her mother and her own childhood.

Charlotte had been blind for years, but now she could no longer remain indifferent to the tragedy hanging over her time, which weighed so heavily on the lives of Thomas, of Gabin, of Frédéric—even when she was very small she had railed furiously against the injustice of the world. Somehow this integrity had kept her from falling too low, in spite of all the excesses she had indulged in. She recalled what Thomas had said to her one day about the cult of money and unbridled ambition. The Delobelles, selling their daughter to the highest bidder, Louise, wrecking her life by turning down honest suitors, Étienne's death and the wretchedness of Aurore and Delbrèze, Roslin's frenzied respectability, Horace Binet's passion for his *guinguette*—and all the rest of them, all those who flaunted their wealth or scraped a living in dire poverty, Frédéric with his useless education and Gabin wearing himself out tragically for his painting.

The world turned sour. She was conscious of the aftertaste of living, like the child's sweet that leaves a taste of acid on the tongue. She was torn by anger against the strong and pity for the weak. When she thought of Gabin she could have wept.

This knowledge of the world must have come to her slowly, unawares. It broke upon her suddenly, at the sight of Thomas's suffering, and at the sound of Aurore's tinkling voice repeating the facile, thoughtless mockery of all that was good and pure and which only served to cover her own shame.

All at once Charlotte wanted more than anything else to get out of the carriage and walk alone among the crowds on the boulevard. The feeling came as no surprise to her, although there had been a time when she hated and feared the thought of being lost in a crowd. But she stayed where she was, incapable of making the move to get out. Old habits of good manners instilled from earliest youth have more effect on the course of men's lives than the great events. Charlotte allowed herself to be carried on, too embarrassed to face Aurore's amazement if she fled. She told herself that in any case it made no difference where she was, realizing in her confusion of mind the difficulty of making any choice in this torn world of shadows.

4

CHARLOTTE COULD not bring herself to seek news of Thomas the next day or in the days that followed. She knew she lacked the courage to go to him herself, and was reluctant to beg her information from the concierge at the house in the Place Furstenburg, who was at best an unreliable source. And so she waited, hoping that time would be on her side. In a week or ten days Thomas might be better. He would have heard that he owed his release largely to her efforts, and how she had been behind Paul Boucher's determination to get him out of prison. She could not have said exactly what it was she hoped, perhaps that as he recovered Thomas would feel grateful for the fervour with which she had espoused his cause and would realize at last how much she loved him. Then when she saw him again, all the old grievances would have vanished, or at any rate faded, and they might at least start again as friends.

She hoped he would be grateful, or at least impressed. It seemed to her that from then on anything would be possible. But when, over a week later, she made up her mind to go and ask for news of him she was stunned and surprised to learn that he had left the Place Furstenburg. The concierge said he had gone away. Charlotte plucked up courage to go and ring his bell, but there was no answer. Completely at a loss, she went back to the concierge and was told that Léone Carier was on holiday and had probably gone to her relations in the country.

This came as a severe shock to Charlotte. The picture she had built up of a romantic reconciliation was shattered. She had got through those past days only by telling herself that she was certain to see Thomas at the end of the week and this time he would not dare to send her away. The thought had eased her pain and kept her love within reasonable bounds. But he was not there. His unexplained absence was like a rejection.

Where could he be? The old haunting sense of lost love returned.

To her own longing to see Thomas was added a morbid desire to know where he was and why he was hiding. Curiosity and jealousy worked on her mind to such a pitch that there was no room in it for anything but her obsession with seeing him.

She dogged Paul Boucher's footsteps in the hope that he might know something, but Paul disclaimed all knowledge and she had to accept that he was sincere. After this she determined to go the rounds of all Becque's friends. She made Paul take her to see Chaptal, who was kind but could tell her nothing. Next, she wanted by any means to see Daguerran who, according to Paul, was Thomas's closest friend. He might know where he was.

Frédéric had gone away to Provence. His father had died and he had to attend to his small inheritance. As far as Frédéric himself was concerned, his journey came at an opportune moment, for he felt a strong need to get away from Charlotte for a while and take his bearings after his bitter disappointment in her, and the kind of dead-end which their relations had now reached. So, released from all scruples on the absent Frédéric's account—not that his presence would have prevented her—Charlotte decided to go and find Joseph Daguerran.

This was a delicate proceeding. She knew very little of him, having only seen him once or twice with Thomas. She dared not go to his home and decided instead to look for him in Belleville, in the offices of *La Marseillaise* in the rue de Flandre. She knew that Daguerran worked there as editorial secretary. He was one of the few members of the staff who had escaped arrest on the night of 9 February.

Her courage was not equal to walking into the newspaper's busy main office, which was as noisy and crowded as a cattle market. She waited in the street listening to the babble of voices and watching the figures that crossed and re-crossed the open windows. Every now and then one would pause for a breath of fresh air and stand puffing his pipe at the open window.

Someone noticed her and a dozen curious heads appeared behind the glass. Charlotte stayed where she was, determined not to budge and before long they tired and went away.

At about five o'clock, a group of men came out for a drink. Charlotte thought she recognized Joseph Daguerran among them, a young man of medium height with a pleasant open face, framed in a short beard. She darted after them.

"Forgive me, messieurs—"

They all turned at the sound of her voice. Five pairs of eyes regarded her with interest. But already Daguerran had recognized her and stepped forward. His friends withdrew reluctantly, their disappointment clear on their faces.

Daguerran knew Charlotte by sight from seeing her with Thomas at the small café in the place Saint-André-des-Arts. However, he studied her with intense curiosity. Until now his ideas about her had been based on gossip. Before he met her, he had pictured a much more striking figure but from the very first he had been deeply attracted by her piquante little face with its fine features and delicate colouring and the expression of almost childish earnestness. He liked women like her. She was a little like his own wife, but prettier.

"Forgive me for intruding on you—" she gave him a shy smile, and he was conquered afresh by her charm. Daguerran was a simple, straightforward person but he had great intuition. He knew this woman as if she had been his sister. Charlotte, for her part, looked at him with liking, thinking that he was not unlike Gabin, only smaller and neater. He was a much more unusual person than a first glance might have suggested. To begin with, his beard was almost blond while his hair was dark. There were freckles on his nose, his brown eyes were alight with intelligence and the dimple at the corner of his mouth lifted him out of ordinariness and made him irresistible, like sparkling champagne. He looked what he was, gay and gallant. They were standing on the pavement directly in the path of the porters who were carrying bundles of copies of the paper to a hand-cart. Daguerran took her arm and they walked a little way round the corner. As they went, Charlotte talked to him quietly about Thomas, confiding her worries.

"I do not understand," Daguerran said with some surprise. "I thought he was at home. Are you sure that what you heard was the truth? Though I cannot conceive why it should not be. It is very strange. In fact I had been meaning to go and see him this very evening—surely he must have gone into the country to recuperate? But I have no idea where he might have gone."

"So you know nothing—I am sorry—"

This was by no means an adequate description of her feelings, and yet she had expected it, at least she believed so now. Perhaps she was merely protecting herself. Now her grief had ripened and become unbearable.

They had come to the canal Saint-Martin and stopped beside the sluggish waters in which the reflections of the near-by houses were distorted as though in a pewter mirror. Some children were throwing stones, cracking open the opaque surface of the mirror and momentarily dissolving the pale faces of the tumbledown dwellings which lined the canal, making them gape and writhe in a silent nightmare.

It was a bleak and dismal place. The only color came from a ray of sunshine striking the surface of the canal and turning the water there a brilliant green.

Daguerran looked curiously at Charlotte. She was biting her lip nervously. She was staring into space, apparently unable to break out of her unhappy trance and return to the real world. There were green lights in her eyes, like those in the canal.

He wondered where Becque could be. He was worried but disinclined to say so. His keen intuition told him that the love between Becque and this young woman was doomed, trouble lay like a tangible shadow over them.

Daguerran wanted to say something to comfort her but could think of nothing. He recalled Becque's face as he had talked about her on the night of the fire at the printers. Becque, he was sure, had erased her from his life completely. *This woman is dead to me*—and the look of tragic earnestness, the hatred in Thomas's eyes, not for his enemies alone, though they had brought about the death of one of his friends, but for life, for love, and for everything that made them worthwhile.

That night Daguerran had felt a gulf which divided him from Becque as clearly as he had felt Becque's own pain, the dragging weight of his past and his revolt. Such destructive fury frightened him. He saw suddenly that they lived in different worlds, and from then on his deep friendship for Becque became touched with fear. Daguerran fought the Empire because he was an idealist and an intellectual. He was a natural pacifist, a musician, a man of sense as well as sensibility. He loved his wife and his two children and looked forward to the time when he would be able to live in peace with them.

Becque, on the night of the fire, had sown the seed of doubt in Daguerran's beliefs and whole way of life. Even his marriage and his love for his wife and children began to seem suspect. In his heart, Daguerran had never really suffered deeply. Happiness came easily to him and so did hope. Becque's fury had revealed to him a degree of suffering he did not know existed. Daguerran had fought with words, but Becque with his life's blood.

Charlotte gave a weak smile. "Forgive me," she said, "I have troubled you for nothing."

He wanted to say that it was his pleasure to have been able to know her better, but the words would not come.

"I have probably been upsetting myself for nothing. No doubt our friend has gone to the country to recuperate, as you say, and will most likely return very soon. When I see him I shall be ashamed of having made such a fuss."

She made an effort to speak lightly but her face was still troubled and her eyes bright with tears.

"We quarrel a little sometimes you know," she said, feeling the need to say something in case Daguerran might know of her break with Thomas, "—but we are very old friends."

No, Daguerran thought, as he shook the hand she offered, no, you will never be friends. He has taken a path where there is no room for you. He thinks the road will be his salvation, but it may well prove his ruin.

She refused his offer to escort her to the omnibus.

A fortnight later, Charlotte learned from Aurore that Thomas had been seen in Paris at the offices of *La Marseillaise*, that he had apparently left again for the country, but would almost certainly be at Tours for the trial of Prince Bonaparte on 21 March.

Frédéric did not return from Provence until 19 March. He had been detained by some distant cousins who had tortuous designs on the young man's already minute inheritance. This consisted simply of the paternal house, considerably the worse for wear after standing for a hundred years in the mistral, a few decrepit olive trees and a vineyard situated some three miles away from the house. It was this circumstance which prompted the cousins to try and acquire it for a modest sum. They were really hoping to marry their daughter to the student, but Frédéric was bent on staying in Paris for a number of reasons and, lacking the least understanding of money matters, was prepared to let them have the land in return for an ancient sporting gun which he wanted, and did not know what to do with once he had got it.

The family, unable to account for his willingness to let the property go were convinced he must have some hidden motive and their attitude to their young relative became more suspicious than ever. Frédéric was supremely indifferent. He was delighted to be back in that sun-drenched landscape. To love Provence is like loving a woman. Frédéric loved the scorched, aromatic scent in the air and, above all, that smell of bare earth caressed by the sun, of sun-dried herbs and grasses and the dry river-bed turned by the heat into a snaking pathway of stones and baked clay, with here and there a patch of mud, running between the grey trunks of the willows.

His cousins, the Bédarious, could not understand his enthusiasm. They themselves were so deeply rooted in the land that they no longer saw it. Even their daughter, Ferdiline, a slim dark girl with calves burnished by the sun until they seemed a part of the very ground she trod, had her parents' nature, the tenacity of an olive tree clinging to the rocky earth. She liked Frédéric but was shocked by his wild ways. On the whole, they all decided, he was a little peculiar. Now that the vineyard had been secured to their own meager property they would be glad to see the back of him. Frédéric, realizing this, moved back to his father's house, which had been patched up a little by the local council for use as a posting station, since the real village was some way off. In any case, the house was so old and ruined that it would cost a great deal to repair. Frédéric abandoned it without too much regret.

However, he spent more than a week there by himself in perfect contentment. He loved the moors which stretched around him, the intense loneliness and warm melancholy of dwarf woods. He spent long hours walking with his shirt over his shoulder and his trousers tied round his ankles like a shepherd. He slept in the open and washed in ice-cold water. And he thought. Once again words began to have a whole meaning for him, round and crisp as the new bread delivered fresh from the baker's cart.

And, just as words began to have a real meaning for him again, so did his own life and feelings. He still thought about Charlotte for hours on end. She lived in him as a counter-point to the rhythm of his days.

He took stock. Never before had he loved and understood her so well as he did during his solitary stay in Provence. He wrote several letters to her but received no reply. This did not disturb him. He was alone, and his love was complete.

Even so he had to think about going back. Idiotically, he slipped a sprig of mimosa into his notecase, knowing quite well that he would never look at it and that it was a pointless thing to do because Provence would be gone from him as soon as the last olive tree was out of sight.

He arrived back in Paris on the evening of the 19th. His first action was to go and see Charlotte, up the front stairs this time. He felt like a different person, bolder and more forthright.

Charlotte was not at home and he would not wait although Annick, who opened the door, had asked him to come in.

On the fifth floor there was nothing for him to do. Millau was out somewhere. The house was very quiet. It was raining. Frédéric went down to see Valerie, dragging his bag with him.

Valerie was at home, of course. Clarisse was having her supper, her nose almost buried in her plate and her little head moving watchfully from side to side like a small dog at some forbidden meat. She went on flinging the soup into her mouth, her eyes fixed warily on Frédéric.

"You're back," said Valerie, "and you have not eaten. Do you want some soup?"

She questioned him about his father's death and his inheritance. He answered her in monosyllables. He asked where Charlotte was and Valerie said she did not know. After this there wes a certain constraint between them and in the end they went out for a stroll.

At last Frédéric saw Charlotte on her way home. He hurried upstairs two at a time, and caught up with her on her doorstep. She looked surprised to see him and opened the door quickly.

She was surprised to see how well he was looking, as bronzed and wild as a shepherd boy, his eyes startlingly blue in the tanned face. Charlotte seemed to dread being alone with him and made the excuse that she had to go out and do some shopping. Frédéric went with her, pretending not to notice her agitation and telling her all the things he had been attempting to tell Valerie not long before. He was very calm. Not she. He thought she was looking ill. On their way back, she paused in the gateway and leaned against the wall. Her face was very pale.

"You are not well," he said.

"A little tired, that is all." But on the stairs she suddenly admitted that she did feel unwell and said apologetically that she wanted to be alone, to sleep.

"I will see you tomorrow," he told her.

But the next day Charlotte was not there.

"Valerie, tell me where she is."

"I am telling you she has gone to Niort."

"Just like that, without a word to me?"

"She had family business—"

"You are lying."

"Don't be so silly."

The date was the 20th. Charlotte had gone without a word to Frédéric and he sat in Valerie's workroom for half an hour tormenting her with questions.

"Floquet lady not gone to Niort. Gone somewhere else. Heard her talking to my mamma. Said she was going to Tours."

Clarisse, who had been quietly playing with her doll in the corner of the room, suddenly proffered this information.

"Be quiet, you naughty little tell-tale. You will be punished for telling stories."

"Valerie, tell me the truth. You are the one who is lying."

"She did go to Tours. Not making it up."

Clarisse faced her mother squarely with stubborn defiance.

"Valerie, I must know."

"Very well, she has gone to Tours. Now are you satisfied? They all went to gape at the trial of Prince Bonaparte. You'd think it was a sight-seeing trip, like going to a wedding. She's not doing any harm, just a little amusement. After all, she's young, isn't she? And she can't wait until you've got the price of a shirt!"

He stared at her, noting her flushed face and uncomfortable air. After a moment's silence he asked:

"What train is she catching?"

"How should I know? Do you think I've got a timetable?"

He went out and slammed the door without answering. Valerie watched, frowning, through the window as he walked away then caught the child to her and hugged her while Clarisse dried her eyes on her pinafore.

In the train, Charlotte was to share a compartment with Aurore and Delbrèze.

The two women were alone. Delbrèze was still smoking a cigarette on the platform before getting into the stuffy train.

"You do not look well," Aurore was saying, although the face she was studying in the pocket mirror was her own.

Charlotte said nothing. She was unusually pale. Disturbed by her silence, Aurore persisted. "Really? There's nothing wrong? You are not sorry you came? It is a chance to see something of the countryside and anyway, all Paris will be there—"

"It is not all Paris I am going to see."

"I know, I know. It is Thomas Becque you are going to see! Confess that it is the thought that he may be in Paris and may take this train which is making you behave like a cat on hot bricks. . . ."

"I am sure he will not be on this train," she said.

"But he will be there, Boucher told me that for certain only yesterday."

"I dare say."

Charlotte was on edge and kept looking at the small silver fob watch she carried. She turned to the window just as Delbrèze got into the compartment.

She saw a man in the distance, running, thrusting his way through the barrier in spite of the protests of the railway employee at the gate.

It was Frédéric. He had not seen her. She shrank back a little, peeping to see what he was doing without being seen herself.

He was running but the train was already pulling out and gathering speed. He was obliged to stop, panting, while she stayed motionless and angry in her seat.

To picture what Tours was like during those few days of the trial of Pierre Bonaparte one would have to conjure up the picture of that glorious renaissance when all the dazzling luxury and splendour, the revels and intrigues of a leisured and decadent court, could be transported to the banks of the river Loire to gratify a French king's whims.

It was as if the soft, rich landscape of Touraine awakened from a long sleep. The aristocratic city of Tours, with its restrained and elegant architecture, was thronged with carriages and the jostle of a colorful, light-hearted crowd. People from all walks of life, from the capital and from the other large provincial cities, were gathered there.

The hotels were full to overflowing. People were paying exorbitant prices to sleep five in a room, in outhouses and even in stables and empty carriages.

The core of this tourist invasion was the horde of journalists who formed a race apart, filling two hotels and rending the air with their clamorous and contradictory opinions.

Despite the most optimistic preparations, the bakers slaved incessantly at their ovens and still there was a shortage of bread. Cellars were ransacked and hotel proprietors had no qualms in venting their ill-humor on their clients, certain that these were in no position to take their custom elsewhere.

Aurore Dumoulin had taken the precaution of writing the previous week to reserve three rooms in one of the hotels in the best part of the town, on the boulevard Heurteloup, very near the Palais de Justice. It was a wise precaution, because the hotel was packed and late-comers were being turned away remorselessly.

It was late when they arrived, after a journey of more than twelve hours. The foyer was filled with new arrivals, and for all the apparent comfort of the hotel, the dinner was poor.

The hotel trade in France was still in its infancy. Only the rich travelled at all extensively, to Normandy or to the various watering places, although the first commercial travellers were beginning to take over the railways and overnight hotels. Hotel proprietors were not accustomed to full houses and not organized to cope with them. Once out of the major cities, the traveller might think himself lucky, just as in the old, perilous days of the diligences, to find a bed with no bugs where the innkeeper would not rob him.

Although the hotel where Aurore, Charlotte and Delbrèze were staying in Tours had some pretensions to grandeur, this did not prevent the proprietor obliging them to pay two days in advance for fear they might abscond without settling the bill.

They were dead tired and thoroughly out of sorts.

Charlotte dropped miserably on to her bed and sank into a feather quilt placed on top of two soft mattresses. Before very long, discomfort forced her to get up again. It was very hot. She opened the window. She was not sleepy and wandered about vaguely examining the room, inspecting the water jug on the table and the battered chamber-pot concealed in a tiny cupboard beside the bed.

She began to unpack, scattering her belongings about the room. She was tired to death and yet felt no desire for sleep. Despite the lassitude of her movements she was a prey to a strange, restless excitement.

She went to the window, seeking fresh air. The weather was oppressive for the end of March, and stale smells of cooking rose up from the kitchen region, which opened on the yard below her window.

She could see figures moving about the open doorway. A man was standing at a big brownstone sink clattering vast piles of dishes. Charlotte stayed where she was, soothed by the darkness and familiar noises.

Suddenly, in the soft Touraine night, the man below at the sink started singing *O Sole Mio* in Italian. He had a fine, resonant voice with all the operatic qualities common to Italian tenors.

He must have finished his work. There seemed to be a number of people down there, because the tremulous notes of a mandolin soon joined in, accompanying the singer.

Charlotte listened, unexpectedly moved by this exotic serenade. At the end of every verse of the song, the mandolin played a little trill, a theatrical sobbing like a woman's melancholy laughter. The Italian words of love flowed like honey in the rich voice and with the warm, masculine tones and the trembling notes of the mandolin, touched her heart with a gentle sadness for the ways of love and all its sweet complaint.

To Charlotte, standing at the window, it seemed as though all the harlequins of Naples were moving past below, strutting in sunlit streets to the sound of tambourines among shouting, barefoot children and girls with languid eyes.

Listening, she saw in her mind's eye the Italy Louise and Étienne had never reached, where she herself had never gone with Thomas, and experienced all the bitter-sweetness of an unattainable journey. Below her, the Italian tenor was still singing. Italians, she thought, knew more about love and betrayal than any other men and would sing on until the end of time. The Italian language was filled with the intoxication of love. Her heart swelled and her eyes filled with tears of happiness and regret.

She spoke Thomas's name softly, overwhelmed by the sudden conviction that he was here, in this town, perhaps even close by. She could feel his presence like a wind from the sea. She had fled from Paris without one word of explanation to Frédéric, rejecting all compromise. Now her life was bounded by the narrow limits of this city of Tours which, until today, had been no more than a name to her. Now it held her fate. She had thrown in all her past life.

The sound of the mandolin died away, leaving an aching silence. The kitchen smells returned, and the night was made fast once more in its ordinary, humid surroundings.

The trial opened the next morning. The streets of Tours were noisy with carriages and the clip-clop of horseshoes playing swift arpeggios on the cobbles. A motley crowd had invaded the city and the bright colours of the women's dresses gave the scene the barbaric splendor of a Mexican religious procession. Parisiennes, dressed in the latest fashion, clutched one another and tittered at the outmoded crinolines of the provincial ladies. More than one country housewife had got out her best silk dress, kept hanging in dust sheets and brown paper all year round in the loft, with its stiffening hoops of steel or basketwork, to honor the occasion.

Now, dressed up to the nines, they had come 'to the trial', as once or twice in their lives they would go to the city to see the unveiling of a monument, to catch a glimpse of the emperor or an important wedding. Country life was not so full of excitement that they could afford to miss a splendid opportunity like this. But though they might have spent five hours the night before starching their ruffles and ribbons, stiffening their petticoats and adorning their bonnets and had thought themselves so fine, brought face to face with these daring Parisian clothes, gowns moulded smoothly to the figure in front and flaring into an audacious little bustle behind, they experienced a sudden, painful disillusionment.

The crowd was concentrated along the two broad avenues which divided the town and ended at the Palais de Justice. This edifice, which was situated in the main square at the corner of the boulevard Heurteloup had been built in 1840, in the austere style suited to its function. It had never been meant to hold such a crowd. Cavalry pickets did their best to control the mass invasion.

Even so there was a stampede. The pickets were swept aside and the crowd poured into the building only to be halted and turned back to the doors by those already inside. It was as if the building disgorged its human contents, which then returned again to the assault. Inside, the corridors echoed with the sound of an assembly in session. Supporters of opposing sides, meeting in the passages, exchanged loud opinions and insults.

In the main hall itself, the witnesses, those supporting Prince Bonaparte and those defending the memory of Victor Noir, had been kept apart, forming two hostile and angry groups.

Delbrèze, as a member of the Press, had been able to get Charlotte and Aurore into the building but once inside they were jammed into a corner at the back of the chamber behind a densely packed crowd. Charlotte could see nothing. Catching sight of an empty place at the end of the back row, next to a good-looking, youngish man with a waxed moustache, she elbowed her way towards it. She had thought he might be keeping the place for a friend but when he saw her eyeing it, the man immediately moved the carefully brushed hat which he had placed on the bench for safey. Too surprised to do anything but take advantage of the unexpected blessing, Charlotte sat down.

Her seat did not afford her a good view of the packed court and she soon discovered that her neighbor had in fact been laying a subtle trap for some unsuspecting lady in the hope of finding some distraction in case the trial should pall.

She gazed at the many black-clad backs before her,

especially at the ranks of the journalists, and after a moment was almost sure that Thomas was not there.

It was suffocatingly hot and there was an incessant buzz of conversation.

The judges took their seats. The noise died away and silence reigned. Most of those standing had found seats.

The chamber was too small to give the historic trial quite its due of grandeur. All that could be seen of Prince Bonaparte, seated in the dock between two gendarmes, was a hunched, dark-clad back view and a semi-profile. He was fidgeting nervously.

The charge was read through at great speed and the Prince's examination began. It passed without incident. Pierre Bonaparte was very pale and his hoarse voice with its strong Corsican accent sounded squeaky and uncertain.

He was clearly making an effort to control himself. His whole appearance announced a man of outsize appetites and dangerous temper. He looked easily roused and of uncommon strength. His voice grated unpleasantly on the ear, betraying the violence and inner conflict of a man at war with his own nature, and he aroused little sympathy. He avoided looking directly at anyone.

Victor Noir's friend, Ulric de Fonvielle, came forward to describe the crime and related how Pierre Bonaparte had fired on his friend and himself without warning or provocation on their part.

The court held its breath. Pierre Bonaparte gazed around the room in an attempt to challenge Fonvielle, but finally dropped his eyes and turned his head aside.

There was a low murmur from the audience. Next came the evidence of Paschal Grousset, the journalist who had taken up Victor Noir's cause, uninvited. His statement evidently annoyed the accused. Grousset appeared flanked by two gendarmes and he, like Rochefort and his friends and a number of other journalists accused by the government of subversive activities, was under arrest.

Charlotte's neighbor was eager to point out to her the chief personages. He indicated Rochefort, standing on the right. At the mention of a name she knew was associated with Thomas, she looked up quickly. She recognized Rochefort from cartoons and caricatures she had seen. He too had a gendarme on either side of him. He was being held in Sainte-Pélagie and had come to the court under close watch by special permission.

The first session came to an end. The crowd began to melt away and still Charlotte had not set eyes on Thomas. She clung to the hope that he might have arrived late and been unable to get in. Boucher, from whom they had their information, had certainly told them he would be at Tours.

The evening seemed endless. Delbrèze, who had a knack of meeting everyone in Paris, had contrived to meet every important visitor from the provinces. No one could have had more acquaintances and fewer real friends. But his acquaintances were useful to him and filled a void in his empty life, in which appearances made up for the absence of real feelings. For at bottom, Delbrèze disliked and feared solitude.

Consequently he had a ready-made invitation to offer his companions from a local landowner, Monsieur Richet, who had some pretensions as a leader of intellectual society in Tours, on account of some early experience with a local newspaper which he had abandoned to take up the more promising career of a "man of letters."

Delbrèze had met him at the time of the Universal Exhibition of 1867, when Richet had visited Paris and scraped acquaintance among the journalistic circles of the capital. He had been attracted by Delbrèze's flow of conversation and his elegant cynicsm. Given a comfortable income derived from family estates and vineyards, which paid for the upkeep of his house in Tours and provided dowries for his daughters, Richet was able to leave his property in the more capable hands of his tenants and play at the aesthete among the leading lights.

Delbrèze had written to Richet the previous week, reminding him of an invitation which the latter had somewhat incautiously delivered when carried away by his experiences in Paris.

Charlotte was rendered speechless by the information that this letter had been answered promptly by an invitation from Richet to his house. It seemed to her that she would never understand Delbrèze. He was capable of a littleness quite unexpected in one of his cynical and world-weary disposition.

She was thinking of this as she sat with Aurore in Richet's handsome drawing-room. The house was a renaissance-style building with tall windows and wrought-iron balconies. The room had been divided at some time but still retained something of its former splendor. The lighting was by candles. Outside, the great trees arching over the drive seemed listening to the quiet of a provincial night.

From time to time, a carriage passed, breaking the silence which belongs to such houses, and to the virtues and regrets which ripen within their walls. But the carriage was a visiting one and on other evenings the only sounds to penetrate this panelled room with its chimney-piece of white stone would be a man's belated footsteps in the street outside, or the light piano pieces played by the two young daughters of the house.

They were playing just then. A duet by Mozart. It was sweet, childish music, swelling towards the end like a rippling stream swollen with spring rains.

The girls were twins, just eighteen. Both had fair hair and gentle faces, with high round foreheads and the rosy cheeks of youth.

Charlotte, seated beside Aurore on a sofa, forgot the cup of chocolate she held in cramped fingers. She gazed vacantly at the two girls and at their identical, small plump hands, each with the same dimples and rings, dancing lightly over the keys of the piano. How good they looked. A tall, brown-haired youth, sporting a pair of would-be ferocious side whiskers stood by them, turning the pages of their music.

Neither his whiskers nor his ferocious expression could disguise the extreme youthfulness of the boy's countenance. Spots of acne vied with the shadowy growth which lay, like a veil, over his somewhat receding chin.

Aurore was yawning, concealing her boredom behind her fan and smiling whenever she caught anyone's eye on her. Delbrèze, very much at his ease, was chatting to Richet and two other men at the far end of the room. The portly Richet, in a loose, flowing tie, his white hair artistically tousled, had the cheerful, bloated appearance of a man who lived well, gorging himself on small, everyday pleasures. Madame Richet was like her daughters, and looked almost as young, with the same mild, self-effacing air. She was watching them as they played, head bent in an attitude of worship.

Charlotte looked at them all. Just as she had thought of Italy the night before, so now tonight this salon in Tours, with its dark casements looking out over the broad, quiet avenue, reminded her of Niort. When the shutters were closed, she heard again behind closed eyelids the remembered clang of metal on metal. She was back again in Niort. The boy, standing there, might have been Étienne turning over the music while she played and Louise sang. She wondered which of the two girls he was in love with, or perhaps he loved them both.

A wave of nostalgia swept over her, enveloping her like a shroud. One lived each hour more than once, now and in the memory.

She would have liked to stay for a long time at the Richets' because she was really in Niort, not Niort as it was but Niort as it had been. She had a heady sense of being young again with all her life before her.

But they had to go. All the way through the quiet streets, Charlotte walked in a remote and gentle dream while Aurore beside her took her arm, stumbling on the uneven stones and cursing the town and all who lived in it. Delbrèze walked ahead impatiently, pausing at every corner to wait for them so that they did not miss their way in the ill-lighted streets.

"Is anything the matter?" Aurore asked, disturbed by Charlotte's silence.

She shook her head.

Her thoughts were far away with Thomas, not Thomas as he was at that moment or as she hoped to find him but as she had known him long ago in Niort, in her father's house, talking about God in a mocking, sardonic way that made her blush for shame. In her recollection he was younger, and his eyes unbelievably blue. He had loved her at first sight.

He had called her sweetheart the first time they met. He was laughing at her. He had always laughed at her, or perhaps at himself—because he loved her.

Oh God, she thought, how can we stop ourselves throwing away what we have? Do we ever learn? Or, when we have, must it always be too late?

The streets of Tours by night had a sad, provincial charm.

EARLY THE next morning, they made their way to the Palais de Justice for the second day of the hearing. The session was disappointing. Thomas did not appear.

That night, Charlotte was determined to go to bed early and sleep at all costs.

The next day was the 23rd. People in the courtroom were beginning to know one another and exchange smiles.

Two journalists got into an argument in one of the corridors. A blow was struck and cards exchanged but immediately their friends intervened. All that could be seen were two groups of men in dark clothes waving their arms and legs in a grotesque pantomime, and shouting at one another in deep, resonant voices.

But the indifferent crowd passed them by, drowning their voices in the soft murmur of taffeta and silk. Gentlemen found their dignity somewhat impaired by the constant obligations to bend and retrieve perfumed handkerchiefs dropped by their ladies. Little girls craned their necks with innocent coquetry to inspect the cherished whiteness of their shoes.

Charlotte carved her way through the crowd like a knife through butter, leaving a swathe of riveted masculine eyes behind her. Her hope of seeing Thomas had revived with the morning, as fresh as if the day before had never been.

"He's not here, I can't see him," Aurore whispered in her ear from time to time, as her head pivoted this way and that.

As if Charlotte did not know. She seemed to have eyes in the back of her head.

They had almost to fight their way into the courtroom.

Members of the Press entered through a side door, the bulk of the crowd by the main entrance. Although the doors were wide open, the crush in the doorway was made worse by the fact that no one was willing to give way an inch. The ushers did their best to control the flow.

"Patience, ladies and gentlemen, if you please. There will be room for everybody, one at a time, now, please." The crowd swept by unheeding, the men crushed back against the walls like so many helpless beetles by an irresistible many-coloured tide of hooped skirts.

Those still outside stood on tiptoe and craned their necks to get a sight of what was going on within. Aurore thrust purposefully forward dragging Charlotte with her. Charlotte, who had always hated crowds, felt a momentary surge of panic. Only the hope of seeing Thomas inside prevented her from turning back.

Aurore was in front. In the angle formed by one of the pillars, three young women were chatting vivaciously, their swaying bustles giving them the air of three young female centaurs, curvetting in front of the man who was half-hidden by the pillar. One of them stepped aside and Charlotte found herself gazing with astonishment into the face of the young man who was with them. It was Worski.

He stood with his back to the wall, his body rigid and a faint smile at the corner of his lips, but his black eyes shone with all the provocative brilliance of a pair of diamonds in a maharajah's crown. He was studying the crowd with a brooding, ironical gaze which belied the slight smile with which he honored his companions.

He had discarded his old black frock coat and was wearing a suit of dark or royal blue. The clothes looked new, and the waisted coat was moulded across the shoulders without a single wrinkle, like a second skin. His trousers, unnecessarily tight even for a fashion which left little to the imagination, followed the outline of his legs and dropped carelessly over the heels of his light, pointed shoes. From the side, his long, slender figure with sharply accented calves made him look like a dancer.

People, the women especially, turned to look at him as they passed with swift, predatory glances. He undid his jacket a little because of the heat, revealing, over his high-necked white shirt, a tight-fitting, violet waistcoat with silver buttons. He turned to survey the crowd and then turned half back again to face his companions. His ash-blond hair, worn rather long, curled thickly over his collar.

There was something feminine in the attraction of that fair hair brushed negligently back on the man's neck, which caught the eye of those women who saw him and filled them with a dreamy sense of protectiveness. Women who demanded from their husbands the utmost correctness in matters of dress, melted at the sight of this cox-comb with his barbaric features and his girlish hair. But then, most women are defenseless when men turn their own weapons against **them**.

Worski was like a miracle to them, a living miracle of even greater perfection than the romantic heroes of their dreams, whose stereotyped good looks would almost certainly end by boring them in real life, and of whose ultimate absurdity they were secretly well aware.

But for the present, their eyes reverted to him constantly, following his slightest movements. Dawdling in the corridor, waiting for the crush in the doorway to clear, they soon saw that he was really alive and their amazement changed to interest and excited curiosity. Timid glances grew bolder and more lewdly speculative, estimating his size and strength and lingering appreciatively on the sturdy legs revealed by the clinging fabric, with the unrestrained frankness common to even the most respectable women once the time of their first modesty is past.

Worski standing hemmed in by the crowd pretended not to notice the attention of which he was the object. But Charlotte, hidden behind Aurore, was aware of it and suffered from a kind of shame at the Pole's flamboyant charm which made him such a dainty morsel for feminine eyes.

It was not just that he was handsome. A search among those present would have revealed a good many men with faces which, for delicacy and harmony of features, might have rivaled or outshone Worski's according to the classic notion of beauty, or the fashion of the day. The Pole's magnetic attraction lay precisely in that contrast of sweetness and savagery which his face revealed: the high, flat cheek-bones and huge, black eyes, the straight nose with its flaring nostrils and the beautifully chiselled mouth with a tendency to fullness in the lower lip ... these, with his boyish fair hair, powerful neck and the languid grace of his elegant form, and the brooding sensuality of his gaze made Worski pure provocation.

Suddenly Charlotte found herself hating Worski as though he had been standing there naked. More than anything, she hated the remembrance of those feelings he had once aroused in her. Obsessed by the thought of her love for Thomas, her hopes of seeing him took on a kind of religious fervor. Like any woman very much in love, she experienced a saintly revulsion at the thought that any other man could bring her pleasure.

Except for Frédéric, whom she never succeeded in regarding as a lover, Charlotte had lived since Thomas's release from Sainte-Pélagie in a state of total absorption in him and complete renunciation of all others.

Her color had risen, despite herself, and she hoped that Aurore hid her from Worski's eyes. Her heart thudded uncomfortably. And yet the fact that Worski should be there, in Tours, against all expectation, was like a malign stroke of fate. One could go for weeks without meeting someone, only to come face to face with them just when one was with someone else. Suddenly, Charlotte was certain that the miracle which had brought Worski to this corridor in the Palais de Justice heralded some such stroke of fate. Because Worski was there, she knew that Thomas would come.

The crowd surged towards the door. Charlotte tried to slip past unobserved by Worski. Then it all happened very quickly. He saw her. Their eyes met over a sea of flowered hats and with a stiff bow to his companions who were clearly no more than chance acquaintances, he began thrusting his way towards her. For a moment she thought that he would not succeed, that there were too many people in the way and she would be able to slip quickly into the chamber. The purpose which had brought her to Tours made any company undesirable, and especially that of anyone as striking as Worski. A cowardly impulse made her want to melt and disappear into the crowd.

But she had reckoned without the effect of the Pole's charm. The crowd parted to let him through. With a muttered word of apology here and there, Worski passed through like a flame.

He caught up with Charlotte and clutched her arm in the crowd. As they went through the door a hundred pairs of eyes turned to watch them.

"Good morning," Charlotte said coldly.

She tried to free herself from Worski's grip on her arm. He appeared to think she needed protecting because he forged a path through the crowd, shielding her with his body with an aggressive masculinity which Charlotte found ridiculous, the more so since his blue-clad shoulders blocked her view of the room.

She wished she could escape and glared firmly in the opposite direction to demonstrate that their companionship was pure chance and that she wished to be alone. He appeared not to understand and regarded her amiably.

"What are you doing here?" he asked.

His eyes were warm and glowing, full of calm certainty. His face was too close to hers. She felt for him the loathing one feels for a foreigner at a time of patriotic exaltation. She was furious with him for being so close. She hated the sound of his voice and the deep, foreign accent which made people turn to look at him.

"Won't you tell me why you are here, in this town?" he asked again.

"Why are you?" she asked, to avoid the necessity of a reply. She could have screamed with fury at the loudness of his voice, but only the unnatural brilliance of her eyes betrayed her anger. She pretended to be busy thrusting back the sea of people still flowing in through the door. The room seemed packed, and yet, somehow they were still managing to get in.

Everyone found a place at last. Charlotte was jammed up against the wall between a woman in a crinoline and a bearded man whose watch-chain dug into her ribs. There was no way out. A wave of misery swept over her. Her fear of crowds made her feel terribly helpless. Worski was standing in front of her, straining against the pressure of the crowd, but from time to time he was pushed against Charlotte and for an instant she was aware of the warmth of his body and of the forgotten smell of him, an unfamiliar, musky smell of amber and cologne with a hint of mustiness which still seemed to cling to his clothes for all their apparent newness, taking her mind back to the dank house in the Marais.

She wondered desperately whether Thomas was in the room. She could see nothing but backs and heads and hats. The president of the court was examining a witness. His voice came muffled, as though through ten feet of water. Charlotte leaned back against the wall feeling suddenly faint.

"I came to Tours to make a report on this trial," Worski was saying. "I have a specific—no, I mean a special interest, in this trial, in this affair. Sometimes I have difficulties with your French language. It is—deceptive—" He brought his words out slowly, as though he were offering a gift of rare pearls which that rasping voice with its foreign intonation had fashioned specially for his hearer.

But to appreciate Worski's voice it was necessary to be in a state of grace such as Charlotte had known on that long ago evening in his house. Today Charlotte was not in a state of grace. The thought of Thomas obsessed her to the exclusion of all else. Stuck there behind this wall of humanity, hemmed in by this man, it seemed to her that something terrible must be happening outside, and that she should be there, running with the rest, seeking for Thomas in the maddened crowd.

She raged against Worski as she might have raged against the part of herself which kept her there, against all her frivolity and her old unworthy self. Worski, with his beauty, was transformed in her mind into a pagan idol to be worshipped and destroyed.

"I came to see you," he was saying, "I wanted to see you again. I thought of you day and night. I would not fight it because to be strong it is not enough to conquer the desire of something. Discipline is simply a kind of pride, is it not?"

She did not answer and tried to slide away, pretending she was being pushed. He held her back.

"What I am trying to say is, discipline without consent—which does not make us grow—you understand—it is not the sacrifice which matters, it is the reason for it. I was thinking of you. You know—I am sure that you know. It has never happened to me before, to live with the thought of another, of a woman—one does not speak of these things, I know, and yet I am telling you—I am not ashamed to tell you."

He paused and went on: "I came to the rue Monsieur-le-Prince. I waited but you did not come. I dislike waiting. Meekness is something that does not come easily to me."

"You over-estimate your own importance," she said coldly.

He gave her a long look.

"Yes. I know."

He was silent before going on. "I am important because I exist. Everything that lives is important. I do not cling to life, you know that, do you not?"

For a moment she was disarmed by the sudden seriousness of his voice. He looked at her gravely, and his beautiful eyes were like a cloudy sky, a vast, warm universe, without beginning or end.

"Everyone clings to life," she said.

"Why? Life means hope! But hope means doubt and suffering. I do not wish to hope—"

She was silent. She wished she need not listen to him, but he was not someone one could ignore. He demanded attention. Anger. There was a kind of simple nobility in him which she did not understand but which was once again having its effect on her. It was, almost, respect.

But she did not wish to restore him to favor too quickly and said indifferently:

"You are fortunate, you have everything. You must be loved, adored even—"

She hoped the tone of her voice was enough to show how little it meant to her.

"They do not love me," Worski said. "Women love not

me but an idea of me which is not true. And I have no men friends."

He was probably telling the truth. He shocked and disturbed people. His pride looked like conceit. He was not likely to achieve real human contact. He must have many enemies. Wherever he went he was a reproach to the ugly and a temptation to women.

"Why have you come to Tours?" he asked again.

"I came to look for someone."

"Who is he, this someone?"

He was staring at her earnestly, holding back the crowd with one arm braced against the wall.

"Someone—a man," she said, resenting his question.

"Are you in love with him?"

She did not answer, but made a hopeless attempt to elude his rock-like arm.

"Are you?" he said again harshly.

"Yes," she said. "Yes, yes, yes—"

She fell back against the wall, still repeating the word yes with a hysterical intensity, as if it were some terrible obscenity she were hurling in his face.

"Yes, yes, yes, yes, yes, YES—"

She was rocking herself backwards and forwards against the wall, careless of her neighbors. "Yes, yes, yes—" Somewhere beyond the wall of people was the court, laughter and shouting, the trial going on in another world. "Yes, yes, yes, yes—"

"Quiet," Worski said.

She met his eye and was silent. Her silence hung between them, dividing them, although he continued to look at her, with his body touching hers as he stood protecting her from the crowd. They were divided by worlds of incomprehension and estrangement.

He looked at her but there was nothing he could say. He might have been carved from hard metal. She did not understand his feelings and yet she sensed that she had hurt him. But if so, how? He was out of reach of pity and yet the very density of his tense figure, his warm, steady gaze, was a pain.

He knew she thought him hard and unfeeling. He had encountered too many reactions from people like this young woman to make any mistake. He was not hard. He was a foreigner, an exile, an expatriate, divided between two nationalities and any number of races. He was Polish but no more so than he was German or gypsy, like his mother's remote forebears. There was even Asiatic blood in him through a grandfather whose origins lay back in some far-eastern place. For all his white skin, he was a half-caste in blood and being.

He was torn between the tortured patriotism of the Pole and the spartan upbringing of his German boyhood, when in his fourteenth year, after the Russians had put down the Warsaw rebellion of 1863, he had joined his father in Prussia.

An impartial observer would have said that Worski was lacking in intelligence. He had no critical sense and his stoic principles were strongly imbued with romanticism. None the less, that greatness which women felt in him was real and placed him above mere heroics. His idealized love for his mother, combined with love of his unhappy country, a religious mysticism and longing for drama had made him until now an exceptional and lonely being with a deep and abiding hatred of all promiscuity, of all relations in love or friendship which fell below the ideal.

For all his narcissism, he both hated and feared his own beauty, and this dual conflict drove him to withhold himself rather than commit himself to any love which sprang from his unworthiest self. His rather superstitious faith in God only helped to strengthen this attitude.

On leaving his Prussian university, he had lived in Paris doing practically nothing to earn a living before embarking on his amateur attempt at journalism with *La Marseillaise*. He had gone there out of his need to enter the struggle at the side of those men he admired but his ideas were too confused and he was still too young, not yet twenty-one, although generally taken for older than he was. Until then, he had lived with the Countess Lievitz, who until his legal coming of age had control of the modest fortune left by his mother, the Countess Worska. Madame Lievitz herself was rich and had made Frank her heir since her own son was dead, but although she made believe to love Worski like her own son, the poor woman was in fact tormented by very different emotions which she did her best to conceal even from herself. As for Frank, he traded on her kindness and patience as any real son might have done, while at the same time half unconsciously allowing a hint of the gigolo creep in his manner towards her, for which in his more honest moments he reproached himself bitterly.

Worski looked at Charlotte. The pressure of the crowd thrust him against her, isolating them in their own corner, cut off from the people on either side. He looked at her. He had longed to see her again. He could be as mad loving her as he had been two months before in vowing he would not love her. ...

They were pressed close together and quite simply he bent his head and set his lips on hers.

She shrank away, her whole body filled with a vast, formless revulsion and loathing. He felt her stiffen but he did not let her go. It was the first time he had kissed a woman like this, a woman who was not a casual street-girl or one of those students' whores to be found in any university city.

And so he held her, firmly yet gently, almost timidly not daring to press too close. His eyes were open. To begin with, he touched her lips reverently and awkwardly but then, as his natural sensuality got the better of him, his mouth covered hers with a soft, abandoned languor and his lips nuzzled hers as silkily as the curled petals of a rose.

She dared not thrust him away because of the people all around them, for fear that they would turn round and see them and also from a kind of cowardice and monstrous fear that Thomas might be in the room and see her.

The idea that Thomas might be there pounded in her brain, overcoming her revulsion and loathing at the Pole's kiss. At that moment, she was thinking of Thomas's stubbornness and how she had lost him on account of Alphonse and of how he would condemn her now, with that withdrawn, brooding expression of a jealous man, incapable of distinguishing between what was important and what was not, or even of trying to understand. He was a normal, healthy man with an irritating rightness,

112

and narrow views of faith and happiness. He was far removed from the sophisticated decadence of a man like Delbrèze, or from the problems of one like Paul Boucher. Thomas was a rock, oppressive in his maleness, and yet she wanted him, she cried out for his hardness and his obstinacy. If he would only come and beat her, force her to be faithful or else kill her—

Worski released her. Charlotte turned away her head, refusing to look at him, wishing he would disappear. People had noticed and were looking at them. Girls in flowered hats were feasting their eyes on Worski, imprinting him on their memories for the long, lenten life to come in the rain-sodden countryside, with a husband, perhaps, who never spoke except on Sundays.

For the first time in her life Charlotte wished she were plain, to be lost and overlooked in a crowd. She had frittered away all her youth and hope. What was the use of anger now? It was her own fault that Worski was beside her. Two months earlier she had done her best to win him, he would have every right today to retort that she did not know what she wanted.

Worski continued to look at her with a new expression in his eyes, a sudden weariness which invaded her body. She was conscious, with a kind of indifference, of his foreignness, of the hidden elements of his nature which he must have inherited from some distant race, perhaps not even from Poland, but from Asia. There was something slow and cat-like about him. It was in the way he stood and in the droop of his eyelids. She sensed that to be with him would be like initiation into the forbidden rites of some strange creed. These differences might have made her reject him wholly, but Worski's youth and purity commanded respect and forbade any contempt. She knew it would not be so simple to erase him from her life.

The session was at an end and the crowd beginning to filter out of the door. Already Charlotte knew that Thomas was not there.

The trial lasted seven days. On the first six, Charlotte went and sat through the long, boring sessions while her hopes of seeing Thomas slowly dwindled in reality, while in her mind they retained the painful clarity of dreams that will not be forgotten.

On the fifth day—the trial was generally expected to last eight or nine—Aurore and Delbrèze, tiring of the arguments and interested chiefly in the verdict, proposed visiting some of the châteaux of the Loire but Charlotte would not go with them. She wanted to attend the court for fear of missing a single chance of seeing Thomas, should he come.

On the seventh day, tourists who had fallen off somewhat on the fifth and sixth flocked back once more and the court-house was again packed to suffocation.

On the three preceding days, Charlotte had seen Worski but he had merely bowed without daring to approach her. He was accompanied by a thin, dark young man with a pale face who seemed vaguely familiar to Charlotte. She was sure she had seen him once before, the day when she had so foolishly gone to look for Worski in the Châtelet square. From his accent, he seemed to be Polish.

Although she had arrived early, Charlotte was tired of the crowd and that day she found herself once again at the back of the room, after managing to find herself a seat on the other days. The session had begun and she was listening with half an ear when she saw Worski with his friend enter and come towards her. She was tired of standing and waiting and no longer felt even the desire to escape. Moreover, since Worski had dared to kiss her, she was less afraid of him because fear is generated by ignorance and suspicion. Worski had lost his mystery.

On this particular morning she was so depressed that she almost welcomed the young man's company. She smiled and asked him about his friend who, seeing him about to join her, had left him. Worski said his name was Vladimir Lojko and that he was Polish like himself. He said little more and seemed anxious to change the subject.

They were again close to the wall but this time side by side and the young man made no effort to decrease the distance.

The trial had reached the evidence of a certain Monsieur Touchet, a retired captain who was to testify to the

114

courage of Prince Bonaparte, accused, among other things, of having deserted his post before Zaatcha.

"I knew the Prince in Africa," Touchet stated with military precision, "and he was much admired for his courage and for the eagle stare common to his family."

There was a roar of laughter from the court.

"If that happens again, I shall have the court cleared at once," boomed the president, very red in the face.

The laughter died away slowly.

Touchet returned to his seat and Prince Bonaparte turned to the prosecuting counsel.

"You laughed just now, sir, at the words of the gallant Captain Touchet, who was wounded in the chest at my side. He may not be much of a hand at rhetoric, Maître Laurier, but at least he has more courage than those of your faction can be credited with."

There was a low murmur. The lawyer rose and declared that the accused had insulted him, without provocation.

The Prince sprang to his feet.

"You laughed at my comrade Touchet who had his chest smashed in by a ball fired by the enemies of France."

A voice spoke in strong, measured tones from the back of the court.

"And you murdered Victor Noir."

The uproar in the court was indescribable. Everyone turned to the back of the room where Ulric de Fonvielle, who had spoken, had already risen furiously and climbing on to the bench hurled cries of "murderer" at the accused. In an instant, everyone present was on their feet, shouting and waving, some calling for Fonvielle to be taken out and others the accused.

The gendarmes closed in on Fonvielle, who was already being led out by the guards, while the police captain escorting Prince Bonaparte was also preparing to leave the court.

At length, order was restored. The procurator general, Grandperret, asked for Monsieur de Fonvielle's action to be recorded for further consideration at a later date.

When Fonvielle returned to the room a number of those

sitting on the right-hand benches rose threateningly, and began shouting: "Kill him! Kill him!"

Fonvielle recoiled instinctively, appearing not to understand at first that these threats were directed at him. Then one of the men sprang forward with a raised fist and he saw the hatred on his face. Fonvielle parried the blow. He did not know this man, or any of them. He had seen them earlier merely as faceless members of the crowd. He tried to face them, but, taken by surprise, he stumbled and fell heavily against the bench.

By now the whole room was in an uproar. The man who had tried to strike Fonvielle was struggling to seize him by the collar. Behind him was a tall, fanatical-looking fellow of a type common to all revolutions everywhere, who held his right hand buried in his pocket in a gesture so overwhelmingly sinister that it seemed as though at any moment there would be the dull gleam of a knife between his fingers, an impression confirmed by the ominous expectancy of his whole attitude and expression.

The excitement had risen to such a pitch that people were beginning to climb onto the benches as though about to pour down into the body of the room. The guards formed a chain to keep them back but already the chain was giving way. The gendarmes surrounding Ulric de Fonvielle did their best to hold off the troublemakers who grappled with them, shouting abuse, regardless of their uniform.

Glandaz, the president, hammered desperately on his desk but his voice was lost in the general uproar, while the lawyers, gesticulating wildly, their black gowns flapping about them, joined in the shouting.

Slowly order was restored once more. The attackers, beaten off by force, seemed to melt back into the crowd. People rescued their seats. The heat was such that the ushers opened the doors to let in a breath of air. Charlotte felt dead on her feet. She stood first on one foot then on the other, like a heron, in a vain search for relief. She had with her a little fan made of painted cardboard which she had bought in the street outside and which was now crushed to a pulp between her hands. She amused herself snapping the frail wooden spines with her fingers, taking a perverse pleasure in the idiotic act. The nervous, rhythmic gestures soothed her and at the same time exerted an almost hypnotic effect.

She heard the fresh outburst of shouting. One of the men who had attacked Fonvielle had gone for a member of the jury. Charlotte was in a bad position to see what was happening and had in any case long ceased to care, but Worski, beside her, was craning forward intensely and the strange, rapt light in his eyes gave to his expression something she had not seen there before, something which revealed beneath his apparent indolence forces of hatred and passion kept fiercely battened down.

"I know these men," Worski said. "I saw them like that at the trial of Berezowski."

"Who is Berezowski?"

"A Pole. He shot at the Czar in Paris in '67. For us, his countrymen, he is a hero."

"Because he killed the Czar?"

Worski looked at her oddly.

"He shot at him but he did not kill him. Do you really not know whether or not the Czar was shot dead in your own country three years ago?" She flushed, mortified more by the idea that she had made a fool of herself than by the fact that she really did not know. The Czar of all the Russias was nothing to her. There had been a time when she had held the history of the whole world in supreme contempt.

"I was not listening," she said stiffly.

But already he had forgotten her blunder. Once again his eyes were fixed on the scene in the court, still burning with that frightening inward fire.

"There were men like that at Berezowski's trial! The same men! They sought his death. Hang him, they were shouting. And yet they had no real reason to hate him. They were not Russian, and what did they care whether the Czar lived or died? But they hated Berezowski all the same. Yes, they bayed like a pack of hounds, that is what they were like, a pack of hounds. They hate liberty and courage and that is why they wanted our friend to die."

Some spirit of contradiction moved her to say: "Was it

117

heroism to fire at the Czar, to try and shoot a man in the back?"

"He did not shoot him in the back, and it was heroism because he had no hope of getting away with it. Can you understand that for us, the Czar is a tyrant? He is responsible for the sufferings of our country! My mother was raped by the Czar's soldiers in '63, in the Warsaw risings. I saw children shot—"

"Death and destruction," she said, sickened. "Is there nothing else in the world?"

Worski had suffered. With what dreadful matter of factness he said: "My mother was raped by the Czar's soldiers—" Once again, she was aware of how alien he was.

He was silent, leaning stiffly against the wall beside her. He had this gift of withdrawing into himself, of suddenly liberating himself from the presence of others, which was disconcerting. She was almost grateful to him for his detachment and conscious of a fleeting admiration. People in the crowd were looking at them. Every now and then a face from the anonymous mass would turn from the trial to look at them. People whispered and nudged one another.

And so, in the end, as the long session dragged on, the presence of Worski, careless and indifferent beside her, conferred on her a kind of consequence. The thought of Thomas grew and swelled almost unbearably within her. The present moment, the noise, the crowd, her own hopes, were all sublimated and her expectation took on the garb of tragedy. Her love had become the stuff of legend, something outside and theatrical.

Daylight waned. Inside the court, the lamps were lit. Suddenly the room took on an air of grandeur and solemnity. The audience became hushed and respectful as though conscious of grave events in preparation. The trial had gone more quickly than expected and it was possible the verdict would be brought in that very evening. The court was already rising with a rustle of gowns and moving towards the door.

Pierre Bonaparte was taken out.

"There is a smut on your face," Worski said. He offered

Charlotte an embroidered handkerchief, impeccably folded. She took it and scrubbed furiously at her face.

"Here, on your forehead."

He took the handkerchief and did it himself. The gesture was a perfectly ordinary one but it had a caressing quality which she hated. She had to make an effort not to push him away, she felt like treading on his toes.

When he had finished, she turned away quickly so as not to look at him and suddenly, without warning the sea of heads parted for a moment and she saw Thomas standing by the door.

She could see his face quite clearly. He was looking towards her. Had he seen them? Another instant and he had vanished into the crowd.

Charlotte tried to thrust her way towards him but she was hopelessly caught up in the crowd, trapped between a young couple and the mother of one of them who made a solid barrier between the benches.

She tried to push past but encountered a sharp stab in the ribs from the young woman's elbow and seeing that they would not let her past, she gave up the attempt, feeling suddenly unutterably tired and helpless.

Outside, it was gray dusk. The lights of the Palais de Justice shone brightly through the tall windows. The room was hushed and expectant.

The members of the court took their seats once more. The president read the verdict. Pierre Bonaparte was acquitted.

Ulric de Fonvielle, on the other hand, was sentenced to ten days' imprisonment for contempt of court.

In the trial of Victor Noir's murderer, Fonvielle was the only man found guilty.

The public reaction was a howl of anger. The fact that Prince Bonaparte was ordered to pay the sum of twenty-five thousand francs damages to Victor Noir's family, did not lessen the shocking leniency of the court and the unfairness of such an acquittal.

The evidence of the doctor who certified that, on examination, the Prince had proved to have a bruise on his cheek as a result of his fatal quarrel with Victor Noir had made it possible to sustain a plea of self-defense, and claim that Noir had provoked Pierre Bonaparte by striking the first blow.

Despite their own competence and the justice of their cause, the counsel for the prosecution, Maître Laurier and Maître Floquet, were ultimately bested by the accused himself whose influential connections had inclined his judges to clemency and, still more, to prudence.

But to the vast majority of the crowd, the acquittal was a scandal which meant nothing more or less than letting a murderer go unpunished. An angry murmur ran through the room. From where he sat, Maître Laurier, white with anger, was heard to utter the word *Borgia* in the direction of the Prince who was rising to depart.

The doors were open but the crowd did not disperse at once, and voices were still heard raised in anger.

Hemmed in by strangers, Charlotte allowed herself to be borne along unresisting by the movement of the crowd.

She found herself outside on the steps, but though she stared about her with fierce concentration, everything seemed to dissolve before her eyes. People came and went in the square but she could not make out their faces. Only the tall, unmoving trees across the street seemed real and solid.

As she grew accustomed to the fresh air, her eyes cleared and she saw that there was a stir in the square. Prince Bonaparte had just emerged from the Palais de Justice to return to the prison where he was a guest of the governor.

A wave rose up and swept towards Pierre Bonaparte. Whistles, jeers and catcalls rose from the crowd and the dark mass of people swept menacingly towards him. The Prince, flanked by his friends and supporters, continued to advance, his head held high but his small bloodshot eyes roved anxiously from side to side and his face was deathly pale.

The insults grew louder. The crowd closed in. There was still about ten yards to go. At the far end of the narrow lane was the group of journalists and Charlotte recognized Rochefort standing a little apart, a gendarme on either side of him. Thomas was with them.

It was getting dark but every now and then the heavy

clouds which rolled overhead parted to give a glimpse of a pure, forget-me-not blue which drove away the night. Pierre Bonaparte and his friends had come to a halt a few steps away from the group of journalists from the other side. They stared at one another. Someone shouted: "Murderer." Neither Bonaparte, nor his friends moved a muscle. Slowly, and with evident reluctance, the others stepped aside. It seemed as though at any moment the undercurrent of anger would break forth and spread throughout the square.

Charlotte stayed where she was on the steps, seized again by her superstitious fear of the crowd. Her eyes sought the figure of Thomas for comfort. He was still there, talking to Rochefort. As always when she saw him with other people, she was struck by the sheer size of him. His empty sleeve stood out against the neat overcoats of his companions like a hussar's uniform, a sombre flag which would always have power to tighten her heart strings.

The groups of men in the square were breaking up. Prince Bonaparte reached the carriage which was waiting for him. There was a stir in the crowd and Charlotte saw Thomas coming towards her.

She stood as if paralyzed, incapable of movement. She had taken one step forward but that was all, she could do no more.

She was wearing her canary yellow dress, edged with black braid, the tight fitting frogged jacket flaring over the skirt. People turned to look at her, struck by her unusual slenderness. A tiny cocked hat was perched on her chestnut hair and her long black gloves reached to the elbow.

Worski, who had followed her unnoticed, saw her white face and the sudden alteration in the profile that was towards him in the dusk. He stepped towards her.

"Are you not well?"

She had not heard him approach. She had believed him gone. He was looking at her with great concern.

"Go away—" she said, "leave me, I beg you—"

"Are you ill? You are so pale."

She was very pale, white to the lips. She stared at Worski vaguely, aware that it was too late to send him away. Thomas was coming towards them. He would see them together. She could not make Worski go now, she no longer had the time or the strength.

She took two steps forward, with Worski close beside her. Too late, too late to drive him away now. She felt his youth and beauty, like a cruel, blinding light beside her, echoing her own so that the two of them stood out, a focus for all eyes against the dark background of the Palais de Justice. Behind them, the visitors were throwing crumbs to the pigeons. There was an old man there who had lured the birds by putting pieces of bread in his hat and they fluttered round him, heavy, greedy things, settling on his shoulders and his head. The man was covered with them and people were laughing. Charlotte and Worski were enveloped in a fantastic aerial ballet, framed in a surge of frenziedly beating wings, as though in some pretentious allegory of youth and patriotism.

Charlotte had the uncomfortable sensation of moving in one of those moments when life itself achieves a kind of symbolic perfection. The birds, the slanting rays of the setting sun, Worski's youth and her own—it seemed to her that he should always stand like that, with the birds flying up behind him. She knew that they were beautiful, Worski and herself, in the evening light that filled the square with the pigeons whirling madly around them, and her heart contracted because Thomas was coming towards them and because he, for his part, was maimed.

She wished desperately to be ugly, lost in the crowd. She felt a stab of fear that, seeing them, Thomas would be hurt, not because she was with another man but because they were both so remorselessly young. All at once, it seemed to her, that this was the only thing that mattered.

For what did Worski matter! Oh, if Thomas only knew. Not Worski, nor any man meant a thing to her. Youth and beauty had torn her apart before and would do so again, even more perhaps, but for today, it could not touch her. She would willingly have been old and ugly, if that would comfort Thomas. She would have cut off her own arm.

The burden of Worski at her side weighed on her like the guilty burden of her own youth, and yet she made no move to evade the inevitable. In that instant, time stood still.

"Thomas," she thought wildly, "I love you. I am yours. Do with me what you will."

He was almost on them. He could not help seeing them. There was an almost imperceptible hesitation. Her eyes sought his, aware of their clear blue, like the blue of a spring sky.

There was no time to take in every feature and she retained only an overwhelming impression of familiarity. He bent his head. He was not ten yards away. He had entered the dizzying orbit of their love.

She reeled under the impact of his presence and a thousand little wounds of pleasure and submission opened before him. All that he had ever brought her of happiness and grief seemed to press down on her at once.

Then they were face to face. For a brief instant, she stared into his eyes, devoid of all expression.

His hat was already in his hand. He merely nodded briefly in her direction and then passed on. He did not look at Worski.

Charlotte stood, petrified, her cheeks flaming, fighting off the evidence of her own eyes, seeking to make his very neutrality a reassurance. Farther on, a man was waving to Thomas. He went towards him and the two of them moved away round the corner.

Worski and the need to pretend in his presence blunted Charlotte's suffering. The people strolling to and fro across the square smothered her private tragedy in their carefree promenade.

She wanted to walk with them to force herself to believe that nothing had happened. She turned, unconsciously, towards the river and, with Worski following her, walked on and on until she had left the bridge far behind.

At last she stopped and stood for a long time staring at the broad expanse of the Loire with its scattering of islets. It was nearly dark but a last glimmer of light joined sky and river obscuring the natural boundaries of the still, watery world.

"You do not like me to be near you? You wish me to go?" Worski asked.

She looked up. She had forgotten he was there. A light breeze off the river stirred Frank's fair hair. He was looking at her with deep earnestness and she realized with amazement how much she mattered to him just then, and how unimportant he was for her. In the midst of her own distress she was suddenly afraid of hurting him, because she knew he was sincere.

She gave him a sad, resigned smile.

"You are so handsome, Frank, and young—so young—so very young."

She had a sudden respect for him, for his dignity. He stood out against the darkening landscape, a splendid, tragic figure with his wind-blown hair, pale face and dark eyes. She had believed him inhuman, but the sight of that anguished gaze told her that he was suffering on her account with all the poignancy and astonishment which comes with the first experience of pain. She thought that she would never forget Frank's face etched against the chiaroscuro of the river. She took pity on his youth.

"Before I knew you," he said, "I believed that one could live on dreams. Now, I know the dream is nothing. That it is an escape, like all dreams." He moved closer. "I have dreamed of you. I wanted to see you again. I think of you as I have never thought of any woman. You could drive me mad, you know that, don't you?"

The fine dark eyes glowed with sincerity. She knew that he meant what he said and that for him, it was a tragic admission and that if she accepted him now he would give himself, body and soul, to this love, and yet it could not move her. It was too late.

"You love another man, tell me his name," Frank said.

"What is the use."

She began to walk again and there were tears in her eyes. He caught her up, gripping her arm and shaking her fiercely.

"Tell me his name. Is it Thomas Becque?"

"How do you know him?"

She drew back, recoiling instinctively from the thought of any connection between these two.

"I know him."

"How?"

"I work for the same paper. Or, to be more precise, I am trying to convince myself that I can be of some use to it. But I am not useful. To them, I am what you call a dilettante. Odd is it not?"

He was still gripping her arm.

"Tell me—is it Thomas Becque, the man in your life?"

"Do not speak of it. Do not speak of him. I do not ask questions of you!"

"Then ask me. I will tell you all you want to know. You could make all my past life nothing. For me, you are France. Do you love France?"

"Yes," she said. And looking out over the drowned landscape she was conscious of a sudden limitless pride in France and of a strange love.

"Becque loves you, does he not? He must love you!"

"I do not know any more," she said.

She walked on again. Worski overtook her and then stopped. She waited. It was quite dark now.

Frank was standing with his back to her staring into the shadows over the river.

"Answer me," he said fiercely. "If you had not loved this man, do you think you could have loved me?"

He turned abruptly, covering her with his mysterious gaze.

"Yes, Frank," she said softly, and knew that it could have been true.

He looked at her for a long time and let her go at last while he remained behind, brooding alone on this love that might have been.

At length he rejoined her and without a word, escorted her back to her hotel.

6

AFTER DINNER, alone at the hotel with no one for whom to pretend, Charlotte did not resist the temptation to go in search of Thomas. With no witness to condemn her behavior, she gave way to her folly. She had reached the stage where the obsession had become unbearable.

She made up her mind to go round every hotel in the town to find him. Something must come of their meeting and it was the certainty of this which still held her in some kind of precarious happiness. She went first to the hotels where she knew the journalists were staying. Neither the first nor the second had any record of a Monsieur Becque, but they suggested a third, a little farther from the center, where some late arrivals were known to have found rooms.

The town was strange to Charlotte; she wandered down the broad arteries where the cafés were displaying an unusual gaiety. There was a chill in the night air, but even so the terraces were crowded with men and women, sitting and standing in animated conversation, while snatches of tunes from operettas came from the orchestras within.

She had been directed to a street on the right. She passed a small private house, brightly lit and decorated with strings of dancing chinese lanterns. Half Paris seemed to be disporting itself within.

Charlotte hurried on down the now dark and empty street. This was the second time she had set out like this to look for Thomas since their parting. It would be the last. This was her last chance. If he rejected her now, it would be the end. She dared not think what might become of her then, even though the moment was almost upon her. She found the hotel a short distance away, behind the church. There was an entrance hall with a tiny desk and from there two steps covered in threadbare carpet led up to a cramped and faded lounge.

The man at the desk told her Monsieur Becque was staying there but that he had just gone out. She explained that she was a relative and was invited to wait.

The lounge smelled unpleasantly of stale tobacco. The small tables held an assortment of religious tracts and farming papers, and she guessed that in normal times the hotel catered to the clergy and to peasants with business in the town.

Through the doorway into the hall, Charlotte could see people coming and going. There were quite a number of them and every time the door opened she tensed herself for a shock, increasing the strain on her already stretched nerves.

Guests returned from dining out or from the café and paused to collect their keys and exchange a word with the man at the desk. Suddenly the door was thrown open and she heard a voice.

"Becque, you owe me my revenge!"

She rose and moved to the door. She dared not call out. He was talking to the receptionist. His companion had gone on ahead and was standing at the far end of the L-shaped corridor, examining two antique maps of the region which hung on the wall.

Thomas mounted the two steps and saw Charlotte. He hesitated and then advanced more slowly.

"Good evening—I had not expected—"

She had hoped he would come into the room to meet her but he stood facing her in the doorway.

"Thomas, I had to speak to you—"

His words had been formal but she could not bring herself to match his tone and this put her at a disadvantage.

"Indeed? Is there anything to be gained?"

The face that met hers was without expression and yet every detail filled her with unbearable regret.

A crowd of people came in and stood talking loudly a yard or two away. Their noisy presence deadened Charlotte's fear and compelled her to one last effort at dissimulation. She strove to speak with a lightness in accord with the cheerful buzz of conversation around her, and with the hurried, temporary feeling of the narrow hallway, with travelers coming and going and a boy in a striped waistcoat staggering under a load of baggage.

But all the time panic was fluttering inside her, though she fought it off and clung to that one brief moment as if she had a lifetime of happiness before her.

"I am sure you're busy—I will not detain you—I should have liked to see you for a moment—"

Her eyes were on the corridor with a pretense of interest in what was going on out there. When at last she looked at him, his unexpected nearness broke down all her assurance and she could not meet his eyes.

When he still said nothing, she went on: "Have you a moment?"

A moment! When her whole life was at stake! She felt a rush of self-pity.

Thomas stepped back in the doorway, glanced out and made a sign to the friend who stood at the end of the passage. Half of him was already outside and the pain was almost more than Charlotte could bear. This was worse than a rejection. She sensed in him a kind of physical haste to be gone, not to escape but simply to go away, to be somewhere else, a healthy masculine desire to be on the move, to return to the men who were his friends.

There was nothing more she could say. Her eyes were huge and anxious. Still standing in the doorway, Thomas turned back to her.

"I am deeply sorry—I am not free. A friend is waiting for me. I am sorry."

The other man was actually coming back and calling: "Becque, you will join me in a *fine*—"

For an instant they faced one another. He avoided her eyes and she saw it.

"Can you really not leave your friend for a moment?"

She was insisting, terrified to feel that time was running out, and finding nothing to say in this brief interview amid the noise and bustle around them that would be strong enough to rouse him to interest, desire or anger; to anything rather than this terrible nothingness that lay between them.

The moment passed. The journalist who had been with Thomas had retraced his steps and was waiting beyond the glass doors which Charlotte had thrust quickly to behind them. But the doors remained slightly ajar and the man was standing there with his back to them, puffing complacently at his pipe.

"Send him away," she begged. "Tell him you will join him in a little while."

"I cannot do that. This man is a friend. He has come from Belgium especially to see me."

Suddenly she hated everything to do with this man's life and with his work. She had never thought about it before, because in those days he had been in love with her and she could afford to ignore such things. But now she was bitterly jealous of everything in his life which she sensed alien to herself, his work, his connections and the incredible number of his friends. She stared at him in blank dismay, cut to the quick by the way in which he had said "a friend," as though she herself had never been his friend, she who today would give him anything, who could still hear his voice pleading, had known him in passion and afraid—

For a moment the hope came to her that he was deliberately trying to hurt her but no, he did not appear to have said what he had with intent to wound. He was quite firm, as though upheld by some inner strength which she did not understand but could feel, and against which she was helpless, as though he had become a monk. Only the blue eyes which would not meet hers directly, left room in her for one last spark of hope, and because beyond the words and what they seemed to say there was still the old feeling that she had when she was near him, that made her simply want to close her eyes.

This hunger for him was no mere passing titillation of the senses, but rather a slow combustion, almost an intoxication which overcame her in his presence. It did not seem to her humanly possible that Thomas did not feel the same insidious torment when he was near her. And she knew that the need of him would haunt her for days and nights on end, eating into her blood like a disease.

She told herself, "I cannot bear it." But there was nothing she could do.

"Very well, I understand," she said in a low voice. "I am going. I would not wish to keep you—"

She was consumed with the desire to touch him, to kiss his hand, his face, fling her arms round him and hold him close to her. It was this desire which kept her standing there against all reason although his eyes were already wandering away, simply in order to see him there, living and breathing, abandoning all demands, one by one except for the one thing, now that all else was lost, only to be near him for a moment longer.

She thought she knew him and for the first time she saw the man he really was, the force of his personality, his careless charm, his importance in his own world and his stature in the eyes of others.

She was at the door.

"Well, good night then." Her eyes sought his in a last glimmer of hope.

She held out her hand. He did not take it. His face was very stern. Color flamed in her cheeks, she averted her eyes and her quickened breathing betrayed her feelings.

Somehow she got herself out of the room, conscious that he had already rejoined his friend and must be walking down the passage deep in conversation. The waiter was outside shifting tables. Charlotte stood by the door. She saw the board with the room keys hanging on it and had an instant's wild temptation to bribe him to give her Thomas's key. The idea became an obsession. She must try everything. She had the whole night before her with all that it might bring.

Suppose she were to go up to his room and wait for him. What would he do? He was a man, after all. He would give in.

Her heart thudded and she was almost ready to try but the waiter came in. He walked past. More people entered.

She went back to her own hotel and wrote to him, a passionate letter declaring all her love and her guilt. It was a letter of confession, of expiation, of crawling humili-

130

ty. She plucked up courage to take it to the hotel desk herself and then walked back again through the unfamiliar and now almost silent streets of Tours.

The next morning she woke at seven and washed and dressed in a dream. She knew she would go back there, she had to see Thomas once more. He would have read her letter. He would have to see her. The things she had said, the way she had humbled herself, would have changed him. No man could have been proof against them. She was beyond pride now. This was her last throw.

At the hotel, she was told that Monsieur Becque was not there, had left early that morning. No, he had left nothing for her, no letter, they were very sorry.

She walked back, feeling suddenly sick. Once in her own room, she was obliged to go to bed. Her despair was such that her whole body revolted.

She was ill for two days. Worski, who knew where she was staying, came and nursed her. Emotional wretchedness turned to physical disorder and she was very ill. Worski made her tisanes and remained obstinately by her side. She gained strength from his presence and although she could not have said quite why, was not ashamed that he should see her in this abject state. In between whiles, he played cards with acquaintances he had made in the city.

During these two days when he came to visit her at her hotel, she never once felt the least uneasiness at this enforced intimacy, or was conscious of any risk of being alone with him. His nearness engendered no familiarity. He was more like a brother. In the end, she realized that he was the only man who had ever given her this precise sense of her own individual worth, made her aware of herself as a woman without any heightening or diminution of her value as a human being, such as she felt in her love for Thomas, or in the soothing affection of Frédéric.

On the third day, as she was getting ready to settle her bill and leave, a message came that someone was waiting to see her. It was Frédéric. For a week, he had waited in Paris, keeping abreast of the trial in the Press. When Charlotte did not return after the verdict, he had grown anxious and finally, unable to bear it any longer, had caught the train for Tours.

His arrival came as a shock to Charlotte. It reminded her of a relationship which, in her own mind, she had already been thinking of as ended, although there had been no actual break between herself and Frédéric, and he was fully entitled to call her to account. It was annoying. She had regarded their affair as finished, if it had not been a mistake from the start.

But this was not something she could say to him outright, and the obligation to conceal the real nature of her feelings forced her to dissemble in a way that would not have been necessary had she been less fond of him and which, inevitably, placed an increased strain on their relations. Frédéric was clearly unhappy and, to make matters worse, Worski arrived unexpectedly while they were together. It was the first time the two men had met and as he waited for Charlotte to introduce them, Worski eyed the student warily. Frédéric was white-faced. The sight of Worski had filled him with a dreadful doubt. He had been well aware that Charlotte's reason for coming to Tours was to find Thomas Becque and had accepted it. Now he suspected her of worse duplicity. Had she really come to meet Worski?

"Let me assure you, Frédéric, Monsieur Worski is a good friend, nothing more," Charlotte said coldly, guessing what was in his mind. "Frank has been more than good to me."

With a curt bow, Worski left them and Frédéric dared not say more.

They caught the train for Paris in a mood of mutual resentment. Worski did not travel with them.

Charlotte could not bring herself to break with Frédéric but neither could she go on with the affair. She was at her wits' end. Her life seemed to have sunk into a desperate state from which she could see no way out. She was still waiting for an answer to the letter she had sent to Thomas, and she knew that if he did not answer, after all that she had said, all the admissions she had made in it, it would be the final rejection and she would never get over

132

it. Her whole life, everything she had suffered for him and through him, would become as nothing.

It was the beginning of May. The walls of Paris were plastered with loud notices concerning the referendum to be held on the eighth by which Napoleon III asked the French people to accept or reject his government once and for all.

This was the Emperor's last attempt to establish the order and authority of his régime, undermined by social unrest and general discontent. The choice was a straightforward Yes or No.

In fact, although everyone knew the plebiscite was to decide the acceptance or rejection of the Empire, it was nominally a matter of saying yes or no to the new constitution promulgated by Napoleon III, the avowed object of which was the liberalization of the Empire.

The truth was that the new constitution offered to the country was nothing more than the old authoritarian constitution of 1852 with a few minor reforms. More serious was the fact that these reforms did not touch on what was, for France, the most important question, the right to dictate war and peace, which remained the prerogative of the Emperor alone. Napoleon II retained complete control of the constitution with his ministers and so-called advisers doing no more than carry out his orders.

At a period when the possibility of war with Prussia was uppermost in all men's minds, this question of the right to decide war or peace was of vital importance to the country. Those with foresight could not ignore the danger. Moreover, Napoleon's minister, Monsieur de Persigny, who was more royalist than the king, was rejoicing openly that in spite of the constitution the Emperor retained all his powers.

Another minister, Emile Ollivier, drew moving pictures of the Emperor labouring for the good of his people. Newspapers in the pay of the régime did their best to sway public opinion.

The opposition, knowing where the Emperor might lead the country once his position was assured, reacted violently in the fear of what might follow if the referendum proved an affirmative. Committees were set up in the rue de Rivoli and the rue de la Sourdière, aimed at making the electorate aware of the traps concealed in the new constitution.

Wednesday, the 4th of May, four days before the plebiscite, was a fine day. The weather was warm, the air was crisp and the sky a soft pale blue. The walls were bright with posters. Groups of people stood arguing beneath them. Students strolled with their girls and Frédéric and Charlotte made their way along the boulevard in the wake of one such couple. The night before, Frédéric, at the end of his tether, had asked her to marry him. She was weary of it all and said yes. Now they were going to the post. Frédéric had written to the authorities of his birth-place asking for the necessary papers.

Charlotte watched the young couple ahead, and all the old restlessness of love stirred in her heart. She stopped and then moved on. She could not go on. How much longer, for how many years yet would she find herself caught like this, in the street, anywhere, seeing Thomas everywhere, in every dark figure—there was one with the girl over there. By screwing up her eyes against the sun, she could almost have believed it was he—

"Charlotte—" Frédéric said.

"No," she said desperately, "no, Frédéric—I cannot marry you—I will never marry you!"

He was staring at her in silence.

Her eyes were wild.

"I will never marry you, Frédéric. You are leading me down a road which is not right for me. My life is Thomas."

"Very well, go and find him!"

His jaw set grimly, he was very pale.

"Go then," he said bitterly, "I do not wish to marry you. I have tried to convince myself but I detest marriage. What do you think I feel posting this letter asking for my papers? I'd like to run away from it all."

Now she was as white as he. Frédéric thrust his face into hers.

"Can't you see I'm doing my best to persuade myself that I am a man, that I must act like a man? All that stuff

134

about virility and the human conscience! But marry you, have a child as weak and helpless as myself? A failure, my dear! That is what I am and if you marry me, it will be out of pity. In fact, if you conceived a child of mine, I'd rather you got rid of it."

For a moment, they stared wildly at one another, then Charlotte began to walk quickly down a turning leading to the rue Cujas.

He ran after her and gripped her by the arm.

"Come with me!"

"No."

He tightened his grip, unconscious that he was bruising her.

"Come. I am a wretched fellow, you know that. If you reject me, you take away my right to live. Stay with me. Marry me. It is true I am afraid, but I love you."

She shook her head obstinately.

"Come," he said pleadingly, "I will not let you go. It is not right for you to be alone either. You have borne too much and it may be that soon our lives will not be our own to choose. If war comes we shall be caught up in it and what we decide will be of little account. I do not want you to have to face life all alone."

He stood before her, a tall, thin figure with dark eyes hollow in his sharp face. She had an impulse to stroke his thin, brown cheeks and soothe away the anxious, haunted look on his face.

But she could no longer bear the thought of binding her life to his. The idea filled her with such revulsion that she could not understand how she could have accepted him before.

Abruptly turning her back on him, she began to walk rapidly away and had soon left him behind. At first he had no longer the will to follow and dogged her footsteps, mechanically, from a distance. The colors and the sunshine of the boulevard Saint-Michel danced before his eyes in a dazzle of bright light. The street had that particular animation which comes just before midday when students pour out of the Sorbonne and the law schools. Some waved or called out to Frédéric.

He stood miserably on the edge of the pavement letting

the noise sweep over him, ringing in the bright spring air like the clamor of horns and trumpets, like the noise made by children coming out of school. It irritated Frédéric beyond bearing.

Ever since his return from Provence, he had found himself hating the artificial gaiety of the Quartier Latin, and now all this ostentatious youth affected him more painfully than ever. He was alone in the midst of a crowd where names and faces were known to him but in which he had no friend. His heart chilled at the thought of the terrifying indifference which really underlay the easy friendships and the ready acceptance which had seemed so wonderfully intoxicating when he first came to Paris. He knew now that everyone was alone, and that a man could die of hunger and misery without a single hand stretched out to help him.

Never had Frédéric felt so small and doomed as in that moment. He seemed to hear, beneath the light chatter of human voices which filled the boulevard, an eternal tragic silence, ever on the watch. The brooding silence of the high walls of the schools and the aged stones pressed down on the boulevard, blind masses against which down the centuries so many young men had dashed their fragile hopes in vain.

Listening to that silence, it seemed to Frédéric that the voices were hurling themselves against it. He could have cried out, caught up once again in the nightmares which had haunted his childhood.

He had crossed the road and stood now in front of a draper's. He could see himself in the glass, hollow-cheeked, his thin face eaten up by a pair of huge eyes like bottomless wells, filled with the cloudy convolutions of the sky.

He was afraid, afraid above all of the flight of his own imagination, the way he walked so often on the extreme edge of reason, letting his nerves control his thoughts and undermine the sane, practical side of him. But then he saw reflected in the glass the blind wall of the Lycée Louis-le-Grand and once again he was a miserable pawn, crushed as he had been ever since he could remember by the burden of college walls.

The thought gave him a salutary shock. He was appalled at his own self-abnegation; he was a human being, like any other. He sensed that he was losing his grasp of life and must do something to redress the balance. Again his mind turned to the war which obsessed him. He could not bear it. The hopelessness of all effort, of all progress was so terrible that he began to run towards the rue Monsieur-le-Prince to find Charlotte, come what might, only so long as he rejected failure, rejected that negative voice within himself which cried that all human effort was in vain and there was no hope for mankind.

He ran up to the third floor and knocked on Charlotte's door. She was inside, pressed against the jamb, listening, but she did not open it.

"Let me in," he cried.

He went on knocking. The blows echoed dully through the building. Charlotte opened the door a crack.

"Go away."

He was breathing hard. "Becque will not come back, Charlotte."

"You know nothing about it. He will come back."

"You fool," he said sadly. "You crazy fool. Listen to me. Becque married Marie a month ago."

She stared at him but he could not see her clearly against the light. "Becque is married, Charlotte. He is married to Marie. That was why he went away after his illness. They went to London. At present he has rented a house at Neuilly."

"You are lying," she said in a strangled voice.

"No. I have said nothing because I did not wish to force myself on you. But now you must know, you must stop ruining your life."

People were coming up the stairs. Charlotte came out on to the landing, pulled the door to and clattered downstairs with Frédéric at her heels. She did not pause until she reached the steps leading to the street.

"How did you know?" she asked suddenly.

She was looking past him as though he were not there, but she held herself stiffly and the knuckles of the small hand grasping the iron stair rail were white with strain.

"We cannot stay here," he begged her, "people are looking."

Madame Delobelle was emerging from the bakery opposite.

"Tell me," Charlotte said.

But for the unusual tension in her voice, the exaggerated care with which she phrased her words, as a deaf person speaks, he might have thought she did not care. Her face was calm, and she seemed to be watching the people pass in the street, although in reality seeking an air that she could breathe to save her from the slow suffocation creeping over her.

Frédéric hesitated and at last he said reluctantly: "It was—it was Ferrat who told me. He ran into Becque recently—"

"Ferrat has a broken leg. He has been bedridden for two months."

Charlotte spoke sharply. She rounded on him in terrifying fury, and her eyes scorched him.

"You lied! Why? Why, Frédéric?"

Ferrat had his leg in plaster and it was clearly impossible for him to have gone out and met Thomas by chance. The lie was clumsy and obvious, too clumsy even for her to take comfort in the fact. There was nothing in Frédéric's nature to suggest that he would stoop to such tactics as that. He stood before her, stubbornly refusing to meet her eyes and then suddenly seized her arm and began dragging her across the road as though from a need to create some kind of diversion, and she was conscious of a vague fear due not simply to the lie he had told but to his whole attitude, his embarrassment and the sudden feeling that he was somehow strange and dangerous.

"Tell me," she said, fighting down her panic, "why should you lie? I want to know, Frédéric!"

"Listen—" his hand gripped hers quickly. "Listen—I may as well tell you—it's true it was not Ferrat! I heard it from Gabin. Why should I hide it from you? He saw Aurore, last week, and she told him Becque was married."

The face she lifted to his seemed at first sight still under control but it was as though some kind of paralysis had struck it. Frédéric had to force himself to meet the anguish in her eyes. Charlotte's mind seemed to have lost control. Her whole being recoiled from Frédéric's final explanation. She had not seen Aurore since her return from Tours. It was not unlikely that Aurore should have had news of Thomas from Paul Boucher—

Nor was there anything improbable in Gabin's meeting Aurore. A dealer having finally shown some interest in his pictures, he had sold three canvases the month before, and as a result had received several invitations to exhibitions and varnishing-days. What she could not understand was why Gabin, hearing this news about Thomas, should not have told her himself and still more why Frédéric should have felt the need to tell that lie about Ferrat.

"There is something wrong about this story. What is it, Frédéric?"

She was utterly lost. Apart from the actual pain of the ultimate blow which Thomas's marriage was to her, she was conscious of something which did not ring true, something she did not understand. This instinct of betrayal, of a barrage of lies around her only increased her misery and loneliness.

"I am going to Aurore," she said wildly.

She did not look at him and he dared not stop her. His hand gripped her shoulder but she wrenched herself violently away.

At Aurore's house the door was opened by a servant who tried at first to tell her that Madame was not at home. But Charlotte had seen Aurore's gloves and parasol on a table in the hall as though she had just come in. The evident discomfort of the servant confirmed her suspicions.

"You mean Madame is not alone. That does not surprise me, I shall go up."

Trained to accept even the most eccentric conduct from his mistress's friends, the man dared not deny her.

Charlotte walked past him and made her way upstairs. Aurore was clearly at home and equally clearly not alone, for the sound of voices carried half-way down the stairs. Then the bedroom door above opened and Aurore appeared, her face hastily powdered, wrapping a lace robe round her.

"Darling—you at last! Where have you been? What have you to say for yourself?"

They met on the stairs and Charlotte, looking up at Aurore's rather faded beauty, had the conviction that she was naked under her robe. Aurore failed to meet her eyes.

"You are—engaged—I suppose Paul is here—" Charlotte said in a voice carefully without expression.

"Darling, how can you? Well, yes, Paul is here. If I had an atom of modesty I'd lie to you but after all you know how matters stand. In any case, I'm not in the habit of hiding my feelings and our affair is hardly much of a secret, is it?"

She seemed quite at ease, indeed delighted to be able to tell. Her robe, carelessly fastened, revealed a glimpse of bare skin.

"If Paul is here, I should like to see him," Charlotte said.

Aurore looked up sharply.

"Indeed? What for?"

"I must speak to him about Thomas."

Aurore came down two steps. Despite herself, she looked faintly alarmed.

"Surely, my dear, it cannot be so very urgent?"

"Aurore, is it true that Thomas is married?"

Charlotte spoke quietly. She felt unpleasantly calm, prepared for anything. For a tenth of a second, Aurore was silent, staring intensely at Charlotte with the round, shining eyes of a naughty child caught in the act. She held this wide, unblinking gaze, as if determined to assure Charlotte of her complete good faith and then all at once she began to talk in a high, rather unnatural voice to demonstrate the relief she genuinely felt.

"So you know! Well, perhaps it's better that way. I have done all I could. Oh, my dear, I know how you must feel. But do not despair, you will forget, you know! He was not worthy of you.'"

"Was it Paul who told you?"

"Yes," she said and this time her voice was matter of fact. "Paul heard almost at once. Such news travels fast, you know, in a tight circle like theirs. Especially when there has been a good deal of talk."

"May I see Paul?"

Aurore fluttered her eyelashes.

"Darling, you really are being rather indiscreet! It's not like you."

"I want to see Paul." Charlotte interrupted her curtly, putting her foot on the next step.

"Are you mad?" said Aurore.

"Aurore, who is with you?"

The other woman laughed shrilly, her nervousness increasing.

"Paul, I told you. Why this inquisition?"

"It is not Paul who is up there."

"Call me a liar?"

"Who is it with you that you are so afraid I will see him? Who, Aurore? You are so white and trembling, is it Thomas Becque?"

Aurore gave a shriek of hysterical laughter.

"Thomas Becque! She is mad! Passion has driven her crazy! My poor dear, do you think everyone shares your desire for that cripple's embraces? Do use your head, my pet. You're behaving like a child."

Charlotte blushed, so wounded both for herself and for Thomas that had Aurore been within reach she would undoubtedly have slapped her face.

She was angry as she had not been for a long time but Aurore had stepped back, leaving the way open. Charlotte darted upstairs.

"You little slut," Aurore shrieked. She was about to follow but Charlotte had already reached the top and flung the bedroom door violently open. The bronze door handle crashed against the wall—

Charlotte stared in horror at the man who stood in the middle of the room, hurriedly buttoning his waistcoat. It was Gabin. Now it was Charlotte's turn to blush. The avenging fury which had driven her so far, collapsed to utter confusion.

She gaped at her brother, the sense of shock increasing as she took in all the implications of his presence in this room. She had surprised a secret which did not concern her. Her shame was for Gabin, but still more for herself for bursting in on him.

Now she understood what had been behind Frédéric's revelations. In some part of her she had known it all along. The picture dealer, the invitations to exhibitions, all these had been engineered by Aurore as a means to gratify her own desires. She had been taken with Gabin from the first, and once she had set her heart on a man she could be restrained by no other consideration from using all her wiles to get him. In many ways a frigid woman, Aurore compensated for this by a tireless quest for new sensations and in her the normal female appetite to possess and dominate was carried to an abnormal pitch.

Now Charlotte began to remember the little intimate secrets Aurore had confided about this man or that. The bitch, she thought.

And so Gabin had given in at last. And not simply from motives of self-interest, she had only to look at him to tell that. His attitude held none of the defiance he would have shown if money alone had driven him into this man-eater's arms. Charlotte knew her brother well enough to be sure that if that were the case he would have challenged her proudly, daring her to judge him.

Instead, he stood there looking embarrassed with all his weaknesses written on his face. Aurore had had him. Charlotte's picture of Gabin as invulnerable, faithful to Illa, his art and his ideals, had been merely childish.

Now she understood it all. Gabin had known of Thomas's marriage from Aurore, probably in the course of one of those intimate pillow talks in which lovers are all too prone to compare their fortunes with those of others. Aurore herself must have heard of it from Paul in the same way. The tale of Thomas's marriage whispered from pillow to pillow! Had Gabin told Illa? And who had told Frédéric?

A little dry laugh escaped her. Aurore, who had come up behind her, had recovered her dignity.

"Think what you like," she said. "You are in no position to judge me. Your own conduct in my house, my dear, has been hardly exemplary."

Charlotte did not move.

"Don't let her fool you, Gabin," Aurore cried. "Ask her

what she was doing with that Spanish boy one night in my small drawing-room—"

"Whoring," said Charlotte icily, "is something I learned in your house, Aurore!"

"Charlotte," Gabin begged helplessly.

"You need not worry," she said without looking at him, "I shall keep quiet. Illa shall know nothing. It's no concern of mine."

"Listen—"

But already she was half-way down the stairs. Gabin's voice made her pause and she stopped in her tracks.

"Wait," he called after her desperately.

But she did not wait. She ran headlong down the stairs, her small feet drumming on the treads with all the long-forgotten fury of her old, childhood tantrums.

The door slammed behind her. She sped out into the street, searching for a cab. Gabin dashed out after her, shouting.

A cab stopped. Charlotte got in and tapped on the glass, shouting an address to the driver, then flung herself back on the seat with her heart beating wildly and her head on fire. She saw Gabin running like a madman alongside the cab, striving to get a grip.

He managed it as last, leaped up and hung half in and half out of the door fighting for breath. His shirt collar was undone. At last he pulled himself inside and sat down beside Charlotte. For a few moments she heard nothing but his harsh breathing. Then there was silence. They had nothing to say. She did not look at him. She sat so still that it seemed to her she must even stop breathing. She sat bolt upright, immutable, like a lead soldier. To Gabin, who like most men in the wrong regarded dignity as an injustice, it was unendurable. He would rather she had stormed or wept.

"Say something," he implored her.

Charlotte sat like stone.

"Almighty God, why don't you go for me? You're the plaster saint, I'm in the wrong, make the most of it."

"Your affairs are not my concern." She looked away.

"I heard what you were saying to Aurore you know—about Becque—did Frédéric tell you? I'm glad. You had

143

to know, someday—I was terrified I'd have to tell you myself—"

"So you told Frédéric?"

Still she did not look at him. Her face was a mask. She was thinking that Frédéric must also have known about Gabin's affair and that was why he had lied to her at first.

"Yes. One evening—I wanted you to know in the end."

Silence.

"Is that all?" he asked violently. "Is there nothing else you'd like to know about Aurore and me? Haven't you passed judgement on me yet? I'm a disappointment to you, aren't I? Go on, I'm waiting—I'm surprised you have not said it yet! You know nothing and yet you dare to judge. You will not even try to understand what made me do it. I was desperate, utterly alone, and then at last found someone who understood—Aurore cared about me. For Aurore I am someone, I exist."

She would not look at him but she could see his face, rather flushed with a faint shifty look about the eyes.

"You also existed for Illa," she said.

"What do you know about it? A man and a woman sleep together, what does that prove?"

For the first time she turned to look at him.

"It proves someone is lying!"

"You cannot understand."

"No, I cannot understand."

"Listen," he said, "stop fighting. Don't look so tragic. Forget Becque. You can't be such a fool. You are young. Things pass, you will see—you must marry Frédéric. If only for the look of it. The boy was good enough to be your lover, surely you can marry him! I am not blaming you of course, you are quite free—but think of your reputation. I know you are a widow, but you are too independent you see, you need to organize your life—oh God, there has to be a compromise!"

"You tell me that," she said bitterly.

"I don't know what you mean."

He spoke stiffly. She remembered the Gabin she had known as a boy, making impossible demands on himself and others, and now here he was urging respectability on her, worrying what people might think. Now that he had a mistress it seemed he was also acquiring morals. It was something that came to married men with maturity, like a taste for good wine.

Charlotte looked at her brother. He seemed to have put on weight. Aurore must be feeding him too.

Once again silence divided them. Gabin felt uncomfortable, not knowing how to resume the conversation. There was a hardness in his sister's attitude which made him vaguely uneasy, like an adult trying to explain some simple social expedient to a child.

Charlotte said nothing. There was a dreadful silence inside her. Thomas was married. She knew that she would never marry Frédéric. Something in her life was finished forever.

She knew she lacked the courage to die of it and wondered how she would find the courage to live.

THE PLEBISCITE was held on 8 May. The result was in no doubt. 7,335,434 in favor and 1,560,709 against. A crushing defeat for the Republicans. France had given the Empire a new lease. There were armed guards outside the Luxemborg. Valerie came to tell Charlotte that Gabin and Frédéric had gone out to join the bands of students who were roving about there in the hopes of starting a fight. Worried, they went out to look for them. Gabin and Frédéric were loitering outside the railings with the rest, but although there were angry looks there had been no direct provocation. What good would that do, in this day and age?

The two young men saw them and came reluctantly to meet them. Frédéric had no words for Charlotte. He had suffered more on her account in those last few days than he would have believed possible. He had not slept and had lived through every stage of grief, jealousy, anger, self-disgust and hatred for all the world. He had suffered too much in those three days. He was almost cured. Sometimes it is like that, indifference comes quite suddenly. A kind of self-protection. Life must go on.

The whole building was woken next morning by screams coming from the Delobelles'.

"Woman!" Joseph Delobelle was roaring. "You're raving mad!"

His wife's voice screamed back at him.

Everyone came out to see. The newest arrival, a Swiss, Jean Corta, who had taken the apartment vacated by the Arnauds, attempted to part the couple, and Louis Combatz was hanging on to Delobelle's arm.

"Let me go, you fool," Delobelle told him.

146

"Gentlemen, calm yourselves," Jean Corta said in his deep voice.

"Do you know what my wife has done?" cried Delobelle, taking in all those present with a sweeping gesture. "She thought she could make our daughter better by slaughtering a pair of doves on top of her. Of all the foolish, ignorant, superstitious—my little girl all covered in blood!"

He lifted his arms to heaven, his eyes wild with horror, and he had just wrenched himself free of Corta's restraining hand on his arm when Delphine suddenly appeared on the landing in her nightdress, like a tragedy queen, covered in pigeon's blood, with her hair hanging loose on her shoulders. An appalled silence greeted the apparition. Delphine looked like the escaped victim of some grotesque, heathen sacrifice. Spectators crowded onto the staircase and landing round the Delobelles' front door. Ferrat and his cousin from the fourth floor, the Combatz, the Cortas and the concierge and Valerie from downstairs, gazed in astonishment at the scene that met their eyes. Their chief reactions were of intense curiosity coupled with a kind of ghoulish enjoyment of the whole ridiculous business.

To her parents, Delphine's appearance was the last straw. Madame Delobelle, wild-eyed and frantic, was hardly recognizable as the same woman. All her genteel affectations had deserted her.

With a childish wail of "Papa," Delphine held out her arms and ran to her father. The scene was turning to farce. Ferrat, embarrassed, turned to slip away but a creaking stair betrayed him and his cousin's claw-like hand descended on his arm. She, at least, was determined to stay to the end.

Delobelle, acutely conscious of how grotesque they must appear, could not bear to see his daughter an object of ridicule.

"Go inside," he begged her. "People are looking at you. You are only making a spectacle of yourself."

Mortified, he felt their critical eyes upon him. But Delphine seemed to have no intention of going in. She stared vacantly round her at the neighbours crowded upon the staircase. Her lips trembled. She must have witnessed the whole dreadful quarrel between her parents, for her face was tear-stained and there were blotches on her cheeks as if she had been fighting.

The sight of that ravaged face moved even the neighbors to pity.

"Come, my little Delphine," her father coaxed her in lover-like tones which made them blush for him.

Suddenly, Delphine tore herself from her father's arms, made a dash for the stair well and began calling Frédéric's name.

"Be quiet!" hissed her mother. "Will you shame us all?"

"You leave her alone," Delobelle roared, holding his wife back by main force. This was getting interesting. They listened breathlessly to the revelation of the Delobelles' prviate lives and secret passions. Again, Delphine flung back her head and called: "Frédéric" up the stair well.

"Calling that good for nothing—has she no pride?" muttered Madame Cazingues between her teeth. Jean Corta, standing beside her, heard the words. His eyes, of a curious liquid golden brown color, rested on her for a moment and the concierge moved uncomfortably under his clear gaze. She had devoted a good deal of energy to cultivating the new arrival's good opinion.

Corta guessed what was passing in the concierge's mind and smiled almost imperceptibly. He was not deceived. While behaving with equal courtesy to all, he was none the less capable of decided judgment of his own, and there were a good many cases in which his pleasant manner concealed a strong dislike. He was a strange man, Jean Corta, a ready talker with a strong but very mixed personality. He drank heavily, to his own disgust, but his real good nature, his love for children and his zest for life in general acted like an infusion of fresh blood to counteract his faults.

Delobelle was still trying to drag his daughter back inside but she clung obstinately to the banisters. Every three seconds she flung back her head and screamed Frédéric's name in a piercing, siren wail. Just so, Corta reflected, must the mourning women have screamed in ancient funeral rites.

A door slammed loudly on the fifth floor and a voice called impatiently down the stair well, dominating the hubbub below.

"What is going on down there?"

Frédéric's face peered down, sardonic and detached.

Delphine called his name again. Frédéric shrugged and skidded rapidly downstairs, appearing among them with dramatic suddenness, a lean, untidy figure, eyes shining with the cold luminescence generally found in deep-sea fishes.

"What is it? To what do I owe—"

He broke off at the sight of Delphine and the Delobelles.

"My God," he said dazedly, "what is she? A human sacrifice?"

"Insolent wretch!" exclaimed Madame Delobelle.

Frédéric did not deign to look at her. He was gaping at Delphine incredulously. Suddenly he began to laugh and turned to Ferrat with a helpless gesture.

"No, surely—they've not been trying to murder her? I know they're mean and stupid but even so, a daughter cannot cost so much!"

His words fell like a stone into the awkward silence. His was the advantage and clearly he intended to make the most of it. They could only stand by while he wallowed in sarcasm, each wishing privately that it had not been necessary to involve him. For all its peculiarity, this little crisis of the Delobelles threw an uncomfortable light on their own middle-class lives and even those who had condemned them without mercy a moment before now felt themselves ill at ease when called upon to face the judgment of this starveling student, this latter-day Villon from the fifth floor.

"I beg you," Ferrat broke in hastily, "have some pity for the child—"

For a fraction of a second, Frédéric paused then he came down the last few stairs, his eyes moving from Delphine to the rest of those present. He made a movement which included them all.

"What are you doing here? Is this a theatre? Go on, be off with you! The play is over. The curtain's down."

"The impertinence!" Madame Cazingues bustled furiously downstairs.

Frédéric turned to Delphine.

"You called me? What is it, Delphine? You need me? How can I help you? Who must I kill?"

Delobelle made as if to push the student away but Frédéric had already taken Delphine's arm in a gentle grip. She clung to him like a leech.

"Tell me, Delphine. Are you hurt? Who would want to hurt you? Trust me. I am not one of them. They would never have me. I am an outcast, a pariah, I've references to prove it!"

He laughed bitterly but the arm around Delphine was sympathetic. The girl leaned against him, apparently incapable of movement. Frédéric had a momentary vision of the grotesque couple they must make, with Delphine in her blood-stained nightdress and he with his dishevelled hair.

"Come," he said. "We must go indoors, Delphine."

It was not easy. The girl's one instinct in her shocked state, seemed to be to cling to Frédéric and not go back to the apartment.

Fortunately, the labors of Madame Cazingues had seen to it that the floor was polished smoothly and he was able to slide her to the door. The moment they were inside, Frédéric promptly slammed it behind them, leaving Delphine's parents outside.

Joseph Delobelle stood for a moment staring at the closed door, glanced shiftily round at his neighbors, and then, without a word, made for the stairs and hurried down. His wife did the only thing left to her and fainted.

The noise in the building died away. Frédéric found himself alone with Delphine. She was still lost and distracted. Not knowing what else to do, he made her sit down on a low chair in the salon. She kept repeating the same thing: "They will kill me in the end with their quarrels, they will kill me—"

She said that she was cold and Frédéric took the gold-embroidered cover off the piano and draped the red taffeta folds around her shoulders like a bishop's robe.

He went and drew back the curtains. Delphine blinked

as sunlight streamed into the room. She was a little calmer now, and began to seem to him a little less ridiculous, a little more pathetic. The embroidered cloth partly hid her hair and made a frame for her face which Frédéric saw properly for the first time. The features were plain with nothing to give character to her expression. The general impression was one of disproportion with the high forehead and the heavy jaw. Her large eyes had the melancholy of a sodden plain and when she spoke, her lips drew back to show her gums.

She began to thank him for coming. She was sorry she said she could not offer him any refreshment but her mother kept everything under lock and key—as if he were paying a social call. Frédéric would have wanted to laugh had he not seen her bloodless face and the small, repressed shudders which shook her body as though with some chronic nervous spasm.

To hide his discomfort, he began looking round the room. It was identical with those in the other apartments, but the rather exaggerated elegance of its furnishings in the style of Louis XV gave a hint of wealth and good taste to the room. But the fragile tables, the delicate china and the stiff, low chair in which she sat only served to emphasize Delphine's heavy, awkward frame. She clashed violently with her surroundings. Nothing in this apartment was designed for her and Frédéric wondered how it was possible for a person to spend years of her life tied to such an unsuitable background. Surely, in the end, it would develop into an unbearable torment?

"Tell me about yourself," he said to Delphine. "Relax—talk to me."

She had dreamed so often that he was sitting there, talking to her, dreams she knew could never come true. From time to time her mother had made scathing remarks about the penniless student, remarking that she would rather die than let him have her daughter. But Delphine, for her own part, knew very well that Frédéric would never enter her house because he would not want to, and that her mother's contempt was nothing compared to the utter indifference with which he regarded all her family.

But now he was there. It was all so simple she was

151

happy. She forgot her terrible fatigue. She talked to him, yes, talked, told him everything. Where to begin? There had always been her mother. Her parents. They and she. Always.

She told him things she had never told to anyone. All that had been choking her, for years. How her mother watched her, questioned her, her wild ambitions. The hatred which, little by little, had come between her parents. Her father's love, equally stifling. Their dreadful quarrels. Her own ill health. When she had a hemorrhage, they had stopped arguing for two whole days—and for the sick Delphine, it had meant peace.

They heard Madame Delobelle returning. Frédéric went to the door and shut it firmly and the mother dared not interfere.

He remained until late in the evening and no one dared disturb them. Darkness fell. Frédéric felt very peaceful, there being nothing so soothing as solving other people's problems.

The slight physical revulsion which Delphine had formerly inspired in Frédéric gave way to an infinite pity for the girl. She had begged him to return and return he did, almost every day, disregarding Madame Delobelle's dislike. She, on her side, dared not contradict her husband when he ordered her to let the student in.

Frédéric came to know the mean, secluded life the girl had led. He would never have guessed that these secret tragedies could exist, so well concealed beneath the apparent comfort of such bourgeois homes. He learned of the domestic hell in which Delphine had grown up, of the hatred of her parents, their quarrels, of frenzied ambition, the worship of money and the petty sadism which developed between two people with little power to hurt.

At last, Frédéric was discovering the existence of forms of suffering other than his own, and by comparison his own thwarted childhood spent in dim colleges seemed to him almost free and full of pleasant memories.

When he came in he would find Delphine lying on the sofa wrapped in shawls. Her eyes would light up when she saw him, reminding Frédéric irresistibly of some provincial scene in a novel by Balzac. He dwelt, with a certain sardonic pleasure, on the quick blush which colored her innocent cheek, the chaste flutter of emotion on her pure soul.

But all this was in reality no more than a cover for his own feelings, as though he had to justify himself for taking pleasure in these visits, he, the ragged bohemian, who until now had worn his poverty like a blazon and whose only glory had been in the contempt of fools.

And yet it was precisely this poverty, this freedom of thought born of his student life, which he now had to offer to Delphine Delobelle. This was the thing she needed. He had thrown open a window and let her breathe. At last he was useful to someone.

Delphine painted little water-colors, taken from postcards, to show him on his visits. There were poems, too, of her own composition, copied into a school exercise book with the titles underlined in red.

> *True feeling is a dying into sense,*
> *Oh, Holy Virgin Mary, sister, friend,*
> *The heather breathes an odour of incense,*
> *To God, the church's flower to the world's end.*

To his amazement Frédéric found in these poems aspirations to a life of purity. He could see well enough how her mother's obsession for money could have produced in Delphine this yearning for a monastic simplicity. He almost wondered why she had not become a nun. Probably her mother had opposed that too.

Delphine had blushed, all the same, at Frédéric's surprise.

"Did you think me so stupid that I could not make two lines rhyme?"

"No," he said, uncomfortably, "no, it was not that. Plenty of girls of your age, brought up as you have been, are by no means fools, either. But it is the kind of background which tends to make girls, well—more practical."

He thought for a long time that night about her poem,

153

finding in its childish rhymes something curiously akin to his own magic world.

"Would you like to live away from Paris?" he asked her one day. "Away from your parents? Think of a village far away. Sheep for your only neighbors! The postman three times a week. The loneliness of heath and torrent. But books in plenty, a wide hearth and red clay in the garden to make little figures with—"

"That would be a wonderful life!" Delphine said earnestly. She had raised herself off the sofa. "To leave Paris. Never again to hear the traffic and sound of windows shutting, not to be stifled any more—"

"Would you go without your parents? Would they agree?"

She did not answer at once and for the first time her blank, doe's eyes rested on Frédéric with a strange expression. Then she said regretfully: "Do not make me hope—there are some things which should not be said. Today, I can bear this life, but if I had to renounce the hope of escape then I should die."

He understood and did not speak of it again.

But at the beginning of June he asked after Charlotte who had been away for a fortnight.

"She must be at Juvisy," Gabin told him. "At least, I suppose so. We have been too busy to go."

The next day Frédéric went to Delphine and told her he had things to tell her about himself, asking her to forgive him if what he said must hurt her.

Then he poured out to her the story of his life, his love affairs and all the sorry history common to any poor student living from hand to mouth. He told her of his moodiness, his bouts of causeless depression, all adding up to the word failure. He said as much to Delphine.

They talked for a long time that day.

The next morning he wrote and told Charlotte of his intention to marry Delphine.

At the time Frédéric wrote his letter, Charlotte was no longer in Juvisy.

She had arrived at her mother's house in a state of

154

uncontrollable depression. They nursed her and left her alone.

They even took away Elise when she came running into the room ferreting about hopefully for sweets. Charlotte hugged her ferociously until the child began to wail at this outburst of maternal affection.

Charlotte had difficulty in controlling her tenderness, brooding anxiously over the mischievous, untidy girl with her dimpled cheeks and bright brown eyes.

When she was better and went into the garden, Charlotte was able to visit Horace Binet's little café, which now stood at the bottom of the orchard by the river. There was a veranda running out over the water. Veranda was an impressive name for the rickety platform below which the greenish water could be seen lapping at the rough supports.

Binet had cut back great armfuls of reeds and left them rotting by the water's edge, attracting flies.

This was clearly not the only grudge which people had against Binet, and hence against Charlotte Floquet. She was quick to notice a coldness on the part of the inhabitants of their little village.

The little wooden café with its red and yellow paintwork exhaled, inevitably, a smell of white wine and frying. During the week it might not offend the eye too much, having few customers, but on Sundays it was very different. Sunday evenings were shattered by the common music of an accordion, and couples roamed along the path wreaking havoc with the river bank and leaving a litter of sandwich papers which attracted rats. They flattened the grass and the Morels' fence bowed beneath the weight of leaning bodies.

Charlotte was inclined to fight back. Let them boycott her family, much good might it do them, she had nothing to gain from the Seuriots or the Forestiers. The only one who mattered at all was Roslin, and he for Louise's sake continued to call on the Morels. But Madame Morel enjoyed a good moan and moreover suffered pangs of conscience at the vulgar display which took place every Sunday. As soon as Charlotte was well enough, Madame

Morel began to complain, even going so far as to talk of suicide. Louise was actually considering a convent.

"What do you expect me to do?" Charlotte cried. "You know it is too late now and we can certainly do with the money here."

They begged her to be quiet, to remember that ears could be listening behind the hedge. Charlotte looked hopelessly at the sagging roof, the unweeded garden. The fence was falling down. Strangers wandered in with no regard for damage.

It was at this point that Madame Morel received a final installment for the sale of her second tannery, and decided that they should go away for a holiday.

It was not sensible, because there was a good deal to be spent on the house at Juvisy, but it was exactly what Charlotte needed. She set aside her problems for the moment. She was already trying to let the soothing influence of the countryside do its work. She must go on, and wait. Wait for what?

Roslin was delighted and offered to accompany the three women. They decided to take Elise, but not little Jeanne who was to be left with Lucia. Charlotte suspected Lucia of more than friendly relations with Binet because she had taken to going out each evening as soon as the washing-up was over, with the promptness of a woman going to meet her lover.

Louise cared for her daughter conscientiously, without apparent excess of mother love. The idea of leaving the baby at Juvisy presented no problems.

And so it was that after two days of planning and poring over maps of France they decided to go to the Basque country.

It was the first time Charlotte had had a holiday. In her childhood such things had been practically unknown. The ladies took with them two trunks, parasols and quantities of lace. From Toulouse, they took the diligence.

It was raining but this did not prevent them from admiring the landscape. They were to dine and sleep at Cambo. The Basque countryside was beautiful and they saw it at its best the next morning in warm sunshine. Charlotte, bouncing up and down in the diligence with the others, hung out of the window breathing in the unfamiliar pure air and looking at the green valleys with their hundreds of white farm buildings where children played in the muddy yards, calling forth cries of "Oh, how picturesque," from Louise.

Their main stop was to be at Biarritz, which was then very fashionable. They stayed at a modest hotel, although not too modest because Madame Morel had no wish to demean herself, or to demean Louise in the eyes of Roslin. There were a good many summer visitors and the tourists enjoyed pointing out in the street this or that friend of the Empress Eugénie who had a villa at Biarritz, this or that lady of the court, or even Prince Metternich, passing through on his way to take the cure at Bagnères.

One afternoon, while they were taking tea at a smart confectioners' in town—Roslin was paying—their attention was taken by an elegantly dressed woman, accompanied by a man older than herself. What drew Charlotte's notice particularly was that the man had lost one arm below the elbow.

His hair and moustache were light brown and in spite of the severe cut of his coat, he carried himself like a soldier. There was a stiffness in his bearing which suggested the habit of command as well as hinting at old wounds bravely borne, but this abruptness in his manner was belied by the singular tenderness and affection of the smile he directed at his companion.

Madame Morel could not take her eyes off them and quite forgot the *religieuses à la crème* she had been eating.

"Someone very distinguished, I'm sure," said Roslin, determined if he could not achieve distinction himself at least to appear knowledgeable.

When they had finished their tea, Madame Morel could bear it no longer and giving a coin to the expressionless waiter questioned him in a whisper about their mysterious neighbors.

"The lady and gentleman are the Prince and Princess Orloff," he informed them with a condescending smile. "His Highness lives in Paris but spends the summer at Biarritz."

157

Madame Morel, never having set eyes on a prince, was overcome with joy, a fact which caused Roslin some irritation. Charlotte, who had met a good many, both genuine and otherwise, at the house of Aurore Dumoulin, took the announcement perfectly calmly.

None the less, Prince Orloff, although no longer very young, was still a very attractive-looking man. His wife wore a simple, full-skirted blue dress but when she turned her head in their direction, Charlotte was struck by the fair, delicate beauty of her face, lit up by a pair of remarkably fine eyes. It was an intelligent face with clear-cut features.

They had decided to try the sea bathing and went to hire costumes. The women appeared in daring suits made up of short skirts over long pantaloons, revealing to the world at large that they had legs, a thing of which men ought strictly to have been in ignorance until that time. Charlotte discovered the sea with rapturous enjoyment. The tempestuous ocean called up an answering violence in her own nature but she swam like a lump of lead for all that and Roslin, decked in long black drawers dazzled them all with his performance, having learned to swim while on military service.

Princess Orloff was forgotten. Charlotte had no idea in what circumstances she would meet her again.

The weather had turned sullen and Madame Morel, Louise and Charlotte shared its mood. Only Roslin, playing idly with a few shells, and Elise, paddling in and out among the small waves with delighted screams of terror, seemed content.

The weather was not the only thing responsible for their mood. The resort lay on one of the main roads through the Basque country and constant streams of people passed by on their way to take the cure at Bagnères-de-Bigorre. Rumors spread quickly, and war was as common a subject of gossip as lunch-time's stale fish.

The abdication of Queen Isabella of Spain had still failed to secure the Spanish throne for her son. The royalists of the peninsula wanted a king. It was rumored that Don Juan, count of Reus, marquis of Castillejos, an ambitious officer who would not have been averse to gaining the throne for himself, had long been looking round for a suitably docile king through whom to rule. Word had already got about that the candidate he favored was Leopold of Hohenzollern, a relative of the king of Prussia and also of Napoleon II, through his mother, a Murat. Leopold's father was also said to have refused the throne on behalf of his son, who was still serving as a major in the Prussian Guard.

There were no tangible facts to go on but rumors of war wheeled in the air like gulls and Biarritz in that third week of June was thick with them. The farther from Paris the greater the alarm. They felt as though in exile.

Morever, the seaside had its bad days as well as its good ones. When the beach lay cold and drear under a grey sky in which hordes of gulls shrieked mornfully, it seemed as if the deep sadness of that limitless expanse of sea and sky penetrated their very souls.

We must be sensible, Charlotte told herself, as fear and anxiety tightened round her ribs like a corset; good lord, there is nothing to be afraid of for the present!

"If Leopold's candidature is accepted," Roslin hastened to inform them, "France will never countenance the thought of a Prussian prince on the Spanish throne."

"Why not?" Charlotte asked irritably.

"Well, er—" Roslin said uncertainly, "it is a matter of honor."

"Would this affect our honor?"

"Well, consider the possibility of an alliance between the two countries. German supremacy is already a danger to the power of France—"

"Spain has troubles of her own, do you really think she will be in such a hurry to make a military alliance with Prussia? Soldiers must be shod."

"Admirably put!" Roslin almost danced to show his appreciation. "Very witty, indeed. Was that your own, my dear? The seaside obviously sharpens women's wits! But you are forgetting, you know, our armies fought barefoot in 1792."

"And I have heard," Charlotte retorted sweetly, "that

your ragged French soldiers only won at Valmy because the Prussians had colic."

"Charlotte!" said Madame Morel.

"It has also been said that Danton purchased the victory of Valmy from the Prussians with the jewels of the crown of France," Roslin countered smoothly. "You see, my dear, who does one believe?"

"Even so, surely men do not make war for such stupid reasons," Charlotte cried, her face very red. "Simply because a Prussian cousin goes and sits on the Spanish throne! Or do the Prussians want war even more than we do and is there nothing, absolutely nothing we can do about it?"

"I am sure there are reasons which you do not understand, dearest," Madame Morel said confidently, "and you may be certain that France will be on the right side. Is not that so, my dear Ernest?" she added turning to Roslin and using his Christian name to add force to her appeal.

Roslin hesitated.

"You do not think so, Monsieur Roslin?" Louise asked anxiously.

He looked at the two women sitting on the sand, their faces raised to his with a world of confidence in him and in their country, and felt slightly ashamed of the big words he had used when all the time he knew quite well that nothing but the excuse was needed to provoke a war which both France and Prussia wanted. Not that it was the French people who wanted it, But the Emperor, his wife and those around them, and the industrialists—but how could he explain that to these women when he himself was having to struggle against patriotism, vanity and common sense?

"Naturally," he said stiffly, "we shall be on the right side."

Charlotte rose and walked along the beach where the gulls wheeled like evil omens on the wind. There was a weight of bitterness on her heart, for nothing is so bitter as the evil one sees coming but cannot prevent, especially when—however ill-informed—one can discern the hidden motives of self-interest underlying the slaughter.

She thought of Thomas, of Frédéric, of Gabin and of

others like them. Would they be killed? She could not imagine Thomas not going to the war. She saw him as a soldier. Danger threatened him, and Gabin, Frédéric, herself, her mother, her little girl—

This last thought was more than she could bear. She could endure anything, but not to see Elise suffer. She turned, her eyes searching for the child, but Elise was out of sight, playing near a tiny cave a few yards away from the group seated on the beach.

For a fraction of a second, Charlotte was afraid. A big wave broke. There was a scream. Charlotte bounded forward. People were running over the soft sand, making for others coming up from the sea below. A woman, then a man. In his arms the man held the soaking figure of Elise.

Terrified, Charlotte reached out and pulled the young woman on to the narrow path. Elise was breathing. They put her down on the short grass.

"She had no time to swallow much," the woman was saying, "we were sitting close by the cave and we saw the child picking up shells. She went too far out. There is a strong undertow and it knocked her over. But it is nothing, she is more frightened than hurt."

"How can I thank you, madame—I'm so grateful—oh, what a fool I am! If anything had happened to her—" Charlotte was almost beside herself with anxiety.

"It is nothing," the young woman said again, "a hot drink, and she will have forgotten all about it."

Madame Morel and the others were hurrying towards them with worried faces. A young man appeared from the dunes and came quickly to the man who had carried Elise.

"Give me your coat, Karl," the man said. "Wrap it round the child, she is shivering."

His voice roused Charlotte from her dazed condition, and brought her back to the world. While the young man was taking off his neat coat and wrapping it round the soaking Elise, she took another look at his companion and saw to her surprise that she was looking at Princess Orloff.

"Madame," she said, "thank you, thank you again—"

She would have seized her hands and kissed them but the young Princess withdrew them gently. She looked closely at Charlotte, studying the lovely face still white with shock.

"You are staying here? Close by, perhaps—"

"At the Hôtel du Midi."

"I'm afraid the town is somewhat crowded." She smiled. "I can hardly think you have come here for the cure at your age," she added. "Certainly you do not look like it. But there are few amusements. If you would care to be my guest this evening, you and these ladies—"

"My mother and sister—" Charlotte murmured vaguely.

"Very well then, this evening let us say, all four of you. We will have some music."

With a brief nod of farewell she took the arm held out to her by her companion, who also bowed stiffly, clicking his heels.

"Well, my goodness, that was an adventure," Madame Morel said as they walked back to the town, Roslin carrying Elise, who seemed only too happy to be made a fuss of.

"I shan't go," Louise said. "I have nothing to wear."

"Oh do stop whining! You have your pink dress!"

"Why not my grey dust-coat? Do you want me to look ridiculous? The Princess will do very well without me!"

"If you do not go, then I shall not go either," declared Madame Morel, who was in any case quite overwhelmed at the idea of spending a whole evening in such exalted company.

Louise, who had hoped to find herself alone with Roslin, had to put up with this. Good manners obliged Charlotte to honor the invitation.

She made apologies for the rest of the family, conscious of some embarrassment at arriving alone at this luxurious villa, full of an unobtrusive elegance where each individual object seemed a miracle of good taste.

"Come," Catherine Orloff was saying. "Do you like sweets, a syrup, or can you face a liqueur without flinching? I want you to enjoy yourself, please."

Charlotte was enjoying herself. Her training in Aurore's salons had taught her not to flinch at a liqueur.

Catherine Orloff questioned her about herself. Charlotte answered with the complete frankness and naturalness which had always served her well. She succeeded in making Catherine laugh and wondered how old she was, this enchanting little princess married to a hero so much older than herself.

Catherine Orloff told her merely that she had been a Countess Troubeskoy before her marriage, and that when she had met Prince Orloff theirs had been a love match.

Then Charlotte remembered the other man who had been with Catherine that day on the beach, and who had not been her husband. At first she had been too terrified to notice him but now she wondered who he could have been, the upright man with the hollow cheeks and hard blue eyes. He was not immediately attractive, but there was a fascination about him and Charlotte had sensed a firmness of mind indicating strong character, which was always one of the first things she noticed about people.

She lacked courage to ask Catherine Orloff about him, especially since she remembered that the couple had been coming from a lonely part of the beach and reflected that she might well be committing an unforgivable indiscretion.

"Do you play the piano?" Catherine asked.

"I used to once. But not any more—"

"I will play for you, in a moment. My friend is very fond of music, and as he must leave tomorrow—"

Charlotte was surprised when Catherine Orloff offered her tiny cigarettes in gold papers.

"I'm sure you do not smoke. It is only my own indulgence makes me offer them," Catherine said smiling.

Charlotte realized suddenly that the tall man with the high forehead and blue eyes had come into the room. He bowed. Catherine took him familiarly by the arm. He was relaxed and smiling.

"I am going to give you some Schumann preludes," Catherine said laughing as she went to the piano, "unless you would rather have Beethoven. Your romantic Pathétique sonata?"

"The sonata," he said, his eyes on her.

His look at that moment told Charlotte that this man loved Catherine Orloff. Catherine was a gifted pianist, but throughout the recital she gave them Charlotte continued to watch the mysterious man. His bearing and accent were German and he was much older than the mistress of the house, but everything about him, for all his careful correctness, spoke of a love that was slow and patient but very deep.

He saw her watching him and for a brief instant smiled at her. The steely eyes were almost soft. He was beating time with his hands and Charlotte noted he had good hands.

As she was taking leave of the Princess, Charlotte heard noises on the stairs of the big house, the sound of heavy footsteps and the clatter of trunks. Catherine Orloff stood in the wide hallway, a candlestick in her hand to light the way and smiled at Charlotte as though to cover the untimely noise.

"Thank you, madame, thank you again," Charlotte said. "Today, I owe you my little girl's life. I am greatly in your debt."

This time, she succeeded in taking her hand and kissing it quickly.

"I live in Samois for most of the year, I should be happy to see you there," Catherine said. "I have few friends, so very few—you might come—with the child—"

With a last wave, they parted. Charlotte stepped outside the bright zone of light.

The next morning, she naturally had to answer questions on the evening but said little, not willing to broadcast her memories.

"But surely, she must have said something? At least she gave you something to eat or drink—"

She had to tell them, a little. Not too much. Some things she kept to herself. Just then a former fencing champion, who was staying at the hotel and engaged to play shuttlecock with Roslin that morning, came up to their table. Clearly, he knew all about it. In such a small town, everyone knew everything.

"So you spent the evening with the Princess, I hear, Madame Floquet. You are indeed honored. Although she is certainly more hospitable when her husband is away from home." He laughed, as if at a private joke.

"A pretty woman, Madame Orloff," he said appreciatively. "And not one to put on airs, for all her title. She's certainly given them something to talk about here; round about '57, it was, and then in '62 and '63 or was it '66? I can't remember. That was the year—no I'm wrong, well anyway there was talk about her. With the exalted company she keeps it's hardly surprising tongues were wagging."

"What company?" Charlotte asked sharply.

"Why, didn't you know about her friendship with Bismarck? They met here, in this very town I'm telling you, in about '57 it was. Love at first sight on the old man's part, even if he was twenty years older than she. Head over heels in love and the husband the only one who didn't know. They were always together. Though, mind you, I'm not saying there was anything wrong in it! In fact I'd be willing to bet with that Prussian gentleman it was never more than 'kiss your hand.' But he loved her for all that. And the husband closed his eyes to it, because he couldn't do otherwise."

There was a silence, then he added thoughtfully: "All in all, she might have done better to make him happy. It makes you wonder if there'd be all this talk of war now if that man had got what he wanted. When a man's disappointed in love, what else is there but politics?"

"The Chancellor Bismarck! But he is a married man!" said Madame Morel as though that clinched the matter.

"Indeed he is! A wife in Germany, and they say she has big feet!" The fencer chuckled hugely. "Oh, yes, he's faithful! But there, with all due respect to you ladies and gentlemen, the world would certainly be a more peaceful place if men thought more of love and less of statesmanship."

"Oh, be quiet, you dreadful man!" Madame Morel protested shrilly.

Louise rose abruptly from the table. "Where is Charlotte?" she asked suddenly.

"She is outside. I can see her in the square."

Out in the open, surrounded by pigeons and sunshades and all the familiar noises of a holiday town, Charlotte felt her heart contract. The man she had seen the night before with Catherine Orloff had been Bismarck. She was certain

165

of it now. He must have come, just for the day, almost in secret, to leave again almost at once for weightier business. He was in love with her, he must love France a little also, since he came so often to the Basque country. How could anyone not love France? She could have wept as she remembered the stern, cold man, whose features she could recognize now. Nothing he had said or done held any comfort for her. And now, at that very moment, he must be in the train that was bearing him back to his native Prussia.

To her horror, Charlotte found that all the happy memories of the pleasant evening she had spent were spoiled. Everything was spoiled.

For the first time in her life, it came to her that it was possible to hate one's country and the thought was intolerably painful.

She was frightened. This time, the threat of war seemed very close.

8

THEY RETURNED to Juvisy earlier than they had intended. There, Charlotte found Frédéric's letter telling her he meant to marry Delphine Delobelle.

She read the letter three times, unable to take it seriously. She looked at the date: two days after their departure for Biarritz.

More amazed than hurt at first, she read the letter again. It was short and to the point, both cynical and honest. Frédéric also talked of Delphine and of the life she had led. He made it clear that this was not a case of love, or even of friendship, but of a feeling at once much greater and more selfish, of being comrades in misfortune. We are both outcasts. She loves me. We shall go and live in Provence. Her father has offered me money. He wants to see her settled. That does not matter. The important thing is that, together, we shall try to get out of this—

For two days Charlotte was unable to take this letter seriously. Then it began to haunt her. Like all women, she found it hard to admit that anyone could stop loving her or, worse, be misguided enough to seek happiness elsewhere. She was careful not to examine her feelings too closely, feeling conscious that she could claim no right over Frédéric. In the end, she managed to convince herself that he was doing this from a spirit of sacrifice and blamed herself for leaving him so suddenly alone. She could have helped him, she thought.

"I shall go to Paris," she told herself. "He cannot be allowed to commit this folly."

end of the same week, she saw Delphine and Frédéric

But when she reached the rue Monsieur-le-Prince at the

outside. They had leather bags and were dressed for travelling. Joseph Delobelle was with them.

With a dreadful feeling that events had already moved on, she stopped to speak to them. Quickly, without mincing words, Frédéric told her of his marriage which had taken place that morning. Charlotte heard herself make the conventional congratulations but she seemed to be floating miles away from the real world.

While they waited for the cab, they talked at random with a desperate nervous energy which only served to point the gulf between their words and what was in their minds.

Charlotte was chiefly conscious of an overpowering curiosity, and she found it hard to take her eyes off Delphine's muffled figure. Frédéric avoided her eye. He looked thin and nervous. He, like Delphine, had dark rings round his eyes.

Charlotte might have continued to believe that he had acted out of some motive of defiance, but she sensed a subtle undercurrent running between the two of them, some sort of bond she did not altogether understand. It troubled her. She would have given a great deal now to talk to Frédéric alone, to extract from him some admission of the part which she herself had played in his life, for the disagreeable truth seemed to be that he had won free of her.

"I've forgotten my pipe," Frédéric said suddenly.

"Go and find it, quickly," Delobelle said, "I will hold the cab."

Charlotte's eyes met Joseph Delobelle's. Neither was deceived. They knew that Frédéric had not forgotten anything, that it was merely an excuse to allow Charlotte to go after him.

Delobelle looked away. He cared nothing for Charlotte Floquet. He knew all about her and her connection with the student. Heaven knew his wife had talked enough about it. But he did not care. Nothing mattered for him except his daughter Delphine.

He could not face the thought that Delphine would die. And she would have died in the end, of a simple decline. He had lived and worked for Delphine. He had come to hate his wife for her determination to get their daughter off their hands. He knew Delphine loved Frédéric. He had done his utmost to promote the marriage. Financially, he had been more than generous, had held out tempting offers. It was all a long way from the splendid match and smart society wedding Madame Delobelle had hoped for, and she had wept. Her dislike of the student was intensified by her suspicion of his motives.

But Delobelle cared nothing for Frédéric's motives. He wanted his daughter to be happy before it was too late. He told himself fiercely that he would pay any price to buy that happiness for her, however short, however illusory. He would have given all he had. There was nothing left for him in any case. He wondered if he would ever have the courage to climb the stairs to his apartment and take up his old life again. Was there somewhere, away from money and from the town, where he could find peace? He felt a need to find out things he had never known, to learn to understand nature. He could almost hear his wife's laughter, that unending, strident laugh of hers that was worse than any abuse and yet was not the laughter of contempt or of mockery. Her laughter was a denial, the defiant laughter of ignorance known but unacknowledged.

He could see little Clarisse, Valerie's daughter, running towards them waving her arms. She must have found a cab. Delobelle watched her hurtling past the tall grey buildings, skipping with practised agility between the passers by, already adept at side-stepping the teasing street arabs. But while he watched Clarisse, Delobelle was thinking of his wife. After twenty-six years of marriage, it was the first time he had ever really thought about her. I do not love her, he thought, or it is so long since I did so that it comes to the same thing. Yet I am sorry for her. It seems odd, but I am. I know her insecurity, her fear of failure. It must be a blow to her to see her daughter go off into the wilds with a poor student. Even when she had given in and agreed to the marriage, she wanted to keep Delphine here. But that student swore he would never live in the same house with her. What he said was dreadful, unforgivable. He is young and cruel and must have

169

wounded her for life. But I'll back him up because of Delphine, I'll always back him up, because of my daughter—

Delobelle would not turn round although he knew that Charlotte had run after Frédéric. She found him in Valerie's room off the courtyard. They faced one another like enemies.

"Why have you done this? Nothing can come of it. She is ill, you know that. You never cared for her. You do not love her."

"One loves where love is given."

"Frédéric, this is a desperate solution. You are making a gesture, just to convince yourself that you are real. Listen to me," she went on urgently, "I am not thinking of myself, I have no right to any claim on you, nor anything to offer you. But this senseless utopian idea of rushing off into the wilds of Provence with a sick girl for company! How will you live?"

"I have money. For as long as this lasts, that will be provided."

"Have you done this for money? I cannot believe that of you."

"Why not? You know of me only what you wish to know. I have suffered from lack of money like a shameful disease, without your knowledge. You did not even see it, the malady I carried with me like a shade. That is what money was for me. Delobelle will give it to me. He has given me back my dignity. Do you know what I did with my old jacket? I dragged it down the street in the mud and stuffed it down a sewer for the rats."

"No," she said angrily, "you were young and carefree. Now you are simply dramatizing. No one suffers on account of an old coat."

"No?" he said holding her eyes.

"You are marrying for money," she cried, clinging to her argument. "You detest these people and everything to do with them."

"I am marrying for reason, or trying to. I am trying very hard to live as I think right, in a country I love with a girl who can understand."

"I suppose I could never understand!"

170

"You no longer enter into it," he said simply.

"This marriage is madness," Charlotte repeated, shaking her head. "You will make Delphine unhappy."

"She loves me," he said shortly. "I shall play the game. And whether you believe it or not, it has already ceased to be a game. In a very little time, I have really come to know her. Love, friendship, understanding, these are nothing to do with time, I have told you. We are alike, like two exiles. And was it not you yourself who urged me to live?"

He was a different being, strange and curt, already engaged in a new life. It was terrifying how in so short a time this could have happened, everything had been destroyed and built up again, turning him almost into a stranger, a person over whom she had no rights, not even any claim to know or help him.

Throughout this exchange, Valerie had continued quietly with her sewing. They were suddenly conscious of the silence in the room. A blue feather drifted lightly to the floor. Clarisse was coming into the courtyard, her feet echoed on the stones. Instinctively, they tensed themselves for the shock as she flung open the door.

"Well," Frédéric said, "I'm going! No need to look like that, both of you. You know quite well you will have forgotten me in two months."

He shrugged. "Goodbye and thanks for feeding me all these years."

He stood for a moment by the door, then shrugged again and bowing deeply, opened it and closed it firmly behind him.

The two women were left staring after him. Valerie rose and looked through the window. Charlotte had a nervous inclination to laugh while at the same time she was hurt and angry, knowing that with his departure something else had gone out of her life. But she thrust away the new loneliness, refusing to think of it. Her grief would keep. Life must go on.

"You only came to see Frédéric, did you not?" said Valerie. "You wanted to help him—"

"Yes, I truly believe that."

"You do not know him very well. You thought you were

acting for the best but you were wrong. This marriage is right for him. He has found a wife; he is going back to his own country. This girl loves him. She understands him better than we do."

"What do you know of it, Valerie?"

"I know. He has been at peace, in these few days."

She went back to her birds.

"He never found it easy to be happy."

Charlotte looked at Valerie, remembering that she had once loved the student and they had had a brief affair.

"Were you angry with me, Valerie? Because of him?"

"No. Oh, I am no saint! I have my faults. But I am not jealous. He was not for me. He was too young. He had his romantic notions, but I was like a mother to him, I could not help myself."

She picked up a feather and smoothed it between deft fingers.

"Besides, he was happy with you. I could not have given him that. You are younger, and more beautiful." She looked up at Charlotte frankly. "You see," she went on, "I think with him I felt old for the first time and I was not even thirty. I dared not even look in a mirror beside him. I was afraid he would see the difference. There was a fire in him, you know, burning him up as if he were drugged with his own youth." She made a small, affectionate movement. "I was very fond of him. He, he never thought of anyone but himself. He said he would be a failure. I told him not to be so silly. I never took him seriously. He thought I did not understand but I could see he was driving himself to death with words. When I think of the future, that is when I am afraid for him, when his youth is gone—do you know, at the beginning, when he first came to Paris, he used to come in here and sit for hours just looking out of the window. He always believed something would happen, a miracle! He really believed it. It passed and he stopped looking, but he always wished he would see one."

Valerie had never talked so much about Frédéric and their past and, listening to her quiet voice, Charlotte thought it was like a funeral speech, and equally distressing. She knew Valerie could not have understood the

172

student, any more than the student could have understood Valerie, with her strong, down-to-earth nature and very real courage.

Charlotte said she must go. They had little more to say. Their talks always ended like this, with the sudden awkwardness that came between women in different walks of life, even when they had been closest.

"Will you go to Juvisy?"

"Yes."

"Doesn't it bore you, out there in the country, even with your little girl? To a city person, all that greenery gets dreary in the end."

"I have enough to keep me occupied."

Nothing important, she knew that, but still she had to cling to it, keeping herself busy, to prevent herself from thinking.

"Here comes your sister-in-law."

Illa had come to see Charlotte. She told her Gabin was ill in bed with a sore throat. To avoid going up, Charlotte said she had a train to catch. Ever since the meeting in Aurore's house, her relations with her brother had been strained. It was not that she despised him. She no longer felt she had the right to judge others. But she was afraid that he might think she was judging him.

One evening early in July, the 6th to be exact, Charlotte was in what remained of the orchard at Juvisy picking raspberries when all at once she found herself in the grip of a violent reaction, like an actual physical shock, a dangerous compound of old memories with a sudden uprush of new life. She stood up and eased her basket, feeling her face flush, her heart pounding, her thoat dry with terror at the strength of her own vitality and will to live. She looked round her at the house, her house, which she had once wanted so much and which seemed to her suddenly shabby with its untended garden. Fruit had dropped from a forgotten cherry tree onto the heaps of rubble left there by Binet. Rain water dripped from an overhanging gutter into the water-butt.

The place had the depressed sadness of somewhere so familiar that one ceases to see it at all. Something vital is missing here, Charlotte thought. There is no peace for me. I cannot live without love. Even if it cannot be Thomas. I'm only a woman. I was not made to spend my life just with my mother and sister.

Without realizing it she had been walking down towards the guinguette. She felt like talking to Horace Binet, perhaps because he was the only person in this place with whom she could be herself. It was a week-day evening and there was no dancing or accordion music. There had been rain. Charlotte paused beneath the rickety porch which sheltered the back door, looking at the rubble, the dripping roof of corrugated iron and heaps of old bottles.

It was ridiculous to stand there in the open. The sensible thing was to go inside but there are times when the body takes command and Charlotte stood in a kind of uneasy trance watching the water drip down the lopsided wooden porch.

At last she did go in. A solitary fisherman was staring at his drink. The room was damp and sawdust clung to her shoes.

"I tell you no lie, Monsieur Horace," the fisherman was saying at regular intervals. "Big as that, it was." He held out his hands to indicate the size of the one that had got away.

Binet was at the far end of the counter reading a paper, his stomach resting against the edge of the zinc which was the one bright thing in the whole dank, dismal room. He was wearing a clean shirt, yellow tartan waistcoat and cotton over-sleeves like a clerk. He still aspired to a certain cosmopolitan elegance, his clothes were neat, his hair shone as though in pursuit of some boyhood dream of the Anglo-Saxon tourist.

For all his suspicious manner, Charlotte thought Binet could be rather too smooth when it suited him. Binet's watchword was, and always would be, "Look out for number one." He was a rogue whose only religion was himself, but he stuck to his principles and could be generous when the mood took him.

He looked up at Charlotte's greeting, but to her surprise

he did not answer. Instead he got out a glass although she had not asked for anything.

"Drink? It's cold out."

He seemed in a hurry, as though something were wrong. However, the fisherman had noticed nothing. He was still gazing vacantly into his absinthe, his rod still on his shoulder.

"It has been raining," Charlotte said, "it is certainly not very hot. If it is like this on Sunday—"

"Sunday—" Binet grunted.

"What is it, Binet? Is something the matter?"

He looked at her as though wondering if she had taken leave of her senses.

"You are soaked," he said. "I'll make you a hot rum."

"Please don't bother."

"Well, good night," said the fisherman, a hand to his cap.

Binet watched him go. "Pickled as a newt," he said.

There was a heavy silence. Charlotte, accustomed to his usual unending flow of conversation, found it disturbing. "Something is on his mind," she said to herself, "perhaps the local people are making trouble for him. But, that doesn't usually worry him. Unless it could be Lucia. A lovers' quarrel?"

"I'm having a drink with you, M'dame Floquet, you can join me or not as you please."

He tossed back a drink without lifting his elbows from his side, put down the glass, picked up his paper and relapsed into silence. After a while he wiped his mouth, slowly.

"Have you got a good settled income, something behind you, M'dame Floquet?" he said suddenly, looking at her.

"No. Why, you know we've put almost everything into this place. I work—"

He held out the paper. "Read that."

Startled but uncomprehending she followed his pointing finger.

"Well?" he said. "This time it means war—"

"What?" Charlotte's voice was blank.

"My God, you know what's been happening! You have

read about this damned business of Prince Hohenzollern and the Spanish throne?"

"I never read the papers. But I have heard a little. There was talk of him at Biarritz."

"How did you know? You only came back on the 31st, and I read it in the *Journal des Débats* on the 1st or 2nd."

Binet was in the habit of buying serious newspapers. He felt they added to his commercial status. In any case, he preferred them.

"I tell you everyone down there was talking about it. Things always leak out."

"Well, they announced it officially three days ago. The Spaniards have not answered yet. You can imagine the rumpus among our Bonapartist friends! They have been howling for three days and now, today, we get the comeback. Listen to this. This is the 6th, eh? Well, listen: This is from the Spanish Ambassador to the Minister for War in Madrid: "Far from diminishing the effects of their initial reaction, the declaration of the government and the attitude of the legislature"—he means the fellows in the French Government," Binet explained, " '—may be regarded as a promise of certain war with Prussia if a Prussian prince becomes King of Spain.' And it's signed: 'Olo-gaga'."

"Oh surely not," Charlotte said impatiently. "That proves nothing."

"Oh yes, it means that our fine friends in the Legislative Assembly have been standing up making warlike speeches, that's what that means. Here, look at yesterday's paper. A deputy from the Loire by the name of Cochery tabled a motion about the Hohenzollern affair, calling for caution. M. de Gramont more or less told him to mind his own business."

"M. de Gramont! Our distinguished Foreign Minister," he sneered. "By God, to think he took up office in May! A pity he didn't break his neck first! Conceited, power-hungry oaf! Of all the pompous old women who govern us, he takes the biscuit."

"Binet," Charlotte said mildly, "you must not be so

ready to abuse people you do not know. It is easy to be right when there is no one to answer back."

"We know him all right. Have you heard what they call Gramont? The biggest fool in France! They're not far wrong, or I'm a Dutchman!"

"Binet, is it really serious, this Spanish business?"

He glanced at her quickly with a kind of animal suspicion that she had not seen in him before.

"Is it really serious?" she asked again. Her voice was normal, but she was in an abject state of nerves.

"Yes. Very serious, little lady. They sit there in the Assembly, prating on about the greatness of France. Here, read this, this is today as well: 'May I offer my warmest congratulations. All France is behind you and will follow where you lead.' M'sieur de Persigny was the chicken who laid that one. The honorable Minister of the almighty Emperor of the French. You see what that means—"

"No," Charlotte said. "They cannot go to war for *that*." She could not believe it. She clung to her woman's common sense which insisted that war was a tragedy which only grew from tragic events.

"This business of the Spanish throne is only the spark to set it off, M'dame Floquet. You listen to Binet. He may be ignorant and uneducated but he can read and understand, he can tell! They've got it all worked out, an affront to our honor! What an excuse to have a go at them!"

"It will blow over," Charlotte said earnestly. "It must."

"My eye! Not likely. They'll have *their* war. They've been brewing it for a long time. I must have been daft to go on as I was, working for the future. I've sunk ten years' capital in this business. For what? Fine lot of dancing there'll be when all their sweethearts are at the front! I'll be ruined. Ten years' work for nothing. Why me? I'm sick of being rooked by the government. They finished my father and my brothers, cut down like dogs under the Turkish sabres. And all for what? And the Prussians are all ready to go! Before you can say knife, we'll all be Germans, I'm telling you." He came out from behind the counter and began to shout.

"And I'm buggered if I care. I'll be a bloody Prussian so long as my pockets are full. What's patriotism to me! Fine words! This is where my country is—right here—" He plunged his hand into the open till and ran the coins through his fingers.

"What have their bloody heroics got to do with me?" he mumbled.

"That's enough, Binet." Charlotte's voice was like breaking ice. "You go too far."

Binet looked at her evilly, his hands still in the till. "France!" he said bitterly. "Honor and glory and right! All big, hollow words leading to ruination. And you'll die for such stupidity!"

"That will do, Binet. I said be quiet." After a moment she went on quietly: "I am only a woman, Binet, and I do not know much. But I know that if you lack the innocence to believe in honor, you must not be so ignorant as to suppose our enemies are saints, and ourselves monsters. There may be people in France who want this war. But Prussia wants it too. You do not know everything, Binet. Others have thought of these things before you. You think yourself clever, but in matters of policy and state secrets you know as little as I or anyone, but I do know because I have been told, that Prussia means to be the first power in Europe and will do anything for that."

She left him abruptly and went home, wondering how she would break the news to her family. But Madame Morel and Louise had heard it already from Roslin.

Madame Morel was weeping in the drawing-room. Charlotte was horrified. Her mother's grief struck her as a foretaste of what the war would bring to many thousands of women.

Louise took refuge in a stubborn refusal to believe a word of it. She insisted that the rumors about the Spanish throne were nothing more than malicious gossip.

For some time now, Louise had adopted an attitude of advanced cynicism which was highly irritating to her family. As befitted a woman whom life had treated cruelly, she had renounced her youthful errors, but had unfortunately taken it upon herself to renounce at the same time those of other people. It was equally unfortunate that her sharpened critical faculties should have been exercised solely upon others so that, little by little, she came to distrust any but the most conventional behavior and feeling.

Viewed in the light of this arid common sense, coupled with Louise's talent for ignoring anything she did not like, the war became merely a fantastic joke in very poor taste.

This attitude drove Charlotte into a heated argument. but even though she knew Louise was talking from pure ignorance, she could not help feeling a small surge of relief at hearing her say war was impossible. Slowly her sister's arguments, uttered with no knowledge but with perfect confidence, succeeded in undermining the structure of her fears so that they shifted and crumbled like a stone wall, letting in a shaft of light.

Next day, however, the fears were still there. The feeling of the country had altered. People stood in doorways talking, and business was slow. Madame Seuriot greeted Charlotte at the market.

Charlotte bought all the newspapers. Her heart beat quickly as she took them, skimmed over the main points of the news and put them down again.

On 7 July, it was known that the French Ambassador in Germany, Monsieur Benedetti, a Corsican and a Bonapartist, had been instructed to seek an interview with King Wilhelm and request him to "Advise Prince Hohenzollern to renounce his claim to the Spanish throne."

On the 9th, the newspapers announced that King Wilhelm had received Monsieur Benedetti *cordially*, although he made clear his displeasure at the things said by Monsieur de Gramont, the originator of this move.

"Everything will be all right," Madame Morel said constantly, "if King Wilhelm has received our ambassador—"

She had a touching faith in authority and placed confidence in what she called "a little man to man discussion."

The fear lifted, but only for a while. The next day, it was learned that Monsieur de Gramont, not content with King Wilhelm's courteous reception of his ambassador, now wished Monsieur Benedetti to return and extract from him a written order concerning the famous renunciation.

The country was appalled. Everyone was aware of the folly of such insistence.

9

On 12 July, as Roslin left his house to go to the newsagent in search of the latest information, he met Charlotte Floquet in the street. She was apparently going shopping and explained that Lucia was unwell. A cold, she said.

"May I accompany you? Perhaps I could carry your parcels?"

"Thank you, you are very kind. But I prefer to go alone."

Roslin bowed with a good grace, summoning up a rather sallow smile.

It was a beautiful morning. The air was warm and the sky blue above the hedges bordering the lanes which ran between the main street and the river, while here and there gaps in the green afforded glimpses of the sparkling water.

"One ought to be happy in such weather, not afraid," Charlotte sighed. "We should have life, not war."

Roslin was watching her. She would not look back, his presence in these days made her feel uneasy, and she wished he had not been there.

She was seeking for some phrase which would prevent his accompanying her when a cart swung round a right-angled bend into the lane, and ran into the thick-set laurel hedge of a garden opposite.

The driver got out, swearing energetically. He was a huge, robust countryman in corduroy trousers and a patched checked shirt.

He backed his vehicle out of the hedge and then came towards them leading the horse and touched his peaked cap.

"Excuse me, but can you direct me to a house by the name of Maréchal. It's on a corner, that's all I know. But I've been driving around here for half an hour with nothing to show for it."

"Maréchal? Over there, the house on the corner of the next street but one. But you'll find no one there."

"And why won't I? I've a wagon-load on order for them. They're expecting it. You don't think I'd lug this lot all the way from home before I was paid for it?"

He spat a long stream of tobacco juice.

"The Maréchals are away," Charlotte said. "A relative of theirs in the country has died and they will not be back for at least a month."

She glanced at the man, a beefy, red-faced fellow whose looks suggested he did not starve himself of alcohol.

He cursed expressively. "Got me all the way here, with a load of potatoes in this hot sun and then what? Not there! And what am I supposed to do, eh? Carry this bloody load right back again—blast all city folk!"

He felt for the bottle hidden beneath his seat and swallowed a draught regardless of them. It calmed him a little.

"You see, I farm at Courcouronne. You wouldn't know it. But it's a fair way and the roads! It's all right for them as can travel in style, with leather cushions and all, but when it comes to the rest of us—even the cattle won't use 'em. Take a look at this cart! And the way that bag-of-bones is sweating she'll never make this hill."

"Your horse is thirsty," Roslin said.

"You've said it, sir. Thirsty! How did you guess? You're a sharp one and no mistake. Been abroad in the service perhaps?"

Charlotte went for a bucket of water. The man spat, stuck another quid in his cheek, drank, and went on: "But where can I dump these 'taters? I'll never get 'em back with this broken-winded old bleeder between the shafts. I suppose you don't know a shop round here might need 'em. One hundred and ninety kilos there are—but I'll take a lower price seeing as how the potatoes have been

181

sweating a bit. In fact, I'll be only too glad to be rid of 'em."

Charlotte considered. A hundred and ninety kilos of potatoes. Why not? They would be something to fall back on, if there was a war— For the first time it occurred to her that war might not be simply a drama of death and separation, but of shortages, of hunger, even of famine as in the old days. No bread. Stories of armies with no bread. Famine, the age-old terror.

Instantly, she pictured what it would be like. She thought of the garden; they should have planted vegetables. They would have to buy chickens, rabbits—whatever happened, Elise should have enough to eat. Nothing else mattered.

"I will take your potatoes," she said to the peasant.

"That's what I like, a lady knowing her own mind!"

"A hundred and ninety kilos, Madame Floquet!" Roslin stared at her in horror. "What will you do with them?"

"Make soup," Charlotte said grimly.

"But, I say—only think—what a bother for your mother!"

"Listen, Roslin," she said, regarding him earnestly, "if there should be war—if there is famine—"

"What an idea! If there is a war the Germans will be defeated in two months."

"Roslin, do not deceive yourself. We do not know. I have a family, a daughter to feed, do you understand? I *must* be prepared for anything."

Roslin quailed before the determination on her face.

"I understand, but—hoarding—isn't that rather alarmist? Suppose everyone did so, then there would be famine before there was any fighting."

"I am thinking of the future. I am a woman. Nothing will stop me looking after my daughter's safety. This is not for myself. I do not give a jot for myself. Will you understand that?"

"Very well, I merely thought to warn you. You have your reasons and it is none of my concern."

Telling the man with the cart to wait, Charlotte ran home. Madame Morel protested, appalled at the thought of one hundred and ninety kilograms of potatoes. There would be no room in the cellar for anything else. Charlotte overrode her arguments.

"You are out of your mind," Madame Morel said at last.

"Try and understand," Charlotte cried. It dawned on her that she was shrieking like a mad thing, so that her voice could be heard in the next-door garden or in the street.

Madame Morel gazed at her in horror.

"It is some kind of a joke," said Louise from the doorway.

"Yes, a joke! Naturally," Charlotte said dully, shooting a venomous glance towards her sister. Turning to her mother she took her arms urgently. "Listen. Try and understand. I do not want to upset your household-but think, maman, think if there is a war. Suppose there is nothing to eat, suppose you and the children are dying of hunger—"

She could picture it all too clearly. Elise, roaming hungrily round the house looking for something to eat, grizzling, the way she did sometimes, and whining for her maman, her one refuge in distress. Charlotte's imagination revolted at the thought of the child going hungry. It was so blatantly unfair as to be inconceivable, its very melodrama saved it from becoming real. And yet, at that moment, Charlotte could feel the child's hunger within herself and she knew that the thought of it would haunt her more than any other, more even than the fear of violence.

She sensed that her mother was conscious only that her talk of famine was outrageous. It took time to accustom oneself to the notion of tragedy. To begin with, one was capable only of everyday fears.

"Give me the money, maman—it is there on your desk—please."

She picked up the little leather bag which held their small reserve.

"No," Madame Morel was saying. "No, I will not let you. You cannot indulge this childish whim."

"Leave the money alone," Louise said, "it is from the sale of our fruit."

"I am aware it has not come from the sale of your charms," Charlotte retorted.

"You nasty cat!"

"Go on, Louise."

"Mother," Louise appealed. "Take the money away from her."

"Give it back, dear," said Madame Morel, "it will leave us nothing to fall back on."

"Nothing for your little tea-parties, you mean. You can't give them up, for the sake of appearances. You've always sacrificed everything for appearances. The good opinion of your stupid neighbors has always meant more to you than our security."

"Take your money then, and buy your silly potatoes," Louise flashed at her, with a flounce like a ruffled bird.

"What money, everything I had I have put into the house. I have mended the roof, the drains—"

"No one asked you to! If that is your attitude—"

For an instant, Charlotte found no reply. She was conscious that her voice was breaking and there was a lump in her throat. She alone knew the seriousness of what she was saying. Louise's deliberate refusal to understand hurt her far more than her mother's protests, which were no more than those of a good housewife seeing money spent on useless stores that would only take up good space. But Louise—with her sly insinuations reducing Charlotte's earnestness to a silly, childish whim—was too much. She opened her hand and let the coins drop to the ground, hearing the chink of metal on the tiles. It was true, no one had asked her to do anything. She had been over-generous, to the house, and to her family, but even today she could not be entirely certain that her motives were admirable. Louise accused her of wanting to hold it over her, but she was judging by herself. One always saw oneself reflected in others.

"No," she thought, "I have done it all for the house, for Elise, and for them, too. They will not let me be generous."

The last coin fell to the ground. Charlotte stood with her hands apart, fingers spread wide in what she was conscious was a theatrical gesture. But it was not resignation which kept her standing there in that attitude of renunciation. As Madame Morel picked up her pinafore and bent down, she saw her mother, careful, homely woman that she was, down on her knees on the tiles picking up the money with quick, anxious movements as though afraid someone would take it from her. Charlotte was suddenly seized by a rush of anger.

"A cartload of potatoes—I could have had it—it was security, I could have slept in peace. The word 'potato' offends them, it's too banal. It's funny. But I don't care what you think. I will buy stores, we shall have provisions here whether you like it or not. Ten cartloads, a hundred cartloads of potatoes. I'll smother you in potatoes, but I'll have enough to eat for five or ten years if necessary!"

"Before you start throwing money away, you might wait until this war has become something more than newspaper gossip," Louise argued airily. "For my part," she added, "I do not mean to let either them or you upset me."

"Of course, you can tell!" Charlotte trembled with fury. "You are omniscient, infallible!"

"At any rate I do not fly into a panic over nothing!"

"You are stupid and ignorant!"

"Indeed?" Louise answered, flushing. "Stupid, am I? Well, if there was going to be a war, there would be something more to show for it than a lot of high-flown tittle-tattle. Look at it sensibly, Charlotte. Look at the stock exchange figures, for a start. Do you think prices would be the same if we were on the brink of war?"

"You are simply repeating Roslin's argument, parrot-fashion," Charlotte said harshly. Louise was a fool, and she was a fool to have listened to her for so long. She cast about for some crushing remark that would put Louise in her place once and for all so that she would never dare open her mouth again, but nothing came. She felt quite unreasonably angry and disappointed, and now only an outburst of sheer temper would match her feelings. It occurred to her that this kind of raging anger was only possible with her family.

It was odd how such domestic quarrels could reach greater intensity than even a white-hot passion, and always over something so utterly stupid and meaningless.

Louise, she thought, was preternaturally gifted for such domestic drama. She had a gift for inserting poison into every quarrel, driving it to its height and forcing a conclusion. She could reduce you to shouting like a maniac so that the room re-echoed and the blood pounded in your head. And every time, she, Charlotte allowed herself to fall blindly into the trap. For one intolerable instant, she glimpsed the terrifying world of resentment which divided them.

"I wish you were dead," she told Louise and meant it.

Louise's face froze. She rolled her eyes at the ceiling, even at that moment noticing the crack above her head, and her lips moved in a prayer which was lost in her high buttoned collar. Seeing her fingers make the sign of the cross, Charlotte guessed she was addressing God and gave a hysterical shout of laughter.

"Now she is praying for me! Saint Louise! Well, keep your prayers for yourself. I know what your religion is worth."

"Harpy," Louise said calmly.

"You hate me—we hate one another more than men fighting a battle," Charlotte said with horror. "It is hideous—it ought to make you weep. One's own family, one's worst enemies. Here we are, nursing our grievances from years back. Mother remembers things I did when I was twelve, I know she does. And I have not forgotten either. We are not brave enough to hate one another properly, families don't do that. But do we love each other? No! Yet here we are, together because that is how things are. Yet what do we know of one another? You misjudge me and I long for friendship so much that I would beg for it on my knees. Oh, my friends, where are you, why did I leave you?"

Louise shrugged. "Hysterical," she said. Charlotte rounded on her mother, her eyes glittered and her face was on fire.

"I was better off with my friends, Mother, do you know that? With those disreputable friends I thought I despised. At least I was warmed. They warmed me by at least trying to understand me—"

"Hussies," said Louise. "We know what they are worth."

"My darling," begged Madame Morel, stretching out

186

her hands to Charlotte, with a bewildered expression, as though afraid of understanding her daughter's meaning. Her whole life was based on the comfortable conventions of the family and she was deeply shaken by the thought that such passions could enter it.

Charlotte went out. The warm air brought her to her senses. She must go and tell the peasant she did not want his load after all, and find some excuse to escape from Roslin. She was impatient to be alone. She took the path along the river.

Suddenly she heard the sound of footsteps in the field behind her. She was separated from it by a thin screen of young trees and a narrow path. She got up and saw a group of men coming towards her. They were strangers, dressed for hunting and carrying horns. It was a most unexpected sight at that hour of the morning.

Charlotte thought they looked ridiculous but at the same time was intrigued by the odd group. There was something fantastically comical and at the same time sad about the little cohort, gleaming in purple and gold, striding down the little pathway in their high boots.

They halted abruptly as though on parade. A big fellow with a great deal of hair approached Charlotte.

"Madame, pray do not let us disturb your walk. Be pleased to take the path while we hurl ourselves into the ditch. Far be it from us to discommode a lady. It is much honor for us, meeting French lady, as I think you are? Please excuse, my French not good. I present myself: General Poliakoff, officer of His Supreme Majesty, the Czar of all the Russias. At your service. I am in France for my health, after long sickness, pardon, trivial and unimportant woundings. I have been your neighbor."

He bowed and his companions followed suit. He had a martial dignity which overcame the oddity of his words. He had the stiffness of a soldier and the youthful geniality of a well-fed baby. Poliakoff. Charlotte vaguely remembered hearing her mother speak of a Russian colony which had recently taken up residence in the neighboring village.

Poliakoff bowed again. They stood facing one another on the path and the situation seemed likely to continue.

187

Charlotte made a move to depart but the Russian was bowing again.

"I pardon—please excuse my bad French—do you speak English? It would be preferable to explain—we are a party, you understand? In French, also, is not? My friends and me, we are lovers of music, we—we make group for music, you understand?"

Charlotte said nothing. She had seen Roslin emerging from the path beneath the trees. He joined her, explaining hastily that, hearing an argument had taken place at her house, he had refrained from calling.

"I feared to intrude."

"You would have done," she said drily.

"Forgive me for spying on you," Roslin added softly, "but I heard what this fellow was saying to you. I found myself in the most unfortunate position. There I was and dared not emerge. Do I understand these heroic representatives of the Czar's army are seeking Roncevaux from their horns?"

"Don't speak so loud, they'll hear you."

They had moved a little aside. Roslin was whispering while the Russians stood in the middle of the path conferring together.

"These are our new neighbors," Roslin said, "General Poliakoff, if my information is correct, has taken the Château de Monteleau."

"What are we to do?" Charlotte said irritably. "This is ridiculous."

Her irritation was equally for the intruders who had disturbed her solitude and for Roslin who lost no opportunity of hounding her.

"Sit down here, on this rock," Roslin said. "When these Russians see you doing nothing, they may understand and go away."

Just then Poliakoff came towards them and bowed.

"Madame—you are French—we love France, we wish to play for France now—for the glory of France—"

"Roslin! Stop them." Charlotte said, horrified.

"But what can I do?"

"We play for glorious France and you sit there just as you are on that stone and listen," said Poliakoff.

Charlotte repressed a nervous desire to giggle. Poliakoff performed a military salute.

"Do not move, you listen. We play for France, land of good liquor and noble thoughts. We play for her victory in war."

There was no stopping them. They formed a group and, their horns at the ready, stood waiting a sign from their General before breaking into an overture so deafening that the echoes of it rang far beyond the tree-lined river path.

As luck would have it, they broke into the Marseillaise, it being the only French tune that they knew. Some men who had been fishing a little farther on were drawn by the noise and stood, rigid with embarrassment, at this display of patriotic feeling in mid-week. Roslin stood as if turned to stone beside them, conscious of the emotion which betrayed him but unable to choke back the pure torch-like flame in his heart.

Charlotte beheld him, a tiny, absurd figure, his shoes and trouser bottoms coated with mud from paddling through the wet grass. But she could not find it in her heart to laugh. For all his ridiculous appearance, there was something moving about Roslin, as about those other ordinary men standing rooted to the path. It is too late, she thought, much too late to try and understand if France is right or wrong. I love my country better than my mother.

She ran down the field and followed a small pathway through the corn which was already high. It ended in a lovers' nest where the ground was still trampled from the previous Sunday. Charlotte flung herself down, her head on the spiky stalks.

Suppose I were to lose everything, she thought, and keep only one thing, what would I choose? Elise, of course. She would go away with her, somewhere far away. A mother with her child has no country. But I love France! France, with its blue sky wheeling above her head through the yellow-green corn. Her mind went back to the wet riverside at Tours. Would I be capable of sacrificing myself for my country?

The sky turned turtle as she rolled over on the ground

and buried her face in the damp, warm earth, filling her hands with the soil of France. I must be mad, she thought, with a mixture of shame and exultation.

Late that afternoon, Roslin called on the three Morels to tell them that news had come during the day that the Hohenzollern had withdrawn his candidature for the Spanish throne. This done, the apparent cause of war seemed to be removed.

"So, it is peace, after all?" Charlotte asked dazedly.

"Yes, it is peace," Roslin said smiling.

"Peace! Are you sure? You could not be mistaken?"

"These dimplomats, they don't know what they want," sniffed Madame Morel.

"I am not mistaken," Roslin said. "The news is certain."

"Oh God, peace—peace—peace, do you understand? We can all live again without this hideous fear—"

The next day it was announced in the Press that the duc de Gramont, not content with the withdrawal of the Hohenzollern prince, was further demanding a guarantee from King Wilhelm to the French Ambassador, Monsieur Benedetti.

Public opinion was thunderstruck. Fear returned, and with it the agony of waiting. Charlotte insisted on being driven to Courcouronnes to purchase a cartload of vegetables.

On 13 July, Wilhelm of Prussa again consented to give audience to the French Ambassador, and explained politely that, as far as he was concerned, the Hohenzollern affair was at an end. This was a confirmation of peace, but Gramont, still seeking a pretext for war, sent Benedetti back, yet again, to bother the King of Prussia.

On the next day, 14 July, Benedetti telegraphed from Ems: "Ems, 3:45 p.m. I have just seen the King at the station. He told me simply that he had nothing more to say and that any further negotiations would be carried on by his government."

Monsieur Benedetti regarded this as an insult. He demanded another interview with the King of Prussia. This was, undoubtedly, a great mistake, the kind of mistake which that highly intelligent man would never have made in a drawing-room. However, he insisted on seeing Wilhelm. Wilhelm, bored and irritated, sent word that, for him, the incident was closed.

It was at this point that Bismarck intervened. If France wanted war, he was not the man to deny it. Immediately, he sent the following dispatch to his diplomats abroad: "After Prince Hohenzollern's withdrawal had been communicated officially to the French government, and to the Spanish government, the Ambassador requested His Majesty the King, at Ems, for authority to telegraph Paris to the effect that His Majesty pledged himself to refuse ever to countenance it if Prince Hohenzollern should go back on this decision. His Majesty declined to receive the Ambassador ever again and conveyed to him, through his aide-de-camp, that he had no further communication to make."

This dispatch, which twisted the truth sufficiently to inflict a severe blow on the French pride, roused a storm in the Assembly on 15 July. When the Prussian dispatch was read the duc de Gramont declared that in these circumstances any further attempt at peace would be foolish and unjustifiable. "We have left no stone unturned in our efforts to avoid war," he went on disingenuously. "Now we can only prepare to face it when it is forced on us."

The Senate burst into fanatical cheers. Rouher, the Minister, cried: "Let God and our own courage make the sword of France victorious."

Emile Ollivier, who had been sufficiently rash to declare in an earlier Assembly that he would go to war *with a light heart* was clearly not the man to make counsels of reason and prudence prevail. Already his mind was busy with the necessary financial calculations. The left and the centre did not stir. They seemed shocked. The extremists on the right, led by Granier de Cassagnac, were rubbing their hands. Thiers rose to speak.

With the support of Gambetta and the passionate determination of the left to strive for peace, he endeavored to prove to M. de Gramont that he had won his point and France had gained what she wanted in the withdrawal of

Prince Hohenzollern. He might have been speaking to deaf ears.

The declaration of war was voted by an overwhelming majority.

The first news appeared in Paris and its outlying regions on the same day. Before the end of the afternoon war was regarded as a certainty.

Roslin called on the Morels and found them sitting in appalled silence.

"Elise, where is Elise?" Charlotte asked suddenly.

"What is the matter?" Madame Morel said sharply, as though waking from a dream.

"Nothing." But Charlotte's voice rang with sudden panic. She ran into the passage, banging doors and pushing past Lucia who was sitting on the stairs sobbing. She found the child and, catching her in her arms, carried her upstairs hugging her tight and kissing her with a kind of desperation. Only the child's small body clutched against her, could soothe the terror and rebellion in her heart.

Naturally the child struggled to be free and Charlotte, setting her down, realized that she could not stay at Juvisy waiting. There was a train for Paris that evening at half past six. She would catch it. She must see Gabin, Valerie and her friends.

Madame Morel began to cry again when told she was going but she would always be crying now.

She found herself in the rue Monsieur le Prince at last. The streets were full of people. Madame Cazingues, the newcomers, Ferrat's cousin were all outside, but not Valerie or Gabin, or Illa. Charlotte was cold and went upstairs. She kept Annik part-time when she was away to keep the place clean, but even Annik was not there.

There were some letters. Charlotte was about to throw them all down when the writing on one caught her eye. It was a letter from Worski. A long letter. She forced herself to read it, fascinated by the bold, elegant handwriting. What he said she scarcely understood. It was not important. She saw that he was speaking of the Countess Lievitz, who was very ill and dying. He wrote: "*It is over*

PUT ON A LITTLE MUSIC AND LET IT PLAY

MUSIC—the lively new fragrance from Fabergé.
It's a song. It's a scent. It's a twist of lemon, flowered with wild geranium,
spiced with a whisper of Indian sandalwood and patchouli.
Put on a little MUSIC and let it play.
Cologne, Dusting Powder and Gift Sets—only 2.00 to 5.00.

Lancers
Vinho Branco
means
white wine.

Who knows
what it will
mean to
you.

IMPORTED
LANCERS.
Vinho Branco
A WHITE DINNER WINE

LANCERS® VINHO BRANCO. WHITE DINNER WINE.
SOLE IMPORTERS, ©1972. HEUBLEIN, INC., HARTFORD, CT.

a year now since I applied for my French naturalization. I have not spoken of it to you. My friend Madame Lievitz has connections which may obviate any difficulties attached to my foreign status. Since I am German through my father, the first thing was to obtain Russian citizenship—my mother was Polish as you know but there is no longer a Polish state, only a martyred Poland to remember—and as a Pole, I am technically Russian and shall find it easy to obtain French nationality. In times like these when no German could obtain naturalization, such matters are important. . . ."

There followed a somewhat confused paragraph which Charlotte skipped. She failed to grasp what he was trying to say or why he was writing to her. At the end he wrote: *"I have been thinking of you more than my country. I want to marry you in the sight of God and of your country and, as your husband, to become as truly French as you and the land of my choice, both in my heart and by adoption."*

The letter fluttered slowly to the floor, Frank, the Pole—the expatriate. It was so long since she had thought of him that she found it difficult to recall him. He wanted to marry her. She was not indifferent to him, certainly, but so far from any such thoughts that they seemed to belong to some past history, near yet unattainable, before the declaration of war. Now everything was different. All values had altered. She stood, in the current of air from the window, staring down into the empty courtyard. What would war be like? As yet it had no reality. It was the present that should bring comfort and reassurance.

Scattered shouting came from the thin crowds that were abroad. A voice cried: "Berlin—"

10

As soon as war was officially declared, England, Italy and Austria at once set about trying to hold back the course of events but to no avail. The official declaration was handed to King Wilhelm on 19 July at 1:30 in the afternoon.

In France itself, the fever continued to rise. In Paris, people flooded in from the outlying districts and crowded the main squares and thoroughfares of the city.

The recruiting offices were filled with young volunteers, many of them escorted by their families. An exotic touch was added to the scene by the *zouaves* on sentry duty, the famous *turcos* who were the pride of Paris. They had cashed their savings and given them with their watches to their families or sweethearts.

The news spread quickly that the army had received weapons and ammunition for the campaign, including the many-barrelled *mitrailleuses*, which were to spread terror in the ranks of the enemy.

Word went round that Napoleon III had agreed, in the interest of national morale, to allow the Marseillaise to be sung in public after being banned throughout the period of the Empire on acount of its republican associations. "You may authorize the song," the Emperor's private secretary telegraphed on 15 July, "but it would be advisable to warn the prefect of police."

Was Napoleon III as optimistic as he would have it believed?

Nothing was left now of the ambitious projects of his youth. He was a man weakened by long illness and harassed by the pressure of those around him. What was in the mind of this utopian dreamer at this, the vital turning-point of his life?

He was at Saint-Cloud when war was declared. Marshall Leboeuf joined him there. The Emperor trusted him but none the less decided to take command of all military operations in person and to set out for Metz accompanied by the Prince Imperial.

Before they left, the Empress took her son to the Invalides and made him kneel before the tomb of the victor of Jena. White-faced and brave, the boy knelt in silence before Bonaparte's tomb. He had been raised on thoughts of glory. If courage were demanded of him, they should have good cause to be proud.

But there, beneath that cold, inhuman dome, it seemed an empty glory, or one too great for him. He knelt on, pale and still, as though he could not tear himself away and the Empress, close beside him, saw him square his shoulders beneath the military coat which made him seem all at once so young and vulnerable. For an instant, she felt fear. She was a proud woman but her pride was not for herself. Politics had made her a queen and mother love had made her a schemer for honors for her child. An unhappy married life, frustration and disappointment in her life as a woman, had only increased her determination to succeed through her son.

Suddenly, seeing his youth and slenderness, Eugénie had a fleeting vision that she might be working for his harm. The easy triumph she had pictured for his future swayed and crumbled before it.

She could no longer bring herself to look at her son, he too had forgotten her, rapt in contemplation of the glory for which he had been sedulously trained. He was young and pure, and he loved his country. Everything was very still.

Napoleon III travelled to Metz with his son. In order to dissuade him from passing through Paris on his way from Saint-Cloud, the prefect of police warned of the risk of damage from an overenthusiastic crowd. The Emperor may even have believed it. He had been told so many lies about his popularity.

Instead, he travelled by train to the Strasbourg terminus. The station had been cleared and filled with police.

The Emperor said little. His movements, once quick and decisive, had become slow and hesitant as though he were seeking to conserve his strength. His body was heavy, not with the genial corpulence of those who have lived well but with a general thickening and sagging of the abdomen which were the signs of his ill health. His attitude was one of utter weariness, but it was his face which was most striking. Even through rolls of flesh, it still contained the swollen nobility which had come to him with age, a decadent, imperial mask, worn for posterity by a living man.

The Prince Imperial copied his father's silence. He was very pale. The train moved off and Napoleon III looked at his son, a nervous figure pathetically imbued with the idea of the noble part he was to play for France. The Emperor loved his son but he had always regarded him as a child. What would the future hold for the young prince if the morrow should prove a disappointment? This was not the moment for fears or regrets. He could only go forward as he had always done, trusting in his stars.

The train pulled out. The Emperor, like all the rest, gazed out of the window.

At Metz, the Emperor's welcome was a cool one. The cries in the streets were not *Vive l'Empereur!* but *Vive la France!* Napoleon understood. His misgivings increased. He took up residence in the city itself and passed his time re-examining the same problems for the hundredth time, sometimes alone, sometimes with his officers. They did their utmost to reassure him but the Emperor was afraid. On one occasion he was seen to weep at the thought of the coming war.

The truth was that for the first time, the tragic facts of the situation had come home to him. They had thought themselves prepared for this war but they were not. The confidence at his headquarters was based simply on ignorance. Negligence and confusion reigned in military administration. Self-interest and petty squabbles over prestige blocked every attempt at coordination.

Worse still, before war was declared, Napoleon III had believed firmly but misguidedly in the lack of internal solidarity among the German states. He believed that Prussia would be his only adversary. But almost at once most of the German States joined with Prussia. Plenty of enlightened statesmen had long endeavored to warn the Emperor that this would happen, but they had been ignored. Now France was fighting not only Prussia but a unified Germany.

While the French mustered some two hundred and fifty thousand men, the Germans had nearly a million, six hundred thousand of them already in fighting form. Ahead of them went fifteen hundred cannon.

The French army was made up basically of recruits who had been unfortunate in the draw and paid for their misfortunes with several years' training. Seven years' service for a small minority while the majority of able-bodied men could not hold a gun. Finally, it emerged that there was practically no money for war, most of the budget having gone up in smoke on such costly mistakes as the ill-fated Mexican expedition.

"If the French do not reach Mayence by the twenty-fifth of August," General Moltke, commander-in-chief of the Prussian army, had said, "they will never reach it."

The French army was made up of eight corps commanded by MacMahon, Frossard, Bazaine, Ladmirault, de Failly, Canrobert, Félix Douay and Bourbaki. The Emperor was for attacking immediately, penetrating the German lines by a frontal attack using the bulk of his forces.

The first men were leaving for Alsace and the front. At 6, rue Monsieur-le-Prince, Millau was the only conscript. Gabin had drawn a ticket exempting him from military service. He said nothing of enlisting and even avoided any encounters with his former friends which might have led him into discussion of the war. Charlotte dared not broach the subject with him. Illa, Gabin's wife, was German and the war had placed him in a terrible dilemma.

Illa scarcely appeared at all. She was pregnant and near her time and she talked to no one, giving Charlotte only a faint, sad smile when they chanced to meet. Charlotte was nervous of going out and offering help. She knew that

Gabin was often absent, much too often, and this added to her awkwardness.

Valerie could not let Millau go to the station alone and persuaded Charlotte to go with her. No bohemian girl friends appeared and the boy from Arles looked suddenly very lonely and lost. His uniform jacket was too tight and he had not managed to fasten his gaiters.

Millau had dumped his kit in the hall and taken his midday meal with Valerie. The day was hot, without a breath of air, and they had left the door open. Valerie had cooked a chicken and invited Charlotte to join them.

Millau ate little and after three hungry years in Paris it was the first time they had seen him refuse food. The women were not hungry either. Valerie attempted to keep up some kind of conversation. Millau, in his tight jacket, suffered particularly from the heat. His red trousers made an unexpected splash of color in the shabby, grey workroom.

Valerie had purchased a bottle of good wine and Millau drank heavily. The wine went to his head. He set back his glass and tipped back his chair, forgetting that he must go. He remembered suddenly and the front legs of the chair struck the ground with a thump. The sun, striking the worn stone threshold and paved yard, was so bright that he might have been sitting in the doorway of his father's farm in Provence, but for the fact that no grass grew between the dusty stones. The gutter which ran down to the drain in the center was dry now, but it was impossible to look at it without seeing the thin trickle of greenish water that seeped down it all through the winter.

It seemed to Millau that in all his three years in Paris it had done nothing but rain. He searched desperately for a memory of sunshine but could not find one. Damn, he told himself, I'm drunk. His mind refused to function. He stared out at the blazing sunshine and saw only a vision of dismal grey and wet. His eyes went to Valerie's, hopelessly seeking reassurance.

"When I think we have spent three years sitting in cafés in this benighted *quartier*, talking about ourselves, thinking we were important," he said bitterly, "what fools we were. Well, that's all over now—"

It was time for him to go. He went out into the yard and everyone leaned out of their windows to watch him. He was a sight worth watching, staggering under the unfamiliar kit bag, in his blue jacket and red trousers with his cartridge belt awry and his kepi perched on his springy hair.

Ferrat and Louis Combatz came down to shake his hand. Madame Cazingues was in tears. They set out to find an omnibus to the station, but they were all full and they found themselves on the boulevard among the crowd of men in uniform waiting for their trains.

Near the gare de l'Est, the crowds were even thicker. The way was blocked by cabs and horse-drawn omnibuses. Private carriages, piled high with baggage, endeavored to force a way through.

It was no secret that a number of affluent persons, anxious to be out of the way of danger, were taking refuge in England. Many of these last-minute travelers were foreigners who had no desire to remain in France while hostilities lasted, but there were French families as well, and this caused a good deal of comment, especially in the Press.

Inside the station, the crowd was dense. A sustained hum of voices rose to the glass roof and the air was thick with smoke.

Charlotte and Valerie with Millau hunted for the right platform. There were several trains in, one already getting up steam. People were rushing backwards and forwards.

Millau was thirsty and they looked about for the buffet. They tried to get him some sandwiches but there was nothing to eat. Soldiers were everywhere. At last, they found the train and Millau clambered into a carriage already full of soldiers. Once there, he seemed at a loss. They stayed talking to him, stretching upwards while he leaned down from the window, jammed against it by the press of men behind.

The noise around them continued at the same unvaried pitch. Mothers were saying goodbye to their sons, urging them to take care. A girl stood beside Charlotte, her arms round her soldier sweetheart's neck.

The confusion went to Charlotte's head. The voices

throbbed about her in a continual, vibrating din. It was as if a plague, or cyclone, had struck the city. She looked up at Millau and wondered what she was doing here, seeing off a boy who was almost nothing to her. It was an odd twist of fate which made him the only person she had to say goodbye to. She lived in the same building with him all these years without even knowing that, but for the war, he would have been faced with seven years' military service when his studies were finished. He had never mentioned it. Now, here they were with nothing to say and anything they might have said doomed to remain unheard through the noise.

Then, without warning, the barriers were opened and a horde of zouaves swarmed onto the platform, shouting and waving their sabres, their black eyes gleaming like coals. The crowd on the next platform recoiled in terror and some ladies screamed. The zouaves scrambled over the rails, regardless of orders, and their barbaric cries echoed in the dim spaces beneath the roof.

Their shouts were answered by the conscripts in the next train and the crowd, a little reassured, burst into modified applause. Ignoring the doors, the turcos hauled themselves in through the windows, with a great kicking of red breeches and buff boots and waving of swords.

Millau's train began to move. The crowd flowed back and the men reeled and staggered inside the wooden carriages. Hands waved and one by one the men at the windows turned back and struggled for a place among the packed human cargo. Bottles were opened and voices raised in song. Some sat in silence, their kits between their knees, their eyes blank, shaking with the rhythm of the train.

The next day Illa was sick and complained of abdominal pains. Charlotte went for Doctor Marthe who feared the possibility of a premature birth. However, the pains might be due to nothing more than nerves and he could not say for sure.

Illa's condition frightened Charlotte. She was exhausted, her thin face wasted with suffering and her eyes huge and dull. She seemed to have given herself up completely to sheer animal terror. Charlotte was sorry for her because she was German, but could do nothing to help. Illa suffered in silence, with mute acceptance.

Gabin was not at home. Charlotte knew where he was. He was with Aurore. Not a day went by without his going there. Until now, Charlotte had tried not to judge her brother harshly but Gabin's absence at such a moment epitomized, more than his own frailty, all that was mean and pitiful in the human heart, a prey to lies and prevarication and incapable of sacrificing even its least pleasures.

It horrified her to think that the war would make no difference to all this. Was the war to be nothing more for those who remained behind than to endure the petty round of daily life, just as before? She had never thought of that. This vision of war was grimmer than any battle.

She went home in terror, thinking that she must do something, make herself useful in this war, whether for France or for someone, or go mad. The post brought her another letter from Frank. Briefly, he told her of his desire to see her and asked her to meet him in the place de l'Opéra at four o'clock in the afternoon. He said he had "something serious" to tell her. He begged, he even demanded, that she come.

Charlotte stood with Frank's letter in her hands, listening to Annick in the kitchen talking to the concierge who had brought up the letter. She looked down at Frank's writing. It was flowing and sensual, like himself, betraying a quivering, nervous energy in the formation of the letters.

The sight of his writing troubled her more than the sense of the actual words. She put the sheet down on the table and went quickly into the next room, then she came back and studied it again. Again the virility of the writing struck her like a physical blow. Her heart beat faster and she was astounded that he could so affect her, even from a distance.

She had lived too sequestered in these last weeks, trying with vain self-deception to forget love.

For a moment she gave herself up to the pleasure of thinking about Frank. She told herself it did not matter, for she did not love him and did not intend to see him, though if she were to go—

She struggled but youth and her appetite for life betrayed her.

In the afternoon, Madame Cazingues came panting upstairs to tell Charlotte that a gentleman was asking for her but did not like to come up. Charlotte was surprised to see Daguerran.

She asked him in and he was joined after five minutes by Paul Boucher.

"Madame," said Joseph Daguerran, "we have come to you with a somewhat delicate request. Indeed, it needed all the urging of our friend Paul, who is acquainted with your generosity, to make us even consider—"

He seemed to be suffering from some embarrassment. Boucher, a vague smile on his face, had settled himself comfortably in an armchair and was engaged in polishing his heavy spectacles, revealing a pair of wicked, monkey-like eyes.

"To cut a long story short, madame, we have come to ask your help for a friend in great trouble. His name is Jean Hertz. He was deported to Guiana for political reasons—"

He explained Hertz's plight. Having escaped and returned to Paris, the former convict had believed that since the term of his sentence had expired even before he had completed his hair-raising escape through the Brazilian jungle, he was entitled to the benefit of an amnesty. The outcry raised by his book on Guiana which Thomas had published in *Demain* had called attention to him once again, with the inevitable search for a new pretext to re-imprison him.

The reasons were purely vindictive. Hertz's state of health made the idea of the journey to Guiana unthinkable. He would die before he got there. It was only his amazing will-power which had kept him going so long, earning a living writing exotic stories for a provincial publisher. At least his experience in the tropics was proving of some value.

Hertz's friends had had the idea that they must hide him, at least until they saw how matters were going. It was Boucher who had thought of Charlotte's half empty apartment.

"I know what an immense sacrifice we are asking you," Daguerran was saying, overcome with embarrassment at having made such a request. Boucher's idea had seemed to him a good one to begin with. It would never occur to anyone to look for Hertz there. But now, looking at the young woman, he wondered how he could ever have considered it.

He looked round. The apartment seemed much smaller than Paul had implied. Then his eyes went to Charlotte. She had made an attractive impression on him before and once again he felt the appeal of her charm to his heart and mind. He looked at her more keenly than he had done the first time and found himself inclined to resent the thought that Hertz might live here with her. He decided to draw back, telling himself they had been mad to think of it. Boucher, enigmatic and cynical, was already going from room to room gesturing with the point of his umbrella.

"It cannot be done, Paul," Daguerran said furiously.

"Why not?" said Charlotte. "I use only the two rooms, surely I can help you."

"He would be too much trouble. The whole idea is absurd."

"But surely you did not come here only to change your mind so quickly. Come and see the room. It is arranged as a study but there is a closet that we can hang a curtain across. Your friend can use the back door."

She caught Daguerran watching her and smiled shyly. He had an open face, eyes bright and sympathetic, and his fair, wispy beard looked soft to touch. As they stood together in the narrow passage Charlotte's heart began to thud again, the nearness of that masculine form, those virile shoulders made her dizzy. She could not help it, she was too much alone.

Dageurran left soon afterwards, leaving Paul to arrange the details.

As soon as she realized they would be alone together, Charlotte knew they were bound to talk of Thomas. With a vague sense of self-preservation, she took the initiative.

"How is your friend Becque? Have you seen him recently?"

203

"Not much. He is married. You know that."

Paul was roaming round the room as though looking for spiders under the furniture. Charlotte found herself obliged to carry on with the pretense.

"He is well?" she asked with difficulty.

"As well as possible, I suppose, since that idotic marriage."

She intercepted a quick glance from him so keen and knowing that it suddenly came to her, with shattering force, that there was little he did not know about the two of them, little of the truth that his sensitive, unhappy nature had not guessed.

She experienced a keen discomfort at the thought. She wished she could have known all that Paul knew of Thomas. It seemed to her suddenly that this bitter little man held her fate, all that life held for her of hope, within his twisted brain. She tried to speak but her throat was dry. At that moment she both loved and hated Paul. Her very existence depended on him and she could not draw back, could not suppress the wild hope which seemed all at once a thing apart from herself.

Paul was still speaking in the same light tone. "You know my views on marriage, my dear. I like my women married to other men."

Charlotte forced herself to speak. "What do you want of life, now, Paul?"

"I wait—suppressing my heroic inclinations."

"You?"

"Yes, me! Amusing, is it not? I suffer from an unrequited patriotism. I have resisted the temptation to enlist. Can you see me as a soldier? I should cut a sad figure in uniform. It would be unfortunate were I to be killed. Heroes should not appear ludicrous."

"Would you really fight?" she asked, astonished that this disillusioned cynic could harbor thoughts of greatness or of duty. Was he, perhaps, less selfish than she had believed? He was certainly a sensitive and unhappy man.

"No, I would not fight," he told her with a sardonic chuckle, "I only said that to impress you. Of all fatal passions that for military glory seems to me the most dangerous. I love my mother but I doubt if I would kill for her."

"But one's country, Paul, surely that means something?"

"I do not know, Charlotte, I swear to you I do not know. Love of one's country too often means hatred of one's neighbor." He paused and smiled at her. "You are lovely tonight, my dear. Tonight, Charlotte, I am in love with you. What a pity I did not realize it sooner. I have an idea Daguerran finds you to his taste. In fact, I quite thought he was going to kiss you—"

"Be quiet. Do not say such things."

"Do you dislike him?"

"I have not thought about it."

Paul laughed. "Don't be cross. I thought he was the kind of man you liked—"

Charlotte said nothing. He guessed all her thoughts but she felt too weak to fight him.

"My dear, I know that Aurore is sleeping with your brother," Paul said suddenly.

"What do you expect me to do about it?" she burst out hopelessly.

"Nothing. If I put up with it is for one of two reasons: either I love her too much to have any pride or I do not love her enough. Do you mind being deceived?"

He picked up his umbrella. "I am going. You are beautiful, Charlotte. Do not waste all your life in fighting your mistakes. Live, little one. Forget Becque, or rather do not froget him, the experience of loving has put a bloom on you."

"Paul, is he happy?" Her voice was unsteady.

"*La Marseillaise* has folded, you know that? Becque is going to the front as a war correspondent for Zola's paper. His hatred of war made it necessary to be in the front line. I knew he would do it. He cannot bear to be useless. Had he two arms he would already be either dead or decorated."

"His wife—"

"I do not know her well—"

"You were going to say something else, Paul."

"Was I? Very well then. You may as well know. She is

205

expecting a child." He frowned. "You are torturing yourself. Do you still love him?"

"Was it for that he married her?"

"It may have been. He has a strong sense of duty. But do not deceive yourself. I dare say he is happy. At all events he does not tell me. He does not talk much at all, in fact he's damned unapproachable."

For a moment Charlotte was silent and when she did speak it was with such visible effort that he was appalled.

"Goodbye, Paul—I will do what I can for your friend Hertz."

She went with him to the door. He turned at the stair head and saw her still in the doorway.

"I lied to you in saying that Becque was happy. But then, I do not really know. Marie is not easy to live with it seems. But rumor has it—"

He started down. "I will come again. Until then, goodbye Charlotte. I enjoy seeing you suffer."

At the beginning of August, Joseph Daguerran himself brought Jean Hertz to Charlotte Floquet's apartment. The weather was fine and Paris looked almost normal. One scarcely noticed the little knots of people, gathered here and there in shop doorways or on pavements, talking over the news. It was not very good. Those who had looked for instant success by the French army were beginning to experience a slight anxiety.

"I shall not know what to say to this young woman," Hertz said to Daguerran for the hundredth time. "Perhaps, after all, we had better give up the scheme?"

"I understand your scruples, Hertz, but she has already agreed. And do not worry, officially she knows nothing. She has simply let you a room in her apartment for the sake of the money, that is all. For her and everyone else you are Jules Payen, a noveliest recuperating from a long illness, at least that is what we have decided. There need be no question of her good faith. And you will be safe here."

He glanced at Hertz who was walking quickly at his side carrying the small traveling bag which contained his more than modest wardrobe. Never having seen Hertz dressed in anything but his present ancient, black overcoat, Daguerran even wondered for a moment whether the poor fellow had not purchased the bag simply in order to appear more respectable. It seemed brand new and almost empty. Daguerran noted, with a mixture of amusement and pity, that Hertz was also sporting a new cravat which, with his outsize shirt collar, was his only vanity. The loose satin bow was tied with such meticulous care that it made him look like some sad, superannuated, first-communicant.

Charlotte was not at home but Annick brought the two men into the salon to wait. At last she came, the men rose to their feet. Hertz, hideously embarrassed, managed to get himself tied up in the tablecloth and knocked over his bag. By now, even Daguerran was nervous. On the last occasion, the presence of Paul Boucher had helped to disguise his natural shyness, but now their presence here struck him as wholly out of place. The more he looked at Hertz, the more he was conscious of the embarrassment his friend inspired.

Charlotte was as nervous as they, and in a way this made things easier for them all, because she went straight to the point and as soon as the introductions were over showed them the room and the closet leading off it which she had prepared for Hertz. This part of the apartment gave on to a tiny hallway leading to the service stairs and into which the kitchen passage also opened. The other part of the apartment had its entrance onto the main staircase.

Charlotte had hung a curtain across the entrance to the kitchen passage to give Hertz some illusion of privacy. He was at liberty to use the kitchen when he liked; Charlotte saw no objection.

"Thank you, madame," Hertz said. "I am tormented to impose on you like this."

Daguerran grinned into his beard at this characteristic phrase but the unhappy Hertz clearly saw nothing funny in his words. Charlotte glanced at him covertly, greatly intrigued by his appearance. After her initial agreement to the request made by Paul and Daguerran, she had felt some qualms at having committed herself so readily to shelter a stranger sought by the police. Heaven alone knew how she had pictured the ex-convict. In any event, Hertz's appearance not only reassured but touched her. He was so pale and thin, all his movements so precise. His candid nature shone through the marks of suffering on his face. It was obvious that here was an incurable idealist who, for one reason or another, had failed to defend himself against a dishonest society.

At last, Hertz deposited his bag in the room. A table had been put there for him to write on. As Daguerran had said, it had been agreed that as far as the world and the concierge in particular were concerned, he would be Jules Payen, which was the pen name under which he wrote his adventure stories. They decided it would be a good thing if he went out occasionally to avoid rousing suspicion among the neighbors. It would be easy enough to put it about that he had come from the provinces in consequence of a bereavement and indeed his neat, yet lugubrious appearance constituted practically a passport to widowerhood. This, at least, was Daguerran's opinion, although he refrained from mentioning it to Jean himself. Hertz was not what is normally meant by a humorless man, it was simply that with his innocent desire to believe all that was said to him he often failed to recognize humor. Besides, he had suffered too much for his sufferings to be a fit subject for mirth, even in the cynical world of newspapers.

The afternoon was far advanced and Charlotte, not quite certain how to embark on her experiment in parallel living with Hertz, retained Daguerran to dine. She busied herself helping Annick in the kitchen, glad enough not to be alone.

Hertz, still suffering under the effects of paralyzing shyness, ate daintily. It was all they could do to drag a word out of him and when he did speak, conquering his nerves, they were surprised at the grave resonance of his voice coming from such an apparent dreamer. Charlotte gazed with interest at Hertz's grey eyes. They were filled with a bland and total innocence that was very strange. She could not help comparing those eyes with Frédéric's, grey too, but different. The glow in Frédéric's eyes was the glow of rebellion, that in Hertz's the illumination of a virgin soul. She thought that Hertz was more like Ferrat and a closer observation convinced her of this. They might have been brothers.

Daguerran and Charlotte bore the brunt of the conversation, conscious of tossing the ball back and forth as though in a theater, leaving no awkward pauses. Nor was this play of words altogether an act. It was all part of a curiously light-hearted understanding which seemed to link them both above the head of poor Hertz. Daguerran sat opposite Charlotte. She could see him better tonight but she still felt the same sense of equilibrium which he had always given her. Everything about Daguerran spoke of a classic moderation. He was of middling height, although beside Hertz he seemed small, and well proportioned with regular features and the warm and lively brown eyes which went with his kind of face.

He was typically French. Auvergnat, Poitevin, Béarnais, he could have been any of these but Charlotte remembered him saying he came from Brittany.

She wondered about his life. He talked of his childhood in a remote Breton village where the ghosts of the Chouans rose to haunt the long winter evenings. The son of poor parents, he owed his education to the charity of the local squire and the kindness of the parish priest.

The stories of his childhood made Charlotte laugh. He described its characters with affectionate humor and she did not find it difficult to picture the wild, scapegrace boy he must have been.

She began to notice him in a way she had not expected. A closer observation revealed his classic features to be more apparent than real. Certain significant irregularities emerged. His thatch of hair, for example spoke of an energetic and aggressive nature. The lower part of his face was heavier than it looked under his beard, the mouth strong and determined with a full lower lip. A realist, but one who suffered from the demands of a nature perhaps over-generous.

All this disturbed her a little. She liked him but it was really no more than that. He had none of the surface attractions which sent young women wild but she felt relaxed and friendly in his company. It seemed to her that she had always known him. He had good hands, she noticed, and the cuffs and collar of his shirt were spotlessly white.

He was looking at her, his eyes alight with laughter and friendliness. She told herself it was natural, unimportant. They were both young and healthy and in a little while he would go away leaving to both of them the memory of one of those countless embryonic friendships which never go beyond a smile and a feeling of mutual esteem.

And just because she believed he would soon be gone, she let her friendship show in her face more than she would ordinarily have done, as though trying in some measure to compensate for a future in which they would be nothing to one another.

But then Hertz, who did indeed look very tired, suddenly asked their leave to retire. Daguerran and Charlotte were left alone. They followed Hertz, mentally, down the passage and through the curtain archway leading to his room. For a moment, their minds dwelt on the thought of him alone amidst the unfamiliar objects.

Time passed and soon they grew conscious of the silence between them. Daguerran should have left then. They were both aware of the dangers which lay in wait.

CHARLOTTE was the first to break the silence, talking of
the war and asking what were his plans for the future.
Daguerran answered that, not being a trained soldier, he
would not be going to fight. He hesitated a little and she
realized that he was unwilling to speak frankly on the
subject. Then he told her that he expected to go to Alsace
as a war correspondent and was actually due to leave in
two days time. That very day he had seen his wife and
children off at the station for an indefinite stay with
relatives in the country. He told her of the difficulties
which faced journalists trying to obtain reliable information at the front, and of the obstacles erected between
them and the troops by a headquarters which clearly
regarded them as nothing more than a nuisance. He
worked hard to distract her but all at once Charlotte
seemed very tired and her face bore a look of strain. She
did not ask the name of the paper he was going to serve.
She feared it would be Thomas's, and then again that it
would not be. It seemed preferable to remain in doubt,
deceiving herself once more with the thought that Daguerran would join Thomas at the front, that he was
going to see him. He was Thomas's friend, he might see
him tomorrow, with the image of her fresh in his mind—

Even as the thought came and went, the moment was
marred. Thomas had come between them like a distorting
mirror, twisting whatever was between them and giving
them, while still almost strangers, a whole past intimacy in
common. Daguerran ought to have left but still Charlotte
lingered, warming herself with the presence of this man
who was Thomas's friend.

He too knew that he should leave but was in no hurry

to go back to his empty home. He looked at Charlotte, seeing her resemblance to his wife and knowing quite well that this was the worst possible reason for staying. In the light of the lamp which stood beside her he could follow the play of emotion on that lovely face. Not once, during the meal, had he mentioned Becque's name, but he knew that she was thinking of him and that she loved him still.

The thought of Becque filled him with a slight sense of irritation. Even now he could not admit Thomas's marriage to Marie. In his view it was no more than an escape, a way of using duty to escape from life and its problems. While he had nothing in particular against her, Daguerran did not like Marie and it seemed to him that she would ruin Becque's life. He had even managed to persuade himself that Thomas had only gone back to Marie and given her a child as an excuse to break with his old way of life. The real truth was that he was afraid to take the risk of more demanding love and, looking at Charlotte, Daguerran was more than ever inclined to believe this. He ran away, he told himself, but can one truly blame him? He is not a whole man and has much to suffer. He hides his infirmity so well that we have never thought of it but every woman must. And now it is all too late. What a waste! A waste of his life, of this woman's life and now, with the war, of all our lives. What will tomorrow bring for all of us? Shall I ever see my wife and children again?

He should have gone and yet he could not. Outside, the loneliness would have overwhelmed him. He knew that Charlotte was prolonging the evening to the same end. He smiled at her again across the uncleared dinner table.

She smiled back in quick response. Although no word or gesture had passed between them, every second brought them nearer to understanding. They were a man and a woman, facing one another alone in the presence of war and an uncertain future. The evening was a moment of calm before whatever was to come.

Charlotte sighed and leaned back in her chair, tired of fighting her own instincts and clinging to impossible memories. She acknowledged her own weariness, her need of love.

She could show her weakness to Daguerran. They were

a man and a woman, that was all. They would not be betrayed into love. He was her friend, even, to some extent, her accomplice. He could understand. He was still looking at her, disturbed by her increasing languor and by the dangerous web of solitude being drawn ever tighter around them while neither lifted a finger to break it.

He rose and moved round the table towards her. Her head was tipped slightly backwards, her eyes closed. He bent over her and from behind closed lids she could see his face close to hers, smiling gravely.

She tensed, feeling his hand on her neck, then yielded to the caress. She dared not open her eyes. His fingers caressed her throat and she knew that he was still watching her intently. It was the first time she had encountered such warmth of friendship in desire. Was it just because they were free of any emotional obligations to each other?

The touch of a man's hand made her more strongly aware of her recent loneliness. She could not bring herself to fight him, she could only accept and acknowledge her weakness. Any man she could respect was better than that empty solitude.

He stroked her neck and face and she responded to the firm pressure of his fingers. They were both terribly conscious of their actions, as though this slow, voluptuous mime contained the whole complicated ritual of love.

No other woman had ever given Daguerran this dazzling awareness of perfection. The pleasure which united them, and through them every other man and woman thrown together by the hazards of this world, was like a solid bastion against loneliness and death.

At last, she opened her eyes and looked at him. He smiled back, a slight, mocking, self-deprecating smile and in spite of the stiff collar and white cuffs she saw in him the same sardonic detachment which belonged to Thomas.

And suddenly, that crooked, ironical smile said more than any words. It was a sign of surrender, dismissing any regrets for what might come.

Turning up her face, he imprisoned her mouth beneath his own in a kiss so long that when at last he let her go they had already traveled more than half the way that lay before them. Drawing her to her feet he held her to him, smiling into her face. His body against hers was already seeking those points of contact which would stimulate their senses and inflame their nerves with intimations of delight. He read her feelings in her ravaged face and, taking it gently between his hands, he studied it with infinite curiosity, devouring the tragic beauty born of her need for love.

Then, as though even now he could not quite believe that it was to him she looked for peace, he seemed to give way suddenly to a desire too strong for him and crushed her lips roughly beneath his own.

Any remaining thoughts of caution vanished. He was not smiling now and in his arms she felt again the force and urgency of Thomas. Daguerran made love well. He had the understanding and control of a man past thirty and also the slightly teasing tenderness of a married man, familiar with the ways of women.

The bedroom was in darkness with just light enough for them to make out one another's faces in the gloom. Charlotte's head was clear and with her heart beating wildly at this excursion into love-making without love, she gloried in the presence of the man's body beside her. In Daguerran her dead love seemed to live again.

It was nearly three o'clock when Daguerran tore himself away at last. They stood, smiling a little awkwardly at one another. He dared not take her in his arms again.

"What will you do now?"

"Wait—for the war to end."

"I meant—how will you live?" He put his hands gently on her shoulders. "You cannot go on ruining your life like this. The end of the war is not an end in itself. You must try and live, Charlotte, and soon a wind will come and sweep away the clouds."

She smiled. "I will try."

Still he could not bring himself to leave her.

"I have no regrets," he said abruptly.

"One should never have regrets."

"This is the first time I have ever deceived my wife, does that seem odd to you?"

"Of course not," she said awkwardly.

"I have no regrets. There is no cause for any. We need not have done what we have done but there are moments when life has its own laws—you also believe that, do you not?"

He was trying to justify himself. He must love his wife and feel some regret, for all that.

Charlotte was grateful to him for his honesty but she could not know that it was not only of his wife that he was thinking, but of Thomas also. Daguerran had thought a great deal of Becque in these last hours. The very fact that Becque had loved Charlotte before himself had given him a persistent sense of sacrilege while he explored her, slowly, almost fearfully in spite of his ardor, knowing beforehand that she would be lovely and good to love.

She pushed him away, gently. "You must go," she said. "Go now." She stroked his cheek.

"It is absurd for us to part like this," he said wretchedly, struggling against an unfamiliar sense of desolation.

"You know we must."

"To leave you like this—not knowing what may happen to you—"

"You cannot return here, you know that," she said in a strained voice.

"Yes, I know—"

"You are married—"

"Yes," he said, "I am married."

There was a moment's silence, then Daguerran said urgently: "Forget Becque!"

It was the first time that night he had mentioned the other man's name. Charlotte shrugged lightly. Everyone she knew seemed to be telling her to forget Becque.

"Forget Thomas," he said again. "Do something with your life. I am not saying any marriage is perfect but I am married and I can tell you it is still one of the best ways of finding happiness, of keeping one's head above water. Live, marry, have more children. There must be other men in your life. Many men must love you."

So many men, Charlotte thought, that they had almost ruined her life among them.

"Is there anyone else?" he persisted. His efforts to return

215

to their former friendly footing was belied by the look in his eyes.

"There is someone?"

"Yes," she said, "of course—"

"Would he marry you?"

"He believes so, but whether he really knows what he wants—"

"You think too much. Everyone has doubts at first, but afterwards it is all right. Who is this man?"

"A young man." She could not help it and he sensed it.

"Who is he?"

"Nothing can come of it," she said. "He is too young and unstable."

She almost laughed to think of Frank, the idealist, as a potential husband, Frank married and living like other people. None of the ordinary rules applied to him. As though she sensed the terrible loneliness underlying the cloak of nobility which made him different, she was suddenly afraid for him.

"Do you like him?" Daguerran demanded.

"He is handsome," she admitted.

In those words she expressed all the anguish she had suffered in the past for the sake of unattainable beauty. What she felt for Frank had always been something worse than love. She looked at Daguerran.

"Go now," she said in a low voice.

He gave her his roguish smile.

"I hate to leave you. You will have to throw me out."

She went to the door on tiptoes so as not to wake Hertz who was sleeping at the other end of the apartment.

The next day, Charlotte made a niche for Daguerran in her thoughts as one might place an object in a museum. She wanted to think of him simply as a friend and kept telling herself all day long that he was a good man and she valued him as such.

She dined early, sent Annick home and took some soup to Hertz who had caught cold and had kept to his bed. He was wearing his everyday shirt, the front of which showed grey without its floppy bow. The room had already acquired a stale, bachelor smell, made up of dead tobacco, clothes and old leather from his worn writing-case. He himself looked, if anything, more pale than a handkerchief. The thin stubble on his chin accentuated the impression of a sad child overcome by premature senility.

Charlotte did her best to make conversation, but their mutual embarrassment soon put an end to her well-meant efforts and she left him, feeling only a dull sense of pity.

A little before nine, the bell rang. It was Daguerran. She stared at him in horrified amazement, incapable of forbidding him entrance.

He followed her into the dining-room and then stood for a moment in silence.

"Why have you come?" she said at last in a voice full of reproach.

"You know very well why."

"You should not have come."

"Perhaps—I do not know—"

"You should not—" she was almost in tears.

"Why not?" His voice was low and intense.

"It is wrong. You have ruined everything."

"I leave tomorrow for Alsace. I could not go without seeing you again." He moved towards her.

"What is the good of making rules to prove our virtue? What use is it forcing myself to be without you tonight when I have been thinking about you like a madman all day long?"

"You have ruined everyting—" she wailed again despairingly, appalled at his failure to respect their tacit understanding.

"Why have you come? Why?"

"I had to come."

"Go away, I beg of you."

"I cannot."

"Why did you give in to it, why? Why?"

Charlotte was panic stricken.

"I want to do it again, Charlotte."

She hated this frank admission and the sensual, fatalistic smile which went with it.

"Nothing has changed. We are still the same. I am your friend as I was yesterday. I want to be with you tonight. I want to, that is all. It is so stupid. I cannot be in Paris, so close to you, wanting so much to see you and just to sit there like a fool until I leave tomorrow. I had to come—" He paused and added softly: "You know you do not want to send me away. It will make no difference to what we have decided."

His coolness only increased her disappointment. She had hoped, in her heart, that he might be falling in love with her.

It seemed intolerable to her not to be loved. What was life, after all, but the projection of oneself onto others, the casting of the spell whose power proved one's own existence? When the spell failed it was like a star going out, a bird dropping from the sky, a funambulist falling soundlessly. Daguerran's words had cast her back into a self-doubt and loneliness even greater than before.

She drew back quickly when he tried to take her arm. The comradeship of the night before now seemed to her only one more proof of man's cynicism and of the foolishness of her own illusions about love.

Daguerran was looking at her anxiously. What an admission! What a comment, on himself and her. Stripped of their clothing of sentiment, their relations stood out in all the crude light of truth. He wanted her and so he came. That was all. But because he was too honest and intelligent to shirk the implications of his acts, he had come in full knowledge of his motives.

He was still looking at her. He had not come lightly. Rather, he had obeyed his instincts, allowing them to lead him, without a struggle and without regret. Far from it. Perhaps it was the war which destroyed all values. He was not an unsophisticated man but, until now, he had always lived according to certain voluntarily accepted principles. His concept of faithfulness to his wife had been sacred to him, the very foundation of his happiness and of the character of the man.

Now, the war had torn his private world apart. The idea of keeping faith with his wife no longer had the same meaning and he realized that what he had always striven to preserve by a determined loyalty often at odds with his violent, undisciplined nature and his strong taste for women, was his home itself. In time of war, all virtues were turned upside down. Killing became an act of heroism and men got drunk in order to forget and took a barmaid when they could, as a kind of reward. The old morality was gone and those who had believed in man no longer believed in anything. And Daguerran was conscious of this disruption. Their own petty problems of a man and a woman were nothing.

His eyes were on her, his face tired and drawn with strain. She did not want to yield but already she found her thoughts turning to him and the longing to touch him, to lose herself in him, was like a galloping hunger inside her.

"Go away," she said.

He shook his head. They seemed bound together by a terrible force of sexual attraction and Charlotte knew there was no reason why it should cease tomorrow, or afterwards, whenever they were together and she knew too that they would give way to it whatever ties their lives might hold at the moment.

No, she thought, I will not give way to it. But it was her pride that spoke, her will not to destroy the idealistic vision of love that she had carried as a banner through her life. But Daguerran caught her swiftly to him, slaking his desire on her lips in a long kiss, gradually weakening and cracking that defensive shell which had barely hardened since the night before, and molding her anew in obedience to the slow workings of desire.

Even then she still tried to fight it, her spirit rebelling against the disorder which Daguerran had brought into her life. But he was unaware of her anger. He only wanted to touch her, to offer his own warmth, his strength and weakness. He was no longer conscious of anything beyond the need to saturate her with happiness through every pore, rooting and burrowing with the fury and concentration of some woodland animal in a joyous orgy of rediscovery.

Who had taught her to make love? He knew too well. Becque. At that moment he hated Becque. He was even on the verge of jealousy. Anything might happen. He could easily love her, too easily, love her and suffer torments for her sake. He loved everything about her.

"Oh, you are beautiful!" He exulted fiercely. "Beautiful! Beautiful! I am in love with loving you! What a fool Becque was to leave you. Let me look at you. You will drive me mad, you lovely woman. I wish I could show you to everyone!"

Charlotte could have killed him. She thrust him away from her so viciously he thought she would have scratched his eyes out. He drew back and stared at her and quailed at the cold, murderous look in her eyes.

"Get out!" she hissed between clenched teeth.

Instinctively, before he could stop himself, he slapped her face. Anger took hold of him.

"Have you gone mad? What made you do that?" He was shaking her hard.

"I never want to see you again."

"Why are you like this? Tell me. Why do you hate me all of a sudden? Confound it, I've hurt you—"

He saw that she was crying. He let her go and sat down on the edge of the bed and waited in silence.

"Stop crying," he shouted at her at last. "I can't bear tragedy!"

"Why don't you go away?" she moaned hiding her head in the pillow, still shattered by the happiness of the moment past. Daguerran was beside himself with rage and bewilderment. He got up and began to dress.

"Who are you fooling? Do you even know yourself? You are mad, mad and irresponsible—nothing else can explain it."

She lay, like a board, while he raged at her. At last she said: "I do not love you. We are not in love."

"To be sure. I was engaged in proving it to you."

"That is not what love is," she said tragically. "I know it is not."

"Ah!"

"No. One might as well die at once—"

He gazed at her for an instant and then went for her furiously.

"Then what is love? You tell me."

"Go away."

"Don't worry I'm going."

He finished dressing. Charlotte told herself she would have peace when he was gone, and there was no longer any hope beyond such as lay in her old, hopeless dreams. At the same time, it occurred to her that Daguerran was reacting exactly as Thomas would have done. It was because he was so like Thomas that he had made her so happy.

"Come here," she murmured faintly when he was ready. "Sit by me, at least say goodbye."

He gave a short laugh. He had seen it coming. None the less, he took her hand. It was very cold.

"I thought I was your friend."

He ground his teeth to keep himself from hitting her.

"Idiot!"

Then, overcome with rage and misery, he took her in his arms and buried his face in her hair.

"I am very fond of you," she said sadly.

"And I shall end by hating you." He let her go, and paced angrily across the room and back to her.

"Tell me. What do you want out of life? Do you mean to go on living like this? You sit here crying for love, but you had love! Becque loved you, and you let him go. And even now, your happiness is in your own hands. Good God, have a little courage! Wipe out all that. Look life in the face." He paused. "I can do nothing for you; to my sorrow, I am not free. But I told you yesterday. Marry this boy who loves you and you are fond of, or at least live with him, it does not matter. It is the same thing!"

She shook her head. She could never accept that. Never. Better be alone. Her love for Thomas was the only thing that mattered to her. She said: "There will never be anyone else for me."

He forced himself to keep calm, and questioned her again about the other man, asking his name, his occupation. He was not jealous. He was trying to understand. Suddenly, he was very tired, telling himself that he had to help her, that it was all he could do for her now, while the happiness which she had destroyed left an evil taste in his mouth.

Charlotte told him something of Worski. Daguerran

remarked that he knew a Frank Worski who worked occasionally for *La Marseillaise* and who had recently been in trouble with the police on suspicion of being concerned in treasonable activities.

"It cannot be! It cannot be the same man!"

Charlotte's face betrayed the shock she felt. Daguerran described Frank. The matter was beyond a doubt.

"It is the same," said Daguerran. "They arrested him four or five days ago at the office. He was one of a nest of Germans hanging out at Belleville."

"That proves nothing. Besides, he had just obtained his Russian papers and was applying for French naturalization. In any case, he is not a German. He would never be one! He is Polish. He was born in Warsaw!"

"How you spring to his defense."

"I believe in him, absolutely! I will never believe him capable of treachery. Never!"

To Charlotte it was inconceivable that Frank could be accused, his youth and honor besmirched. He was finer than all of them. They could not understand him, they would hurt him.

"You are in love with him," Daguerran said.

"No."

"Don't deceive yourself."

"No. I know what I am saying."

"He is attractive. Women are bound to fall for him in one way or another. Even you. Why should you shy like that? It is nothing to be ashamed of."

"You do not understand—"

"Better than you think."

"He has no friends. I want him to know that I am his friend." She thought sadly how many people hated Worski instinctively for his beauty and his pride. If he were in trouble, he would never make them understand. He would attract suspicion. He was incapable of compromise, incapable of self-preservation.

"If you believe in him, then you must help him. If he is innocent, go and find him. Go and live with him, marry him."

His arms were round her. "You must stop this pantomime of living. See things as they are. Like a real woman.

I wish there were more I could have given you. If at least I could have helped you in this, I would be happy. Tell yourself that if you hesitate, you are lost. You will grow old and everyone will weary of you. You will become one of those lonely old women whose emotional poverty makes them a laughing-stock for others. You! When you have such a gift for life! What a waste."

He sought her lips and kissed her unashamedly. She was in tears. He said goodbye and left her quickly, while it still hurt, before he could feel sorry for her.

ON THE evening of the 5th, Illa gave birth to a 7-lb baby girl who was named Marthe. She had been in labor since the night before, but in the end everything went off better than the midwife had hoped. Gabin appeared stunned, as though he had not yet come to terms with the fact of being a father. Mother and child were both asleep. Charlotte, feeling that there was nothing she could do, left her brother with his wife.

The evening papers contained disturbingly little news. But on the 6th, the morning brought a sudden announcement of a dispatch reporting that MacMahon's army had attacked the Prussian forces near Fröeschviller, routed them and taken prisoner the Prussian prince and thirty-five thousand men. It was also said that the French had taken Landau.

The news went round the capital in a wave of enthusiasm. Everyone was in the streets. Charlotte, going down with Annick, found all the tenants of the building, Valerie among them, gathered outside.

"While I think of it," Madame Cazingues told Charlotte, tapping her forehead wisely with one finger, "I've got something for you." She disappeared inside.

"Here, a letter. It came this morning by messenger."

She stood by, eagerly watching the young woman's face as she opened the envelope. The message was a hasty scribble in pencil.

"According to latest news, your friend Worski was not held for questioning for more than twenty-four hours. He is now at liberty and probably out of danger. Either good sense or partiality must have given you second sight.

Marry him. I leave tonight. Good luck. I think of you as I had hoped to think. Your friend. Daguerran."

Charlotte put the letter in her pocket feeling happier than she had done for a long time and gave herself up to the mood of joy which infected the town. Crowds were gathered at every crossroads, and flags fluttered from every window.

As she and Valerie went down the boulevard, people seemed to be pouring from every side street. The city was like an octopus, there was singing in the place Saint-Michel with a tenor and a soprano from the Opéra thumping out the Marseillaise to a frenzied crowd. Banners streamed in the wind, licking the ancient stones like the wings of so many warrior angels.

Charlotte stood watching the great flags writhing and cracking in the rising wind. She shivered in the moist chill coming from the river. The sky was becoming overcast.

Charlotte had foreseen this moment when excitement would give way to exhaustion worse than the anxiety of the previous night. There had been too much singing, too many flags. There was something terrifying in so much rejoicing. Why this sadness she felt when she should be rejoicing for her country? Did she no longer believe in the victory? Or had there been such an excess of patriotic feeling that now it could no longer touch her?

There was a movement in the crowd. A man detached himself from it.

"Frank!"

She could not stop herself. She began to run towards him. There was no mistake. He had seen her. He was running away. Uncomprehending, Charlotte saw him turn into the rue Saint-Sévérin.

Valerie was some way off, separated from her by the crowd. Charlotte began to hurry after Frank, trying not to lose track of him through the press of people who blocked her path.

She ran on blindly with only one thought in her head: Frank. Never had she been so desperate to reach anyone.

She came to a breathless halt and called again, but her voice was lost amidst the uproar of the crowd. The noise of singing and brass bands came to her, heightening her awareness. She knew that this was one of the great moments of her life and that every detail of the crowded boulevard would be imprinted on her memory forever.

She began to run again. She could no longer see Frank, although she thought she caught another glimpse of his dark figure ahead. He went into a house at the end of the rue Saint-Sévérin. The noise was fainter here but even this deserted alley had about it a warm, relaxed summer holiday air. There was a smell of frying in the air from the dark doorways of oriental eating houses, and a small boy, about three years old, as black as the ace of spades, was sitting paddling his feet in the gutter.

Charlotte could see the door which Frank had entered, but he himself had vanished. She contemplated the dingy entrance with its antique timbering and crumbling staircase, clinging by some miracle to the greasy wall. The whole wretched building reeked of poverty and disease.

Charlotte started up the stairs. Once past the first flight, the smell of cooking became unbearable, mingled with other noxious odors.

She had heard a door slam and it seemed to her to come from the top floor. On the last but one landing, the door stood open, apparently flung back by the wind. As she passed, Charlotte caught a glimpse of a couple sprawled on a mattress, a bottle of wine beside them on the floor. She tightened her lips and went quickly by. On the top floor there was a low ceiling and skylight. The door was shut. Charlotte knocked with determination. There was no answer. She waited, peering through a tiny window looking out onto a courtyard. The sun shone on a whitewashed wall, transforming it into the terminus of some eastern alley. Somewhere a woman was singing an Arab lament.

Charlotte knocked again, more loudly, disappointment and annoyance making her careless of the neighbors. Here, in the heart of Paris, she was faced with an unknown country, with the Algerian poverty which haunted these lost alleyways. And her heart, too, was faced with one more stage in the mystery which surrounded Frank, his strange, secret life, and the real dangers which surrounded him. Charlotte could feel the danger. Life and death roamed abroad in this building, behind this door. Who is he? she thought. What is his mission in life? Suppose he is a German spy?

She had never put much faith in spy stories, but now she was afraid. For him. He is capable of anything, she told herself, it is in his soul!

Still no one answered. She went down a few steps, not leaving, simply tempting fate, and stood on the grimy half-landing. A cat, mewing plaintively, was rubbing its mangy back against a rough place in the wall, which must once have been a door, perhaps hastily plastered up to conceal a crime.

Inside, behind the door on the fifth floor, lay a small, airless chamber, more like a chicken hutch than a room. There was no window, only a skylight set in the low raftered ceiling bisected by one great angular beam. The ventilator in this skylight was rusted up but one of the panes was broken, letting in a gust of air laden with whatever odors were in season, a whiff of the bazaar in summer and icy blasts in winter.

Frank was there standing on a chair to bring his eye in line with this narrow spyhole. Outside, instead of the vista of empty sky which should have rewarded the climber to this otherwise sordid eminence, a dismal and monotonous landscape of roofs spread all around. It was a strange, disturbing sight, this zone of tiles and rusty iron with the occasional zinc sheet gleaming like a pool of silver in the sunlight, and as Frank's gaze roamed over the wretched no-man's-land before him, he had to fight down the vertigo which always attacked him when he stood at that window.

For this was not the first time he had been in the room. It belonged to a girl named Rachel Beulant. She was behind him now, standing in her petticoat ironing the ribbons on some female undergarment. Frank could hear the regular thump of the iron and smell the moist, warm smell rising from the old clothes which Rachel had spread upon the table for her work.

Rachel was thirty-five or so, and admitted to twenty-eight. Beulant was her father's name, but her mother had been Egyptian, and her beauty was wholly of the East, dusky eyes, heavy brows, a strong nose and legs rather short for her height. Yet for all that there was a look of Paris in the pert, rounded figure compressed into the tight-laced stays.

"You had better open up, it will cause less of a stir," Rachel advised, showing her displeasure by a certain increase in the force with which the iron descended on the ribbon. She glanced at Frank, standing with his back to her in shirt-sleeves and his old blue trousers. What did he find to interest him out there on the roof? There was no knowing. He was a strange boy.

Rachel bit back her anger, knowing it made no impression on Frank and conscious, as always, of a certain humility in his presence. She was not worthy of him. From time to time, his beauty troubled her and yet, after all, he knew that she was older, much older. What did he want of her? She shrugged, resigned alike to incomprehension or ultimate suffering. Men were like that. Life was like that. When he had come back without warning, a week ago, she thought, it wasn't just because he wanted me, it was to hide his friend. And that in itself was quite a thing to ask.

Frank had not moved. He still stood looking out and listening. Listening to the sounds which came from the passage on the other side of the door. He knew Charlotte had followed him. He had heard her footsteps. Had she gone away now, or was she still there waiting on the half-landing? He pictured her waiting, so near. He knew she would not have gone away so quickly. She must have been disappointed when he fled from her and, still more, desperately curious. He knew just what she would be feeling. He always knew what others felt about him, it was all part of his awareness of himself.

Charlotte had followed him. She must be still waiting. Frank had a terrible longing to open the door. He felt his hands shaking as they gripped the edge of the skylight. He looked at them and in doing so caught sight of his unbelievably dirty shirt-cuffs. He hated being dirty. It was three days since he had changed. They had released him from the prefecture that morning after thirty-six hours' interrogation.

She must be there, he thought. I shall not open. He had a will of iron. He could force himself not to give way to temptation. His hands clenched. Where was the discipline on which he had based his life? He knew he had to find himself, to find the logic he had worked out long ago for being what he was. If not, he could not go on. There was a shame on him from the contempt and humiliation they had put upon him in the course of his interrogation. . . .

His mind went back to the commissioner's dull, unremarkable office. The commissioner himself was a small man, neat and bald. The clerk, at the next desk, had spectacles and wore over-sleeves to protect his cuffs. A shaft of dirty sunlight moved round the room, throwing a faint yellow glow on the black ranks of files. The man held a bronze paper-knife in his hand and had a habit of tapping the desk with it absent-mindedly.

They had questioned him for thirty-six hours. No, he did not know a German citizen, Charles Harth by name, convicted of spying. No, he had no connections with any network of German spies at Belleville, nor, to his knowledge did any such network exist. The questions had gone on. His father was German? Yes. He had studied in Germany from his thirteenth year? Yes, his parents' marriage had been annulled and he had recently obtained Russian papers as a Polish national on his mother's side. "A somewhat belated access of patriotism, surely?" the commissioner suggested blandly. "You would appear to have taken no great interest in Poland all these years. You will admit that in view of the present relations with Prussia, your decision to change your nationality looks suspicious."

Frank hated the commissioner's voice. His eyes glowed darkly as he answered, and he was very pale. His very youth and intensity condemned him in the eyes of his inquisitors, and he knew it but he had to speak to them. No one could say he had not cared for Poland.

Frank had cried aloud at the name of Warsaw, a name inseparable from that of his mother. His voice shook and he was aware of being ridiculous as some kinds of tragedy are always ridiculous. The commissioner listened, looking bored and tapping his paper-knife idly. He told Frank to keep his histrionics for the court where they might carry more effect. Frank's voice died away in a dreadful, choking sob, and he bowed his head hopelessly on to the wooden arm of the chair. The commissioner's boredom increased. "That's enough," he said sharply.

Frank raised his head. His eyes were dry but the look in them was terrible.

"Play-actor," said the commissioner.

Commissioner Leuleu was not an evil man, but he was convinced that Frank knew Harth and that he belonged to a group of Prussian spies, all young men, operating in France. He hated dealing with matters of this kind, believing they were the province of the military. Spying had always struck him as a peculiarly unsavory crime. He thought he knew Worski's type: a narcissistic little gigolo who probably lived off women. His dossier said twenty-one, although he looked more. At all events, he was too young to be the chief operator in this business. Probably only small fry.

It should not be difficult to extract a confession. The commissioner had a low opinion of delinquents of this class.

Finally, however, Worski's extreme good looks became a source of irritation. There was something almost indecent about them.

"You have been living in the house of Countess Lievitz?"

Frank said the Countess was a friend of his mother's. The commissioner smiled with polite incredulity.

"What is your source of income?"

"My father sends money to me, my mother had a small private fortune, which came to me when I was twenty-one."

"Your female connections?"

"What has that to do with your inquiries concerning Harth?" Worski said white-faced.

"In your own interests, m'sieur, I would advise you to be more respectful." The commissioner gestured wearily, and his voice, as he repeated his question about the women Frank knew, was an almost inaudible murmur.

Again Frank refused to answer. His pallor elicited a gust of laughter from Leuleu.

"Very well—I understand. You should have said so at once."

"I beg your pardon?"

The other shuffled his papers and said in a voice grown suddenly brisk: "So, you admit that for this past year you have lived under the roof of Madame Lievitz and compounded for your bed and board. You deny associating with any other women. You admit to being an invert—"

"What do you mean? I do not understand."

Frank had risen to his feet. His face had hardened and any resemblance to the gigolo had fled. Well, well, thought Leuleu, the villain has woken up. Our bird is not the small-time rascal I took him for, that look proves it. How easy it is to be mistaken. This lad could be capable of anything. Aloud he said:

"I think I have been mistaken in you. You are an adventurer. And I will tell you what I think. I think you arrived in Paris penniless. You had some vague acquaintance with Madame Lievitz, and you took advantage of it, and of her age and weakness. You became involved with the secret goings on in Belleville and acted in one way or another as a go-between for the German agents. That was your major source of income. You spent the money gambling, we have proof of that from circles where you are known. No women. You prefer men. That is your business, it only completes the picture of what you are."

Frank stood leaning so heavily against the massive desk that the edge of it bit into his thigh. Leuleu drew back nervously before the fury in his face. Frank's color had risen, his eyes glittered dangerously and his mouth was a hard line. He was sick with disgust.

"If we were anywhere but here, in this building, in this office, I would kill you for that," he said in a choked voice.

Leuleu frowned, doubt putting an additional sting in his voice. Frank sat down and closed his eyes. The questions continued. Frank felt he could stand no more. He felt dirty and despised himself because he was weak and helpless in the face of these two men, and others who

231

came and went. They told him: "You love Germany." He did not answer. Four times Leuleu repeated the statement. Frank looked at him wildly.

"No. It is my father's country. I did not love my father."

"That tells us a great deal."

"I have chosen my mother and Poland. There are moments in life when one has to choose." His voice was hoarse with the effort to explain. He had applied for his French naturalization papers as soon as his Polish nationality was confirmed.

"I have chosen France." His voice was almost a scream.

"One of the most curious aspects of this case is that your naturalization should in fact have gone through so quickly when in the normal way this may take years. You must have powerful friends—whom I should be glad to know. You will no doubt understand my reasons. Your organization has threads everywhere. Your associates must be induced to betray themselves."

Frank said nothing. His eyes were closed, he might have been asleep. The growth of beard covering his pale, young face, stopped short when it reached the neck, whose smoothness had something about it so irredeemably boyish that, in the honesty of his heart, Leuleu was ashamed at so torturing one who was no more than a child. In spite of himself, he was stirred by pity for the tears which crept down Frank's cheeks into that youthful beard. He was ashamed because Frank might have been his own son, because suddenly it seemed to him that this was a dirty man's business with which such youth as Worski's had no concern. He could not be held responsible for the ugliness of the adult world.

"Years"—Frank said without raising his head—"years one must wait unless one has, as you say, friends. You say it so naturally but do you know—do you know what it is like to be a foreigner?" He stood up slowly, like a man paralyzed. Leuleu turned his eyes away from the young man's ravaged face.

"Do you know, monsieur? Years of trying—for those who choose France. Do you think it easy to choose? You do not know. You are a Frenchman. You did not need to be.

It was not your choice. It was your mother's doing. You were born French. It was not something you aspired to—"

"I am indebted to you for the lesson," Leuleu said pleasantly, but he shifted uneasily in his seat and was disagreeably conscious of the presence of his fool of a clerk, Rousseau, sitting, pen at the ready, as witness of his discomfiture.

As Frank stood there confronting Leuleu, pride and anger had brought out the Asiatic character of his face. To the commissioner he seemed foreign, even barbaric, and his eyes were the eyes of a warrior of the steppes. It came as a shock to hear him speak of France, and yet he, for all his sincerity and sense of duty, never felt as deeply the things Frank was saying. He is a savage, Leuleu told himself. One cannot talk to him.

"You are a weak man, monsieur," Frank said. "You know nothing. For me, I weep for those who look to you, or men like you, for their right to be Frenchmen. And you will never understand how hard it is, how much one must love France in order to desire her, so much more than she loves us."

Worski's head was spinning like a top. He had not eaten since the day before. He fainted.

The questioning continued the next day. This time it was not Leuleu but another, milder, more unconcerned man. The same questions: No, he did not know the German, Charles Harth. In the end he found himself repeating the words mechanically, without effort, in time to the rhythm of the traffic outside.

"Harth has ten, even twenty aliases. Among others, he has passed himself off as an Austrian, and also as a Pole. One of the names he uses is Wladimir Lojko."

"That cannot be. I have known Lojko for ten years," Frank cried. "I can vouch for him."

"He may have lied to you."

"No. I would lay my life on it. If Harth has used that name, he must have stolen it from my friend!"

"Have you seen Lojko recently?"

"—No—"

"Worski, you hesitate."

"No, I say."

He was not aware when the session ended and he was taken back to the cell he shared with a petty trickster.

The next day, they had released him and it had not occurred to Frank that this might have been to watch him more closely and perhaps discover a lead from him. He was free and for the moment, that was enough. In his miserable state he was ready to clutch at the least straw of happiness. It was still early. He went into a shop and bought a brioche and the woman looked at his soiled collar with kindly pity. Then, still eating his brioche, he went on to where Rachel lived in rue Saint-Sévérin. Never had he walked more slowly.

The news of the fall of Landau was sweeping through Paris, sending a rush of banners and triumphant singing into the uncertain August sky, torn between rain and shine. Frank had turned back to get a shave and it was then that he had seen Charlotte.

"All the same," Rachel said, "you ought to open it. What gets into the hussies to run after you like that? Think they could eat you."

Frank did not answer. His eyes were on a tiny alcove, covered by a red curtain, at the far end of the room. Just visible behind it was the head of a young man asleep.

The sleeper was his friend Wladimir Lojko, Polish like himself. For a week now, he had been hiding in this room, because the police were searching for him as the man also known as Harth and he had no means of proving his innocence.

Rachel had agreed to hide Wladimir Lojko. She would have done anything for Frank. "Holy Mother of God," she thought, as she looked at him, "but he is beautiful!"

The first time he had come to her she had thought, with amazement, that he was a virgin and ascribed it to timidity. She had asked him and his answer had been a silent laughter that had something unkind in it. "Well, that's all right with me," she had retorted, vexed. She had a limited grasp of masculine psychology, which, however, she believed covered every kind of client from the schoolboy to the dandy.

But she had been mistaken in Worski to a degree which

234

shook her confidence in the superiority of her own profession.

For the first time in her life, though she had been hardened to her trade by eighteen years' experience, Rachel had been made conscious of the precise nature and condition of women of her kind, and their function in the eyes of the men who paid them.

Afterwards, she had gone back to her old routine, telling herself he would not return but the wretchedness of a prostitute's life had come home to her as never before. Rachel was a simple girl and in the long run more lazy than grasping. Before she met Frank, she had been innocently proud of her position as the local odalisque, parading her succulent byzantine charms between the rue Saint-Jacques and la Maub.

Now, she felt old and her district seemed small and cramped but still she stuck to her beat within the strict limits of the quai behind her room, though she no longer joined in the banter of the other girls or took her accustomed glass of wine with the charcoal merchant. It was not that she had hoped for Frank's return, it was simply that since his coming she knew she had no hope at all.

But Frank did return, three, four, five times. Always without warning. She was never able to understand why he came. She had seen the women's eyes on him in the street and could not imagine he really needed her services.

Once, at the beginning of April, some three weeks after that first meeting, he had knocked at her door in the middle of the night. Rachel was naturally timid and in any case she was at heart a conservative and home-loving creature and generally asleep at that hour.

She got up sleepily and found herself blinking at the vision of Frank, elegant in evening dress, standing in the doorway. She had caught her foot in the loose thread hanging treacherously from her worn and shabby mattress and, swearing, thought for the hundredth time that it was time she bought a new one. It was little things like that which could give a woman a bad name. In fact, she was careful, almost close, where money was concerned.

Nervously, she pulled the door open wider. For all her naïve infatuation, she could not help feeling there was

235

something absurd in the sight of Frank poised in her dingy doorway, like an archangel in a dress-coat. It was all wrong, he looked so out of place. His clothes unnerved her too, especially the stiff, shiny shirt-front. That hard shell, put on for the evening, made her think of rich men, stony hearted, men of steel.

"Well," she said at last, "I don't suppose you're here to take me to midnight mass."

She was freezing, standing at the door in her nightdress. Since no one was expected, she had put on an old, washed-out shift in which she felt comfortable. Snatching up her shawl, she wound it round her waist like a sarong.

"What do you want? After all, this is hardly the time to call." She was stuffing combs feverishly into her tousled hair.

"Go back to bed, you'll catch cold."

Rachel sat with her legs tucked up, clasping her knees shivering between the sheets and eyeing Frank as he stood by the window.

"What's up with you anyway? Can't you make up your mind? You don't exactly look short of money!"

Any illusions she might have held about his social status were gone now. Before, she was able to cherish some faint hope that, while not born to poverty like herself, his origins were not so far above her as to put him altogether out of reach. The cut of his present garments, the coat extravagantly double breasted with a cut-away collar turned up negligently at the back, proclaimed the dandy, one of the class of elegant exquisites who idled arrogantly between Tortoni's and Rond-Point, flaunting the challenge of their paradoxical private world and matching it with their own outrageous style of dress.

To Rachel, they were the gilded youth and the thought that Frank belonged among them gave her a further jolt. She was within an inch of giving him up forever. However, her infatuation was such that his presence, owed initially to accident, had become essential to her. She told herself he must have a respectable home, servants to clean his shoes, and that he came to her, like any other gentleman, only for a low debauch. She little knew Frank, with his independent and fastidious nature. But little as that was, it was still more than she could have learned by trying and, in the long run, her vague uncomprehending instinct was probably right. At any rate, she did not throw him out but continued to watch him reflectively as he stood by the window with his back to her.

"It doesn't matter if you've got no money. Not this once. I can give credit. But come on, I'm freezing."

"I have money. I won some." He produced a fistful of gold coins from his pocket.

"All right, all right. I don't want to see. All those shiners make me feel bad, as if I was dirty or something." She bowed her head on to her humped knee and shivered.

"Why don't you go? You've no business here with scum like me. All that cash! It's not fair, that's what, it's not fair!"

Rachel began to cry suddenly. Going up to the bed, Frank began dropping the gold coins one by one about her feet.

"What d'you think you're playing at?" she asked in a muffled voice.

"Take them."

"You won't want them back?"

"I won't."

"You're crazy. You'll be sorry. It's not right. I don't want them. I bet you stole them."

She snatched up the coins and let them fall back on to the counterpane, because her fingers shook too much to hold them.

"Keep them, I tell you I won them. I came to give them to you."

She gaped at him. "You going to be a monk or something?"

He shook his head, unsmiling. Rachel understood at last what it was that seemed so unnatural about him tonight. She had never seen him like this. The strong lines of his face were blanched and wasted, reduced to a pair of glowing eyes. Rachel was aware of a burden of sorrow hanging on him.

"You'll need the money? Keep it anyway."

"No."

Shocked, she let the coins fall. It came to her that Frank was rejecting far more than the money and that in this he was utterly sincere. Standing there in the dark coat and dazzling shirt-front, which were like symbolic attributes of his own youth, he seemed to her an image of purity, isolated in an ideal world which she could guess at but not understand.

There was a tightness in her throat. She was filled with respect for Frank and at the same time afraid for him. She, who had never had it, felt the terrible burden of money, money which could buy nothing because only when free of it could one be young.

She got up, leaving the money lying where it was; she no longer felt the least desire to touch it. She went to Frank, where he stood at the window, feeling the cold bite into her shoulders.

"What is it, Frank? There's something. Tell me. It will do you good."

She stood in her bare feet and waited but he did not answer.

"You mustn't let it get you down."

Still his eyes did not leave the window.

"Why did you come to me?" she asked again, unable to leave the question.

"Because I had nothing to gain, or lose."

She dared not press him further. At last, he dropped into a chair, and sat there, unmoving, his head in his hands, oblivious of the cold blast from the window. Rachel, exhausted, fell asleep wrapped in her shawl.

And still Frank sat thinking. He was thinking of the Countess Lievitz who had cut her wrists three days before because of him.

Two years earlier, the Countess, who was an old friend of his mother's and now administered her fortune, had written to Frank in Germany inviting him to come to Paris. He had quickly fallen in love with France but had refused at first to make his home with Madame Lievitz. His mother's fortune would not come to him until he was of age and he did not wish to be a burden to her. He had lived variously with Polish friends, or gypsies, or in hotels, giving lessons in fencing or in German. He had learned to handle a sword at an early age from his father, who was himself a master of fence.

When his financial problems had been partly solved by a monthly allowance from his father, he had finally agreed to accept her hospitality. He liked the damp, dilapidated old mansion in which he occupied one wing. The early tragedies of Frank's life had occurred when he was eight years old. Childhood suffering strikes deep and leaves its mark on the character forever. Frank had grown up with these hurts and, even as a man, he still saw everything in black and white, with no shades in between.

He had accorded Madame Lievitz all the instant, open-hearted devotion of his Polish nature. She swept into his theatrical world like a queen.

He was quite unaware of the strain which their relationship placed upon her. She had fought it at first but she felt the burden of her widowhood and little by little she succumbed to his fatal charm, until she began to live for Frank's coming, for his footsteps echoing in the flagged hall, his laughter and the unconscious attacks mounted by his beauty upon her peace of mind. She tried to convince herself that he was only a child and be amused by such theatrical tricks as his habit, whenever she found occasion to scold him, of catching up the hem of her dress and kissing it reverently.

In anyone else, the gesture would have been absurd and familiarity with the more restrained manners of Paris and London had made Madame Lievitz forget the excesses of the Polish temperament.

But Worski had a way of going down on one knee, or kissing the hem of a dress, that was all his own. In anyone else it would have been absurd, but not in him. His walk, the way he plucked a rose or threw it down, his long hair and general air of old-fashioned aristocracy excited and enthralled her. Sometimes in the evening he would sit with her and there was something about her gentle figure in the limelight, expecially about the brown hair, carefully coiled, that reminded him of his mother's long ago. It roused in him a desperate filial affection very far from her thoughts and which, on his part, soon waned into impatience. She knew his reckless nature. He could not sit still in one place for five minutes without discomfort. He did not know what to do with his legs. He had to get up and roam about the room or go and kick the logs in the hearth with the raised heels of his half boots.

If he did manage to stay seated, he would sit slumped in his chair, his chin on his hands, his shoulders hunched like a beast about to spring. Sometimes, he would prop his legs on a small table and although Madame Lievitz scolded him for form's sake, she could not help noticing the muscular legs, the shapely calves and high instep moulded by boots of supple leather.

She lay awake at nights, imagining Frank beside her; her waking dreams were part prurience, part schoolgirl fantasy. She went to confession but gave it up when her spiritual adviser offered only such radical solutions as erasing Frank from her life. It was a woman's way of dealing with the sin.

In the end she sank to spying on him, unashamedly, through a crack in the wall when he was alone in his room. But these stolen glimpses only added to her torment.

The tragedy occurred before Frank could do anything to prevent it. He had been conscious for some time of an increasing strain between them. Madame Lievitz no longer troubled to hide her feelings but Frank, fixed in his concept of maternal saintliness, still refused to understand.

Like many Poles in exile, he belonged to a small network of so-called resistance organizations, for the most part as ineffectual as they were high-minded.

Some of the most active of these were in contact with organizations of a revolutionary kind in France and hitherto Frank had joined in their activities in a spirit of romantic exultation, oblivious of the practical implications of their aims.

One day, he made the acquaintance of two Poles, a man and a woman, who were deeply involved in the part anarchist, part revolutionary groups of which Paris was full.

The man, Joseph Kaliz, was a big, strong fellow of about forty, dark swarthy, hot-tempered and ready to make any sacrifice for Poland. His companion, Nathalie Warga, was as dark and hot-blooded as himself.

It was through certain members of one of these French secret societies, with whom his actual acquaintance was slight, that Frank had originally met Rochefort and plucked up courage to offer his services to *La Marseillaise*. However, not being entirely without common sense, he had soon dropped the connection, having summed up the members of this organization as dangerous fanatics, not to be compared with the able and efficient men who fought at Rochefort's side. But he had continued to see Kaliz and Nathalie Warga, both of whom he liked.

One day, an inspector of the French police had called on Madame Lievitz asking for information about Kaliz, on the grounds that his activities constituted a threat to public order. The real reason was that the government, haunted by the fear of a *coup d'état*, was furiously hunting down revolutionaries of every kind.

Believing that Frank might be incriminated, and terrified at the thought of losing him, Madame Lievitz had answered that she had seen Kaliz once or twice as a fellow countryman but that she knew nothing of his activities. She had given his address, which she knew, and so delivered up both him and Warga to the French police.

Frank had been present for the latter part of the interview.

"Madame," he said, when the inspector had gone, "you have betrayed our friends and Poland."

"I could not let them take you. You have been mad and foolish. This Kaliz is dangerous, and Warga too. I have been watching them for a long time. They will compromise you, Frank."

He stared at her in bewilderment. This ruthless, energetic woman was not the gentle, meek person whom he loved, the image of his mother.

"You have betrayed them!" he said again harshly. "I will never forgive you. You have made me share your guilt."

"Enough of these heroics, Frank. Listen to me."

What she did not tell him was that it was not fear of the law alone which made her act as she had, but jealousy. Nathalie Warga was very pretty. She and Kaliz came very often to the part of the house where Frank lived. In her besotted state, it was inconceivable to poor Madame Lievitz that every other woman was not as desperately in love with Frank as she herself. Moreover, Warga was like Frank. They were both of them like a pair of unbroken horses.

But in this she was mistaken. The stern and lovely Warga would have given her life for her Kaliz. Madame Lievitz pursued Frank into the passage.

"Frank, I will not let you ruin yourself. Poland is dead. You must see that—and what do I care for Poland if you must die for it, or rot in prison?"

"You are allowing your fondness for me to lead you astray. I am nothing. Only Poland and liberty are important."

Frank had reached the stairs leading to the ground floor of the house. Unable to bear the thought of his going, Madame Lievitz ran after him, twisted her ankle on the second step and fell with a cry.

Frank turned and at the sight of her white face and agonized expression sprang back to her assistance. Feeling his arms about her, she lay limply against him while he carried her. She lay, half unconscious, with her face against his chest while he bore her to her room. Her one thought was that his arms were like steel.

He dumped her somewhat unceremoniously on her bed and said he would summon her servant. She cried out at once that her leg hurt her, and made him feel her ankle. He probed it none too gently, conscious of embarrassment now and in haste to get away. She had thick ankles. Hating this thing that had come between them, he controlled himself with an effort. His fingers worked steadily. He had a skill in such matters. He gave a sharp wrench and there was a click. Madame Lievitz gave a little shriek and then bit back her tears. Her face, contorted by the fear of pain and by a dreadful spasm of pleasure, appalled him.

She began moaning and writhing on the bed. He let her go, and rose, white faced. She called his name and seized his hand and kissed it.

He stood in dumb silence, conscious, as any man in his position, of the ridiculous figure he must cut. They strove in silence, then she began to speak, telling him softly of her love, revealing all her secret obsessions with the lack of modesty of a woman no longer able to keep silent.

He stood like an iceberg, unapproachable, leaning against the bedhead, tormenting her with his youth.

For his rejection of her was absolute, unpitying; even cynicism she could have borne, but he said nothing and that was worst of all. He stood there, in the barren, inhuman glory of his youth, rejecting her, as though he were a martyr and she his executioner.

This, for her, was the ultimate misery. To have wept, to have abandoned every shred of pride for love's sake and then to be confronted with this unseeing youth. She was old. Her love was abject and ridiculous and therefore she was old.

Frank was ashamed, but he was thinking of himself. He had brought her to this. She had renounced her faith in God, her country and her friends for him. He felt soiled, wounded in his ideals of greatness. For him, this love was a thing incestuous.

He told her he was leaving and that night she had slashed her wrists. She had recovered, but after that he had not dared to go. For three days he had lived in the same house with that pallid woman with her bandaged wrists and staring eyes. He could not even ask forgiveness, since his only crime was his rejection of her and he knew that she still loved him.

Frank thought of all this while Rachel slept, drugged with weariness. She did not even hear him go.

And now, here they were again. Frank had left Madame Lievitz's house in order to help Lojko and hide him. Madame Lievitz had fallen ill shortly after her attemped suicide. It was thought to be cancer of the throat and there was a suggestion that she had brought it on herself with her desire to die. Frank saw her every day but he was unwilling to take Lojko to the house in the Marais.

He and Lojko had met at Basle where Frank had gone

to study after rejoining his father in Germany. What had first brought them together was the fact that Wladimir Lojko was also half Polish.

They had met again in Paris and renewed their friendship. On Frank's side there was admiration and a great devotion. It seemed to him that in Lojko he had found the brother he had never had.

In daytime, Rachel's room was a sordid enough place. It shamed Frank that he should be there. Before the two days he had spent in prison, he had scarcely noticed, but now whatever shame surrounded him, he took it on himself. He had been humiliated and rejected, suffering for himself and for all those like him. There was no longer the same sympathy in France for Polish exiles as there had been in 1830 after the first Warsaw rebellion.

It seemed that men grew tired of heroism. What were they, he thought bitterly, but a lot of penny revolutionaries down on their luck? Had they really believed that one day they would liberate Warsaw? It had needed all Frank's youthful idealism to take them seriously. And that golden-hearted giant Joseph Kaliz and his faithful Warga, what would become of them? They too would probably be arrested and thrown into prison.

And Frank himself, what hope was there? A life of degradation of one kind or another, with a Lievitz or a Rachel. Weakness was a habit easily acquired. He was a man without a country, a displaced person, and he belonged where he was, in the gutter with the rest of his kind.

A footstep on the stairs. They listened. Frank's heart contracted.

"Your lady friend is still waiting." Rachel spoke lightly, but her heart as she bent over the damp ironing was heavy with the fear that Frank would leave her. He might pretend indifference but she knew what it was like, that sick longing to see someone.

"Don't go, Frank. This is not the moment—"

Frank was sweating. He was afraid to open the door. He had been hurt before and now he was afraid. But he too sensed that Charlotte was outside.

He opened the door and pulled it shut behind him. He and Charlotte stood face to face on the narrow landing. Both were acutely conscious of their cramped surroundings, forcing them into a position of intimacy which pride would have forbidden either to seek deliberately. Charlotte saw, without registering the knowledge, that he was dressed in a white shirt and the trousers he had worn, brand new, at Tours, were now soiled and crumpled. Her eyes were not for his clothes but for him, her memory busy with every little half-remembered detail of his face. The vague elusive picture vanished from her mind as she beheld the living reality that was Frank.

"Come," he ordered curtly. He gripped her arm and she realized that this was something else she had forgotten, the almost unbearable tension and magnetism of a young body.

As they reached the next landing, the door above, on the fifth floor, opened and a woman's voice cried: "Frank, come back!"

The woman leaned over the banister as though she meant to throw herself down and Charlotte saw her face upside down, misshapen and formless, with the starting eyes and the straggling hair. Frank stopped dead. They stood in a recess and the woman did not see them. "He is her lover," Charlotte thought. "And she is jealous."

"Come on," he breathed in her ear. But Charlotte sensed that it was something other than complicity which had made him keep his voice low. Even so, she could not resist asking:

"Who is that woman?"

"A prostitute," Frank answered simply.

Charlotte blushed, feeling foolish. Outside, in the street, a little dark-skinned girl ran up to Frank and he spoke to her in some foreign language. A man with a horse and cart selling crockery came by and he spoke to him too. Frank patted the horse.

Charlotte stood and waited, feeling still more foolish and knowing she could not go away but wait, however long he might be.

At last he rejoined her and, taking her arm, began to lead her towards the river. Now she was able more fully to take in the oddity of his appearance. She was conscious of the hardness of his arm, the sheer solid bulk of him. She thought: "He is a man now."

He took her down to the river, near Notre-Dame, where there was a little backwater. There was no one about except for two tramps under the bridge.

THE *quai* stretched before them, empty and deserted, towards the Pont de la Tournelle. They strolled on, automatically. The air was foul with the smell of refuse underfoot, like the bad breath of Paris itself.

When they had walked a little way Frank stopped.

"What are we doing? Is there any way you want to go?"

How like a man. Charlotte had guessed that some such unanswerable question was coming. If she said: "Let us walk on, where we shall be quite alone," it would imply that this was what she wanted, so she could only say that she was quite happy where she was, even if this were quite untrue and the place was thoroughly uncomfortable and draughty.

The result was that they stood awkwardly where they were. Frank's careful avoidance of seeking her eyes only made matters worse. Charlotte could sense, beneath his veneer of detachment, such a feeling of confusion about herself and their relationship that she knew, if she were to leave him now, she would leave something of herself with him.

She did not look at him directly but she was aware of his presence and of the droop of his young body close to her, as he kicked idly at the cobbles underfoot.

The movement irritated her. Suddenly the whole of life seemed too much trouble.

A dog trotted by. Frank, whistling through his teeth, shied a stone at it, following this up with another into the river. He seemed on the point of walking away and putting an end to the whole uncomfortable interview.

He stood there, chucking stones into the water, and his

whole attitude expressed a boyish truculence that seemed to carry them both back into a past where boys and girls were natural enemies.

This time, she knew, it was absurd to stay. She made up her mind to leave him and go home. She saw herself going up the street. She would not be unhappy. France was at war. That was much sadder than any private grief of her own.

The dog came back, leaping and barking like a mad thing. Frank snapped his fingers, caught and muzzled the animal with his hands and the dog submitted. Then it leapt up again, growling and worrying until at last it flung itself on the ground, panting and exhausted, and licked his hands with a look of abject devotion and even then ready at the slightest sign to begin leaping and bounding again.

To judge from the foolish, blissful expression with which he rolled on his back displaying his pink underparts, he could not have been more than six months old. Frank tickled him and he rolled in the dust, showing the whites of his eyes, rigid with ecstasy.

Frank laughed, a loud, carefree laugh that made him seem suddenly free and invulnerable. Charlotte forgot herself and thought only of watching him.

Without taking his eyes from the dog, he asked abruptly:

"Tell me, why did you come today?"

The question caught her unawares. It was too late now to explain that in following him she had simply followed her impulses. Now if she said that it would be almost hurtful. He might not even believe her. And so she said:

"You wrote to me—"

He looked up then and his face was softer.

"Yes, and you did not come—"

"I wanted to. I could not—"

"I wrote twice—"

"I swear to you, Frank, I could not come."

"I do not believe you."

There was bitterness in his tone.

"But it is the truth."

"No, the truth is you did not want to come."

His eyes glowed darkly as he looked at her. "I put all

my hopes of you into those letters. You know how much you mattered to me. I made you an offer of marriage and you did not so much as trouble to refuse. Do you think I would offer my life to anyone, like some poor half-wit not knowing what he does? Are you so shallow, or do you hold me in such contempt that you scorn me in this fashion?"

She gazed at him in horror, unable to collect her thoughts. Only some vague consciousness of disaster seemed to warn her of the enormity of what she had done in not even answering Frank's letters.

"Frank," she managed to say at last, "I did not understand—I did not truly believe—"

"Why did you not believe?"

She stood convicted. Frank was regarding her steadily and her very inability to meet the light of those clear eyes condemned her. He stood stiffly before her, trembling a little, not bothering to hide his mortification.

"I wrote twice. I told you how important it was for me that you should come. I would not go to you because I wanted you to come of your own free will. For me, it mattered terribly that this should be your choice, your decision. More than anything, I hoped that you would come. I waited for you a long time, until eight o'clock that night. It was the first time I had waited for a woman I loved and she had not come."

The bitterness in his voice was a condemnation of her and the whole frivolous world she represented. A world of grown men and women without honor.

In a last effort to excuse herself, she began enumerating the reasons why she could not come. Her mind went back to that grim evening when war had been declared, when she found Frank's first letter with its proposal of marriage. She had shared in the sorrow which weighed on the city. She tried to convince herself that her treatment of Frank's letter as something unimportant had been justified by the greater miseries of her country.

But she knew it was not true. The truth was that she had not believed Frank's letter. She had been not so much indifferent as unbelieving. For three months she had not set eyes on him and three months in her vain, shallow world was worse than a lifetime. She had forgotten that sincere hearts still existed and might be simple enough to believe in her.

What could she say to him? Frank was still looking at her. The anger had gone from his eyes which shone instead with a kind of painful, barely repressed hope that all might yet not be finished between them. She thought that his youthful pride had given him no defense against love's disappointments and for that reason was perhaps the more vulnerable. She did not want to ruin his life for her. She saw now how much admiration she had always had for him. She did not want to see it spoiled by life.

She felt too weary and disillusioned to deserve this love. She had neither the desire nor the courage for it. Yet even so, she stayed, held captive as always by the strong spell of his charm.

"Frank," she said. "Listen to me—I must tell you why I could not come. The second time—I was going to come. It is true. And then—a friend called. He happened to say something about a man I care for deeply. You know him, Thomas Becque. And after that it was ridiculous, I did not want to go out. I simply stayed there, brooding on my memories."

For all the note of self-mockery in her voice, she was deliberately dwelling on her love for Thomas, the follies she was capable of committing for his sake, showing quite clearly that she preferred an evening of old, worn-out memories to a meeting with Frank.

He shrugged. "I guessed it was Thomas Becque."

"I shall not see him again. He is married."

"I know that too."

Suddenly Charlotte wanted more than anything to go home, to be left alone. There was nothing more to hope for now. Thomas would not come back. There was no one who could understand. She could not understand herself. There were women like that, she knew, half-crazy old maids, living with a man in pure imagination, talking to him, laying his place at table, falling asleep with their own arms for comfort. Such love was monstrous, and absurd, and yet sublime, a lonely burden affording only the bitter daily relish of self-destruction.

She sounded almost happy as she said: "You must forget me, Frank. I have nothing to give you." She took his arm and shook it earnestly. "You must forget me, do you hear?"

He shook her off. "Then why do you not forget?"

She recoiled, flushing deeply at the contempt and irony in his voice. Her persistence in her hopeless love left him quite simply surprised and scornful. The painful memory of the same words uttered by another voice came back to Charlotte with overwhelming force. She had talked too much of her sorrow. At first her friends had understood but they had expected more courage of her, some attempt at recovery. Now they were beginning to weary of her.

She smiled unhappily at Frank.

"I am sorry. I have never wanted to hurt you. You, more than anyone, Frank—I am not trying to make excuses. I only want you to know that, however it may seem, I have never, no never, played lightly with you. My feelings for you have always been sincere. I am not offering you my friendship, that word has been too much debased, I only know that I care for you very, very much—that I love you more than my brother, Frank."

She clasped his hand. Frank stood, unmoving, his jaw set. She told him she must go. He took her arm and they walked together up the ramp leading to the street. But when they reached the top, Frank turned in the opposite direction, towards la Tournelle. Charlotte dared not protest. She thought that he must let her go. She felt utterly weary.

Still walking, he began to speak.

"Why do you want to go? To be alone? You do not know what it is to be really alone. But I know. Alone because one has nothing, no home, no country. Alone because one has always been alone, from a child, even one's mother's smile forgotten because she died when one was too young. And so you invent her smile on the faces of other women. And even that is an illusion. Still one is alone and there is no one who can understand."

In a little while he stopped and leaned on the shady parapet. Charlotte said nothing, not knowing what to say. In a moment, she thought distressingly, she would feel sorry for him and this she did not want. She looked at his dirty shirt and saw it suddenly as the inevitable mark of his position as a social outcast. She recalled his trouble with the police, a subject she had not yet dared to broach, and guessed with a pang that he had suffered.

"Did they hurt you, Frank?" And when he did not reply at once, she added: "I heard that you were in trouble. I hope it is all over now?"

Not daring to ask who had told her, he simply thanked her for not doubting him, and explained briefly the reason for his arrest. Charlotte listened excited by this dramatic aspect of Frank's life and at the same time afraid for him. That it was serious, she guessed but, not wishing to show her anxiety, she forced herself to be sensible.

"But why should the police think your friend Lojko might be this Charles Harth?"

"Harth is known to have used a number of different aliases. I imagine he must have used my friend's name, which is by no means as uncommon in Poland or among Polish refugees as the French believe. Either my friend or myself may even know this Harth by sight without being aware of his identity. They suspect us because we have connections with the German community at Belleville, although most of those are old acquaintances from the university."

Charlotte dared not ask how far he could trust his friend Lojko. Frank's friendship was clearly absolute and any doubt cast on his friend would be like a personal insult. But she had some inkling of what he must have suffered at the hands of the police, and that was more than enough.

He said sadly: "Once, I was proud of being Polish, today, I am ashamed. They have made me ashamed. Today, I know what I have tried for years to forget, that my country has been beaten and enslaved, its people ignorant and down-trodden, and I cannot bear it. I think of my friends in Poland, intelligent, sensitive people—and most of them cannot read. Their children will not be able to read—"

At the thought of how he loved and suffered for his

country, Charlotte longed to stretch out her hands to comfort him.

"There was a time when I used to think of nothing but sacrificing myself for my country. Now, I know it would do no good. My French friends laugh at us, the Polish heroes who do nothing. Fine heroes, are we not?"

"No, Frank—"

He glanced at her, touched by the gentleness in her voice. She stood there, in her green dress, against the darker green of the leaves, with her soft hair and sweet childish face and that smile which was the thing he loved best of all in her. He said with great intensity:

"You are France and I love you."

His hand moved along the stone balustrade to clasp Charlotte's strongly.

"Will you be France for me? Will you be my country?"

Charlotte was silent. The pressure on her hand increased and she knew he would go on squeezing it until she answered. She stared unseeingly at the river, incapable of uttering a word. To say yes meant to renounce Thomas and the hope which lived like a premonition of some future time when she and Thomas would be reunited.

She was half out of her mind. She did not want to accept Frank, she did not want to. He took her in his arms, unexpectedly because the place where they stood, though lonely, was still a public street. She made a little move to free herself which only brought her more closely into his arms.

"Won't you try and live? Always, there comes a day when we must choose. We are alive and we cannot escape it. I am willing to forget my country and cleave to yours, but it is not a piece of paper that will make me a Frenchman but you—if you will—"

Charlotte knew that in making this choice, the country he was really rejecting was not Poland but Germany, his father's country. Whatever his choice, he would still suffer. France would have real meaning for him only if she became his wife.

He held her gently, his arms young and firm about her, their foreheads lightly touching in the way of very young lovers. Then his arms tightened and she felt the strength and sinewy tautness of his chest and thighs. The sense of well-being she experienced frightened her. She had forgotten how beautiful he was. Already she was falling under the agonizing spell of his beauty, a spell that was something apart from her love for him. It was almost as though she was jealous of his beauty.

His passion for her was something total, unlike the desire of other men. His was the whole-hearted devotion of the very young.

For the first time, she had encountered a man seeking to give rather than to take. Frank could not envisage love without marriage because he could not love unless he gave himself entirely. When he murmured in her ear: "This is the first time I have told a woman that I love her," she knew it was true. She felt that to give oneself completely to such a useful love meant an absolute forgetfulness of self, it meant becoming the other person, feeling like them, identifying oneself with them. This was something Charlotte had never known before Frank. Her idiotic marriage to Étienne had spoiled the miracle of first love for her.

No, she could not marry Frank. In years their ages were the same but she had lived through too much. She felt it would be wrong to accept him.

She made a move to draw back.

"No, do not go," he begged her. "Please, if you go it will be all over."

"I know."

"You are afraid. Why?"

"I am not afraid. I cannot marry you. It is too late, Frank, much too late—"

To live with Frank she would have to wipe out ten years of her life. It was too much. It could not be done. Frank would find happiness with another, a younger woman, but not with her.

For a moment, neither spoke. Charlotte looked away.

"It is too late," she said again. "Much too late."

People were coming towards them, in a group, chattering excitedly. In their midst, a newsboy precariously perched on a bicycle with enormous wheels, was waving a printed sheet and shouting:

"False report of the fall of Landau. Enemy agents suspected. Read all about it—"

The cyclist swooped from one side of the street to the other, like some strange Don Quixote on wheels.

In spite of themselves Charlotte and Frank watched, fascinated. The boy waved his newspaper like a flag, without any apparent intention of stopping to sell any. But the group of people on foot were nearer now, still talking excitedly. A young girl detached herself from the group and started across the street towards them calling out:

"Landau has not fallen. It was a false rumor spread by spies."

Frank and Charlotte looked at one another in bewilderment. The child, for she could not have been more than thirteen and was clutching her music-case in one hand, was clearly thrilled to be the bearer of tidings. Just then, her mother, who had been walking a little ahead, turned round and missing her, came back and seized the child's arm.

"Yes, I am afraid it is true," she said in answer to Charlotte's question. "We have been deceived, madame. French troops have not taken Landau. Nor is there any news from the front and it seems that things may be going badly at Wissenbourg."

Charlotte walked on beside Frank in a stunned silence. Thir own problems were lost in the general air of anxiety which hung over Paris. A crowd had collected outside the War Ministry, waiting for news but as yet the Ministry itself had none. A rumor began to spread that the false news had been traced to a group of speculators hoping to make a killing on the stock market, and the anger of the citizens knew no bounds.

It was not until evening that a bulletin appeared stating that the announcement of the capture of Landau by French troops had been the result of a wicked hoax and that the culprit was now behind bars. An appeal was made to the people to keep calm.

The name of the supposed culprit was never revealed.

Charlotte and Frank found themselves outside Notre-

Dame. Organ music floated out through the open doorway into the deserted square. Low in the sky, a blood-red sun was setting, its ominous glow as yet unquenched by the onrushing shadows of the August night. The windows of Notre-Dame seemed on fire. A good many people had come to pray. Charlotte and Frank stood outside the doors. Charlotte felt dwarfed by the majesty of the cathedral, which only served to increase her wretchedness.

"Suppose France were to lose this war," she thought. "What will become of us? What shall we do?" She, like everyone else, had lived all her life in the belief that her country was inviolate. "What have I ever done for anyone?" she asked herself.

And now, there was this war and no news from the front in Alsace. What would decide the fate of the French armies? Was God French? God must be on their side, he must make them win. France was the eldest daughter of the Church. Her soldiers could not die in the mud for nothing. God must step in to make them saints and heroes.

She began to pray fervently. They left the church. For the past two hours they had said not one word about themselves. Surely, they could not part now, knowing they would never meet again.

Sensing the approach of a parting which, by her own wish, would be final, Charlotte abandoned the struggle against a growing anxiety. It seemed inconceivable to her that she would have the courage to say goodbye and watch him go.

He was so close to her, so real, a handsome poetic figure with his white shirt and fair hair and his young face. She could not bear to cut these things out of her life and the staggering thought that nothing forced her to do so, began to form like a comforting, insidious hope within her. All at once she knew that she could not and would not do it. Released from the burden of Frank's suffering, she was conscious only of her own sorrow, the bitter-sweet ache of a sacrifice she might regret as long as she lived but never as much as she would regret letting Frank go, for ever, through her own fault.

"Frank, I will marry you—"

His eyes transfixed her.

"Why this change of heart? You do not want to."

She closed her eyes.

"All I know is that I cannot let you go, I cannot bear to think of you alone and unhappy."

"I do not want your pity."

"It is not pity, Frank. It is something else, a form of loving. I mean it. Do not make it more difficult. Listen—"

Her eyes searched his as though in this way she could find the truth. "Listen, we must give ourselves time. We will talk of it again. Will you meet me tomorrow?"

He hesitated.

"Frank, answer me—"

"Yes. Very well. I will wait for you here, outside the church, at a quarter past four."

"I am your friend."

He took the hand she offered and gripped it as though he would crush it.

Charlotte went home alone. Next day there was still no news from MacMahon's front. The weight of anxiety was overwhelming.

Charlotte was almost glad to be meeting Frank. Her mind was full of him. At about three o'clock, there was a ring at the door. Annick went to open it and called Charlotte. It was a messenger-boy with a letter.

Charlotte gave the boy a tip and opened the letter at once. It was addressed in a strong, masculine hand that was strange to her. She glanced at the signature: *Thomas.*

With the feeling that her legs would not support her, she went into her sitting-room and sat down. She was bathed in sweat. At first, she could not even read the letter.

"I make no excuses. I am on my way back from the front. I want to see you. I will be in the little tea-room facing Saint-Germain-l'Auxerrois at four o'clock."

She was conscious of an immense weariness, she doubted if she had the strength to get up. When at last she did, it was only by leaning on the arm of her chair.

"Thomas, my love, my love—" She blundered round her room, looking for her dress, wondering what Thomas wanted of her. Not that she cared, she would go wherever he willed, her own desires were nothing, he might mold her as he wished. Only to see him, that was all. To see him just once and then die.

She was outside. She did not even know where she was going. All she knew was that at each step her heart seemed to be torn apart by the violence of her hope.

The confectioners and tea-room in the Place Saint-Germain-l'Auxerrois faced the squat, black side of the church. It was a quiet, respectable neighborhood. The shop had net curtains over the windows.

Charlotte closed her eyes as she always did when trying to capture some fleeting moment of life. Then she pushed open the door, hearing the expected little tinkle of the bell. The room was full of strangers, ladies with unknown faces, and a smiling waitress.

She found it hard to breathe. She knew that there was someone waiting at the far end of the L-shaped room because of the eyes which, at her entry, went automatically to that corner. She moved forward.

There was a man, there—

It was Frank.

Charlotte stopped dead in the middle of the tea-room, incapable of moving another step. She stared at him, not needing to understand, knowing instinctively that she had been betrayed.

Their eyes met with no words spoken. Charlotte was beyond speech. Frank had risen. He saw her, suspended in mid-motion. The sunlight threw a pattern of tiny flowers from the muslin curtains across her elegant figure. She was wearing a lilac-colored dress he had not seen before which made her waist look absurdly small, with a lace jabot at the neck and a skirt that fell in little pleats below the knees at the back. She wore an Italian straw hat and long white gloves.

Frank's face was very pale, his eyes reproachful and defiant.

Charlotte's own soft, childlike features, so gentle in repose, so animated when she was excited, had thinned into a rigid mask of horror. Frank saw her lips move but no sound came. At last, in a slow, almost inaudible whisper, she managed to say: "You ... should ... not. ..."

She turned blindly, knocking into one of the tables, and fled back across the shop. Frank hurried after her and caught her up. She struggled like a beast caught in a trap. Her whole mind was bent on flight. But his, with the same blind obstinacy, was bent on capturing her. He hurt her but she did not even feel it.

"Hate me," Frank shouted at her. "Insult me."

The hand that gripped her arm was trembling.

"Speak to me. I want to hear your voice. I implore you, do not leave me here alone."

She shook her head helplessly.

"Look at me—yes, I did it. I sent that letter, and you have every right to hate me."

"How could you do it?"

How dared he set this vulgar snare for her? Disguising his writing, signing Thomas's name! The thought of her high hopes of a moment before nearly overcame her.

Thomas in a confectioner's! The very idea was grotesque. That alone should have warned her. Now, she would never forget this teashop, the waitress, and the women sitting there, their faces fixed in expressions of astonishment, as though the wind had changed and left them frozen like that.

But Frank, how could he have indulged in this farce, fit only for some jealous, provincial husband? The absurdity of the trap he had laid only added to Charlotte's distress.

"I had to do it. I could not let you marry me out of pity, Charlotte. Hear me, if I have hurt you, I have hurt myself a hundred times more. I prayed that you would not come, yet all the time I knew you would, I knew you would forget me, waiting for you at Notre-Dame."

He was still gripping her arm, careless, whether or not he hurt her.

"You do not answer. You hate me. And I hate myself for bringing you here with a lie. I did it because I love you and because I deserve something more than the leavings of your affection. I had to know what you would

259

do if Becque came back to Paris tomorrow and called you. Now, I know. Now, you have chosen."

"You might have saved yourself the trouble. I made my choice long ago."

Her voice cut like a whip and her eyes stung him. Frank's face went a shade paler. He stood before her stiffly. Even in despair, his eyes shone with a last brilliant flash of pride. He felt cold, in spite of the sunshine. To Charlotte, his youth, his pallor, his melodramatic stance, seemed equally absurd.

And yet today he was resplendent. Charlotte had not even noticed the care with which he was dressed, his dark-grey suit and dazzling white shirt, immaculate cuffs and collar setting off the smooth texture of his skin.

He stood there in his pathetic attitude of defiance.

"You are making yourself ridiculous," she said.

But at the same time she knew that there was nothing sacred about her love for Thomas Becque. The claims of Frank's love, of Frank's motives, were as strong as hers.

"I shall never forgive you, never!"

She walked away without looking back, leaving him standing there on the pavement. She was utterly wretched.

Frank stood for a long time just as she had left him. He watched the passers-by without seeing them. People came out of the church and began crowding into the now peaceful tea-shop. Their conversation was all about the news from the front.

It was late when Frank returned to the rue Saint-Sevèrin. It was almost dark. He had spent the time roaming the streets, his steps turning automatically to Rachel's house.

Suddenly he stopped short, catching sight of Rachel lurking in the narrow doorway. She had seen him and was trying to hide from him.

She darted away quickly down a side alley. Frank ran after her but she was already out of sight. She must be hiding somewhere. Someone opened a window and in the light from it he saw Rachel quite close to him. He gripped her arm.

"Why are you running away? Are you afraid of me?"

She tried to jerk herself free and they struggled violently in the shadows.

"What is the matter?"

"Spy!" she gasped suddenly. "You nearly had me all right."

"What?"

"All right, I know all about it. I've had my eye on your Lojko for a long time. Little Rachel's not so stupid. There was something about your pal—"

"What is this nonsense?"

"How could you lie to me? And to think that I believed you!" Hurt, angry tears were streaming down her face. Still Frank did not understand.

"That friend of yours," she sobbed, "he is Harth, Charles Harth! He's no more a Pole than I am!"

"You are raving!" He clapped his hand across her mouth to silence her. Rachel, thinking she was about to be strangled, gave a little moan and collapsed limply in his arms, her head resting on his shoulder.

"You didn't know—you must have, you're not that stupid. Anyone can see he was a wrong 'un. I watched him, when he thought he was alone. Once, when I was in the yard, I saw him call a boy out of the window and give him an envelope. I managed to get hold of it."

Rachel had opened the envelope and found inside it a suspicious-looking coded message. She had searched Lojko's belongings while he was behind the curtain, washing. She was especially interested in a black leather wallet which he kept in his overcoat pocket. Inside she had found three passports made out in different names. Neither Lojko nor Harth appeared on any of them. But there was a letter in German, probably from his mother, which began *"My dearest Charles."* Rachel had learned enough German in the course of her trade to learn that.

"What are you going to do?" Frank asked, retaining his grip on her arm.

"Fetch the *flics*, of course."

"You can't do that!"

"You see if I can't!"

With a swift wrench, she tore herself free and ran like a hare down the alley.

Frank began to run in the opposite direction. He dashed up the stairs and flung open the door of the room. Lojko was asleep. Frank shook him roughly. He opened his eyes and saw Frank standing at the foot of the bed. Picking up the overcoat, Frank took out the black wallet and emptied it. The passports fell to the ground. The colour left Lojko's face.

"You are Harth," Frank said. "You have deceived me."

Lojko did not move.

"Get out," Frank said between his teeth. "Get out before I kill you!"

Lojko rose, sallow-faced, and began grovelling in his shirt for the papers. Frank tossed him his trousers, saying that Rachel had gone for the police. Lojko asked why Frank himself had not given him up.

"Because you do not give up a man who has been your friend, even if he has betrayed you."

Lojko was clumsily gathering up his things. Frank watched him, a chill in his heart.

"I regret nothing. What I have done, I have done for Germany."

"France gave you hospitality, Harth, and you betrayed her. And to betray France, is more than to betray a nation, it is betraying liberty, betraying mankind. The home of all man's hopes, the land deserving all our gratitude, that is what you have betrayed."

"For me there is only one country, Germany."

They were coming. Harth glanced round in terror. There was only the skylight. He had to climb on a stool to haul himself up and for a moment he hung suspended between earth and sky, his legs dangling.

Frank saw his figure apparently sucked out into the night beyond. He himself had made no move. He heard the footsteps on the stairs. There was still a fraction of time in which he too might escape. So little time, yet long enough for a lifetime in retrospect.

He thought of Charlotte. She had never understood how he loved her.

The door was flung open. Frank let himself be handcuffed and led down the stairs. Rachel hurtled down after them, screaming wildly.

"It's not him, I tell you. It was another one who got away! This one had nothing to do with it. Frank, tell them! Don't let them take you. They'll shoot you. You are innocent, innocent—" In desperation, she was banging her head on the stair-rail. The men continued their descent in silence. At last she raised her tear-stained face, staring about her with dazed, unseeing eyes and murmuring:

"Frank, Frank, my darling—" On an impulse of superstitious fear, she crossed herself.

Charlotte learned the news of Frank's arrest from the newspapers. The Press as a whole was by no means hostile. It was stated that Rachel, the prostitute who had denounced Harth, persisted in her assertions of Worski's innocence. Worski himself maintained a disconcerting silence in the face of all questioning, as though indifferent to whatever fate awaited him.

Charlotte began to have dreams. For three nights in a row she had the same terrible dream. There was always a man with bound hands and bandaged eyes, standing in the silent, empty courtyard before a firing squad. As though in a theatre, she saw him fall and saw the blood on his shirt.

Then she knew that Frank would die. He would be condemned to death as Harth's accomplice. Yet he was innocent, she knew. He would let himself be condemned. He wanted to die. God knew what need he felt for heroism, unless it was from sheer indifference and disgust for life.

She spent hours talking to Jean Hertz, who knew him well and had a great respect for him. He told her:

"You do not understand him. What boys like that have need of is simply ordinary love."

She made him talk to her about Frank because it seemed to her that while Hertz was talking, Frank must still be safe. The affection which she had denied him before she was beginning to give him now, a little more each day. As she learned to know him, through Hertz, she began to understand herself how much she cared for him. She could not let him die. Frank, so young and beautiful, his young body riddled with bullets. A deathly shudder shook her at the thought.

"What have I ever done for anyone?" she cried to Hertz passionately. "I must do something, I cannot let Frank die."

Hertz said he did not think the police believed in Frank's guilt, that they were holding him in the hope that it would lead Harth to give himself up.

"They'll let him go. Frank will not die."

"He will die unless I do something for him," she said desperately, knowing how she herself had helped to push him towards death on that terrible day in the tea-shop.

On August 10, the government passed the emergency law authorizing the conscription of all Frenchmen between the ages of twenty and thirty-five.

On the 12th, the newspapers reported that Charles Harth had been arrested near Gien.

A few days later, when Charles Harth had exonerated Worski completely, claiming sole responsibility for his actions, and since the police had failed to produce any evidence of Frank's connection with the German spy ring, the case against him was dropped and he was called at the trial only in the capacity of a witness.

Charlotte discovered the day of Frank's release by calling on Rachel.

When he saw her waiting for him, he stopped as though in doubt. She thought for a moment that he was going to reject her, that he did not trust her any more. But he was too straightforward for that. He had thought about her too much to reject her now. For him the bitterness between them had ceased to have any meaning, except perhaps to draw them closer together.

She ran to him and he held her gently in his arms without a word. He did not look like a failed hero. He was not even haggard. He was just a boy, a young and healthy boy, in whom the force of life was all powerful. Charles Harth was shot on the 27th. He died bravely.

Charlotte and Frank were married on the same day in the

town hall of the fifth *arrondissement*. Frank had received his naturalization papers at the same time as his discharge. The mayor was accustomed by now to such hurried ceremonies pushed in before the young men left for the front, so as to regularize the union before it was too late. He pushed them in at dinner time between courses.

It was all very quick and gay and rather casual. They had their names inscribed in a big book and were out in the street again in ten minutes. It was raining. Frank drew Charlotte close to him in the shelter of his overcoat. They walked down the rue Soufflot, stopping on the way to buy ham, foie gras and wine, and went home loaded with small packages.

They insisted on Hertz coming to eat with them. The dinner was a trifle scanty but they did not care. Hertz left early and went out so that they could be alone.

They did not speak at first. Frank played a thin, tinkling tune on a row of glasses arranged before him filled to different levels with water. He held his ear cocked against the glass. He stopped suddenly and looked up at Charlotte and smiled. It was only then that the full meaning of Frank's presence in that room came home to her. The setting did not suit him, any more than it suited her. The apartment did no more than offer a shelter for their own rebellious youth. The incongruity of their presence in these cramped, humdrum surroundings, made Charlotte aware for the first time that with Frank she was young. They were like two children left at home by the family on a Sunday afternoon, romping together in some faded drawing-room.

That tonight he would be lawfully her lover was a thought which had not yet occurred to her. She would be his. She looked at him tenderly, wondering when he would dare to come to her, how they would dare to love one another and what would happen then.

All the same, she thought, she was no longer a child. What was this extraordinary shyness which had come over her? Frank rose, annihilating the stuffy room where in times past she had seen Étienne fade and Thomas flee. For a moment he stood looking at her with shining eyes.

"I can't," she whispered. "I am frightened of you."

Frank's eyes were alight with mocking laughter. She flung herself into his arms, beseeching:

"Hold me, hold me!"

"I was waiting for you to ask me." His arms closed vice-like about her, crushing the tiny buttons on her dress. They stood quietly for a moment while Charlotte's inner voice said:

"How will we ever dare? We cannot do it." But she saw that he was holding her too fast for her to free herself in any other way. He was the only way out. Frank, Frank. . . .

He left for the front a week later. He had enlisted without telling her, doing his duty towards his adopted country. She went with him to the station, as she had gone with Millau.

They stood with their arms round one another until the last moment. Charlotte could not believe that he was really going. While he was there, everything was easy. She loved him as she had never loved anyone before. They were simply two young people, very much in love; now at least, she believed that that was possible. She would be faithful to him always. With him, she was good and virtuous.

He hugged her tightly and she felt the special softness of his lips on hers. The agony of a last kiss which tastes so wonderful just because it is the last. She felt him tear himself away from her and climb into the train with the rest. She wandered desolate along the platform, looking for him among the crowds of men in uniforms. They had shaved his head, two days earlier, so that he looked like a Russian peasant. But just then he must be wearing his kepi. She searched for his black eyes among the eyes all around her but saw only the anonymous crowd.

The train drew out. Charlotte stood waving at nothing in particular. Now that she no longer had Frank's hand in hers, all her wonderful new faith in life faded into an almost unattainable memory. The war will end, she thought. We shall be happy. We can only live in hope. Then why did she have this conviction that some quite different destiny was before her, a destiny infinitely more tragic? Why this ridiculous certainty that she, that all of them, were born for something else?

Frank, my young love. I will be faithful to you.

She ran into a crowd of soldiers and civilians alighting from a nearby train. Men jostled her and she found herself apologizing to them for disturbing their packs. Their ravaged faces bore the scars of battle and defeat. France could not lose the war, she must not. Could one lose a war and not lose hope?

She bumped into a muscular arm and turned with a word of apology, only to find herself face to face with the portly Chaptal and Thomas Becque.

They seemed on the point of boarding a train. She had thought Thomas was already at the front. Was he only just leaving, or was he going back a second time?

Neither was in uniform. Dimly, she heard herself speaking to Chaptal. The crowd reeled about her. She staggered against Becque's good arm, her eyes never leaving his face. He gripped her firmly, reassuringly.

"Come, over here. Listen, wait for me at the station buffet. I will join you there. All right? You will wait?"

She nodded. Bells were ringing in her ears. She was aware of the roughness of Thomas's sleeve and she made no attempt to resist the terrifying knowledge that she loved this face, this curly hair and these blue eyes, more than life itself. Mindlessly, she let him lead her. They were like wreckage in a storm. Chaptal was some way ahead. Thomas still had a hold of Charlotte's sleeve, but the pressure of people around them was slowly driving them apart. As the crowd parted them she heard him say:

"Go to the buffet, I am coming." She went. Chiefly because she was incapable of doing anything else. The buffet was almost empty and she saw herself, where she had no business to be, reflected in the fly-blown gilded mirrors of this place of a thousand meetings.

Barely a quarter of an hour since Frank had gone. She could not betray him in this way without destroying all her hope in human goodness. She would keep faith. At least she would have given that to someone. She would go, would give up Thomas. It would not be so hard now.

Not so hard to give him up as to abandon the utopia of his returning.

As she left the café, she saw Thomas in the distance. It was this crowd that had thrown them together. Anywhere else, he would never have wished to speak to her. This did not mean anything. She thought of Frank.

Thomas was coming towards her but was caught up and carried away by a rush of soldiers coming from the platforms and making a maelstrom round the café door. Charlotte found herself thrust back against a wall, already a long way from the buffet. She had lost her hat. A gentleman in civilian clothes gallantly picked it up and offered it to her. She thanked him and, seeing his eyes on her, dared not stand there any longer like a street walker. She made her way towards the exit, hurried along by the crowd of people on her heels.

14

BETWEEN THE 4th and 6th of August, the second German army marched into Alsace at Weissenburg. Marshal MacMahon concentrated his troops on the Strasbourg road, some ten miles south of Weissenburg. His army took up a position on a foothill of the Vosges mountain overlooking the little river Lauter. Below the hill were the two small towns of Fröschviller and Wörth. This meant that forty-one thousand men and a hundred and nineteen cannon were disposed along a front six miles long with Elsasshausen and Fröschviller in the center.

The attack began on the 7th, earlier than expected, owing to the activities of a Prussian reconnaissance party. At first, the German attempts to gain the plateau of Elsasshausen were unsuccessful and the French pursued them actually into the streets of Wörth, but they did succeed in overrunning the French right on the plateau of Morsbronn.

The French had no more infantry. MacMahon decided to sacrifice a brigade of Cuirassiers. The two regiments drew into the attack. After a terrible advance across hop-gardens interspersed with deep ridges, under a rain of fire, they charged into the village to meet with point-blank fire from the Prussians barricaded inside the houses. In the maelstrom of terrified horses, the Cuirassiers fell one after another.

The French right, dug in up near Elsasshausen, parallel with the Reichshoffen road, had to fall back before the Prussian drive which swept over the plateau. To defend the road and cover the retreat, MacMahon brought up his remaining forces, one division of Cuirassiers and a regiment of foot, the 1st Algerian infantry.

The Cuirassiers charged first but were mown down by sustained machine-gun fire. Then it was the turn of the infantry. Nothing could stand before them. They had fought the day before at Luxembourg. They advanced, all seventeen hundred of them, drawn up as though on parade, holding their fire and shouting: "Bayonets at the ready!"

The Prussians simply abandoned their guns and their positions and fled in terror. The Algerians recaptured Elsasshausen and gave chase as far as the outskirts of a near-by wood. The mist, so common in that region, had dispersed, giving way to a fine drizzling rain that streamed down the mountain and turned the ground into a bog. The foot soldiers hurled themselves blindly after the Germans who had taken refuge in the wood. Many fell, the rest dived for shelter in the shell-holes or behind any projecting bit of ground. The rain soon turned any open ground into a sea of mud.

In this nightmare of mud and powder, the Prussians saw the dark faces of the Algerians coming at them through the wood, their bayonets flashing white amid the undergrowth.

Eight hundred of the French died. The Germans suffered enormous losses. The bodies of men fallen into ravines were caught and held among the branches of the sodden pine trees.

Meanwhile, the German 1st army had entered Lorraine and defeated General Frossard at Forbach. Marshal Bazaine was still holding out in the fortress of Metz. But this bastion of Lorraine, called the "key to France," far from forming an impenetrable gateway to the country, was liable to become a danger if it immoblized too many troops.

It was vital, once the defeats were known, for Bazaine's army inside Metz to leave the city and fall back with the remnants of MacMahon's forces on Châlons and Verdun, so as to bar the route to Paris.

However, Napoleon III was clearly reluctant to give the order for withdrawal to the garrison of Metz. The emperor's indecision paralysed his headquarters staff. In the end, the order for the evacuation of Metz was not given until

14 August, when it could have been made four days earlier. Napoleon's half-hearted orders were often countermanded almost immediately without warning. Confusion and apathy were general.

After Forbach, the retreating army passed through Sarreguemines on 7 August. The inhabitants watched with horror as the ragged troops stumbled by, the enemy hard on their heels. The men went through these villages with empty stomachs, their eyes still smarting with powder and rage in their hearts. They hauled their supply wagons across the sodden fields, stopping now and then to take on a hasty load of provisions from the farms.

That Sunday was a day of first communion. The peasants in their Sunday best gathered at the roadside to watch the haggard troops go by, bewildered by this evidence of disaster coming in the midst of their holiday.

"Run for your lives," the soldiers told the gaping villagers. "The Prussians are coming. They are shooting all those who resist."

On the same day, part of General Frossard's force was also on the run, having lost most of its strength. The men had abandoned their carts and their supplies. All they had left was their bulky packs, too heavy and awkward to permit of rapid movement and one of the causes of the superiority of the Prussian army over the French.

The rain had stopped an hour before and the day was almost warm. The men were exhausted and wanted to rest. They were passing through a roadside village. Near the church there was a green with dogs and chickens on it. The fowls scattered at the approach of the soldiers. The bells were ringing for vespers. One of the soldiers, unable to go any farther, dropped his pack in the shade and his example was at once followed by the rest. The village people coming out of church came up and stood looking at them nervously.

"You must get away," one of the soldiers told them. "Get away, understand. The Prussians are coming. They will take you all—commandeer the houses, scrounge everything—in the name of all that's wonderful, these peasants haven't a notion—"

He flung himself back on the grass. One of the peasants to whom he had been speaking gaped at him in silence.

"Here, you clod-hopper, have you understood a word of what I have been saying?"

The peasant just stared like the rest at the strange sight before them. The soldier let his weary head fall back onto the grass with a sigh, swearing aloud that he was wasting his time talking to these yokels. His neck ached and he would never have believed his head could feel so heavy. What was he doing in this damned war anyway?

His name was Farrenc, Eloi Farrenc. He was the grumbler of the unit, a strapping young Parisian labourer, with a straight nose, fair hair and chubby cheeks. Next to him was Louis Richet, a cunning, broad-shouldered fellow from Touraine.

Not far from Farrenc and Richet, a young lieutenant whose name was Willaert lay spread-eagled face down where he had fallen.

"Well, *mon lieutenant*," Farrenc said, "if anyone had told us a fortnight ago that we should all find ourselves back here tonight! Still, here we are!"

Willaert rolled over on his back and stared up at the sky with his mouth open. Ferranc eyed his slim, almost girlish figure and wavy blond hair and thought that he was a nice little gentleman.

One of the peasants came up to them and began saying something in guttural patois. Farrenc chuckled uncomprehendingly.

"Carry on, mate. It's all Greek to me."

The old man went away. Farrenc discovered a blister on his heel. One of the village girls, a strapping wench in her best Sunday muslin, approached timidly and offered her handkerchief.

"Thanks, darling, I'll let you have it back next time you're in Montmartre," Farrenc said kindly giving her cheek a pat. The girl blushed, not understanding a word of what he said.

"You pretty girl—very pretty," Farrenc said in an effort to convey his meaning. The girl continued to smile uncomprehendingly.

Farrenc slumped back on the grass in disgust. "Fine lot

of heathens they are. No one's going to tell me this lot are French!"

"Ask your sister," Richet told him.

"And what about my sister?"

"She'll tell you Lorraine is in France because if Lorraine isn't France then where would France be?"

"Are you trying to tell me people who can't even speak French are more French than you and me?"

"I'm telling you nothing, but Lorraine is France and without Lorraine France wouldn't be France."

"I don't like the idea of people who can't speak French being more French than me," Farrenc said decidedly. "And you can't answer that one."

"That's enough," said an old soldier lying near by. "Can't you shut up and let us have a snooze?"

But it was too late, already it was time to go. The soldiers scrambled up slowly. The village women brought them some fruit. The rain was beginning again. As they tramped off through the wet a boy galloped up on a horse shouting that the Prussians had swept past Sarreguemines that very morning.

The villagers who, a little while ago, had been reluctant to believe, were seized with panic. The soldiers went on their way stolidly through the rain while the hens pecking in the village street ran screeching before them. One man, a tall, red-headed fellow with a limp and a wild look in his eyes, turned his gun on the hysterical fowls. Shots spattered in every direction and the soldier with his torn red breeches and flaming beard kept pressing the trigger like a madman.

The peasants stood by, watching the slaughter of their hens in stricken silence. At last the soldier stopped firing and began picking up the dead chickens which he fastened by the feet to his belt. As there was no more room in his knapsack he stuffed the last two inside his shirt before going on. After five minutes, however, his skin had begun to itch intolerably as the chickens' countless fleas transferred themselves to him. At last, unable to bear it any longer, he dropped the birds one by one along the roadside, tearing open his shirt to scratch himself and swearing like one possessed.

With no time in which to move his hundred and fifty thousand men, Marshal Bazaine was cut off below Metz by the German army. On 14 August, the German 1st army mounted an attack at Borny. The attack was repulsed, but the French wasted precious time. On the 16th, the Germans attacked again, at Rezonville. This time, they were numerically inferior and might have suffered a resounding defeat had not Bazaine, for reasons best known to himself, forbidden any counter-offensive.

On the 18th, at Saint-Privat and at Gravelotte, the biggest battles of the war were fought. Two hundred and twenty thousand Germans and seven hundred cannon against a hundred and twenty-five thousand Frenchmen with four hundred cannon.

The French defended themselves heroically against an attacking force of almost twice their number. But by evening the course of the battle was decided. The far right of the village of Saint-Privat, which Canrobert was defending, was attacked by seven thousand Germans. When these were mown down by the French rifle fire, the Germans launched a massive attack with a hundred and sixty-eight cannon. By eight o'clock, the French had no more ammunition. They waited for relief from Bazaine. It never came, although the Marshal was holding in reserve the imperial guard and a further twenty thousand men able to fight. So Privat was in flames and Canrobert, under attack by thirty thousand foot, was forced to evacuate. The cost of the battle to the French was twelve thousand men, to the Germans, twenty thousand.

Bazaine was still isolated outside Metz. However, Marshal MacMahon's idea was to fall back towards Paris so as to organize an effective defense of the city. The minister Rouher, a fervent supporter of the Bonapartist régime, was terrified of the effect on public opinion if the army fell back on the capital. Appearances must be kept up and the prestige of the Empire, which had already suffered grievously, must be maintained at all costs. The private ambitions of Rouher, one of the emperor's evil geniuses, a general fear of the people's anger and the anxiety to preserve the régime, were all allowed to outweigh the nation's good. The Empress took the minister's side and managed to dissuade the Emperor from falling back on Paris. But MacMahon received orders to join Bazaine in his defensive position outside Metz.

Unfortunately, the French army moved slowly. It wasted ten days crawling between Châlons and Montmédy, where it was to join up with Bazaine's forces. In the meanwhile, Moltke learned, as the result of an indiscretion by a Parisian journalist, of the existence of the Châlons army. The German 1st and 2nd armies, then advancing towards Paris, were ordered to move as fast as possible to meet the French army. They took it by surprise on 13 August at Beaumont.

Acting against the orders of MacMahon, who was anxious to push on as quickly as possible to Mouzon, General de Failly had bivouaced his troops in a field at Beaumont, where they spent the night of the 29th. The next morning, the general and his staff breakfasted with the local mayor.

An inspection had been ordered. The soldiers had taken down the guns, some were polishing their weapons, others doing their washing. No one had any idea of an enemy attack.

The three survivors of Forbach, Eloi Farrenc, Richet and Paul Willaert, after a fortnight's idleness in camp at Châlons, were now with the rest in their exposed position on the open ground. Willaert, stripped to the waist after rinsing his shirt in a near-by stream, was busy trying to dry this garment by stretching it between two bayonets. Richet was greasing his rifle with the same stuff with which he was accustomed to anointing his moleskins and the soles of his feet. Farrenc, who was less particular, was idly polishing his weapons. The sun was shining.

A shell exploded without warning in the middle of the camp. As the dust subsided, the men gazed in horror at the huge hole in the ground. Projecting from it were one or two twisted rifle butts and a human leg.

The silence was absolute. No one had noticed the direction of the shot but it must have come from the woods close by. The attack had come as a complete surprise, catching the French troops literally with their trousers down, their guns dismantled and their gun-carriages unprepared.

The artillery was not in position. It would be a massacre. In an instant, all was panic and confusion with men running for their weapons in all directions. Battalions formed up hastily, in no kind of order. Some of the men were running for their officers. The shells were now falling heavily all over the field, leaving great gaping holes in the ground and empty gaps in the ranks of the men.

The eleventh, forty-sixth and sixty-eighth battalions, with the fourth Chasseurs, managed to reach the high ground and drove the Prussians back into the wood before they could enter the village. But the enemy returned to the attack. The German artillery pounded the French troops as they struggled to get their own guns into position. After that it was a rout. The Germans outflanked the French and had them almost encircled.

The Cuirassiers made one last heroic charge. The marines threw themselves hopelessly against the enemy. But the main body of the army was utterly routed. The men turned pale and fled as though the devil were after them, throwing away their kit and swarming down the roads leaving a litter of abandoned cannon and small arms behind them.

On the same morning of 13 August, military supply trains and official convoys poured into the small town of Mézières. The streets were jammed with traffic, while in the main square the market was in full swing, filling the air with a smell of sun-warmed fruit and vegetables. The wide-brimmed hats and blouses of the peasants contrasted with the red and blue uniforms of the soldiers waiting to be ordered to the front. Field kitchens had been set up where buxom women, each with a flock of children clinging to their skirts, wielded great iron stew-pots.

The town hall had been taken over as army headquarters. The officers were billeted on the local inhabitants. A host of civilians, the majority of them French or foreign journalists, were to be found in hotels and officers' messes alike.

These war correspondents were to be found in every garrison town on the eastern front. Dressed with military smartness in fur hats and heavy, caped overcoats, they bustled about like so many incipient Byrons, recording the glories of French heroism and, incidentally, presenting the world with the edifying spectacle of their own disregard for danger.

This, at least, was how they were viewed by those of the higher-ranking officers whose duty it was to deal with them. The officers performed this duty with a noticeably bad grace, due to their well-founded suspicions as to the discretion of some of these reporters, for whom the war was simply another sensational story for their columns.

There had, in fact, been so much of this at the beginning that the general staff had finally forbidden press men to go with the army. It was the correspondent of *Le Soir*, Edmond About himself, who, when a general denied him the privilege of observing operations at first hand, promptly reported:

"Is that your last word, General? Well, I'm afraid you may regret it, because if that is the case, we, for our part, have quite made up our minds not to give your war the benefit of our publicity."

By the end of July, the government had decided that the public was to be kept informed only through official channels. The journalists from all quarters had to fall back on some unofficial rumors, and information gleaned from whatever sources they could find to eke out the meagre official dispatches.

Those journalists who had gone to the front with the honest intention of carrying out their task of informing the public suffered like the rest from this decree. Some even made up their minds to go through the campaign with the soldiers in the ranks in order to obtain first-hand information.

At Mézières, on the morning of 13 August, the large officers' mess which had been established in one of the town's hotels was crowded. In one corner, the *Figaro*'s correspondent, Alfred d'Aulnay, was arguing with a colonel in uniform.

D'Aulnay, a brilliantly controversial talker, had actually been subjecting this officer for the past quarter of an hour to a bold inquisition on the army. The colonel, a heavy, plethoric man, visibly ill at ease and unaccustomed to such argument, was content to nod his head and clear his throat by way of agreement. He kept glancing at the door, as though expecting someone. Charles Hugo, the young correspondent of *Le Rappel,* who happened to be standing near by, listened appreciatively to his colleague's conversation.

"D'Aulnay is an incorrigible bluffer," he remarked to his neighbor, another journalist, although from his dress he looked more like a lawyer.

"Listen to him, Massé," Hugo went on, "giving that old bureaucrat a lesson in strategy. He's got a nerve. He even called his scheme of fortification d'Aulnay's lines. He has a positive genius for blowing his own trumpet."

"I'd hardly call it genius," Massé said crossly. "A bit of a talent at the most."

"If you knew the things he says about you, you'd be even harder on him," Hugo retorted with a laugh. He was a young man who enjoyed a set-to were it not that he blushed too readily. Massé shrugged and glanced up over his misted glass of beer to contemplate with idle curiosity d'Aulnay the celebrated journalist and man of the world.

Alfred d'Aulnay was known to have come to the front as representative of the *Figaro* even before war was officially declared. Alone, he had undertaken an *inspection* of the fortifications. The inhabitants of Valenciennes, confused by his extravagant mode of dress, which corresponded in their eyes to that of no known nation, and seeing him strolling on the ramparts offering cigars to the soldiers, had taken him for a Prussian spy. It was a mistake which nearly turned out badly for him.

Hugo was watching d'Aulnay with interest and admiration, that were not entirely without a touch of amusement. D'Aulnay's dress was clearly calculated to attract the notice of a rural population. His appearance was designed to get him recognized at first glance as the traveling intellectual, whose social status could be gauged from the cut of his overcoat and the tilt of his wide-brimmed felt hat.

The door opened and an officer came in. He wore the insignia of a general, but his cap was pulled down over his eyebrows and there was dust on his coat. He was very tall with clear, commanding blue eyes set in a weatherbeaten face, a large nose and a neat moustache. He looked as though he had traveled some distance and seemed amazed by the laughter and cigar smoke which filled the crowded room. His expression was such an obvious rebuke that the chatter ceased and all eyes were turned on him.

The colonel, who had been d'Aulnay's captive audience for the past twenty minutes, left him with a curt nod and hurried up to the newcomer.

"General—" from his busy nervous movements he might have been about to pick up a pile of imaginary luggage. The rumor went round: "It is Wimpffen, General de Wimpffen."

The two officers passed quickly through the room and out into the corridor, where they entered a small office and shut the door behind them.

"Top brass," said Charles Hugo.

"—General de Wimpffen—back from Africa, and promoted apparently—of course I can't say for sure—replacing de Failly as Commander-in-Chief of the 5th Corps—mind you, don't quote me—"

"I say," Hugo interrupted with a glance at the door, "there's Becque and Daguerran. I thought I saw them in the town yesterday."

"—Came by the afternoon train yesterday—direct from Paris—Becque's working for *La Cloche*, you know. Daguerran's either taken Machin's place on *L'Avenir National* or else is acting as his second string."

"You're a mine of information, Massé."

Hugo waved to the two men who had just come in and they nodded back. Although it was still early in the morning, the restaurant was doing a brisk trade. By about ten o'clock, the room was full. The noise was deafening. In spite of the defeats suffered at Alsace and Lorraine, no one as yet believed that France was beaten. Everything was sure to turn out all right in the end. There were a great many journalists present, both from Paris and the provinces, and a good many lively arguments were in progress.

The main idea of most of these journalists was to hitch a lift with some officers leaving for the front, a thing which was by no means easy, as they were not popular with the army. The only reason they were allowed into the hotel lounge, which served as the officers' mess, was that the room was divided into two parts, and they could not very well be prevented from using the first while the military had no intention of depriving themselves of its amenities.

Standing near the journalists at the moment was an enormous, bullet-headed colonel, who might easily have passed for a Prussian. The plainness of his uniform contrasted strongly with those of the more traditionally dandified French officers. He was typical of those risen from the ranks by dint of their courage and their prowess at poker. He was talking very loudly in a resounding, parade-ground voice. His neighbours were two more officers sipping small glasses of spirits. The colonel was describing at the top of his voice how, a couple of weeks before, he had been obliged to lead his troops from Nancy to somewhere in the region of Metz without so much as a map of the region. After the event, it sounded like a tall story and a good joke.

"Such negligence shames the whole army, Colonel." The words came from a lieutenant standing near the group, but not of it. He was a small, thin, rather pompous-looking young man, but that his indignation was genuine could be seen from his pale face and the uncomfortable brightness in his eyes. His fanaticism seemed out of place in that good-humored atmosphere, and his observation was a barely concealed insult to his superior officer.

There was a general turning of heads as the journalists stopped their own conversations to watch the colonel's reaction. The officers present looked embarrassed. The colonel himself had reddened and seemed uncertain how to take the attack which, although not addressed directly to him, came sufficiently close to it. Could he call the man to account before the Press? The colonel felt that he had been taken advantage of by this little whipper-snapper, who insisted on treating seriously what had been no more than a bit of fun.

The colonel's color deepened. He was a man who had always found it difficult to get on with the unfledged products of the staff colleges. For all his courage, he knew that they cared little for his scars. "It's not maps the general staff need, it's brains! And meanwhile our men are dying." The taunt came from one of the journalists.

At once, the colonel's anger became directed against the Press. He glared at them, purple in the face, and bellowed:

"I'll arrest the next man who casts aspersions on the army, gentlemen of the Press!"

"He'll have a heart attack!" someone said softly.

Another voice answered. "The only sort of attack he's capable of at present."

"Who said that?"

"When you go to war as though it were a holiday, you must expect criticism," observed Charles Hugo, who happened to be one of those closest.

The colonel glared at them with bloodshot eyes.

"I'll have you court-martialled for this," he shouted.

"I should be careful of your own accusations, Colonel," said Becque, who, with Daguerran, was standing next to Charles Hugo. "I was standing beside my friend here and I can bear witness that it was not he who spoke before."

"Attacking soldiers in time of war is treason!"

Unable to vent his fury on the lieutenant who had spoken first, the colonel had turned his anger instead on the group of men in civilian dress before him.

"We are not attacking soldiers," Becque said, "for my own part, I know better than any the herosim of which they are capable. I was at Weissenburg."

"You in your white shirt?"

"Precisely. But there are some pleasures denied to you by reason of the pips on your arm."

"You Press men, you are nothing but a parcel of scoundrels!" The colonel blustered, losing all control. "If I had my way I'd shoot the lot of you!"

"So this is what we have come to," the lieutenant said,

white-lipped. "The army is slandered in public and the sacrifices of our men are forgotten while we squabble with professional gossip-mongers. What has become of France when her honor is in the hands of men like this? When any journalist can come and flaunt his mistresses under the very noses of our troops!"

"Take care, that is slander," a journalist retorted angrily. "We are here to do our job as war correspondents. You are not making our task any easier. We will not put up with abuse!"

"So far as I know," put in another, "the ladies we see in the hotel lounge do not belong to any journalists. I have even heard them referred to as the *headquarters' tarts.*"

A young woman was in fact to be seen at that moment, observing them curiously through the glass doors leading to the lounge. She was elegantly dressed with a good many feathers and jewels.

Tempers rose higher until, at one moment, it seemed as though the lieutenant would challenge one of the journalists to fight. The unexpected entrance of General de Wimpffen, followed by his subordinate, produced a sudden silence.

The general took in the situation at a glance. With his upright bearing, his skin tanned by the African sun and an air of hard practical experience, Wimpffen stood out clearly from the other officers. They were all conscious of the force of his personality. The calm, even mild blue eyes held the uncompromising directness of a man of unquestioning courage, accustomed to wide open spaces. As Massé had whispered to Hugo, Wimpffen had returned from Africa to take over the command of the 2nd Corps from General de Failly. Now, addressing himself to officers and civilians alike, the general politely requested an explanation.

The big colonel embarked on a confused account. Cutting him short, Wimpffen asked him, with the lieutenant, Charles Hugo and Becque, who were standing a little in front of the rest, to go with him into another room.

When they had removed themselves to a small conservatory, Wimpffen asked the names of the two journalists. He was better informed about the controversies of the

Press than might have been expected. Among other things, he recalled certain none too friendly criticisms Becque had made two years earlier, in his paper *Demain*, concerning some events in Africa in which Wimpffen had been involved. He looked at Becque thoughtfully, recalling that, at the time, these attacks had annoyed him because in his opinion the journalist did not know enough of what he was talking about. It was not the moment to discuss that now but Becque met the general's keen gaze without anger, but with a certain firmness. Wimpffen studied the man's strong face and powerful body, noting that he was taller than himself. It was only then he noticed what he had failed to see before, that Becque had only one arm.

His voice, when he spoke, was calm.

"The general staff has good reason to fear the indiscretions of the Press. You must be aware of the harm that can be done by irresponsible reporting. Nevertheless, it is inadmissible that the army's secrets or its shortcomings should be the subject of vulgar bragging—"

The last hit was clearly directed at the big colonel, who stood bolt upright against the wall.

"We have no intention of discrediting the army," Becque answered. "We know as well as the officers, the danger of il-considered judgments put before the public. But French people are paying heavily for this war. They have the right to know more about what is going on than they can learn from brief dispatches."

"What paper do you work for?"

"*La Cloche*, an opposition paper. I have no reason to deny it."

Here the second colonel, who had accompanied Wimpffen, remarked that it was Monsieur Zola's newspaper, and that there had been some trouble, a week or two before, about the tone of its comment on the war. Wimpffen's eyes met Becque's across the narrow room but he seemed disinclined to pay great attention to his subordinate.

"To denounce the errors of the Imperial government and its criminal hesitation that costs the lives of our soldiers is perhaps a way of loving France that escapes you," Becque told the colonel stiffly.

"The Press must be brave enough to tell the truth," put in Charles Hugo. "Today, more than ever, the Press must act as the conscience of the nation."

Once again Wimpffen studied the journalists. His eyes were keen and for an instant Becque sensed that the general was not so much their enemy as they might have thought; that he too might, like them, dislike the confusion resulting from the Emperor's accumulated mistakes, which had roused the anger of the country and threatened to cost them the war. But Wimpffen had already turned away and the flash of warmth in his eyes had given way to the cold impersonal stare of the soldier trained to control his feelings at all times. At that moment, Becque hated the man for that inhuman shell, for the conventional officer's mentality based on the hollow creed of professional heroism, and the beauties of danger. Thomas Becque was no soldier. He was a cripple. A man like the rest, less than the rest, to be despised by this general because he wore no uniform. In spite of the real sympathy he felt for him as a man, he hated Wimpffen. Hated him for being what he was. His whole being revolted against the idea that this man could despise him. Never had he been so miserably conscious of his missing arm.

"Well, gentlemen," Wimpffen said after a silence, "if you wish to give the French people information, I will give you a chance to do so. Such facts as an officer may know, any Frenchman has the right to demand. And if you cannot tell them of a victory, you can at least assure them we have saved the honour of France."

They looked at one another.

"You will travel with me," Wimpffen said. "My carriage is a large one. I can take two or three men and we shall do very well if we are prepared for a little discomfort. I am joining the 5th Corps somewhere near Mouzon."

"I shall not trouble you," Charles Hugo said. "I have to leave tonight for Sedan with Lieutenant Duval. Besides, you are with Daguerran, Becque."

They left the room. Some fifteen minutes later, General de Wimpffen's party set out for the region of Mouzon where the general was to find the army. Behind came the supply train, baggage wagons and field kitchen.

In the event, there were six in the carriage. Wimpffen, besides his staff officer Captain d'Héricourt, Becque and Daguerran, had agreed to take with him an American journalist from the *New York Times*, who was covering the Franco-German war in spite of the semi-official prohibition placed on foreign journalists. Some English journalists had been sent home two weeks earlier, but the Americans were more welcome. There was also an ultra right-wing journalist, Eric Massé, whom Becque and Daguerran knew well. They disliked and despised one another equally, but for the moment the war served to neutralize their mutual animosity and they were content with ignoring each other. The American Kirk Bogart was of the classic type, slow of speech and indifferent to danger. He was a big man with straw-colored hair cut short and irregular, and mobile features. He had studied at university in France and spoke the language perfectly apart from a slight accent.

They were crammed into the berlin, which was designed to hold no more than four. This did not seem to bother Wimpffen, whose only interest appeared to be in their route, which involved a number of stiff climbs. Several times they had to get out to lighten the carriage. Although it was now midday, a thick mist had got up.

They talked little. From time to time Wimpffen gave an order to the coachman. He had a pleasant, decisive voice which brooked no argument. Now and then, the general's eyes met those of Becque or one of the others. They were clear blue and quite expressionless. Wimpffen's face was strong and square-jawed, with firmly marked features that spoke of courage and stubbornness. Only the mouth, gentle behind his soft beard, hinted at a man that women, or one woman, might love.

But in spite of his other worries, the general was conscious of the presence of these men in his carriage and especially of Becque. The two men felt for one another a vague hostility coupled with a kind of involuntary respect which they could not ignore.

The American fidgeted constantly. Daguerran seemed to be dozing. Looking at him, Wimpffen thought that here was a man with both arms and of an age to fight who had taken care to avoid enlistment. In fact this was not true. Daguerran had tried to enlist. When he found out he was to be sent to guard a level crossing in the Pyrenees he had preferred to go back to his newspaper reporting. He had been glad to leave Paris. His brief affair with Charlotte had left him filled with doubts about himself. He had learned of her marriage to Worski and although, at the time, he had been morally pushing her into the marriage, it left him with a feeling of defeat. He had not expected to find himself with Becque in Wimpffen's party, although he had been pretty sure of seeing him at Mézières. The two men were unlikely to discuss Charlotte Morel for the good reason that for both she belonged to a different part of their lives, unrelated to the other. For Becque she was the past and for Daguerran she belonged to a comparatively recent experience. Because of this, he felt no guilt about her in relation to Becque, even though he knew that his whole relationship with Charlotte began and ended with Thomas. But this was something Daguerran preferred to forget and, in his heart of hearts, he did not greatly care, since ultimately his concern had been for himself.

General de Wimpffen was thinking that he had been recalled from Africa to defend his country but was it not already too late? He was fully aware now of the criminal neglect of the national defenses. He knew the army had practically nothing. Wasn't it too late to win this war?

Suddenly, above the moisture in the air, they smelled a sharp, distinctive smell of powder. It seemed to be everywhere.

"Something is happening," Wimpffen cried. "Whip up the horses!"

The vehicle bowled down a steep slope. Below them, on the level ground, they could see the tiny figures of hundreds of soldiers running to and fro. As the carriage drew nearer, they could clearly see it was a rout. The men were fleeing from an invisible enemy. Now they were plunging into a wood, still firing a few random shots.

The general stopped the coach and tried to shout to the soldiers. They looked up at the sound of his voice, then went on running. Wimpffen and his companions got back into the coach and drove on to intercept another group of fleeing men.

"Stop," Wimpffen called to them. "Where do you think you're going? Look behind you, there's nothing following."

Haggard and panting the men collected on the slope below the road. They stood, not knowing what else to do. More soldiers joined them. They suffered themselves to be formed into some kind of order on the edge of the wood, sitting on the grass, submitting blindly to military authority.

From their incoherent accounts, the general learned of the shambles of Beaumont. He was gripped by a sense of irreparable disaster. He turned and saw the baggage wagon lying on the road behind. The officers were struggling to sort out the men and regroup them according to their regiments. The blockage on the road was growing worse at every moment.

Darkness was falling when they saw a civilian convoy approaching. They were the wagons of the Imperial suite and the Emperor's kitchen. Those in charge demanded that the road be cleared.

"Tell them to get back before I open fire," Wimpffen bawled at one of his officers, beside himself with rage.

His face was a brick red and running with sweat.

"I order you to get back," he thundered, hurrying up to the Imperial convoy. "Clear the road! Take another route."

Soldiers dashed about trying to make the convoy move back with the result that a number of vehicles got stuck in the ditch and the scene became one of utter confusion.

Daguerran approached Wimpffen. "May we be of any assistance, General?"

The general turned to look at him and Daguerran and his companions sensed that he had forgotten all about them.

"No, thank you," he said briefly.

"We would be glad to be of service," Becque put in,

piqued by the officer's attitude. "It is the least we can do after inflicting ourselves on your convoy."

"Thank you," Wimpffen said again in a tone indicative of polite refusal.

Becque, Daguerran, the American and Massé stood looking at the vehicles which comprised his majesty's Imperial kitchen sunk in the muddy road while scullions struggled to free the wheels. A few guns which had survived the battle were beginning to appear on the road behind the convoy of carts, drawn by haggard-looking men. Abandoned weapons were strewn about everywhere and there were more carts filled with wounded.

It was a heartbreaking sight. The dismal countryside of Lorraine had become a scene of desolation of disorderly retreat. Darkness was falling on the beaten army. They guessed what Wimpffen must be feeling faced with these rags of the army he had come to command.

Finally, tired of seeing them standing there, Wimpffen ordered them briefly to go to the next village and try to find help. They were to call in the constabulary if possible. They came back bringing the local police force and a few peasants who placed themselves at the general's command. The evening was well advanced before they were on the move again. They reached Sedan in the middle of the night with the remnants of the 5th army. Leaving the general at the camp, the journalists set about finding lodgings. All the hotels were full because Napoleon and his numerous entourage, civilian as well as military, had taken over every habitable building in town.

Sedan at night looked like any small provincial town in the throes of some unusual activity. At last they found a school which offered at least a roof over their heads.

Next day, General de Wimpffen inspected the camp and went to pay his respects to Marshal MacMahon, who received him without enthusiasm. After this, he was granted an audience with Napoleon III.

"But, General," said the Emperor of the French, his eyes filling with ready tears, "tell me why are we being defeated? What, in your opinion, was the cause of this disastrous business at Beaumont?"

In the presence of the stern and active Wimpffen he was conscious of a feeling of inadequacy and guilt.

Wimpffen stood as though made of ice. What was there for him to say except that this and all the other defeats were the result of sheer disorganization and culpable negligence?

What Wimpffen did not know as yet was that the Germans were already on the point of encircling Sedan. The only way to save the army would have been to pull out of the town on the 30th and the morning of the 31st of August while there was still time, and fall back on Mézières. This was not done and by the evening of the 31st it was too late. The circle was closed. The French army was imprisoned in Sedan.

Still, some attempt had to be made to save the trapped army. It was decided to attack the following morning. The 7th Army Corps under the command of General Douay took up a position in the woods at Garenne, on the heights above Sedan. The 5th Army Corps under General Wimpffen, or what was left of it, held the center and the heights of Givonne with General Ducrot's 1st Corps. General Lebrun's 12th Corps together with the marines took up a position facing the enemy at Bazeilles.

It was four o'clock in the morning and the fog was dense. Fierce fighting broke out almost at once. On the level ground, a detachment of the 5th Corps, thoroughly demoralized since Beaumont, fought alongside General Ducrot's men. Becque, Daguerran, the American, Bogart and Eric Massé found themselves with the men of the 5th Corps close to the main road. This time, few of the war correspondents from Paris or the provinces had waited for official permission to join in the battle. None of them had been able to sit quietly in Sedan and await the outcome. They were all in the forefront of things. Besides Becque and his three companions, there was a journalist from Lyons, an excitable youngster whose dandified clothes were already covered with red clay from the ground on which they were obliged to throw themselves down every few yards on account of the sustained artillery fire.

Around them, French soldiers were being mown down

by a fire five times heavier than their own. It was a massacre. They were all drunk with the horror of it.

The five journalists, including the American, were lying pressed against the low bank beside the road. Not far off they could hear the crackle of machine-gun fire from General Wimpffen's 5th Corps.

"This is murder, they will all be killed," gasped the man from Lyons. In his light shoes, slithering in the mud, he looked like some strange figure out of a comic opera. But the fog was so thick that none of them could have known their own mothers.

Before he had finished speaking, a group of Saxon horsemen loomed up out of the fog. They halted on the road, ghostly figures, their horses dancing and curvetting with fright.

The French guns cracked a moment longer and fell silent. French soldiers were running back and shouting:

"Get down! The Bavarians are in the trees."

From where they lay, behind the bank, their faces pressed to the stony ground, Becque and his companions could see the abandoned machine-gun, the soldiers killed at their posts. One of them fell right beside Bogart, face downwards, a gaping hole in his head. Bogart pushed the corpse away from him. He put his hands to his face shivering, as he wiped away the mud and blood, the dead man's blood which splashed him as he fell. Suddenly without warning, he sprang up and made for the abandoned gun.

"I'll get the sons of bitches!"

He was half-crazy, bare-headed and covered with mud.

"Bogart, are you out of your mind?" Thomas cried. "What are you doing?"

But the American was in no state to hear him. He had flung himself full length against the bank and was trying to get hold of one of the big machine-guns, half buried in the mud. He slipped. Thomas leaped after him and landed with the full weight of his body on top of the American.

"Bogart, don't be a fool. Do you want to get yourself shot as a sniper?"

The two of them rolled to the foot of the bank, Becque struggling to hold down the lithe American. At last, they lay half-dazed and panting, their faces pressed to the ground. French gunfire rattled not far off. Two of the Saxon cavalry on the road dropped as neatly as toy soldiers from their saddles. A third was so close to them that they could see the boyish face framed by his helmet. A fresh burst of firing dropped him like the other two. He fell and was dragged by his horse along the stony road. The others turned and disappeared.

"Bogart, what the devil came over you?"

He had let go of the American and the two of them crouched, red-eyed and gasping, feeling the sick clutch of fear in their stomachs, in the inadequate shelter of the bank. Not far off, the big gun was still firing at regular intervals. The firing from the woods had ceased. They could see French soldiers running between the mist-shrouded trees.

Bogart said nothing. Nothing was needed. Becque understood. He too had felt that desperate urge to fight. The impotent rage that came of watching helplessly while other men were killed.

"This battle's done for," Thomas thought. "We are going to lose this war."

They got up and rejoined Daguerran, the Lyonnais and Massé. Soon, they came across a handful of soldiers of the 5th Corps who had been driven back across the road. Among them were Lieutenant Willaert, Richet and Farrenc, survivors of Frossard's army who had been attached to the 5th Corps. Willaert was wounded in the head and had made himself a temporary bandage with a piece torn from his shirt. More blood was still pumping from the wound, spreading an even stain across his bandaged forehead.

There were a few other men with them. They had become separated from their officers and the main body of their regiment and had no idea how the battle was going.

"We'd better try and rejoin General Wimpffen," Massé said. He turned to the lieutenant. "Do you know where he ought to be?"

"On the heights of Givonne," Willaert answered, pointing to a point somewhere on the thickly tree-covered slopes from which smoke was rising.

They set out to climb the hill. To do so it was necessary to cross the line of enemy fire. All around them were smoking craters, splintered trees and the bodies of dead soldiers, flung at random up the banks and into the undergrowth. Their faces were mostly unrecognizable and their limbs sprawled helplessly.

They met men coming from all directions. Some told them of a complete rout at a place called Illy. Others insisted that Marshall MacMahon was dead. All were hungry and exhausted, having eaten nothing since the morning. Nothing had been provided, as much owing to the chronic disorganization of the commissariat as to the confusion of the battle itself.

General de Wimpffen had gone down to the level ground in order to inspect the battlefield as best he could. He looked at the bottom of the Givonne, pock-marked with craters, and at the countless dead lying all over the field. Wimpffen had met Napoleon III also on his way down from the heights of Bazeilles. The Emperor was going to lunch.

He was still thinking of the Emperor when he saw the little group of soldiers from his command coming along the road. With them were the journalists.

"Ah," said the general. "Here are the heroes of the Press safe and sound. Well, gentlemen," he went on in a harsher voice, "now is your chance to castigate French incompetence. We are losing the war because we have no equipment. The Germans have five times as many guns and rifles and we have nothing for our men to eat."

"There are times when it can do no good to complain," Becque answered. "We have said enough already and no one has listened. When we wanted peace we were accused of being traitors to our country. The traitors were those who were determined to fight, knowing they lacked the means to do so."

They faced one another without hostility but in their hearts they were strangers. Captain d'Héricourt, who accompanied Winpffen, stood rigidly with an expression of fixed disapproval. Thomas saw, with a stab of irritation, that his own words to Wimpffen must strike a dedicated soldier such as d'Héricourt as an unpardonable liberty. The words of a popular song crossed his mind: "So long as there are soldiers—" The memory of his own impoverished childhood came back to him with redoubled force, his passionate desire for justice and for happiness for himself and others.

Not a word of this conversation was lost on Bogart, standing beside Thomas and examining the French officers with undisguised curiosity. He sensed Becque's instinctive defiance of all authority and saw that, for all his superficial polish, he was still the boy of the people, quick to take offense. Becque's attitude to General de Wimpffen was a little like that of the delinquent child finding an adult who at last seems to deserve his admiration and fearing disappointment.

All this took only a few seconds. The cold wind of the Ardennes struck their faces. Wimpffen was unaware of Becque's and Bogart's scrutiny. He was an officer, unaccustomed to gauging the reactions of the men under his command. Already, his eyes had moved on. His thoughts were on the battle. Was it lost? Was there still a chance? What was left of his army was only an exhausted remnant. There was nothing to eat for the next day. It looked as though they would all die uselessly on the Givonne hills.

A silvery sunshine was beginning to pierce the fog and light up the plain. The Prussian batteries were still firing incessantly. General de Wimpffen made his way back to the heights. The others followed. They climbed a steep path between oak woods where sharp stones clattered underfoot. They found a shepherd's hut in a small meadow inhabited by an illiterate old shepherd who had refused to be driven out by the war and had penned his sheep as best he could in a wooden stockade.

By this time other groups had joined Wimpffen and his companions and, terrified by the soldiers, the sheep trampled down the barriers and escaped. The old shepherd whistled frantically to his dog and set it running after the flock. Scattered groups of soldiers were caught up in the tide of panic-stricken beasts. They were bowled over, left and right, slipping and sliding in a torrent of frightened sheep and clutching at the damp grass to save themselves, while their comrades who were out of the way leaned on the wooden hurdles laughing and shouting encouragement.

Sergeant Farrenc was one of those knocked off his feet by the sheep and tumbled the whole length of the sloping meadow. Whenever he tried to stand up, his feet were knocked from under him. He clutched at the greasy wool of one old sheep, but as the tide of beasts moved on was forced to let go and found himself rolled into the hedge at the bottom. Through the gaps in the leaves he could see down to the plain far below, where tiny shells burst in puffs of smoke. There were men in those explosions, the poor bastards. Up here, the ground was moist, smelling of earth and grass with a powerful odor of sheep mingled with the sharp, sweet smell of some wild flower whose name he did not know. Smoke from the bursting shells drifted upwards from below. Farrenc thought he would be content to die there among the earthy smells. He lay still where he was. He felt at peace.

Soldiers were appearing from all sides and forming a group around General de Wimpffen. They lay on the grass propped against the rocks and waited, wounded and unwounded alike. An hour went by and the battle seemed certainly lost. General Ducrot came to join Wimpffen. He proposed making a desperate last sortie towards Mézières.

Wimpffen said firmly that it would be madness and forbade any such attempt. Illy, scene of the massacre of most of the French army, seemed to be overrun. The remaining forces would never get through the German lines north of Sedan. Their only chance, said Wimpffen, was to try to make a breach to the south in the direction of Carignan, and then turn and take the Germans in the rear.

Wimpffen's plan was a bold one but involved fearful risks. Ducrot set his face against it. The two generals were at loggerheads. Finally, angered by Ducrot's persistent refusal, Wimpffen took out of his pocket his appointment as Commander-in-Chief and ordered the general to obey. Ducrot stood to attention.

In spite of the risks, Wimpffen was determined. The French army must be got out of the trap at all costs and the only way was to attempt a sortie towards Carignan, but for this the Emperor's authorization was necessary. That meant at least two hours wasted, even supposing the messenger ever got to Sedan. Wimpffen gazed anxiously at the lower slopes of the Givonne, ploughed up by artillery fire. Confusion and terror were all around him. He had only a single staff officer, d'Héricourt. Almost the whole of the headquarters staff had been shut up in Sedan since the morning, following the wounding of MacMahon.

Wimpffen was on his own. The responsibilities he carried were too great for one man to bear. He told Captain d'Héricourt that he was going to send a message to the Emperor and that d'Héricourt must carry it.

"You'd better send a duplicate, General, supposing I don't come back," d'Héricourt said.

"You are right."

But who was there to send? He had no more staff officers, indeed, very few officers of any description and he was going to need all he had. In any case, they were all too tired to undertake such a mission. His eye fell on the journalists standing a little way off.

"You wouldn't think of sending a civilian, General?" d'Héricourt frowned, following his glance.

"They are gentlemen of the Press. I can trust them with an official mission more readily than some inarticulate sergeant. Besides, they will only be there in case you fail. You must reach Sedan, d' Héricourt, you must."

"Yes, General."

"The fate of the battle depends on it. The fate of us all."

"Yes, General."

Wimpffen made his way over to the journalists.

"Can any of you ride a horse?"

"I can," said Becque.

"You never told me," Daguerran ribbed him.

"Don't worry, I learned on a broken-winded hack on the wasteland at Gentilly as a kid."

"Are you willing to be of service?" Wimpffen said. "Will you carry a message to Sedan as second to Captain d'Héricourt? If anything happens to him, you will take both papers as proof of identity."

"I am a civilian, General. How will I obtain an audience?"

"I am enlisting you."

Daguerran whistled. "There, you've been wanting to be a hero ever since the war began."

"I warn you, your chances are slim. You can refuse."

"I will go, General, and we will come back."

"Then go at once."

It was a desperate attempt and they could all sense the tension in the general.

Thomas and d'Héricourt set their horses at the steep track down the Givonne. They had to make their way through heavy shell-fire, and the animals were wild with terror. The open ground was strewn with dead. The torn and ravaged earth spewed out human limbs and torsos and everywhere the nameless corpses lay in their uncounted thousands.

Horror itself was silent before such horror. The eyes of the two men burned with unshed tears.

The gates of Sedan were blocked by the pathetic remnants of the army, pouring into the city with carts and wagons. The tattered and mud-covered soldiers looked like men who had been set upon and robbed. The civilians stood and gazed at this rabble with unbelieving eyes. The walls of the town glowed yellow in a sickly sunlight and even the river Meuse carried its toll of dead men, and horses with grotesquely swollen bellies.

It took them some time to find the hotel where the Emperor and his staff were staying.

The scene inside was like something out of an operatic farce. Officers in uniforms plastered in gold braid came and went. There were many pretty women. No one seemed aware that less than two miles away men were screaming and dying. The hall was filled with pot plants and tapestries and there was the smell of cigar smoke in the air.

The Emperor himself was nowhere to be seen. A colonel informed d'Héricourt stiffly that the Emperor would see no one but that he would have Wimpffen's message delivered, although it could do no good.

"There must be some mistake," Captain d'Héricourt insisted. "I tell you, General de Wimpffen—"

"General de Wimpffen has acted without orders. The Emperor has decided to ask for terms of surrender."

"Surrender?" d'Héricourt's face was white.

"And what terms do you think the Germans will give us?" Thomas spoke uninvited to the colonel who had so far ignored his presence completely. "Or do you even give a damn?"

"The Emperor will take steps to avoid unnecessary slaughter—"

"Unnecessary slaughter! You should have thought of that before you declared war. If you surrender now you might as well deliver France up to the Germans bound hand and foot. You are letting them walk straight in. Next, our industries will be paralysed and the misery of the people will be greater than ever."

The colonel controlled himself with difficulty.

"It is defeatists such as you who have brought France to this pass."

"At least we did not fling France into a war she was in no condition to wage."

Already people were beginning to look at them and it seemed as though at any moment there would be a public scene. Captain d'Héricourt was like a cat on hot bricks.

"Monsieur," he said to Becque in agonized tones, "this is neither the time nor the place for a private argument. Our country is in danger. Come, General de Wimpffen is waiting."

One of the Emperor's aides was dispatched to go with Captain d'Héricourt and carry his Majesty's answer to General de Wimpffen. It was already nearly an hour since they had left the heights of the Givonne before the three men found themselves once again in the crowded streets of Sedan. Word had already spread to the crowd that the Emperor meant to surrender. The people were shocked and horrified. Old men were shaking their fists.

One old soldier limped along with tears in his eyes. "So

297

Bonaparte means to surrender; he'll wave the white flag over the roof tops—"

The streets had a heart-rending air of defeat. The entire civilian population was out of doors, adding to the confusion of the stricken army. The sun was still shining, bathing everything in a lurid yellow light. So it was that Thomas always remembered Sedan during the siege, a yellow city, like something from another planet, heaving and straining with the press of people within.

Becque followed the two officers as best he could as they forced a passage for themselves on horseback through the cluttered streets. The sun was hot on his coat and on his forehead, making him sweat. The light was unbearably bright. Thomas was drunk with fatigue and crammed full with horrors. He traversed the streets of the town as though nothing had happened, but he was not the same man he had been that morning. He had seen things in the carnage of Sedan that he would never forget. There were no words to describe what men had done to men. It was no good looking for someone on whom to lay the blame. They were all to blame for failing to prevent such horror. But they would not forget and nothing could ever be as it was before. Now, all they could do was survive. When they reached the main square, they found the troops of General de Wimpffen's 5th Corps pouring in from the Givonne. The general had finally grown tired of waiting and, fearing encirclement, had come to Sedan to receive his answer in person. General Lebrun was with him. The Emperor's aide went up to him and saluted.

Daguerran and the other journalists were sitting on the steps of the town hall when Becque joined them. Becque recognized Massé, the right-wing journalist who had come with them in Wimpffen's carriage from Mézières, and been their constant companion for two days.

"Well, Becque, I hear your name is to go down in history! Your friends on *La Cloche* won't be best pleased to hear of you saving the day."

"Save the eloquence for your readers, Massé. They'll need it. And I'm too tired to fight you."

Meanwhile, the Emperor's aide-de-camp had given

Wimpffen the note. Wimpffen read it without a word and tore it up. Then he turned slowly to the officer.

"Tell your master I do not recognize his right to surrender my country."

The words were uttered with biting deliberation. The officer gaped and then saluted.

Daguerran sat down beside Thomas. "Wimpffen's risking a court martial," he remarked.

Seizing hold of a French flag, Wimpffen sprang on to the statue of Turenne which stood in the middle of the square and waved it strongly. Then he spoke to the soldiers, calling on them to resist and urging them to drive a wedge through the German lines towards Carignan. The wind seized his words and carried them away. The soldiers were tired and hungry. They had eaten nothing since the morning. Would Wimpffen's voice be able to rouse them? The square was a patchwork of glaring yellow light and sombre shadows. It was three o'clock in the afternoon, the dead hour when all the morning's hopes disintegrated. But the soldiers were slowly getting to their feet and pressing forward. Wimpffen went on speaking, seconded by General Lebrun.

"This is madness," Daguerran said. "He'll lead them all to their deaths."

"It is all up, in either case," Becque said. "If Sedan surrenders the whole army will be taken prisoner and whatever the gentleman at headquarters may say, the Prussians will not spare us. Wimpffen may have a chance of succeeding and turning the tables."

"There are no more ardent patriots than your men of the left," Massé observed with a laugh, his eyes on Thomas. "Touchy as girls where the honor of France is concerned."

"I am going with Wimpffen," Becque said without answering him. "You can do what you like."

"We're coming," Daguerran said, "although something tells me I shall not get out of this stinking war alive. You coming, Yankee?"

"O.K.," said Bogart who had been following the scene with interest.

There was a rush to follow General de Wimpffen. Two

thousand soldiers marched after him out of Sedan in the direction of Balan. They included men from all regiments, a motley assortment of infantry, hussars, zouaves, militiamen and even civilians of Sedan itself, dragging with them through the cobbled streets their last remaining guns.

Caught unawares by this unexpected resistance, the Germans fell back towards Balan. House by house the French fought their way back into the little town. In this way they reached the church where the curé was holding out with some of his parishioners.

Pigs were wandering in the rustic town square with its low houses backed by a small copse. Suddenly, an astonishing sight amid the rubble and destruction, a number of the village women appeared, walking along in single file with parasols held over their heads, picking their way carefully among the shell-holes. Among them was a young woman with child, very near her time.

The little fat curé had put down his gun to let everyone into the church. There were a dozen or so children who looked more curious than frightened. The women were afraid and the pregnant one was crying. Her mother, a stout, masterful-looking woman who sat beside her, spoke firmly to her.

"Stop grizzling like that. It's not due until October." This did not stop her daughter crying. The mother was at her wit's end in front of so many grinning soldiers. Thomas saw her twisting and turning in her seat. He thought of Marie, who was also about to have a child. He did not think about it much as a rule because the thought of the child was not yet real to him. But just then it seemed to him that it might have been Marie sitting there. He smiled kindly at the girl whose name was Ethel. Ethel looked back with frank curiosity at the filthy one-armed figure smiling at her. He was covered in mud and had a revolver stuck in his belt, one of the weapons being handed round by the curé. Ethel seemed fascinated by Becque and stared continually at the tall man with the missing arm, dirty face and bright blue eyes. He seemed to her frightening and reassuring at the same time. Other soldiers and civilians came into the church, Massé among them. The

300

officers had set up their headquarters in the sacristy. The journalists kept watch from the windows. Soldiers and wounded were lying in the nave. The women did what they could for them. Thomas saw the curé get more guns out of a cupboard.

"It seems that the Lord will indeed provide, monsieur le curé, but are you sure God is on our side?"

"I hope so," the curé replied simply.

"We can only hope that God will not follow your example, Massé," Becque said to the journalist who sat near by loading an ancient rusty rifle. "If he sides with the strongest, then we are done for."

Becque watched Massé blowing down the breech of his old rifle. At heart, for all his sybarite airs, he was a careful, meticulous man. Even now, his neat clothes were hardly soiled after all they had been through. Becque reflected that there was something unwholesome about bachelors of his type, but he knew he was only searching for reasons to dislike the man. He found none. In fact, at that moment, he rather liked Massé.

"If anyone had told me I should ever find myself firing a gun beside you out of a church window, Becque," Massé retorted, "I should have said I'd rather not have been born. Tell me, seriously, where does this leave us, us and our convictions? Tell me you still cling to your principles at this moment and I'll not believe you. Do you know what you're doing here? We are fighting against a common enemy. But if we have a common enemy, then we are allies, brothers. Admit it, Becque, you'd never have believed we could be brothers!"

Becque did not answer. He was listening to the firing. It was near now. The Germans were returning to the attack. It was too late to get out of the church, but they lacked the strength to defend it. Were they to die there, caught in a trap? General Ducrot's hoped-for reinforcements had not arrived. Ducrot had been reluctant to obey Wimpffen's orders. What if he did not come? What if he went to Sedan and surrendered with the rest?

Was this to be the end of everything, here in this church? Thomas looked round at the companions fate had set beside him and with whom he was perhaps to die. He

301

looked at Daguerran and thought that they were friends and had been through much together. Daguerran had been like a brother to him in these last years but had he ever looked at him as he was doing now? Did he even know his face? Becque, he asked himself, have you really loved Daguerran as a brother or have your friends been merely useful adjuncts for your own work and ideas?

"If we are not going to get out of here—" Daguerran said suddenly. He was leaning against the sacristy window and outside the sun was shining on a low wall. "If we are not going to get out of here, I want you to know about something that happened between Charlotte Floquet and myself. I made her my mistress. I thought I loved her, and maybe I did. She got under my skin in a way that gave me no peace. It was not love, but something more than that. I think she made me take stock of my life for the first time. I realized that before her I had not been fully alive and what I thought was loyalty to my wife was really a kind of moral laziness. She turned my whole world upside down. The virtues on which I prided myself were only weakness and vanity. I am not telling you all this because I believe I owe you any account, I do not think I owe you anything where Charlotte is concerned. She is nothing to you now and you deserted her at a time when she should never have been left alone. Since then, she has made a mess of her life and you are to some extent to blame. But that too is none of my business. When I made love to her she was a free agent and I do not feel guilty towards you. But if this is to be the end, then I wanted you to know. I wanted someone to know the truth about me, that in a way I have ruined my life by refusing to live."

Thomas stared out of the window in silence.

"Charlotte has married young Worski. They are both young. They have their lives before them," Daguerran said.

There was a pause. "Why are you telling me all this? It can do no good," Thomas said. It might have irked him to be forcibly reminded of something that already belonged to the past, but that he realized Charlotte's name still had the power to hurt him. Charlotte and Daguerran, Charlotte and Worski. He was too tired to form a judgment. His judgment had been at fault before. His thoughts went to Charlotte, how young she had been when he first met her. He realized now that what he had felt for her was not so much passion as a desperate tenderness.

Time passed and still the reinforcements did not come. They would be surrounded, captured and shot on sight. They would be put up against this very wall and shot before the day was over. Thomas was suddenly conscious of the sun prickling on the back of his neck. He still loved life, his life. They could not let themselves be shot like dogs.

But it was all over. Wimpffen had realized that the reinforcements would not come and that more resistance was vain. He made up his mind to go back to Sedan. When he announced his decision to the soldiers in the church they heard him in silence. The door was opened and they went out into the little square.

"Let's make a dash for it," said Daguerran. "We can't go back to Sedan and be rounded up by the Germans."

At the thought of freedom, the blood seemed to run quickly in their veins. Everything was not lost. Their hearts warmed to the thought that life still lay before them.

"Try and get through the Prussian lines?" Massé said doubtfully. "Thanks, but I'm going back to Sedan."

"You've little to fear from the Prussians," Daguerran told him cynically, "but I dare say we of the opposition would be running our heads into a noose."

"For once, Daguerran, I think you are right," Massé said. "You've everything to gain by running."

"If you are going, then I'm coming with you," said Richet, who had stuck close to them ever since Sedan. "I can't see myself rotting in a Prussian prison."

Eloi Farrenc and Lieutenant Willaert also agreed to try. If they succeeded in getting across the Meuse they would press on until they came to a railway station or met up with some French troops.

They plunged in among the trees. The firing was still going on but for the moment did not seem to be coming any nearer.

303

They ran through the meadows towards the river. A grey dusk was falling and before long they could smell, above the reek of gunpowder, the moist, slightly rotten smell of the river. It spurred them on. The American, Bogart, had come with them. There was no need for him to do so but he was a born gambler. It occurred to them all suddenly that the priest had refused to leave his church and would be shot.

Two hundred yards from the river they were caught in a sudden burst of fire.

"The bastards must have changed their line of fire," Farrenc swore. "Do you think they've seen us?"

Almost before he had finished speaking, the ground at his feet exploded in a shower of earth and liquid mud.

"Farrenc!" Richet screamed, his eyes blinded with mud.

Becque flung him down and held him pressed to the ground.

"Keep down, it's too late—"

Farrenc had been literally blown to pieces before their eyes. Richet was sobbing like a child.

"Farrenc—God damn them—"

"Come on—there is nothing you can do—"

"Let me alone—"

"Get up, you can't stay here." Bogart, coming to the rescue, helped Becque haul Richet to his feet.

"Bastards," sobbed Richet. "Bastards, leave me here and let me die—"

There was a fresh burst of firing. They flung themselves to the ground, while, a few feet away, the earth gaped.

"We are done for," someone said. "We'll all stay here."

"Come on," Daguerran shouted, "we've got to run for it."

He had run only a few yards when Becque saw the ground beneath him open in a vomit of fire and smoke. Daguerran disappeared. He and Bogart ran forward shouting but could see nothing for the smoke. At last, they saw Daguerran's body half buried in the shell hole. Both his legs were smashed. He was unconscious.

Becque and Bogart, helped by Lieutenant Willaert, struggled to free Daguerran. Richet sat dazedly on the ground, still calling Farrenc.

"Cheer up, old lad," Thomas said, tears running down his face. "We'll soon have you out of there—"

They got him out at last and lifted him on to Thomas's shoulders. With eyes blinded with mud and smoke, they staggered on. Daguerran's mangled limbs jolted at Thomas's back. He was dying. When they reached the river bank and put him down, Daguerran's eyes were closed, his mouth hung open. His legs were a mass of torn and bleeding flesh. He was dead.

"Oh God," Thomas thought, "you poor boy. If your mother were to see you now."

The guns roared again. They left him there and ran down to the river as night was falling.

15

NEWS OF the disaster at Sedan reached Paris on September 3. The legislative assembly was summoned at one o'clock in the morning. Jules Favre called for the Emperor's abdication but the deputies showed some hesitation in following his lead. Count Palikao tried to suggest that the surrender was the work of the army but this led to chaos. Napoleon himself was undoubtedly responsible.

All that night, the fate of France hung in the balance. While the deputies remained undecided, outside the crowds were gathering round the Palais Bourbon. Even so, the session ended without a decision being reached. Everything was put off until the morrow. The Empress Eugénie still clung desperately to a belief in her destiny. It was not of the Emperor she was thinking but of her son. She had dreamed for so long of his reigning. Even with the Emperor dethroned her eyes were still on the regency.

The next day was Sunday. The crowds around the Palais Bourbon were thicker than ever. Eventually, growing impatient with the length of the debate, the people broke through the police cordons and burst into the chamber. Only when Gambetta rose to speak did the crowd fall silent, impressed by his manner. The people of Paris dearly loved a touch of magniloquence. Also they needed information and recognized in Gambetta a man qualified to give it to them. Not in the least averse to this, Gambetta paused impressively before announcing that the deputies had just proclaimed the Emperor's deposition. The audience broke into frenzied cheers. Everyone was shouting for the Republic.

Jules Favre spoke up. "This is not the place to proclaim the Republic."

The crowd streamed out into the streets, following the deputies as they made their way to the Hôtel de Ville. The scene was one of frantic enthusiasm. The red flag waved above the building. The left-wing deputies retired to form a government of national defense. There were eleven of them, including Gambetta, Jules Favre and Jules Ferry. General Trochu was appointed governor of Paris. While the crowd besieged the Hôtel de Ville, the *blanquistes*, accompanied by an excited mob of supporters, went to the prison of Sainte-Pélagie, broke down the doors and released Rochefort and all the other prisoners. Rochefort was carried in triumph to the Hôtel de Ville where Jules Ferry took the precaution of removing him from the hands of his over-enthusiastic followers. He preferred to have Rochefort with him rather than against him. Rochefort suffered this. He was a tired man and had always been afraid of crowds and mob violence.

The crowd in the square outside the Hôtel de Ville was growing restless. They had overthrown the Empire and inaugurated the Republic. But had this wholly bloodless revolution really been a revolution at all? What next? While it reassured some, this provisional government based on compromise did not satisfy the majority of the people of Paris. It contained too many names which had been familiar under the Empire. The people wanted new men. The country was in danger. Paris itself was threatened. They knew that what they needed was not compromise. They needed heroes, men who were pure and uncorrupted. Only a government of uncompromising honesty could save Paris, could save France while there was yet time.

And so, that night, while the crowd sang in the streets, drunk with patriotic fervor, each individual was aware of the approaching danger and ready to defend their city to the death. And as evening came they watched the colors fading from the sky, the shadows beginning to gather in the east. Paris, a city carved in the soft grey of centuries, lay like a vessel at anchor between the river and the sky. The people going home from the Hôtel de Ville crossed the Seine to the Île Saint-Louis, lovelier than Venice in the twilight, and looked with pride at the formidable bulk of Notre-Dame crouched beside the quiet river. Each one, looking, was conscious of a deep love for his city. No, Paris, the Prussians shall not take you. You are the head and fount of Europe, your greatness and moderation challenging time itself. There will be as many soldiers to defend you as you have citizens.

Even so, the militant revolutionaries who had returned to the Hôtel de Ville also had their doubts about the provisional government so hastily set up. Committees of vigilantes were formed in every district.

On the 13th, a parade of the National Guard took place in the main boulevards. Patriotic fervor was at its height. Trochu, the governor of Paris, had agreed to preside over the government in place of Jules Favre, who was now only vice-president. The choice was a ridiculous one because Trochu was an indecisive and naturally pessimistic person. Although ignorant as yet of where events would lead him, the future already filled him with dread. Between this nervous man and the people of Paris, swept by waves of passionate enthusiasm for the defense of their city, there was a complete lack of understanding. Trochu was faced not so much by a population divided in accustomed differences of class but by Paris itself, welded into a living, breathing entity by the love and sacrifice of its citizens. This lack of understanding was to prove fatal.

On 15th September, at about four in the afternoon, Thomas Becque, the American Bogart, Lieutenant Willaert and the soldier Richet crossed the Seine by the old bridge at Corbeil. After their escape from Sedan, they had traveled by an unlikely route which took them through Bar-le-Duc and Vitix-de-François, travelling sometimes on foot and sometimes with military convoys and supply columns they encountered on the way. They had reached Melun at noon that day and had walked from there. They were tired, dirty and very hungry. They had heard the news of 4 September, of the Proclamation of the Republic, and they knew too that they could not be more than a little way ahead of the German army. They could feel the growing anxiety in the countryside through which they passed. The rumor was rife that Prussian advance guards had been seen near Melun that morning. At Corbeil, the disbelief of the past few days concerning the exact position of the German armies had given way to acute anxiety. The people had begun making preparation to flee to Paris. It was the same in all the country around the capital and the great exodus was already under way. Becque and his companions walked in silence. They would have given a great deal for an omelette and a glass of wine. For the moment, their blistered feet took precedence even over the horrors through which they had so recently passed. When Thomas thought of Sedan, and of Daguerran whom they had been forced to leave, a poor broken corpse beside the river Meuse, in order to save their own lives, he experienced a dull ache of shame. It seemed to him unjust that he should still be alive when Daguerran and thousands of others—why them?—were dead in payment for the past errors and vanity of a whole people. Thomas felt personally guilty of Daguerran's death. Not responsible, but guilty. There could be no real justification for the death of men in war, because the blame for it lay squarely on all mankind, on men's intolerance and pride. For the first time Thomas was aware of his own selfishness, vanity and intolerance.

They were walking along the Seine, and the river banks at this time of year in early autumn reminded him of Juvisy, which was not far away. Memories leaped up until past and present seemed to co-exist. He did not have to think deliberately of Charlotte, she was always present in him, in his remorse and his regret, but suddenly and with a kind of humility he found her closer to him.

Where was she now? What had become of her? Thomas still found that affair with Daguerran, of which his friend had spoken in a last rush of honesty so short a time before his death, somewhat unreal. As unreal as Charlotte's supposed marriage to Worski. In his mind, everything she might have done since they parted belonged to some kind of fiction. Because he knew how much, how terribly, she had loved him, it seemed to him that nothing she did apart from him had any meaning.

Why had he judged her and rejected her for one night's

folly, a small betrayal that might have made their love the greater if he had been able to forgive? She had been so young, so vulnerable. He was older than she, he should have understood. It was his masculine pride which had been hurt, his vanity, and also a sense of social inferiority, which he had held against her from the beginning. Now, he was ashamed that he had not been able to forgive her for her youth, for that was what it was.

He hated this mental picture of himself, the noble cripple, standing in judgment when he had only been injured in his dignity, steeped in his own private resentment. At this moment, he did not feel worthy of her love.

The road they were following took them along the Seine until they came to Juvisy.

"I'm all in," Richet said suddenly. "You'll have to go on without me, I can't go another step." He sat down on a gnarled root and began undoing the cloth wrapped round his boots. He rested for a moment, barefoot, staring into space, then went and sat on the river bank, letting his feet dangle in the water among the reeds.

"We may not get a train tonight," Thomas said in a worried voice. "If rumor is true, we shall be lucky if the line is still open between Juvisy and Paris."

Richet took his feet out of the river. "Well, we can't spend another night in the open."

Thomas thought of Charlotte's mother, Madame Morel. Her house, if his memory were correct, could not be far off. He could see the slate roof of Roslin's miniature castle through the leaves. The idea of asking Madame Morel to take them in followed naturally. There was a war on, she could scarcely turn them away.

Thomas explained the situation to the others who welcomed the proposal with joy. Accordingly, they set out.

Thomas had more trouble than he expected in finding the right street. Most of the houses belonged to Parisians who came there only for week-ends, and nearly all were shut up. At last Thomas saw the *guinguette*.

It, too, was closed. They passed the rickety wooden jetty where an old chair was rotting quietly. Then Thomas saw the Morels' garden, lit by the last rays of the setting sun. The lawn, the old veranda, and the weeping willow were all as they had been. The four men followed the fence round towards the front of the house.

Charlotte was standing in the road outside, talking to a neighbor, a basket of fruit on her arm. Her face was towards them and she saw them coming but went on talking to the other woman because there was nothing else she could do. But her eyes remained fixed on Thomas. The four men stopped as though by common consent a few yards away, and waited. The other woman was talking now. Charlotte was still looking at Thomas, her thoughts in a whirl. At last the woman noticed her intense gaze and turning, saw the four men.

"Ah," she said with a smile, "I see you are expecting someone. Well, I will leave you—"

Charlotte said goodbye and went towards the four men because there was nothing else she could do.

"Good day to you," Thomas said quickly. "I was not expecting to find you here. In fact, I was coming to beg your mother's hospitality."

"Yes, of course—"

She was incapable of putting two thoughts together. Thomas, to whom her presence had come as an equal shock, found himself embarking on a hasty account of their experiences as though he had to explain himself at all costs.

"We were at Sedan. It was horrible, Daguerran was killed—"

He had not wanted to blurt it out like that, in the street, but he found he couldn't help himself.

"Daguerran was killed!" she repeated, stunned but clinging to that as the one possible point of contact between them. Then she pulled herself together.

"But come inside, you must be in need of rest—of food—"

They followed her up the garden, then through the hall and into the living-room. Charlotte pointed vaguely to the sofa and armchairs, and told them to sit down and make themselves comfortable.

Bogart, who still had some reserves of strength, sat down at the piano and ran his fingers lightly across the keys, adding to the strangeness of the atmosphere. But

311

they were all exhausted and soon fell into a stupefied silence. Charlotte came and went between the kitchen and the dining-room, her thoughts in a ferment. Thomas, at a loss to know how to behave, helped her carry plates, explaining again with acute embarrassment:

"I had no idea you would be here. I thought I should find your mother and we were all so tired—"

"My mother and sister left for Niort yesterday with the children. We thought it wiser. It seems the Prussians will reach Juvisy tomorrow?" Her eyes made the words a question and he sensed her hope that he would contradict her, that he had some authority to deny it.

"It is true," he said.

"But they will not take Paris," she said fiercely, "we will drive them back—"

Thomas said nothing. He was very tired and could have wished himself anywhere else. He could hardly bear to look at her. She was quite different from the way he remembered. He was vaguely aware that she was wearing a plum-colored dress open at the neck showing tanned skin, with an apron tied round her waist. He had an impression of a sun-reddened face, flushed with health. Once, as she came from the kitchen carrying some glasses, he plucked up courage to look her in the face. Yes, she was a little sunburned. She looked hot, her eyes were unnaturally bright and her hair hung damply, like an adolescent tomboy's. But her manner was grave. She held herself stiffly and her movements were neat and precise. She did not meet his eyes.

The atmosphere mellowed somewhat over the food and the men began to talk. Bogart offered to help with the washing-up. After the meal they moved into the salon but throughout the evening Charlotte was conscious of Thomas's eyes upon her. They followed her everywhere as though he could not help himself. She found herself riveted by his presence, although their conversation remained formal.

But all the same there had to come a time when they would find themselves alone and this occurred when the others said good night and retired to the rooms Charlotte had prepared for them. She realized that Thomas had not deliberately sought an interview but that it was bound to happen. She went towards him where he stood at the far end of the room, thinking suddenly how nice he looked.

"Tell me about Daguerran," she said. Even now she could not believe that he was dead. She would never be able to believe it. He had already gone out of her life and this would make no difference.

Thomas had already told her all there was to tell and soon silence fell between them. Charlotte said: "You know that I am married?"

"Yes, Daguerran told me."

She glanced quickly at him, wondering perhaps what else Daguerran might have told him, but it did not seem to worry her and she very soon relaxed. She knew, with all her being, that she must be brave and good and loyal to Frank.

"We are in love. We are very happy," she said with pride. She might have added, "He is young and handsome and I admire him for it." But there was no need for Thomas had guessed.

Ever since Frank had gone away Charlotte's thoughts had been centered on him, on Frank's youth, his love for her and hers for him. It was almost a kind of pride, of gratitude that he could have loved her and have lifted her out of the senseless, unwholesome life she had been leading in that time before she found him again. By marrying her, he had given her the finest gift of all, the gift of self-confidence. She had grown by it. Not for anything in the world would she have betrayed him even for an instant, even in thought. She clung to that with a strength of feeling that was like daily bread to her. She looked on her own past aberrations with loathing and would have given anything to be as pure and clean as Frank himself, who had never loved any other woman and had never given himself wholly and completely to anyone but herself.

Tired as he was, Thomas could feel the flame within her, putting her beyond his reach. This loyalty to another man filled him with a weary jealousy. And yet, at the same time, he could feel that nothing had changed between them, no harmless emptiness had come between

313

them. There was the same shock of reality. He felt tired to death. He longed to hold her close, to lose all his weariness in her, deluging her with a hopeless torrent of words in a quest for warmth and womanly tenderness. But he made no move. Could she ever understand the horror that was in him, his shame and sense of abject failure? If only she could at least understand and forgive him as only a woman could forgive.

He felt utterly hopeless. Tomorrow, he would go to Paris and see Marie. Marie held no future for him. He could scarcely believe that he was to have a child, and even that frightened him. And then there was the newspaper; what could he write now?

"We have lost the war," he said in a tired voice.

"Why have we? They have not taken Paris. They will not take it, we shall fight to the death."

To the death. She would fight. She was cut out for heroism. She would probably nurse the wounded or run a kitchen in the front line.

He found he could not bring himself to point out to her the extent of the disaster and the miracle that would be required if anything were to be saved. He was sorry for her and for the disappointment in store. She had not yet had to test her courage against the horrors and vileness of war. He hoped that she would never be broken as he was tonight. He knew she could be strong and brave at need. She would not weaken. Without taking his eyes off her, he began to think that she would probably despise him if she knew the tenderness and strong desire he felt for her just then, in spite of all that divided them. It was the humble and passionate love of a man for the one thing that had ever given a meaning to his life. If she were only his again tonight she would give him back all his strength, restore him to hope and life again.

But still he made no move. He had rejected her before and for that too he longed to ask her forgiveness, yet he would do nothing and say nothing. There was Marie and there was Frank. And even if there had not been, he could not bear the thought that she might refuse him at the very moment when he had at last accepted the reality of his love for her. Yet he could not escape the feeling that fate had bound them together, as though they were moving towards some inevitable end that would bring them together in spite of everything. But still he only smiled at her and said nothing.

Charlotte turned her head away so as not to see the torment in his face, the blue eyes proclaiming all that there had been between them. What those eyes begged of her was more than love, it was the total gift, of mind, heart and body. No, she told herself, no. She almost hated him. She loved Frank and she would be faithful. Love, repentance for her past life, shame, pride and devotion all prompted her to be faithful. She turned her head away, her eyes filling with tears, and bade him good night.

He left her and flinging himself on his bed was instantly asleep.

Charlotte did the same. She had come to Juvisy only in order to see her mother and sister off to Niort with the children, and to pick the last of the fruit, and was to return to Paris the next day. She thought it would be a long time before she came to Juvisy again. The next day was fine. Juvisy was full of rumors that Prussian scouts had passed through early that morning and had been seen later at Athis-Mons. Charlotte closed up the house and locked the orchard gate and that leading to the street.

Her four companions were still tired and spoke little. It was midday before the train to Paris left at last. After they had passed Athis-Mons it stopped again. A railwayman came running down the track calling to the travelers to get out because the line had been cut between Athis-Mons and Ablon. The Prussians were advancing everywhere.

The train was packed. The people got out, dazed and terrified, not knowing where to go. They could not go back now. Charlotte decided that they would have to make for the main road, which ran close by, and make for Paris on foot. It was a matter of ten or twelve miles. They would not be there until late in the afternoon, supposing they made it at all.

Around them, everyone was in a state of panic, although there had been no firing within two miles of them. They began climbing the hills and swarming through the neighboring properties to reach the road.

Night was falling as they came in sight of the *barrière* d'Italie. They had not seen a single Prussian but the entire population of the near-by suburb seemed to be making for Paris all at once. Charlotte had kept firmly in front of Thomas all the way, walking beside Paul Willaert. He was a head taller than she and his white bandage made him easily conspicuous. Thomas himself was well aware that Charlotte was deliberately avoiding him. She was creating a gulf between them and it was significant that she should have chosen to walk with Willaert, who was young and handsome like Frank, making it obvious that she was doing so. She wanted to hurt Thomas and she succeeded. It did hurt him that she could behave like this when they must part so soon, as though she had not understood what he had tried to tell her the night before. He knew that if Charlotte had wanted him back, he might have been weak enough to leave Marie in spite of the child she was expecting. He was not proud of it. But that was how it was. He had discovered, in the depth of his being, a truth so absolute that it overcame all scruples. And truth was all that was left to him.

Everywhere along the road, they passed crowds of poor people making for the capital in the hope that Paris would offer safety. At the entrance to the city itself, the crush was indescribable. Peasants from all around were arriving continually in carts loaded with chickens, pigs and even cows, as well as innumerable children. The way into the city was blocked and traffic filtered through drop by drop.

For a moment, Charlotte and her companions despaired of ever entering Paris. The panic was increasing and arguments were constantly breaking out in spite of everything the overworked police could do. The thought of all these extra people streaming into Paris was a disquieting one.

As they passed the barriers, Thomas, Charlotte and their friends found themselves caught up in the press of people and swept past. Thomas called to Charlotte. He tried to keep hold of her long enough to tell her that he would always be her friend, but the crowd forced them apart and carried her away beyond recall.

On 19 September, Paris was completely surrounded by the Prussians. There were many people in the city who feared that the government might decide to enter into secret negotiations with the Germans. The vigilante committees in every district met and passed a resolution that the Republic would never negotiate with an enemy occupying her territory, and that Paris would fall in ruins rather than surrender. The people were sustained by a fierce wave of patriotism. The anger of the citizens knew no bounds when, on 21 September, it was learned that the vice-president of the provisional government, Jules Favre, had gone to Ferrière on the 18th to negotiate secretly with Bismarck. A delegation from the vigilante committees demanded an explanation. Jules Ferry swore the government would never treat with the Prussians.

The problem of supplies made itself felt dramatically almost at once. Very soon there was no more milk. The price of eggs rose from three to five sous, and no butter was to be had except at exorbitant prices.

Charlotte had gone back to her apartment in the rue Monsieur-le-Prince, which she was still sharing with Jean Hertz. The little maid, Annick, had gone back to her native Brittany at the beginning of the war. Charlotte could not bring herself to ask Hertz to leave although, with a republican government in power, he no longer had to hide. But the erstwhile political prisoner had almost no money. Charlotte learned on her return from Juvisy that he managed to write some small items of news for Vallès' paper. It was almost nothing, barely enough to keep from starvation. Charlotte was sorry for him. Hertz's physical and mental condition had not improved in these last months. He was not insane, but he was in a highly nervous state almost verging on the mystical and becoming more and more of a recluse. His experiences in Guiana and the tragedy of his wife's marriage had left him a broken man.

When the restrictions began, Charlotte was glad she had sent her daughter to Niort with her mother and Louise. At least, it was a comfort to know that they were safe from bombs and famine. Soon the distribution of food became such a problem that the committee for the fifth arrondissement decided to make the concierge of every building responsible for making a list of tenants and seeing to the allocations of rations in order to prevent hoarding. People were asked to denounce hoarders and prevent the growth of a black market. This decision had its own repercussions. The tenants of the building where Charlotte lived gathered together angrily to express their distrust of Madame Cazingues, whom they considered wholly unfit for such a responsibility. As for Madame Cazingues herself, the addition of a little power immediately made her as unpleasant as she had previously been obsequious. The atmosphere in the house became one of misery and mutual suspicion.

The people of Paris had been urged to join the National Guard and on October 27 the enlistment of volunteers began in the place du Panthéon. A stage decorated with tricolor flags was set up to receive the volunteers. Crowds flocked to join and there were more volunteers to defend the capital than there had been at the beginning of the war. The atmosphere of patriotic fervor was at its height. People held their children up on their shoulders so that they should miss nothing of a sight they would remember all their lives.

Gabin joined up. Illa had given birth to a little girl and Gabin's position with his young German wife was as delicate as ever. It was made worse by the fact that as national feeling grew their neighbors in the building and the surrounding streets were not particular about finding an object for it, and vented their feelings on the German girl. People no longer spoke to her and the shop-keepers would barely serve her. Charlotte was obliged to do her shopping for her, and before long it became almost impossible to obtain her proper share of the rations, which Madame Cazingues handed out with all the contempt of a corporal in charge of prisoners of war. This general hostility certainly played a part in Gabin's decision to enlist in the National Guard. Charlotte thought he was probably sorry that, being exempt from military service, he had not joined up at the beginning of the war; now he lacked the self-confidence necessary to support his wife. In Charlotte's view, he was behaving rather weakly in the face of the general attitude to Illa. She knew that his affair with Aurore had come to an abrupt end when she, like many other members of her set, had departed hastily for England even before war was declared. As for Paul Boucher, however much in love with her he may have seemed, he showed no disposition to sacrifice his honor for her sake. He had enlisted and returned to Paris with that part of the army which had remained at Mézières and so escaped the disaster of Sedan. He was on friendly terms with Gambetta who had persuaded him that he would be more usefully employed as an under-secretary in his ministry than serving as a junior army officer. Paul had been convinced and was now, indirectly, a member of the government. With his brooding, cynical intelligence and the curious contradictory mixture of opportunism and generosity which made up his character, Paul had made friends in all parties and was still to be found haunting fashionable salons. If his heart was with the people his morbidly sensitive nature was repelled by the thought of revolution. He was a clear-sighted person with few illusions about himself or others.

Gabin joined up, partly as a sop to public opinion, partly to quiet his own conscience. The National Guard had uniforms, certain civil advantages and thirty sous pay. It soon became apparent that for most of the poor people who had enlisted this was far too little to buy food and lodgings for their families and themselves. In the end the municipalities had decreed that no tenant could be evicted for non-payment of rent and similar regulations were brought into force in the case of tradesmen whose business had suffered from the war.

On October 15, meat rationing was introduced in the fifth arrondissement. The women began organizing themselves into committees for mutual aid. Valerie asked Charlotte to join the committee for the rue d'Arras. Charlotte, with too little to occupy her time, was glad to have something definite to do. She had not heard from Frank since the disastrous defeat in Alsace and, like thousands of other women, interpreted this silence to mean that Frank must be a prisoner. She was not unduly worried. Such was her faith in Frank that it never occurred to her that anything could have happened to him. And so she waited patiently, but the days of the siege dragged on very slowly. Frank had left her money in the bank, where he had deposited the whole of his mother's fortune and part of what had come to him on the death of the countess, the remainder of which was in Switzerland. The fact that she had only to draw on this money gave Charlotte a sense of unreality. It did not seem to her that it was or ever would be properly hers. It was a present from Frank, just one of the many undeserved gifts which this extraordinary young man had showered on her and as such she accepted it.

Glad to feel useful, she began work for the committee in the rue d'Arras with other women of the locality from all walks of life. She and Valerie were concerned with the distribution of food to the local schools and for the temporary hospitals and first-aid posts which were springing up everywhere. There was one close by, at the Odéon theater. The clubs had begun to reappear and in the absence of any other form of entertainment, people gathered there to talk over events. In them beat the real pulse of the city. Already, as the siege closed in, Parisians were beginning to feel their isolation. The government was divided between the dynamic optimism of Gambetta and the hesitation of the governor, General Trochu.

Gambetta had one idea in his mind, which was to make contact with the provinces so that forces could be organized to come to the relief of the city. In mid-October, he escaped from Paris by balloon, and made his way to Tours to begin organizing resistance. Trochu for his part was set against any idea of a mass sortie from the city and determined instead to try a number of smaller forays, all of which failed. The Italian patriot, Garibaldi, appeared spectacularly to offer his services to France. Gambetta received him without much enthusiasm, but gave him command of a small force of irregulars and militiamen.

Then came the surrender of Metz. Ever since Sedan, Bazaine had remained in Metz with an army of a hundred and seventy thousand men and four thousand officers. Despite this considerable force at his disposal, he made no attempt to break out. He was waiting for peace. He utterly refused to recognize the validity of the republican government and was secretly hoping for the return to power of Napoleon III. When Prince Frederick Charles sent a request for him to negotiate, he did not refuse outright but he wanted to consult the Empress Eugenie, who had fled to England, and the former Bonapartist ministers Rouher and Persigny. The Empress refused to commit herself.

Bismarck was furious, seeing the collapse of all chance of a restoration of the Imperial power in France, which would have facilitated his own ambitions. He thereupon rejected any compromise and demanded an unconditional surrender. Bazaine, who had believed everything settled, gave in. Some of his officers begged him to make one last attempt to break out but after seeing all his most cherished hopes annihilated in the space of a few days, Bazaine refused to fight and surrendered. The entire army was taken prisoner.

This took place on 27 October but the news did not become known in Paris until the 31st, at the same time as that of the loss of Le Bourget and the arrival of Thiers at Versailles with a view to arranging an armistice.

Anger and despair seized the capital. The people of Paris felt betrayed. While the citizens were ready to suffer any peril of siege and famine to resist the invader, an army of a hundred and seventy thousand men had surrendered without a fight, a marshal of France had negotiated with the enemy to satisfy his private ambitions. Trochu, the Governor, became increasingly cautious, keeping a firm grip on the National Guard, which asked nothing better than to fight. Finally, Thiers, more concerned with checking the rise of republican feeling in France than with resisting the German invader, concentrated on reaching a settlement as quickly as possible to take the Republic out of the hands of the republicans before they could do any further damage.

Paris was wild with resentment. The people were hungry. They were prepared to suffer and they felt their courage and heroism had been set at nought. They swarmed into the streets, forcing their way into the Hôtel de Ville for the second time and demanding municipal

321

elections. The forces charged with maintaining law and order mutinied outright.

That afternoon, the socialist Flourens burst into the chamber and, acting on his own authority, arrested the ministers. Blanqui, completely out of his depth, rushed about giving orders to which no one paid any attention. The confusion lasted well into the evening. But the attempt at a revolutionary coup was ultimately a failure. The government of National Defense survived but the day had been won at great peril and repercussions were immense.

Food became increasingly scarce. The shops had nothing left to sell. There was no heating. People were selling rats at anything from thirty to thirty-five centimes apiece and one after another the animals in the Jardin des Plantes were sacrificed for food. The elephants Castor and Pollux were shot and bought by a butcher in the boulevard Haussmann. The weather grew colder and before long there were outbreaks of disease. But worst of all, the Prussians intensified their bombardment of the city. The whole of the left bank was under fire and several districts were evacuated.

Charlotte was frightened of the guns. When the firing was at its heaviest, everyone took refuge in the cellars. These were terrible hours. It was cold and the tenants huddled together in the semi-darkness, lit only by a few candles. Tempers were short and quarrels broke out over nothing. Illa refused outright to take her baby down there and face the hostility of her neighbors. Hertz, too, insisted upon remaining at his open window, occasionally showing a light, although this was now against the law and punishable by a fine.

He would stand there, gasping for breath and gazing out at the fiery sky, occasionally muttering fiercely to himself.

At the beginning of December, the bombardment became heavier still and Charlotte formed the habit of leaving the house during the more prolonged bursts of firing and offering her services to the hospital set up in the Odéon theater, where she was already concerned with the allocation of beds and food. She helped with the registration of the injured who came to them from all the near-by districts and, if necessary, with getting them into bed. Working in the faint light of darkened lamps and wholly absorbed by the fears and sufferings of the injured people around her, she forgot her own fear, her dread of the future, Frank's silence and her own loneliness. She ate little and worked fourteen hours a day but she was only one of many and she did not complain. Yet there were times when she wondered how long Paris could hold out, waiting and suffering like this, and she was afraid that in the end courage and hope would fail. She longed desperately for something to happen, something to break the monotony, and she sensed that it would come and when it did their fate would be decided.

Several times, her work brought her into contact with Thomas, although never for very long. He was working for Vallès' newspaper and at the same time running a committee for his own district. This brought them together, but they were never alone. Thomas behaved perfectly naturally towards her when other people were present but his eyes sought her in silent question. The fact that they were not alone made Charlotte feel safe and she was glad to know that they were both doing their duty.

She knew that Marie's time was near and that the baby would be born sometime in December. One night, when the bombardment of the left bank was worse than usual, a bomb fell on the Musée du Luxembourg, just behind Charlotte's apartment.

They heard the noise of the explosion and saw smoke and flames bursting from the damaged buildings. Charlotte had been on her way to the Odéon and had barely time to fling herself on the ground beside the Luxembourg railings. She felt the earth heave beneath her. A soldier of the National Guard who happened to be near came and helped her to her feet. She was severely shocked but terror gave her the strength to run home. She hurried upstairs and found Hertz standing before the open window. Every pane of glass in the building and in those nearby had been shattered by the blast. Hertz looked at her strangely but said nothing. For some days now he had been in the habit of following her with his eyes and after a while Charlotte had begun to feel increasingly uneasy under that pale yet penetrating gaze, which seemed to see right to the bottom of one's heart.

"Stop it," she cried irritably, "don't look at me like that or I shall hit you, do you hear, I shall hit you." She was still half crazed from her recent fright. She rushed at the broken windows and pulled them shut with a bang, pushing Hertz out of the way. Then she stood where she was with her hands over her face and began to cry weakly.

"We shall all be killed. The whole of Paris will be blown to pieces! We must get away, I can't stay here right under the Prussian guns. I want to go away—"

Hertz looked at her calmly. "You are upset," he said. "It will pass. You've had a fright—"

Suddenly calm again, Charlotte dropped into a chair and sat there without another word while Hertz returned to his post at the window. Explosions were crashing outside. Suddenly they heard hasty footsteps coming up the stairs and there was a knock at Charlotte's door. She got up shakily and went to open it. It was Thomas.

"It's Marie. Her labor has begun. I can't keep her at home, there is no doctor and she is terrified of the guns. I came to see whether you could find her a bed at the Odéon."

He was clearly very worried. Charlotte thought it unlikely there would be a bed but said she would do what she could.

"We will go there at once."

She was quite calm again now that she had something to do, and went out into the streets with no thought of the bombardment which was still going on. For the present, she was thinking of nothing but finding a bed for Marie. She was glad to be able to do something for her, to be able to offer Thomas this act of friendship by which to deserve his gratitude and esteem.

Close by the Odéon, the Musée du Luxembourg was still burning fiercely and firemen were fighting to quench the flames. The patients in the hospital were almost frantic with terror and the doctors and nurses were having some trouble calming them.

At last, Charlotte found a bed, though not without

difficulty as fresh waves of injured were coming in all the time. Thomas's friends brought Marie. Her face was like wax, drawn with pain and fear. She clung to Thomas's hand and he wanted to stay with her, but the doctor on duty at the hospital insisted on his leaving because it was to be a forceps delivery. Charlotte went to the kitchen and asked for some soup for Thomas and for herself. But Thomas was too agitated to keep still and soon he went outside and walked up and down outside the building. The fire across the road was burning itself out and the firing had stopped.

The child was born during the night. It was a boy. Marie was as well as could be expected. When she had gone to sleep, Thomas went to find Charlotte, who was dozing in the pantry. Both were exhausted by their night of sleepless anxiety.

"It's a fine boy," he told her, tired but triumphant. "Eight pounds and the living spit of me."

Charlotte could see the pride in his face, his blue eyes shone with a glow of sheer boyish delight such as she had never seen in him before and for a moment every other feeling was submerged in one of unbearable pain. Somehow she managed to congratulate him. She should have left then but she stayed where she was, terrified by the appalling sense of grief and jealousy which welled up inside her.

Since Marie was sleeping, Thomas wanted to escort her home, thanking her again for her trouble and kindness, but she declined hurriedly and left him as quickly as she could for fear he should see her anguish.

Charlotte tried, in the three days that followed, to pull herself together but without success. The birth of the child, whom Marie had insisted on calling Thomas after his father, had affected her so deeply that it seemed to have struck at the very roots of her new life. She had not known that Thomas could still cause her such pain.

It left her completely shattered, beyond hope of recovery. She tried in vain to recall the single-minded purity of her passion for Frank. The ache within her was incurable and only made worse by the fact that she could speak of it to no one.

She went to church and prayed as she had never done before, kneeling in one of the small side chapels with the tears streaming down her face. Eventually, at some kind of peace with herself, she went back to the rue Monsieur-le-Prince, thinking fervently of Frank, and of Thomas with feelings of friendship. The next day she found Valerie in the little office of the Odéon theater where they were accustomed to do their accounts. She had not dared to visit Marie. She could not bring herself to see Thomas's child.

"Bad news," said Valerie. "Three cases of scarlet fever and two of typhoid among the injured. The worst of it is that Marie Becque has the infection and will not be able to nurse her boy."

Charlotte's distress was greater than ever at this news. Towards noon, as she was leaving the hospital, she saw Thomas going in and stepped back quietly so as not to have to speak to him. She could guess how wretched he must feel but for the moment everything in her refused to share his unhappiness. She knew she could not help him without suffering herself and that any help she gave him must be all or nothing. The thought frightened her. Even so, she could not stop thinking about it all that day. If they took the child away from Marie, where could Thomas put it out to nurse? A new-born baby needed so much care, and there could be no question of going out of Paris and finding one of the nurses who were usually available in the countryside. That night, she could bear it no longer and walked down to ask Valerie, who had been at the Odéon all day, whether there was any further news of Marie. Valerie told her that typhoid had now been confirmed but that she did not know what was to happen to the child.

"Surely we could have him here," Valerie said, following Charlotte's thoughts. "Your sister-in-law is already nursing her own little girl, couldn't she take another as well? Just for a few weeks, until Marie Becque is better—"

The thought that Illa might take the baby had been with Charlotte all day. She was torn between her own good sense and genuine friendship for Thomas and the purely selfish longing to take the child under her own roof. She saw already how this could be done. Illa would come and live in her apartment, which would certainly be no worse than continuing to freeze in her own room on the fifth floor, where she and the baby were already sufficiently cramped. It was true that Charlotte herself was no better off for fuel but at least her apartment was more comfortable. They would put up a bed in the sitting-room and then Hertz could keep the little room at the end because they could not throw him out into the street. In this way, Illa would be able to breast-feed Thomas's baby while Charlotte herself did everything else that was necessary. It would be too tiring for Illa to nurse both children and take care of them at the same time. This, at least, was the excuse she gave herself but already she desired passionately to look after Thomas's child. Once she had got the idea firmly into her head she wasted no more time and went straight up to talk to Illa. Motherhood and her other troubles had made her little sister-in-law so pale and thin that Charlotte felt a moment's pity for her and was afraid that her plan, after all, might be impossible. At the same time, she felt a little guilty, because she knew how much the German girl had suffered from the hostility of her neighbors. She thought that she would never dare ask such a service of her but Illa came to meet her at once.

"Charlotte, how kind of you to come. Did you want to see me?"

She spoke with a slight accent and was such a gentle creature that Charlotte wondered how anyone could find it in their hearts to be unkind to her, and how Gabin could ever have deceived her, forgetting for a moment the ease with which she had once broken her own marriage vows. Illa had always been fond of Charlotte, who had never been anything but kind and friendly to her and had an intuitive awareness of her strength and vigor.

"You have something to say to me?"

Charlotte stood looking at Illa and Gabin's little daughter, Marthe, who lay asleep in her cradle. Then, without further hesitation, she plunged into her story, giving a

327

graphic description of Thomas's position of having no one to look after the baby.

"And—do you really think it would work? That I could do it?" Illa asked in her soft voice. In her present pitiable state she was only too glad to be able to do anything for a Frenchman in order to justify her own existence.

"You have plenty of milk?"

"Yes, but so little to eat."

No matter, Charlotte would give her what they could find. Illa agreed, and Charlotte, unable to wait, went out at once to see Thomas.

His former housekeeper had left his service and there was no one at home. The concierge told her that Monsieur Becque had gone to the brasserie Glaser in the rue Saint-Séverin, where the members of his committee were in the habit of meeting. Charlotte went there. The place was full of people and the air thick with smoke. Thomas was in the back room with his friends. The table was littered with papers. He rose when he saw Charlotte and went out with her into the street. She could read the lines of care on his face.

"I had to see you. Marie is ill, isn't she?"

"Yes. I am very worried, they have had to isolate her. The typhoid is spreading." He took her arm and she could feel how tense he was.

"Let's walk a little," he said. "If you only knew the good it does me to see you."

They walked on a little way. He did not loosen his grip on her arm.

"Oh, Charlotte, if you only knew—I was so happy with this baby. My courage had come back and I felt strong again—now, if Marie dies—" His voice broke.

"Don't say such things. One must always hope—"

She was gripping his hand now, filled with pity for the helplessness of a strong man in the hands of fate. There were tears in her eyes and, not knowing what to say, she only gripped his hand in silence. She saw all at once that she had never really expected Marie to recover and the thought appalled her.

"What will you do with the child?"

"I don't know. It is dreadful."

"Will you let me take him? My sister-in-law is nursing a baby—I will look after him—"

"You?" He did not understand at first but already he looked more hopeful and a light had come into his eyes. "You would do that for me? Oh my dear, how can I ever thank you. I love you for that. What a friend you are—"

He kissed her hands, reverently. Charlotte, at a loss to know how to react, was almost sorry she had made the suggestion. Now she wanted nothing more than to escape. It shocked her that he had accepted her offer so quickly, almost as though she owed it to him, as though it was perfectly natural for her to take his child, as though she would always be there for him to fall back on

But these last selfish instincts were soon gone. She was really thinking of the child. They walked on side by side.

"Everything will be all right now," Thomas said with conviction. "Marie will get better, you will see, and we shall emerge victorious from this interminable siege. The people of Paris will conquer and we will found a real Republic with equal rights for all men, and we will do away with war forever—"

Why was he talking like this? He knew the odds against a victory over the invaders, just as he knew how many were the enemies of the Republic, even those who claimed to serve her, and the pointless differences which divided even men of the same party, his own friends. He knew all their selfishness, their lack of common purpose, their private ambitions and yet, knowing all that, he could still talk in this exalted strain about victory and equality. Perhaps the reason lay in his need to believe that Charlotte had done what she had out of pure goodness of heart. He admired and respected her for it. A single act of real, disinterested generosity might be enough to restore one's belief in all humanity.

"We will come and fetch the baby, tomorrow."

The eyes that thanked her held more than gratitude. He made no attempt to conceal the love in them, the more so in that he was truly grateful and because of their conscious innocence. Indeed, so virtuous had their love become that it was almost a right. At this point Charlotte hastily took refuge in memories of Frank. She stiffened as Thomas took her hand to say goodbye.

Valerie and Charlotte went to fetch the child the next morning. They did not see Marie, who had been placed in an isolation ward with the other typhoid cases. Charlotte's heart beat faster as the baby was put in her arms. He had a mass of dark brown hair that went strangely with his little round crumpled face. His tiny arms ended in a pair of fists like plump pink sea urchins. When he opened his eyes she saw that they were exactly the same blue-grey color as Thomas's. He was so lovely that she could not help falling in love with him at once.

She carried him back to the house and put him to bed with hot water-bottles. Illa fed him and Charlotte saw to him again that night and in the days that followed, temporarily giving up her work for the committee in order to care for the baby properly.

She had thought of everything except that Thomas would come every day to see the child, which she could scarcely prevent, and that however short a time he stayed and however formal his behavior, his presence, even with Illa and Hertz close by, was more than she could bear. Even the safeguards of Frank and Marie could not destroy the ties which still bound them together. Their innocence, however genuine, was only skin deep, and Charlotte wondered desperately if she had not, in the belief of doing him a service, in fact been only binding them closer together through her love of the child and whether they were not being more unkind to Marie than ever.

Then, telling herself she had no right to rob Marie of Thomas's gratitude or to take her child away from her, she made up her mind to give up the baby, find another nurse and make Thomas understand why they must never see one another again.

She prepared herself to tell him when he came that evening and immediately launched into her speech with no attempt to soften the blow. She confessed all the scruples which had bothered her and said at last that he must go. He was sitting in a chair, staring at the ground,

330

and seemed to take so little interest that at last Charlotte was silent.

"It doesn't matter," he said, "Marie died this afternoon."

Charlotte tried to speak and could not. The house rocked on its foundations as a bomb fell on the Panthéon.

Paris waited. The news was catastrophic. One after another, Gambetta's three armies, in the north, the east and the Loire, suffered an unbroken series of defeats in spite of the courage of the French soldiers. Wearying of this dogged resistance, the Germans bombarded Paris incessantly, hoping to force the capital to surrender.

In his anxiety at the restlessness of the National Guard, General Trochu decided to attempt a sortie in the direction of Buzenval. The attack was a failure owing to the dilatoriness of General Ducrot on the right wing, which enabled the Germans to rake the French lines with deadly fire, and to the short-sightedness of General Trochu himself. He engaged only two of the nineteen battalions of the guard, the oldest ones which had been enlisted under the Empire and whose loyalty was not in question, and then sent no relief to the wretched forces at Buzenval. It might have been part of a deliberate plan to reduce the National Guard.

The people of Paris were horrified by the news of the defeat at Buzenval. General Trochu did his best to explain that the defeat was inevitable. Unfortunately, he made the mistake of adding that in his view defeat had been inevitable ever since 4 September. This was a clear admission that he had never really believed in the possibility of victory, even at the time he took command. By permitting the massacre of the National Guard at Buzenval, he had been deliberately trying to break its spirit. The people felt betrayed. There could be no more illusions about the state of mind of a large section of the government. The members of the National Guard roamed the city with cries of "Resign! Long live the Commune!"

On 23 January, Jules Favre at Versailles agreed with Bismarck on the terms of an armistice. On the 26th, hostilities were suspended on all fronts for a period of twenty-one days during which the National Assembly was to discuss the peace terms offered by Prussia. Paris was to surrender her forts and her guns, and disarm the National Guard, with the exception of twelve thousand men who were retained for the purpose of keeping order. In addition, the city was to pay the sum of two hundred million francs.

The reaction in Paris and throughout France was one of total and indignant astonishment. In the provinces, public opinion was in a state of utter confusion. Yet it was this public, a public whose political freedom had already been suppressed for twenty years of Bonapartist rule, that was now asked to go to the polls on 8 February.

The capital was to elect forty-three deputies and among the men its votes put into the Assembly were Louis Blanc, Victor Hugo, Gambetta, Garibaldi, Delezcluze and Félix Pyat. All of these were men who had never ceased to oppose surrender, to advocate resistance to the last and to support a socialist republic. The provincial vote, on the other hand, went mostly to monarchist or moderate candidates. Adolphe Thiers, who came only twentieth in the list of candidates for the Seine, chose to stand for Paris. The assembly, meeting at Bordeaux, elected him "Executive leader of the French Republic." The republican assembly had a large monarchist majority.

This assembly, elected for the purpose of dealing with the German peace proposals, did not attempt to hide its dislike of the representatives of the capital. Thiers himself said that the assembly abhorred Paris. And there was Paris, touchy and resentful, still full of its sufferings during the siege and deeply conscious of betrayal. Peace might be necessary at this point but the people of Paris still felt betrayed. Under the Empire there had been great poverty among the working classes and the hasty, ill-prepared declaration of war had been only the first betrayal of the French people, who had given willingly of their courage and their lives. Then, even when all might have been saved, those who had nothing to gain from a continuation of the war had turned and stabbed the soldiers in the back by conniving at the country's surrender. Alongside the emotional mood of Paris, heightened by the feeling in the clubs and the high-flown rhetoric beloved of the orators of the day, there was a very real poverty and resentment among the people.

And so, on the one hand, there was Paris in this critical mood and on the other, Adolphe Thiers, an old man of seventy-three and a former minister of Louis-Philippe. Thiers was a clever man, perhaps too clever. He had already dealt with the revolution of 1848. A man who had been able to handle one revolution could cope with another. But what Thiers had not understood was the emotional intensity of feeling in Paris. He believed that firmness was all that was needed when in fact a little diplomacy, taking account of the susceptibilities and recent sufferings of the people of Paris, might have soothed their feelings, given them fresh cause for hope and averted civil war. But Adolphe Thiers was an obstinate man and a bureaucrat, and no psychologist.

Consequently, on 10 March, the hostile assembly withdrew the concessions which had been made to tenants and tradesmen in difficulties during the siege. Any money owing was to be paid by 13 March, leaving little enough time for those whose financial problems, owing to the war and to the isolation of the capital, were in effect insoluble. on 11 March, General Vinoy, the new commander of the armed forces in Paris, closed down six democratic newspapers. Lastly, the Assembly decided to cease payment of the daily wage to national guardsmen except on presentation of a certificate of need. In practice, this meant that the major source of income was abruptly withdrawn for many humble families whose normal means of livelihood had been cut off by the siege and who were generally inclined to regard this daily wage as proper compensation. Resentment in the capital ran higher still.

At this point, Thiers decided that he could never succeed in establishing his authority unless he first got hold of the cannon which Paris had refused to surrender to the Prussians. A date was fixed which had to be before 20 March, when the Assembly was to meet at Versailles. Thiers himself would be there on the 14th.

The atmosphere in Paris on the 17th was restless. There were soldiers in the Luxembourg and the gardens resembled nothing more than one vast encampment laid out beneath the bright brown buds of the chestnut trees.

On the evening of the 17th, Paul Boucher called on Charlotte. He had already been to see her once since 4 September to offer her his help through his official contacts, should she need it, but Charlotte had made it clear she desired no special favors. Paul was both amused and somewhat impressed by Charlotte's rather childish determination to be heroic in this, as he was amused and impressed by anything he could not have done himself. He found Charlotte altered by the four months' siege, thinner and tired about the eyes.

"Paul, how nice to see you."

Paul explained the reason for his visit. He thought there was going to be trouble in the city and his sources of information suggested that it would come in the next few days. He urged Charlotte to leave Paris.

"I mean it, Charlotte. Everything points to serious trouble. Go and join your family in Niort."

"I am grateful for your trouble, Paul, but it is quite impossible," Charlotte said firmly.

His coming surprised her, all the same. She knew that underneath his cynical manner he had a very real friendship for her, but that he should have made the journey half-way across Paris, after four months, simply in order to tell her to leave suggested that the future might look very black. She looked at him closely, although she knew that Paul rarely allowed his innermost feelings to show in his face.

"I want to stay here," she went on, "and besides, I am needed."

"I know. I saw Becque the day before yesterday. We spoke only briefly but he told me you had taken his child. His wife's death has affected him very deeply, I believe?"

"Yes."

She averted her eyes, conscious that Paul was watching her.

"Do you see him often?"

"He has come since Marie's death, but only now and then to see the baby. He spends all his time writing, or with his committee. He is working himself to death."

She did not add that he was also avoiding her, that Marie's death and Thomas's reaction to it had made their own situation intolerable. To his regret that he had never attempted to make Marie truly happy was added a certain contempt for his own past selfishness, so that what he felt was less the conventional widower's grief than a deep sorrow for the life he had allowed to pass him by, for his own want of generosity, and a desperate need to cling to everything that was real and true in himself now. He had never paid much heed to appearances, now he hated them. It maddened him to think that he was exposing Charlotte to gossip by visiting her and letting her take the baby. He needed Charlotte, needed her desperately, but it had to be openly, honestly, without hypocrisy.

Charlotte asked Paul if he would like to see the baby and he agreed without much interest. The baby was asleep in Charlotte's room. Illa, who was sewing by the window, stood up timidly as they came in.

"Forgive this intrusion, madame, we will stay only a moment." He looked at the child. "Becque can't deny this one! He's the image of him. But surely, my dear, you are putting yourself in a rather delicate situation—this adoption looks very like adultery."

"Paul! How dare you!"

"Forgive me, pet," he took her hand and kissed it slyly. "I meant that this adoption could mean more than adultery. Be careful, Charlotte, sometimes there may be more in an act of friendship than meets the eye."

Charlotte shrugged indifferently. Paul's cynicism, which had wounded her once, could not touch her now. He saw this and smiled.

"Take no notice of my tongue. It has become a habit with me. But seriously, Charlotte, go away, leave Paris. There is bound to be trouble between the citizens and the forces of the law. God knows what will come of it."

"But surely, respectable people need have nothing to do with it," she said confidently.

Paul gave a short laugh. "Respectable people! I like the way you say that. So according to you, my dear, neither the vulgar uneducated revolutionaries nor the hypocrites of Monsieur Thier's government constitute respectable people. Respectable people are the ones who hold no opinions, like yourself. Well, my dear, some people might call that indifference."

"Oh Paul, not now."

He could see that she was tired and anxious and he wondered what was the root of her anxiety. Certainly, having taken Becque's child she could not change her mind now whatever complications it might bring.

"At all events," he said seriously, "even if you have no political affiliation yourself, your connection with Thomas labels you whether you like it or not. And God knows what the future may hold for those who bear that particular label."

"What do you mean?"

Paul's insistence had begun to alarm her. She had never really thought of things in this light, and although she was aware of a certain amount of local hostility, some sixth sense warned her that it was not as simple as she had believed, that Thomas had other enemies besides her gossiping neighbors.

"God grant I may be wrong," Paul said slowly.

"You seem to be talking a lot about God."

"I shall need Him. Ah well, my dear, I must leave you—"

Just as he was on the point of going, Hertz came in and Paul was struck by the obvious deterioration in his health.

"There are troops in the Luxembourg gardens," Hertz said feverishly. "The city is completely hemmed in."

"There is no doubt something is going to happen. People in a position to know think it will be this week at the latest. Thiers thinks he will get back the cannon without bloodshed and that the guard will give in at the first demand. But Thiers is wrong. He does not know the real strength of Paris or the real state of mind of the people."

"Do you really think it will come to civil war?" Charlotte asked in a choked voice.

"I am afraid so. That is why I was so anxious for you to leave. The Guard will not give way."

Paul looked at Hertz, who kept his eyes fixed on some distant point on the wall and said nothing.

"Mind you, Hertz, I will not disguise from you that I

336

personally am against the use of force, not only because I am a coward when it comes to violence but because, in my view, the republicans are not sufficiently united. The left is divided against itself. I will even go further and say that to my mind feeling in Paris is not ripe for a real revolution. I grant you the people are starving, as usual but as for the result! There are a good many citizens who look to the committees to protect them and have no desire to change society. All they are concerned with is their own immediate problems and they will follow anyone who will take care of them. But what will happen next?"

"They will be slaughtered," Hertz said. "Herded like cattle."

"I'm sorry, Hertz, but that is your obsession. On the whole, people are not sent to Guiana nowadays."

"They will be shot in the streets in broad daylight, women and children—free men will be dragged in the dust and men will spit in their faces—"

"That's enough," Paul said angrily.

"Corpses, thousands of corpses," Hertz went on hysterically, "we shall all be damned—"

Paul led him to a chair. "Calm yourself, Hertz. Charlotte, give him a glass of water."

Charlotte obeyed but Hertz did not drink it. He sat where he was, without moving, as Boucher led Charlotte into the hall.

"Is he often like this? Is his mind really affected or is it a pretense to attract attention?"

"I do not know. But he gets on my nerves. If this goes on, he will have to go."

The truth was that she was worn out and for weeks now a gnawing anxiety had been working on her like a disease. She was not so much afraid as oppressed by a growing sense of unease.

"Hertz has had some kind of premonition, Paul. He knows what is going to happen, I'm sure he does!"

"Stop taking such nonsensical ideas into your head. Well, now I really am going. But seriously," he added, unwilling to leave her in this troubled state, "won't you go to Niort?"

"I've told you, no."

"What are you waiting here for? Becque or your Pole?"

"Paul, I forbid you—"

"My apologies. But you know I am your friend." He opened the door. "Have you any news of Worski?"

"No."

"Has there been any news for the families of those taken prisoner by the Germans since the armistice?"

"Paul, what are you driving at?"

"Nothing. The two men you love are both fools. Goodbye."

Charlotte, having an errand to a near-by shop, decided to go with him. When she returned it was already dark and the camp fires were burning in the Luxembourg gardens, and soldiers standing guard at the gates. The sound of a mouth organ floated on the fresh March breeze. As she passed a young soldier whispered to her through the railings.

"Tomorrow, tell them it's tomorrow."

An officer appeared and the soldier said no more. Charlotte stood on the pavement feeling as though she had lost all contact with reality. A shadow had brushed by her. She shuddered as though for the first time the cold wings of death had touched her soul.

The next day was 18 March. Thiers was still convinced that he would have no trouble gaining possession of the guns and that the handful of National Guardsmen defending them would not stand up against regular troops. But what Thiers did not know was that however carelessly the guns might seem to be guarded, the whole National Guard and all the people of Paris would rise in their defense. He did not know that all three hundred thousand of the National Guard were solidly behind their central committee, and he did not know that it was not only the workers who were angry but the middle classes as well, that the sense of outrage was shared by all Paris.

Not for one moment did it occur to Thiers to make the smallest concession to public feeling in the capital. Instead of disarming a city which had already suffered so much during the siege and was bound to look upon any such disarmament as an insult, he could have temporized and made some attempt to soothe the more violent monarchists in the provinces. But Thiers was afraid of the people, he knew little of their feelings or their strength and he dreaded 20 March, the date he had fixed for the Assembly to meet him at Versailles. He was moreover under pressure from those who were eager to get business going again, and especially from the members of the stock exchange, the very people who had urged the declaration of war and now wanted to put an end to the rebellion in Paris.

Consequently, Thiers had decided to take possession of the guns and, in order to have the matter settled by the 20th, he had fixed upon the 18th for doing so. At three o'clock that morning troops began to move all over Paris from the Buttes-Chaumont, to Belleville, the Faubourg du Temple, the Bastille, the Hôtel de Ville, the place Saint-Michel and the Invalides. In fact, using the guns as an excuse, Thiers was really aiming at military occupation of the capital and at neutralizing the National Guard.

To begin with, General Lecomte's brigade had little trouble dispersing the National Guard on duty by the guns but when it came to dragging the heavy pieces of artillery along the outer boulevards to the Invalides, matters became somewhat more difficult. Day was breaking and the tocsin sounding the general alarm called the companies to arms. The crowds around the soldiers were growing minute by minute and the men broke ranks and joined the people. All over Paris things were much the same.

In the Place Pigalle, a sharp clash occurred between the cavalry and the insurgents. In Belleville and Ménilmontant, the brigade led by General Faron was forced to retreat before the angry crowd. Everywhere the regular troops were being hemmed in by the people of Paris and the National Guard or else the soldiers themselves were joining the crowd.

It was a morning of total failure for the government. Thiers, who had gone secretly to the Quai d'Orsay, heard the news with horror and at once decided to abandon Paris and transfer his headquarters to Versailles.

The real truth about the morning was that neither the central committee nor the National Guard had been prepared for this sudden action and nowhere was the resistance properly organized. Unfortunately, at about four o'clock in the afternoon, the Generals Lecomte and Clément Thomas, who had been arrested and taken to the command post in the rue des Rosiers, fell into the hands of the crowd. Clément Thomas was not loved by the Parisians, who held him partly responsible for the defeat of Buzenval. The crowd was already excited by the day's events and the officer in charge, Herpin-Lacroix tried in vain to prevent the tragedy. His voice went unheard and the crowd dragged the two generals out and shot them, there and then, against a wall in the rue des Rosiers.

16

PAUL BOUCHER had succeeded in gaining admission to the Ministry of Foreign Affairs where he had learned that members of the government were meeting. He was obliged to show his credentials but he was known there and no one made any difficulties. He was standing at a window looking down at a handful of soldiers guarding the ministry when he saw three battalions of the National Guard approaching the building with a brass band at their head. Unless they did not know of Thiers' presence there was going to be trouble. Paul was waiting in a corridor when he saw the leader of the Assembly himself come quickly out of one of the rooms and hurry off accompanied by Le Flô, one of his ministers. Avoiding the main staircase, they slipped away by a small back stair giving on to the rue de l'Universite where a carriage was waiting. Glancing out, Boucher saw Thiers climb in quickly, hiding his face clumsily with his hands to avoid recognition. He was followed by his companion who seemed, if anything, in an even greater hurry and the vehicle drove off hastily along the river.

Paul began to laugh softly. Thiers' flight by the back door appealed strongly to his sense of the ridiculous. He thought that it would make a good story, but at the same time it sickened him to think that he would have to dress it up for the public with all manner of satirical comment and feigned indignation. In fact, he did not feel in the least indignant. Thiers' escape and obvious terror of the vulgar, unclean mob only made him want to laugh. He was almost sorry for the man. No, he would not write the piece. It would be more amusing to keep the memory to himself.

Paul walked back to the Latin quarter and made his way to the brasserie Glazer where he found his friends talking eagerly about the day's events. At five o'clock or thereabouts, he saw Thomas Becque come into the café and make his way to the next table, where Vallès was sitting with a group of friends.

"There's been an incident in the rue des Rosiers. The guard have got out of hand and shot General Lecomte and General Clémont."

There was a horrified silence. Everyone in the room stopped talking. Vallès looked thunder-struck.

"The fools! The stupid fools! Now, there can be no hope of an agreement with Versailles. It will mean civil war."

There were some who disagreed with Vallès, thinking his attitude too abstract and intellectual. The excitement grew.

Vallès asked Becque if he had been there and if he had seen how the thing had happened. Thomas, who had arrived at the end, told what he knew, describing the violence of the mob and the inability of the officer Herpin to prevent an execution as useless as it was unjustified.

"This is madness," Vallès said gloomily. "An act of violence like this does away with any hope of coming to terms with the government at Versailles."

"Well," someone else broke in, "they need not have begun it after all. Who attacked Paris this morning? It took everyone by surprise. We were not expecting a civil war. No, Vallès, if this war comes it will be the fault of the government and history will judge!"

Still shaking his head sadly, Vallès left the café accompanied by Becque, Boucher and Chaptal. None of them spoke. They were all conscious that now that events had begun to move nothing could stop them. Vallès, most of all, was appalled at the prospect of civil war. Could it really be too late?

Vallès, who lived close by, left them first. Thomas walked up the boulevard Saint-Michel with Paul Boucher. The weather was crisp and clear and the air already alive with a sharp, acid sense of spring. The season promised to be a fine one. Even now, there was something of summer in the fading light, a reminder of long evenings when the sun-warmed walls and close courtyards of the city were filled with the unending murmur of voices and laughter late into the night. The two men looked at the familiar streets, bright in the almost summery light. The people talking over the day's events seemed casual and apparently unafraid, as though not even imminent tragedy could ruffle the calm surface of Parisian life. Tragedy might strike but still, a few streets away, people would sit chatting at café tables as they were doing tonight. The soft bustle of movement and conversation gave to the scene a reassuring sense of permanence, of something everlasting and unfailing in human life. And yet death was present even here, it was all around them and tomorrow it might touch them too. Perhaps it was that which gave to the spring evening its quality of timelessness.

Charlotte, like everyone else, had heard something of what had happened. The troops had been coming and going all day around the Luxembourg. By about five, however, things had quieted down and Charlotte decided to go out, and try to get some bread. She was just coming out of the baker's on the corner of the boulevard and the rue Monsieur-le-Prince with her loaves under her arm when she turned and saw Thomas not far away. He had just parted from Paul, who was dining with a friend near the Panthéon. Thomas hurried up to Charlotte and took her arm.

"I must talk to you."

"Come home with me."

It was a month since she had seen him and she had been expecting him each day to come and see how little Thomas was getting on. She began telling him about the baby, how he could smile now and say *coo*. He had his father's eyes exactly. She was quite desotted about the child and cooed over him all day with no attempt to control her need to give her love to something.

"He's good, is he?" Thomas was looking at her. Whenever she talked to him about the baby she saw him swell with the same masculine, almost boyish pride.

"You do not come and see him very often," she said

timidly, unwilling to blame him. She turned away as she spoke rather than meet Thomas's direct blue eyes. They made her feel disagreeably small. It was as though her own mother love had been called into question, as though simply by virtue of being the child's father, he could be more, do more, know more for and about the child than anyone else, even when he did not come and see him. This was something she had not met before in any other man. Étienne had been a proud but somewhat indifferent father, Gabin was a reticent one. She knew no one who was at all like Thomas, no one in whom she could feel the same fierce male pride, the same strong yet gentle love for his child.

Once again, she felt a sudden spasm of revolt as it came to her just how much this child demanded of her and how her own great love for the baby seemed to be leading her into accepting the same standards for herself. It would have been reassuring if Thomas had behaved to her like a grateful friend, if he had shown some concern for her own life, at least inquired if the baby was not a nuisance, taking up too much of her time. But no, he seemed to take all that for granted, as a right justified by the love between them.

Ever since Marie's death he had shown this determination to have everything plain and clear cut. In his absence, Charlotte might still deceive herself into believing she was entirely free but when he was there before her, she was appalled by the state of dependence on him which emerged naturally from their relationship.

She wished she could have talked to him about Frank. If only she had had a letter from him, that would have been an excuse to recall his existence, but there had been nothing. Thomas had taken her arm and they walked back together, talking over the events of the day. Thomas hid his real thoughts as to the gravity of the situation.

Why did he have to hold her arm to cross the road? Wasn't she perfectly capable of doing it by herself? She did not want him to protect her! But she dared not pull her arm away and kept her inward feelings of resentment to herself.

They entered the gate. Two women were standing talking to Madame Cazingues. Charlotte caught a glimpse of Madame Delobelle. The women turned and looked at them as they passed.

"All the fault of these scoundrels," Madame Cazingues was saying loudly, clearly referring to the day's events.

"They can say what they like. I don't care," Charlotte muttered through clenched teeth, conscious of their disapproving glances.

"Listen," Thomas said once they were inside. Illa was in the kitchen and Hertz in his own room. They were alone.

"Listen, Charlotte, I must speak to you. I cannot go on compromising you like this. Those old women with their malicious gossip drive me mad. You know what they say, don't you, that I am your lover. You are a married woman. And if you were to be mine again it would not be like this, but openly, for all to see, none of this hole and corner business. I cannot bear their dirty minds on us. You must understand, my love for you is something which matters to me, I will not let people spoil it. That is why I have come."

"What are you trying to say?"

"I want to take the child away. I will find a nurse—"

"No!" Terror forced the words from her. "No, I beg you—"

"Sweetheart—"

His hand was on her arm, gripping it hard but she did not struggle. The thought that he was going to take the baby seemed to have robbed her of all her strength.

"Sweetheart, my darling," he said. "I am grateful for all you have done, you know that, but you must see that this cannot go on. You know the situation. Anything may happen and I am afraid for the future. I shall be easier in my mind if the baby is out of Paris. And besides—"

He drew her close to him and kissed her gently on the forehead. Charlotte began to cry and was appalled by her own physical weakness.

"Understand, you must understand—Marie's death has altered nothing and it would be hypocritical to hide my feelings. I need you, you are the one person I really do need. And you know precisely how much I need you. But, seeing you like this, with this pretense at friendship, hiding everything that is real between us—I cannot do it. And what is the use? I am a man and you are not a child. You know that I love you."

"Then why take your child away from me? Leave him a little longer—"

"But don't you see what you are doing?" he broke out angrily. "Can't you see the impossible situation you are creating for us both? It is all false. You are deceiving yourself. Do you really believe there is nothing between us any more and that you took the baby out of simple kindness, can you make yourself believe that? You love this child, sweetheart, and each day you love it a little more. What would Frank say if he were to come home and find my child here and see how you have come to love it? Listen to me, darling, I beg you. When I saw you again at Juvisy and you told me about Frank, I accepted it. First because there was Marie and also because I thought that you no longer felt anything for me but kindness. Now, today, I know that is not true and that without realizing it you have betrayed yourself with the baby. I understood at once because I was watching you. I have watched you, you know. I wanted to know the truth and when I understood it I was happy, very happy. By giving your love like this to my child, you have given me more than you have ever done—you betrayed yourself, sweetheart, every time I saw you with the child, without ever realizing it—"

"No, no, it's not true. You are wrong. I love Frank—"

"If I had really thought that I would never have come back, Charlotte, never, do you hear? But that was not what I saw."

She would not look at him. There had been too much truth in his words, truth she did not want to hear. He saw that she would never accept it.

"Frank is a kind of redemption for you isn't he?" he said wearily. "Absence has made him sacred, and you love him in much the same way that you used to love God in Niort. You sacrificed me to your fears once before, sweetheart, when you married Étienne, now you are making me a sacrifice again, this time to Frank's youth. But take care that you are not doing it because it is easier to cling to an ideal than to face life. Life is never perfect, it is tiresome and incomplete like me. Well, you need not worry, I do not intend to come between you and your loyalty to Frank. That is why I want to take the child."

The thought that he was going away made Charlotte feel suddenly immensely tired. Some part of her was obscurely aware that it was easier to be faithful to Frank when Thomas was there because his presence gave some tangible reality to Frank's existence. Already, to her horror, she could foresee a time when that faith would be no more than an empty ideal, when even Frank himself would be only an idea.

In the days that followed, the situation in Paris remained tense. The conflict between the Central Committee and the mayors of the capital ended in the capitulation of the mayors.

The Central Committee of the National Guard, acting with the support of the mayors and deputy mayors, believe that the only way to avoid the bloodshed of civil war in Paris and at the same time strengthen the Republic is to hold municipal elections—"

Paris went to the polls in an orderly way on 26 March. It was a fine, mild day and many people were up early to vote. The streets were gay and crowded and the cafés doing a roaring trade. The next day's results showed an easy victory for the Commune.

On 28 March, the Commune took office in the capital. The occasion became one of popular celebration with a crowd of two hundred thousand or more men, women and children flowing into the center of the city. There were people at every window and the square outside the Hôtel de Ville was hung with red flags as though for a bullfight. It was a gay, colorful scene. The bayonets gleamed in the sunshine.

The excitement reached its height after the solemn proclamation of the Commune. The guard marched past, the soldiers waving their rifles in the air and shouting for joy. The members of the brand-new government waved proudly from their seats.

There were the newly elected members in all the dignity of their tricolor sashes. There were the people of the *faubourgs* with all their children in tow, glowing with pride and optimism because they might be poor but they still had their rights. The middle classes, tradesmen and shopkeepers, were there too, and moderately enthusiastic on account of their financial preoccupations. The very rich had mostly left Paris immediately at the end of the war, those that remained were largely indifferent. On that 28th of March, the people of Paris themselves thronged the city's streets and windows, marching and waving in an orgy of innocent self-congratulation.

The Commune had been in power in the capital for only five days, when on 2 April, there was a rumor of attack from troops at Versailles at the Rond-Point des Bergères. A general alarm was sounded but too late. The supporters of the Commune had been literally cut to pieces by the troops, two divisions of which, with the addition of General Galliffet's cavalry, had converged on the Rond-Point with the object of attacking Courbevoie and Puteaux. The Federates fought valiantly but they were heavily outnumbered. The result was a massacre.

In the end, the troops fell back across the bridge at Neuilly. The affair would not have been serious in itself, and might even have been regarded as victory for the Federates since the other side had finally withdrawn, but the massacre had been complete. The crowd which made its way to the Rond-Point in answer to the summons of the tocsin gazed in horror at the sight that met its eyes. Every single prisoner taken by the enemy had been shot. Their bodies lay in heaps where they had fallen; it was a scene of indescribable carnage. Hospital wagons were brought and they began the task of loading the bodies for the journey back to Paris.

Reprisals of this kind, which were against all the laws of war, the mass shooting of prisoners and anyone else who happened to be on the spot, became henceforth the hallmark of the Versailles army, making the name General Galliffet hated for all time.

In the next few days the Commune made a number of unsuccessful attacks on the outskirts of Paris. Two of their leaders, Flourens and Duval, were taken prisoner and summarily shot. As a result of this execution, the Commune decided to take hostages. These included a number of churchmen, among them the Archbishop of Paris, Monsignor Darboy. At the same time a decree was published separating Church and State. The result was a certain confusion in some people's minds, since the two things were seen to be connected whereas the seizure of the hostages, while not unrelated to the anti-clerical feelings of certain members of the Commune, was in actual fact the result of the summary executions carried out by the Versailles forces. Further rumors of executions were spreading all the time, creating an atmosphere of terror and loathing towards the enemy. Thiers was hated in Paris. He figured in an endless succession of cartoons and was known by a variety of grotesque nicknames.

But in spite of all the alarming stories which circulated, making any agreement between Paris and Versailles seem more remote than ever, the capital did not give the impression of a city living in a state of fear. The city was so large and varied that it was not long in developing a kind of complacent self-absorption. Besides, it was spring and the weather deceptively bright and warm. The Commune began to busy itself with schools and other institutions, but calmly, without undue haste, as though it had a lifetime before it. It was all very different from the revolutionary fury of 1789. There were no Robespierres or Saint-Justs in the Commune. Instead, there were a number of earnest, worthy men, not particularly united among themselves and too different in temperament and background to form a united government. Moreover, to take control of the city after one siege against the Prussians and immediately to be involved in another against the French was a dispiriting task, even if the enemy had not made it their business to infiltrate as many spies, agents, agitators and rumor-mongers into the city as they possibly could.

On 16 May, the Commune at last got round to removing the Emperor Napoleon III from his pedestal in the place Vendôme, providing an excuse for a public holiday and calling down on themselves the anger of Versailles. Some, though not all, of the churches were closed, the theaters re-opened despite a shortage of good actors, and there were regular public concerts at the Tuileries.

The real object of the Commune, however, was to form a genuine alternative government to Thiers' Assembly at Versailles, one capable of maintaining the fundamental rights of the Republic and providing a real as well as a symbolic government of the people in opposition to that at Versailles.

If Thiers were to fight Paris, he needed more than his present ragged army. In order to obtain it, he bargained with Germany for the repatriation of eighty thousand French prisoners of war in return for an undertaking to use them only to restore order within the country. The men were encamped at Satory and Marshal MacMahon, the unlucky commander of Sedan, was appointed to lead this formidable army intended solely to intimidate Paris. Thiers could not accept the idea of a Paris Commune, and in spite of the elections which had brought it to power, he refused to recognize that it had any legal force. In his mind, it had to be destroyed at whatever cost, even if it meant giving Paris over to fire and slaughter and killing thousands of people.

The situation in Paris was extraordinary. Surrounded for the second time, it was facing its second siege, against a second enemy within the space of six months. The news from the provinces was disturbing. No sooner had the news of the revolutionary movement in Paris become known than Communes had sprung up spontaneously in Marseilles, Lyons, Saint-Étienne, Le Creusot, Limoges, Toulouse and Narbonne. One after another, they were crushed by the government forces. Everywhere there was the same tale of death and executions. The capital stood alone, even more isolated than it had been during the Prussian siege, its future bounded, in space if not in time, by the proximity of Versailles, and yet all the time the mild spring weather continued with its deceptive promise of eternity.

But the sorties beyond the city limits took a high toll in lives and there were few districts which did not already have their dead to mourn. In the rue Monsieur-le-Prince,

Charlotte and Valerie learned of the death of Millau, killed under the guns of Mont Valérien on 3 April. He had enlisted in the National Guard at the same time as Gabin after returning, on 4 September, from the camp at Châlons where he had spent the entire period of the Alsace campaign without firing a single shot. They had seen little of him since then as he spent all his leave with a girl friend in Montmartre.

The news of Millau's death came as a real grief to both women but especially to Valerie who had known him better. It was difficult to grasp the fact of his death at second hand. There seemed no connection between Millau, the stocky bull-like boy from Provence, and Millau dead at Mont Valérien.

Charlotte had stayed in Paris despite the fact that she could have gone to join her family in Niort or even to Juvisy for the summer. What kept her there was partly Thomas's child, but equally the hope of a letter from Frank, which never came, although she did not give up hope. It seemed to her that by leaving Paris she would be renouncing that hope once and for all.

Despite what he had said, Thomas had not yet come to take the child. He had written to Charlotte twice excusing himself and asking her to be patient because he had not yet found a suitable nurse.

Illa and Hertz were still living with Charlotte. Gabin was in barracks not far off and came from time to time. Charlotte found their presence more and more trying, but she was even more afraid of sending them away and being left alone. The days fell into a monotonous, unvarying rhythm. Hope came in the morning with waking, faded towards noon, died altogether by three and was reborn with the dusk. It was always the same wild, impossible hope that today he must come. Whenever there was a ring at the door, the hope that it might be Frank made her heart leap painfully. He had not written and therefore it seemed to her he must come unexpectedly. The hope both justified and sustained her in the long, disappointing wait for a letter from him.

But the hope was short-lived. It was never Frank, only a neighbor or the concierge. The illusion passed but the violence of her hope remained, like a physical pain. And yet, as time went by, her memory began to fail her from constantly picturing Frank standing there at the door, how he would look, with his fair hair and strange, foreign air. In the end it hardly seemed to her possible that this Frank of her dreams could ever have set foot inside her humdrum apartment. Had he ever been there? If so, why had he left no tangible trace of himself behind to haunt the rooms? Perhaps, after all, he was only a figment of her exhausted imagination?

And so, each day the hope that Frank would come came and went like some fleeting state of grace. It was then she wanted Thomas and waited for him in a fever of expectation, although she knew that he too would not come. It was the only living moment of her day.

Paris in the spring seemed to her calm and carefree, too carefree perhaps. Many people had gone away. In the middle of the day, when most people were having their meal, there was hardly a soul to be seen in the streets apart from a few Federate soldiers hanging about the Luxembourg Gardens. It might have been any small garrison town. In the empty squares, footsteps echoed in the sunshine.

Posters were everywhere. There were women's clubs which met in the churches. At Saint-Sulpice, there was a club in the daytime and services in the evening. All over the city, women were to be seen dressed as Federates with trousers, caps and guns. Time stood still with danger all around. Paris waited. Charlotte and Hertz roamed the apartment, Hertz seeming to withdraw each day a little more into an ever-diminishing series of concentric circles, except for his one window on the sky. Charlotte believed him almost totally insane. She knew she should persuade him to seek treatment but she did nothing, half conniving in his madness.

One evening when Charlotte came home, Illa told her that a young man had been there asking for her. He had left his name, Jean Frémoy, which meant nothing to her. It appeared that this was the second time he had called. He wanted to see Charlotte and he had been very insistent that she should call on him in the rue des Écoles where he lived, saying that it was very important. Charlotte was surprised because she had heard nothing of his first visit. She asked Illa whether he had given any hint of what had brought him. No, he had said nothing, but he had been very pressing. He had seemed quite a presentable young man and Illa suggested that the next day they should leave Valerie to look after the children and go together to the rue des Écoles.

It was a fine day and there were plenty of people in the streets. The rue des Écoles was a quiet, provincial-looking street just off the busy boulevard Saint-Michel. The buildings here were new and rather depressing. Jean Frémoy lived in a furnished student hostel, its hallway adorned with two enormous bronze torch-bearers. Frémoy lived on the third floor. Young men came and went. Suddenly, as Charlotte knocked, the anxiety which had been with her since the night before and which had made her come so quickly in answer to the summons, took on a keener edge. She was not only worried now, she was afraid.

Her eye took in the small, untidy room, the corner of the street just visible through the open window. Jean Frémoy, who had opened the door, was a small, dark young man with a moustache. He looked uncomfortable and kept running his hand through his hair. All this she took in. It seemed harmless enough and yet she knew that what this ordinary-looking boy had to tell her was something terrible.

"I took the liberty of calling on you, madame," he said when she told him her name. "That is I had already called, in September or the beginning of October, I can't remember exactly—you see, I was worried that I had not given the letter into your own hand. Not, of course, that I doubted that the gentleman would have given it to you but you know how it is, madame, afterwards I thought to myself: suppose anything happened and the gentleman was not able to give you the letter. How could I know —because you see—but please, won't you come in, sit down I expected to hear from you. I thought you would want to know—it would be only natural. But then you did not come. And, well, in short, I was worried. I had to know—"

Charlotte stared at him with huge eyes. She knew already, instinctively, what he was going to say. She spoke in a faint voice.

"I did not receive the letter, monsieur."

"I feared it must be so. You will need all your courage, madame. I have something very dreadful to tell you."

Her eyes widened with horror.

"It's Frank, isn't it? He's dead?"

"Yes. God knows, I would have given anything not to have to tell you this so brutally. Frank Worski was killed in August at the battle of Saint-Privat, madame. I was not in his regiment myself, you understand. I had it all from Mathias, who was taken prisoner with me at the beginning of September as we were being taken into Belgium. Frank Worski died in his arms but before he died, he made Mathias promise to write to his wife. I had made up my mind to run for it, to escape, you see, and my friend Mathias wrote this letter and asked me, if I managed to get as far as Paris, to deliver it to you. I did this, madame, and I promise you I have no idea why you did not receive it."

Jean Frémoy was clearly out of his depth with the tragedy taking place in his room. He felt he had become involved in something that was no concern of his and, while earnestly protesting his good faith, he was embarrassed and at the same time intrigued by the reactions of the young woman sitting opposite him. She neither moved nor spoke and the sight of the two women sitting there so calmly in his anonymous student lodgings made Frémoy feel absurdly like an executioner.

"To whom did you give the letter?" Illa asked timidly at last, seeing that Charlotte said nothing.

"I gave it to the person who opened the door, madame. I asked for Madame Worski and the gentleman said this was the place and that he would give Madame Worski my letter when she returned. I understood him to be a relative of yours, Madame—"

Charlotte rose. She had to go. Out in the street, Illa moved to take her arm but Charlotte refused. She walked on in silence. Frank was dead. He would never come back now. Frank, the orphan, the man without a country, had died for France. But it was not what he died for that mattered. Frank had not been made for life and now, thinking of him, it seemed astonishing that such an unquiet, flamelike spirit should ever really have lived among the dull, complicated lives of ordinary people. She saw him again, as she had seen him those first times, serious, unstable as a child, prevented by his race and his unhappy childhood from reaching any compromise with his own nature. Even about his beauty, there was something strange and unusual in a world where men's faces showed the marks of appetite even in youth.

Charlotte turned her back on Frank as he was. She did not ask herself what might have become of him had he returned. Just as, in absence, she had idealized him, so now, in death, she fixed him in one unalterable image. It did not occur to her that she had nothing really to remember him by, none of the many little personal things on which memory feeds. There were no frenzied, youthful ambitions, no wrongs to forgive, no lies or weaknesses such as Frédéric had had. Frank had had none of those. He was like a rough diamond. He had all the brilliance of youth but none of the contradictions which make it bearable. Frank's youth had been unbearable and it was the fascination of the angel which had made Charlotte suffer for his sake.

But Charlotte was incapable of judging Frank. He was dead. He would never return. For her, Frank's death was an outrage and her grief was boundless. She walked the streets, seeing the world around her with Frank's dead eyes, as a world of insubstantial light where life was no more than a fleeting shadow.

When they reached the rue Monsieur-le-Prince Charlotte went quickly upstairs without speaking. Illa stood trembling in the passage while she rapped on Hertz's door.

His first reaction, when he opened it, was to stare in astonishment at Charlotte's frozen countenance.

"Give me my letter, at once."

Her tone brooked no denial and Hertz did not attempt one. He turned and began fumbling in a drawer. Charlotte watched him, standing with his back to her searching, with shaking hands, among the tumbled linen.

"Why did you do it, Hertz?" she asked him tensely.

He did not answer but went on with his search. She saw that his shoulders were shaking violently.

"Why did you do it? You are mad, Hertz, mad!"

"It is not true. He is not dead. There is no official proof, only that letter from some stranger who could say anything. He could be wrong—even official sources can be wrong—you cannot trust it, it's only a piece of paper—they brought my wife a piece of paper saying that I was dead and she married again, just as you will no doubt marry Becque without waiting—are you in such a hurry to believe that letter, to wipe Frank from your life?"

She stepped towards him threateningly. "You are mad, Hertz, utterly mad!" she told him fiercely. Hertz was sweating and there was a wild look in his eyes. He was afraid of her. "Leave this house—take your things and go. I never want to see you again—"

With one hand she snatched the letter and with the other she began tossing the clothes out of the drawers and throwing them on the ground. Hertz fell on his knees and began gathering them up wretchedly.

Illa stood in the doorway almost in tears.

"Charlotte, do not send him away, I beg you. Where will he go? You know he has no money."

Charlotte's anger was immediately transferred to her sister-in-law, whose gentleness at that moment seemed an intolerable crime.

"No," she cried furiously. "Hertz is right, Illa! No one is to be trusted. I betrayed Étienne and Étienne betrayed me. Gabin has deceived you, too. It is the same everywhere. We are all liars. Our whole lives are made up of lies and treachery. We are weak and faithless, through and through. But now I have done with it all for ever. I shall be faithful to Frank as long as I live and that he is dead makes no difference. He should never have married me! I was no better than a whore!"

Her anger dropped from her suddenly. The words had lost their power. She felt only astonishment at what she had said to Illa and she was ashamed to see Hertz crouching on the ground picking up the clothes which she had flung there. The days of her grand youthful tantrums, half-way between tragedy and farce, were long past. Frank was dead and there was something in her which wanted only to be quiet.

"Forgive me, Illa, that was a stupid thing to say and you know I did not mean a word of it."

Illa's green eyes were limpid pools untroubled by emotion but her face had gone a shade paler. She forced herself to smile. "Yes, Charlotte, I know—Gabin has deceived me, too, but that is over now and forgotten and we are happy as we were before."

Charlotte felt suddenly humble. She thought: she is better than I. I have always thought her a fool when all the time she had more real goodness than I have. And there must be thousands and thousands of people in the world who are better than I, who thought herself so superior.

This was a truth that only yesterday her pride would have refused to face. Yesterday she still believed in her own value. But Frank was dead, and by his death had taken away her chief claim to glory. Now, there was nothing left but the endless months of war, the humbling daily round. Without Frank, all her spirit was gone. Now she was only a woman like all the rest, tired, frightened and alone. She began to shiver and to feel a dreadful pity for Hertz, scrabbling on his knees on the carpet, dreadful because it was on the extreme verge of that sense of the ridiculous which is the death of pity.

But Hertz had passed that line too often since coming to live with her. Poor man. Charlotte understood and forgave the motive which had driven him to keep the letter from her. Obsessed as he was by the defection of his own wife, he could not help identifying the situation with his own. He could not be accused of opening a letter not addressed to him because Jean Frémoy had been explicit as to the reasons for his visit and the contents of the letter he had to deliver.

"Get up, Hertz. Of course I don't mean to throw you out. You can stay."

It crossed her mind that outside they would put him in

an asylum. She would keep him, indeed she was almost a party to his delusions. He too was an outcast, with his insane ideas, his whirling heavens, and perhaps because of that she would protect him, because Frank too had been to some extent an outcast from society.

Charlotte took the letter which Frémoy had given to Hertz to her room. It was, as he had said, written by someone called Mathias from a prisoner-of-war camp in Belgium. There were four pages torn from a school exercise book written in a careful, unpractised hand, describing Frank's death at the battle of Saint-Privat on 8 August. Frank had acted with outstanding courage and heroism against the Prussians, encouraging his companions by his example and continuing to hold his part of the plateau against vastly superior enemy forces, while the bulk of the French army was beginning to fall back.

Frank had died a hero's death as he was bound to do. All or nothing was his nature. But Charlotte read and re-read the letter, searching poor Mathias's labored prose, this vision of some allegorical figure of Frank offering up his youth before the German guns, for some small human weakness, some detail to which her grief might cling. But every line of Mathias' letter breathed admiration and a kind of devoted memory which almost precluded sorrow at his death. Mathias must have written that letter so that she, Charlotte, should be proud, as he was proud of the matchless and unforgettable comrade whom fate had set beside him to his everlasting astonishment. Frank would live on in the memory and admiration of this loyal, unknown Mathias at least, and it was this thought which finally broke down the barrier and made Frank's death real to her.

Throughout the whole of April, Thomas did not set foot in the rue Monsieur-le-Prince. He had still not found a nurse for the baby. The matter had proved too difficult, although he had written to Charlotte constantly saying that he would find one. This, however, began to seem daily more problematical as he rejected one after another. He was reluctant to go and see Charlotte again from a feeling that, little as such inflexibility appealed to him, he could not go back on his last words to her. The war and Marie's death had combined to break his pride but now it was Charlotte who did not wish to see him. He understood this when she let him know that she would send the child to the square with Illa at certain fixed times and he could see him there whenever he wished. Illa, who was in the habit of taking her own small girl, would now take both children.

Thomas went several times to the Luxembourg Gardens and once or twice Illa came as far as the place Furstenberg. They stood and chatted while Thomas looked at the baby who, at four months' old, was quite amazingly like him for all his infant plumpness. Thomas did not attempt to make Illa talk about Charlotte. In any case, she seemed to him very shy and a little awkward in his company. However, Illa saw a good deal more than she appeared to. Once, when Thomas did permit himself to ask news of Charlotte, he had the impression that Illa was going to tell him something important but she changed her mind and afterwards he wondered if he had been mistaken.

Thomas himself had recovered a certain hopeful outlook on life which Illa found attractive. She liked him very much and sensed that he was a man who needed happiness. She never mentioned Frank's death because Charlotte had forbidden her to do so, but although she lacked the courage to go against Charlotte's expressed wishes it troubled her that there should be this lie between herself and Thomas. She would have preferred him to know the truth.

At the beginning of May, Thomas told Illa that he had found a nurse at Gentilly who would probably serve the purpose but as he was very busy and had no time to go and see her, there the matter rested. It also happened that just then the baby had a slight cold and Illa did not take him out for a fortnight, while Thomas could not bring himself to call on Charlotte in person. On 20 May, he was surprised to meet Illa in the place Furstenberg. The German girl was pushing the baby carriage and had brought a letter from Charlotte. Thomas read it quickly. In it, she said that she was obliged to leave Paris for a while and that she wanted to see him in order to settle the matter of the monthly allowance he was paying her for the child's keep. She asked him to meet her the following evening in a café on the boulevard Saint-Michel.

Thomas was surprised at the curt tone of the letter and angry with Charlotte for going to such lengths to create a mystery about nothing.

"She has to go to Niort to see her family," Illa explained.

"She has every right to go!"

He was bitterly angry and disappointed. He knew then that he had not ceased to hope, even though she was married and despite his earnest endeavors to be no more to her than a disinterested well-wisher.

The next day, 21 May, was a fine, spring day and life in Paris went on as usual. In the latin quarter, the day wore on quietly towards evening. Thomas was to meet Charlotte at half past six. In the meanwhile, he went to the brasserie Glazer in the rue Saint-Séverin intending to write. There he met Paul Boucher and Chaptal. Boucher seemed nervous and on edge. At six, Thomas left telling Paul he was meeting someone at the café de Cluny.

A calm, mild evening. The strollers on the boulevard and people sitting at the café tables, gave it an almost carefree air. Thomas reached the café de Cluny and saw Charlotte. She had not come alone. She was with Gabin and Illa. He greeted them civilly. Gabin rose and Charlotte held out her hand. He thought she was looking pretty, thinner, but with a tight little face that he did not like. He was conscious from the first that she seemed very remote and although he had promised himself to behave towards her purely as a friend, he found himself unexpectedly hurt by her attitude. To begin with, they talked of nothing in particular until Gabin, who seemed to have no great relish for the meeting, went off to watch a game of billiards in the back room, leaving Thomas alone with the two women. It was after sunset but the street lamps had not yet been lit. The café was filling up and people were strolling up and down the boulevard in the deepening twilight. Illa sat quietly. For all the comfort that her presence brought them, Thomas and Charlotte might as well have been alone. Charlotte explained that she was going to Niort and that she must ask him to take the child back next day. Thomas agreed.

"And thank you again," he said, "for everything you have done. I will never forget. I only wish that I could do the same for you—" He spoke with real warmth. He felt a strong desire to take her hand, to try and imbue her with some of his own strength and hopefulness. What was the matter with her tonight? Surely the past was dead? Surely, now at last they could be friends?

He talked about the baby, purposely trying to draw her into a discussion of humdrum, everyday affairs. He hoped the thought of the child would disarm her but it did not. Then he turned the talk to current events, to the Commune and what plans could be made for the future. He had a kind of optimism now, a will to be happy. He had changed. He saw things more simply. He wished he could make her see that life was simple, that with just a little care, happiness could be there in your hands. At all costs he wanted to break down this shell of indifference which divided them. He did not want their last meeting to be this fiasco. He did his best, he did everything he could have done but Illa, watching and listening, could see that, little by little, his impatience was breaking through.

At last he broke out suddenly:

"What is the matter? Why are you like this?"

He had reached the end of his patience. It hurt him that she should insist on spoiling everything to the very end.

"Nothing. We were talking about the child—"

"No, you were not talking about the child. You are miles away. You are not even listening. You cannot do me the favor of a smile and you will leave me like that, with nothing, without a word. Do I count for so little in your affection? Is even common kindness forbidden us? What is it, Charlotte? I cannot believe that it is Illa's presence that embarrasses you."

Charlotte looked at him blankly, as though not seeing him at all.

"You have no right to behave like this," he said furiously. "I have been your friend, Charlotte, do not forget that."

Surely she could see the pain she was inflicting? Her mind was wrapped up in Frank. It was quite natural to her to sacrifice Thomas to Frank, to let him suffer and give himself away clumsily like a man wounded in his pride.

He stared at her grimly in silence.

"Very well. I wish you happiness and I hope for your sake, my dear, that your Frank comes back soon because let me tell you you are doing yourself no good—"

Another minute and this sudden hatred and contempt would make him unforgivably vulgar and cruel.

"Frank will not come back," Illa said suddenly. "He was killed in Alsace, in August."

Thomas turned and stared at Illa, then his eyes went back to Charlotte. She met his gaze in silence. She saw that he had aged in these last weeks. The fragile skin below his blue eyes, while not exactly wrinkled, looked creased. It was the look of a man who had suffered. The eyes which had been so warm a moment before were hard now, almost menacing. There was a pause and then he said: "How long have you known this?"

He was suddenly sure that she had known for a long time. He remembered Illa's unaccountable embarrassment when they met in the gardens and the way in which, weeks ago, Charlotte had coldly set about erasing him from her life. He had believed she was merely respecting his wish not to frequent the house.

"How long?" he said again harshly.

"What does it matter?" she said uncertainly. Her face was very pale.

"Can you ask?"

The reproach in his eyes flayed her. She rose, trying to put an end to the interview. Her feelings made speech almost impossible.

"Frank is not dead to me. He will never be, do you understand?" When he did not take his eyes off her she repeated the word: "Never, never."

Thomas knew that "never" was meant for him, for his demands and his determination to make her live with him at all costs, any kind of life so long as it was with him. Charlotte's eyes were fixed on the sky above the café terrace where one lone star was rising slowly above the roof tops. She watched it, fascinated. She had seen it once before.

Now the star was over the chimney pots. Charlotte leaned so far backwards that she had to grip the table to save herself from falling. When next she looked at Thomas, there was a visionary light in her eyes. He stood before her, as pale as she.

"You are killing us both, and this time you are doing it deliberately."

He had not thought she could still make him suffer like this. The longing to slap her face hard held him paralyzed. He hated that ecstatic expression of hers, hated Frank's memory and all the unbridled romanticism of her nature, her foolishness. And hated them both for the hurt their youth had done to him.

This was the end. This time, he was going for good. But not yet. She had dealt him a staggering blow and now he had his chance to see just what ties and what passionate hopes still bound him to her. Worse, he could see how irrational those hopes had been.

He was on the point of saying that he would take the child tomorrow when there was a sudden bustle out in the street. The glass door was flung open and Thomas saw, to his astonishment, Paul Boucher making his way hurriedly towards him.

"The Versailles forces are in Paris. A courier has just got through with the news. They carried the porte de Saint-Cloud at four o'clock. The news only reached the Hôtel de Ville an hour ago. There seem to be two columns making for the center of the city, one by the avenue de Versailles the other by the porte d'Auteuil."

The news had spread the length of the street in an instant. The traffic was brought to a standstill and companies began forming up in the middle of the roadway.

"This time," Paul said, "it's serious."

Thomas looked at Charlotte.

"At any rate, it is too late now for your plans for

leaving. I must ask you to keep the child a few more days—if you will."

He spoke coldly. Charlotte gave her consent with a nod. She felt Thomas suddenly removed from her, caught up again in a life where she had no place, while the noise and bustle in the street seemed to cut her down to her own infinitesimal size. Thomas, seeing the apparent indifference with which she reacted to the new situation, thought that surely not even Frank's memory could hold her so apart from the world around her. How could he ever have thought that she could be truly his wife when they were united by no common ideals, when she did not know even what he was fighting for? Did she even know that in the days to come they might be called upon to die? He wondered in sudden contempt if she could even cook. He brushed past her to the door without so much as a word of farewell. She saw him go up the boulevard with Boucher and some others. Voices were crying: "To the barricades!" Already, people were tearing up the cobblestones at the crossroads. The whole district was in a ferment as carriages were overturned and furniture brought out from the houses to form barricades. Gabin told the two women to go home. He himself was returning to duty with the National Guard. Charlotte and Illa made their way back to the apartment, stopping first to pick up what milk they could find in the shops. It was too late now to think of flight and in any case there was nowhere they could go. They had to stay where they were with the children. Barricades went up during the night, one across the rue Soufflot, another in the rue Gay-Lussac opposite the Luxembourg. There were others on the Montagne Saint-Geneviève, the rue des Écoles, the rue des Boulangers and elsewhere. Everywhere there was a constant nervous activity. Vallès shuttled back and forth between the fifth and sixth arrondissements.

The night seemed very short. The next day brought bad news for the defenders. The Versailles forces had captured and held the gare Saint-Lazare and carried out hideous reprisals. Thiers' armies gave no quarter and shot all prisoners and civilians indiscriminately. At Montparnasse, five women had been shot.

There were now barricades along the whole length of the boulevard Saint-Michel. By midday, the enemy had reached the observatory.

The first night, Thomas and Paul Boucher fell asleep at last a little before dawn in a room at the Mairie. The next day, the guard were encamped in the place du Panthéon.

On the 22nd, the attackers overran a large area of the right bank. The next day, a flanking movement threatened to encircle the latin quarter. Wherever they went, the advancing forces left a trail of dead behind them. In the frenzied blood-lust that was on them even children were not spared.

On the day, those of the local inhabitants who had not taken the precaution of leaving Paris together, spent the day in the cellars, emerging in the evening when they found that there was no immediate danger.

On the Tuesday morning, Charlotte went out to try and buy some food, and in particular milk for the children. She was alone with Illa and the two babies, Hertz having gone off to fight, no one knew where. Once outside, she found herself in a strange city of empty streets. There was no movement except for the wind blowing up the dust and fallen plaster in the roadway, but there was an ever-present feeling of some secret life going on behind the barricades. The shops were all shut, with metal shutters drawn across the windows. Charlotte walked aimlessly for a long time. The day was hot and the latin quarter like a dead city, with now and then a perilous hive of activity in the roadway where death lurked in waiting. It was this waiting silence, more than the sound of gunfire or galloping horses, that was most horrifying. Charlotte had lived within herself in these last weeks, now she found herself useless and bewildered in a deserted city. She made her way up the boulevard, pausing at the far end in sudden panic, wondering where her brother Gabin was, or Paul, or Thomas, in this empty desert. She loosened the neck of her dress. She felt as though she were suffocating. Suddenly, she began to run, half hoping to hear the dreaded hoofbeat of the enemy galloping behind her, to feel the bayonet slide into her back. But it was only a cart clattering by, carrying weapons to the defenders. Charlotte watched it go from the shelter of the doorway. She crossed herself and began to pray. Then she saw the figure of another woman waiting in the doorway by herself and saw with surprise that it was Delphine Delobelle, who had returned from Provence the previous month. She was pregnant and Frédéric, who had enlisted at the beginning of the war, was a prisoner in Belgijm.

Delphine stared at her with her huge brown eyes without a word. Charlotte left the doorway and began to run again. Struck at last by the absurdity of running aimlessly about this empty city, she stopped dead in a gateway and got her breath back; but she reached home empty-handed. Luckily, Valerie still had a little milk left and later on Jean Corta gave them some food from his reserve store. They thanked him effusively. What they feared more than anything else was having no food for the children.

Everyone knew this respite could not last. All that day, the advance continued. The defenders fell back, time and again. Then suddenly, the first shots were fired from the Luxembourg barricade. It sounded dreadfully heavy. They went down to the cellar.

The men watched from behind the barricade in the rue Soufflot as the enemy troops advanced. They included a detachment of the National Guard and a handful of civilians. Gabin was there. With the first volley they had succeeded in making the enemy fall back. Gabin watched with interest. It was the first time he had fought. He was afraid but his fear only seemed to heighten his awareness.

There came a lull and for an hour the rue Soufflot basked in apparent peace. The young leaves on the trees showed pale green in the bright spring sunshine. At about three o'clock, Gabin saw reinforcements coming from the Montagne Saint-Geneviève. Among them were Thomas and Paul Boucher and one or two other civilians whom he knew.

By the end of the afternoon the situation had become grave. The enemy were infiltrating throughout the latin quarter. There was fighting in the place de la Sorbonne, at the junction of the rue Champollion and the rue des Écoles, and as far as the rue des Boulangers and the rue Monge. The barricade in the rue Soufflot, which commanded the whole of the roadway by the Panthéon and included two *mitrailleuses* and a number of other weapons in its armory, held out against the advancing troops. One attack was beaten off but before long the situation began to look less hopeful as agents of Versailles slipped in among the Federates, sowing discord and spreading rumors of disaster.

Fierce fighting went on long after nightfall, until it was too dark to see. The defenders had many wounded and hardly any medical aid. A doctor was carrying out urgent amputations in a room at the *mairie* with the help of two nuns.

The remaining tenants of the rue Monsieur-le-Prince were all down in the cellar. Besides Charlotte, Illa and the children, there was only Valerie and her little girl, the Delobelles with the pregnant Delphine, and the Cortas. For light they had two hurricane lamps and the children had been put to sleep on makeshift beds between the racks of bottles. All afternoon, they had listened to the continual fusillades from the barricades by the Luxembourg and the rue Gay-Lussac. It was too dark in the cellar for them to have any idea when darkness fell outside and it seemed as though they must stay there all night. Charlotte wanted desperately to take the children upstairs. After all, it could make little difference.

The Delobelles were in their own part of the cellar which happened to be next to Charlotte's. Delphine was asleep on the ground, wrapped up in a coat. Madame Delobelle sat bewailing her fate while her husband walked up and down the passage outside with its smell of coal dust and stale wine. Jean Corta had been sitting for hours with his nose in a huge book. His womenfolk were very quiet. Madame Cazingues was sitting on a folding chair in the passage with her cat on her knee, talking to it from time to time. It was a large black tom with a collar fastened tightly round its neck, and it spent much of the time yowling and struggling to escape from its mistress's frenzied grip.

Delobelle was depressing everyone by his insistence that the Versailles forces would blow up the Panthéon.

"They'll take us all out and shoot us," Madame Cazingues wailed piteously, "and you, Quiqui, they'll kill you too."

"Oh, be quiet," Jean Corta told her irritably.

"It's all very well for you," Delobelle rounded on him sharply. "I should be looking just as relaxed if I were Swiss. But don't be too sure, they may not bother to ask for your passport before they shoot you."

Corta glanced up at Delobelle.

"I should be surprised if they shot you for sympathizing with the Commune, Monsieur Delobelle," he said sardonically. "You have made no attempt to conceal your feelings towards these 'ruffians,' as you term them."

"And why should I?"

"Then you will not expect us to believe that you are in any danger from reprisals."

"Anyone may fear for his life in such circumstances."

"And with the company some people in this house are not ashamed to keep, no one is safe," his wife muttered through her teeth.

Charlotte heard and knew the gibe was meant for her but she said nothing and glanced across at Valerie, who was in her own section of the cellar with Clarisse. Neither could see Madame Delobelle but they could picture her behind the partition. The little individual cubicles were very small and every word could be heard through the open doors. Delobelle was silent. He was badly frightened but not prepared to support his wife's intervention. Besides his dislike of her domineering nature, he felt a sneaking sympathy for Charlotte, and even for Thomas Becque, in whose sharp and effective writing he found much to admire. Unlike his wife, he was not by nature aggressive. He was a mild little man of moderate opinions and he had only one secret vice, his obsessive love for his daughter Delphine. The sight of her pregnant was a continual torment to him.

The firing had begun again in the direction of the Luxembourg. The guns seemed to make a fantastic noise, a staccato barking that rent the night air. They were followed by an icy silence. Charlotte wondered what time it was. She wished she could go upstairs but she dared not wake Illa and the babies, who were asleep.

"I want to go upstairs," she said quietly to Valerie.

"It's not a bad idea. My legs have gone to sleep on this stool."

Valerie stretched out her long legs. At that moment the cellar door, up at the foot of the stairs, opened noisily. Delobelle flattened himself against the wall.

"Who's there? If it's them, don't provoke them. You women pretend to be asleep. They'll see we are doing no harm—"

They listened. Youthful footsteps clattered down the dank steps. Two young men emerged into the fading light cast by the lamps. As far as they could see, the first, who wore the uniform of the regular army, was tall, fair and untidy.

Charlotte was the first to recognize him.

"Frédéric—"

The name alone was enough to rouse Delphine Delobelle from sleep. She sprang up and ran forward with a cry. Delobelle stared in horror.

"You, here? But I thought you were a prisoner—"

"Yes, Monsieur Delobelle, but I was taken over, together with thousands of other poor bastards in the same situation, and carted off to Versailles. There, they put guns in our hands and told us to start firing on you poor sods in Paris. I can tell you, I took the first chance of skipping over to the other side. Not that I've much truck with politics, I just naturally support the rebels, and anyway I don't like shooting men in the back. That's a good enough reason."

"Frédéric, you were at Versailles and you never came to see me," Delphine said reproachfully hugging him. He stroked her hair gently.

"I couldn't, my sweet. We weren't allowed out. But I've come for you, Charlotte—"

"For me!" Charlotte said in alarm.

"It's Gabin."

"What is it? What's happened?" Fear gripped her, sudden and unreasoning.

"I was with him in the rue Soufflot. He has been wounded, Charlotte—badly. They took him into a near-by house. You must go to him—one can still get through by the rue Cujas without too much trouble."

"I am coming."

"Do you want me to come with you?" Valerie asked.

"No, stay with Illa and the children. I shall be happier knowing you are with them. And thank you, Valerie, thank you—" She was so close to panic that she no longer knew what she was saying.

"Frédéric, take me with you," Delphine wailed pathetically.

"In your condition, are you mad! You'll stay here," her mother screamed at her, holding her back by force. But Delphine in love was a force to be reckoned with. The last Charlotte and Frédéric saw of her she was fighting desperately.

Outside the firing had died down. They slipped along the rue Cujas under cover of darkness. One or two isolated shots rang out in the crisp air. It was not very long before they reached the Panthéon and slipped in through a breach in the barricade which was opened for them. Charlotte saw civilians and National Guardsmen resting behind the sandbags. There were dead and wounded also. Gabin had been carried into one of the buildings and put in the room belonging to the concierge. It was very small and dark. Gabin was lying on a bed set in a narrow alcove, half his face smashed by a bullet. A second ball had perforated his lung. He was unconscious and his breathing was harsh. Charlotte stood looking at her brother. She could not bring herself to touch him. The concierge, a very old woman, was boiling water but there was nothing they could do.

"Gabin," Charlotte said softly, but she knew he could not hear her.

"There is no one to take care of the wounded," Frédéric said. "Only the surgeon at the *mairie*, who does what he can. There is nothing we can do."

"But we must go and fetch him, we must try and find someone—" She could not bear it. She had to do something—as though their fate were still in their own hands and brotherly love still counted for something. But that was the horror of civil war. It killed brothers. It struck like a curse, the curse of Cain. All this Charlotte felt and she reacted less in the hope of saving Gabin—she knew in her heart he was already lost—than a last desperate gesture of revolt against this divine punishment visited on all alike.

Her brother was dying here in this strange room without ever recovering consciousness. Had he even known the hand that struck him down? Had he known what he lived for, or what he left behind? A brother who was like a part of one's own body. Looking down on him as he lay dying, Charlotte could feel all the myriad invisible links of their childhood running between them like a tangible, unseen thread, binding them together again. There, in that small room where nothing was familiar, brother and sister seemed to be enclosed together in some subtle, uniting membrane. She was surprised the others did not see it and she wondered what this thing was that had joined her life to Gabin's for as long as she could remember, and what it would be like when he was dead.

Everything that had come between them in these last years was pared away, leaving only the kernel of their common childhood and the love they had felt for one another then. He turned his head and moaned and she saw the horrible gaping wound in his right cheek. She could not bear it. She could not stand hearing him moan. Her own helplessness appalled her.

"I am going to try and find someone," she said to Frédéric. She thought he was still standing behind her but there was only the old woman. She hurried out. Her terror at the thought of Gabin's death was an agony in her own flesh. Her whole body reacted to it. The moral and physical lethargy in which she had lived these past months was violently ripped apart and the fear of death gave her a shuddering, gasping lust for life such as she had not known since adolescence. She began to run along the street. People were coming and going in the pale light. Soldiers lay wounded and dying behind the barricades. But Charlotte was alone amid the crowd. Everything about her seemed real and yet unreal at the same time. The mood of the defenders was a strange mixture of horror, exultation and despair, of people determined to hold out until death. The atmosphere was both solemn and febrile and to Charlotte, in her panic, it held out no hope of individual safety.

She walked on, thinking of Frank dead and aware of Gabin's death as of some dreadful injury, the pain of which she could not yet wholly feel. She tensed herself, as though she sensed that death had not done with her yet. Her thoughts reached out blindly to her daughter, her mother, her family, mentally taking stock of everything that was left to her. Suddenly, she thought of Thomas, fighting somewhere in these streets. Suppose he, too, were to die. This was something she had never thought of, even once. She could bear the thought of leaving him, of his going far away from her, because what mattered was that he was still there, somewhere, that he still existed. That he might cease to exist was something wholly inadmissible. All the time they went on fighting and destroying one another, he was there. If he died, she too would cease to exist.

This was something she had never thought of. She had accepted Frank's death as natural, even logical. She had believed herself alone. But it was only if Thomas died that she would be truly alone forever.

She had to find Thomas. Several men were standing outside the Hôtel des Grands Hommes opposite the Panthéon, and among them Charlotte recognized one fat man as a journalist she had seen several times with Thomas. It was Chaptal. She asked if he had seen him. Chaptal told her that Thomas had been fighting that afternoon at the barricade on the Montagne Saint-Geneviève behind the École polytechnique.

"But don't go there. It's not safe."

But Charlotte was not listening. The only thing possible for her to do now in this desert where she roamed was to find Thomas. There was no point in going home.

The barricade was behind the church of Saint-Etienne-du-Mont. Someone helped Charlotte to scramble over.

At first, she could make out nothing more than vague, shadowy figures in the moonlight. There were Federates and civilians, as well as women and children who had come to join in the defense or to bring food to the defenders. Some were sitting, others moving about behind the barricade. The firing had ceased and would probably not begin again before dawn. Charlotte had begun to despair of ever finding Thomas when suddenly she saw Paul Boucher and realized at the same moment that Thomas was with him. Paul was propped against the bags of plaster which formed part of the barricade, gnawing at a piece of sausage. Thomas was half-sitting, half-lying on the ground. Paul saw her first.

"Well, here's Cassandra wandering among the ruins of Troy!"

Thomas looked up. He was exhausted, covered in dust and in no mood for speech. He watched in silence as Charlotte clambered over the bags and torn-up paving stones towards them. He could see in the moonlight she had been crying. Her face was streaked with tears and dust, her hair tumbled on her shoulders and she had lost her shawl. He guessed that something dreadful had happened. He and Paul had been at the barricades since early afternoon. Nearly all their reserves of ammunition, and of hope, were gone. The enemy would probably attack in force tomorrow morning and they would be too few to beat them off again. The dead lay everywhere. Theirs was the calm acceptance of despair.

Thomas looked at Charlotte and felt a fierce spasm of joy. He did not move. He felt too tired to get up but his eyes fastened on her as though by right. Paul offered his hand and she dropped to her knees beside them, covering her face with her hands.

"Gabin is dead."

The cobblestones bruised her knees and her back was bowed under a burden of grief. Thomas drew her to him and let her head fall on his shoulder, her face pressed into his grimy coat. He did not speak. He was resigned to the death that was all around them, to his own death, if it came, and to Charlotte's also if that were to be.

"Try and eat something," Paul said. "Hunger is stronger than death."

She shook her head. She sat down between them and Paul brushed her cheek gently.

"I am very fond of you, little one," he said. "And Thomas is very fond of you too. Aren't you, Thomas?"

His mocking laugh relieved the tension. Thomas took Charlotte's wrist and drew her closer until their cheeks touched.

"Thank you for coming. Stay like this. It's good to feel your cheek against mine."

"You are hurt," she said in alarm, feeling something warm under her hand.

"Nothing, a scratch."

"You can't stay here. Come home with me and rest. We can still get through the rue Cujas."

Paul made a show of making himself comfortable in the roadway. "You go on, I'm fine where I am."

"You'll come too," Charlotte said anxiously.

Thomas had risen.

"Yes, come on Paul."

Paul looked at Thomas and Charlotte standing awkwardly side by side, and burst out laughing.

"I do believe they are afraid to be alone! You are cowards, my children. But I think I will come after all. It will do me good to sleep in a bed."

In fact, they met no one on the way back through the rue Cujas. They went in silence, keeping close to the wall. Thomas and Charlotte both felt comforted by Paul's presence. Even now, they did not trust one another. They were horribly afraid of the happiness that could be theirs. Not for an instant could they turn their thoughts away from what tomorrow's dawn might bring, but now their love went with them, cutting them off from everything, from death and fear, and leading them into a state of grace and hope almost unbearable.

Charlotte made up beds for them in the salon and in Hertz's room. Hertz had been somewhere on the barricades, no one knew where, for two days now. She expected them to wake her at dawn but in fact they were up by two. They had thought to leave without waking her but she was a light sleeper and she heard them. She was up in an instant. It was still dark. Fear gripped her.

"Don't go. Thomas, I beg of you, don't go—you do not

374

stand a chance. You will all be killed. Stay with me, please—"

But even as she said it she knew he would not stay and let Paul go and face his fate alone and that, even if Paul were not there, he would still go.

"What is the use of risking your life now? There are too many of them and you have nothing—it is a useless sacrifice that will do no good to anyone." She knew that she had little right to talk of sacrifice, she who had never sacrificed herself for anything, and that they knew what they were doing.

"Thomas, come back," she cried desperately as they opened the door. There was no answer. He and Paul disappeared down the stairs. Charlotte was left murmuring to herself: "He will come back. I know he will. He must—"

The attack came even before daybreak. The barricade in the rue Soufflot fell at last and the defenders withdrew to the Montagne Saint-Geneviève, where one or two barricades were still holding out, and to the École polytechnique. The streets near the Luxembourg were strewn with corpses, men, women and children, soldiers and civilians, mown down indiscriminately. Bodies lay huddled in doorways and piled high in the Medici fountain and in the place Saint-Michel.

By eleven o'clock, the barricade at the Montagne Saint-Geneviève was also about to fall. The troops poured through. Becque and Paul Boucher were there with Frédéric and a thirteen-year-old named André, who had attached himself to the group of journalists and was loading Thomas's gun for him. He was a real street arab, vulgar, cocky and very brave.

By noon, the enemy had managed to get into the street and take the barricade in the rear. There was a cry of warning as the fusillade poured into the defenders' backs. They flung themselves to the ground, but they were outnumbered by ten to one. They were overwhelmed, disarmed, and driven out from behind their improvised ramparts with blows from rifle butts.

The sun was at its height and it was very hot. The prisoners were herded into the place du Panthéon where they joined other captives taken in the rue Saint-Jacques already lined up against the walls of the church of Saint-Etienne-du-Mont. Thomas and Paul, still dazzled by the brilliant sunshine in the square after the deep, shaded streets, blinked at the spectacle which met their eyes.

A hundred or so Federates, some fifteen of them women, were lined up against the wall in the full sunlight, while facing them the soldiers were already taking aim. Seen like that, with the wall for a background, they looked a multitude. Even now, Thomas could not accept that it could happen. They cannot shoot, he thought. The soldiers fired. The prisoners fell, like dolls. It all happened so quickly that there was barely time to glimpse the face of even one of the victims. One felt rather than saw the white faces staring for one shocked instant into the eyes of their killers, before it was all over. There were only the anonymous bodies. The very speed only added to the horror and contempt of these summary executions.

"This time," Paul said tonelessly, "it's all up. We're done for."

In a few minutes they would be dead, yet even now their minds refused to grapple with the dreadful end that awaited them. Just for an instant, Paul's short-sighted eyes met Thomas's. Paul had always boasted himself a coward but if in that moment he was afraid, he did not show it. His face was calm, almost too calm. He had already accepted death. It was the sight of this resignation in Paul's expression which produced in Thomas a sudden violent revolt.

"No," he muttered to Paul quickly. "I will not let myself be slaughtered in cold blood like some unclean animal."

He thought of Charlotte. He wanted to see her once again, at least. Paul, still looking at Becque, saw one of the soldiers raise a rifle butt and strike him in the face to make him move on. The prisoners were crowded too closely to allow for movement. Thomas stepped back suddenly and with one massive blow from his right arm, sent the soldier sprawling.

It was the confusion that followed that saved Thomas. Other soldiers fired into the crowd and began thrusting the Federates up against the wall to make an end of the business. Two sprang after Thomas, firing as they ran. Paul hurled himself at the legs of one of them as he aimed. The soldier turned his weapon and killed him instantly with two shots in the head. All the soldiers were firing now and the bodies fell on top of those that died before. Thomas ran straight along the wall of the church and, without thinking, plunged in through a side door. The soldiers had already entered through the main doorway and the building rang with the sounds of pursuit. Thomas started down a passage at the back of the nave leading towards the sacristy.

The abbé Huet was there and saw him. Thomas knew the man because he had been pressed into service by the communards to help with the wounded.

"They are after you?" the abbé asked.

"Yes."

"Get in there." The abbé thrust him towards an alcove filled with ecclesiastical vestments.

There was the sound of footsteps in the vaulted passage. The abbé went out and Thomas heard voices. The soldiers were accusing the abbé of Federate sympathies. He had been seen associating with them. The Abbé said that he had had no choice, which was true, but he was taken out and shot. Thomas, in the sacristy, felt the sweat break out on his forehead as he heard the shots.

Still no one came. Thomas listened to the unexpected silence, amazed to be still alive. He went back into the nave, almost ready to give himself up, but there was no one there. The pursuit must have passed on towards the rue Monge. Thomas slipped into a corner and waited, dazed by the silence in the church, which was in agonizing contrast to the firing which was still going on in the square outside. It continued, volley after volley, all afternoon. At last they must have grown tired of killing because the guns fell silent.

Still Thomas did not move. His cheek was bleeding from a blow from a rifle butt. He felt sick. If it had not been for the desire to see Charlotte at least once more he would have walked out openly and let himself be mown down with the rest.

He went back to the sacristy and settled himself in a

377

niche in the wall to wait for dark. As soon as the light had gone he left his hiding place, prepared to risk capture. It was bright moonlight like the night before. There were still troops in the square but they had gathered at the other end because of the corpses, some of which were still lying where they fell, and the light from their camp fires did not reach the church.

Crouching and hugging the walls, Thomas made his way across the place du Panthéon, running from one patch of shadow to the next. There was blood on his face and every now and then he stumbled against the corpses which lay with outstretched arms, one upon another on the pavement. The moonlight gleamed on dead eyes, waking them to a hint of madness. The horror of this murdered multitude was something inhuman. Like a curse. Forgive them, Lord, for they know not what they do. Thomas ran on wildly, as though nothing could stop him. He reached Charlotte's house alive, dashed wildly up the stairs and rang the bell. Charlotte opened the door. When she saw Thomas, she clung to him without a word, then dragged him inside. She saw the blood on his face and made as though to fetch some water but he held her back. He was past speech. His eyes were still full of the horror they would never forget.

"I knew you would come. I was waiting for you."

She stroked his cheek softly, soothingly.

"Say something, anything, just to hear the sound of your voice. And it will do you good."

He could not speak. He could not even sit down. He stood there, mute and paralyzed. But it was warm and quiet in the apartment and suddenly he heard his child crying. Thomas caught Charlotte to him and held her fast.

"You are here, my love—we are together, you and I." Their eyes met as though for the first time. Their faces were drawn with suffering and only their eyes seemed alive.

"They killed Paul and the kid. They killed them all. An orgy of hatred. Why? Why?" The tears ran down his face.

"It is all over. There is no escape. But you are here, my

love—hold me and let me feel you are alive—sweetheart, let me hear you say my name."

Misery had made him almost drunk. After the hell that he had been through, to be with her was too much happiness.

"I don't think I shall even have the strength—oh, sweetheart—one needs so much strength to love, so much strength to be happy." His hand shook as he caressed her face. The body which used to make her feel so small and weak lay like a dead weight against her.

"You need rest, come and sleep," she said.

He shook his head. Their hours were numbered. This might be the last night they would have together, and in a sense it would also be their first. They lay close together, feeling a mutual weight of love and tenderness. Nothing could come between them now or disturb the perfect sweetness or fulfilment of the love that lay between them.

"My love, let the night be long and may the dawn never come."

But dawn came at last. The window showed white between the undrawn curtains. The sky above Paris was red, red with the flame of the Commune. That bloody sky put an end to any hopes of the new day. Standing together, at the window, they watched the dawn break. Their love was proof against anything now. It was the end and the beginning of a new life.

The clatter of booted feet on the stairs. They did not move. They knew already. There was a knock. Charlotte closed the bedroom door and went to open. The officers were outside.

"This is a search. You are hiding a Federate here."

They pushed past her. She watched as they began kicking open the doors. Thomas was ready for them.

"You are Thomas Becque, journalist?"

"I am."

"You must come with us."

"Thomas—" He pushed her away firmly.

"Stay there."

But she ran down the stairs after them. The other

379

tenants were out on the landing watching. On the floor below the officers paused in front of Madame Delobelle.

"This is the man Becque you described?" Madame Delobelle's face was grey. It was she who had denounced Thomas. He was led away.

When they reached the Luxembourg Gardens, Thomas understood. He was to be shot now, without trial. There were corpses in the Medici fountain and more bodies lay scattered about the gardens.

"Thomas!"

Charlotte's scream rent the air. She too had understood. The soldiers tried to tear her away from Thomas but she clung to him with superhuman strength.

"I want to die with you, they shall not drive me away—"

Thomas freed himself violently.

"You must live," he told her fiercely. "For my child's sake—if you love me—"

His arm was round her in one last, desperate embrace.

"My sweet, I love you. You have been the best part of my life—the best—farewell, sweetheart, until we meet again. Sweetheart!"

Charlotte heard him cry out as they thrust him away from her. She fell. She saw them drag Thomas over to a low wall. One last glance from those devastating blue eyes and then the soldiers took aim and fired. Thomas stood upright for an instant longer, then his body seemed to crumple and he fell face downwards on the ground. One of the soldiers stirred Charlotte with his foot where she lay.

"Kill me too," she begged. "For pity's sake, kill me—"

They were not going to leave her there with Thomas's body. Her fingers clawed frantically at the gravel path. An officer hauled her roughly to her feet and marched her before him down the broad avenue to the gate.

She knew now where they were taking her, to camp Satory. She began to scream wildly. Thomas! Where would she find the strength to live without him? It needs too much strength, Thomas, too much courage. Men made wars and then left it to the women to live on and bring up their children and make way for the future. She was a woman. And it was her duty to be practical, not heroic.

380

Future generations depended upon her good sense. "Oh Thomas, my love, you took from me the right to die with you and now you are asking me to do what is so much more difficult. You ask me to live, Thomas, for your baby's sake. No, they are taking me to hell, to camp Satory but I will come back, yes Thomas, I will come back. I will be free and I will care for your child. That is the only proof of love I have to give you. Oh, so many mornings wasted, so many days when we have turned our backs on happiness, Thomas, your soul and mine are one. I can wait a little while, here on this earth, but one day, you will see, summer will come again and we shall be together. Thomas. It is spring now. See the new green leaves on the chestnut tree, feel the sun on my face. My love, we shall be happy, these are our familiar streets, we are in love and the future will be good for us, beloved. Oh, my beloved, give me your hand to cross the road—"

Elisabeth Ogilvie

writes about the tempest-torn Maine coast, its highly individual people, and the dramatic, often beautiful lives they lead.

"Elisabeth Ogilvie is an excellent technician and she writes about the Maine sea coast with knowledge of, and delight in, the background."

Baltimore Sun

THE FACE OF INNOCENCE	N433	95¢
NO EVIL ANGEL	N442	95¢
THE SEASONS HEREAFTER	V2278	75¢
A THEME FOR REASON	W327	$1.25
WATERS ON A STARRY NIGHT	N411	95¢
THE WITCH DOOR	W325	$1.25

Coming soon:

ROWAN'S HEAD

THE DAWNING OF THE DAY

DAZZLING RAVES FOR
SUE-ELLEN WELFONDER
AND HER NOVELS

UNTIL THE KNIGHT COMES

"To lovers of all things Scottish, [Welfonder] writes great tales of passion and adventure. There's magic included along with the various ghosts and legends only Scotland could produce. It's almost better than a trip there in person!"

—RomanceReviewsMag.com

"Welfonder's storytelling skill and medieval scholarship shine in her latest Kintail-based Scottish romance with magical elements."

—*Booklist*

"A fun fourteenth-century romance. Mariota is a fascinating protagonist. Kenneth is her ideal counterpart. Readers will enjoy this solid historical starring two never-me-in-love individuals falling for one another."

—Harriet Klausner, *Midwest Book Review*

"Will win your heart. It's a romantic treasure. If you love Scottish tales, this one is for you."

—FreshFiction.com

more . . .

ONLY FOR A KNIGHT

"Hooked me from the first page . . . larger-than-life characters and excellent descriptions bring this story . . . to vivid life."
—*Rendezvous*

"Captivating . . . fast-moving . . . steamy, sensual, and utterly breathtaking . . . will win your heart."
—FreshFiction.com

"Four-and-a-half stars! Enthralling . . . Welfonder brings the Highlands to life with her vibrant characters, impassioned stories, and vivid descriptions."
—*Romantic Times BOOKclub Magazine*

"Wonderful . . . Kept me glued to the pages."
—RomanceJunkies.com

"A book I highly recommend for those who enjoy sexy Scotsmen. A wonderful tale of love."
—TheRomanceReadersConnection.com

"Terrific . . . [a] fine tale."
—*Midwest Book Review*

"As usual, Welfonder gives her many fans another memorable historical read."
—ReadertoReader.com

"Such a sensually romantic read . . . enticing."
—HistoricalRomanceWriters.com

WEDDING FOR A KNIGHT

"TOP PICK! You couldn't ask for a more joyous, loving, smile-inducing read . . . Will win your heart!"
—*Romantic Times BOOKclub Magazine*

"With history and beautiful details of Scotland, this book provides romance, spunk, mystery, and courtship . . . a must-read!"
—*Rendezvous*

"A very romantic story . . . extremely sexy. I recommend this book to anyone who loves the era and Scotland."
—**TheBestReviews.com**

MASTER OF THE HIGHLANDS

"Welfonder does it again, bringing readers another powerful, emotional, highly romantic medieval that steals your heart and keeps you turning the pages."
—*Romantic Times BOOKclub Magazine*

"Vastly entertaining and deeply sensual medieval romance . . . for those of us who like our heroes moody, *ultrahot*, and *sexy* . . . this is the one for you!"
—**HistoricalRomanceWriters.com**

"Yet another bonny Scottish romance to snuggle up with and inspire pleasantly sinful dreams . . . a sweetly compelling love story . . . [with a] super-abundance of sexual tension."
—*Heartstrings*

more . . .

BRIDE OF THE BEAST

"Larger-than-life characters and a scenic setting . . . Welfonder pens some steamy scenes."
— *Publishers Weekly*

"A wonderful story . . . well-told . . . a delightful mix of characters."
— *RomanticReviews.com*

"Thrilling . . . so sensual at times, it gives you goose bumps . . . Welfonder spins pure magic with her vibrant characters."
— *ReaderToReader.com*

"Four-and-a-half stars! . . . A top pick . . . powerful emotions, strong and believable characters, snappy dialogue, and some humorous moments add depth to the plotline and make this a nonstop read. Ms. Welfonder is on her way to stardom."
— *Romantic Times BOOKclub Magazine*

KNIGHT IN MY BED

"Exciting, action-packed . . . a strong tale that thoroughly entertains."
— *Midwest Book Review*

DEVIL IN A KILT

Bride
for a
Knight

SUE-ELLEN
WELFONDER

FOREVER

NEW YORK   BOSTON

Copyright © 2007 by Sue-Ellen Welfonder
Excerpt from *Bride By Seduction* copyright © 2007 by Sue-Ellen Welfonder
All rights reserved. No part of this book may be reproduced in any form or by any electronic or mechanical means, including information storage and retrieval systems, without permission in writing from the publisher, except by a reviewer who may quote brief passages in a review.

Cover design by Diane Luger
Typography by Ron Zinn
Illustration by Craig White
Book design by Giorgetta Bell McRee

Forever is an imprint of Grand Central Publishing.

The Forever name and logo is a trademark of Hachette Book Group USA, Inc.

Forever
Hachette Book Group USA
237 Park Avenue
New York, NY 10017
Visit our Web site at www.HachetteBookGroupUSA.com

Printed in the United States of America

First Printing: September 2007

10 9 8 7 6 5 4 3 2 1

In loving memory of Elizabeth "Lizzy" Benway.
Passionate reader, enthusiastic supporter of romance,
and much-loved friend to many authors,
a hurricane tragedy ended her life way too soon.
Lizzy loved Duncan, the hero of DEVIL IN A KILT,
and I will never forget the fun we had when she launched a
contest for that book on her popular John DeSalvo Web site.
Above all, Lizzy will be remembered for her big-hearted
goodness and the unbridled joy she poured into
everything she did.
I miss you, Lizzy, and thank you for making
my early-author-days so very special.
A brilliant light went out in the romance community
the day we lost you.

Acknowledgments

Scotland is a land of great beauty where ancient tradition, legends, and lore are still alive and appreciated. Those who dwell there are privileged; those who visit are enchanted, forever spellbound by Scotland's magic. No place is more soul-claiming, more difficult to leave. Scotland is also my secret elixir, the wellspring of my inspiration, and every time I visit, I am renewed. Repeatedly awed by how easy it is to walk there and feel and glimpse the past. Or, too, to believe that in such a special place, dreams truly might come true.

While researching this book, I happened across quite a few heroic James Macphersons, each one larger-than-life and leaving their own bold legacy on Scotland's past. One in particular touched my heart for he lost his life unjustly, succumbing to a corrupt hangman's noose in the very moments a racing horseman arrived waving a pardon.

Known as the "Gypsy Outlaw," this James Macpherson was a gifted fiddler. Like the Jamie in this book, he was also said to have been quite tall and of incomparable strength. Roguish, dashing, and full of charm, he was only twenty-four when he died, his dream of rescue shattered when the town clock was set forward, sneakily enabling his execution before salvation could reach him.

The charming young fiddler should not be forgotten and perhaps some of Scotland's magic blessed him after all, for he outwitted the authorities one final time, his legacy living on in his music, appreciated to this day whenever "The Macpherson's Rant" and his other beautiful tunes are played.

I would also like to remember three women who lend their own special magic to my work, offering much appreciated advice and encouragement. Roberta M. Brown, my best friend, agent, and greatest champion. My wonderful editor, Karen Kosztolnyik, whose insight and guidance I appreciate so much. And Michele Bidelspach, who I have adored since *Devil in a Kilt*.

As always, my deepest love and appreciation to my very handsome husband, Manfred, for not complaining (too much) each time I run off to Scotland. His support and enthusiasm means so much. And my little dog, Em, faithful companion and much-loved friend, the whole of my world revolves around him.

Bride
for a
Knight

❦

BALDREAGAN CASTLE
THE WESTERN HIGHLANDS, 1325

Devil take your tsk-tsks and head-shakings." Munro Macpherson, a lesser Highland chieftain of scarce renown, clenched his fists and glowered at Morag the midwife. He refused to look at the wraith on his bed, focusing his fury on the bloody-handed old woman. "Dinna think to tell me she's dying. No-o-o, I willna hear it!"

He took two steps forward, another when the midwife cast him a sorrow-filled stare. The same kind she'd been sending his way ever since he'd burst into the birthing chamber.

A stare that said more than words.

Told him things he didn't want to accept.

Shuddering, he glared denial at her, willed the sympathy off her lined, age-pitted face. "'Tis you and no other who'll be meeting your Maker this night if you do not soon restore my wife's vigor!"

"'Tis God's will, sir." Morag sighed, made the sign of the cross.

"Then call on the old gods!" Munro shouted, his mouth twisting. "All in these hills know you're familiar with 'em!"

The old woman pressed her lips together and rubbed more herbed oil onto her hands. "Your own eyes saw the piece of cold iron I laid in her bed. And I told you the water my niece is using to blot the sweat from her brow comes from St. Bride's own well."

"Then use devilry!" Munro all but choked. "Try anything!"

He narrowed a scorching stare on Morag's timid-faced niece, the dripping rag clutched in her hand. Rage scalded him that such a pale wee mouse of a female could live and breathe while his lady, so lush, golden, and until yestereve, so alive, could lay dying.

Consumed by fever, already long out of her senses.

Unable to bear it, he whirled away from the two women, the pathetic shadow that was his life. All that remained of her were incoherent moans and the tangled spill of her glorious hair across the soiled bedsheets. A magnificent cascade of rippling bronze, but already matted and losing its luster. Just as her creamy, rose-tinged skin, always her pride, had drained of all color.

Haggard and spent, she no longer even thrashed when the birth pangs gripped her. She simply lay there, her sunken eyes and the waxy sheen of death signaling her fate.

Her destiny, and Munro's doom.

Entirely too aware of his inability to do aught about it, he planted himself before an unshuttered window and frowned out on the bleak autumn night. Hot tears rolled down his cheeks, but he fought them, drew in a great breath of the chill, damp air.

But no matter how hard he stared into the rain-washed darkness, or welcomed the furious thunder cracking in the distance, he felt impotent. Small and inept, as if he were no longer the tall, powerfully built man who strode so boldly across the hills, but a quivering nithling ready to drop to his knees if only pleading might help.

Instead, his blood iced and his entire body went so taut he wondered it didn't crack and shatter into thousands of tiny ne'er to be retrieved pieces.

Tight-lipped, he kept his gaze riveted on the dark of the hills, his hands curled around his sword belt. "Hear me, Morag," he said, his tone as humble as one such as he could make it, "for all my moods and rantings, I love my wife. I canna bear to lose her."

The words spoken, he turned, his gut knotting to see the old woman peering beneath his wife's red-splotched skirts, her wizened face drawn into a worse scowl than his own.

Munro swallowed, tightened his fingers on his belt. "Name your price if you save her. Whate'er it is. I will be ever in your debt, and gladly."

But the midwife only shook her head again. "The babe is too big," she said, easing his lady's thighs farther apart. "And she's lost too much blood."

"Meaning?" Munro's temper resurfaced, his eyes began to bulge. "Speak the truth, woman, lest I pitch you and your sniveling niece out the window!"

"Your wife will die, sir," Morag answered him, "but

there's a chance the bairn will live. His head is already emerging. Strong shoulders, too. Be thankful—"

"*Thankful?*" Munro thrust out an enraged hand, yanking up his wife's blood-drenched skirts in time to see a large, coppery-haired man-child slip from between her lifeless thighs.

"Thankful for a tenth son?" he roared, glaring at the wailing babe. "The child who killed my Iona?"

"He is your son, my lord." Morag cradled the babe against her chest, splayed gnarled fingers across his wet-glistening back. "And a fine, strapping lad, he is. He will make you forget. In time—"

"I will never forget," Munro vowed, staring past her, watching the horrible glaze coat his wife's vacant eyes. "And I dinna need a tenth mouth to feed. I didna even want this one! Nine healthy sons are enough for any man."

"Sir, please . . ." The midwife handed the babe to her niece, hastened after him when he made for the door. "You must at least name him."

"I must do naught!" Munro swung around; he would have hit her were she not so old and bent. "But if you would have a name then call the lad Jamie—James of the Heather!"

The midwife blinked. "*'Of the Heather'?*"

"So I have said," Munro confirmed, already stepping out the door. "'Tis there he was spawned in a moment I'll e'er regret, and 'tis there he can return. So soon as he's old enough. Baldreagan has no room for him."

Chapter One

✦

FAIRMAIDEN CASTLE
NEAR BALDREAGAN, AUTUMN 1347

"*The tenth son?*"

Aveline Matheson paced the length of the high table, her father's startling news echoing in her ears. Equally distressing, her sister's red-rimmed gaze followed her and that made her feel unpleasantly guilty.

She took a deep breath, trying hard to ignore the sensation that her world was spinning out of control.

"To be sure, I remember there was a younger son, but . . ." She paused, finding it hard to speak with Sorcha's teary-eyed stare boring holes in her.

Indeed, not just her oldest sister, but every kinsman crowding the great hall. All of them were staring at her. Swiveling heads and narrowing eyes. Measuring her reaction as if the entire future and fortune of Clan Matheson rested upon her shoulders.

And from what she'd heard, it did.

Wincing inwardly, she stopped in front of her father's

laird's chair and stood as tall as her diminutive stature would allow.

That, and Alan Mor Matheson's fierce countenance. A look her plaid-hung, bushy-bearded father wielded with as much skill as he swung his sword.

Seeing that look now, she swallowed, wanting only to escape the hall. Instead, she held her ground. "For truth, I am sore grieved for Laird Macpherson," she began, scarce able to grasp the horror of losing nine sons at once, "but if you mean to insist upon a union between our houses, shouldn't Sorcha be the bride?"

Upon her words, Sorcha gave an audible gasp.

Alan Mor's face hardened, his large hands splaying on the high table. "Saints of glory!" he boomed, his choler causing his eldest daughter to jump as if he'd struck her.

Ignoring her distress, he leaned forward, kept his attention on Aveline. "Your sister was to be the bride. She was to wed Macpherson's eldest son, Neill. As well you know. Now, with Neill and the others dead, only Jamie remains."

He paused, letting the last two words hang in the smoke-hazed air. "Sorcha is more than fifteen summers the lad's senior and your other three sisters are wed. I willna risk the alliance with Macpherson by denying his only remaining son the most suitable bride I can offer."

Aveline lifted her chin. "Be that as it may—"

"It doesn't matter. Not now." Sorcha touched her arm, blinking back the brightness in her eyes. "'Twas Neill who should've been mine. I-I . . . would have followed him to the ends of this earth, even through the gates of hell," she vowed, her voice thick. "I've no wish to wed Young Jamie."

"Even so, I still grieve for you." Aveline released an uneven breath, a surge of pity tightening her chest. "And my heart breaks for the Macphersons."

Alan Mor hooted. "Your sister is a well-made young woman with fine prospects. Another husband will be found for her," he declared, glancing around as if he expected someone to gainsay him. "As for that cross-grained old goat, Macpherson, that one has e'er claimed the devil's own luck. His hurts will lessen once he remembers the bonny bit of glen he'll be getting to graze his precious cattle. Not to mention the well-filled coffers he wheedled out of me."

A chill slid down Aveline's spine. She said nothing.

If her father had brimming coffers to offer Munro Macpherson, he'd likely filled them with stones—or empty words and bluster.

Sure of it, she watched Sorcha whirl away and move toward the hearth fire. With her shoulders and back painfully straight, the older girl's face looked pale in the torchlight, her eyes shadowed and puffy. Worse, her stony expression voiced what every Matheson knew.

Neill Macpherson had been her last chance to wed.

Few were the suitors willing to accept Sorcha's large-boned, overly tall form for well made. And even Alan Mor's most cunning double-dealing and swagger couldn't transform her plain face into a pleasing one.

Indeed, not few were those who shook their heads over Neill's acceptance of her.

But he'd agreed for the sake of an alliance.

And now he was dead.

Shuddering, Aveline curled her fingers into her skirts, the image of the MacPherson brothers' last moments flashing across her mind.

Not that she'd been there.

But everyone born of these hills knew the treacheries of the white-water cauldron known as Garbh Uisge, the Rough Waters. They filled the deep, birch-lined gorge that divided Matheson and Macpherson lands.

A danger-fraught chasm, alive with a wildly plunging waterfall and splashing, boulder-strewn burn, the surging cataracts and clouds of spume now posed a forever reminder of nature's wrath. Leastways when served by the splintering of damp, age-warped wood.

The unexpected collapse of a narrow footbridge neither clan had been willing to refurbish, each laird insisting his neighbor made more use of the bridge and ought to dole out the coin for its repair.

A hotheaded foolhardiness that had taken a grim toll, and now sent Aveline striding across the hall, away from her father's black-browed arrogance.

"You err," she said, keeping her back to him as she wrenched open the shutters of the nearest window. "Naught in this world will ease Laird Macpherson's pain."

"Mayhap not," Alan Mor shot back, "but the man's a good deal more daft than I thought if he isn't at least comforted by the boons he'll reap through this alliance."

To Aveline's dismay, an immediate ripple of assent swept the hall. Murmured agreement swiftly followed by the clinking of ale cups and boisterous cheer. Alan Mor's own self-pleased grunt.

Aveline tightened her jaw and stared out at the misty, rain-sodden night, the outline of rugged black hills and the glimmer of distant stars twinkling through gray, wind-torn clouds.

"God grant you have the rights of it," she said at last, welcoming the evening's chill on her face. "Nevertheless, I would speak out against taking advantage of a man who is down and foundering."

"*'Taking advantage'?*" Alan Mor's deep voice shook the hall. "You'd best speak plain, lass. And hie yourself away from that window."

Stiffening, Aveline kept her gaze on the silvery glint of the river winding through the trees not far from Fairmaiden Castle's curtain walls. Older than time, the slow-moving river gave itself much more placid than the white-watered Garbh Uisge that had claimed so many innocent lives.

And brought others to this unexpected pass.

Herself included.

Her temples beginning to throb, she turned from the window. Sorcha now stood in a darkened corner, her ravaged, tear-stained face shielded from the reach of torchlight. Everyone else was turned her way, her father's face wearing an even darker scowl than before.

Aveline squared her shoulders, then took a step forward.

"Well?" Alan Mor demanded, his stare almost searing the air. "Are you accusing me of trying to deceive Macpherson?"

"Nay, I—" Aveline broke off, unable to lie. Her father's famed sleights of hand and well-oiled words were known throughout the Highlands.

Coming forward, she sought a way to cushion her suspicions. "I would not accuse you of aught," she ventured, hoping only she heard the cynicism in her tone. "And to be sure, I am willing to wed, am even eager for the day I might have a husband and household of my own."

"Then why are you looking as if you've just bit into something bitter?"

"Because," Aveline admitted, "I do not think Munro Macpherson will appreciate us meddling—"

"So now I'm a meddler?" Alan Mor shot to his feet, the movement scattering the parchments spread before him. "Helping the old fool is what I'm doing! Did you not hear me say tongue-waggers claim he's taken to his bed? That he fears leaving his privy chambers because he thinks the ghosts of his sons have returned to Baldreagan? Are haunting him?"

Alan Mor glared at her, his nostrils flaring. "Munro isn't yet in his dotage, but he soon will be if no one takes him in hand. He needs Jamie."

"Since when have you cared about Macpherson's well-doing?" Aveline challenged, stepping onto the dais. "You and Munro were ne'er friends."

"We are neighbors." Her father looked down, took a sudden interest in examining the colored string tied around a rolled parchment. "Knowing he's right in his head is a lesser evil than annoying the bastard."

"I vow you'll vex him mightily if you persist in this fool plan of yours." Aveline snatched the parchment scroll from her father's hand and held it out of his reach. "Munro Macpherson ne'er spoke fondly of Jamie. He's even been heard to call him a dirk thrust beneath his ribs."

Alan Mor sucked in his breath, his surprise at her bluntness all the answer Aveline needed.

Neither the Macpherson nor Young Jamie knew her father still meant to uphold the proposed alliance.

"Word is, Jamie's grown into a fine, strapping lad. A knight." Alan Mor recovered quickly, thrusting out his chin. "He even fought alongside King David at Neville's Cross last autumn, his bravery and valor earning him much acclaim. Munro will change his mind about the lad once he's home."

"Still . . ." Aveline tightened her grip on the parchment. "I do not think this should be sent to Jamie until Laird Macpherson is fit enough to decide if he, too, still wishes a union between our houses."

To her horror, her father laughed.

As did his inky-fingered scribe.

"Too late!" Alan Mor's eyes lit with mischief. "That scroll in your hand is naught but a letter to your sister in Inverness, asking of her health and thanking her for the casks of wine her husband sent to us. The many jars of their heather-tasting honey."

Aveline dropped the parchment. "You mean you've already sent word to Jamie? Without informing Macpherson?"

The look on her father's face turned smug. "Someday you'll thank me. You, and that blethering fool, Macpherson."

"And Jamie?"

Alan Mor snorted. "Him most of all—once he sets eyes on you!"

His foul temper forgotten, he beamed on her. "What young loon wouldn't be pleased with such a delicate bloom?"

But Aveline wasn't so sure.

Glancing down, her gaze skimmed over her thick braid, not acknowledging how it gleamed like gold in the candlelight, but rather settling on her tiny hands and feet, the smallness of her breasts. Anything but a full woman, lushly curved and ripe, she doubted any man would find favor with her.

Or the distasteful circumstance that would propel her and Young Jamie into a marriage bed.

No man liked being duped.

Long-lost son, or no.

Across miles of darkling hills and empty moorland, thick with bracken and winter-browned heather, Clan MacKenzie's Cuidrach Castle loomed above the silent waters of Loch Hourn, the stronghold's proud towers and that great sentinel, the Bastard Stone, silhouetted against a cold, frosty sky.

A chill night; icy stars glittered in the heavens and knifing winds whistled past the windows, rattling shutters and making those within glad for the leaping flames of the great hall's well-doing log fire. Eager-to-please squires circulated with trays of hot, spiced wine and steaming mounds of fresh-baked meat pasties. Men crowded benches drawn close to the hearth, jesting and jostling amongst themselves, their rich masculine laughter rising to the ceiling rafters, bawdy good cheer ringing in every ear.

Only one of Cuidrach's residents shunned the comforts and warmth of the hall this night, seeking instead the privacy of a tiny storeroom filled with wine casks, blessed torchlight, and James Macpherson's mounting frustration.

Holding back an oath that would surely curl the devil's own toes, Young James of the Heather, sometimes teasingly called Jamie the Small, glared at the tiny red bead of blood on his thumb.

The fifth such jab wound he'd inflicted on himself in under an hour.

And, he suspected, most likely not the last. Not if he meant to complete his task.

Sighing, he licked the blood off his finger, then shoved his stool closer to the best-burning wall torch. Perhaps with brighter light, he'd have a better chance of restitching the let-out seams of his new linen tunic.

A birthday gift from his liege lord's lady.

And the finest tunic he'd e'er possessed. Softer than rose petals and with a bold Nordic design embroidered around the neck opening; just looking at it brought a flush a pleasure to his cheeks, and even made his heart thump if he thought about the long hours Lady Mariota had spent crafting such a gift for him. A gift he was determined to wear to his birthday revelries later that night.

He would, too.

If only the tunic weren't so tight across the shoulders, the sleeves a mite too short. And his fool fingers so damnably clumsy.

Frowning, he picked up his needle and set to work again. Truth be told, there was nothing wrong with the tunic . . . it was him.

Always had been him.

He was simply too big.

And, he decided a short while later, his hearing a bit too sharp. Leastways keen enough to note the sudden silence pressing against the closed storeroom door.

He tilted his head, listening.

But his instincts hadn't lied.

Gone indeed were the muffled bursts of laughter and ribald song, the occasional barks of the castle dogs. The high-pitched skirls of female delight. Utter stillness held Cuidrach's great hall in a firm grip, the strange hush smothering all sound.

A deep kind of quiet that didn't bode well and even held sinister significance—if he were to trust the way the fine hairs on his nape were lifting. Or the cold chill spilling down his spine.

Curious, he set aside the unfinished tunic and his needle and stood. But before he could cross the tiny storeroom, the door swung open. His liege lord, Sir Kenneth MacKenzie, stood in the doorway, flanked by Sir Lachlan, the Cuidrach garrison captain, and a travel-stained man Jamie had never seen.

The stranger's rain-dampened cloak hung about his shoulders and his wind-tangled hair bespoke a hard ride. But it was more than the man's muddied boots and bleary-eyed fatigue that made Jamie's mouth run dry.

It was the look on the stranger's face.

The undeniable impression of strain and pity that

poured off him and filled the little storeroom until Jamie thought he might choke on its rankness.

Especially when he caught the same wary sadness mirrored in Sir Kenneth's and Sir Lachlan's eyes.

Jamie froze. "What is it?" he asked, his gaze moving from face to face. "Tell me straight away for I can see that something dire has happened."

"Aye, lad, I'm afraid that is so. Would that I could make it otherwise, but . . ." Kenneth glanced at the stranger, cleared his throat. "See you, this man comes from Carnach in the north of Kintail. Alan Mor Matheson of Fairmaiden Castle sent him. He brings ill tidings. Your father—"

"Of a mercy!" Jamie stared at them. "Dinna tell me he is dead?"

None of the three men spoke a word, but the tautness of their grim-set expressions said everything.

Jamie blinked, a wave of black dizziness washing over him. Sakes, even the floor seemed to dip and heave beneath his feet. It couldn't be true. Naught could have struck down his indomitable father. Munro Macpherson was honed from coldest iron, had steel running in his veins. And after a lifetime of the man's indifference, Jamie shouldn't care what fate befell him.

But he did.

More than he would have believed. So much, the roar of his own blood in his ears kept him from hearing what Kenneth was saying. He could only see the other man's mouth moving, the sad way Sir Lachlan and the courier shook their heads.

Jamie swallowed, pressed cold fingers against his temples. "Tell me that again, sir. I-I didna hear you."

"I said your father is not dead, though he is faring poorly and has taken to his bed. That's why Laird Matheson sent his man to us." Kenneth came forward to grip Jamie's arms. "And there has been a tragedy, aye."

Jamie's heart stopped. He could scarce speak. Breaking away from Kenneth's grasp, he searched the men's faces. "If not my father, then who? One of my brothers?"

The three men exchanged glances.

Telling glances.

And so damning they filled Jamie with more dread than if someone had leveled a sword at his throat. For one sickening moment, the faces of his nine brothers flashed before his eyes and he thought he might faint. But before he could, Sir Lachlan unfastened the hip flask at his belt and thrust the flagon into Jamie's hand.

"Drink this," he urged, his face grim. "All of it if you can."

And Jamie did, gulping down the fiery *uisge beatha* so quickly the strong Highland spirits burned his throat and watered his eyes.

The last softly-burning droplets still on his tongue, he squared his shoulders. Prepared for the worst. "Tell me true," he entreated, his fingers clenching around the flask. "Which one of my brothers is dead?"

"It grieves me to tell you, lad." Kenneth drew a long breath, slid another glance at the courier. " 'Tis not one of your brothers, but all of them. They drowned in the swollen waters of the Garbh Uisge when the footbridge collapsed beneath them."

"Christ God, no-o-o!" Shock and horror slammed into Jamie, crashing over him in hot and cold waves as eerie silence swelled anew, its damning weight blotting all sound but a high-pitched buzzing in his ears and the keening wind.

A low, unearthly moan he only recognized as his own when lancing pain closed his throat and the wailing ceased.

And so soon as it did, he staggered backward and sagged against the stacked wine casks, disbelief laming him. His knees began to tremble and his vision blurred, his entire world contracting to a whirling black void.

A spinning darkness made all the more terrifying because it taunted him with glimpses of his brothers' faces, cold and gray in death, but also as they'd been in life.

Neill, the oldest, with auburn hair bright as Jamie's own and the same hazel eyes. Confident and proud, he was the most hot-tempered of Jamie's brothers. After Neill, came Kendrick, the most dashing with his roguish grin and easy wit, his ability to create a stir amongst the ladies simply by entering a room.

Then there was Hamish, the dreamer. A secret romantic, good-natured, quiet, and most content when left alone to ponder great chivalric myths and tales of ancient Gaelic heroism. And six others, all dear to him, brothers who'd been his lifeblood in the years his father had shunned him.

His heart's joy and only solace right up to the day he'd struck out across the heather, found a new home and purpose as squire to Duncan MacKenzie, the Black Stag of Kintail, his liege lord's uncle.

And now his brothers were gone.

Jamie closed his eyes and swallowed. He couldn't believe it; wouldn't be able to accept the loss so long as he had breath in his body. But when he opened his eyes and looked into the troubled faces of the three men standing just inside the storeroom's threshold, he knew it was true.

Still, he tried to deny it.

"It canna be. My brothers knew every clump of heather, every peat bog and lochan, every stone and hill face of our land," he said, willing the room to stop spinning. "They crossed that footbridge every day, would have known if it was near to collapsing."

The courier shrugged, looking uncomfortable. "'Tis thought the recurrent rains of late weakened the wood. The planks were aged and warped, some of them rotted. My pardon, sir, but you've not been to Baldreagan in years. The bridge truly was in need of repair."

Jamie struggled against his pain, gave the courier a long, probing look. "You are certain they are dead? All nine? There can be no mistake?"

"Nay, son, I am sorry." The man shook his head, his words squelching Jamie's last shimmer of hope. "I saw the bodies with my own eyes, was there when they were pulled from the river."

Jamie nodded, unable to speak.

The words tore a hole in his heart, stirring up images he couldn't bear. With great effort, he pushed away from the wine casks and moved to the storeroom's narrow-slit window, welcomed the blast of chill air, the heavy scent of rain on the raw, wet wind.

He curled his fingers around his sword belt, held tight as he looked out on the night mist, the dark belt of pines crouching so near to Cuidrach's walls. Swallowing hard, he fixed his gaze on the silent hills, willing their peace to soothe him. But this night, the beauty of Kintail failed him.

Indeed, he doubted that even the sweetest stretch of heather could calm him. Wondered how moments ago his only concern had been restitching his birthday tunic, and now. . . . He tightened his grip on his belt, let out a long, unsteady breath just as Cuillin, his aged dog, nudged his leg, whimpering until he reached down to stroke the beast's shaggy head.

In return, Cuillin looked up at him with concern-filled eyes and thumped his scraggly tail on the floor rushes. Neill had given him the dog, Jamie recalled, a shudder ripping through him at the memory. But so soon as the tremor passed, he turned back to the room, his decision made.

He cleared his throat. "I've ne'er been one to thrust myself into places where I am not welcome," he began, standing as straight as he could, "but I shall ride to Baldreagan, whether my presence suits my father or no. I must pay my respects to my brothers. 'Tis a debt I owe them."

To his surprise, the courier's mouth quirked in an awkward smile. " 'Tis glad I am to hear you say that," he said, stepping forward. "See you, as it happens, I've brought more than ill tidings."

He paused, puffing his chest a bit. "Truth be told, I have something that might prove of great interest to you."

Jamie cocked a brow, said nothing.

Undaunted, the courier fished inside his cloak, withdrawing a rolled parchment tied with colorful string and sealed with wax. "Something that might give a lift to your aching heart. See here, I've a letter from—"

"My father?" Jamie asked, incredulous.

The courier shook his head. "Och, goodness, nay. Your da is in no form to be dashing off letters. 'Tis from my liege, Laird Matheson. But he sends it in your father's name, and out of his own wish to do well by you."

Jamie eyed the letter, suspicion making him wary. "My father and Alan Mor were e'er at odds. It is one thing for Matheson, as our nearest neighbor, to send word of my brothers' deaths if my father was unable. But to pen a letter in my da's name? And out of courtesy to me? Nay, I canna believe it."

"On my soul, it is true." The courier held out the parchment. "Much has changed in the years you've been away. As the letter will prove. You might even be pleasantly surprised."

Jamie bit back an oath, not wanting to take out his pain on a hapless courier. "I'd say this day has brought enough surprises." He folded his arms. "I'm not sure I wish to be privy to any more."

But after a moment he took the parchment, ran his thumb over the seal. "Though I will admit to being curious."

"Then read the letter," Kenneth urged him. "What the man says makes sense, Jamie. Now might be a good time to mend the breach with your sire and put the past behind you."

I have tried to do that the whole of my life, Jamie almost blurted. Instead, he found himself breaking the wax seal, unrolling the parchment. He stepped close to a wall torch, scanned the squiggly lines of ink, an odd mix of astonishment and dismay welling inside him.

A brief flare of anger, too. That he should be welcomed home only now, under such grievous circumstances. As for the rest . . . he looked up from the parchment, shoved a quick hand through his hair.

He started to speak, but the words caught in his throat, trapped there by the irony of his plight. If Alan Mor weren't playing some nefarious game, everything he'd ever wanted now lay within his reach.

If he did what was asked of him.

Seemingly in high favor for the first time in his life, he turned to the courier, trying not to frown. "You know what is in here?" And when the man nodded, "Is it true that my father and Alan Mor have entered into an alliance? One they meant to seal with the marriage of my brother Neill and Alan Mor's eldest daughter?"

The man bobbed his head again. " 'Tis the God's truth, aye. So sure as I'm standing here." He accepted the ale cup Sir Lachlan offered him, taking a sip before he went on, "Your father is in sore need, asks daily if you've arrived. He's failing by the day and won't even set foot outside his bedchamber. 'Tis hoped your return will revive him."

Pausing, the man stepped closer, laid a conspiratorial

hand on Jamie's arm. "That, and seeing the alliance between the clans upheld."

"Through my marriage to this Aveline?"

"Tchach, lad, which other lass would you have?" The
courier drew himself up, looked mildly affronted. "Poor
Sorcha is heartbroken o'er the loss of her Neill, and too
old for you by years. The other daughters are already
wed. It has to be Aveline—she's the youngest. And still a
maid."

Jamie eyed the man askance, would've sworn he could
feel an iron yoke settling on his shoulders.

It scarce mattered to him if Aveline Matheson was tender of years. The state of her maidenhood concerned him
even less.

He remembered the lassies of Fairmaiden Castle.
Regrettably, not by name. If memory served, there wasn't
a one amongst the brood he'd care to meet on a moonless
night. And with surety nary a one he'd wish to bed.

One nearly equaled him in height and build. Another
sported a mustache some men would envy. And one e'er
smelled of onions. Truth be told, he couldn't recall a single redeeming feature amongst the lot of them.

Binding himself to such a female would prove the
surest and quickest route to misery.

But he did want to see his father. Help him if he could.

Jamie sighed, felt the yoke tightening around his neck.
"I ne'er thought to see my father again in this life. For
certes, not because he claims to need me. As for taking
one of Matheson's daughters to wife—"

"Och, but Aveline is more than pleasing. And spirited."
The courier stepped in front of him, blocking the way

when Jamie would have paced back to the window. "She brings a healthy marriage portion, too. Prime grazing lands for your da's cattle. I say you, you willna be sorry. I swear it on the souls of my sons."

"I will think on it," Jamie offered, doing his best to hide his discomfiture.

"Why don't you hie yourself into the hall to get a meal and some sleep?" Kenneth clamped a hand on the courier's elbow, steered him to the door. "Jamie will give you his decision on the morrow."

Turning back to Jamie, he arched a raven brow. "For someone who spent his life yearning to win his father's favor, tell me why you lost all color upon hearing of the man's sudden need for you? Surely you aren't troubled by this talk of a desired marriage?"

Jamie folded his arms over his chest again, felt heat creeping up the back of his neck. Damn him for a chivalrous fool, but he couldn't bring himself to voice his misgivings.

Admit he'd rather have his tender parts shrivel and fall off before he'd find himself obliged to bed one of Alan Mor's daughters.

If he even could!

"Ach, dinna look so glum." Sir Lachlan took the letter, glanced at it. "There is nothing writ here that binds you," he said, looking up from the parchment. "You needn't do aught you find displeasing."

And that was Jamie's problem.

Returning home, even now, *would* please him. So much, his heart nearly burst at the thought. And once there, he'd be hard-pressed to disappoint his father.

Or Aveline Matheson.

If indeed such an alliance required his compliance. Truth was, he lived by a strict code of honor. One that forbade him to shame an innocent maid.

Even if sparing her feelings came at the cost of his own.

And besides, arranged marriages were more common than not. With few exceptions, only the lowest-born enjoyed the luxury of wedding for love.

Heaving a sigh, he snatched up his new tunic and donned it, unfinished seams or no. "We all ken I shall wed the lass if my da wishes it," he said, moving to the door. "I'll ride for Baldreagan at first light, and visit Alan Mor so soon as I've seen my father."

His intentions stated, he stepped into the great hall, pausing to appreciate its smoky, torch-lit warmth. The comfort of kith and kin, a crackling hearth fire. Everyday pleasures his brothers would never again enjoy. Indeed, compared to their fate, his own struck him as more than palatable.

So long as Aveline wasn't the sister almost his own size, he'd find some way to tolerate her.

Or so he hoped.

Chapter Two

❧

Jamie knew he was in trouble the moment he drew rein on a lofty, gorse-covered ridge and surveyed the dark hills spreading out all around him. Mist curled in the higher corries, the sight stirring his spirit and squeezing his heart.

Welcoming him with arms flung wide.

An embrace in the old way of the hills and one that clutched fiercely, holding fast until his breath caught and he would've sworn he'd only left these northern reaches of Kintail that very morn.

Wishing that were so, he blinked against the heat stinging the backs of his eyes. Now as never before, he recognized how the lure of hill and moor could make even the deepest cares seem far away.

Behind him, his dog, Cuillin, stirred in his wicker saddle basket, almost as if the ancient beast also sensed a subtle change in the air.

Knew, like Jamie, that they were home at last.

And for certes, they were.

Already deepening twilight, he could just make out the distant yellow-gleaming lights of Baldreagan. Little more than weaving pinpricks of brightness from his vantage point, but home all the same.

The one place on earth he'd ne'er thought to see again.

The place he'd expected to miss till his dying day.

"God in heaven," he breathed, a strong sense of belonging sliding around him.

Duthchas, the feeling was called. A Highlander's fierce attachment to his home glen, a soul-deep sense of oneness with the land of his blood.

A pull Jamie now felt to the bone.

His chest tightening, he found himself sorely tempted to swing down from his saddle and kiss the peaty, moss-covered ground. He might have, too, but did not wish to frighten Cuillin.

Instead, he simply looked round, wishing his reason for returning had been a happy one.

But even here, a good distance from the Garbh Uisge, the roar of the rapids tainted the night. A dread sound that hollowed him, gouging an emptiness he doubted could ever be filled again.

Blocking his ears, he swore.

Then he clenched the reins so tightly his knuckles gleamed white.

As did the moonlight spilling across the dark roll of the hills. Bright, slanting bands of shimmering silver, rippling on the night breeze, the beauty stilling his heart.

Especially when one of the iridescent silvery bands proved to have a most pleasing feminine form.

Jamie blinked.

Ne'er had he seen the like.

But he wouldn't be a Highlander if he didn't recognize the wonder before him. A sight as ancient as the rocks and heather, but so rare, his whole world tilted.

His breath catching, he slid a hand behind him, curling his fingers into the scruffy fur at Cuillin's shoulders. "Saints o' mercy!" he marveled, his eyes widening. "A faery!"

There could be no doubt.

Only one of the *Daoine Sìthe* could be so delicate and fair.

More exquisite than any female of this earth, the fey beauty slipped through a moon-silvered glade, her dainty feet not seeming to touch the ground.

Saints, she looked so tiny he doubted she'd come up to his chest were he to stand before her. Small-breasted and slight, she moved with a grace that bespoke lithe, slender legs. And she wore her hair unbound and flowing, a glistening sheaf of palest silk so beautiful he would've groaned did he not wish to risk drawing her attention.

But he did catch her scent on the chill night air.

A fragrance reminiscent of summer, violets, and fresh, dew-kissed green.

Truth tell, she must've bespelled him.

Even watching her from a distance, Jamie was seized by an irresistible urge to ride after her and touch her moonlit hair. To tangle his fingers in its silkiness, seeing for himself if the shimmering strands felt as soft and glossy as they looked.

See if her eyes really were the deep sapphire he

suspected. And if the tips of her eyelashes would appear as if dipped in gold.

Perhaps he'd kiss her, too. If a mortal man could even touch such a creature.

Jamie's brows snapped together at once, the spell broken.

A hot flush swept up his neck and the racing of his heart began to slow. Big as he was and fragile as she looked, his very breath would likely bruise her.

And his cheek for having such thoughts about a *Sithe* maid would surely land him in the depths of some faery knowe, bound by inescapable golden bonds. Or, equally unpleasant, see him plunged into a charmed sleep for a hundred years or more.

Such things were known to happen.

He shuddered, reached up to rub the back of his neck.

But then the moon vanished behind a cloud and when it reemerged, the broad sweeps of moor and hill loomed empty, the night still and quiet as it'd been.

"By glory!" He released his breath, peering hard at the little glade, but the faery was truly gone.

Nothing moved through the shadowy birches and scrub but the dark ribbon of a tumbling burn.

"Och, mercy me—did you see her, Cuillin?" He twisted around in the saddle and ruffled the old dog's ears, not missing that Cuillin's rheumy gaze remained on the very spot where the *Sithe* maid had disappeared.

Or that the old dog's tail was wagging.

Not that Jamie needed proof of what he'd seen.

Nor did he blame Cuillin for being smitten. The faery had been a vision of loveliness. Truth be told, she couldn't have been more beautiful had she been wrapped in cloth of gold and moonbeams, her shimmering hair dusted with stars.

And thinking about it, he decided that was a reasonable description of her.

He'd also wager she tasted of nectar and moon-spun temptation. He wasn't a man known for pretty words, only his great size and the skill of his sword arm. Yet this faery inspired him to such courtly verse.

Even so, he released her from his mind, his gaze falling on another glimmer of brightness. This one as earthy and real as the Highlands, welcome enough to flood him with memories. Bringing salvation, and again, the eye-stinging tightness of chest and throat that had plagued him every heather mile since leaving Cuidrach.

A malaise that worsened the farther north he'd ridden.

Setting his jaw, he sat up straighter and swiped the dampness from his cheeks, his stare fixed on the thick, whitewashed walls of a small, hump-backed cot house just visible through a copse of ancient Caledonian pines a bit farther down the long, rock-strewn slope. Peat smoke curled in thin blue tendrils from the cottage's stone-hung thatched roof and if he listened hard, he was certain he'd hear the bleating of sheep. Perhaps even a few faint strains of fiddle music.

And if he really concentrated, he might even catch a savory whiff of beef marrow broth or mutton stew.

For the cot-house was Hughie Mac's. A man already older than stone in Jamie's youth, Hughie Mac's gnome-like body was as twisted and gnarled as the Scots pines sheltering his cottage. But Hughie also had twinkling, smiling eyes. And he'd once been Jamie's grandfather's favored herd boy; a lad prized for his herding talent, but even more for the magic he could make on the strings of a fiddle.

The warm welcome and ready smile he'd always had for Jamie, especially when his world had seemed at its darkest.

For two pins, Jamie would ride there now, hammer on Hughie's door, and if the grizzled herder answered, he'd crush him in a hug that lasted till the morrow.

Hughie would greet him kindly.

His da's reception remained to be seen.

And it made him mighty edgy. Especially since glimpsing the faery. So he squared his shoulders and rode on, eager to be done with it. Digging in his heels, he sent his garron plunging down the rough, broken hillside and straight through his da's cattle, his passage startling the lumbering beasts.

A tall, hooded figure stared at him in horror from the edge of the protesting, scattering herd.

A tall, hooded *female* figure.

Jamie's jaw slipped and for one crazy mad moment, he wondered if she, too, was of the fey. Or if Hughie Mac still had a way with bonny lassies. But as he spurred toward the woman, he could see she was mortal as the day.

And without doubt the plainest creature he'd e'er set eyes on.

She was also the most terrified.

"Dinna come near me!" she shrieked, backing away. "No closer—I pray you!"

Jamie prayed, too.

His heart thundering as the most unchivalrous corner of his soul pleaded the saints that this Valkyrie wouldn't prove to be Aveline Matheson.

The proximity of Fairmaiden Castle made it a distinct possibility.

Nevertheless, he pulled up in front of her and swung down from the saddle. His honor demanded no less. But to his amazement, her eyes flew even wider and she flung up a hand as if warding off a horde of flying banshees.

"Have mercy!" she wailed this time, her face blanching in the light of the rising moon. "I—"

"You must be one of the Fairmaiden lasses." Jamie took her by the arms, seeking to soothe her. "You've no need to fear me. See you" —he jerked his head in Cuillin's direction—"what fiend o' the hills would ride about with an aged, half-blind dog? I am James of the Heather, come home to—"

"Praise God!" She blinked at him, her color slowly returning. "I-I thought you were Neill."

Jamie swallowed hard on hearing his brother's name. He'd been thinking about his brothers ever since crossing onto Macpherson land.

Speaking about them, even just one, was something he wasn't sure he could do.

Not yet.

But his knightly vows and Valkyrie's misted eyes had him reaching to brush the tears from her face.

"You knew Neill?" he probed, the name costing him dearly.

She flinched and bit down on her lip as she nodded.

Then her eyes filled anew, her reaction suggesting her identity.

"I am Sorcha," she said, confirming his guess. "I was Neill's betrothed and until a short while ago, the most light-hearted maid in these hills."

She looked at him, her eyes dark pools. "He was tall and bonny. A bold, forthright man who should have had all his days before him. But who could have foreseen . . ." She clapped a hand over her mouth, unable to finish.

Jamie drew a deep breath. "Saints aid me, lass, I dinna ken what to say to you." Having never mastered the courtly skills of proper wooing or even comforting distressed damsels, he did think to take her elbow and pull her with him to his garron. "I'll see you to your sire's keep," he suggested, trying to avert any further talk of his brother. "You can ride and I'll walk alongside."

But she backed away when Cuillin lunged forward to sniff her, his tail thumping against the wicker of his basket. "You are as goodly as Neill e'er said you were, but I wish to be alone. Fairmaiden is not far and the walking is a comfort to me. I've already come from Baldreagan this e'en, a few more paces willna—"

"From Baldreagan?" Jamie stared at her. "But that's well more than a few paces," he said, striding after her as she moved toward the trees. "And no journey for a maid unescorted. 'Tis nigh dark and the Rough Waters . . ."

He left the warning tail off, but she must've understood because she stopped, turning around to face him. "I know better than to go near the rapids. They are still in spate and there are ghosts there," she said, a dull flush spreading up her cheeks. "Only a fool would set foot there of a night."

She lifted her chin, fixed him with a piercing stare. "Truth be told, I doubt I'd even go there by day. The ghosts have been seen by many, they—"

"*Ghosts?*" Jamie looked at her, hoping he'd misunderstood.

She nodded. "Your brothers' spirits, aye. 'Tis why I thought you were Neill. He's been seen down at the cataracts. They all have."

Jamie folded his arms. "I dinna believe in ghosts."

The *Sithe*, aye. There wasn't a Gael born and walking who'd deny the existence of the Good People.

But bogles?

And of his own brothers?

Nay, he couldn't believe it.

Frowning, he drew himself to his full height and put back his shoulders—just to emphasize his denial. "Nay, lass," he repeated, shaking his head, "that canna be. Not Neill. Not any o' my brothers, saints rest their souls."

"I canna say I've seen them, but others have." The Valkyrie gave him a long look. "At the rapids and up at Baldreagan," she added, brushing at her cloak. "Your da sees them most often and they frighten him. That's why I was there tonight. My sister and I take turns looking in on him."

Jamie rubbed a hand down over his face. "The sister you mention, is she Aveline?" he asked, looking back at her.

But she was gone.

Or rather, he could just make out the dark swirl of her

cloak as she disappeared through the trees in the direction of Fairmaiden Castle.

Her father's keep, a sister bound to him by an alliance he had yet to fully believe, and a tangle he wasn't sure he cared to unravel.

But at least Aveline wasn't the Valkyrie.

And nary a jealous *Sithe* princeling had yet appeared, enchanted blade flashing and ready to escort him to his doom.

His plight could have been worse.

Or so he thought until a short while later the vast sprawl of Baldreagan loomed before him. A proud demesne, its sturdy towers rose dark against the surrounding hills. And, as at Hughie Mac's cottage, curling threads of bluish smoke drifted from the tower chimneys. No one could be seen on the parapet walk, nor did anyone shout a challenge as he drew near, yet he could feel wary eyes watching him.

And with reason, for lights shone from some of the higher windows, including the one he knew to be his da's private bedchamber.

But the welcoming effect of the flickering torchlight and the earthy-sweet scent of peat proved sorely dampened by the sprays of red-berried rowan branches affixed to the castle gatehouse.

Red-ribboned and ridiculously large, the rowan clusters stared back at him. A mute warning of what he'd find within, for red-ribboned rowan was his family's special charm.

An ancient cure bestowed on the Macphersons by

Devorgilla, the most respected wise woman in all the
Isles and Western Highlands.

A charm the cailleach had assured would safeguard
the clan's prized cattle, keeping them fat and hardy
throughout the long Highland winters.

But also a talisman said to repel evil of any kind.

Including bogles.

Ghosts.

Jamie frowned. Thinking of his brothers thusly was
not the homecoming he'd envisioned.

Even the weather was less than desirable, for the night
had turned foul, with a thin drizzle chilling him and thick
fog sliding down the braes to creep round Baldreagan's
walls. An eerie, shifting gray shroud that minded all too
easily of his reason for being there.

Refusing to be daunted, Jamie pulled his plaid more
closely around him and peered at his father's empty-
seeming gatehouse. Not surprising, the portcullis was
lowered soundly into place. And since his brothers had
e'er taken turns at sharing the castle watch, there'd be no
telling on whose shoulders such a duty now rested.

He found out when the shutter of one of the gatehouse
windows flew open and a less-than-friendly face glared
down at him.

A young face, and one Jamie didn't recognize.

Even though the lad's freckles and shock of red hair
marked him as a Macpherson.

A herder laddie, Jamie was certain, for when the boy
leaned farther out the tower window, a distinct smell
wafted on the night breeze. As if the lad had just returned
from mucking out the cow byre.

"Who goes there?" the stripling demanded, his suspicious tone lacking all Highland warm-heartedness. "You're chapping unannounced at the door of a house in mourning and I've orders not to open to any."

"Not even to a son of this house?" Jamie rode beneath the window. "I am James of the Heather," he called up to the lad. "I've come to see my father. And pay my respects to my brothers. God rest their souls!"

The herd boy stared at him, disbelief in his eyes. "My laird's youngest son occupies himself in the far south of Kintail, in the service of a MacKenzie, last we heard. He hasn't been to these parts in years."

"That may be, but I am here now and would have entry to my home," Jamie returned, his temples beginning to throb. "It is cold, dark, and wet down here. Too wet for the old bones of the dog I have with me." He reached around and patted Cuillin's head. "We are both weary from traveling."

The boy hesitated, his gaze flicking to Cuillin then back to Jamie.

"You do have the look o' Neill about you," he allowed, still sounding doubtful. "What if you're his bogle?"

"His—" Jamie began, then snapped his mouth shut, unwilling to discuss ghosts twice in the same evening.

Instead, he cleared his throat. "I am my father's son James, so true as I'm here," he said, his head aching in earnest. "Now raise the portcullis and let me in. I would see my da before he sleeps. I was told he's ailing."

"Hah!" came a second voice as a stern-faced old woman appeared at the window. "Aye, and so he is unwell," she confirmed, peering down at Jamie. "He's in a bad way and he willna be troubled this late of an e'en. These are dark times with many ill things afoot. We canna trust—"

She broke off, her eyes rounding. "Jesus wept—it *is* you!" she cried, clapping her hands to her face. "Wee Jamie come home at last. Ach dia, how I've prayed for the day."

Jamie blinked, staring open-mouthed. He scarce trusted his eyes. But the silver-gray curls framing the well-loved face and the sharp, all-seeing eyes were the same.

His indulgent childhood nurse, a woman who'd filled every hour of his earliest years, shielding him from his da's temper and spleen. Soft-hearted for all her bluster, she'd been the mainstay of his youth, lavishing him with warmth and love, salving his boyhood hurts.

And now she stood clutching the window ledge and gawping at him with such moony-eyed astonishment, Jamie felt a surge of warmth and pleasure.

He shook his head, his heart clenching.

"Ach, Morag, is it yourself?" he managed, but then his throat closed and her beloved face blurred before him.

Not that he minded, for in that moment, she whirled from the window and, almost at once, the great spike-tipped portcullis began rattling upward.

That sweet sound ringing in his ears, he spurred beneath, riding straight through the gatehouse arch and into the torch-lit bailey, the chill, cloudy night and even the red-ribboned rowan promptly forgotten.

He was home.

Nothing else mattered.

And if his father's welcome stood in question, Morag was clearly pleased to see him.

Swinging down off his garron, he lifted Cuillin from his basket, then caught the old woman to him in a close embrace.

"Holy saints, Morag, you do not look a day older," he vowed, holding her tight until she pulled away to beam at him, tears spilling down her face.

"Come away in," she urged, dabbing at her eyes, then grabbing his arm and pulling him toward the keep where the massive double doors stood wide. "Praise God, you came," she added as they entered the great hall. "Your da grows more muddle-headed by the day and all in this hall would agree with me."

She squeezed his arm. "'Tis more than his fool ghost talk and losing your brothers that ails him," she confided, lowering her voice. "He's old and knows he split this clan asunder the day he sent you away. He yearns to make peace with you, even if he doesn't know it."

Jamie stopped.

He drew a deep breath and let it out slowly. Across the hall, on the wall above the high table, two well-flaming torches framed the Horn of Days, his clan's most prized treasure, and he had the most uncomfortable sensation that the thing was staring at him.

Waiting.

Or, better said, assessing and challenging him.

Exquisitely carved and banded with jewels, the ivory horn had been given to Jamie's grandfather by Robert the Bruce after the great Scottish victory at Bannockburn. A gift made in appreciation of the clan's support and loyalty.

A celebration of days spent in faithful service to the crown and days filled with prosperity in the clan's future.

Recognition, too, of each new clan chieftain, with the horn now passing with great ceremony from one laird to his successor.

A family tradition that should have honored Neill.

Now the horn would be Jamie's.

Staring at it now, its gleaming jewels still seeming to bore holes into him, Jamie put back his shoulders. He'd accept the horn's challenge and prove himself worthy.

Even, no *especially*, to his father.

Turning back to Morag, he addressed his first hurdle. "So it's as I thought?" he pressed, not forgetting she'd stated his father wished reconciliation even if he didn't know it. "My father did not send for me?"

Morag glanced down, fussed at her skirts.

The clansman crowding around them averted their gazes and even those clustered before the hearth looked elsewhere. Those sitting at the nearest trestle table busied themselves making a fuss over Cuillin. Others took great interest in their ale cups or the wisps of smoke curling along the blackened ceiling rafters.

No one met Jamie's eye. But, he would've sworn their cheeks flushed crimson.

He lifted a brow. "So it was Matheson's doing?"

To his surprise, his kinsmen's bearded faces turned an even brighter shade of red.

Only Morag had the steel to look at him.

"His doing and ours," she admitted, leaning heavily on

her crummock, the same hazel walking stick Jamie was
sure she'd used in his youth. "Alan Mor had the idea after
your brothers . . . *er* . . . when his eldest daughter no
longer had a betrothed. And we"—she waved a hand at
the clansmen suddenly hanging on her every word—
"agreed for your da."

Jamie's eyes flew wide. "You agreed for him?"

Morag nodded, a touch of belligerence tightening her
jaw.

"What else were we to do?" She tilted her head. "Your
da isn't by his wits and willna leave his bed. So we held
a clan council. God kens, he'd reached a fine alliance
with the Mathesons and he needs the grazing grounds that
would've been Sorcha's bride portion. Alan Mor offered
a way to uphold the agreement—"

"By seeing me wed to Matheson's youngest daughter?" Jamie stared at her. "Da knows nothing of this?"

"He does now," Morag owned, still looking too uncomfortable for Jamie's liking. "He's agreed to honor the
alliance."

"And I wouldn't be standing here were I not willing to
meet my obligations," Jamie returned, his gaze sliding
again to the Horn of Days, the great looping swath of his
grandfather's plaid hanging so proudly above it. "He
needn't worry I would unsay his sacred word."

Rather than answer him, Morag fidgeted. "A man of
your da's ilk is ne'er so easily pleased."

Jamie looked at her with narrowed eyes, but she'd
clamped her lips together and he knew the futility of trying to pry them apart.

So he glanced about the smoke-hazed hall, keenly

aware of his kinsmen's speculative stares and the telltale shifting of their feet. The revealing way the tense silence throbbed in the air.

Curling his fingers around his sword belt, he frowned against his suspicions. Morag was keeping something from him and there was only one way to find out what it was. Not that he should care, all things considered.

But another glance at the dais end of the hall, this time at the empty laird's chair, twisted his heart. Much as he didn't care to admit any such weakness.

Sentiment was a dangerous thing.

A pitfall he'd learned to avoid whenever his father crossed his mind.

Giving in to other emotions, he grabbed Morag one more time and planted a smacking kiss on her cheek. "Dinna you worry," he said, lifting his voice so all could hear him. "I am not here to set Da's plan to naught. And I'll do my best to mend the rift between us."

His declaration made, he snatched up a platter of hot, cheese-filled pasties—a savory favorite of his da's—and strode from the hall, swiftly mounting the spiraling stone steps to his father's bedchamber.

A room steeped in darkness and shadows for the shutters were securely fastened and none of the torches or cresset lamps had yet been lit. The only light came from a large log fire blazing on the hearth and a lone night candle.

Munro Macpherson lay asleep in his bed, the covers pulled to his chin, one arm flung over his head.

And the longer Jamie hovered on the threshold gaping at him, the harder he found it to breathe.

So he stalked into the room and plunked down his peace offering on a table beside the hearth. "Cheese pasties just as you like them," he said, his da's snores telling him he hadn't been heard.

"You're looking fine," he lied, wondering when his great stirk of an irritable, cross-grained father had grown so old and frail. "A bit of sustenance in your belly, a hot bath, and you'll be looking even better."

"I dinna want a bath and I told the lot of you I'm not hungry!" Munro's eyes popped open and he glared at Jamie. "I only want—holy saints!" he cried, diving beneath the covers. "Would you jump out of the dark at me again?"

"I'm no ghost." Jamie crossed the room and pulled the covers from his father's head. "I'm James of the Heather, come home to help you set things aright."

"You!" Munro pushed up on his elbows, color flooding back into his face. "I gave orders you weren't to come anywhere near me," he snapped. "And that trumpet-tongued she-goat of a seneschal and every man below-stairs knows it!"

Jamie sat down on the bed and folded his arms. "Mayhap if you'd eat more than the untouched gruel and watered-down wine on yon table, you'd have the strength to better enforce your wishes?"

"I don't have any wishes." Munro glowered at him. "Or can you bring back my sons? And I dinna mean as bogles!"

I am your son.

Jamie left the words unspoken, knowing now what had troubled Morag and his kinsmen.

His da may well have aligned him in marriage to Alan Mor's daughter, but he did so believing he'd be spared any contact with the son he'd e'er considered a bone in his throat.

Even so, a wave of pity for the man swept Jamie.

Pushing to his feet, he crossed the room in three quick strides, pausing before the nearest window. "Fresh air will chase the bogles from your mind," he said, sliding back the latch and throwing wide the shutters.

A blast of cold air rushed inside, but Jamie welcomed its bite. He braced his hands on the window's stone ledge and stared out at the rain-chilled night.

A quiet night cloaked in drifting mist so thick even the hills beyond Baldreagan's walls were little more than dark smudges in the swirling gray.

Somewhere out there Aveline Matheson slept.

Or perhaps she stood at her own window, wondering about him.

Just as chivalry deemed he ought to be thinking of her.

If not with eagerness, at least kindly.

Instead, it was a single glimpse of a dazzling will-o'-the-wisp he couldn't get from his mind. A faery maid so delicate and fine he knew he'd barter his soul if only he could touch a single finger to her shimmering flaxen hair.

Jamie frowned, shaking the notion from his mind.

Other, more serious matters, weighed on his shoulders and in the hope of tending them, he turned from the window and plucked a cheese pastie off the platter on the table and returned to his father's side.

"Eat," he said, thrusting the savory into the old man's hand. "Bogles are more likely to come a-visiting those with empty, growling stomachs than a man well fed and sated."

Munro sniffed. "Dinna you make light of what I see nearly every e'en afore I sleep," he grumbled, scowling fiercely. "And my wits aren't addled as a certain clack-tongued scold surely told you."

"I am glad to hear it," Jamie returned, pleased when his da took a bite of the cheese savory. "Finish that pastie and I'll leave you to your peace. Eat two more and I'll send up a fresh ewer of ale to replace that watery wine."

"Had I known what a thrawn devil you've grown into, I'd have ne'er agreed to Alan Mor's plan," Munro carped, between bites. "Broken alliance or no. And to be sure not to satisfy a snaggle-toothed old woman and a pack o' lackwits who call themselves a council."

"Then why did you?"

Munro tightened his lips and glanced aside. He'd finished the cheese pastie so Jamie went back to the table and retrieved two more.

"Can it be you agreed for the pleasure of seeing me yoked to a Fairmaiden lass?" Jamie lifted a brow, betting he'd latched on to the truth. "'Tis no secret those sisters—"

"The Lady Aveline deserves far better than the likes o' you!" Munro blurted, snatching a savory from Jamie's hand. "And I was cozened into the match, led to believe a groom would be chosen from your cousins. The *council* only saw fit to tell me yestermorn that Alan Mor specified you!"

He all but choked on the savory.

His eyes bugging, he leaned forward. "I'll not besmirch my name by having Matheson and his ring-tailed minions claim I reneged on my word," he vowed, wagging a cheese-flecked finger. "And, to be sure, you're the lesser evil, much as it pains me to say it. I'm right fond of the wee lassie and I'd see her away from her da. He's a scourge on the heather and I dinna like how he treats her."

Jamie stared at him, his mind whirling.

All knew Munro Macpherson had little time for women, save bickering with Morag or shouting orders at serving wenches. Tongue-waggers even claimed he hadn't once lifted a skirt since losing Jamie's mother.

Yet his agitation indicated he genuinely liked Jamie's intended bride.

"Dinna gawp at me like a landed fish," he groused, reaching for the third savory. "Now keep your word and leave me be."

"As you wish," Jamie agreed, moving to the door. He looked back over his shoulder, not at all surprised to see his father still frowning at him.

But at least he was eating.

Jamie smiled. "I'll send up someone with the promised ale. See that you drink it."

But as he made his way back to the hall, the victory in getting sustenance into his da's belly warred with the revelation that his cantankerous, hard-bitten father had a soft spot for Aveline Matheson.

It remained only to be seen why.

Chapter Three

✦

Jamie's good humor lasted until almost noontide the next day. But every shred deserted him as soon as he arrived at Fairmaiden Castle and two of Alan Mor Matheson's burly stalwarts escorted him into the stronghold's great hall. Whether the louts appeared friendly or not, he stopped just inside the shadowed entry arch, planting his feet firmly in the rushes and folding his arms over his chest.

The back of his neck was prickling and that was never a good sign.

Indeed, it was all he could do not to put his hand on the hilt of his sword. Perhaps even draw his steel with a flourish. But he'd come to Fairmaiden as a friend and had thus far seen no true reason for wariness.

Even so, the fine hairs on his nape were stirring and it wasn't the two fool-grinning loons crowding him that caused his discomfiture.

Big as he was, he towered over them and every other

clansman milling about the aisles between the hall's well-filled trestle tables.

Truth was, he'd surely stand head and shoulders over the table-sitters, too.

Though were he to heed the urge to wheel about and leave, he knew he'd be pounced on. Not that he minded a good, manly stramash. Even if Alan Mor's underlings weren't known for fair fighting.

Minions his da called them and Jamie had to agree.

Ne'er had he seen so many different plaids under one roof. Or such a large assemblage of wild-eyed, lawless-looking caterans. Broken and landless men, some were even said to hail from Pabay, a tiny islet off the Isle of Skye and home to any Highland undesirable able to make it safely to that isle's ill-famed shores.

But with generations of Fairmaiden lairds proving unable to sire more than overlarge clutches of daughters, there were few in Kintail who'd rumple a nose at where each new Matheson laird harvested his men.

"Ho, lad! You look like a doomed man standing before the gallows and trying to ignore the dangling noose!" The crooked-nosed giant to Jamie's left clapped him on the shoulder, flashed a roguish smile.

Leaning closer, the brute lowered his voice, "You've no need to fear dipping your wick in aught unsavory," he said, wriggling his brows. "There isn't a man in this hall save Alan Mor himself who'd not give his very breath for one hour with the Lady Aveline beneath him."

Jamie frowned. A nigh irresistible urge to rearrange the oaf's already crooked nose seized him.

But he'd rather not start a melee in Fairmaiden's hall

before he'd even come face-to-face with its laird, so he
ignored the temptation.

A word of warning, however, was certainly due.

"I'll own Laird Matheson wouldna take kindly to any
fool who'd attempt to dishonor his daughter," he said,
flipping back his plaid to display the stout, double-edged
battle-ax thrust beneath his belt, the hilt of his equally impressive sword. "Nor, my friend, would I."

His threat set the men back; his way now clear to enter
the smoke-hazed hall.

He strode forward through the throng, the back of his
neck prickling more with every step he took.

And then he knew.

It was the *hall* that unnerved him; not Alan Mor's
milling horde of cutthroats. Nor was it the reason for his
visit—a neighborly call to confirm the alliance and to
meet his intended bride.

Nay, it was Alan Mor's hall.

A hall like any other, if notably filled with boisterous,
weapon-hung men. And with nary a skirt in sight. Not the
sad-eyed Sorcha or any of her sisters so far as he could
see. Truth be told, Fairmaiden's hall could be anywhere
and anyone's. Its lime-washed walls were well-hung with
the usual banners, weaponry, and a few moth-eaten stags'
heads, and was filled with enough peat smoke to mist the
eyes of noble and baseborn alike.

The expected number of dogs scrounged beneath the
trestle tables and a well-doing fire of birch logs blazed in
the massive double hearth. And speaking for his host, the
floor rushes appeared newly spread, their freshness giv-

ing the black-raftered chamber a cleaner appearance than most.

Alan Mor clearly appreciated his comforts.

But something bothered Jamie all the same.

A queer sense of familiarity he couldn't put his finger on. Something faint and elusive that slid around him, teasing his senses and making his pulse race, his breath come rapid and uneven.

An indescribable something that unsettled him so much he didn't realize he'd returned to the hall's heavy, iron-studded door until his fingers closed over the latch.

And other, equally determined fingers clamped on to his elbow. "Young James Macpherson, I'll wager," boomed a voice deeper than sin. "If you're looking to refresh yourself after your journey, you'll find what you need just off the first landing of the stair tower to your left."

Releasing him, Alan Mor eyed him with mock reproach. "Or were you after leaving before even meeting my daughter?"

"Och, I wasna going anywhere," Jamie lied, stepping away from the door. "I just thought to retrieve my betrothal gift for Lady Aveline," he improvised, remembering the silver gilt mirror and comb his liege lord's friend, Sir Marmaduke, had once pressed on him.

Gewgaws, Kenneth had called the gifts, but Jamie liked them. And he praised the saints he'd been so gripped by his arrival at Baldreagan, that he'd forgotten to fetch them from his saddle pouch.

An oversight that salvaged the moment for Alan Mor slapped his thigh, beaming approval. "So you are the gallant I heard tell you were," the man said, and with fervor. "Not at all like your ill-winded, stiff-necked father."

"My da says much the same of you," Jamie returned, measuring the other. "He—"

"Your lout of a father is blessed to have a son with a more honest tongue than his own!" Alan Mor barked a laugh, then threw an arm around Jamie's shoulders. "Come, lad, and meet your bride. You can fetch whate'er bauble you've brought her later."

Setting off toward the raised dais at the far end of the hall, he shot a sidelong look at Jamie. "If there even is a bauble?"

"Och, aye, that there is," Jamie confirmed. "A mirror and comb of finest silver," he extolled, hoping the other man wouldn't guess he'd had no intention of making the items a betrothal gift.

Truth be told, he'd thought to present them to Baldreagan's cook—in the hope of securing extra portions. A necessity for a man of his size and appetite.

"The mirror is well crafted," he offered, maneuvering around a sleeping dog. "It's thought to be from an ancient Celtic horde or perhaps of Viking origin. The silver is—"

"*A silvered mirror!*" Alan Mor enthused, his voice ringing as they stepped onto the dais. "Heigh-ho! Did you hear that, lass? I told you Young James would do you proud. Such finery! Now what do you say?"

"I say him welcome," came a quiet voice from the far end of the high table.

A softly melodious voice, calm and steady, but edged with a definite trace of reserve.

Jamie's brow furrowed.

Alan Mor barged forward, seemingly oblivious.

"And you, lad?" He nudged Jamie toward the lass. "What do you think of my Aveline?" he boomed, waving an expansive hand. "Is she not fine?"

Jamie looked at her and drew a sharp breath, his world upending.

Aveline Matheson was more than fine.

She was his faery.

And recognizing her almost stopped his heart. As did her perfume of violets and sun-washed summer meadows. A sweet, fresh scent that went to his head so quickly he'd swear it was making him drunk.

It also let him know what had bothered him upon entering Fairmaiden's hall.

It'd been her scent.

He'd recognized it.

Jamie swallowed. Saints, he felt so light-headed the floor seemed to roll and dip beneath his feet, letting him feel almost as unsteady on his legs as the one time he'd had the misfortune to cross the Irish Sea.

Even worse, his birthday tunic, donned especially for his visit to Alan Mor, seemed to have grown even tighter. So uncomfortably tight, he was tempted to slip a relief-spending finger beneath his shirt's fancily embroidered neck opening.

And all the while the Lady Aveline sat watching him, an unreadable expression on her beautiful face.

Her unblinking eyes the very sapphire shade he'd imagined.

Not that it mattered whether she blinked or not.

He was surely blinking enough for the both of them.

And, the saints pity him, the whole of his great, hulking body tingled beneath her steady gaze.

Alan Mor grinned. "Well?"

"She is beyond lovely," Jamie managed, his heart thudding. "A vision."

He started to reach for her hand, but thought better of it and gave her a low bow instead.

He'd crushed more than one knightly bravo's fingers with the firm grip of his overlarge hand. His intended bride had the tiniest, most delicate-looking hands he'd ever seen.

Unthinkable should he forget himself and clasp hers too tightly.

Nor was it wise to touch her silky smooth skin, however innocently. Not with that blue gaze locked on him and her bewitching scent of summer violets wafting so sweetly beneath his nose.

"Lady, you bedazzle me," he said, powerless but to speak the truth.

Her lashes—gold-tipped as he'd suspected—fluttered in surprise. "And you, sir, should have allowed yourself time to catch your breath before coming here." She slid a glance at her father and her lips tightened ever so slightly. "My sorrow that we could not have met under more auspicious circumstances."

She stood then, placing her dainty fingers on Jamie's arm. "I am ever so sorry for your loss."

Jamie nodded, her sympathy warming him.

She stood proud before him, for all that she barely reached his shoulders and that the wildly flickering pulse at the hollow of her throat revealed the nervousness she strove so well to hide.

An edginess her father dismissed with a loud *hrumph*.

"'Fore God! An auspicious meeting!" He clapped a hand on her shoulder, pushing her back onto the trestle bench. "What more favorable way could the man begin his return home than coming here to meet you?"

To Jamie's astonishment, a flash of hot anger flared in her eyes and she lifted her chin, the stare she fixed on her da every bit as challenging as any foe he'd e'er faced down on a field of battle.

"Aside from some quiet time to mourn his brothers, some might say a more propitious beginning might have been to count the coin in those coffers you delivered to his sire," she declared, holding her father's gaze. "My marriage portion, you'll recall?"

Jamie arched a brow, her cheek secretly pleasing him.

Alan Mor laughed. "Ne'er you worry about Munro and his siller. That old he-devil e'er gets what's a-coming to him and he cares far more about the sweet grass in our grazing lands than what's in those strongboxes."

Jamie looked from his intended bride to her father and back again.

He cleared his throat. "If several large, iron-bound chests in my da's bedchamber are meant, I dinna believe he's opened them."

"Hah! Just what I meant!" Alan Mor hooted another laugh. "The man has other worries these days and that's why I'm of a mind to help him turn his thoughts elsewhere."

The words spoken, he thrust a hand beneath his plaid,

fumbling inside its folds until he produced a small leather pouch.

"Let no one say I'm no' letting this alliance cost me," he announced, slapping the pouch onto the table with a flourish. "I sent clear to Inverness for these, had them fashioned by the most skilled goldsmith known to do business in that den of robbers and money-pinchers."

The Lady Aveline turned scarlet.

Jamie eyed the small leather pouch, suspicion beating through him.

Alan Mor turned a pop-eyed stare on them both. "Well, it *would* be inauspicious to use the rings meant for Sorcha and Neill now, wouldn't it?" Grinning, he snatched up the pouch and opened it, letting two gold and sapphire rings tumble into his hand.

Jamie stared at him, his amazement only greater when Alan Mor plunked his treasure on the table and beckoned to a man hovering in the shadows of a nearby window embrasure.

A man Jamie hadn't noticed until now.

A dark, heavy-set man with hooded eyes and garbed in the robes of a monk.

He strode forward, his intent writ all o'er him.

"Baldric of Barevan," he announced, inclining his head to Jamie. "I am well acquainted with your sire. He's gifted our humble church with more than one fine stirk down the years."

"Has he now?" Jamie folded his arms.

"Och, aye." The monk flicked a glance at Jamie's bride, his slitty-eyed gaze holding a shade more appreciation than suited a man of God. He returned his attention to Jamie. "Your union with the Lady Aveline will surely raise your sire's spirits."

"Say you?"

"Ahhh, to be sure." Brother Baldric lifted his face heavenward, made the sign of the cross. "He knows God's hand is in the match. Why, just the other e'en he told me how much he's looking forward to grandsons."

Jamie arched a brow.

The man was a bald-faced liar.

And if Barevan church in distant Moray did lay claim to a Macpherson bull, they'd paid out their noses for the privilege. Like as not double what Jamie's da usually wheedled out of cattle buyers.

"Good sir," he began, "everyone in these hills knows my father has gone out of his way to avoid churchmen since my mother's unfortunate passing, claiming he'd prayed his last and lost his faith that ill-fated night."

Baldric of Barevan shifted from one foot to the other.

He said nothing.

Jamie went on, regardless. "See you, my father would sooner walk naked through a blizzard before he'd gift a wee church clear across the Highlands with one of his prized stirks. Truth be told, before he'd make *any* church such a gift."

This time the monk slid an uncomfortable glance at Alan Mor, but that one only shrugged. "I've no idea what Munro does with his cattle," Alan Mor claimed, settling back in his laird's chair. "I only know he agreed to this alliance."

"Aye, that he did," Jamie confirmed, if only for the sake of Lady Aveline.

Honor and tact forbid him to add that his father was anything but pleased about seeing the lass tied to him. 'Twas a match with one of Jamie's many cousins he'd agreed to.

Munro Macpherson had been cozened.

Just as the smooth-tongued, hand-rubbing monk and Alan Mor were now attempting to do to him.

So he wasn't about to argue about bulls, or his feelings about his sainted mother's death. Not with two such obvious blackguards.

And with other serious matters bearing down on him. Namely which sensation plagued him more—the one that felt like a noose slipping over his head or that his knightly spurs seemed to be getting weightier by the moment.

Putting back his shoulders, he eyed the monk and his smug-looking host. The ever-growing circle of grinning, sword-hung Matheson henchmen crowding around them. Most especially, the Lady Aveline. Saints, the maid was tiny enough to ride a milkweed for a steed. And she had the most lustrous hair he'd ever seen.

Jamie took a deep breath, deliberately turning his mind from her beauty. At the moment he needed his wits about him.

Refusal or chivalric duty.

Those were his choices.

And if his guess about the holy man's presence proved accurate, he'd need to decide soon.

Unfortunately, his annoyance at being duped must've shown because his bride-to-be's eyes rounded as her gaze flitted between him, her da, and the monk. And unless his own eyes were failing him, she even looked a little faint, all color draining from her face.

Worse, she'd begun to tremble.

But she surprised him by leaping to her feet and wheeling on her father. "You swore he knew the betrothal ceremony was this noon!" she accused him. "You've made a fool of me—letting me dress in my best gown and braid silver ribbons into my hair! You looked on when Sorcha left the hall, telling her you understood why she couldn't bear to be a witness, reminded of the day she pledged herself to Neill."

"Now, lass." Her father raised a hand. "You ken I ne'er do aught without good reason."

Ignoring him, Aveline jammed her hands on her hips and aimed an equally livid glare on Brother Baldric. Likewise the rough-looking clansmen who'd crowded onto the dais.

"All of you knew!" she railed, her blue eyes snapping. "Everyone knew save the most important soul beneath this roof. James of the Heather!"

She glanced at him then, both sympathy and agitation pouring off her.

"He wasn't told. Just look at him. 'Tis plain to see he knew naught of this." She pressed a hand to her breast, drew a great breath. "I will not be party to such a deception! I—"

"You are beset by the womanly fears that seize every bride on such a day," Jamie declared, her distress making his decision for him.

That, and the endlessly heavy weight of his spurs.

Feeling that weight pressing on him, he stepped closer

to her, using the width of his back and shoulders to shield
her from curious stares. If there was one thing he couldn't
tolerate it was seeing a woman mistreated or shamed.
Blessedly, in this instance, he had the means to salve her
embarrassment.

He straightened his back, steeling himself to lie for the
second time since entering Fairmaiden's hall.

"For truth, I swear to you I knew about the betrothed
ceremony," he vowed, certain a lightning bolt would
strike him dead on his ride back to Baldreagan. "My da
told me of it when I arrived yestereve."

She looked at him, disbelief clouding her eyes.

Jamie slid a finger beneath her chin, lifting her face toward his. "Think, lass. Why else would I have brought
you a fine mirror and comb as betrothal gifts?"

On his words, she bit her lip and blinked, clearly struggling to keep tears from spilling down her cheeks.

And just looking at her, Jamie knew himself lost.

Knew he'd made the right choice.

Even if the lie someday found him sharing a pool o'
brimstone with Alan Mor and his shifty-eyed monk.

He narrowed his eyes on them now, not at all surprised
when they squirmed. For truth, they had good reason to
do so. If either of them e'er exposed him for speaking
falsely, he'd forget his size and strength and give them
such a pounding they'd wish they'd ne'er been born.

Unfortunately, Lady Aveline still looked doubtful.

And more than a shade unhappy.

"Is this true?" She slipped from Jamie's grasp and
turned back to her father. "He did know the ceremony

was set for today? This is not one of your schemes to force him into a plight troth he doesn't want?"

Before Alan Mor could respond, James Macpherson stepped close and placed his hand on her shoulder. "I would not be here did I not wish to bind myself to you, my lady. Dinna you think to doubt it, for I have ne'er spoken truer words," he said, his voice soft and low, the warmth of his fingers spilling all through her.

"You don't even know me," Aveline couldn't help but protest, his touch unsettling her. "And I do not know you. We have ne'er even seen each other before this day. We—"

"We both know that isn't true," he said, his fingers tightening ever so slightly on her shoulder. "I *do* want you."

Aveline's breath caught, his words setting her heart to fluttering for he'd dipped his head to her ear and spoken them just for her.

Equally pleasing, he kept his hand on her shoulder in a reassuring way, his touch more welcome and pleasurable than she would have believed. Especially when his thumb began moving in ever so light circles up and down the side of her neck, each tender caress soothing and melting her.

"Hah!" Alan Mor slapped the monk's back with a resounding whack. "Will you look at that?" he cried, his mirth scarce contained. "I coulda searched miles through the rock and heather to find the best husband for my wee lassie and here's my arch-fiend's youngest, smitten as the day is long!"

He rocked back on his heels, his face splitting in a

grin. "Suffering saints! And to think the girl doubted me!"

"There is e'er reason to doubt you," Aveline grumbled beneath her breath, watching her da's mummery with suspicion.

But she couldn't deny that he appeared genuinely pleased.

And like as not, he was. Even if his reasons would be his own self-serving ones and not his professed concern for Munro Macpherson and that one's well-doing.

To be sure, he didn't care a jot if Laird Macpherson's strapping son found favor with her or nay.

Even less that she thought he was the most powerfully handsome man she'd e'er set eyes upon. His great size and similarity of feature revealed his kinship to his brothers, but she was quite sure he'd top even Neill by an inch or more were they to stand side by side.

His shoulders looked wider, too. Definitely more impressively muscled. And though Neill had been a pleasure for any lass to rest her eyes upon, he'd worn his pride and station like a crown and Aveline had ne'er felt wholly at ease beneath his stern, sometimes arrogant stares.

No matter that Sorcha e'er insisted there hadn't been a vainglorious bone in his undeniably comely body.

But *this* Macpherson had his clan's far-famed looks and a good heart. That, she could already tell. It'd been especially apparent in the way his voice had softened when he'd spoken of his mother. And she'd seen it, too, in his readiness to comfort her.

She suspected he had a dimple, too. Something she'd

watch for as soon as he ceased frowning at her father and Brother Baldric.

And, saints preserve her, but she was certain she'd also caught glimpses of glistening, coppery-colored chest hair at the neck opening of his tunic.

Aveline moistened her lips, the notion exciting her. Would such hairs prove as soft and glossy as they'd looked? Or would she find them wiry and crisp?

That she even wanted to know astounded her.

As did the tingling warmth that spooled through her the longer she thought about such things. Aye, she decided, watching him, he was the finest, most magnificent man she'd ever seen.

And the most valiant from what she could tell.

Proving it, he stepped forward and took the two rings from the table, lifting them in the air. "Let it be known that this betrothal ceremony is both binding and desired," he said, raising his voice so all could hear.

Saying the words before his good sense kicked in and sent him hastening from the hall to seek a bride not burdened by a sire he knew to be more slippery than an eel.

Instead, he cleared his throat and concentrated only on her beautiful sapphire eyes, the scent of summer violets.

"I, James of the Heather, take you, Aveline of Fairmaiden, as my betrothed bride," he said, a burst of boisterous approval rising in the hall as he slid the smaller of the two gold-and-sapphire rings onto her finger.

Not surprising, so soon as the ruckus died down, Brother Baldric began rattling off his assets. And one quick glance at Alan Mor's beaming countenance told him where the monk had gleaned such knowledge.

But before he could comment, the second ring was gleaming on his own finger, his *Sithe* maid's soft voice accepting his plight troth and offering her own.

And then the deed was done.

The faery was his bride.

About the same time but across a few mist-draped hills and the wild torrent of water known as the Garbh Uisge, Munro Macpherson tossed in his curtained bed, trying to decide between the perils of falling asleep and risking another fearing dream or staying awake and listening for the heavy breathing that always heralded the arrival of his sons' ghosts.

"Ach—for guidsakes!" Scowling fiercely, he punched down his pillows for what had to be the hundredth time since chasing Morag and her fool meal tray from the room. "Beset by bogles and bowls of gruel in my own bedchamber!"

Flipping onto his stomach, he squeezed shut his eyes and resisted the temptation to jam his fingers into his ears. Whether or not anyone could see him, sequestered as he was behind his tightly drawn bed curtains, scarce mattered.

He was still a man of power and consequence and should maintain at least a semblance of lairdly dignity.

And to that effect, fearing dreams seemed less treacherous than staring into the gloom of his enclosed bed, his ears peeled for any sound he shouldn't be hearing.

Not comfortably ensconced in his own well-shuttered and barricaded privy chamber.

Pursing his lips, he reached to part the bed curtains just

a wee bit. Only to make certain that fox Alan Mor's strongboxes of stones were still piled against the bolted door. Blessedly, they were. And they provided sound proof against further intrusions from his long-nosed she-bat of a seneschal and any lackeys she might send abovestairs to pester and annoy him.

He almost snorted. That was something they all seemed ever good at, bedeviling him.

Alan Mor, by thinking him so simpleminded he'd be fooled by a thin layer o' coin spread oe'r a coffer filled with rocks.

Morag and his kinsmen, by repeatedly sneaking into his bedchamber when he slept to throw open the shutters, nigh blinding him. Or expecting him to eat pig's swill they called gruel and believe such a sorry excuse for victuals would replenish his strength.

His strength, a goat's arse!

He hooted his scorn, sending a last glance at the iron-bound coffers. Saints, he would've smiled were he not so concerned about bogles.

But he was, so he let the bed curtains fall shut again and frowned into his pillow.

Truth was, a whole teetering tower of strongboxes wouldn't keep out a ghost. But the three heavy chests he'd managed to pile on top of each other at the door did prove he hadn't lost his muscle.

That he knew the coffers' contents without peeking inside showed his wits were still with him as well.

If Alan—*fox-brained*—Mor possessed even half his own cunning, the lout would know the Fairmaiden grazing ground was more than enough to satisfy him.

That, and the flap-tongued fool's precious wee lassie.

And thinking about her brought a smile to his tired, angst-fraught heart, so he snuggled more deeply into his bedcovers, certain that, for once, his sleep would prove untroubled.

Regrettably, instead of dreaming about sitting before the fire, his feet up and a bouncing, red-cheeked grandson on his lap, it was the sound of water that invaded his sleep.

Swift, swirling water plunging wildly over tumbled rocks. A churning cauldron of froth and spume, its thunderous roar echoed inside the confines of Munro's curtained bed.

A refuge no longer framed by the dark oak of his great bed's canopy but the wind-tossed branches of the skeletal birches rimming the Rough Waters.

The dread Garbh Uisge.

The cataract-filled gorge where his sons had lost their lives.

Sons he could see now, their broken bodies shooting over the rapids, their death cries carried on the wind. Some of them already bobbed lifelessly in deeper, more quiet pools near the gorge's end.

But others still suffered, their battered bodies crashing against the rocks, their flailing arms splashing him with icy, deadly water.

Munro groaned in his sleep, his fingers digging into the bedcovers as his heart began to race. Sweat beaded his forehead, damping his pillow.

The tangled sheets and plaiding of his bed.

Mist and spray surrounded him, its chill wetness making him shiver and quake. And then the rushing water surged across him, carrying him ever closer to his sons' reaching arms. The facedown, floating bodies of the ones already claimed by their watery fates.

"No-o-o!" Munro cried, his eyes snapping open.

He pulled in a great gulp of air, noticing at once the pool of water he'd been wallowing in.

How wet he was.

And that someone had ripped open the bed curtains.

"Of a mercy!" He sat up, dashing his streaming wet hair from his eyes.

He swiped a hand across his water-speckled beard, peering into the gloom and shadows. Sodden or nay, he wasn't about to throw off the covers. Only a spirit could've brought the Garbh Uisge into his room and experience warned him he'd soon see that ghost.

And he did, recognizing Neill despite the dripping wet cloak he wore, the dark cowl pulled low over his white, hollow-eyed face.

An accusing face, filled with recrimination.

"You did this," his eldest son decried, pointing at him. "You and your insatiable greed."

Munro scrabbled backward on the bed. "Begone, I beg you!" he wailed, his teeth chattering. "I had naught to do with—"

"Aye, you did naught. But you could have repaired the bridge." Neill backed into the shadows, his tall form already beginning to waver and fade. "Now it is too late."

And then the shadows closed around him just as the rushing waters of Munro's fearing dream had swirled around and over him, pulling him ever deeper into the horrors he couldn't flee even in sleep.

Trembling uncontrollably, he somehow crawled from his bed and tapped his way across the chamber, making for his chair. Hard-backed and sturdy as befitted a Highland laird's dignity, the chair was anything but comfortable.

But with a dry plaid draped around him and another spread over his knees, it would suffice as a resting place until his bedding dried.

Loud as he'd roared at Morag the last time she'd poked her grizzled head around his door, she wouldn't be coming abovestairs to see to his comforts for a while. A good long while, like as not. And his pride kept him from calling out for her.

So he dropped down onto his chair, tucked himself into his plaids as best he could, and frowned, in especial at the pile of Alan Mor's strongboxes blocking his door. Weak-kneed as he was at the moment, he doubted he could move them even if he did wish to go seeking a sympathetic ear.

Truth be told, there was only one soul he knew whose strength could push open his barricaded door. Munro's brows snapped together. Och, aye, unnerved as he was just now, he might even be glad to see his youngest son.

Infuriated by the notion, he sat back and turned his face toward the fire.

Then he did his lairdly best to pretend such a fool thought had ne'er entered his mind.

Chapter Four

✣

Jamie stood before the arched windows of Alan Mor's hall, for all intents and purposes legally bound to the Fairmaiden laird's faery-like daughter and about to perform his first act as her personal champion.

Once the jostling buffoons crowding around her drew her away from the high table, he'd have words with Alan Mor. Words that needn't reach her gentle ears.

Some things were best kept between men.

A muscle twitched in Jamie's jaw and he flexed his fingers, waiting.

Her composure regained, his new lady accepted her father's men's well wishes with perfect poise. She joined in their laughter and met their cheers and jesting with a dazzling smile, her sapphire eyes alight and glittering in the glow of the torches.

And the longer Jamie watched her, the more she pleased him.

Her voice carried to him, its low-pitch beguiling, its

smoothness flowing over him like honeyed wine. Saints, but he wanted to touch her. Indeed, just looking at her was almost like a physical touching and he burned to cross swiftly to her and pull her into his arms, holding her close and letting her spill soft, sweet words all over him until he fair drowned in them.

But someone had appeared with a generously heaped platter of fried apple fritters and spiced pears, the tempting delicacies drawing enough attention for Jamie to seize his chance.

The time was nigh.

Leaving the shadows of the window embrasure, he strode purposely toward the high table, his plaid thrown back to reveal the many-notched haft of his Norseman's ax and the leather-wrapped hilt of his steel.

Upon seeing him, Alan Mor grinned and reached for the ale jug, making to pour Jamie a cup of the frothy brew. But Jamie took the cup before his good-father could fill it, setting it deliberately out of reach.

Alan Mor's smile faded.

"Ho! What's this?" he queried, one brow arcing. "Refusing my ale? I'd think you'd be after quenching your thirst on such a notable day?"

"Notable, aye," Jamie allowed. "'Tis also a day for plain speaking."

Alan Mor eyed him. "My ears are open," he said, sliding a glance to where Aveline stood in the midst of a crush of apple-fritter-eating clansmen. "Dinna tell me you are displeased with my daughter?"

Jamie took the ale jug and poured himself a portion,

not taking his gaze off the other man as he downed the ale.

"Displeased with her?" he echoed at last, returning the cup to the table. "With surety, nay. But I am mightily vexed to have been duped. See that it ne'er happens again."

To Jamie's surprise, his words only earned him another smile.

"I would hope to stand higher in your favor, having arranged for you to have such a prize." Alan Mor cast another quick glance in his daughter's direction. "She—"

"Is too great a treasure to be publicly shamed," Jamie cut him off, his voice pitched for Alan Mor alone. "Embarrass her e'er again and be warned that you shall answer to me and there'd be no escaping." Jamie let his fingers curl demonstrably around his sword hilt. "I would be after you in a thrice, on your heels as relentlessly as yon greyhounds curled before your hearth fire."

Again to Jamie's surprise, the older man's smile deepened and he slapped the table, this time even barking a laugh. "Saints, had I known you'd take such umbrage, lad, I'd have been more subtle," he vowed, pushing to his feet. "But I am an auld, gruff man, unused to courtly airs and fine ways."

Unmoved, Jamie plucked a fine-looking morsel of roasted meat off the table and tossed the tidbit to a nearby dog. "Forget what I said about your greyhounds," he said, wiping his hands. "Cause yon lassie a single moment of grief from this day forward and I shall be your shadow."

"'Grief'?" The older man grabbed Jamie's arm, turning him toward the cluster of revelers mid-hall. "Say me she doesn't look happier than any maid you've e'er seen."

And she did.

Jamie couldn't deny it.

"All the same," he said, shaking off the other's grasp, "I would that she remains that way. And I'd have a private word with her now. Somewhere away from your hall and where she may speak freely."

Alan Mor dropped back down into his laird's chair, then waved a casual hand. "Auld and gruff I may be, but no' thoughtless. My privy solar has already been readied for you, and with all the comforts of my house."

Jamie nodded, then turned on his heel. He needed but a few long strides to reach Aveline's side. When he did, he brought her hand to his lips and kissed it.

A privilege entirely his, but dangerous.

Just breathing in her violet scent stirred him. Feeling the softness of her skin beneath his lips proved a greater temptation than he'd expected.

Or needed.

Especially now, when he wished to speak earnest words with her.

"Come," she said, twining her fingers with his and leading him from the hall, "I saw you exchange words with my father and understand you'll wish to speak with me." She looked up at him then, her sapphire eyes long-lashed and luminous. "I would speak privily with you, too. My father's solar has been prepared and awaits us."

And it did indeed, Jamie observed when, a short while later, she led him into the quiet chamber, closing the door soundly behind them.

Little more than a small, low-vaulted chamber just above Fairmaiden's great hall, the room held all the comforts Alan Mor could boast. As belowstairs, the floor rushes appeared freshly strewn and sweet smelling and the walls were recently limed, their whiteness holding nary a trace of soot from the pleasant little peat fire glowing on the hearth grate.

A settle near the door invited with finely embroidered cushions and a fur-lined coverlet, while a small table held a light repast of green cheese, cold beef slices, and honeyed almonds.

And Jamie knew without sampling, that the beckoning ewer of wine would prove as heady as any he'd e'er sampled.

Above all, it was the room's smallness that undid him. Close as it was, the tidy little chamber captured and held his bride's bewitching scent. Even the chill, damp air pouring in through the narrow window arches couldn't dispel her pleasing essence.

Her perfume swirled around him, its hint of summer sun and violets teasing his senses. Truth tell, everything about her was proving almost more an enchantment than he could bear.

Especially when she rested a hand on his arm and peered up at him with such concern that his heart skittered.

"I know what's troubling you," she said, lifting her chin. "But you've no cause to harbor such doubts."

Jamie looked at her. "Doubts?"

She nodded, sure of it. "I told you—I saw you speaking with my father. Your displeasure was plain to see."

"My displeasure had naught to—"

"Hear me out, please," she cut in, touching her fingers to his lips. "If it is my size giving you pause, be assured that just because I may look delicate doesn't mean I cannot run a household."

She peered up him, well aware at least two past suitors had rejected her because she didn't appear robust enough. And equally aware she didn't want such concerns clouding her union with James Macpherson.

But he surprised her by looking at her as if he could hardly believe his ears.

Relief sluiced through her, hot and swift.

Especially when he waved aside her worries. "Sweet lady, nothing is farther from the truth," he declared, and her heart gave a lurch. "I've seen the comforts of your home and know you and your lady sister are responsible. Anyone who'd question your abilities is a fool."

Pleased as well as a bit nervous beneath the intensity of his gaze, Aveline crossed the little chamber and flicked the edge of a wall hanging. Truly exquisite, the colors were jewel-bright, the hunting scene depicted of a quality Jamie hadn't seen since leaving Eilean Creag, the isle-girt castle belonging to his first liege laird, Duncan MacKenzie.

"I stitched every thread of this tapestry," his bride revealed, the touching blend of her pride and vulnerability piercing his heart. "And the pillows piled high on the settle by the door."

"Lass, you needn't prove yourself—"

"I can read and Sorcha and I share the task of keeping Father's household accounts," she plunged on as if he hadn't spoken. "Sorcha and I have even run Fairmaiden on our own, in dire times, when my father and his men have been off warring or visiting allies. And"—she fixed him with a level stare—"I am knowledgeable in the healing arts and do not grow faint at the sight of blood and broken limbs. I—"

"You are everything a man could hope for, and more than this one e'er dreamed of making his own," Jamie vowed, three quick strides taking him to her. "You misread my displeasure in the hall. Your father and I had manly matters to discuss. They had naught to do with your lady skills."

She blinked. "Then you weren't speaking of me?"

Jamie pulled a hand down over his chin. "Och, we had other issues to resolve," he said, hoping she'd leave it at that. "But you were on my mind, aye."

"If not my abilities, then what were you thinking of?"

"This," Jamie said, leaning down to kiss her.

A gentle kiss, so soft and light as he could make it. Until she melted into him and sighed with what could only be called pleasure. Clinging to him, she parted her lips—lips every bit as luscious and honeyed as he'd known they'd be.

Unable to help himself, he angled his head, deepening the kiss he'd been burning to give her ever since glimpsing her in the wood. He let his tongue tease hers, his heart hammering when she slid her arms around him, holding fast to his shoulders and tangling her fingers in his hair.

Hair just as thick, rich, and silky as she'd imagined. Falling free to his shoulders, the cool, smooth strands spilled through her fingers as seductively as the slow, sensual glides of his tongue against hers. Fine, liquid heat began streaming through her, making her feel dizzy and yet wondrously alive.

Shivery and breathless.

Her heart began to pound and she pressed closer, welcoming his kiss, her own greedy woman's need reveling in how she could feel every thundering beat of his heart echoing through her entire body.

Her nipples tightened against his chest and her knees quivered, the hot strokings of his tongue unleashing a maddeningly delicious swirl of fluttery sensation deep inside her.

A wicked, incredibly pleasurable pulsing she was quite certain she shouldn't be enjoying.

Not here, in her father's privy solar and the door not even bolted.

But he was her plight-trothed husband and his sapphire ring did wink on the fourth finger of her left hand. So she took courage from that ring and gave in to the wonderment, letting her tongue tease and tangle with his, again and again until such white-hot fire raced through her she was certain she'd find herself singed when the kiss ended.

There could be no harm in allowing him to kiss her.

Or in kissing him back.

After all, wasn't this what she'd yearned for when she'd slipped away to St. Bride's Well the other night? Hadn't she stripped naked in the wood? Bathed in sacred water and moonbeams just to ensure a pleasing, passionate match?

And hadn't St. Bride rewarded her with a glimpse of him?

Though, at the time, she'd thought the handsome, strapping knight she'd seen sitting on his horse and staring at her had been a figment of Highland magic.

A moonlit whim of St. Bride to console her lonely, aching heart.

Indeed, garbed in naught but the night mist, his wind-tossed plaid, and gleaming mail, he'd looked too resplendent for her to mistake him for aught else.

Yet now he was here and kissing her. Aveline sighed into his mouth, opening her own wider, silently willing him not to stop, to keep up his bone-melting assault of her senses until she could no longer bear the exquisite friction of her naked breasts rubbing against the rough warmth of his plaid.

Her naked breasts?

Her eyes popped open, the languorous heat that had been pulsing through her gone in a flash. "Oh, no," she gasped, looking down to see her left breast peeking over the top edge of her bodice.

Not the whole of her left breast, but her nipple was fully exposed.

Dusky pink, tightly ruched, and pressed flush against James Macpherson's chest.

"Ach, dia!" She reached to adjust her gown, but he moved with lightning speed, gently capturing her wrist and lowering her hand to her side.

"Dinna fash yourself," he said, touching just the tip of his finger to her thrusting nipple. "I have ne'er seen a more fetching sight and willna have this day end with you distressed. I want you e'er certain in the knowledge of how beautiful I find you."

Holding her gaze, he brought his hand to his mouth and licked his fingers. He returned them to her breast, toying so lightly with her still-puckered nipple that the sensations stirred by his touch almost made her swoon.

Her knees were certainly weakening.

But she was so small. Her breasts nothing at all like the swelling globes her sisters flaunted so proudly. Or the even larger, great-nippled teats she'd seen on a few of the kitchen wenches.

She knew how often the garrison knights begged those kitchen bawds to pull down their bodices. And she knew, too, the kind of slack-jawed, glazed-eyed letch that always overcame the men in the hall when, with a bold wink and a smile, the kitchen maids complied.

Men favored large breasts.

Big, well-fleshed women. Curvaceous and buxom.

Hot-eyed, robust creatures whose hips swayed when they walked, their bosoms all a-jiggle, and who were wont to throw back their heads and laugh heartily. Brazens who drew manly eyes, inspired lust, and were everything she was not.

Imagining those women now, Aveline swallowed, her pulse racing. But Jamie only smiled at her, so much appreciation shining in his twinkling blue eyes that for a moment she would've sworn he stood not in the fire-lit solar, but in the midst of a grassy summer meadow with bright sunlight glancing off his coppery-red hair.

A stiff breeze coming in the windows riffled that hair, lifting the red-gold strands about his brow and Aveline moistened her lips as she looked at him, certain she'd never seen a man who appealed to her more.

With surety she couldn't imagine anyone rivaling his great height. And the width of his shoulders stole her breath. But it was his warmth and natural exuberance that undid her. The irresistible sparkle of humor that lit his whole face when he smiled.

Even so, she flushed, knew intense relief when he eased up her bodice, smoothing the cloth over her breast until her decency was fully restored.

"You do not believe me," he said, his smile fading. "You doubt me when I say how beautiful you are."

"I am—"

"You are lovely," Jamie declared, seeking to soothe her.

He may not have been blessed with sisters, but he'd spent enough years squiring beneath Duncan MacKenzie's roof to observe that puissant laird's two daughters at their best and at their worst.

If his wee sweet bride hadn't been about to bemoan the smallness of her breasts, he'd eat a brick of peat.

Jamie leaned down, dropping a light kiss to the top of her head. "You have enchanted me and I've meant every word I've said to you. I do want you."

But she continued to look unconvinced. "You have ties to the MacKenzies," she argued, her chin lifting. "They have broad connections and influence. You could have had a maid of higher blood. The Black Stag of Kintail would have done you proud."

"Done me proud?" Jamie could only gape at her.

Her hair alone would be the pride of any husband. Adorned with silver ribbons and reaching to her hips, her thick braid could well be plaited of moonbeams, so fair and bright were the strands.

The privilege of being the man allowed to undo such fine tresses, then run his fingers through the rippling, silken mass, swelled his heart with a feeling so close to wonder, he'd almost believe she really did possess a touch of the *Sithe*.

"Sweet lass, you do me proud," he vowed, lifting her braid to his lips. "If you do not believe me, then I must ask if you have ne'er peered into a looking glass?"

Her blush deepened, but she held his gaze. "Considering how I was foisted on you, I am pleased if you are content."

Frowning, Jamie scooped her up into his arms and carried her across the room, lowering her onto the settle by the door.

"Precious lass," he began, pulling up a stool for himself, "I am more than content—I am ensorcelled, and I have been since I first set eyes on you. And I dinna mean belowstairs in your father's hall."

She considered. "You mean when you saw me in the wood."

Jamie nodded. "I thought you were a faery. And I lost my heart to you there and then, thought you were the most beautiful creature I'd e'er seen."

"But you were frowning." She leaned back and looked at him. "I could see your face in the moonlight."

Jamie grinned. "Lady, I can see I shall not be able to hide much from you!" Leaning forward, he brushed a light kiss across her lips. "I've said you enchanted me, and that is the truth of it. But I did hold you for a *Sithe* maid. And, as such," he added, lowering his voice to make her smile, "I feared the wrath of a handsome faery prince. An outraged soul ready to leap out of the heather, fiery sword to hand and swinging."

She pulled a cushion onto her lap, her fingers curling into its tasseled edge. "Why did you think a faery prince would be wroth with you?"

"Because everyone knows the fey can see into the hearts of men and he would have known how smitten I was with you."

"And now that you know I am not of the fair folk?" she pressed. "Now that you have seen—"

"Your loveliness?" Jamie's brow shot upward. "What I saw just now only proved that you are even more beautiful than I'd thought. For certes, finer than any faery!"

Her eyes widened at that, but she looked pleased.

And seeing her face brighten pleased him. Truth be told, everything about her was pleasing.

In his mind, he could still see her nipple, was even tempted to tell her so, likening its sweetness to a pink rosebud. But he didn't want to frighten her so he simply twisted around on the stool, taking the wine jug and filling two chalices with the bloodred wine.

She angled her head, appraising him through her lashes. "I am thinking you could make a crone believe she was a sight to fill manly eyes, but I am aware of my limitations," she challenged, now meeting his gaze directly. "There are some who might say you would be better served by a stout maid of the north. A wide-hipped lass able to bear you fine, strapping sons!"

Jamie almost choked.

And promptly downed the wine he'd just poured for her.

"I ken many a warring mates whose wives are just as wee as you and who've birthed scores of braw and healthy bairns," he lied, now certain beyond all doubt that he'd spouted enough falsehoods to spend eternity just there where he didn't wish to land.

"I am glad." She reached to touch his face, letting her fingers glide down his cheek and along his jaw, across the curve of his lips. "Other suitors have objected to a match because of my size and I'd feared you'd wished time alone with me to discuss similar concerns."

Jamie bristled. His fist itched to smash the nose of any lout who'd so insulted or hurt her.

"That was ne'er my intent," he began, seeking the best words. "I wanted us to speak privately because I wished to tell you I'd seen you in the wood. I wanted to reassure you that I desired this match because of you and not because of any alliance arranged between our fathers."

She lifted a brow. "But you would have agreed to the union all the same."

Jamie nodded, unable to lie.

"Such is the way of things," he reminded her, pleased when she took a sip of the wine. "I would have done my duty. Now, I am eager for the match."

"I am pleased, too." She looked at him, her words stroking dark places in his heart, soothing hurts he'd forgotten plagued him. "If you thought I was a faery, I would have sworn you were one of the great Fingal's mythical Celtic warriors. Ne'er would I have believed such a fine, braw man would ride up out o' the mist!" She finished her wine, but kept her fingers tightened around the stem of the chalice. "See you, I thought St. Bride of the Waters had summoned you. That she'd sent an ancient Gaelic hero to—"

"St. Bride of the Waters?" Jamie stood, began pacing.

He knew better than most who St. Bride was. And it cost him all his strength to keep from crossing himself. Not to see ill omens in Aveline's mention of the Celtic saint's name.

His mother's brow had been rinsed with water from St. Bride's well on the night of his birth.

And one of his earliest memories was of his da's rantings about the saint. His threats to single-handedly dismantle the well and sink so many stones into its spring that nary a trickle e'er again saw the light of day.

Tobar na Slainte was the well's true name.

The Well of Health.

A chill shot through Jamie and he stopped in front of the settle to look down at his bride, remembering now how close the well was to Hughie Mac's cottage.

"What made you think St. Bride sent me? Had you been to fetch water from the well that night?"

"I'd been to bathe in the well," Aveline admitted, not liking the way his face had lost color. "I—"

"You bathed in it?"

She nodded. "I bathed and washed my hair. Why else would I have been hurrying through the wood of a night? Half-dressed and my hair unbound?"

"Why else indeed?" He stared at her, his face even more pale than before. "But that still does not tell me why you mistook me for a Fingalian hero."

"A Fingalian warrior or . . . Highland magic," Aveline said in a rush, watching him.

She stood, squaring her shoulders. "See you, I'd asked St. Bride to bless our union. I knew you were coming and feared you'd be displeased. So I took her an offering of oatcakes and honey and asked for harmony in return."

"Naught else?"

"You must appreciate the suitors I've been presented with," she tried again, not quite able to suppress a shudder. "Whether they withdrew their offers or nay, I would ne'er have consented to wedding them!"

Jamie hid a smile. "That bad?"

"Worse."

"Yet you agreed to the match with me?"

She looked down, flicking her skirts as she dropped back onto the settle. "I am no longer so young as I was," she said, looking up again, a spark of defiance in her eyes. "And I'd grown weary of waiting for a hearth and family of my own."

Jamie sat back onto the stool. "I have ne'er seen the wish for hearth and home put such fire in a maid's eyes," he observed, taking her hands between his own. "What are you keeping from me?"

He wasn't surprised when she pressed her lips together.

Truth be told, he would've sworn she put back her shoulders as well. But wee and delicate as she was, it was difficult to tell.

So he did what he could, lacing his fingers with hers and leaning forward, one brow raised until the resistance went out of her and she blew out a hasty breath.

"That's better," Jamie approved, sitting back and smiling at her. "No shame and no secrets."

"As you wish," she agreed, her cheeks glowing.

Jamie released her hands and topped their wine, clinking his chalice against hers. "So, lass, what other favors did you ask of St. Bride?"

"Only one," she supplied, taking a sip of wine. "Something I suspect all maids yearn for if they are bold enough to admit it."

Jamie smiled at her. "And are you a bold lass?"

She nodded.

"Then what did you ask?"

"For a pleasing and passionate match," she said, the blaze in her eyes melting him. "A new life with a man who loves me and will let my heart meld with his."

A man who will teach me the meaning of mindless rapture and fill my days with joy.

Jamie looked at her, not sure he'd heard her say that last—or if he'd only imagined the words. Either way, he'd heard enough.

His bride was a hot-blooded faery.

And of Fairmaiden stock.

Whoe'er in all the hills would've believed it? His heart took up a slow, hard thumping, a thousand provocative images whirling across his mind. But before an appreciative smile could spread across his face, the door swung open and he swiveled round, glancing toward the threshold.

"Sir James, my father would know if you'll be staying for the evening meal?" Sorcha inquired. "He says he'll open a cask of celebratory wine if you are."

Jamie rose, going forward to greet the lass properly.

Not that he knew what to say to her. Hovering on the threshold, she clutched a rush light in her hand, its upcast light turning her long, sallow face into an even more sorrowful image.

"Lady Sorcha." He made her a quick bow. "You were missed earlier," he said, regretting the words immediately, remembering her reason for avoiding the hall.

But she only nodded, her gaze going past him to Aveline. "Father has ordered Cook to prepare your favorite savories. I vow he is ready to plunder the castle larder just to set a grand table."

"He'll be feeling guilty then," Aveline observed, rising. "He's played with the fates of too many people in recent times and will be wanting to make amends." Coming forward, she touched a hand to her sister's sleeve. "I am sorry, Sorcha, he should not be arranging such a feast. Not with you—"

"I do not mind," Sorcha said with quiet dignity. "The revel will keep my mind from straying where it ought not." Turning back to Jamie, she waited. "Will you stay?"

"My sorrow, but there will not be time for suchlike this e'en," he spoke true. "I would be back at Baldreagan before dusk and I'm hoping to pay my respects to my brothers along the way."

Sorcha inclined her head. "To be sure, my lord. I will inform my father and he will welcome you to our table another time."

"I shall look forward to it."

Sorcha nodded again and retreated, closing the door softly behind her. Jamie almost followed after her, her plight compelling him to comfort her, if only with a few awkward words and a gentle pat or two upon her shoulder.

But by the time he stirred himself to open the door and step onto the landing, the narrow turnpike stair loomed empty. His bride's unhappy sister was already gone.

Turning back to the solar, he was heartened to see that the sky seemed to have lightened. He'd be well served to be on his way before the clouds lowered and the cold rains returned.

His bride had other ideas.

"May I go with you?" she blurted, suddenly standing in front of him.

Jamie blinked. "To Baldreagan?"

She nodded. "I have some wax candles for your father," she said, indicating a cloth-covered basket he hadn't noticed. "He keeps them burning of a night and needs more than Morag can supply him."

Jamie tightened his lips and retrieved the basket, not too keen on catering to his da's fool whims. Like as not, if he'd burn fewer candles, he'd sleep better and imagine less ghostly visitations.

But what was one basket of candles when it meant more time spent in his faery's company?

And even if she weren't a true *Sithe* maid, she certainly had the grace of one. She bedazzled him, standing there limned by the hearth glow and with her violet scent rising up between them, teasing his senses.

For one unsettling moment, she appeared clothed in sparkling, misty glitter and Jamie nigh dropped the basket, but then the image cleared and he realized she'd only flashed him a smile.

"I thank you," she said, touching his chest, and despite the cloud-cast afternoon, he would've sworn the sun itself burst into the tiny chamber. "I know your father can be vexing, but the candles soothe him."

"I suspect it is you who comforts him." Jamie stepped away from her, making long-strided for the door.

His father was a sore subject and other, grievous duties lay ahead of him.

But as his bride slipped past him out the door, his father's scowling face rose up before him and he shot out a hand, circling his fingers around her arm.

"My father is overfond of you," he said, looking down at her. "I doubt it's because you take him candles. Yet"—he paused to angle his head—"so far as I know, he hasn't had a pleasant word for any female in years."

Aveline shrugged. "Perhaps he likes me because of the alliance between our clans?" she suggested, lying out her nose.

Jamie could tell because of the way she avoided his eyes, looking down to flick invisible lint from her gown.

Folding his arms, he drew himself up to his fullest height, fairly or unfairly employing his great bulk as his only self-defense against wee, fetching faery lasses, his over-sized body making escape impossible.

"Could it be you treat him too softly?" Jamie lifted a brow, watching her carefully. "Perhaps listening too long to his blabbering and, through your well-meant sympathy, encouraging his foolery?"

She sniffed. "Some might say you treat him too harshly. He is old and should not be made to pay for past sins or regrets. For myself, I would never do aught that would encourage him to frighten himself."

"Hah!" Jamie grinned. "And there we have it."

"Have what?" Her chin took on a defensive tilt.

"You listen to his prattle about my brothers' ghosts. That is why he is so fond of you."

"Nay, that is not the reason," she said, shaking her head. "Leastways I do not think so."

"Then what do you think?"

"That he likes me because I am the only one who believes him."

Jamie stared at her, his brows shooting upward.

And then he laughed.

"Ah, well, letting him think you believe him may well be it," he agreed, pleased to have solved the riddle.

"You do not understand," she said, the look on her face sending shivers down his spine. "I do not let him think I believe, I honestly do."

Jamie blinked at her. "You believe he sees my brothers' ghosts?"

She nodded. "I know that he does."

"And how do you know?" he asked, feeling the walls beginning to close in on him.

"Because I have seen them, too."

Chapter Five

❦

It wasn't just his father.

His bride had seen the ghosts, too. And her words kept gnawing at Jamie. Especially when they reached his family's chapel and churchyard and he spied all the richly carved grave slabs, the tall Celtic crosses, and other signs of lives long past. Each ancient, moss-covered stone bearing tales and stories.

And some, like the mounded stones covering his brothers' graves, weren't moss-grown at all.

Jamie's breath caught as he drew rein and swung down, reaching out at once to help his bride dismount.

He tried to steel himself, striving to appreciate the beauty and stillness of this sacred place, but it was no use. Telling the sun not to rise in the morning would have been easier.

His brows snapped together in a fierce scowl and his mouth went dry.

His heart split.

"We can leave now." A small hand touched his plaid. "It will make no difference to your brothers if you visit them this night or another," she said, the same note of sympathy in her voice that had so touched him earlier, in her father's hall. "Truth be told, I vow it would please them more if you'd spend the time getting to know your father better. He is not the ogre I know you think he is. He—"

"He ought to have repaired the bridge," Jamie said, still frowning. "Had he not been so tightfisted mayhap my brothers—"

"Do you not think he suffers every night for such a remiss?" Aveline took her hand from his plaid, the warm look of understanding in her eyes cooling. "Can you not think more kindly of him?"

Jamie compressed his lips and ran a hand through his hair. He *was* trying to mend things with his da. Leastways, he was trying to help the man.

But at the moment, the nine burial cairns hit him like a fist in the gut. Nine hard-hitting fists cutting off his air and knifing through him like fire lances. His insides churned and he would've sworn hot, smoldering coals burned in his chest.

Now he knew why he'd put off coming here.

The pain was worse than he'd expected. Far worse. Cold rain and blustery winds were sweeping in from the west, but he paid scarce heed to the rough night.

Even so, the finality of the combined scent of rich damp earth, leaf mold, and regret, almost knocked him to the ground. As did the unspoken echoes of words he wished he'd said and now would ne'er have the chance.

"Holy saints." He blew out a breath, more aware of his bride's pitying glances than was good for him. "If only I'd told them how much I loved them."

"They knew," she said, her voice revealing the thickness in her own throat. She stepped closer, reaching to touch him again, this time smoothing a fold of his plaid. "Their fondness for you was one of the reasons I knew I needn't fear our betrothal."

She raised her head and looked at him. "Your father loves you, too. He hides it well, but he does."

Jamie shrugged. Were they anywhere else, he might have hooted his disbelief. Or questioned her, for the possibility did give his heart a jolt.

But here, in the windy dark of the churchyard, he could see only his brothers' graves. He stared at them, feeling the weight of his sorrow bearing down on his shoulders.

A fierce, searing pain he'd endure gladly if only such suffering would undo the cause.

Certain his soul was ripping, he stared up at the heavens, seeking answers but finding only a scattering of cold, frosty stars and drifting, wind-torn clouds.

The night sky stared back at him with all the chill silence of the hills and the thick-growing whin and broom bushes hemming the churchyard. The dread row of low, piled stones he knew held his brothers' bodies until their fine granite tombs and effigies had been readied for them.

Only he couldn't feel them here.

Not his nine full-of-swagger brothers who should have come strolling forward to welcome him home, their eyes alight and their arms spread wide.

Loud, boisterous, and alive as he remembered them.

Jamie's mouth twisted and he clenched his hands, the hot tightness in his chest stopping his breath. He could think on his brothers all he wished, hearing their voices and seeing their smiles. But still they'd be gone.

Already *were* gone—and well beyond where'er he might reach them.

Nothing but oppressive silence greeted him as he forced himself to approach the graves. A black and eerie quiet marred only by the howling of the wind and the drumming of rain on the dark, wet stones.

That, and as a glance across the deserted churchyard proved, fat clusters of red-berried rowan bedecking the narrow chapel door.

He frowned.

His bride curled her fingers around his elbow, gently squeezing. "Your father thought it best," she explained, once again playing his da's wee champion. "What can be the harm if such safeguards soothe him?"

Jamie tamped down the urge to scowl at her. The *harm* was in allowing his da to sink deeper into his delusions. "My father is close to losing his wits," he finally said. "That is the danger."

The maid's chin shot up. "I told you, I have seen the ghosts, too," she reminded him. "And so have others. Just the other day, one of my father's squires swore he saw Neill and Kendrick in the wood near St. Bride's Well."

This time Jamie did scowl.

But he held his silence, not trusting himself to comment on such foolery.

Neill and Kendrick, his two favorite brothers, were

just as dead as the others. Alan Mor's squire had likely seen morning mist drifting near the sacred well.

Not his brothers' bogles.

"'Tis true," his bride persisted, almost as if she'd read his mind. "I saw how upset the lad was when he came in."

But Jamie scarce heard her. He was looking past her to the chapel, his stomach knotting.

Someone had even draped rowan around the splendid carved standing stone that guarded the entrance to his family's ancient, half-ruined sanctuary. Supposedly built many centuries before by a follower of Skye's far-wandering saint, Maelrhuba, the tiny chapel stood on the site of an even older stone circle.

Clan belief held that the remaining standing stone marked the burial place of the chapel's sainted builder. But some graybeards and local henwives insisted the magnificent Pictish stone was all that survived of the original pagan circle, claiming early Christians destroyed the sacred stones, renaming them Na Clachan Breugach, the Lying Stones.

An intended slur against stones once believed to have been prized as the Stones of Wisdom because of their ability to foretell the future. Tradition claimed that any- one stepping within the stones' charmed inner sanctum on the nights of certain moons would be blessed with brief glimpses of events yet to transpire.

Jamie didn't know which version of the remaining stone's past he believed and, truth be told, he didn't really care.

At the moment, he could only think of his brothers as

he'd last seen them. Bold, brash, and mirthful, each one bursting with spirit and vigor.

" 'Fore God," he swore again, blinking hard.

The wind surged then, splattering his face with icy rain droplets, but he made no move to dash at them. Instead, he let them track down his face, rolling over his cheeks like the tears he could no longer shed.

He did narrow his eyes on the little chapel and its hoary sentinel, fixing his gaze on the rowan garland wrapped round the proud stone's venerable height.

Wind whipped at his plaid and tossed his hair, but he stood rooted beside the burial cairns, his fingers swiping at raindrops that suddenly felt hot on his skin, salty on his lips.

Whether or not the stone was a true remnant of the Na Clachan Breugach, the handsomely carved relic didn't need the rowan's protection.

The monolith held magic of its own.

And so far back as he could remember, deference alone would have kept any Macpherson from even touching a finger to such a sacred relic of the clan's dimmest, haziest past.

"Thunder of heaven," he breathed, his heart drumming against his ribs.

He flashed another glance at the chapel door's rowan-draped lintel. In keeping with old Devorgilla's erstwhile instructions, he could see bright red ribbon winding through the berry-rich branches.

Like as not, he'd find the interior of the church equally festooned; the whole wee chapel brimming with charms and foolery designed to scare away his brothers' souls.

Jamie's jaw tightened. He kicked at a clump of rain-speckled, knee-high deer grass. Then he stooped to snatch up a small rock, hurling it into the moon-glinting waters of a nearby burn. Only Aveline's presence and his damned knight's spurs kept him from muttering an oath that would've blistered the night's chill.

An oath that would've made his brothers roar with laughter and jab each other with their elbows as they wriggled their brows at him, challenging him to do better.

But he couldn't.

Not this night.

Not standing in the wind and rain, heart-stricken, and knowing he'd still be missing them even after he'd drawn his last breath.

Then make me proud and prove you have at least a bit o' my charm by seeing your lady out o' the rain. Now, before it's her last breath that concerns you.

Kendrick!

Jamie started, glancing around.

The words still shimmered in the darkness. They'd come from nowhere and everywhere, yet echoed in his ears so real as if his brother stood right beside him. Glowing with vitality and strength, too handsome by a stretch, and ready as ever to boast about how easily he turned female heads.

Make haste. The voice came again, more urgent but fainter. *Do you not see how the lass shivers?*

But to Jamie's mind, he was the one shivering.

His Fairmaiden bride graced the night composed as always, even if she was staring at the Na Clachan Breugach stone with eyes as wide as if she'd not only heard Kendrick, but seen him as well.

Not that he was going to ask her.

He did coil a quick arm around her and sweep her up against his chest, flipping his plaid over her to shield her from the gusting wind.

But as he strode toward the chapel, a rash of shivers spilled through him. And just when he nudged open the narrow, rowan-bedecked door, he thought he caught a glimpse of something flitting through the trees.

A faintly luminous something, moving away from the cairns and aglow with soft iridescent light.

Until he blinked and nothing but mist-wraiths and empty wind curled through the wood and the only glow in sight proved the glimmer of the moon, peering down at him through the clouds.

The strange light was gone.

And for that reason, he left the chapel door open, preferring a clear view of the churchyard and the surrounding wood of birches and oaks. But he did not fear his brothers' bogles. Truth be told, he'd be keen to see them. But he trusted his instincts.

With all respect to his bride, Fairmaiden Castle was known to attract unsavory men. Broken, clanless caterans well adept at hiding in bracken and heather. Brigands he'd trust to skulk through the gusty night, swinging lanterns and rattling chains, whate'er their nefarious purpose.

A possibility he wasn't about to share with Alan Mor's daughter.

But cold chills such as the ones still slithering down

his spine were the only reason he'd come away whole
from the slaughter at Neville's Cross. He doubted there
was any danger of an English arrow storm descending
upon his family's tiny chapel and churchyard, but something equally unpleasant lurked in the nearby wood.

He was sure of it.

And whatever it was, it wasn't his brothers.

They rested quietly beneath their mounded stones. The
only sign of life within the dank, incense-steeped chapel
squirmed and wriggled in his arms. Soft, warm, and far
too tempting for his current mood. Impatient, too, for she
shoved back the hood of her cloak and looked up at him
the moment he set her on her feet on the rough, stone-
flagged floor.

"You needn't peer about with such caution," she said,
watching him scan the church's dim interior. "They aren't
here. Not now."

"Not now?" He arched a brow at her.

Aveline shook her head.

Jamie folded his arms. " 'Not now implies no longer,' "
he said, uncomfortably aware of the many recumbent effigies of his long-dead ancestors.

Proud Macpherson knights, their tombs lined the
chapel walls and crowded the deeper shadows. Colorful
paint gleamed on their armor and shields, making their
stone helms and swords look startlingly real and bringing
their cold, chiseled features to such vivid life that he
crossed himself.

"And 'no longer' implies they once were here," he finished, trying not to feel his ancestors' stony-eyed stares.

Trying especially to forget that farther back in the

chapel, his mother slept as well. She slumbered deeply, hidden away behind the high altar, well beyond his sword-swinging, shield-carrying forebears, her beautiful marble tomb tucked deliberately out of sight.

As if secreting her sculpted likeness from view might undo its reason for being.

"They were here, aye." His bride's words echoed in the half-dark of the chapel, bringing his thoughts back to the present.

She looked down, flicked a raindrop from her cloak. "Leastways, two of them."

" 'Two of them'?" Jamie could feel the back of his neck heating. "Which two?"

"Neill and Kendrick."

Jamie put back his shoulders, looking at her. "See you, lass, since I'm fairly certain my father would rather roll naked in a patch of stinging nettles before he'd set foot in this chapel, I canna believe he's seen any of my brothers here. Not Neill, not Kend—"

"He didn't. I saw them here." She lifted her chin, her sapphire gaze challenging him.

"You saw Neill and Kendrick?"

She nodded. "Here, and other places, as I told you. But it was outside, in the churchyard where I first saw them. I told your father and he ordered your cousins to bring the rowan charms."

"Then my cousins are as addled as my da."

She looked at him for a moment. "They are devoted to him. And, like me, only sought to ease his cares."

Jamie opened his mouth, but no words came out.

Reminding her that there were some who had good

reason to doubt Munro Macpherson had a caring bone in
his body struck him as sounding too unchivalrous to risk.

But his temples throbbed at the thought of his wild and
unruly cousins descending on the clan chapel, their burly
arms filled with rowan and red ribbon; his family's cattle
charms.

But he didn't want to think on such buffoonery or his
cousins just now.

Not when he'd just learned that this was where Aveline
had seen his brothers. His two favorite brothers.

Especially Kendrick.

Kendrick. The name alone gutted him and he glanced
aside, his gaze falling on the holy water stoup set into the
chapel wall. He jerked, but before he could look away he
felt his jaw slide down and his eyes widen as the pathetic
layer of stone dust lining the empty basin suddenly vanished beneath clear, sparkling water.

Holy water teeming with a black mass of squiggly tadpoles, the whole gelatinous lot swimming in the sacred
stoup.

A boyish prank Kendrick once played on Morag—
much to the amusement of his brothers.

And Jamie as well.

But he wasn't amused now. He was frightened; worried his brain was going as soft as his da's.

A notion that instantly banished the tadpoles.

All saints be praised!

"Kendrick and Neill," he began, studying his bride's
face. "Were they . . . did they . . ." He let the words tail
off, unable to voice what he burned to know.

Just thinking of them dead undid him.

Talking about their ghosts was beyond his strength.

Saints, he still couldn't quite believe in . . . bogles.

But he did have questions.

He began to pace, rubbing the back of his neck as he went. "Were you not afraid? When you saw them?" he asked, shooting her a glance. "Not afeared to come here tonight?"

"Afeared? Of your brothers?" Aveline smiled before she could catch herself. "Och, nay, they do not frighten me. I feel blessed to have seen them."

So soon as the admission left her lips, he stopped beside one of the narrow window slits. "My father doesn't feel blessed when he sees them," he said, looking skeptical. And so handsome in the moonlight streaming in through the window, that her breath caught.

His coppery hair shimmered like burnished gold against the cold wall, the raindrops caught in the glossy strands gilded silver and glittering like diamonds. And with his great height and size, he made the tiny, vaulted chapel seem even smaller. Almost insignificant, with its dank stone and shadows, while throbbing vitality and rich, glowing warmth seemed to pour off him.

She started forward, then hesitated, not certain she trusted herself not to blush if she stepped too close to him.

Even standing where she was, she could breathe in his scent, a heady masculine blend of clean leather and linen. Chill blustery winds and the freshness of rain.

A heady mixture she inhaled with pleasure, especially when she recalled the more unsavory smells that had swirled around some of her less appealing suitors in the past.

Shuddering, she rubbed her arms. Truth was, she'd always known her husband would be chosen for her, but she'd never expected him to be so dashing.

Or so valiant, she admitted, remembering how he'd sheltered her from curious stares in her father's hall. How he'd leaned close and lowered his voice, whispering soothing words to reassure her.

She swallowed, half-afraid to trust the emotions he kindled inside her.

The hope that he might be the answer to her most secret dreams, her deepest longings.

The kind of things she shouldn't be thinking about now. Not here in his family's chapel with him peering into the gloom, his jaw clenched and a frown creasing his brow.

Almost as if he expected one of his stone-hewn ancestors to leap up and challenge him for daring to intrude on their eternal slumber.

But then his gaze snapped back to her, his eyes narrowed and assessing. "How can you be so at ease about having seen my brothers when my father—a man many times your size and strength—cowers in his bed at the mere mention of their names?"

She lifted her chin. "He has reason to fear them. They are angry when they appear to him."

"So I have heard." He folded his arms, eyeing her. "Yet they were not wroth with you when you saw them?"

"They did not visit me," Aveline explained. "I simply happened to see them. There is a difference."

She moved to one of the tombs, tracing the sculpted edge of the effigy knight's sword.

She wanted to speak of her dreams.

Her hopes for a harmonious future, one filled with family and sharing. Mutual respect and, if they were blessed, love.

Love and passion. Those were the things she burned to explore with him. Not talk of bogles and things neither one of them could change.

But he was striding around the chapel again, clearly bent on a lengthy discourse. "My brothers did not appear ill-humored when you saw them?" he asked, proving it.

Aveline sighed.

"I have seen Neill and Kendrick twice," she admitted, drawing her cloak tighter about her. "Once near the Garbh Uisge, but at such a distance I canna say whether they looked grieved or nay. And the time I saw them here, in the churchyard, they were anything but angry."

She paused to look at him. "If you would know the truth of it, they were dancing."

"Dancing?" Jamie halted abruptly. "You saw Neill and Kendrick dancing? In the churchyard?"

She nodded. "Aye, in the churchyard. With Hughie Mac."

Jamie stared at her, his astonishment complete. "But Hughie isn't dead. I've not yet seen him, but I asked of his health as soon as I arrived. Morag swore he's fit as his fiddle strings."

She shrugged. "I can only tell you what I saw."

"And what exactly did you see?"

She went to one of the windows, looked out at the

rainy night. "I told you. They were in good cheer and dancing. And Hughie Mac, he was standing in the moonlight, playing his fiddle."

"But Hughie—"

"Och, he's fine," she confirmed. "I went to look in on him the next day. He said naught of your brothers, so I didn't ask. It was enough to know him hale and well."

Jamie shook his head. "You must've been dreamwalking."

"Like as not," she agreed. "But whether I dreamed your brothers or nay, I am glad I saw them happy. I was able to share the tale with your father and I believe it comforted him to know I'd seen them in good heart."

But Jamie only made a noncommittal *humph* and started walking away from her, his entire attention on one of his stone-cast ancestors.

A particularly lifelike ancestor, for even in the chapel's dimness, the vibrant paint decorating the carved stone effigy made him appear jauntily swathed in plaid.

"Ach—for guidsakes!" He stopped before the tomb, his eyes rounding.

His knightly ancestor *was* wearing plaid.

In all his days and a lifetime of Highland weather, he'd ne'er seen a Macpherson plaid as sopping wet and dripping as this one.

"What in the name of glory?" He stared down at it, blinking, but there could be no mistaking.

It was definitely a dripping wet Macpherson plaid.

And on a closer inspection, the thing wasn't draped artfully over the effigy as he'd surmised.

It'd been carelessly flung there.

Half the plaid hung down the side of the tomb, its end pooling in a soggy heap on the chapel floor.

An insult to his name even his wild-eyed and rowdy cousins wouldn't allow themselves.

Anger swelling in his breast, Jamie stared at the puddle of water spreading away from the base of the tomb. He clenched his fists, unable to think who would do such a thing.

He'd e'er suspected some of his randier cousins used the secluded little sanctuary for a trysting place with light-skirted kitchen lasses, but even if a kinsman had indulged in such bed sport inside the darkened chapel, he didn't ken a one of them who'd spread his plaid on the uneven stone floor and leave it there.

And to be sure, he didn't ken a soul who'd toss a wet plaid across the solemn form of a sleeping forebear.

Frowning, he stepped closer, touching a finger to the sodden wool. His suspicious warrior nose noted, too, that the plaid didn't stink.

Its drenching was recent.

Yet the slanting rain now lashing against the chapel walls had only begun after he'd carried his bride inside. The rain that had dampened them in the churchyard at the burial cairns had been little more than a Highland shower.

A wetting rain, aye, but not near enough for the voluminous folds of a many-elled great plaid to absorb such a huge amount of water.

A startled gasp sounded behind him and he whirled around to see Aveline hurrying toward him, her gaze fastened on the plaid-draped effigy, her feet flying all too quickly over the wet floor.

"Dia!" she cried, looking aghast. "What is—"

"Slow, lass! There's a puddle," Jamie warned too late.

"*Ei-eeee!*" Her foot slipped on the slick stone flags and she went flying, her arms flailing wildly. But only for the instant it took Jamie to leap forward and catch her before she could fall.

His heart pounding, he clutched her to him, cradling her in his arms and holding her head against his shoulder. "Saints o' mercy," he breathed, not wanting to think of what might have happened if he hadn't caught her.

If she'd slammed down onto the hard, wet stones of the floor.

Or worse, hit her head on the edge of a tomb.

"Dinna e'er run across a wet floor again," he said, well aware he was squeezing her too tightly but somehow unable to hold her gently.

She twisted to peer up at him, the movement bringing her face dangerously close to his. "I didn't know the flags were wet," she said, her soft breath warm on his neck. "I couldn't see the puddle in the dark."

Jamie frowned. "Then dinna do that, either," he warned, releasing her. "Flying about in the shadows!"

She shook out her skirts. "I wanted to see what was bothering you."

You and all your enchantments are bothering me, Jamie almost roared.

Instead, he allowed himself another *humph*.

Then he looked at her, astounded she didn't know how perilously close he was to forgetting the wet floor and even his dripping-tartan-hung ancestor.

He could ponder such mysteries later.

For now, she looked too fetching and dear for him to care about much else.

Especially considering her skirts had hitched to a delightful degree, plainly exposing her slim, shapely legs and even a glimpse of pale, satiny hip.

And, saints preserve him, for one heart-stopping moment, he'd caught an intimate enough flash of nakedness to know the curls betwixt her thighs looked so silky and tempting he burned to devour her whole.

"You know I shall not be taking you back to Fairmaiden tonight," he said when he trusted himself to speak. "The hall at Baldreagan should be nigh empty by the time we return and I would enjoy sitting with you in a quiet corner, perhaps before the hearth fire."

If the hall proved as private as he hoped.

And above all, if he wasn't mistaking the meaning of the flush staining her cheeks. The wonderment in her soft, wide-eyed expression and the way she kept moistening her lips.

How pliant she'd gone in his arms.

All soft and womanly.

As if she'd welcome another kiss, perhaps even some gentle stroking.

"Sorcha and I have slept at Baldreagan before," she said, watching him. "On nights when your father was restless and wished to talk."

Jamie drew a breath and let it out slowly. "Your sister's plight weighs heavy on my mind," he said, picking up the wet plaid with his free hand. "So soon as things settle and she is in better spirits, I will do what I can to find a husband for her. Perhaps—"

"My sister loved Neill," she cut in, letting him lead her from the water-stained tomb. "She truly grieves for him. I do not think she will wish to wed another."

No one will have her.

Some even whisper that losing Neill has turned her mind.

The unspoken words hung between them, loud and troubling as if they echoed off the chapel walls.

Frowning, Jamie cleared his throat, seeking a solution.

"Even if she does not desire a husband," he began, hoping he'd found one, "perhaps she will warm to the thought of a family? A marriage to a widowed clansman? One with wee bairns in need of a mother?"

To his relief, Aveline smiled. "Oh, aye, that might please her," she said, her eyes sparkling. "Do you have anyone in particular in mind?"

"Och, a cousin or two," Jamie offered, thinking of Beardie.

Recently widowed and a bit of a lackwit, but left with five snot-nosed, bawling sons. Wee mischievous devils ranging in age from less than a year to seven summers if Jamie's memory served.

But even good-natured Beardie might balk at the prospect of taking Sorcha Matheson to wife.

A superstitious soul, the widowed Beardie might worry that ill luck clings to the maid. That fear alone would deter the most ardent Highland suitor.

"I don't think we should say anything to Sorcha for a while," Aveline said, and Jamie almost leaned back against the nearest tomb in relief.

Truth was, his bride's sister posed a devil's brew and

he couldn't imagine what to do about her, much as he'd like to help the lass.

So he did what seemed natural and slid his arms around *his* Fairmaiden lass, pulling her to him and kissing her until she melted against him. And even then, he kept kissing her, absorbing her sweetness and reveling in the way she tunneled her fingers through his hair, clutching him to her as if she, too, craved the intimacy and closeness.

Maybe even needed or welcomed his kiss.

And outside the chapel, the squally wind and rain dwindled and the moon sailed from behind the clouds, its silvery light spilling across the little churchyard with its burial cairns and ancient Pictish stone.

Illuminating, too, the tightly entwined young couple standing just inside the open chapel door and kissing so feverishly.

Feverishly enough to send a shiver through the watching hills.

A cold and deadly shiver.

Chapter Six

✦

In a world far beyond Clan Macpherson's little church-yard, more specifically in the isle-girt castle known as Eilean Creag, just off the shores of Kintail's Loch Duich, Lady Linnet MacKenzie sat near the hearth fire of her well-appointed lady's solar and frowned at the untidy stitches of her embroidery.

Clumsy, careless stitches.

And were she honest, the worst she'd made in a good long while. Though, with her needlework gracing count-less cushions, bed drapings, and tapestries throughout her home, everyone within the MacKenzie stronghold's proud walls knew she'd ne'er mastered a lady's skill of being able to make tiny, nigh invisible stitches.

Her stitches fell crooked and large, easily identifiable at ten or more paces.

A lacking her puissant husband, Duncan MacKenzie, the Black Stag of Kintail, accepted with notable toler-ance. E'er a man apart, he even complimented her most inept efforts, never letting on that her skills were anything but splendiferous.

Forbearance she did not expect when he returned from paying a call to Kenneth, their nephew, and discovered that her dread *taibhsearachd* had once again visited her.

Linnet glanced at the hearth fire and sighed. Even after a long and happy marriage, her otherwise fearless husband still felt ill at ease when it came to her special gift.

Her second sight.

As seventh daughter of a seventh daughter, the *taibhsearachd* was something she'd lived with since birth. And while it was ofttimes a blessing, it was more often a curse.

"Aye, a curse," she muttered, letting out a shaky breath.

Shuddering, she set aside her needlework and wriggled her stiff and tired fingers. It was no use sitting on her hearthside stool, jabbing her needle into the hapless cloth. Her gift had unleashed a nightmare this time, and all her usual distractions were failing her.

She couldn't forget what she'd seen.

Or undo its truth.

The action she'd set into motion because of it; a bold undertaking sure to unleash her husband's wrath.

"O-o-oh, he'll be sore vexed," she admitted, speaking to Mungo, a tiny brown-and-white dog curled at her feet and who belonged to her stepson, Robbie, and his lady wife, Juliana.

Biting her lip, she reached down and tousled the dog's floppy ears, gladly obliging when he rolled onto his back to have his belly rubbed.

With Robbie off with Duncan at Kenneth's recently restored Cuidrach Castle, and Juliana gone at Linnet's own behest, wee Mungo was in her care.

And from the way the little dog trotted after her, never leaving her side, she could almost believe that he, too, possessed a touch of her gift. That he knew how much trouble would soon descend upon her.

Sure of it, she moistened her lips and stood, grateful to stretch her legs and move about the lady's solar. Even if she would've preferred awaiting Duncan's return on the wall walk of Eilean Creag's high-towered battlements, as was her usual wont. A habit she doubted she'd allow herself to indulge for a good, long while.

Not after such a fright.

Shuddering again, she hugged herself, rubbing her arms until the gooseflesh receded.

Only then did she glance at the carefully bolted window shutters, wishing she could risk opening them to the brisk evening breeze.

But she didn't dare.

Sparing herself a repetition of the grim vision she'd seen the last time she'd looked upon the still, shining waters of Loch Duich was more important than filling her lungs with fresh night air.

Air she knew she'd need as soon as the door flew wide and she came face-to-face with Duncan wearing his most thunderous expression.

An unpleasantness that was about to crash down upon her, for she could hear angry voices and the sound of hurrying feet pounding up the turnpike stair.

Two sets of heavy, masculine feet.

Accompanied by two identical glares, for Robbie would be with him and equally displeased.

Then, before she could even smooth a hand over her hair or shake out her skirts, the door burst open and the two men swept into the room. Chill night wind from the stairwell's arrow slit windows gusted in as well, its rushing draught gutting a few candles and making the torch flames flicker wildly.

But not near so wild as her husband looked.

Frowning darkly, he strode forward, sword-clanking and windblown, his eyes blazing. "Saints, Maria, and Joseph!" he roared, staring at her. "Tell me you haven't sent my daughters to the north. *To anywhere.* And without my consent!"

Looking equally mud-stained and disheveled, Robbie shook his head, his expression more of disbelief than fury. "Surely we misheard." He glanced at his father. "Juliana would ne'er ride off without telling me. If she had need to make a journey, she would've waited until I returned from my own."

"She went because I asked her. She—" Linnet broke off when Mungo streaked past her to hurtle himself at Robbie's legs.

Scooping him up, her stepson clasped the little dog to his chest, some of the darkness slipping from his face, washed away by Mungo's excited wags and yippings, his wet slurpy kisses.

Duncan snorted.

His brow black as his tangled, shoulder-length hair, he ignored his son and the squirming dog and glanced around the fire-lit room before heading straight to a table set with cheese and oatcakes, an ewer of heather ale. Helping himself to a brimming cup of the frothy brew, he downed it in one long gulp, then swung back around, looking no less fierce for having refreshed himself.

"God's wounds, woman, I have loved you for long." He narrowed his eyes on her, his stare piercing. "But this is beyond all. I canna say what I will do if aught happens to either of my girls."

Linnet clasped her hands before her and lifted her chin. "Our daughters are well able to look after themselves," she returned, meeting his glare. "They are escorted by a company of your best guardsmen. Juliana"—she glanced at Robbie— "accompanied them for propriety's sake."

"That doesn't tell me why they are gone," Duncan shot back, looking at her long and hard.

"You know I would have known if danger awaited them."

"Faugh." He folded his arms. "'Tis still a bad business."

Linnet held her ground, flicked at her skirts. "I sent them away for a reason."

Duncan arched a brow. "And would that be the same reason you've barricaded yourself in here with all the shutters drawn tight? You, with your love of fresh air and open windows?"

"To be sure, I would rather have the shutters flung wide," Linnet admitted, lowering herself onto her stool. "I—"

"By the saints!" Robbie's voice echoed in her ears, already sounding distant, hollow. "Father, do you not see?"

Vaguely, Linnet was aware of Robbie setting down Mungo, then grabbing his father's arm, shaking him. "She's closed the shutters to block the view of the loch! Like as not, she's had another one of her spells. The *taibhsearachd* . . ."

But Linnet heard no more.

Truth be told, she wasn't even in the lady's solar anymore, but standing on the parapet walk of Eilean Creag's battlements, enjoying the wind in her face and a splendid Highland sunset.

A glorious one, with the still waters of Loch Duich reflecting the jagged cliffs and headlands, the long line of heather and bracken-clad hills rolling away beyond the loch's narrow, shingled shore.

Only then the open moors and rolling hills trembled and shook, drawing ever nearer until the vastness of Loch Duich narrowed to a treacherous defile. A deep, black-rimmed gorge hemming a rushing, raging torrent, all white water, rocks, and spume.

Linnet cried out and reached for support, her legs threatening to buckle as she clung to the parapet wall and stared down at the vision before her, the most-times tranquil loch's dim-shining waters nowhere to be seen.

She saw only the steep-sided ravine and the churning, boiling water. The deadly, racing cataracts and the black, glistening rocks lining the water's edge and thrusting upward through the flying spray.

The tall, well-built Highlander caught in the furious cauldron, his strapping body crashing against the rocks, then shooting onward, downstream, tossing and rolling in the wicked current, his plaid and streaming auburn hair the only notable color in a whirl of frothing, life-stealing white.

But then the white narrowed further, becoming nothing more ominous than the whiteness of her own bright-gleaming knuckles as she held tight to the cold stone of a merlon in the battlements' crenellated walling.

The horror was past.

Linnet drew a great quivering breath and blinked, half-expecting to find herself slumped against the stone merlon, a chill night wind tearing across the ramparts, buffeting her trembling body and whipping her hair. But she was in her tapestry-hung lady's solar, the window shutters still securely latched and the hearth fire crackling pleasantly as if nothing had happened.

Sadly, she knew otherwise.

And from the looks of them, so did her husband and her stepson.

"Holy Christ, Linnet," Duncan swore, proving it.

He knelt before her, holding her hands in a bone-crunching grip, all vexation gone from his handsome face. "Why didn't you tell us straightaway why you were holing yourself up in here?"

He glanced at Robbie, took the ale cup he offered him and pressed it against her lips. "Drink," he urged, looking almost as shaken as she felt. "Then tell us what this has to do with Arabella and Gelis."

"And Juliana," Robbie added, likewise dropping to his knees in the floor rushes.

Linnet blinked again, still dimly aware of the tragedy she'd just seen. And for the second time. She shivered, gratefully taking another swallow of the heather ale.

Seeing the vision twice only underscored its in-evitability.

"Our girls and Juliana will be fine," she said when she could speak. "'Tis Young Jamie that concerns me. He is the reason I sent them to Baldreagan. To—"

"'*Baldreagan*'?" Duncan's jaw slipped. "Every clapper-tongued kinsman belowstairs claimed you'd sent them to visit Juliana's Strathnaver kin and then on to Assynt, to spend time with Archibald Macnicol and his sons at Dunach."

"That you'd hoped Kenneth's wife's father might know of suitable husbands," Robbie put in.

"I may have said something of like," she owned, a bit of color returning to her cheeks. "Archibald is a great northern chieftain and his sons are making distinguished names for themselves."

She sat up straighter on her stool. "The girls are of marriageable age," she said, her tone and the jut of her chin revealing she was now fully recovered. "Some might even say past marriageable age."

Duncan sniffed.

His foul mood returning, he pushed to his feet. "What do my daughters' tender ages have to do with James Macpherson?" He stared down at her, his hands fisted around his sword belt. "You know he quit service with Kenneth to return home to wed, if Kenneth had the rights of it."

To his surprise, his wife shook her head. "He returned home to die," she said, her voice catching.

"*To die?*" Duncan could feel his eyes bugging out.

His wife nodded. "I've seen his death," she said,

sounding so sure of it, his nape prickled. "He is going to drown in the Rough Waters, just like his brothers. That's why I sent the girls. On a pretense to order a new stirk for you, but, in truth, to urge Jamie to be careful."

Duncan's head began to ache. "Have you not always told me naught could be done to alter such things as you sometimes see?"

"Aye, that is the way of it," she admitted, looking miserable. "And I warned the girls not to let on to Jamie what they know. Such knowledge might bring on his doom with greater rapidity."

"Then why send them in the first place?"

"Because they are sensitive enough to know who at Baldreagan they can trust," she said, looking at him as if he were a simpleton. "They'll find the right soul to warn."

Duncan grunted. "If a warning was all you hoped to accomplish, why didn't you just send word to old Devorgilla of Doon? She could have worked a spell or winked at the moon and sped a message to Baldreagan without my daughters needing to traipse clear across Kintail."

His wife pressed her lips together, clearly annoyed. "Devorgilla knows without messengers when her aid is needed," she finally said. "Just as I know some action is required of me when I am visited by my gift."

Getting slowly to her feet, she walked past him to the little table spread with oatcakes, cheese, and ale. "If Devorgilla is meant to help Jamie, she will," she added, looking down at the table but touching nothing. "For myself, I have done all I could."

"And if neither your help nor Devorgilla's is needed?"

Robbie joined her at the table, helping himself to a good-sized chunk of cheese. "What if it wasn't Jamie you saw? But one of his already drowned brothers?"

"By God, he's right!" Duncan flashed an admiring glance at his son. "Those Macpherson lads all looked alike."

Replenishing his ale cup, he drank deeply. "Aye, that will be the way of it," he declared, looking immensely pleased.

"Nay, that was not the way of it." Linnet glanced up from the table; she could feel the heat flooding her face. "It was definitely Jamie. There can be no mistaking."

"No mistaking?" Duncan and Robbie chorused.

She shook her head. "None whatsoever."

Duncan stepped closer. "And how can you be so sure?"

"Jamie squired here," Linnet reminded him, unable to meet his eyes.

"Jamie, Lachlan, and a goodly number of others as well," he shot back, eyeing her significantly. "I dinna see what that has to do with it."

It had everything to do with it—and was something she just couldn't push past her lips.

"Squires and young knights often take their baths in the kitchens," she blurted at last, hoping they'd understand.

But they didn't.

Both her husband and her son stood gawping at her, slack-jawed and owl-eyed.

Totally uncomprehending.

Certain her flaming face would soon burn brighter

than the hearth log, she blew out an agitated breath and said the only other thing remaining: "Jamie is a big lad."

Duncan and Robbie exchanged glances.

Neither spoke.

But after a moment, a pink tinge began to bloom onto Robbie's cheeks. "Oh," he said.

"Exactly," Linnet agreed, grateful at least one of them understood. "And that is how I know it was him. By the time his body reached the deep pools at the end of the rapids, his plaid had been torn from him and he was naked."

"Naked?" Duncan echoed, making it worse.

Linnet nodded. "Naked and tossed about often enough in the water for me to know without a doubt that I was looking at James Macpherson. Young James of the Heather."

The image still branded in her memory, she paced to the nearest window and yanked open the shutters, at last breathing in the brisk, strengthening air she so sorely needed.

"And," she added, staring down at the night-blackened waters of Loch Duich, "if naught can be done to prevent it, he will soon be as dead as his brothers."

Jamie's hope for a pleasant evening spent wooing Aveline Matheson before the hearth fire vanished the instant they rode into Baldreagan's bailey and he spied the chaos.

Anything but emptied and quiet—the castle inhabitants tucked in and snug for the night—the supposed house of mourning appeared under siege.

And he and his bride seemed to have arrived right smack in the middle of the assault.

An invasion by MacKenzies!

Jamie's brow furrowed, but there could be no doubt. He'd spent half his life at Eilean Creag, squiring for the castle's formidable laird. He'd recognize these bearded, plaid-hung clansmen anywhere.

As would any Highlander; leastways those of a warrior bent. The MacKenzies were amongst the most fierce fighting men to stride the heather, commanding respect and awe where'er they went. As generous and open-handed to their friends as they struck dread into the hearts of their foes.

And Jamie knew them as friends. The very best of friends.

"Suffering saints," he breathed, their presence transporting him to another, larger and more imposing bailey.

His heart clenched and at once a flood of memories crashed over him.

Good memories.

These men weren't just any MacKenzies. They were the Black Stag's men, and some of his best, if Jamie's eyes weren't lying to him.

Braw stalwarts to a man. Kintail's pride.

Swinging down onto the cobbles, Jamie looked around. The whole of the moonlit courtyard teemed with men, skittish horses and excited, barking dogs.

He even caught sight of his own beast, Cuillin. Ever in the thick of things, the old dog's shuffling gait and milky eyes didn't stop him from joining in the revel and din.

But the MacKenzies caused the greatest commotion.

There were scores of them and they hastened hither and thither, some hefting heavy travel bags on their shoulders, others helping Baldreagan's stable lads carry extra hay and grain into the stables lining the far wall of the bailey.

Stables with room to house at least sixty horses, though considering the ruckus coming from that direction, he guessed a good many more were now squeezed into its stalls. A few had even been crammed into the sheep pens near the postern gate and if that wasn't surprising enough, light blazed from every window of his father's five- toried keep.

But before he could wonder about the unexpected visit, he felt a touch on his arm. Aveline stood peering up at him, her eyes round and luminous. Her pale, flaxen hair shimmered in the moonlight and she looked so beautiful he almost forgot to breathe.

He *had* forgotten to help her dismount.

Already a stable lad was running forward to see to her riderless steed.

Jamie bit back a curse. "My apologies," he said, jamming a hand through his hair. "I meant to lift you down, but I was so surprised—"

"I don't need apologies." She leaned into him, a fetching twinkle in her eyes. "Just as I didn't melt in the rain back at the cairns, neither will I shatter if I slide off a horse unaided."

She stood on her toes, pressing a quick kiss to his lips.

A quick, soft kiss, and with just enough hint of tongue to make him wish they were still in the sheltering dark of St. Maelrhuba's chapel and not the crowded bailey.

But already she was pulling away.

"Of course, you were surprised," she said, glancing around at the bustle. "Who would have thought we'd find Baldreagan overrun with MacKenzies?"

Jamie looked at her. "You know them?"

Aveline smoothed her cloak, suddenly uncomfortable.

"Ach . . . ," she stalled, her gaze going to the keep's forebuilding with its steep stone steps up to the great hall. "See you, the truth is, men from Eilean Creag have visited Fairmaiden a time or two over the years," she finally explained. "They always came for the same reason—claiming your father's asking price for his cattle was too high and wanting to know if my da could make them a better offer."

"And did he?"

"Oh, aye. Every time." She waited until two gear-toting MacKenzies hastened past, then lowered her voice, "He'd tell them they could have all the cattle they desired and for nary a coin."

"For nothing?" Jamie couldn't believe it.

"Not exactly nothing," she hedged, still avoiding his eye. "There was a catch. They could have the cattle if they took one of my sisters as well."

Jamie almost choked.

The only thing that saved him from laughing out loud at his good father's gall was the sudden appearance of a creature almost as ill-starred as his bride's sundry sisters.

"Jamie! You'll ne'er guess who's sitting in our hall, and why!" Beardie came panting up to them, his broad, pox-marked face flushed with excitement. "Och, nay, you'll ne'er guess," he repeated, his great red beard jigging.

Jamie winked at Aveline then looked back at his cousin. "Could it be MacKenzies?" he ventured, feigning ignorance.

"O-o-oh, aye! To be sure, but *what* MacKenzies!" Beardie rocked back on his heels, gave Jamie a sly wink. "Your jaw will hit the rushes, I say you."

"Then do." Jamie folded his arms. "Say me who is here and causing such a stir."

"The Black Stag's womenfolk! His son Robbie's wife, Lady Juliana, and"—Beardie's eyes lit—"his own two girls!"

Jamie's jaw did drop. "Arabella and Gelis are here? And with the Lady Juliana?"

Beardie nodded. "Who would've thought it? They're looking for husbands." Leaning closer, he lowered his voice. "I think they have me in mind for one of 'em. They've been making moon eyes at me."

"That may well be," Jamie agreed, thwacking the other man on the arm, knowing he couldn't bring himself to dash his bumbling, bushy-bearded cousin's hopes for a new wife. A mother for his five bairns.

A female he suspected would be found amongst the lesser kin of an allied laird. A toothsome, big-hearted lass willing to mother Beardie's brood, but with surety not so fine a catch as Duncan MacKenzie's maidenly daughters.

Lively, beautiful, and high-spirited, the well-dowered MacKenzie lasses were destined for only the highest-ranking husbands.

As Beardie would know if he had even a jot of sense.

Instead, he stood preening. Brushing at his plaid and hitching his wide, leather belt to a more advantageous sit across his round and impressive girth.

"I'm off to fetch my great-great-grandda's winged helmet," he confided, speaking again into Jamie's ear. "The fiery lass, Gelis, was impressed when I told her I had a touch o' Norse blood!"

Jamie opened his mouth to tell him there was nary a Highlander who didn't have a few drops of Viking blood in his veins, but Beardie was already running off, barreling a path through the throng, clearly bent on retrieving his rusted treasure.

A relic the likes of which could be found aplenty at Eilean Creag.

Jamie blew out a breath, looking after him.

The moment Beardie vanished from view, he reached for Aveline's hand, pulling her with him toward the keep stairs. Something was sorely amiss and the sooner he found out what it was, the better.

Lady Juliana might well be escorting Duncan MacKenzie's daughters across the Highlands, but the reason wasn't to find them husbands.

Especially not at Baldreagan.

That Jamie knew so sure as the morrow.

He was doubly sure when they neared the top of the forebuilding's steps and a small, grizzled woman materialized out of the shadows to block their way.

"Saints be praised, you've returned!" She swooped down on them like a black-garbed crow, her eyes glinting in the moonlight. "The whole world's a-falling apart and I'm running out o' ways to hold it together!"

"Ach, Morag." Jamie flashed her his most disarming smile. "I've seen you ready the hall for far more illustrious hosts than two wee lassies and Lady Juliana." He reached to ruffle her iron-gray curls. "Dinna tell me—"

"It isn't them troubling me." Morag grabbed his arm, drawing him into the deeper shadows of the door arch. "It's your da. He's in the hall now, at the high table, making merry with the MacKenzie lasses—"

"He's left his room then?" Aveline stepped forward, the notion pleasing her. "Praise be," she said, smiling at the old woman. "These are good tidings. We've been trying to get him to come belowstairs for days."

She paused, sliding a glance at Jamie.

He'd stiffened beside her and whether it suited him or nay, she was determined to help bridge the gap between them.

"Your da has been missed, see you. Especially of an evening," she tried to explain. "No one feels spirited enough to tell tales or even enjoy their ale, and his hounds mope about with hanging ears and sad eyes."

Jamie surprised her by nodding.

"Aye, his presence in the hall is naught to be fretting over," he agreed.

Morag pursed her lips. "It is when I tell you he's only in the hall because he's vowed ne'er to set foot elsewhere!" she said, wagging a finger at him. "He's *pretending* to be at ease. In truth, he's in a greater dither than he's been since I can remember."

Aveline's smile froze.

Jamie's expression hardened. A muscle began jerking in his jaw.

Seeing it, Aveline edged closer to him. "Did Munro have another visitation?" she asked, lacing her fingers with Jamie's and squeezing. "Was it Neill again?"

Morag nodded.

"Aye, that's the rights of it," she confirmed, her head still bobbing. "And the poor laird took such a fright, he barricaded himself in his room. We found him huddled in his chair, talking gibberish."

She sent a wary look over her shoulder. "Like as not, he'd still be there if four clansmen hadn't put their shoulders to the door," she said, lowering her voice. "And if the MacKenzie lasses hadn't arrived when they did. They're the reason he came belowstairs."

Jamie raised his brows. "And now he's vowing to stay there? In the hall?"

"So he says."

Aveline frowned. "He canna sleep in the hall," she objected, the image of the old laird passing the night wrapped in his plaid in the draughty cold of the hall making her shiver. "For all his bluster, he's old. And not himself of late."

Jamie bit back a snort.

So far as he'd seen, with the exception of his newfound fear of bogles, Munro Macpherson was still very much his crafty, cantankerous self.

But his bride seemed to have tucked him into her heart, so he gave her the most reassuring look he could muster. "Ne'er you worry," he said. "I willna let him bed down in the hall. He'll sleep abovestairs as befits him."

"Tchach! We shall see." Morag clucked her tongue.

"That old goat is as thrawn and unyielding as the day is long. Nay, I canna see him going back to his room."

Jamie shook his head. "Last time I spoke with him, he was vowing ne'er to leave his bed."

"Aye, he was all for hiding beneath the covers," Morag agreed, stepping closer. "But that was before Neill's ghost came a-calling, all wet and dripping from the grave."

Jamie's heart stopped.

Aveline grabbed his arm, holding tight.

"What are you saying?" Jamie stared at the old woman, the fine hairs on the back of his neck lifting. "What do you mean Neill was *'wet and dripping'*?"

"Just what I said." Morag put back her bony shoulders. "Your da won't be going back to his bed because he's afraid of drowning in it. If we want to believe his rantings, the last time Neill appeared to him, he was dripping wet and the very waters of the Garbh Uisge were flowing all around him."

"That canna be," Jamie argued.

Morag shrugged. "Be that as it may, his bedding and the floor rushes were drenched when we found him."

"You saw this?" Jamie asked, though, in truth, he already knew.

The icy chills sweeping down his spine answered him.

Indeed, he didn't even hear Morag's reply. The blood was roaring too loud in his ears. And in his mind's eye, he was seeing only one thing.

The sopping wet plaid flung across his ancestor's tomb.

Chapter Seven

❦

Jamie paused just inside the hall door and immediately found himself surrounded by jostling, rowdy clansmen. Clearly in good cheer, they pushed, shoved, and wrestled in the aisles between the trestle tables. Others stood apart, indulging in that favored Highland pastime of story-telling, the more golden-tongued among the visitors regaling circles of listeners with rousing tales about their ancestors.

But it was another MacKenzie who caught Jamie's eye.

Burly and bearded, the man stood nearby, thrusting a great drinking horn in the air and claiming he'd filled it to the brim with *uisge beatha*. Grinning broadly, he challenged any who'd dare to gulp down the fiery Highland spirits in a single draught.

Jamie frowned at him, thinking he'd borrowed the clan's famed Horn of Days. A treasure only touched when the reigning Macpherson chieftain relinquishes his

authority to his successor. Certain the man didn't know
the horn's significance, Jamie started forward. But on
closer look, the reveler's drinking horn was only a common ox horn.

The man simply enjoyed the carouse—as Gaels are
wont to do.

Even so, his ringing voice added to the mayhem, the
whole commotion proving so crushing Jamie slid an arm
around his bride, keeping her close as he blinked against
the thick, smoke-hazed air. But it took a few moments for
his eyes to adjust to the shadows and torchlight, his ears
to grow accustomed to the raised voices and laughter.

Boisterous laughter, clamor, and song.

A stir and tumult the likes of which he doubted
Baldreagan had seen in years.

Truth be told, the din and disorder almost matched the
chaos in the bailey. And ne'er in all his days had he been
more grateful to lose himself in such a raucous swirl of
noise and confusion.

Every blessed distraction took his mind off the wet
plaid and a nagging suspicion so disturbing it felt like an
iron yoke settling around his neck.

The morrow would be soon enough to ponder such
troubling matters.

For the now, he'd force a smile and the best spirits he
could summon. And for good measure, he'd watch his
back and keep a wary eye on over-dark corners.

Including *corners* well known to him, much as such a
notion displeased him.

But as Kenneth MacKenzie once said, pigs aren't
likely to sing from trees. And neither did sopping wet

plaids sail into dark and empty chapels and fling themselves across stone-faced Highland knights.

Jamie drew a deep breath and let it out slowly. He also tightened his arm around Aveline.

Och, aye, something was amiss.

And until he solved the riddle, his new lady wasn't leaving his side.

"O-o-oh, I see the trumpet tongues spoke true," chimed a female voice just to his left. "You *have* found yourself a beautiful *Sithe* maid!"

Jamie swung about, almost colliding with a glowing-eyed, flame-haired lassie no one would dare call a faery.

"Gelis!" he greeted Duncan MacKenzie's youngest daughter. "Saints, but you've grown."

He looked down at her, amazed at how womanly she'd become in the short months since he'd last visited Eilean Creag. "You are a fury unbound—sneaking up on us when I'd hoped to escort my lady to the dais in style."

The girl tossed her bright head and whirled to face Aveline, eyeing her with open curiosity, but a warm and teasing smile lighting her face.

"Ah, well, then I shall take her," she trilled, grabbing Aveline's hand and leading her away, pulling her deeper into the hall, straight through the milling, carousing throng and up onto the dais.

"He will catch up, dinna you fear." She gave Aveline a conspiratorial wink. "That one needs a jolt now and then," she added, urging Aveline to take a seat at the high table. "He worries too much about propriety."

"And you do not?" Aveline looked at her, certain she'd never seen a more vivid, breathtaking creature.

All burnished coppery hair, sparkling eyes, and dimples, she breathed charm and enchantment.

She was worldly as well. Aveline could see it in her eyes. "You do not care what the glen wives say?"

Gelis laughed and dropped onto the trestle bench beside her. "Not if I can help it!" she said, settling herself. "Worrying is for graybeards and . . . Jamie!"

"Hah! And the moon just fell from the sky," a raven-haired beauty put in from across the table. "My sister worries all the time. Regrettably, too often about things that do not concern her."

Lifting her wine cup, she smiled. "I am Arabella," she said, as serene and self-assured as her sister brimmed with gaiety. "And"—she indicated an older, equally stunning woman farther down the table—"that is the Lady Juliana, our brother Robbie's wife. Like myself, she is along to keep young Gelis out of mischief."

"*'Young'?*" Gelis leaned forward, her plump breasts swelling against her low-cut bodice. "I am not so young that certain braw eyes haven't been admiring my charms!"

Arabella set down her wine cup. "As you can see, she is overly modest as well."

Gelis gave a light shrug. "If you weren't so swaddled in the folds of your arisaid, I vow you'd have a few manly eyes looking your way, too," she quipped, picking up the end of her braid and wriggling it in her sister's direction. "We both know your *charms* are even bigger than mine."

Running a finger up and down the side of her wine cup, she looked through her lashes at a passing MacKenzie.

An especially bonnie one.

"Yours jiggle more, too," Gelis observed, returning her attention to her sister. "Or they would if you'd put them to better advantage," she added, her fiery hair bright in the hearth glow.

Arabella flushed. "We did not come here to flash smiles at hot-eyed guardsmen," she minded her sister, something in her tone sending a shiver down Aveline's spine.

But the dark beauty's face revealed nothing. She sat ramrod straight, the image of polished dignity, her sole attention on the bannock she was smearing with Morag's special heather honey.

Only her flame-haired sister seemed fidgety.

Gelis squirmed on the trestle bench and kept sliding cheeky glances into the main area of the hall, her gaze going repeatedly to a long table crowded with young MacKenzie guardsmen.

And, Aveline knew, several of Jamie's bolder cousins.

She also knew no man had ever looked so hungrily at her.

Unlike the MacKenzie women, she had tiny breasts that would never strain and swell against her bodice, threatening to spill over the edging in a provocation that had surely delighted and stirred men since the beginnings of time.

And in her case, a pitiful lacking that clamped white-hot fire tongs around her heart, squeezing hard and jabbing sharp little green needles into soft and hurtful places she didn't care to examine.

Until she heard someone mention Jamie's name and

remembered how his eyes had darkened with passion when they'd kissed in her father's solar and her gown had slipped, baring her left nipple.

She remembered, too, how gently he'd touched her.

At once, a pleasurable heat bloomed inside her making her almost ache with the need to feel his hands on her again. She'd never imagined a man's touch could be so exquisite. Just remembering sent tingly warmth sweeping across her woman's parts and a deliciously weighty sensation to her belly. She shifted on the bench, hoping no one would guess the reason for her restlessness.

Hoping, too, she might later have the chance to explore such tingles in earnest.

"Baldreagan cattle, eh?"

Munro's booming voice cut into her reverie, and she glanced down the table to see him in deep conversation with Lady Juliana. To Aveline's relief, he looked anything but feeble or frightened. Indeed, she recognized the glint in his eyes. It was a look she knew from her father, as well, but the MacKenzie woman appeared Munro's match.

Well made and exceedingly comely, she had fine glowing skin and a wealth of reddish-gold hair that glistened in the torchlight. And like her two young charges, she'd been blessed with one of the fullest, most alluring bosoms Aveline had ever seen.

"My good father, Duncan MacKenzie, wishes a new stirk come the spring," she was saying, watching Munro over her wine cup as she spoke. "He might even take two if the conditions are amenable."

" *'Amenable'?* " Munro slapped the table and hooted. "My conditions—"

"Will be more than amenable," Jamie announced, his voice brooking no argument. "They will be fair and good."

Munro glared at him. "What do you know of cattle dealing?"

"I know more than you suspect."

Striding up to the table, Jamie nodded to Lady Juliana, then poured himself a healthy measure of ale, draining it in one long draw before setting down the cup with a loud *clack*.

He dragged the back of his hand over his mouth, his gaze fixed firmly on his father.

His bride looked far too fetching in the soft glow cast by the well-doing dais fire and he couldn't allow such a tempting distraction—not with the image of that dread wet plaid looming in his mind.

But he did wish to distract his father. Only so could he squeeze more than rants, splutters, and snorts out of the man.

So he took a seat, snitching a bit of cheese from a platter and tossing it to Cuillin. Then he got comfortable and launched his assault.

"Anyone who can afford blazing log fires in every hearth can also allow a bit of openhandedness when selling cattle to a long-time ally."

Just as he'd expected, his father tightened his lips and frowned at him.

And said not a word.

"I hope, too," Jamie went on, circling a finger around

the rim of his ale cup, "that you've laid an equally fine fire in your bedchamber? It's a chill night and I wouldn't want you catching an ague."

Munro gripped the table edge and leaned forward. "Since I willna be sleeping in that room again, there's no danger of me taking ill there."

Gesturing for Morag to replenish his ale, he sat back in his throne-like laird's chair and treated Jamie to a rare smile.

A smug smile.

Tight-lipped and defiant.

"Indeed," he continued, his self-pleased stare still riveted on Jamie, "I just decided I shall sleep in your chamber. You can have mine."

Refusing to be baited, Jamie didn't even blink. "As you will. Truth be told, I am much relieved as I'd heard you'd meant to make your bed in the hall and I would not have allowed that. Too many men spread their pallets here and I'd not see your night's rest disturbed."

Not when one amongst those men might wear two faces.

And a sopping wet plaid.

Sure of it, Jamie reached across the table, laid strong fingers atop his father's age-spotted hand. "Tell me," he said, speaking low, "when Neill came to you this last time, was he swathed in his burial shroud or wearing his plaid?"

"His plaid, you buffoon!" Munro snapped, yanking back his hand. "His drenched and dripping plaid." He twisted around and shot a glare at Morag. "As everyone in this hall knows!"

"Then I shall offer him a new and dry one if he dares make a repeat visit," Jamie declared, bracing himself for his da's next outburst. "And you shall indeed quarter in my bedchamber. You and two trusted guardsman."

" *'Two trusted guardsmen'!*" Munro mimicked, glancing around. "There's not a soul under the heavens can hold back a flood once the waters start rushing. I near drowned in my bed, and no muscle-armed, smirking guardsmen woulda been able to help me had the waters not receded when they did."

"But such treacherous waters as the Garbh Uisge can be rendered harmless if one avoids them." Lady Juliana picked up a platter of jam-filled wafers, setting it in front of Munro, but turning a sharp eye on Jamie. "There are many who would sleep with greater ease if you vowed to avoid the Rough Waters," she said, something in her expression making Jamie tense.

"Trust me," he said, "I've no wish to go there. If e'er an ill wind blew through these hills, that's where it is. But I do mean to examine the damaged footbridge," he added, feeling every eye at the high table upon him. "The bridge will have to be repaired."

"That devil-damned monstrosity canna be repaired," Munro grumbled, and bit into a wafer. "I've sent every last bit of it to the flames o' hell where it belongs!"

" 'The flames o' hell'?" Jamie exchanged glances with Aveline, but she looked equally perplexed.

"Och, aye. Straight to Lucifer himself," Munro snipped, reaching for a second wafer.

"He means he's burned it," Beardie gibed, elbowing

his way through the throng. "The whole footbridge. Every last piece."

Burned it. Every last piece.

The words circled in Jamie's head, an unpleasant inkling taking seed as Beardie came closer and the red, pulsing glow from the dais fire edged his great, bumbling form.

Jamie looked from his cousin to his father and back again. "Dinna tell me the logs blazing on every hearth grate are bits of the footbridge?"

Munro sucked in his breath and spluttered something unintelligible. But the annoyance sparking in his eyes proved Jamie's suspicions.

His tightfisted da hadn't spent a coin laying in fuel for Baldreagan's scores of fireplaces. The bright gleam Jamie had noticed lighting every tower window were the flames of his brothers' death weapon.

Beardie's beard-shaking nod confirmed it.

Looking pleased to be the bearer of as-yet-unknown tidings, he drew up behind Gelis, his tarnished Viking helmet clutched in his hand.

"Where do you think we've been these last days?" He cocked a bushy brow, indicating a few other kinsmen milling about in the shadows.

Death lurked in those shadows, Jamie would've sworn someone whispered. Someone close behind him, their voice pitched low and full of warning. But when he twisted around and glanced over his shoulder, no one stood near enough to have flustered the words.

Hughie Mac held court on the far side of the hall, playing his fiddle with gusto and flourish. And one of Jamie's cousins had drawn a fulsome kitchen lass into the semi-privacy of a nearby window embrasure, the flickering torchlight revealing the white gleam of her naked breasts and that his cousin's hand was groping deep beneath the lassie's skirts. Other cousins occupied themselves shouting encouragement to two MacKenzie guardsmen enjoying a vigorous round of arm-wrestling at one of the long tables.

And Morag hovered close by the dais steps, her sharp gaze on Beardie's older lads as they chased a few of the more playful castle dogs around the oaken partition that made up the hall's screens passage.

Everything appeared as it should.

Yet he'd swear he could feel malignant eyes watching him.

"Those were dark hours, down at the Garbh Uisge," Beardie was saying, and a few listening kinsmen nodded in shuddery agreement. "Tearing apart what remained o' the bridge and fishing the rest from the water. I wouldn't want to do the like again."

Jamie tipped back his head and stared up at the smoke-blackened ceiling, blew out a frustrated breath.

Wouldn't want to do the like again, Beardie had quipped. A muscle in Jamie's jaw twitched.

Would that it hadn't been done at all.

Wishing that were so, he put back his shoulders and straightened his spine against the chill creeping over him. Ever since discovering the wet plaid, he'd wanted to examine the fallen bridge.

Scour each and every inch of splintered, shattered wood for hints of foul play.

But now the best he could do would be sweeping the bridge's ashes from Baldreagan's hearth grates.

And making certain that the misbegotten sod who was staring such angry holes into him was kept well away from his lady and his da.

Well prepared for a clash of wills with the latter, he reached across the table and slid the platter of jam-filled wafers away from his father's grasp.

"Whose idea was it to burn the bridge's remains?"

"The bogles," Beardie answered him, claiming a seat beside Gelis. "Neill was furious with your da because o' what happened and warned he wanted no reminder left o' the tragedy."

"The idea was my own," Munro insisted, fisting his hands on the table. "Mine, and Alan Mor's. I'm paying for a new bridge to be built and he's seeing to the sculpting of my sons' effigies and tombs."

He glanced at Jamie. "'Tis part of our agreement. A way to appease the bogles."

Jamie frowned and bit his tongue.

Beardie looked doubtful. "But you said they're wroth—"

"And so they are!" Munro shot back, glaring down the table. "Though why they dinna plague Alan Mor as well is beyond me. He bears equal blame for letting the footbridge fall into disrepair. God kens we both made use o' the thing!"

"And did anyone examine the bridge before you turned it into firewood?" Jamie asked, his persistence reaping another of his da's dark frowns.

When nothing but the scowl answered him, he pushed to his feet.

"I'll see Lady Aveline to Kendrick's old chamber," he said, already moving to help her rise. "It's closest to yours, and since I'd relish a visit from Neill or whoe'er else might wish to call, I'll gladly accept your offer that we exchange rooms."

Munro grunted and reached for his ale cup. "You'll be sorry you're jesting about your brothers' ghosts," he warned, tossing down a swig. "They *are* afoot and they willna be pleased with your mockery."

Jamie shrugged. "And I willna be pleased if I visit the Garbh Uisge and uncover one sign of fiddling—and I dinna mean yon Hughie Mac and his music!"

Sliding his arm around Aveline's waist, he drew her against him, feeling a need to shield her. "Whether the bridge is gone or not, there might yet be something left that the *bogles* dinna want us to see. If so, I mean to find it."

He glanced round at his kinsmen and friends, making sure everyone had heard him.

Hoping any *un*-friends who might be about, heard as well.

"And when I do, it won't be me who'll be the sorry one," he added, pulling Aveline along with him as he strode for the tower stair.

But their exit was marred by a feminine gasp, a rustling flurry of skirts as Gelis leapt to her feet and dashed after them.

"O-o-oh, you canna go near the cataracts," she cried, grabbing Jamie's arm. "Say you will not!"

He swung around and looked down at her, the fear in her eyes and the paleness of her face making him all the more determined to go indeed. Especially since she was Linnet MacKenzie's daughter.

He knew better than to discount warnings coming from that direction, but he also recognized the need for caution. So he patted her hand and forced a reassuring smile.

"Ne'er you worry," he lied, telling a falsehood to an unsuspecting female for what was surely the hundredth time in just the last few days. "I willna go near the Rough Waters."

But I might poke around a bit on the braeside over-looking them.

That last, of course, he left unsaid.

"I did not like the way she looked at you."

Aveline blurted her concern the moment they topped the turnpike stair head.

"Gelis?" Jamie shot her a bemused look. "The Black Stag's sassy wee gel?"

Aveline nodded.

She smoothed her hands on her skirts, annoyed by their dampness. Truth was, she hadn't seen anything *wee* on the MacKenzie lass.

Not that it mattered.

She'd liked the girl. And Jamie—clearly hearing with a man's ears—had totally misunderstood her.

Even so, she wished the words unsaid. But that was impossible, so she let him lead her down the dimly lit passage and into the empty bedchamber that had been his brother Kendrick's.

She bit her lip as they crossed the threshold, her own agitation immediately forgotten. Faith, but the room's silence twisted her heart.

Truth be told, she'd liked Kendrick tremendously. Though like her sisters and any female with a whit of sense, she'd known not to take him seriously. A notorious skirt-chaser; laughing-eyed, full of himself, and e'er amusing, he'd been the most dashing of the Macpherson brothers.

Quick to smile, outrageously flirtatious, and able to make even the most withered stick of a crone feel beautiful.

Aveline swallowed, fighting against the thickness in her throat.

Even the few times she'd glimpsed his ghost, he'd looked, well, larger than life.

Anything but . . . dead.

"Come, lass." Jamie looked at her over his shoulder. "You needn't fret o'er Gelis. Or fear this room. Kendrick isn't here."

But Aveline wasn't so sure.

Gelis didn't really bother her, but traces of Kendrick's zest lingered in the chamber and it was all she could do to keep from glancing about, looking for him.

Half-expecting him to swagger over to them, offering refreshments and a lusty, wicked tale, she shivered and clasped her hands before her, looking on as Jamie closed and bolted the door.

He *humphed* as soon as the drawbar slid into place, but

other than that noncommittal grunt, he gave no sign of intending to say more.

Far from it, he strode across the chamber, taking the night candle from the table beside the bed, then lighting it at the hearth. A charcoal brazier already hissed and glowed in one corner and a few of the wall sconces had been lit and were throwing off their light as well, but Jamie continued to move about with the burning taper, tipping its flame to the wick of every candle in the room.

"To better see the *bogles*," Aveline thought she heard him say.

But she'd been listening for other voices, finding it so hard to imagine Kendrick gone. And feeling not quite at ease claiming his quarters. The notion sent chills sliding up and down her spine no matter how many candles Jamie set to blazing.

An unnecessary extravagance, for enough moonlight streamed into the chamber to stretch deep into the room, silver-gilding the elegant trappings, illuminating the sumptuousness.

And the room was sumptuous.

Looking round, Aveline knew she'd seldom seen anything quite so fine.

Rather than the usual rushes, furred skins covered the wood-planked floor and still more furs, softer looking and more luxuriant, made the room's great four-poster bed an almost irresistible enticement.

Her heart thumping, she went to one of the arched windows and breathed deep of the chill damp air. The night smelled of rain, wet stone, wood ash, a soul-lifting hint of heather and Caledonian pine.

Soft mist and dark, lowering clouds.

The silvery sheen of the moon.

Night scents familiar to all Highlanders and not at all unlike she knew from Fairmaiden. But here, in this grand-seeming chamber with its heavy oaken furnishings and arras-hung walls, intoxications that caressed and stirred.

Rousing her deepest, most elemental yearnings. Desires even Kendrick's ghost couldn't squelch. Not with James of the Heather striding toward her, the look in his eyes melting her.

"You needn't fret o'er Gelis," he said again, stopping not a handsbreadth away from her. Lowering his head, he brushed his lips ever so gently across hers. "I think you saw in the wood that night just who enchanted me."

He pulled away to look at her and she drew a shaky breath, the taste of him still heady and sweet on her lips.

"I did not mean—"

"I ken what you meant." He smoothed his knuckles down her cheek. "But you're worrying for naught. Duncan MacKenzie's daughters are like sisters to me. I could ne'er think of them otherwise. Though I'll admit they make fair gazing!"

Aveline glanced aside.

He caught hold of her chin, tilting her head for another kiss. A slow, soft one this time, with just a hint of tongue. "See you," he went on, ending the kiss, "those girls have been spoken for since birth."

He slid his arms around her, drawing her closer. "Leastways, it stands clear that they'll wed highborn husbands. If their father doesn't stop hiding them away behind his stout castle walls."

Aveline blinked. "I thought they were traveling north to seek possible matches?"

"Och, nay, sweetness. They came here for a different reason." Jamie splayed his hands across her back, rubbing her gently. Soothing her. "A reason that has little to do with their weddings, whene'er their da allows the like."

"You know the reason?"

Jamie looked aside, his gaze on the windows and the darkness beyond. "I have guessed, aye."

"And will you tell me?"

He was silent, but a muscle jerked in his jaw and Aveline would've sworn she felt him stiffen.

Och, aye, she could feel the ill ease thrumming all through him. A taut wariness she could almost taste, and troubling enough to make her own heart skitter.

So she circled her arms around his neck and twined her fingers in his hair, determined to hold fast until he told her what she wanted to know.

Needed to know.

"Can the reason have anything to do with the way Lady Gelis was looking at you in the hall?" She peered up at him. "When she ran up to us as we were leaving?"

"So that was the look you meant?" Jamie reached to caress her hair. "You were not jealous? Only concerned about her warning?"

"So it was a warning?"

He shrugged. "I can only guess, but I would say aye. Those three women came here for one reason. To warn me away from the Rough Waters."

Aveline shivered.

He disentangled himself from her grasp and began pacing about the room, peering into corners, eyeing the locked and bolted door.

The air around them seemed to darken, the very shadows drawing near. Until, watching him stride past a window, Aveline caught a glimpse of the moon sailing from behind a cloud and its silvery glow returned, once more filling the room with soft, shimmering light.

A cold light, for even the fine-burning log fire seemed to have lost its warmth.

Biting her lip, she rubbed her arms against the room's sudden chill. "Surely they cannot think something bad might happen to you, too?"

Jamie turned to face her. "Sweet lass, I'll own they *know* something unpleasant will happen," he said, not wanting to frighten her, but thinking it best she hear the truth. "The lassies' mother has the *taibhsearachd*. Her gift is unfailing and so true as I'm standing here. I have seen the proof of her abilities many times."

Aveline's heart stopped. "And you think she's seen something?"

"I can think of no other reason for them to come here." Jamie rubbed the back of his neck. "Even their excuse about the Black Stag wanting to haggle with my da over a stirk or two rings false."

"Because he's always sent his men to do the like?"

"Exactly."

"Then you must make them tell you what they know." She hurried over to him, clutching at him. "If they know you've guessed, they will not keep it from you."

Jamie shook his head. "They've already revealed

more than is wise," he said, catching one of her hands and bringing it to his lips. "Highland as you are, you ought to know it isn't wise to poke and prod into what's revealed to those with second sight. They've given me a warning and I'm accepting it gladly."

Aveline frowned. "But—"

"It is enough. And more help than many receive."

He turned her hand and dropped a kiss into her palm, folding her fingers over it. "You keep that kiss to yourself and let it soothe you when you worry," he said, smiling at her. "And keep whate'er we discuss between us."

Her eyes flew wide. "You fear treachery?"

Jamie put his hands on her shoulders. "After seeing the sky darken with English cloth-yards at Neville's Cross, there is not much left to fear," he said, meaning it. "Least of all anyone cowardly enough to drape themselves in a wet plaid and try to frighten an old man."

But I do fear what such a miscreant might do to you.

Leaving that concern unspoken, he went to stand before the hearth, trying hard not think about what burned so merrily on its grate.

"I do not doubt what you've told me, lass." He raked a hand through his hair and hoped she'd believe him. "I am sure you did see Neill and Kendrick at the cairns, dancing with Hughie Mac. And down at the Garbh Uisge, too. Even so—"

"I did see them. I swear it," she insisted. "And they had to have been bogles. They vanished right before my eyes. Even as I was staring right at them."

She came to him then and he gathered her close.

"Leastways that was the way of it in the churchyard. At the cataracts, they just sort of drifted off into the trees."

"Ah, well." Jamie stroked her hair. " 'Tis not my brothers' spirits that concern me. 'Tis the bastard masquerading as a ghost that's plaguing me."

She looked doubtful. "You truly think someone is?"

Jamie cocked a brow at her. "Can you truly think someone isn't? After what we found in the chapel and then discovered upon returning here?"

And to his relief, she shook her head.

"But what do you mean to do about it?"

Jamie grinned. "What I do best when the need arises," he said, flipping back his plaid to reveal the many-notched haft of his Norseman's ax and the leather-wrapped hilt of his sword. "Assure the safety of those I care about."

"And what about those I care about?" she returned, touching his cheek. "Those I know your father cares about. You are the one who received Lady Linnet's warning."

Jamie captured her hand, kissing her fingertips. "Och, I shall be careful, ne'er you worry."

He smiled again, pleased with the precautions he'd arranged.

"Even as we speak, Beardie and another cousin should be taking up position outside this chamber's door. And" —he winked— "Beardie wields an even deadlier Viking ax than I do. If you haven't yet noticed, he's rather proud of his Norse granddaddies. And he doesn't take kindly to anyone even glancing cross-eyed at a woman."

She peered up at him through her gold-tipped lashes, looking more confused than reassured. "You've set two guardsmen to protect me? Just like the two you ordered to see to your da?"

Jamie grinned again. "I've set two trusted men to guard the door. I shall protect you."

"Oh!" Her gaze flew to the large, fur-covered bed. "So you will be sleeping here?"

Jamie followed her gaze and immediately began to harden.

The very reason he would not spend the night in the same room with her. Especially not in his brother's sumptuous love nest of a bed.

Not just yet, anyway.

Clearing his throat he stepped to the side of the hearth, glad for a means to distract himself before the tightening at his loins overrode his good sense.

"I shall sleep in my da's chamber, as he wished," he told her, whipping aside a heavy tapestry to reveal an oaken door. "This room was once my mother's, see you. That is the true reason for its opulence. And you will be safe here, I promise."

She blinked, her jaw slipping when he opened the door to reveal a small anteroom. And, clearly visible on the other side of the wee chamber, a second closed door.

"The bedchambers are connected," he said, taking a wall torch from its bracket and ducking into the little room. "We'll leave the doors open and the torches burning."

"To scare away the bogles?"

Jamie cocked a brow but said nothing. He knew

enough of lasses to let her think what she would if doing so soothed her womanly mind.

Truth be told, he was the one in need of soothing.

She'd followed him to the open doorway, her beguiling violet scent and the proximity of her soft feminine warmth almost making him regret he'd mentioned the connecting doors.

He could easily have stayed with her in Kendrick's chamber. If only wrapped in his plaid before the fire. The saints knew he'd slept in more uncomfortable places than on his late brother's fur-strewn floor.

Hovering on the threshold of the anteroom, she watched him with great, luminous eyes.

"And you will know if something stirs?"

Jamie jerked as if she'd reached out and curled her fingers around him. If she knew the kind of stirrings her mere presence was causing him, she'd wish him back belowstairs—no matter how passionately she kissed.

She was yet a maid and he meant to go gently with her.

"Lass," he said, his voice thick, "I will know if the night wind shifts a raindrop on your window ledge."

His most courtly reassurance spoken, he touched the smoking torch to the anteroom's two wall sconces, satisfied when they caught flame and the little room filled with the same golden light as Kendrick's chamber.

In a matter of moments, his da's room would be awash with light as well.

But not to frighten bogles.

O-o-h, nay, he hoped they'd come.

Leastways the one who favored dripping plaid.

And if the lout did make an appearance, Jamie would be ready for him.

Him, his Norseman's ax, and his trusty blade—whiche'er death the *ghost* preferred.

Chapter Eight

✦

A sennight later, Aveline paused on the landing outside Jamie's former bedchamber, a well-laden dinner tray clutched in her hands. Munro's dinner tray, for he alone whiled behind the chamber's closed oaken door.

And judging by the silence from within, Aveline suspected he slept.

But when she shifted the tray onto her hip and eased open the door, she found him sitting up in bed, propped against his pillows and rummaging through a great iron-bound chest.

A scuffed and somewhat rusty strongbox that looked very much like the one her father had sent Munro as her bride price, but that she knew contained only stones.

And sure enough, a scattering of stones were strewn across the bedcovers.

Stones and a few rolls of ancient-looking parchments.

Aveline took a deep breath, debating whether to retreat or stay.

"Sir," she finally called. "I've brought—"

"For mercy!" Munro looked up, jerking as if he'd been stung.

He slammed shut the chest's lid and grabbed for the parchments, crumpling one in his hand but sending two others fluttering to the floor.

"Saints, lass," he said, his brow furrowing, "I wasna expecting a meal this e'en." He eyed the steaming bowl of stewed beef and fresh-baked bannocks, but his mind was clearly elsewhere. "Morag said she'd be away, a-seeing to some ailing glen wife and Jam—er, ah . . . *that one* claimed he had business of his own."

Aveline forced a smile. "You should have known I wouldn't let you go without aught to eat," she said, trying not to look at her father's damning strongbox.

Embarrassment heating her cheeks, she approached the bed with the tray. "I know Morag or Jamie usually bring your victuals, but I thought you wouldn't mind if I did in their absence?" she asked, placing the food on a table beside the bed. "I can sit with you while you eat—"

She broke off, a whirl of doubts rushing her.

Her father's chest sat on the floor opposite the bed, its heavy iron lock undisturbed.

"I thought you were looking in my father's strongbox," she said, only now seeing that the chest on the bed appeared much older than the one containing her *bride stones*.

Following her gaze, Munro swore and scrambled to his feet. "This has naught to do with Alan Mor and dinna you tell a soul what you've seen," he said, snatching the fallen parchments off the floor, then trying to scoop up the stones spread across the bedcovers.

Lovely stones.

And as Aveline now recognized, each one was beautifully smooth and rounded, and in an array of striking colors. Some green, some reddish, with a few black ones shot through with sparkling ribbons of quartz.

The kind of stones she and her sisters had collected as children, up on the high moors. Treasures, the pretty little stones had been. And from the way Munro was clutching his, she had a sneaking suspicion he cherished these as highly.

Likewise the tattered-edged scrolls he'd jammed under a pillow.

"Not a word," he warned again, this time inching up the lid of the chest just enough to drop the stones inside. "I willna have that old she-goat belowstairs laughing at me and young Jamie needn't ken—"

"Needn't ken what?" Aveline turned to the table and poured a measure of ale into a cup. "I don't understand," she added, handing him the brew.

"No one would understand." Munro seated himself on the edge of his bed and took a deep swallow. "Not after all these years."

"All these years?"

Munro *humphed*.

Then he pressed his lips together and glanced aside.

Aveline looked closely at him, seeing not only the stubborn set to his jaw but the over-brightness of his eyes.

She also caught a faint whiff of something she hadn't

noticed until now. Not until he'd reopened the lid of his chest.

It was the pungent tang of heather.

Old heather.

Puzzled, she sniffed again, certain the distinctive smell came from the old laird's strongbox.

And then she knew.

Between the scent and the stones, anyone with even a shred of sentimentality would have guessed. Especially anyone from these parts—folk who knew how fond Munro was of walking the high moors.

Especially the heather-grown moor known locally as *Iona's Heath*.

The rumored trysting place of Munro and his late lady wife, Iona, in the long ago days of their youth.

The woman who'd died birthing Jamie.

And, as the tongue-waggers also claimed, Munro was never able to forget.

"Och, nay." Aveline's heart clenched. She took the empty ale cup from him and returned it to the table. "Dinna tell me you've filled that chest with—"

"All I have," he blurted, the stubbornness going out of his jaw, but the brightness in his eyes now damping his cheeks. "My memories," he added, reaching to lift the lid of the chest. "One handful of heather and one stone for each year she's been gone. I collect them every year up on the moors, on the eve of her passing."

"Jamie's birthday." Aveline's own eyes misted as she peered into the chest at the clumps of dead and dried heather, Munro's collection of colored stones.

Swallowing against the sudden thickness in her throat,

she sat beside Munro and hugged him. "It wasn't his fault," she said, hoping she wasn't making it worse, but feeling compelled to speak. "Jamie cares about you. I suspect he always has. Perhaps if you—"

"I'm no dried-up husk without a heart." Twisting round, Munro yanked one of his parchments from beneath the pillow and thrust it at her. "I've kept abreast o' the lad o'er the years."

Her own heart thumping, Aveline unrolled the scrunched-up missive and began reading. Sent by a man she knew to be one of Munro's allies, the parchment was dated about a year before and detailed Jamie's valor during the tragic Scots defeat at the battle of Neville's Cross near the English city of Durham.

She looked at Munro, not knowing what to say.

He humphed again and reached into his strongbox, fishing deep into the clumps of heather until he withdrew another handful of squished and yellowed scrolls.

"There are others—as you can see." He stuck out his chin, his eyes now glinting with a touch of belligerence. "Years' worth."

Aveline set down the Neville's Cross parchment and took a deep breath.

Munro stared at her, his mouth set in a straight, hard line.

"You must show the scrolls to Jamie," she said, disappointed when the old laird's expression didn't soften.

"That they exist ought to be enough," he said. "And you'll say naught about them. I'll have your word on that."

Aveline sighed, but finally nodded.

"As you will," she agreed, her heart aching for Jamie. And his father.

Munro Macpherson was wrong. The mere existence of his scrolls wasn't enough to smooth the rift between him and his only surviving son.

But it was a beginning.

A notion that would not have pleased the shrouded figure standing in the swirling mist high above the Garbh Uisge and peering down at the racing, roaring cataracts.

Healing, justice-bringing rapids. Quiet now, save for the deafening rush of the water; the fitful winds rattling the birches and bog myrtle clustered so thickly on the steep braesides.

Nothing else stirred.

The curses and shouts that had shattered the gorge's peace on a certain fateful day were silent now and those who'd deserved to die slept cold and stiff in their graves.

All save one.

And he, too, would soon be no more.

His father, bluster-headed coward that he was, would do himself in. Fear and guilt were his enemies. No great effort would be required to rid the hills of him.

A few others might follow as well.

If a greater atonement proved necessary.

The beginnings of a most satisfying smile twitched at the corner of the figure's lips. A soft, much-deserved laugh was also allowed. There was no need not to savor the moment. The darkening woods and the frothy white gleam of the water. The pleasure that deepened with each return to the scene of the figure's shining triumph.

Aye, it was a moment to be relished.

And with the exception of the figure's dark and flowing cloak and its shielding hood, there was no need for caution. Enough mist and rain had descended on Kintail in recent days for there to be ample cover to slip inside one of gorge's deep, mist-filled corries should any fool risk a visit to this devil-damned defile.

The figure sniffed. Nay, unexpected intruders were not a concern.

Neither from Baldreagan or Fairmaiden.

The winding deer track from Fairmaiden, especially, was choked with drifting curtains of thick, creeping mist. No one from that holding of reformed cutthroats and new-to-the-soft-life caterans would desire to bestir themselves on such a gray and clammy afternoon.

And if they did, it wouldn't be to trek through chill, impenetrable mist just to gain the treacherous confines of the Rough Waters. Those who dwelt at Fairmaiden relished their comfort too greatly to brave the gorge's steep, rock-lined shoulders save on fair, sun-filled days.

And the fools cowering within Baldreagan's blighted, hell-born walls were too busy poking about elsewhere to pose a serious threat. Too occupied switching bedchambers and lighting candles, thinking smoking pitch-pine torches and bolted doors would protect them.

The figure stared out over the Garbh Uisge, admiring the gloom and flexing eager fingers. Truth was, all the heather and stone in Scotland wouldn't hide them if a *bogle* wished to find them.

Whether they paid a visit to the ravine again or nay.

Though it could be surmised that *he* stayed away because his silly bride dogged his every breath and step.

His faery.

The figure scowled and clenched angry fists.

Only the great flat-footed James of the Heather would come up with such a ludicrous endearment.

Och, aye, that one was too chivalrous for his own good and wouldn't want to take a chance on the wee one trailing after him into the mist and twisting her precious ankle on a leaf-covered tree root.

Or worse.

Like watching a puff of wind blow her away.

Perhaps looking on in horror as she lost her footing on the slippery, streaming slopes and plunged headlong into the icy, tossing waters. Hitting her fair head on one of the many waiting rocks.

Black and jagged rocks.

So deadly.

And utterly innocent. Who could foist blame upon the dark, serrated edges of a rock if a soul was careless enough to fall atop it?

Certainly not the fools who'd gathered the remains of the footbridge and then been empty-headed enough to burn the wood without even noticing the saw marks and gouges it'd taken to cause the worm-eaten, weather-warped old bridge to collapse.

The figure smiled again.

And moved closer to the edge of the ravine.

If one leaned forward a bit and looked carefully enough into the foaming cauldron, it was almost possible to imagine a swirl of pale, streaming hair caught in the tossing waters. A dainty hand, reaching out for a rescuer that would never appear.

Or, even more pleasing, a flash of bright auburn hair and a quick glimpse of a bonnie male face, the eyes wide with terror and the mouth roaring a silent, water-filled scream.

But all the cries and thrashings would prove for naught.

Just as they hadn't helped his brothers when the foot-bridge had given way beneath them. The figure's lips began to quirk again and a warm, pleasant sense of satisfaction banished the afternoon's chill.

The Macpherson brothers had dropped like stones.

And most of them hadn't even struggled, for all their swagger and boasting in life. Their black-hearted gall and deceit. They'd sputtered and gasped for breath, flopping about like hapless flotsam, letting the current speed them to their deaths.

A few had fought fiercely, kicking their legs and flailing their arms, wild-eyed and shouting, cursing down the sun.

But the sun hadn't cared.

And neither had the lone figure standing high above them, looking on with an approving smile.

A smile that had soured just over a sennight ago when happenchance allowed the figure to witness an act of infuriating passion.

A kiss so shamelessly heated even the memory scalded.

And in a holy place, standing on the threshold of St.

Maelrhuba's chapel and in clear view of the Na Clachan Breugach stone.

The figure shivered and stepped back from the lip of the gorge. Not wanting to invoke the older, darker powers that might frown on taking such justice into one's own hands, the figure adjusted the folds of its great, voluminous cloak and slipped back into the mists and shadows.

While St. Maelrhuba's influence might be a bit watered down after so many long centuries, there wasn't a Highlander walking who'd doubt the lingering sway of the ancients.

The mysterious Picts and others.

Shadow folk one would be wise not to rile.

Passing by the Na Clachan Breugach stone each time a visit to the ruinous chapel was required was daunting enough. Kissing in the shadow of such a stone, and then so lustily, was to call up a thousand devils.

Never mind that in the days of the ancients more lascivious acts than kissing had surely gone on within the sacred circle of those hoary stones.

Stones of Wisdom or the Lying Stones, only one remained and the figure was sure it hadn't been pleased to witness such a kiss.

Such passion.

And so, the figure decided, moving stealthily through the trees, measures would need to be taken to ensure such passion didn't flame again.

Only then would the stone be appeased.

And the figure's grievances well met and avenged.

* * *

About the same time and not all that far from the swirling waters of the Garbh Uisge, Jamie followed Alan Mor into his privy solar at Fairmaiden Castle. Once again, he marveled at the little room's cheery warmth and beauty. This time he also wondered if he hadn't misjudged his host.

Perhaps placed unwarranted suspicion on his doorstep.

Truth was, whether he found it hard to believe or not, the Matheson laird looked genuinely outraged and appalled.

And, Jamie couldn't deny, exceedingly innocent.

Leastways of having had anything to do with the deaths of Jamie's brothers.

Alan Mor's indrawn breath and the way he'd leapt from his seat at the high table when Jamie stated his reason for visiting was testament enough to his surprise. Even now, his bushy-bearded face was visibly pale.

Clearly shaken, he raked a hand through his hair and strode to the shuttered windows, then wheeled back around almost as quickly. "I would not be party to such a black deed if my own life depended on it," he vowed. "Or the lives of my fair daughters."

"But you understand I had to come here?"

"Och, aye," Alan Mor owned. "I just canna think who would do such an evil thing."

He started pacing, rubbing the back of his neck as he stalked around the solar. "I'll admit your da and I have had our bones to chew, but any feuding we carried on has e'er been amiable feuding. Anyone in these hills will tell you that. Though I willna deny we keep a wary eye on each other. But see Munro's lads done in?"

He stopped in front of the hearth fire and shook his bearded head. "Nay, lad, I had naught to do with the like."

Jamie frowned.

Ne'er had he accused any man of such a vile deed.

Even by association.

But he'd seen and heard what he had.

His brothers were as dead as dead can be. He couldn't back down. If he hadn't been able to save them, he could at least honor them now with his persistence in uncovering their murderer.

And hopefully, in the doing, prevent more tragedies.

Someone had appeared in his father's bedchamber draped in a dripping plaid—a plaid that selfsame someone later tossed onto the effigy of one of Jamie's long-dead forebears.

Although he'd not discount Aveline's insistence that she and others have seen his brothers' ghosts, Jamie was certain the *bogle* plaguing Munro was a flesh-and-blood man.

Someone well capable of tampering with an age-worn footbridge.

And, he suspected, equally guilty of recently mixing fish bones in a kettle of porridge meant for consumption at Baldreagan's high table.

A near disaster he'd learned of just recently, the almost-tragedy, averted thanks to Cook's watchful eye.

Just now, though, Alan Mor's eyes were on him, waiting. So Jamie put back his shoulders and plunged on.

"In truth, sir, I canna think who would have done it either," he said, speaking true. "I—" He broke off when the door opened and Sorcha entered with a large flagon of warmed, spiced wine.

Jamie nodded to her, gladly accepting the cup she offered him. He also tried not to frown again. But it proved difficult for her presence made him keenly aware of the loss of his brothers.

His reason for visiting Alan Mor.

Taking a sip of the wine, he turned back to his host. "After what I've told you, surely you must see that someone is responsible?"

"So it would seem," Alan Mor agreed after a few moments of brow-furrowing. "But" —he whipped out his dirk and thrust it at Jamie, hilt first—"I'd sooner have you ram my own blade into my heart if you think my hands are stained with your brothers' blood."

Jamie took the dirk and tucked it carefully back beneath the older man's thick leather belt. "I can see it was not your doing," he said, meaning it.

But the matter remained unresolved.

He slid an uncomfortable glance at Sorcha, not wanting to besmirch her father's house and his associations in her presence. But she didn't seem to be paying them any heed.

She was seeing to the fire, jabbing a long iron poker into the flames, and he couldn't help thinking of the hearth fires at Baldreagan, each grate well laid with smoldering pieces of the footbridge.

The notion called his brothers' nine faces to mind and

he could almost feel their stares. They wanted and deserved their deaths avenged.

Something he'd never see accomplished if he fretted about offending those who might have answers.

So he took a deep breath and cleared his throat. "Your men," he began, watching Alan Mor closely, "can there be one amongst them who'd carry such hatred against my clan?"

"My men of Pabay? The reformed cutthroats as the glen wives call them?" Alan Mor waved a dismissing hand. "There's not a one o' them I'd trust to commit such a barbarous act."

"But they wouldn't have come to you from Pabay— the robbers' isle—if they didn't carry a good share of dark deeds on their shoulders."

"Dark deeds, aye. But there are degrees of villainy."

Jamie cocked a brow. "I've ne'er heard the like."

To his surprise, Alan Mor grinned and thwacked him on the shoulder. "Lad, now you see why I've trusted my wee lassie to your care. One look at you and a man knows you'd ne'er do ought to hurt her."

Jamie almost choked on his wine. "To be sure I'd ne'er harm her. I'd kill any man who tried."

"Well, now! Isn't that what I just meant?" Alan Mor grinned at him. "And, aye, there are degrees of villainy, but my Pabay men have put their days of thieving and deceit behind them. Though a few are scoundrels. I willna deny that."

He paused and jerked his head meaningfully at his daughter, waiting until she left the solar and the door closed softly behind her.

"Nevertheless, there isn't a murderer amongst my men," he continued, folding his arms. "That's always been a line I refused to cross. If you knew aught about such men as call Fairmaiden their home, you'd know they'd ne'er do aught to lose their welcome here."

He fixed Jamie with a piercing stare. "See you, I give them a chance to make a new life. They'd be fools to vex me."

Jamie returned the stare. "There's something you aren't telling me," he said, certain of it.

Alan Mor blew out a breath. "Only that there are some in these parts who do bear grievances against your da."

"Who?" Jamie took a step forward. "Name them if you know."

"Ach, laddie, would that I could," Alan Mor returned. "But doing so would mean naming every laird and chieftain e'er to purchase cattle from your father."

Jamie stared at him. "You mean men vexed o'er his cattle prices."

Alan Mor nodded and poured them both new cups of wine. "Munro's haggling and scheming to squeeze the last coin out of his buyers has earned bad blood," he said, handing Jamie one of the replenished cups. "Likewise his gloating when he succeeds. If you'd e'er seen him preen and squawk as he tucks away his money pouches, you'd understand."

"Och, I understand," Jamie assured him.

His da *was* filled with wind and bluster. And he did relish trumpeting his own horn.

"I'm glad you do understand," Alan Mor said.

"Though I still canna see one of those up-backed cattle lairds going to such extremes to vent their spleen. Highland honor forbids such low-stooping, whether a man is rightly grieved or no."

He paused for a sip of wine, then dragged his sleeve across his mouth. "Nay, laddie, I dinna think you'll find the murderer amongst Munro's cattle buyers."

"Neither do I." Jamie took his own wine and went to stand at the window.

Setting down his cup, he unlatched the shutters and opened them wide. The air held a biting chill and full darkness would soon claim the eerie half-light, so filled with shadows and damp, sighing wind.

He stood rigid, staring out at the gray pall of mist. Thick, drifting sheets of it curled across Fairmaiden's bailey and the surrounding woods.

Woods that bordered on some of the finest, most lush grazing grounds in Kintail. Fairmaiden's greatest prize and a treasure he could scarce believe would soon be his.

Leastways a goodly portion of it.

He was quite sure his da wouldn't have parted with an inch of such sweet, rich pasturing lands. No matter how many daughters he might have had to dower.

And that was another question he had to put to Alan Mor.

Once and for all time.

He turned from the hushed silence beyond the window. "I will find my brothers' murderer," he said, willing it so. "No darkness will be black enough for the bastard to hide in for long. But I would ask one more question of you."

Alan Mor shrugged. "I've naught to hide."

"Save the stones weighting down the bride price coffers you gave my da."

To Jamie's surprise, the older man laughed. "A private jest," he said, sounding not at all put out that Jamie knew. "Call it repayment for all the years your da has fleeced me to the bone each time I've been fool enough to buy a stirk or two from him."

He wagged a finger at Jamie. "That'll be the reason the pop-eyed lout hasn't complained. He knows he owes me."

Jamie folded his arms. "What I would know is why the alliance in the first place? Both your daughter Sorcha to Neill, and now giving Aveline to me?"

He glanced at the closed door, wishing it were bolted. Or perhaps even better, opened wide. Simply to ensure curious ears weren't pressed against the wood.

Especially Sorcha's for he had no desire to stoke the maid's sorrow.

"Aye," he went on, looking back at Alan Mor, "I canna wrap my mind around your willingness to forge a bond between our houses. It's bothered me since I first received your missive at Cuidrach Castle, and it still plagues me. Though I am more than pleased to have Aveline as my bride."

"Why shouldn't I wish peace between our houses? A lasting bond?" Alan Mor jutted his chin. "Mayhap I've grown weary of feuding?"

"Amiable feuding," Jamie reminded him.

"So I have said."

"You have the better grazing lands," Jamie pointed out. "By your own admission, you must've bought enough Baldreagan bulls o'er the years to have enriched and strengthened the blood of your own herd."

"Would you believe because your cattle are protected by old Devorgilla's rowan charms?"

Jamie shook his head. "Not for a heartbeat."

Alan Mor curled his fingers around his belt. "Suffering saints, laddie, I hope my wee daughter ne'er gets on your wrong side!" he said, but his tone was amused. "If you'd have the truth of it, there is another reason I sought this alliance. But it has naught to do with your brothers. That I swear."

"Then what is it?"

Alan Mor pressed his lips together, scratched his bearded chin.

And said nothing.

But the faint tinge staining his cheeks assured Jamie he did have something to say.

Jamie waited. "Well?"

"Ach, simply this." Alan Mor swept his arm in a great arc to take in the splendor of his privy solar. The fine tapestries dressing the walls and the costly standing candelabrum with its pleasantly-scented beeswax tapers. The richly carved settle by the door with its sea of welcoming cushions.

Even the flagon of heady spiced wine they'd been sipping. The generously-laden platters of cheese, confits, and sweetmeats spread on a table near the window.

Alan Mor enjoyed his comforts and Jamie couldn't

fathom what the man's high taste had to do with making peace with his long-time feuding partner.

Good-natured bickering or no.

Unless . . .

Jamie's brows drew together. The notion forming in his mind was too preposterous to put in words.

"I canna believe you feel threatened by my da?" he asked, regardless. "Dinna tell me you feared he'd seize Fairmaiden? Take your riches from you?"

"Sure as I'm standing here, that's the reason I wished an alliance with the cross-grained devil," Alan Mor admitted, his face coloring a deeper red. "Though it was ne'er Munro himself who concerned me. The saints know he hasn't roused himself to raid a neighboring keep in more years than I can count!"

Jamie frowned. "That still doesn't explain the alliance."

"Nay?" Alan Mor guffawed. "I'm a-thinking it does well enough. If you think about it! See you, I'm a man who appreciates his leisure. I had my share of warring in my younger days, even traipsed across the land and the Isles with the good King Robert Bruce in his fraught and hungry years before he won his crown."

He started pacing again. "And I've done my own share of devilry, cattle stealing and the like. Why do you think I open my doors to the men of Pabay and other souls like them? Broken men can find a home here, warm themselves at my hearth and drink my ale. They are welcome to make their pallets in my hall."

He threw Jamie a challenging look. "So long as they've put their roving days and banditry behind them.

I want no cause to lose what I've worked so hard to
gain. My peace of a night" —he paused to plump one of
the settle cushions—"and my comforts."

"Begging pardon," Jamie said, "but I doubt my da
cares whether Fairmaiden is filled with luxuries or if
you and your men sleep on straw."

I doubt he cares where and how I sleep.

But he kept that last to himself.

"I told you—it isn't your da," Alan Mor said, helping
himself to a sugared sweetmeat. "It's his fool cattle
dealing and the enemies he's made because of it. High-
placed enemies in some cases and I canna afford to have
such long-nosed snoopers poking around hereabouts."

Taking a handful of the sweetmeats, he dropped onto
the settle, looking suddenly tired. "See you, even though
my men have ceased spreading havoc across the heather,
there isn't a one o' them whose name wouldn't perk ears
in certain lawful places. So it's been my concern that
your father's dealings might cause the wrong souls to
come swarming into these parts one o' these years."

Jamie's brows shot up. "So that's why you wished an
alliance? To keep away the law?"

Alan Mor nodded. "I willna have a grieved cattle
laird sending a sheriff across my land to get to yours
and, by happenchance, discovering how many reformed
cutthroats dine at my table!"

"But how would an alliance prevent such a thing?"

"Because," Alan Mor wiped his mouth and leaned
forward, "your brother Neill had a far sounder head on
his shoulders and knew how to settle a fair deal. I'd
hoped the marriage of Munro's eldest son would see

him managing more of your da's lairdly duties. He would've tempered the dangers and grievances your father seems to stir whene'er he opens his mouth."

"I see," Jamie said, understanding at last. "And you think my marriage to Aveline will bring the same benefits?"

"That is my hope." Alan Mor stood. "Aye, there you have it."

"Then I shall do my best not to disappoint you," Jamie said, the words surprising him.

Ne'er would he have imagined he'd one day be offering a hand of peace to Baldreagan's bristling bear of a neighbor.

And a well-meant hand of peace, at that.

The door swung open then and Sorcha stepped inside. "'Tis almost vespers," she said, glancing at the now darkened window arches. "The evening meal is set in the hall if you care to come belowstairs? And" —she looked from her father to Jamie and back again— "I need to know if an extra bed needs to be prepared for the night?"

"You are kind, but I must return to Baldreagan," Jamie told her, already making for the door. "I've already tarried too long. Though I will stay for a quick bread and ale, aye."

But a short while later, as he pushed back from Alan Mor's table, his words kept circling in his head, haunting him.

. . . *Tarried too long.*

He could think of something else that had lasted too long.

Namely the rift between himself and his sire.

A matter he needed to devote more attention to and would, as soon as he'd rid Baldreagan of bogus bogles and avenged his brothers' deaths.

Hopefully the coming days would bring success.

And since the alternative wasn't acceptable, he'd simply have to ensure that they did.

Chapter Nine

✤

"*Gunna of the Glen?*"

Aveline's fingers stilled, her needle poised over her handiwork. Her question hovered in the hall's smoke-hazed air, almost alive, definitely taunting her. Worse, she could feel her pulse beating in her throat, and so rapidly she was sure the others would notice.

But she'd had to ask.

Something about the way Gelis had said the woman's name struck dread into her heart.

As did the pointed glances Arabella and Lady Juliana turned on the girl. Not to mention the high color now staining Gelis's cheeks and how she promptly lost the ability to meet Aveline's eye.

"Who is she?" Aveline's gaze flitted between the three MacKenzie women.

"She is no one," Lady Arabella finally said, glancing up from her own needlework, but not without sliding another chastising look at her younger sister. "Gunna of the

Glen is a widow, naught else. She dwells in a side glen near our cousin Kenneth's holding, Cuidrach Castle, and is best known for her golden herrings."

Gelis sniffed and began jabbing at her embroidery work with particular relish. "Herrings—bah!"

Ignoring her, Arabella set her stitching aside and stood, pressing a hand against the small of her back. "Prized smoked herrings," she intoned, glancing round as if to dare anyone in Baldreagan's crowded great hall to deny it.

"Smoked herrings and her skill in bed." Gelis lifted her chin, accepting the challenge. "Our own father admits there isn't a man in Kintail who hasn't enjoyed her charms! She has masses of long, silky hair the color of soot and breasts said to bring even the most fierce Highland warrior to his knees at just a glance. Some even say she keeps herself e'er naked and that her voice alone is enough to—"

"You have ne'er seen her," Arabella quipped. "Mother says she has a kind heart."

Gelis snorted. "Mother likes everyone. Have you ne'er heard the glen folk call her St. Linnet?"

"Hush," Lady Juliana admonished them, her own needlework long finished and set aside. "I am sure Lady Aveline has no wish to hear of a Glenelg joy woman."

But Aveline did.

Especially since Gelis had let slip that Jamie had been known to pay calls to the voluptuous beauty. A creature said to be irresistible. Whether Linnet MacKenzie found her kind or no, Aveline didn't like the sound of her.

But the matter appeared closed, as the other three

women had clamped their lips together as tightly as if they'd bitten into something sour.

"Now you see why we must leave on the morrow," Lady Juliana said after a few uncomfortable moments. "Our purpose in coming here has been met. Jamie now knows it would not be wise to visit the Garbh Uisge and you've promised to encourage him to be cautious if he does venture there."

Aveline bit her lip. Having grown up with a bevy of sisters, all of them save Sorcha married and away, she'd relished the company of the MacKenzie women. Even if their stay meant finding out about a well-made joy woman in some faraway side glen, she'd be sad to see them leave.

She slid a glance across the hall to the high table where Munro sat eating his meal. He, too, would regret the women's departure. Even now, occupied as he was enjoying cheese pasties and roasted chicken, no one could miss how his gaze repeatedly sought the lively MacKenzies. The pleasure he took in their company.

Pleasure that meant a much-deserved distraction.

Aveline's heart dipped.

"I will miss you," she said, returning her attention to the visitors. "Everyone will. You've only been here a short while—"

"Trust me," Lady Juliana interrupted, glancing at Gelis, "it is better for us to leave before our welcome frays. A boiling cauldron can be cooled, but once it spills over, the damage is done."

Standing, she brushed at her skirts. "Indeed, we should

retire now and see to our packing. The way north is long and difficult. An early night will serve us well."

"I am not yet tired," Gelis objected, making no move to budge from her stool. "We've not yet told Aveline about our marriage stone ceremony. With her own wedding celebrations set for the spring and Jamie having squired at Eilean Creag, mayhap she'd like to hear of it?"

Clearly warming to the idea, she leaned forward, her eyes lighting. "Perhaps she'd even wish to come to Eilean Creag for the wedding? Use the stone—"

"Only MacKenzies can use the stone," Arabella reminded her. "Jamie squiring at Eilean Creag does not make him a MacKenzie, much as we love him."

Aveline tried to look interested, but what she wanted was to hear more about Gunna of the Glen.

More specifically, Jamie's visits to her.

"Marriage stone ceremony?" she asked, her heart not in the words.

Gelis nodded. " 'Tis a more romantic tale than any French ballad."

But Aveline scarce heard her.

Her ears still rang with the girl's earlier chatter about the raven-haired joy woman with her sultry voice and magnificent breasts. More discomfited than she wished to show, she stole another look across the hall, this time scanning the torch-lit entry for a particularly broad set of shoulders and a familiar flash of bright auburn hair.

But she only saw Hughie Mac making his hunched way toward her, his own auburn hair age-faded and streaked with gray.

He clutched his fiddle in one hand and his horn-handled crummock in the other, using the long walking stick to propel himself to where the women had claimed a reasonably warm and well-lit corner to do their stitching patterns.

That, and engage in female babble.

The latter being an occupation Aveline now wished they'd ne'er embarked upon.

But Hughie Mac had a way about him, with his laughing eyes and good humor. Older than stone and many claimed just as wise, he hobbled forward, his hazel stick *tap-tapping* through the floor rushes, his grizzled appearance somehow lost in the warmth of his smile.

Aveline sprang to her feet, quickly fetching an extra stool and setting it in the warm glow of a nearby brazier.

"The MacKenzies' marriage stone?" Hughie Mac looked round as he lowered himself onto the stool. "I've seen it once," he said, resting his fiddle across his knees and leaning his crummock against the wall. " 'Tis a beautiful and mysterious stone."

"Mysterious?" Aveline echoed, reclaiming her seat on one of the twin facing benches of a window embrasure. "I thought it was a marriage stone?"

"And so it is. In truth, a swearing stone like so many others scattered around our hills and glens," Hughie Mac revealed, stretching his legs toward the warmth of the brazier. "A good-sized standing stone of a fine bluish cast and carved with ancient Celtic runes, the MacKenzie stone is more fair than most such stones but it shares the usual hole through its middle."

"It's the centerpiece of every MacKenzie wedding feast," Gelis enthused, plopping down beside Aveline.

She curled her legs beneath her and grabbed a pillow, hugging it close. "At the height of the feast, four of our brawniest warriors carry the stone into the hall and parade it about for all to admire while our seneschal approaches the high table with a ceremonial chalice of hippocras for the bride and groom to share."

"The happy twain and certain young lasses who have no business sipping such a potent concoction!" Arabella put in, claiming a seat on the window bench facing them.

Gelis rolled her eyes. "Father himself gives me my own wee cup—as you well know!"

"Our father would pluck down the moon if you asked him," Arabella returned, flicking her dark braid over her shoulder. "Like as not, the sun, too. Even if fetching it down would mean forever branding his hands."

Gelis flashed a grin. "Do not fault me if he loves me best."

"He loves you both and none more than the other," Juliana interceded, turning to Hughie Mac with an apologetic shrug. "They are young," she said, and Hughie nodded, looking young as well, for the space of a breath.

His hair thick and rich-gleaming in the torchlight, his weather-worn face smooth and almost bonnie, and his crooked legs straight once more.

"Aye, they are young," he agreed, the moment passed. "They also left out the most exciting part of their clan's marriage stone ceremony."

Aveline looked at him. "The mysterious part?"

Hughie shook his head. "The mystery is the stone's origin," he said, nodding to the clansmen who'd gathered near to listen. One handed him a brimming ale cup and he took it gladly, tipping back a healthy swig.

"The exciting part is the kissing." Gelis leaned forward and swatted her sister with a tasseled cushion. "Is that not right?"

Arabella flushed. "You would enjoy the kissing part."

Gelis stuck out her tongue. " 'Tis the best part," she said, smoothing her skirts. "Even if the silly legend has to be recited first."

"Silly legend?" Aveline lifted a brow.

"The tale of how our clan came to possess the marriage stone," Gelis told her. "But the kiss is better." She turned to Hughie Mac, smiling. "Do you know the kissing part?"

"To be sure, and I do," he said, taking up his fiddle. "After the ceremonial drink-sharing and the telling of the legend, the stone is carried thrice around the high table before the clansmen carrying it stop behind the laird's chair. The newlyweds then join hands through the hole in stone. They vow to honor the old gods and ask for their blessing."

He paused to wink at Gelis, playing a few lively notes clearly meant for her. "Then the groom takes his bride in his arms and the couple kiss—"

"Then they're escorted abovestairs for the bedding!" Gelis exclaimed, her eyes alight and her cheeks dimpling. "Mother won't allow us to join in that part," she admitted, fluffing her skirts.

"Och, indeed." Arabella rolled her eyes. "You've not missed a single bedding at Eilean Creag since you were old enough to realize everyone in the bedding chamber would be too ale-headed to notice you sneaking into the back of the room to watch!"

Gelis wriggled her braid at her sister. "At least I have learned about . . . things! 'Tis more than you can say."

"I am content to learn such things when it is time for my own bedding ceremony," Arabella snipped, her face scarlet.

"What is the stone's mystery?" Aveline asked, noting Lady Juliana's thinned lips and wanting to steer the conversation in a safer direction.

She glanced at Hughie, not surprised when he began playing a slower, almost heart-rending tune. "You said it's stone's origin?"

Hughie nodded. "No one knows the stone's true history or where it came from. There is a legend, aye."

Pausing, he waited until the hall quieted. "Magnificent as the stone is, its base is ragged and cracked as if it was wrested from its original location. All that is known is that the stone washed ashore at Eilean Creag and has been blessing MacKenzie marriages e'er since. 'Tis believed the power and beneficence of the old gods is vested in the stone."

"Then tell the tale," one of the younger MacKenzie guardsmen encouraged Hughie. Pushing through the crowd, he sat at the old man's feet, and soon a few others joined him.

Even Munro looked on from the high table, though he made no move to leave the dais.

"Ah, well . . ." Hughie glanced at Lady Juliana and raised a scraggly brow. "If it is not too late, my lady?"

Lady Juliana looked about to protest, but then smiled

and shrugged. "Those lasses would not sleep now even if I chained them to their beds," she said, the affection in her voice taking the sting out of her words.

Looking pleased, Hughie set down his fiddle and flexed his fingers before he started playing a soft, poignant tune.

"The legend of the MacKenzies' marriage stone hails from a distant time," he began, his voice seeming to swell and deepen on each word. "A time when Scotland was young and the old gods still held sway."

The hush in the hall thickened and those who'd gathered near edged closer. "Some claim the stone comes from the Land of Shadows, the hither side. If so, its true background will ne'er come to light," he said, his words falling sweet now, flowing and golden as his music. "Others say that Mananan, the old Celtic sea god sent the stone as reward for the MacKenzies' valor in battle. But most believe the stone has a more tragic past and that it is the version recited at MacKenzie wedding feasts."

Reaching down to stroke Cuillin's head when the old dog came to lie at his feet, he waited a few moments before he took up the tale again.

"Long ago, in an age before time was counted, a proud Celtic king dwelt not far from where Eilean Creag stands today," he said, his voice carrying to all corners of the hall. "A powerful and bold man, no enemy dared challenge him and 'tis even said the devil avoided him, knowing even he couldn't best such a formidable foe.

"The king had four daughters and they, too, stood in awe of him. Some might even say they feared him. Only his youngest lass laughed at his bluster, doing as she pleased and so sure of his love, she saw no reason to hide her wish to marry a young man she knew her father would deem unworthy."

Hughie slid a glance at Gelis. "This daughter was his favorite. She was also his destruction. So great was his love for her that he raged for seven days and nights upon learning of her betrayal. For even though the maid's sweetheart was a braw and pure-hearted lad, his bonnie face and strapping build would ne'er make up for his lack of prospects; the empty future which was all he could offer a bride of such noble birth."

Aveline slid a glance at Gelis, not surprised to see the girl's stare fixed on Hughie.

He had that kind of effect on his listeners and his ability to weave a tale only seemed to grow richer with age. Only Cuillin appeared restless, but with all eyes on Hughie, that was understandable. Rapt tale-listeners do not usually dole out tasty tidbits to hungry dogs.

Aveline, too, spared him only a moment's glance, then looked back at Hughie, sorry to have missed even a few words of his tale.

"Devastated to see how gravely she'd misjudged her father's favor, the lass and her braw laddie ran away, fleeing to the marriage stone, certain its sanctuary would save them.

"And it would have, for the stone's magic was powerful and true. Anyone gaining the sacred ground on which it stood and then joining hands through the stone's hole, would be blessed, their union sanctioned by the Old Ones." Hughie set down his fiddle, his voice music enough to finish the tale. "Sadly, the father was warned and he chased after them, coming upon them the very moment the young lovers thrust their hands through the stone."

He paused again, looking satisfied by the thick quiet that had descended over the hall.

"The king's rage overcame him and he rushed forward, his fury giving him the strength to tear the stone from its cliff-side base and hurl it into the sea—his daughter's lover with it." Hughie pushed to his feet, using his long hazel stick to lean on. "The deed stopped the old king's heart as he'd ne'er meant to kill the young man, howe'er livid he'd been. Truly repenting, he fell to his knees, pleading his daughter's forgiveness. But the girl's pain went too deep. Not even looking at her father, she followed her sweetheart into death, calmly stepping off the cliff edge to claim in the netherworld the love she'd been denied in life."

"So furious were the old gods by the king's disregard for the stone's sanctuary," Gelis finished for him, "that they took away all he held dear, destroying his stronghold so thoroughly that not even a stone remained to mark where he'd once ruled."

"But all was not lost," Arabella supplied, "for many centuries later the stone washed up onto our little island and has been in our safekeeping ever since." She lifted her chin, looking round. "We believe the stone's magic is even more potent today and we guard it well, considering it our most prized possession. Every newlywed MacKenzie pair clasps hands through the stone and makes the ritual oath, thus pleasing the Ancient Ones and guaranteeing themselves a bond that no mortal man can destroy for the old gods watch o'er them, granting them their forever favor."

"I told you the tale was romantic." Gelis beamed at Aveline. "'Tis the stone's honest history. I feel it here," she declared, pressing a hand against her heart. "There really was an ancient king who threw our stone into the sea after killing his daughter's one true love and seeing her leap to her death. I am sure that was the way of it."

"The stone could have come from anywhere," Arabella countered. "We are blessed to have it at Eilean Creag and that is enough."

But Aveline doubted anyone outside the window embrasure had heard her, for ear-splitting applause suddenly erupted to chants of *"Hughie Mac! Another tale!"*

But Hughie simply smiled and shuffled back to his stool, his energy for the evening clearly spent.

"Another day," he promised, gratefully accepting the hot meat pastie and fresh cup of heather ale one of the MacKenzie guardsmen brought him. "I am glad I had the chance to be present at a MacKenzie wedding many years past. Were that not so, I could not have done justice to the tale, well-known as it is in these Kintail hills."

"We've heard there is a stone of uncertain origin here, too," Gelis chimed, reaching to touch Aveline's knee. "At the Macpherson's family chapel."

Aveline shivered, thinking of the wet plaid.

And how she'd seen Neill's and Kendrick's bogles dancing in the churchyard—along with Hughie Mac.

He, however, was sitting quite contentedly on his stool beside the little charcoal brazier, munching his meat pastie and saying nothing.

Even though, for a moment, she would have sworn he'd looked about say a great deal. Something he'd apparently decided to keep to himself, for his lined face now wore a decidedly shuttered, wary expression.

Aveline frowned and drew her arisaid closer around her shoulders, suddenly feeling chilled. Icy cold and almost certain that someone, or *something*, was watching her from the shadows.

She could feel the stare boring holes into her. An unfriendly stare, almost malignant.

"Is there such a stone?" Gelis pressed, her eager voice breaking the spell.

Aveline blinked, resisting the urge to shudder. "You mean the Na Clachan Breugach monolith," she said at last, speaking to Gelis, but watching Hughie from beneath her lashes.

Whoe'er or whate'er had been glaring at her, she was certain he'd also sensed the malice.

"The Na Clachan Breugach?" Gelis nudged her again.

Aveline nodded. "It stands in the clan burial ground and guards the entrance to St. Maelrhuba's chapel."

"'Tis but a few paces from my cottage," Hughie spoke up, looking over at them. "The churchyard is a hoary old place, with the chapel half in ruin."

Aveline looked at him openly now, but his blue eyes were twinkling again and he continued to eat his pastie with relish, sharing bits of the meat filling with Cuillin and his castle dog friends, seemingly unaware of any reason he should feel uncomfortable at the mention of the stone. Or the little churchyard with its sad row of nine burial cairns, Celtic crosses, and mist.

Far from it, the look he sent her way was anything but sad.

Not that she had time to think about it, because Lady Juliana was bearing down on the window embrasure, the look in her eye brooking no refusal.

She meant to see the MacKenzie sisters to their beds.

Proving it, she drew up in front of Gelis. "You are a sly one," she said, planting her hands on her hips. "You know all about the Macpherson's Na Clachan Breugach stone. We discussed it some nights ago when Morag recounted the stone's deeper past. How it is said to be the last remaining stone of a sacred Pictish scrying circle once known as the Stones of Wisdom. And, too, how it might just be the Lying Stone as later Christians dubbed it."

Juliana folded her arms. "You've no need to hear the tales again. You do need come abovestairs and get some sleep."

Gelis frowned. "It is still early and—"

"It is late for you." Juliana jerked her head toward the nearby stair tower. "Say your good nights and come along."

Arabella rose dutifully to her feet.

Gelis stood as well, but not without casting a longing look at the comfortable embrasure bench with its maze of soft, embroidered cushions and the deep-set window arch, gilded silver with moon glow and rain.

"Aveline saw the ghosts of two of Jamie's brothers near the Na Clachan Breugach stone," she said, gathering her forgotten stitching patterns.

"Many Highlanders see a bogle or two in their lifetime," Juliana minded her, guiding her by the elbow away from the window embrasure.

"He's seen them, too," Gelis blurted, dragging her feet as they passed Hughie's stool. "Aveline said so."

"She spoke true." Hughie looked up from his second meat pastie. "I have seen the lads a time or two. Often enough to ken they are well and content where they are."

Aveline doubted Gelis heard him for Juliana was herding the girls at a fast clip toward the stair foot. But she'd heard him and it took her several moments to notice what was wrong when she glanced over at him.

Cuillin was gone.

Even though Hughie Mac still clutched a goodly portion of his meat pastie in his hand.

E'er ready for a handout, Cuillin would only have left the old man's side for one reason.

Jamie had returned.

Aveline spotted him at once, even clear across the hall. He stood before the wall laver in the hall's shadowy entry arch and was washing his hands. Cuillin, apparently of far keener senses than her own, was pressing himself against his master's legs, his plumy tail wagging.

But even if she'd spotted him second, her pleasure in seeing him was no less exuberant. Not even Munro's scowling face and demonstrative departure dampened her excitement. Already her heart was pounding and the desire to be pulled into his arms and kissed again proved almost overwhelming.

He spotted her then, too, and grinned, lifting his hand in greeting. But the instant she started forward, a vivid image rose up before her, blocking the way.

Transparent, shimmering, and vibrant, the vision-woman hovered in the aisle between the trestle tables.

Aveline blinked, but the image didn't fade.

Instead, she glowed all the brighter. A tall voluptuous woman with a luxurious spill of long glossy black hair. Her heady, musk-like perfume wafted around her like a dark, sensual cloud.

Even worse, she was naked.

Quite happily naked, judging by the seductive curve of her full red lips.

The smoldering heat in her midnight eyes.

Aveline stopped where she was, the hall and everyone in it spinning wildly around her. The floor even seemed to pitch and sway, but when the wheeling and dipping finally stopped, the frightful image was blessedly gone.

Better yet, she found herself where she'd yearned to be.

Jamie must've flown across the hall, because he stood holding her, his chin resting on top of her head.

"Saints, lass, I thought you were going to swoon," he said, tightening his arms around her. "You went chalk white and swayed. You would've hit the rushes if I hadn't run to catch you."

Aveline drew a shaky breath and pulled back just enough to look up at him. "You do that well—as you've already shown me. In the chapel, if you've forgotten."

"I've forgotten naught," he said, capturing her hand and lifting it to his lips for a kiss. "And there is a matter of importance that I would speak with you about if you can give me your trust?"

At once, the sultry-eyed beauty flashed across

Aveline's mind again, but she steeled herself against the woman's persistence and summoned her boldest smile.

"I will always trust you," she said, the words coming from somewhere deep inside her.

She just hoped he would trust her.

That he'd listen when she urged him to treat his father with greater kindness.

But for the moment she let him grab her hand and pull her with him across the hall. Through the throng and past the high table with Munro's empty laird's chair, taking her, she knew, to his brother Kendrick's bedchamber.

Once there, she'd discover whate'er he wished to discuss with her. Just as she meant to voice some of her own cares. Determined to do just that, she straightened her back and let him lead her up the stairs.

If she could summon her daring, she'd also learn just how close he'd been to a certain Glenelg joy woman.

After all, knowing one's enemy was half the battle.

And Aveline wanted victory.

The fullest, most round triumph possible.

Chapter Ten

❧

Jamie stood in the middle of his brother Kendrick's well-appointed bedchamber and tried not to frown beneath Aveline's penetrating stare. He also wondered if his ears were playing tricks on him. Truth be told, he wished they were because he wasn't sure what to do if they weren't.

He did fold his arms over his chest and attempt to feign a look of manly innocence.

There were some things womenfolk were just not supposed to know about and, with luck, pretending ignorance would make the whole matter go away.

But the look in his lovely's eyes and the way her back seemed to be getting straighter by the minute told him this matter wasn't going anywhere until it was aired.

Jamie sighed.

An audible sigh and coupled with an expression that told Aveline exactly what she wanted to know.

Or better said, what she didn't want to know.

Folding her arms, she considered her options. Clearly, James Macpherson was well acquainted with the Glenelg joy woman. Even more obviously, he wasn't keen on discussing her.

Unfortunately for him, she was.

Not that she expected anything good to come of gaining such knowledge. Indeed, thrusting her hand into a wasp's nest might prove less painful. But the sultry beauty's image wouldn't let her go and neither would her own growing awareness of her smallness.

Aveline turned to a well-laiden table near the hearth and poured herself a generous portion of heather ale. An indulgence she regretted almost immediately because the table's silver candelabrum cast its telltale illumination onto her hands, highlighting their daintiness.

A fault nowise near as galling as her tiny breasts.

And much to her irritation, the vexatious candelabrum spilled light across her bodice, too. A lovely bodice, to be sure, crafted of finest linen and decorated with a delicate band of stitchery.

Stitchery designed by her own wee hand for the sole purpose of attracting the eye away from the lack of the great swelling orbs most Highland maids flaunted with understandable pride.

Aveline frowned and set down her ale cup untouched.

The frothy brew wouldn't help her grow a lush bosom. Nor would it solve a jot of her distress.

Sooner or later, Jamie would have to answer her questions about the woman—his paramour from the sound of it.

Resisting the urge to start tapping her foot, Aveline

simply pinned the man with a *look*. As her father often said, what she lacked in physical size, she made up for in patience and calm. Her ability to persuade without words.

But instead of telling her about the bawdy widow, Jamie appeared content to stand before her with a closed expression, his jaw set and his mouth clamped tight.

He did run a hand over his face and wish himself anywhere beside where he was presently standing. Somewhere, where the devil wasn't on the loose and out to get him.

Saints, even Cuillin was fixing him with a baleful, unblinking stare. An accusatory stare if e'er there was one. And coming from a male dog who'd ne'er denied himself his own pleasures, his disapproval stung.

All men visited willing-armed and succoring joy women, and he had a greater reason than most to do so. Ignoring that reason, he crossed the room to where Aveline stood near the hearth fire.

"Who told you of her?" he asked, putting his hands on her shoulders. "Gelis, I'll wager?"

Aveline's chin lifted a notch. "Then you admit there is a Gunna of the Glen?"

Jamie inhaled deeply and glanced at the ceiling. "Of course, there is a Gunna of Glen," he said, releasing the breath and looking back at her.

"See here, lass," he began, "there have always been such women and ever shall be. So long as men have a need, there will be such women as the fair widow of Glenelg."

He winced, realizing his mistake as soon as the words left his tongue.

His wee Aveline was jealous.

Proving it, she pulled free of his grasp and went to the window. She whisked open the shutters and peered out into the streaming night.

"So she is as beautiful as Gelis claimed?" she asked, her back even more rigid than before.

Jamie bit back a curse and followed her. "Most joy women are comely," he said, stopping a handsbreadth behind her but not touching her. "Though I vow some of the older ones are not so savory."

"Older ones?" Aveline whirled around. "Just how many such women do you know?"

"Just one," Jamie told her true. "I only e'er went to see the Glenelg widow. She is the only such woman I have e'er known."

Two spots of color appeared on his bride's cheeks and she looked down, fussing at her skirts.

She said nothing.

Not that she needed to for waves of distress rolled off her, each one lancing Jamie more than the last.

He wanted to soothe and reassure her, not make things worse.

Scowling openly now, he shoved a hand through his hair. He was sorely tempted to forget his chivalry and do bodily harm to the fiery-haired bit of MacKenzie baggage who'd told her of the lusty widow.

Jamie swallowed, misery weighing on him. Even the neck opening of his tunic was growing tighter by the moment. Worse, he was also finding it increasingly difficult to breathe.

Duncan MacKenzie had once warned him that facing

a woman's jealousy was more daunting than crossing swords with any manly foe. And Jamie now saw the wisdom of the Black Stag's words.

Feeling more discomfited by the moment, he glanced around the bedchamber, looking for inspiration. Anything he might seize upon to wend the night in a different direction.

One that didn't feel like a white-hot vise clamping around his chest.

Blessedly, his gaze lit upon a small hole in the deep-set arch of the window. Just a minor fault in the masonry, a place where a bit of stone had fallen or been worn away by weather or years.

But perhaps it was his salvation.

Hoping it so, he put back his shoulders and cleared his throat. "Would you not rather speak of the MacKenzies' marriage stone?" he asked, stepping forward to smooth a strand of hair off his lady's brow. "I have seen it many times and can tell you a few tales of the stone and the good clan's feasting revelries."

Aveline's head snapped up, but her expression hadn't improved at all.

"How long were you in the hall?" She looked at him. "'Tis obvious you know Hughie Mac regaled us with the legend of the MacKenzies' stone."

Jamie frowned, torn between admiring her persistence and wanting to throttle her for being so difficult.

"I heard every word of Hughie's tale," he admitted, not surprised by her arcing brows. "I stood in the shadows, not wanting to spoil the moment, then joined a few kinsmen for some hot roasted ribs and honey bannocks. You caught my eye just as I was washing my hands after our repast."

Her brows lowered at once, drawing together in a frown that surely bode ill. "Since you spent so many years squiring at Eilean Creag, you will know their traditions well," she said, something about her tone letting him know he could expect even more trouble.

"As it happens, I heard enough of their stories tonight to occupy me for months." She glanced down, flicking an invisible fleck off her sleeve. " 'Tis the Glenelg woman who interests me," she said, looking up. "Your tales of *her* that I wish to hear."

Jamie blew out a breath and rubbed the back of his neck. Now he knew the devil was somewhere underfoot, and far too close for comfort.

Certain of it, he considered taking his bride into his arms and kissing her until such fool notions fled her mind.

A possibility he quickly dismissed.

In her present agitated state, she just might reward any such peacemaking attempt by biting off his tongue.

He frowned again.

Truth be told, she was being unreasonable.

After all, he'd not done anything wrong. So far as he knew, all men paid an occasional visit to a joy woman and in most instances to more than one.

Many loftier knights and lairds of his acquaintance kept a veritable string of mistresses, some even favoring their concubines and their offspring above their legally wed consorts.

Something Jamie would never consider; not with such a pleasing bride.

Saints, he was besotted with her.

"You're not being fair," he said, stepping closer to her again. "Surely you know that men have certain needs? Urges they sometimes tend by visiting such women as Gunna of the Glen?"

His bride said nothing.

Instead, she slipped past him and went to stand in front of the fire, staring down into the flames.

"I know of the heat of passion that blazes between a man and a woman—and what they do about it!" she said, not looking at him. "I am not ignorant."

She spun around then, her sapphire eyes snapping. "I *am* innocent. Should you wonder."

Jamie sighed. "Ach, sweetness, the thought ne'er crossed my mind," he said, leaving off how often he had thought about her innocence, but not for the reason she suspected.

Nay, he worried that her purity might remain a permanent state.

He looked down, then immediately wished he hadn't when his gaze fell on his hands. Saints, big as he was and tiny as she was, just holding her might crack one of her ribs if e'er he forgot himself and clutched her over-tight.

Jamie's mood darkened, the mere notion of causing her pain making his head throb. He'd sooner not touch her at all than risk hurting her.

"See here," he started to explain, "my concern is—"

"You said this woman, this Gunna of the Glen, is the only such female you've visited," she persisted, her gaze back on the hearth fire. "Have you then only lain with her? Have there been no others?"

Jamie rammed a hand through his hair.

"Of course, there have been others," he admitted, now feeling the devil's eyes on him.

"And who were they?"

"Kitchen bawds and laundresses. Big-boned, broad-bottomed lasses, light-skirted wenches free with their charms," he explained, his head now pounding in earnest. "I dinna remember the names of any of them. And from the time I went to serve my liege, Sir Kenneth Mac-Kenzie, the Keeper of Cuidrach, I only took my ease with the widow."

"No one else?"

Jamie shook his head. "No one."

"Then you must've been mightily fond of her?"

"I was, and am," Jamie said, smoothing a hand over his chin. "She is a good woman with a big heart. She misses her late husband and the bed sport they shared. That is the reason she welcomes such attention."

"That was baldly put." Aveline slanted a glance at him. "So she is a well-lusted woman?"

Jamie nodded, silently damning whate'er fool saint saw fit to bless him with such an unflagging penchant for honesty. "She is lusty, aye."

And so well-ridden even I can slide in and out of her with astonishing ease.

Something he needed to explain, however awkward. He could already see a slew of other interpretations slipping across his lady's face.

False notions that couldn't be farther from the truth.

So he inhaled deeply and crossed the room. Before she could move away, he seized her chin, forcing her to look at him. "What you are thinking is not how it was," he said, willing her to understand. "I did not seek out the widow because I had heart feelings for her. She suited me well for one reason and one reason only."

Aveline blinked, letting silence stretch between them.

Jamie swallowed. At least she hadn't looked away or tried to break free of his grasp.

It was a start.

Something to build on.

"So you did not love her?" she finally asked, her cheeks turning pink on the question.

"Love her?" Jamie's brows shot upwards. "I am fond of Gunna of the Glen," he spoke true again. "But she is a friend, naught else."

"An intimate friend."

"Aye, that indeed. As intimate as a man and woman can be." Jamie looked hard at her. "I will ne'er lie to you, lass. Dinna ask me questions if the answer will displease you."

Her chin rose. "Will you see her again?"

"Nay, I will not." Jamie shook his head. "That I swear to you. Leastways not for the reason I visited her in the past."

She looked doubtful. "Will you tell me what that reason was?"

"Och, aye." Jamie curled his hands around his sword belt, holding tight. "Truth be told, I must tell you."

Her eyes widened. "You must?"

Jamie nodded again. Then he let go of his belt and

reached for her, sliding his hands down her back and over the curve of her buttocks. He cupped them lightly and drew her to him, holding her just close enough so that she couldn't help but feel the thick bulge of his sex.

A *problem* blessedly at ease for the moment.

Hoping her soft feminine warmth and delicate violet perfume wouldn't alter that state too quickly, he glanced up at the ceiling again and sought the best words.

"Back in the hall, you said you wished to speak to me about something important," she said then, peering up at him, her eyes luminous in the candlelight. "Did it have aught to do with this woman? Or the MacKenzie marriage stone? I ask because Hughie Mac was telling the tale when you returned."

Jamie tightened his arms around her, squeezing her ever so lightly. "It has naught to do with those things and yet everything to do with them," he said, sweeping her up into his arms and carrying her across the room to lower her onto the edge of Kendrick's great four-poster bed.

"The only thing this has to do with the MacKenzie stone is that I needn't clasp your hand through a holed stone to know that our union will be mightily blessed," he said, hooking his hands beneath his sword belt again and pacing before the bed. "All I need is the assurance that I won't hurt you. That, and naught else is troubling me."

Aveline's jaw slipped. "Hurt me?"

She stared at him, confusion spilling through her.

This was the last thing she'd expected him to say. "I do not understand."

He shot a glance at her. "You ken we are now as good as legally wed?" he asked, pausing beside the foot of the bed. "You are aware that we can lie together now, this moment, and no one would raise a brow?"

Aveline nodded. His words caused a flurry of warm, fluttery tingles low in her belly.

She *wanted* to lie with him.

And she wanted more of his kisses.

Mayhap even the all-over kind of kisses one of her sisters had secretly told her about one night after she'd imbibed too much spiced wine, claiming her husband loved nothing better than to lie between her legs and lick her.

Aveline shivered.

The notion had excited her when Maili had shared it. Now, after being held and touched and kissed by Jamie these last weeks, the thought of him doing such an intimate thing to her—actually getting *down there* and touching his tongue to her—shattered her.

Truth be told, the notion filled her with such thrilling heat she had to clamp her thighs together.

"Did you hear me?" he prodded then, watching her. "We are bound now. Before God, man, and all these great hills surrounding us. Naught between us is a sin, even though we will not wed till spring. Our betrothal ceremony sealed our vows. We are as good as man and wife."

"Aye, I know this," she said, the tingles in her belly beginning to spread even lower.

He came closer again, stopping just in front of her. "Then you will not object if we speak freely about certain things?"

" 'Things'?"

Aveline's heart began to pound.

She shifted on the bed, her mouth going dry. Saints

preserve her if he'd read her thoughts. Half-afraid he had, she moistened her lips, sharply aware of his nearness, his clean masculine scent.

She blinked, his braw good looks and his scent distracting her. "What things?"

He stepped closer, so near his knees rested lightly against hers. "Man and woman things," he said, looking down at her. "You have said you know about them?"

She nodded. "My sisters have told me what happens at beddings and I have seen my father's men coupling with the laundresses in the shadowy corners of the hall and sometimes in the stables."

"And you have seen unclothed men?" he asked, watching her.

Aveline bit her lip. Scorching heat shot up her neck. Worse, wicked as it was, talking so openly about such things seemed to increase the hot prickly-tingly feeling between her legs.

And she was finding she liked the sensation.

She drew a slow breath, forcing herself to speak evenly. "Aye, I have seen my father's men undressed. Mostly of an e'en and in the hall as they readied themselves for sleeping."

Looking down, she smoothed a fold in the bed coverlet. "I've also bathed a goodly number of my father's loftier guests."

"But such guests would not have been aroused." Jamie held her gaze, his knees still pressing against hers. "Have you e'er seen a man thus stirred?"

"Only one," Aveline blurted before she lost the nerve. "He was standing behind a tree near St. Bride's Well when my sisters and I once bathed there. He was swollen, aye, and touching himself."

"Men do that sometimes, lass," Jamie said, his tone tight. "It relieves their need. But committing such an act while spying on you and your sisters was inexcusable and I hope he was severely punished."

Aveline curled her fingers into the bedcovers and glanced aside.

"He ran away before we could see his face," she lied, unable to tell him that two of her sisters had flaunted themselves, deliberately lying half-naked in a patch of sunshine beside the sacred well.

Jamie nodded, his fingers itching to curl around the neck of the dastard who'd taken such a cowardly means to find his ease. But he was also relieved his bride was familiar with a man's body.

Not taking his gaze off her, he unfastened his hip flask from his belt and tossed down a hefty swallow of fine and fiery *uisge beatha*. Highland water of life, a potent spirit well known for curing any and everything thought to ail man, including over-tight tongues.

He offered her some, then frowned because he hadn't thought to first fetch a cup for her, but she surprised him by accepting the flask and placing it immediately to her lips.

"So you see," she said after taking a sip and handing the flask back to him, "I know what to expect when we bed and I am not afraid. I also know you will not hurt me—that you'd never treat me as roughly as I've seen some of my father's men use the laundresses and kitchen lasses."

Jamie cleared his throat. "That is not the kind of hurting I meant," he said, not surprised by the flash of confusion in her eyes. "To be sure, I would ne'er treat you roughly. 'Tis my size that concerns me, see you? I fear hurting you because my man parts are overlarge."

To his surprise, rather than widened eyes or a scandalized jaw drop, her lips tightened and she avoided his eye, turning her head away to stare into the fire again.

"Is that why you were so fond of the widow?" she asked, her tone warning him that she was irritated again. "Because she relished your great size?"

Jamie sat down beside her on the bed. "I have told you why I call the woman a friend. She has a good and generous heart," he said, knowing it to be true. "The reason I went to her was not because she was fond of me, but because I needn't worry about causing her discomfort."

"I see." Aveline plucked at the bedcovers.

"I would that you do. My size has brought pain to more than one lass," he explained. "This caused me so much distress that I stopped lying with women and saw to my needs myself in the way you saw the man in the woods touch himself. Though I ne'er did such a thing save when I was certain I was fully alone."

Needing to make her understand, he reached for her chin again, turning her face so she had to meet his eye. "When I was urged to visit Gunna of the Glen, I was relieved to find a woman who could sheathe me with ease, fully without pain, and, aye, even take her own pleasure in the act."

Aveline's eyes rounded. "You are saying you went to

her because you could slide easily into her?" she asked, speaking more bluntly than she would have wished.

"Aye, that was the way of it," Jamie admitted. "There was no other reason. No heart feelings whatsoever, as I told you. I was pleased to have a woman I could lie with and not hurt."

"As you worry about hurting me?"

Jamie nodded. "Ach, lass, you are so wee that I canna imagine truly touching you without breaking you," he said, speaking as plainly as he could. "Even if resisting the temptation of you costs me my last breath, I willna cause you pain. There are other ways we can be intimate together. Other things—"

" 'Resisting the temptation'?" She opened her mouth to say more, but to Jamie's horror, her eyes suddenly started to glisten and she pressed a fist to her lips, blinking rapidly as she stared at him as if he'd suddenly sprouted two heads.

Or, judging by the tremulous smile curving her lips when she finally lowered her hand, looking as if he'd just handed her the sun, moon, and stars on a silver-gilt platter.

"You make it sound as if you desire me," she said, dashing the dampness from her cheeks, then frowning a bit when the tears kept leaking from beneath her lashes no matter how furiously she swiped at them.

"By the Rood!" Jamie gathered her into his arms, holding her as tightly as he dared. "Have I no' kissed you with enough passion for you to know how much I want you? How much you delight me?"

He began stroking her back, soothingly he hoped.

"Have you forgotten how much I enjoyed that one sweet glimpse of your breast?" he reminded her, his voice deep, growing husky with need. "Surely you know I'd love to see such beauty again."

"You want to see my breast again?" The words came so faint Jamie wasn't sure he heard her.

He pulled back a bit to look at her. "Perhaps with both nipples visible this time?"

She stiffened at that, so he slipped a hand between them, allowing himself the pleasure of cupping her breast and rubbing a single finger gently to and fro across her delicate swells. Touching her exactly as he had in her father's solar, only this time through the cloth of her gown.

"M'mmm . . . ," she sighed, melting against him. But she caught herself almost as quickly and reached circling fingers around his wrist, lowering his hand with astonishing strength.

"My breasts are small," she said, her eyes glittering suspiciously again. "That is the reason I fretted so much about the Glenelg joy woman. Gelis described her in great detail and I saw her in my mind, imagining her lush welling curves and huge ripe breasts."

Pulling away from him, she looked down, bunched her hands in her lap. "Nipples the size of my fists—"

"Hah! And so they are!" Jamie threw back his head and laughed, a quick image of the widow's large dark-hued nipples flashing across his mind.

Ah, the hours he'd spent licking and sucking them. Or simply plucking and pulling on them, rubbing and toying, circling a fingertip endlessly around the wonderfully crinkled flesh of her large aureoles.

Memories and images that stirred him not a whit.

His man parts, usually so responsive when thinking of the joy woman's bountiful charms, didn't even twitch.

Aveline touched his thigh. "So her breasts really are large and ripe."

"And yours are straight from heaven," Jamie owned, meaning it. "Do you know, sweetness, that since seeing you in the wood, a thousand full-breasted, well-curved females could come flouncing their wares into this room and I would still see only you?"

She looked aside, the color in her cheeks giving away her doubt.

"'Tis true." He leaned close to brush a feather-light kiss across her temple. "I am quite besotted."

Reaching for her braid, he began undoing it, letting the shimmering flaxen strands spill through his fingers until the whole gleaming mass cascaded about her shoulders, a riot of moon-spun silver tumbling down past her hips.

Looking at her sitting on Kendrick's bed, her unbound hair making such a bold statement of accepted intimacy, Jamie's heart began a slow, hard thumping and his loins tightened.

Not that he intended to touch her.

Not in *that* way.

He still had serious reservations about the like. But he could give her a soft, lingering kiss.

"You are a prize beyond measure," he vowed, finally releasing her.

Holding her gaze, he scooped up a thick handful of her hair, looping the luxuriant strands around his wrist and then bringing his hand to his lips, burying his face in the glossy, fragrant skeins.

"You take my breath," he vowed, kissing her hair, rubbing his cheek against its silkiness.

"And you please me." She traced a finger along his jaw, the wonder in her eyes stopping Jamie's heart.

She was watching him kiss and nuzzle her hair, her lower lip caught between her teeth as he let his fingers glide over the laces of her gown.

"You are lovely," he told her, his hands aching to undo her bodice. "I have ne'er seen a more beautiful maid and will ne'er tire of looking on you."

Smiling now, she brought her own hands to her bodice, her slender fingers deftly working the ties. "If I please you, you can look upon me all you wish," she said, the color in her cheeks deepening even though her words rang bold.

"But I would see you, too," she added, glancing downward.

"Me?" Jamie drew a tight breath, more aware of her than was good for him.

Aware of how much he wanted her.

How easily she could make him lose control.

Especially with the not-so-discreet direction of her gaze letting him know exactly what part of him appeared to interest her.

Proving it, she reached out to touch him. Not *there*, only on his chest. But her fingers warmed him clear through his plaid, the pleasure of her touch stirring him even if her hand hovered well above his sword belt.

"You tell me you're worried you'll hurt me," she said,

challenge thrumming behind every word. "Why not let me decide if I am afeared of your touch or nay?"

Jamie frowned.

"You do not know what you are saying," he argued.

She only smiled and reached again for her bodice laces, untying them until the top of her gown gaped wide and her naked breasts winked in the firelight, all creamy white, her rosy nipples already puckering.

"Well?" She looked at him, waiting.

"Well, indeed." Jamie could only stare at her.

Truth be told, he couldn't even move.

Ne'er had he seen a vision more lovely.

And ne'er had he run hard so swiftly.

So granite-hard, he was certain the slightest touch or movement would cause his shaft to snap in two. But then, he had hoped to begin acquainting her with his body tonight. He'd just envisioned an entirely different situation, had thought they'd progress slowly.

He'd certainly thought to remain fully at ease and then perhaps brush casually against her, letting her feel for herself why such worries plagued him.

Perhaps, too, he might have simply flipped aside his plaid, easing down his hose and braies just enough for her to have a wee peek. Then later, if the sight of him didn't frighten her, he'd hoped to encourage her to touch and explore him—if she'd shown herself so inclined.

Having her sit before him on a bed with her naked breasts all agleam and then expecting him to show himself to her, that was an entirely different kettle of fish.

An unexpected turn of events that set him to reeling

and made him want to clutch her to him so fiercely he feared he really would break her.

"I am not fragile. Nor am I afraid of things that are natural," she declared, moistening her lips in a way that only increased his discomfort. "If you find pleasure in looking at me," she added with a quick glance at her breasts, "then why would I not enjoy seeing you?"

Jamie pressed his lips together and took a deep breath.

She turned a look on him filled with more self-possession than he would have e'er dreamed in such a teeny lassie. But he could see it all over her, and she wore it well. So beautifully that just watching her proved a temptation he'd not be able to resist much longer.

"I will touch you if you wish," she said, as if she knew. "Anywhere it pleases you."

That did it.

Like a man possessed, Jamie sprang from the bed and unlatched his sword belt, tossing it aside to clunk to the rushes somewhere behind him.

His heart thundering, he kept his gaze fastened to the sweetness of her creamy, perfectly formed breasts and undid the great plaid brooch at his shoulder, swiftly sending it and his plaid sailing after his blade.

Grinning now, he reached for the bottom of his tunic and began pulling it over his head. But before he could wrest it fully off, or even think about shoving down his hose, a rude hammering sounded on the door.

"Hellfire and damnation!" He yanked down his tunic and glared across the room. "We need naught," he roared, his brows snapping together when the pounding only increased. "Come back in the morn!"

" 'Tis your da," Morag called anyway, her voice loud and unrelenting. "You'd best come. Now!"

Jamie froze, the old woman's tone icing his blood.

"Go!" Aveline gave him a shove toward the door, began hastily redoing her bodice. "Morag would not be calling for you if aught wasn't seriously amiss."

"That I ken," Jamie swore, already striding across the room to unbolt the door and fling it wide.

"Merciful saints!" he demanded of Morag, glaring down at her. The old woman's eyes blazed and her hair looked wild, its straggly ends poking up in all different directions as if she'd been standing in a fierce winter gale.

Jamie shot a look at Aveline, then turned back to Morag. "Lucifer's knees," he swore, "what has happened?"

"Aye, the Horned One will have had his hand in this!" Morag grabbed Jamie's arm, her gnarled fingers closing on him like talons. "Make haste! And bring your sword and ax," she urged, glancing at his discarded sword belt and blade, the Norseman's ax propped against the far wall. "We're under attack."

Jamie eyes flew wide. "Under attack?"

Morag nodded. "So everyone thinks," she said, turning to hasten back down the dimly lit passage, making for the stair tower as fast as her spindly legs would carry her.

Jamie and Aveline exchanged glances.

"God's bones," Jamie swore again, running back across the room to fetch his brand and the ax.

"Morag—hold you!" he yelled, grabbing Aveline's hand and pulling her with him from the room. "Wait!" he called again, amazed the old woman could move so quickly. "You said it was my da? What of him? Has he been hurt?"

But Morag was already far ahead of them, her tiny form swallowed by the shadows of the turnpike stair, the bobbing, wildly flickering flame of her rush light the only sign they'd even seen her at all.

Until her voice floated back up to them, her words echoing in the stair tower.

"I dinna ken how he is. Only that he's been shot by a crossbow."

Chapter Eleven

❖

O-o-oh, nay!"

"I dinna care how many wounds you've stitched, lassie, you willna be a-sticking that needle in my arm!"

Munro's protests echoed off the walls of the great hall, his bellowing rising above the din and catching Jamie's ear even before he and Aveline reached the bottom of the stair tower and burst into the crowded hall's chaos and turmoil.

A quick glance showed that the entirety of the MacKenzie guardsmen and at least half of Jamie's father's men appeared to have vanished, though he strongly suspected they'd hastened away to man the wall walks.

Those remaining dashed about shouting orders and cursing, some stoking the already blazing fires and heating great cauldrons of water, useful on the walls, Jamie knew.

"Dear saints, Morag spoke true. They're readying for a siege," Aveline gasped beside him, her gaze on a group of garrison men who stood nearby strapping on sword belts and other war gear.

Jamie frowned. "If so, I doubt our attackers hail from the Otherworld," he observed, certain of it.

Everywhere men rushed about snatching up more assorted, wicked-looking weapons than he'd realized his da's men possessed. Some had already taken defensive positions at the windows and doors, and still more were running for the stair towers, their clattering footfalls loud and echoing as they hurried to the battlements.

Aveline glanced at him. "I know you don't believe Neill and Kendrick—"

Jamie snorted. "Ghosts dinna shoot crossbows—or wear wet plaids," he said, tightening his grip on her hand as they pushed through the chaos, heading for the hall's crowded dais end.

Nor did they mix fish bones into harmless porridge he added in silence, not about to frighten her by revealing that particular incident.

A threat that had come to naught but just the kind of nonsense he was determined not to let happen again.

As for shooting old men with crossbows . . .

Jamie set his jaw, his blood heating as they neared the raised dais.

"Wench, be gone with you—you, and your devil's needle!" his da roared again, and Jamie spotted him at once.

He stood behind the high table, his left arm bright with fresh, streaming red blood, his hands in a white-knuckled grip on the back of his laird's chair.

Wild-eyed and furious, he was glowering at anyone who attempted to approach him.

At present, that seemed to be Lady Juliana.

" 'Tis only a scrape, I tell you!" Munro insisted, glaring at her. "I'll heal just fine—without you jabbing new holes into me!"

Ignoring his wrath, Lady Juliana took two steps closer to the dais. "This is only a very thin bone needle," she said, holding it up for him to see.

White-faced, Gelis and Arabella trailed after her, both girls in their bed robes, a pile of clean-looking linens clutched in Arabella's arms, while Gelis carried a bucket of steaming water.

Munro raked them with an equally black-browed stare. "Go back to your bed, lassies!" he yelled at them. "I've no need o' your nursing."

"Or yours." He rounded on Jamie and Aveline, agitation rolling off him. "I like you fine," he said, his gaze latching on to Aveline, "so dinna tempt me to change my opinion. Just stay where you are and leave me be."

"But, sir, your arm must be treated." Aveline started forward. "Like Lady Juliana, I, too, can—"

"You can stop right there and no' be a-joining up with this devil's besom and her needle," Munro exploded, glowering.

"Come you, Sir Munro," Lady Juliana tried to soothe him, her voice calm and low. "My stitches are so fine and quick, you'll ne'er know I've even touched you."

"So spoke the wolf before he ate the lamb!" Munro pulled his dirk from beneath his belt, brandishing it in her direction. "I'll poke any one o' you who sets foot on this dais. Including women!"

He threw an especial glare at Morag. "And no quarter given for age!"

Undaunted, she frowned back at him, her hands planted firmly on her scrawny hips. "I'm thinking that *scrape* will be needing more than stitching," she said, sliding a glance to the hall's massive central hearth where a stable youth held a broad-bladed dagger to the flames.

"Lady Juliana means well, but the wound is too deep and jagged, the blood spilling too swiftly for her dainty stitches to do much good," she added. "More the pity as sealing the wound with a hot blade will hurt far worse than being sewn up!"

Munro thrust his dirk back beneath his belt and whipped out his sword. "God's living eyes, any one of you goons try and bring a fired blade anywhere near me and I'll skewer you through! Be warned!"

He frowned darkly but when he made to shake his sword at the small group of friends and kin gathered before the dais steps, he swayed on his feet and the great brand slipped from his bloodied fingers, clattering to the floor.

Munro grabbed at his chair again, this time leaning heavily against its carved oaken back. "I meant what I said," he vowed, his eyes snapping defiance. "Dinna any one o' you dare come near me."

And then he ran chalk-white and slumped to his knees.

"Damnation!" Jamie vaulted over a trestle bench and leapt onto the dais, Aveline running after him.

"Clear the table," he called to her as he scooped his father into his arms.

"Someone bring *uisge beatha*! We'll need lots—a

good measure for Da to drink and even more to pour o'er his wound. And you"—he looked to the MacKenzie women—"help Morag fetch her salves, bandaging, and whate'er else she'll need. She knows better than any what must be done."

Pausing for breath, Jamie scanned the hall for Hughie Mac. He glanced at Morag when he didn't see him. "Where's Hughie? He'll know what to do, too. He's nigh as good as you at healing."

Morag sniffed. "That one left some hours ago," she told him, taking the steaming water bucket from Gelis. "He hasn't spread a pallet here in a while, fussing that his legs pain him of a night and that he only finds comfort in his own wee cottage."

"Hughie fussing?" Jamie lifted a brow.

He'd ne'er heard the erstwhile herd boy complain about anything. Like any true Highlander, Hughie Mac possessed an inborn imperturbability as solid and unshakeable as the hills he called home.

Jamie looked at his old nurse. "Nay, I canna believe it," he puzzled. "Hughie would ne'er fash about aught."

Morag only shrugged. "Hughie Mac's turned queer of late if you're asking me," she said. "But ne'er you worry. I know well enough what we need to do."

"Ye gods! There isn't aught *to* do." Munro's voice rose to a shout as Jamie held him while Aveline and Lady Juliana spread a clean linen cloth over the emptied high table.

He glared at everyone, his scowl darkening even more when Jamie lowered him onto the tabletop.

"Tell those fools to stop running around like twittering

women," he raged, twisting his head toward the bustle in the hall. "There's no need. Baldreagan isn't under siege. 'Twas Neill's bogle who shot me and no other—as I've already told the lackwits!"

Morag huffed. "I'd sooner believe it was God Almighty. You've e'er given Him ample reason to be vexed with you!"

" 'Twas Neill's bogle so sure as I'm looking at you!" Munro narrowed his eyes on her.

Jamie and Aveline exchanged glances.

"Bogles dinna use crossbows," Jamie said, beginning to ease back the edge his father's blood-drenched plaid. "And lest you've forgotten, so far as I recall, Neill was a master with a blade but he ne'er fired a crossbow in his life."

He slid another glance at Aveline. "If you didn't know," he told her, "most knights frown on crossbows. Neill held them in particular scorn."

Munro sniffed. "How would you ken what he can or canna do now, in his *after*life? Him, being a bogle and all?"

"My brothers may be dead, but I've yet to see proof that any of them are returning here as ghosts. Despite all the reports to the contrary." Jamie bit back his temper and kept working at getting the bloody plaid off his father without causing him more discomfort than necessary.

The man's failing wits were suffering enough. If he had them in better order, he'd recall his eldest son's vaunting pride.

Truth was, Neill had despised crossbows, calling them

a coward's weapon, good only for the lowliest paid mer-
cenaries and brigands.

Neill had loved their father, too. Ne'er would he attempt to harm him. Not in a thousand lifetimes—whether
Munro had neglected to repair the old footbridge or no.

Jamie pressed a hand to his brow. His temples were
beginning to throb again.

"You don't think it was one of my father's Pabay
men?" Aveline stepped close, pitching the question for
his ears alone.

He looked at her. The notion had flashed across his
mind, but he dismissed it now.

"Nay, lass, with surety not," he said, speaking equally
low. "One of your father's reformed brigands would ne'er
have missed their target. My da lives because the shot
was clumsy. A true crossbowman would've had the skill
to send his bolt through my father's heart and not his
arm."

She bit her lip, looking unconvinced.

Jamie shook his head, seeking to reassure her. "I'd
wager my last breath that none of Fairmaiden's Pabay
men did this. Dinna you worry. I only meant to say it
wasn't Neill's ghost, either."

Proud as he'd been, he wouldn't have touched a crossbow, insisting that doing so would've been beneath his
dignity as a noble and belted knight.

If Neill, Kendrick, or any Macpherson stood on the
wrong foot with a man, they'd challenge their foe outright. It wasn't their clan's way to hide in the shadows,
using darkness to cloak their blows.

Truth be told, such wasn't the way of *any* Highlander.

Jamie turned back to his father, that knowledge making his head hurt all the more.

"Tell me, Da, was *Neill* wearing his wet plaid again when he shot you?" he prodded, certain that whoe'er was masquerading as his brother's ghost had also fired the crossbow. "Did you see him?"

"Of course, I saw him." Munro's eyes blazed, but his voice sounded wheezy, hoarse and growing fainter. "Do you think I'd say it was him if I hadn't seen him?"

Pushing up on his elbows, he pinned Jamie with a fierce stare. "I'm no' the only soul hereabouts who's seen Neill lurking about and Kendrick, too. So dinna go a-telling me I'm daft."

Ignoring his da's outburst, Jamie only cocked a brow. "And the plaid?"

Munro clamped his lips together, wincing when Jamie eased away another blood-sodden bit of cloth from the wound. "Nay, he wasn't in his plaid," he finally admitted, pushing the words past gritted teeth. "He— *eeeeeei-ioooow!*"

The scream speared Jamie's heart, hurting him, he was sure, a thousand times more than the old man writhing on the high table.

"I am sorry," he said, hating the tears filling the older man's eyes. "The last bit of plaid and your tunic had to be ripped away."

He didn't mention that still more of the cloth would have to be picked and dug from his flesh. Deep in his flesh, for the iron-headed crossbow quarrel had gone clear through Munro's arm.

Morag, Lady Juliana, or even Aveline would perform

the task with great care, seeing to it as soon as the wound was washed and rinsed, though Jamie doubted his father would appreciate their gentleness.

"I willna have the wound seared." Munro grabbed Jamie's wrist then, staring up at him with glittering, fear-glazed eyes. "Tell them. No hot blade on my flesh."

Looking down at him, something inside Jamie snapped and broke. Hot and jagged, it spun free to whirl ever upward, lodging in his throat, making it thicken and swell, burning his eyes.

He blinked, needing to clear his vision.

When he did, he recognized it was the panic in his father's eyes that twisted his heart. And made him angry. Munro Macpherson had never been afraid of anything.

Saints, Jamie wouldn't have been surprised to hear his da challenge the Horned One himself. A fight to the death and with the devil's own weapons of choosing!

Yet now the old man's every indrawn breath was tinged with fear.

A grievous state he'd lived with e'er since a certain faceless coward began using the tragic deaths of his sons to haunt and break him. A miserable gutter-sweep Jamie strongly suspected might even have caused those deaths.

And whoe'er he was, Jamie would find him. Even if doing so meant overturning every stone and clump of heather in all broad Scotland.

"Mother o' the living God!" Munro bellowed then, flailing with his good arm. "You're both right pests," he added, trying in vain to knock Morag and Lady Juliana away from him.

But with the fortitude born of women, they ignored his

curses and thrashings, only nodding calmly when four braw clansmen appeared to help Jamie hold his father in place as they washed and tended the wound.

"Come, sir, one sip—for me."

Jamie heard his bride's voice in the midst of the chaos, soft, sweet, and soothing as a gentle spring rain. Glancing at her, he looked on as she tried to coax Munro to drink the *uisge beatha*.

A cure he needed as surely as having his wound cleaned because the moment the women finished, the dread sealing would follow.

Whether it pleased Munro or nay.

He'd die otherwise for nothing else would staunch the bleeding.

Jamie shuddered. Having once had a sword cut on his thigh sealed by such hot branding, it was a pain he'd prefer to spare his da, so he nodded to the four kinsmen holding Munro and went to the head of the table, taking the flask of fiery Highland spirits from Aveline's hand.

"Drink," he said, clamping his fingers on to his father's jaw and tipping back his head. He held the flask to the old man's tight-pressed lips, nudging. "As much as you can."

Munro glared at him, tightening his lips even more.

Jamie glared right back at him. "You know I will pry open your lips and pour the whole flask down your throat if you dinna take a swallow—or two."

Apparently believing him, Munro shut his eyes and opened his mouth. Not much, but enough to allow Jamie to send a healthy measure of the healing water of life flowing down his father's throat.

Before he could get him to accept a second gulp, a commotion in the hall drew all eyes.

Beardie came pounding up onto the dais, red-faced and panting, but resplendent in his great-great-grandsire's rusted Viking helmet and his huge and shining Viking battle-ax clutched tight in his hand.

"The siege is ended!" he announced, coming to a skidding, graceless halt. "And without a single scaling ladder being thrown against our walls. No' one enemy fire arrow sent whistling through the air!"

Beaming, he swiped a hand across his glistening brow. "My Viking helmet must've scared them! One glimpse of a true-blooded Norseman hanging o'er the parapet and waving a battle-ax, and the spineless bastards tucked their tails between their legs and ran."

Jamie stared at his cousin. He couldn't believe there really had been attackers.

"You saw them?" he asked, his mind whirling with the consequences if Beardie spoke true.

"Well . . ." Beardie looked down, taking a moment to hitch and adjust his belt. "We had to have frightened them off because there was nary a sign o' them anywhere," he admitted, removing his Viking helmet and scratching his head. "Nary a glint o' steel, no whinnying horses or clink o' armor. Not one insult hurled at us as we looked for 'em."

He jammed his rusty helmet back on, looking puzzled. "Truth is, the castle dogs didn't even bark."

"I told you it was the bogles," Munro said from the table, his eyes popping open. "Neill's bogle. I saw him take aim. He was wearing his burial shroud and he was *in* the bailey. Only a ghost could've slipped past the gate-house."

A ghost or someone who comes and goes as he pleases.

And has a right to do so.

Jamie's blood chilled.

He should've asked where the attack had occurred.

Now he knew.

And the answer was more disturbing than if a whole band of hostile clans had arrived to storm Baldreagan's walls; such foes can be fought. Unseen enemies in one's own midst were far more difficult to besiege.

"But I don't understand . . ." Aveline touched Jamie's arm.

He turned to her. "Dinna understand what?"

She edged closer, her brow knitting. "The bailey," she said, sliding a glance at Munro. "He swore he'd not set foot outside the keep, yet he was attacked in the bailey."

Munro tried to push up on his good arm. "Of course, I was in the bailey," he wheezed. "Neill told me to go there."

"He spoke to you?" Aveline hurried back to the head of the table, smoothed the damp hair back from the old man's brow. "When was this? Why didn't you tell us?"

"He came to me in *his* bedchamber," Munro managed, his gaze sliding to Jamie. "He told me if I took all the candles I can carry to St. Maelruhba's chapel and lit them in penance, he'd ne'er visit me again."

" 'Candles'?" Aveline glanced at Jamie.

Jamie shrugged.

Morag stopped dabbing at Munro's wound long

enough to jerk her head toward a dark corner of the dais. A familiar-looking wicker basket stood there, heaped high with fine wax tapers.

Fine wax tapers splattered with red, as was the basket itself.

"The candles the Lady Aveline brought for him from Fairmaiden," Morag explained, taking the fresh wet cloth Gelis handed her and dropping the bloodied one into a pail.

She pressed the new cloth against Munro's torn flesh, then looked their way again. "We found the crossbow bolt in the basket of candles. He was carrying it when he was hit."

Aveline gasped, clapping a hand to her breast.

Jamie frowned.

He could well imagine why Neill's *bogle* wanted Munro's hands full once he'd lured him outside the keep.

Even old and addle-headed, Munro Macpherson was a hard man to beat with blade in his hand.

And everyone in these parts knew it.

But before Jamie could think on it further, a cleared throat and a hesitant touch to his elbow startled him. Turning, he came face-to-face with the stable lad who'd been holding a dirk in the flames of the hearth fire.

The lad indicated that dirk now. He'd wound several layers of thick leather and cloth around the hilt and was holding the thing as far from his body as he could.

Jamie understood why.

The dagger's broad, two-edged blade glowed redder than the gates o' Hades.

"Holy saints," Jamie swore, his stomach clenching. He nodded to the stable lad, all else forgotten.

He didn't dare look at his father.

But he had to.

Yet when he did, Munro was staring past him, an awed-looking smile hovering on his lips. "Iona," he breathed, his gaze fixed on the empty shadows of a corner.

Chills swept down Jamie's spine and the fine hairs on the back of his neck lifted. Iona was his mother's name. And with surety, she wasn't standing across the dais looking at Munro.

She'd been dead since Jamie's birth. A tragedy his father had ne'er let him forget.

"My Iona," Munro said again, and a tear trickled down his cheek. "Nay, I am not afeared," he added, his strained voice sounding just a shade stronger.

Then his eyes cleared and he looked straight at Jamie. "The searing," he said, unblinking. "Do it now, son, and be done with it."

"So be it." Jamie took the red-hot dagger from the wide-eyed stable lad. He jerked the instant his fingers closed on the well-padded hilt, the throbbing heat from the blade nigh scalding his hand. And he was only grasping layers of cloth and leather! Unthinkable what the fired blade would do to his da's naked flesh.

Wincing, he slid a warning glance to the four men holding his father. At once, Morag nodded and pressed the gaping flesh together. Then, before Jamie lost his nerve, he stepped closer and lowered the blade to the wound.

"Awwwwwwwwggghhh!"

Munro's cry and the loud *zish* of burning flesh pierced the silence. Blessedly, his eyes also rolled back into his head and his body went still, leaving the echo of his pain and the horrible smell of singed flesh to his kin and those others who cared for him.

The deed finished, Jamie stepped back, glad to drop the searing dirk into the pail of water someone thrust at him. Then he wheeled away from the table and stood silent, waiting for the bile to leave his throat.

From the corner of his eye, he could tell that Morag and the MacKenzie women had taken over. His old nurse and Lady Juliana were already spreading a healing salve onto the newly-branded flesh and Gelis and Arabella stood close by, strips of clean bandaging in their hands.

"Come, you, let us be away abovestairs."

Jamie turned and found Aveline peering up at him, an indefinable promise in her sapphire eyes, a pleasing curve to the sweetness of her lips.

She reached for his hand, lacing her fingers with his bloodstained ones. Her gaze went to Munro then back to Jamie. "You can do no more for him. Not this night," she said, leaning into him, her words for him alone. "I would see to *your* needs. If you will come with me."

"My needs?" Jamie cocked a brow, wishing he hadn't let show how deeply branding his father's flesh had affected him. "It had to be done, lass. Sorry though I am to have hurt—"

"You misheard me. That is not what I meant, though I know the searing cost you," she said, her gaze dipping just enough to let a heat of a very different sort begin flickering across a certain sensitive part of him. "I am thinking you might favor a bath?"

The flickering heat became an insistent throbbing. Jamie cut a glance at the hall's large double-arched hearth fires, the heavy iron cauldrons of steaming water suspended above the crackling flames.

Water heated in vain for a siege that wasn't.

He looked back at his bride, his pulse quickening even when his conscience balked at leaving his father.

"He will not waken until the morrow," Aveline said, making him think she'd peered into his mind. When her gaze then slid to the steaming cauldrons, he was sure of it.

"The water is already heated," she added, the soft huskiness of her voice convincing him. "There is surely enough for a long, leisurely bath."

Jamie nodded. He agreed entirely.

His lady smiled and Jamie was well pleased to let her lead him toward the stair tower. He could use a bath. The morrow would be soon enough to renew his efforts to root out the mysterious *bogle*.

Neill's bogle. And a few other things weighing heavily on his mind.

But one of those things resolved itself halfway up the winding turnpike stair, the answer hitting him in the gut with all the punch of a well-aimed fist.

As if someone had reached out and ripped blinders from his eyes, he knew why he'd felt such a wrench when he'd seen the fear in his father's eyes.

That fiery squeezing sensation had been more than mere sympathy.

His heart had heard what he hadn't.

Tell me, Da, was Neill wearing his wet plaid . . .

His own words came back to him and he paused to press a hand against the cold stone of the stair tower wall lest his knees buckle beneath him.

A crossbow bolt and a red-hot searing knife were not exactly the means he would have chosen to come to such a stunning pass. The result was earth-shattering all the same.

And so utterly amazing he was tempted to whoop for joy.

Under any other circumstances, he would have.

As it was, he simply gave himself a much-needed shake before grabbing his bride's hand again so they could resume their spiral ascent to Kendrick's bedchamber.

He didn't need whoops and chest-thumpings to celebrate. Nor even a night of revelry and free-flowing ale. What he'd learned was more than enough.

In truth, more than he'd e'er expected.

For the first time since he could remember, he'd called his father *Da*.

And even more astounding, his father had called him son.

Chapter Twelve

✦

That same night, Baldreagan's kitchen lads filled buckets of hot water from great iron cauldrons and lugged their sloshing burdens abovestairs to the linen-lined bathing tub in Kendrick's bedchamber. And as they went about their task, another very different cauldron simmered and bubbled elsewhere. Across darkening peaks and silent glens, dubiously scented steam rose from this second cauldron. A fine, black-sided cauldron, this kettle's murky waters weren't intended for any lairdly son's leisurely bathing pleasure.

Nor were the nameless objects floating on the water's surface meant to fill anyone's hungry stomach.

A *scrying* cauldron, the kettle served one purpose and one indomitable soul.

And its keeper, Devorgilla of Doon, the most far-famed cailleach in the Highlands, had already made use of its powers earlier that night.

Just as she had every e'en for some while, hoping to

catch a glimpse of a certain faithful friend. A valiant, true-hearted friend who'd been away on a special mission, and was overdue to return.

She'd tried to scry his whereabouts in the soft hour of the gloaming, when the veil between all things of legend and wonder tended to be at its thinnest. But this e'en as on the other nights, she'd failed.

Even the especially powerful charms she'd tossed into her cauldron in the hopes of enhancing her success only turned the usual pungently scented steam into rankly foul smoke. She addressed this nuisance by opening her window shutters and seeking her pallet for an early night of *dream*-scrying. A method nowise as reliable as her cauldron's *seeing* steam, but the best she could hope for if the steam refused to cooperate.

Annoyingly, her dreams denied her as well and rather than the return of her brave and adventurous friend, she only saw Baldreagan's distant walls. Her dreams showed her through those walls and into one of the keep's darkest and oldest stair towers, her sleep filled with images of trudging feet and well-filled pails of heated water.

Churning, racing water, too.

White and deadly.

Blessedly, the tiredness of her bones let her slip into a deeper, dreamless sleep. One not plagued by such devil's waters, though her ears, e'er sharp and keen, still rang with endless, trudging footfalls.

Even though she made her pallet a good distance from Kintail and the deep pine hills of Baldreagan.

Truth be told, anyone seeking her wisdom would have to journey for days over rough and treacherous land, then sail across miles of shining, moon-silvered water to reach the great sea cliffs of Doon. Proud and forbidding, they rose darkly from the Hebridean Sea, their precipitous heights privy to many ancient secrets.

Now, as Devorgilla slept, heavy sea mist clung to those cliffs and the night wind fell light. Especially along the crone's own stretch of the jagged, rock-bound coast. There where the Old Powers still lived and breathed, and only Devorgilla's wee cottage broke the loneliness of the shore.

Few dared follow the narrow stony path to her dwelling's misty hiding, tucked as it was in deep heather and dark, sheltering rock, but of those souls brave enough, most were made welcome.

All were received hospitably.

Even those of darker hearts and ill luck, for such was the Highland way.

Some visitors, of course, were eagerly seen and even greeted effusively.

One such soul arrived now, slipping quietly out of the inky black shadows and into the little clearing in front of the low, thick-walled cottage. Sure of his welcome, the visitor sought the center of the moon-gilded clearing, knowing well that he'd soon be noticed.

He was expected, after all.

And the cailleach had been getting impatient.

He knew that because the thin blue line of peat smoke rising from the cottage's thatched roof carried a tinge of the crone's more powerful spelling goods.

Pleased by such tangible evidence of the crone's

regard, the visitor stretched and yawned, then sat on the night-dampened grass and waited.

Soon he'd be praised for a job well done.

And the crone's eagerness to see him might mean he'd receive a more generous reward than usual—especially when she learned how successful he'd been.

Not that anyone named after the great Somerled, King of the Isles, would be anything outside of victorious.

He was hungry, though. And thirsty. He'd journeyed far and his task hadn't been easy. *O-o-oh, aye,* he decided, watching the moon slide out of the clouds, he could use a bit of the pampering the crone showered on him when he pleased her.

And tonight, she'd be very, very pleased.

So he looked round to make certain none of his friends or kin were about and might see him. Then, once assured that he was alone, he allowed himself a small and seldom-used breach of his usual dignity.

He barked.

Devorgilla's eyes snapped open.

Somerled. He'd returned.

Relief sluicing through her, the crone pushed up on her elbows and peered about, looking for her little friend. Then full wakefulness came and she realized he'd be out in the moonlight.

Somerled favored silvery, moonlit nights, claiming they were as conductive to his magic as Devorgilla's own favorite soft hour when night fell and the mists gathered.

He barked again and Devorgilla cackled with glee, her pleasure helping her to her feet.

"He is hungry," she said, glancing at her other four-legged companion, her tricolored cat, Mab. A creature nigh as old as Devorgilla herself but a deal more crotchety.

Leastways in Devorgilla's view.

Curled at the most comfortable end of the pallet, Mab pointedly ignored her rival's return.

She simply opened one eye, her look of disdain assuring Devorgilla that her feline sleep concerned her far more than a certain adventure-seeking red fox was troubled by an empty belly.

"You, *mo ghaoil*, ate your fill of herrings this e'en," Devorgilla reminded her as she pulled on her boots. "So, my dear one, surely you will not begrudge Somerled a wee bowl of gannet stew?"

Another of Mab's superior stares said that she did. The seabird stew was one of Mab's favorite dishes. And definitely tasty enough to please Somerled.

Even so, Devorgilla hobbled to the door and opened it wide. Her little friend sat silhouetted in moonglow in the middle of her charmed glade, the grassy clearing that shielded her from unwanted, prying eyes.

Somerled's eyes watched her now.

The little red fox had magical eyes.

Beautiful, expressive, and wise, his eyes could tell whole tales with one carefully aimed stare and as he stretched to his feet and came forward, Devorgilla knew that his mission had been a success.

A tremendous success.

"Ah, my precious," she crooned, stepping aside to allow him into the cottage, "I see everything went as planned."

Somerled strolled around the cottage, then chose to sit

in the warmth cast by Devorgilla's charcoal brazier, his expression assuring her that he'd succeeded indeed.

But his task hadn't been without difficulty and as she filled a wooden bowl with the fine-smelling gannet stew, he let her know that he suspected she'd soon have reason to send him back to Baldreagan.

Truth tell, he was so sure of it, he would have stayed and not yet bothered himself with the long journey to Doon did he not know the crone would be fretting about him.

That, of course, he would keep to himself.

Devorgilla had her pride, he knew.

And while she also had a surprisingly tender and sentimental heart, he knew she secretly enjoyed knowing how fearsome some folk considered her.

"We shall not think about that this night," she said, setting down the stew and a small platter of bannocks smeared with honey and bramble jam. "If there is a need for you to return, the Old Ones will let us know."

A large bowl of fresh spring water followed, and a smaller bowl filled to the brim with her very own specially brewed heather ale.

But Somerled deserved a special treat, so she waited until he began eating the gannet stew, then she shuffled to a hanging partition of woven straw that hid a small larder off the cottage's main room.

Shoving aside the straw mat, she stepped into the cool dimness of the larder, quickly gathering choice portions of her best cheeses and dried meats, a generous handful of sugared sweetmeats.

These treats she arrayed on not one but two good-sized

platters, carrying them over to the handsome little fox with all the glory-making ado a woman of her years could muster.

"So-o-o, my fine wee warrior," she crooned, her face wreathing in a smile, "in honor of your triumph, *two* platters of delicacies for you."

Raising his paw in acknowledgment, Somerled thanked her, then made haste to avail himself of his reward.

His just reward, if he did say so himself.

Much pleased, he deigned to ignore Mab's hostile stare and finished off the gannet stew. He'd enjoy his remaining victory victuals—both platters of them—at a slower, more leisurely pace.

As befitted a great hero.

And he had no doubt that he was one.

Indeed, if he had two long legs rather than four short ones, he was quite sure someone would've knighted him for his most recent knight-like accomplishment.

Sir Somerled.

He could almost hear the accolades. The trumpet blasts and horn blowing, the cheers from maidens fair.

Instead, he realized with a start, his horn tooting was only old Devorgilla's fluting snores.

Poor soul, she'd fallen asleep on her three-legged stool beside her cook fire. Not wanting her to waken any more stiff than could be avoided, Somerled fixed his golden stare on her, working his magic until she stirred herself and, still sleeping soundly, returned to her plaid-covered pallet.

A penetrating look at her thin-soled black boots saw

them slide easily from her feet. And one last stare tucked the plaid gently around her, draping her clear to the tip of her grizzled chin.

Satisfied, he decided he really should begin to think of himself as Sir Somerled.

He was, after all, the wisest, boldest, and most magical fox in all the Highlands.

He was the most successful, too.

A true champion, as his two platters of reward delicacies proved.

He just hoped he'd be as triumphant the next time.

Back at Baldreagan, darkest night curled around a certain stout-walled tower and a biting chill slipped through the wooden slats of the bedchamber's brightly painted window shutters. Freezing autumn rain pelted those shutters, but the brilliant, jewel-toned colors shone fetchingly in the candle-and-torch-lit room, their romantic whimsy bearing yet another reminder that the chamber had belonged to Kendrick.

His private lair and love nest.

The scene, Aveline was certain, of many heated embraces and other lascivious delights. Kendrick's bed-sporting exploits were legion, though a thoughtful soul might credit some of the wilder tales to hopeful female hearts.

Boastful female hearts, she suspected.

In truth, Kendrick could ne'er possibly have bedded all the lasses who claimed they'd enjoyed his favor. And ne'er had she actually encountered one of the countless bastards he'd supposedly sired throughout the neighboring hills and glens.

A great red-haired giant, though not quite as big as Jamie, Kendrick's twinkling blue eyes and his quick-flashing smile could bedazzle at a glance. And if his high good looks weren't enough, he'd possessed a merry tongue and a soft Highland voice almost too beautiful for a man this side of heaven.

Aveline shivered, the image of Jamie's roguish brother having his way with angels almost making her smile, had it not been so sad.

He ought to be here still, wooing and winning *living* hearts.

Ravishing byre maids and knights' daughters alike, whisking them away to his high-towered love lair and filling hours with naught but laughter, song, and uninhibited carnal bliss.

The deliciously decadent kind as hinted by the naked images painted into the innocent-seeming pastoral scene gracing Kendrick's window shutters.

At first glance, it seemed a tranquil woodland landscape filled with mythical creatures and a fanciful distant castle. A closer inspection showed unclothed wood and water nymphs in a variety of suggestive poses, some even attended by handsome knights in equal states of dishabille.

Aveline shivered again, seeing the painted images as clearly as if she were standing in front of the shutters and examining them. An undertaking she'd already allowed herself, carefully inspecting each and every depicted pair until the possibilities were emblazoned across her mind.

Erotic possibilities.

Images of lust and bared flesh, limbs entwined and handsome faces awash with rapture. She just hoped her joinings with Jamie would be as joyous.

Willing it so, she pressed a hand to her breast, trying to steady her breathing, the thrilling sensations that spun through her each time she imagined herself and Jamie as one of the mythic pairs depicted on the shutters.

Ach, to be sure, Kendrick's bedchamber revealed a man who'd savored his sensual pleasures. And this night, she hoped, he wouldn't mind if she borrowed his love nest for her own.

A step she'd already taken in ordering a bath for Jamie, then setting out and lighting her finest beeswax candles. Aveline smiled and smoothed her hair. Faith, she'd even tossed a handful of pleasantly aromatic herbs onto the hearth fire. Preparations she'd finalized when she'd bolted the door behind the retreating army of kitchen lads who'd carried up a seemingly endless supply of steaming water pails.

She looked again at the heavy oaken door and the sturdy drawbar now slid so soundly into its socket inside the wall. The bolted door was more than just a shielding barrier for their privacy: it was a tangible sign of her new life. The happy and fulfilling existence she meant to seize for herself as James Macpherson's bride.

His soon-to-be wife.

And in every conceivable way.

Aveline drew a deep breath. His notions about hurting her were absurd. Even innocent, she knew that nary a child would be born if a woman weren't capable of stretching enough to let the babe slide out of her.

No matter James of the Heather's great size, she doubted his manhood was larger than any smiling, gurgling bairn she'd e'er bounced on her knee. And with so many married sisters, she'd seen her share of newborn babes.

She just needed to convince Jamie that if bairns can come out of a woman, a man's privy part will surely always fit in.

To that end, she completed the reason she'd kept her back to him so long, pretending she was waiting until the last of the kitchen lads' loud, pail-clattering descent faded from the stair tower.

In truth, she used the time to undo her stays and laces. Taking her lower lip between her teeth, she mustered her courage and then let her gown slip to the floor.

Jamie's sharp indrawn breath from somewhere behind her, marked her victory.

Her next triumph would come when she turned around and he glimpsed her standing before him wearing nothing but her near-transparent undershift.

And, she hoped, a seductive smile.

A look bold enough to rouse and excite him, tempting him into forgetting the night's horrors and thinking only of the pleasure she wished to give him.

But if his eyes narrowed or clouded with disappointment, she'd retrieve her gown and re-don it. Then she'd bathe him as chastely as she'd tended the worthies who'd visited Fairmaiden Castle.

"They are gone," she said, referring to the kitchen lads and their racket. "And you, my lord, shall now be treated to a bath like no other," she added, turning at last.

Her pulse quickening at her daring, she eased down the straps of her shift, gently lowering the top piece until her breasts were fully uncovered.

Jamie's brows shot upward and his breath snagged in his throat. His reaction seemed to please her for she made no move to cover herself. She simply stood where she was, her shift falling loosely around her hips and her breasts delightfully bared.

And, he saw at once, not just her sweet, rose-tipped breasts. Through the thin cloth of her camise, he could also make out the silky curls of her woman's mound, a tempting triangular shadow just topping her thighs.

"Holy saints." He knew he was staring, but couldn't stop. "Sweet lass, do you ken I can see all of you?"

"To be sure, I know." She looked at him, her chin lifting. "Would I have undressed for your bath if I meant to keep myself covered?"

Jamie hesitated, an unpleasant thought stealing into his mind.

Saints, now *he* was the jealous one.

"Did you bathe your father's friends thusly?" he asked, damning the question, but needing to know.

She shook her head. "Nay, I was e'er fully clothed when seeing to the comforts of Fairmaiden guests."

"I am glad," Jamie admitted, his relief almost a living thing.

Humbling, too, for its portent. Truth was, he'd often lain with Gunna of the Glen on a pallet still warmed by another man's rutting. Yet all he'd cared about was taking his ease.

Aveline was different.

He wanted her body, aye. But more than that he wanted her companionship and caring, her wit and intelligence. The way she could make him laugh. Her appreciation for the beauty of the great hills and moors they called their own. The respect she'd displayed for the Old Ones and the ancient ways by bathing naked at a sacred well, garbed in naught but her unbound hair and the silver of the moon.

Her kindness to his father and Hughie Mac touched him, too. As did the softness that came into her eyes when she knew he was missing his brothers.

And though he'd ne'er admit it, he loved the way she passed the best tidbits from her supper trencher to Cuillin or whate'er other castle dogs might come nosing up to her for a handout.

Jamie drew a deep breath, astounded by the clutch she already had on him.

As if she guessed his thoughts, she glanced at her naked breasts and then back at him, suddenly looking shy. But she recovered as quickly, sending him a bright, dimpling smile.

Stepping closer to the bathing tub, she swirled a finger in the steaming water, then turned away to fill a small earthenware bowl with violet-scented oil, carefully placing the bowl near the hissing, red-glowing charcoal brazier.

"Hot scented oil for after I've bathed you," she told him, moving to the tub again. "That, and more."

"More?"

"You will see." She drew up a low three-legged stool and placed a small jar of soap and washing cloths onto its seat. "But first, I must see you. Out of your clothes and into the water."

Jamie nodded, but he still wasn't certain he wanted her to see him at all. It was one thing for her to be daring so long as his clothes hid the dangers, and quite something else for her to actually see that *danger* hanging heavy between his thighs, long, thick, and swaying.

Blessedly, he was still relaxed, but staying that way was proving a ferocious struggle.

Jamie frowned.

Aveline dipped her fingers into the bathwater again, watching him. "You were about to show yourself to me when Morag came abovestairs," she reminded him.

"Sweet lass, this has naught to do with removing my clothes." He raked a hand through his hair. "I am trying not to run hard, is what I'm doing. Think you I can get naked and into that tub, have you touching me intimately, and not wish to touch you in a like manner?"

She smiled. "Then do."

"I can hardly breathe for wanting you and—" He looked at her, his jaw slipping. "What did you say?"

She studied him, her lovely face turning serious. "You did say we are so good as legally wed, did you not? That because of our plight troth anything we do isn't a sin?"

Jamie nodded, unable to deny his own words, or the truth of them. Leastways to his way of looking at things.

Such as his conviction that she was his the instant he'd seen her gliding through that moonlit glade near Hughie Mac's cottage.

Or that he'd been hers since that moment.

And anyway, come the spring, they would be man and

wife in truth. Their union blessed and sanctioned by man, Church, and God. Until then, he'd personally slay anyone who dared try to come between them.

Be it man, dragon, or bogle.

Especially bogles. Wing-backed and haloed, ring-tailed or horned. He'd have done with whate'er variation of the beasties cared to come at him.

She tapped his chest, looking pleased. "Then," she said, a dimple flashing in her cheek, "if you agree that we are as good as wed, get in yon tub and let us see what happens!"

Jamie groaned. She was the one who needed to be worrying about what would happen. He could already feel what was happening.

Or rather, what was stirring.

But it couldn't be helped. Not with her rosy nipples so tight and thrusting, and her perfect little breasts jiggling so delightfully each time she swirled her fingers through his bathing water.

So he made short work of sword belt and clothes, tossing off every last stitch with a speed that would serve him wonders if he could duplicate it on a field of battle.

Full naked, he fair leapt into the tub. But not so quickly that he hadn't seen her eyes widen in shock, the look of horror that flashed across her beautiful face.

Jamie's heart sank.

She clapped her hands to her cheeks and stared down at him.

"Dear saints in heaven," she gasped, shaking her head. "You—"

"I tried to warn you," Jamie said, his world tipping,

narrowing to her stunned face and the tears suddenly glinting on her fine, gold-tipped lashes.

He sank down into the heated water, damning his uncommon height, his over-long legs that made it impossible to scrunch himself deep enough into the wooden tub to hide what he'd known would shock and scare her.

And it had.

Horror stood all o'er her and he wouldn't blame her if she fainted away in a swoon. Or crossed herself and ran screaming from the room.

Frowning, he grabbed a washing cloth and used it to cover himself. "Sweet lass, please dinna fret," he said, searching for the right words. "I've told you, I will ne'er hurt you. There are ways—"

"Och, Jamie!" She dropped to her knees beside the tub and flung her arms around his neck, kissing him everywhere. His lips, his temples and brow, his eyelids and ears, even his nose. "Jamie, Jamie, 'tis not your size that shocked me," she said, grabbing his face between her hands, her tears spilling freely now. "I knew to expect *that,* and am thrilled and excited to explore you most thoroughly!"

Jamie blinked.

His heart split wide and blinding heat slammed into the backs of his eyes. "By the Rood," he managed, pushing the words past the thickness in his throat, "then whate'er made you go so pale?"

"This." She thrust her arm into the tub and ran her fingers down his hip and farther until she reached the long puckered scar marring the outside of his left thigh. "You ne'er told me you've had a wound seared. It grieved me to see the scar after what happened tonight."

"Ach, lass." Jamie leaned back against the linen-padded rim of the tub. "The scar is one I brought back from Crossgate Moor," he said, blowing out a breath, wishing one great gusty sigh could banish the images of Neville's Cross and its arrow storm of English longbows.

The shattering defeat and the incredible blow of Scotland's young King David being captured and taken prisoner from right beneath the noses of the realm's greatest nobility. And none of them able to do aught but look on in appalled horror as the English routed and slaughtered them, then plucked their hiding king from beneath the span of a bridge.

Shuddering at the memory, Jamie reached for his bride's hand, kissing her fingers one by one, the soft, silky warmth of her inner wrist.

And as he'd hoped, the sweetness of her smooth, white skin helped chase away the shadow images of angry and torn flesh, bright red and streaming. Or cold and gray, once death claimed the countless poor souls who'd left their lives on that devil-damned Sassunach bog.

"I'd forgotten you were with the king at Neville's Cross," she said, her expression pensive.

Jamie shrugged. "Compared to most, I came away unscathed," he said, truly believing it. "What saved me was the good fortune of riding with Robert, the High Steward. He commanded the left of the field and we fared better than most, having the luck of more stable terrain to fight on. Even so, we were still unable to stop King David's capture."

He looked down at his scar, then back at her. "After the carnage I saw that day, I can ne'er think of myself as having even been wounded in the fray. Truth be told, I canna even recall the moment it happened."

"I am glad." She slid her arms around his neck and kissed him, and this time her kiss was leisurely, soft and sweet, and full on the lips.

When at last she eased back, she smoothed her hand down his cheek. "It is best not to dwell on painful things we cannot undo or change. God was kind in letting you forget."

"Ah, but I do remember the searing," Jamie admitted, her caress already taking his mind elsewhere. "'Tis why it grieved me to brand my own da. I knew the pain I'd be giving him."

"You also gave him life, did you not?" Aveline stood. "I vow he will be right pleased about that when he comes to his senses again."

To her surprise, Jamie laughed. "Not pleased enough to apologize to Lady Juliana and Morag for threatening them with his sword, I'll wager!"

Smiling back at him, Aveline leaned forward and kissed his cheek. "Then I shall apologize to you for looking so shocked upon seeing your scar and making you think the reason was otherwise."

He cocked a brow. "You truly are not frightened by that particular 'otherwise'?"

"Frightened?" Aveline dipped one of the washing cloths into the little jar of soap and began to scrub his shoulders. "My only fear is that you might withhold yourself from me and"—her gaze slid to Kendrick's painted window shutters—"I find myself eager to share pleasure with you."

"Eager enough to remove your shift and join me in this tub?" He arched a brow at her again, the simmering heat in his eyes and the way his voice deepened sending delicious thrills all through her.

Making it impossible to say no.

"O-o-oh, aye," she agreed, already reaching to shove down the camise.

But he shot out a hand, strong fingers encircling her wrist. "After you've finished bathing me," he said, flashing a wolfish grin.

"Of course," Aveline agreed, slipping away to fetch a flagon of sweet, spiced wine.

Returning to the tub, she handed him a filled chalice, watching as he sipped. Two heavy wax candles burned on a nearby table and the bright flames illuminated his naked body, casting an alluring pattern of flickering light and shadow across his broad shoulders and back.

Rivulets of water trickled down his chest and she followed their path, admiring the fine glint of his chest hair and how some of the droplets caught there, clinging to the smattering of wiry red-gold hairs and hovering like glittery little diamonds before breaking free and rolling lower.

Her gaze drifted lower, too, but this time he smiled and made no attempt to hide himself. Or his pleasure. The steadily increasing beat of the pulse in his throat bespoke his excitement, as did the rise of his maleness.

An answering pulse quickened inside her. Her heart thumping, she dipped her hand deeper beneath the water, letting her fingers glide across and then tangle in the thick coppery curls springing at his loins.

Her own loins went molten at the intimacy, especially when the backs of her fingers brushed against the smooth, silky skin of his thick, swollen shaft.

Aveline's breath caught and her hand froze, her fingers curling deeper into his nether curls as his manhood twitched and jerked against her. And though she could scarce believe it, swelled and lengthened even more.

"Dear saints," she whispered, looking down at the large, plum-sized head. Jutting well above the still-steaming water, a tiny glistening droplet of moisture appeared on its tip. Dewing moisture she knew had naught to do with the water droplets trickling down his chest.

She swallowed and wet her lips, fascinated. Aching to stroke and fondle him, yet too awed to touch such magnificent male perfection.

He must've sensed her hesitation, for he shifted in the tub, opening his thighs a bit more to give her a better view. Or greater access. Tingly heat swept her at either notion. Nay, he was definitely not hiding himself now.

Not that he should.

She was quite sure he was the most beautifully made man she'd ever seen.

Watching her, he reached to capture a loose tendril of her hair, curling it slowly around his finger. "Touch me," he said, firelight reflecting off his own vibrant, auburn hair. "I'd meant to wait, would've abstained totally—or tried! But it is too late, sweetness."

His gaze went to her little bowl of warming oil, its

heady violet scent already rising. The drifting fumes perfumed the air, intoxicating his senses.

" 'Tis too late for warmed oil massages, too," he added, his voice turning husky. "Too late as well for the removal of your shift."

He flashed her a smile, one that quickly spread into a roguish grin when her sapphire eyes deepened with her own desire and she stood to retrieve the bowl of oil anyway.

"There is another use for the oil," she said, placing one foot on the stool and easing up her shift's dampened skirt, her position leaving her fragrant woman's curls but a handsbreath from his face.

"Sweet Jesu!" The two words escaped between Jamie's teeth as he realized her intent. "Where'er did you learn such a wanton's trick?"

"From my sister, Maili," she explained, already dipping her fingers into the bowl. "Her husband is also quite well-proportioned, though I canna believe he is so large as you. Maili told me if e'er I were to wed such a well-favored man, I might rub myself with warmed oil before the first few couplings and thus ease the joinings."

Jamie swallowed.

She touched glistening fingers to her sex. Holding his gaze, she began gently rubbing the oil between her legs, even applying some to the tender flesh of her smooth inner thighs.

It took Jamie all of a heartbeat to know what he wanted to do.

"Nay, lass, let me," he said, thrusting his fingers into the bowl of heated oil. "I will rub you."

*And in ways that would make her far more ready for
him than any scented oil, heated or otherwise.*

"Come closer," he urged her, "and part your legs for
me. Just enough so that I can see and touch you."

And she did, stepping so near that her sweetness hovered just above him. The rich musk of her arousal flooded
his senses, making him drunk with desire.

He touched his fingers to her then and a startled gasp
broke from her lips. Pleased by the sound and the flare of
desire in her eyes, he rubbed her, carefully massaging the
oil onto her most tender, sweetest flesh.

She trembled beneath his caress, her own fingers digging into the folds of her shift as she held the bunched
material well above her thighs.

"Holy saints," she breathed, a great rippling shudder
streaking through her when he ceased his feather light
strokings and began sliding a slow, probing finger up and
down the very center of her.

"Ach, lass, you are just beginning to explore pleasure."
At last, Jamie flicked lightly at her most sensitive spot.
"This will melt you as naught else," he told her, circling
his finger over her quivering flesh.

Slow, deliberate circlings he kept up until she closed
her eyes and began to rock her hips. She arched her heat
against his hand, her hitching breath and the slick moisture damping his fingers letting him know it was time.

"I can wait no longer," he vowed, seizing her by the
waist and lifting her into the tub. "I am sorry, lass, I
would that it could've been otherwise."

"It is perfect," she cried, looking down to where he

held her poised above him. "You are perfect. Fully magnificent, and I would have no other."

She wriggled against him, her slick female heat slipping across the swollen tip of his shaft, a sensation almost blinding in its exquisiteness. Jamie threw back his head and clenched his teeth, unable to keep his hips from lifting in response, the tip of his iron-hard shaft sliding right into her.

Not the long fluid thrustings he burned to give her, sure, deep, and smooth. This was only a first tentative sheathing, her slick and tight wetness taking only a few throbbing inches.

Or so he thought until she flung her arms around his neck and, kissing him, slid the rest of her sweet, clinging tightness right down over him.

"*Mother of God!*" he cried, his seed shooting into her even as he tore through her innocence. Her own precious little body jerked and tightened against him, the glory of her pleasure cries shattering him even more than the power of his release.

A wonder he would ne'er have believed possible.

Even if, in truth, she'd only taken half of him.

There would be time later to accustom her to more. And he knew now that she'd welcome each joining with him, for there could be no mistaking that her passion had burned as hotly.

But his wonder was the greatest, he decided, reveling in the feel of her, all soft and silky warm in his arms. His heart clenched, and he was certain he'd ne'er be able to have enough of her.

Never be able to hold her closely enough or slide

deeply enough inside her, kiss her long enough or explore every sweet inch of her with his hands and lips and tongue. Live enough days to love her as endlessly as he wished to do.

And, in time, he hoped, make her love him.

She consumed him and ne'er had he felt such a burning need to make a woman his.

She was also still straddling him. Her sweet rose-puckered nipples pressed into his chest and her sleek female wetness proved an irresistible delight. He'd thought to wash and tend her, making certain he hadn't hurt her. But already he was swelling again, each hot slick glide of her softness over his shaft, causing him to pulse and throb anew.

"You dinna ken what you're doing, sweetness," he warned, pushing to his feet and sweeping her up with him. "I can no longer be responsible for what happens between us behind closed and barred doors."

"And beyond those doors?" She stepped out of her dripping camise and kicked it aside.

"Beyond them?"

She stepped closer, trailing her fingers through his glistening chest hair. "I know a fine woodland glade," she began, letting her hand glide lower as her gaze slid to Kendrick's erotic window shutters.

She looked back at him. "You did say there are many ways for us to be intimate?"

Jamie nodded, his throat too thick for words.

He'd followed her glance and knew full well what stood painted on Kendrick's shutters.

The notion of enjoying even one of the shutters' sensual pleasures with her almost robbed his breath.

"There are many ways for a loving couple to enjoy each other," he said when he could speak. He watched her carefully, waiting to see if she'd respond to his unspoken question.

And she did, the comprehending light in her eyes nearly bringing him to his knees.

Her gaze flew once more to the shutters. "I hope you will show me all of those ways."

"As you wish it," he agreed, silently thanking Kendrick for acquiring the shutters.

She need never know how much he and his other brothers had ribbed Kendrick about his choice.

"Aye, lass, so it shall be," he said again, just because it pleased him. "There is naught I would deny you."

Chapter Thirteen

❖

Y̶ou did say there was naught you'd deny me."

Jamie's words came back to haunt him just a few days later. In fine Highland tradition, he put back his shoulders and folded his arms, determined to maintain his dignity. Even so, he couldn't quite keep his lips from twitching and only the solemnity of the day kept him from laughing out loud.

That, and the great press of kinsmen and friends crowding Baldreagan's bailey.

"Naught, you said," his lady reminded him.

Jamie gave a noncommittal *humph*.

He should have known better than to trust a woman with such a broad and all-encompassing statement.

Aveline Matheson included.

Nay, her in especial.

Blessedly, she'd leaned close, pitching her voice soft and low so that only he could hear her. Still, knowing what sharp ears the MacKenzie lasses possessed, he was quite sure they'd heard her, too.

Likewise their puissant father's hovering, ever-present guardsmen, however busy they were dashing about with travel coffers and all the other goods the Black Stag's cosseted daughters deemed essential to their well-being. Jamie's own da had surely heard as well, along with Morag and anyone else who'd gathered to bid farewell and good journeying to Baldreagan's departing guests.

"It would be so nice to see them again," Aveline persisted, watching the bustle.

Jamie slid a glance at her, bracing himself for more carefully crafted persuasion. They were standing in the shadow of the keep's forebuilding and he stepped closer now and hooked his fingers under her chin, lifting her face so she had to look at him.

"The MacKenzies have already promised to come here for our wedding revelries in the spring," he told her, lowering his own voice.

Not because he cared if Gelis Long-nose and the MacKenzies heard what he had to say, but because he did not relish his father hearing him.

Even though the thrawn old goat stood a good distance away. Looking more stubborn than usual, he leaned heavily on Morag's arm, having stoutly refused to use a crummock for support. But walking stick or no, Jamie knew there was nothing wrong with Munro's hearing.

Truth be told, he'd often suspected the man could listen through walls.

Indeed, for all Jamie knew, such a feat might well be how he always managed to get the better of his fellow

Highland cattle lairds, e'er seeming to know what the men said behind his back or when they believed Munro out of earshot.

"I have ne'er sailed the Hebrides," Aveline pressed him then, hooking her hand through his arm and squeezing. "Lady Gelis says her father or his friend, Sir Marmaduke, would surely take us on a grand sailing adventure. Perhaps even as far south to the Isle of Doon? We could visit Devorgilla—"

Jamie laughed despite himself. "The wise woman of Doon? For truth, lass, that one ne'er misses a wedding feast anywhere in the Highlands and the Isles," he said, secretly certain the indomitable cailleach could even appear at two celebrations at the same time if she wished it. "You will surely see her in the spring as well. Without—"

"But—"

"Without us having to make the long journey to Eilean Creag and even farther to Devorgilla's fair isle," he finished for her, looking pleased with his logic.

Aveline cast a wistful glance at the MacKenzie pannier ponies. Well-burdened and restless, they appeared eager to be on their way. Excitement began to beat through her. Lifting her chin, she gave Jamie her most hopeful smile.

"Visiting the MacKenzies would be an adventure," she said, certain of it.

But Jamie only shook his head.

"Nay, lass," he disagreed, speaking close to her ear, "it would be a strenuous excursion that would push my da past his limits."

"Oh." Aveline's face fell. "You are right, of course. And he would ne'er stay behind."

"There you have the way of it."

Jamie sighed, sliding a quick glance at his father. Although he kept his bearded chin proudly lifted and was even making an effort to be halfway gallant and charming to the three MacKenzie women, Jamie was certain he was leaning even more heavily on Morag's arm than he had been moments ago.

Most troubling of all, the sparkling glint in the old man's eyes that Jamie knew most would mistake for a host's laughing good cheer, wasn't the like at all.

Munro's eyes were misting with emotion.

He was sorry to see the girls depart and Jamie worried that without their light and laughter, their lively and spirited chatter filling the hall of an e'en, his da's spirits would grow even bleaker.

To be sure, he cherished Aveline. As, it would seem, did everyone at Baldreagan. They'd heartily welcomed her into their midst. But she'd become family; the MacKenzies had provided a distraction.

A most welcome distraction. And a needed one, especially for Munro.

Jamie ran a hand through his hair and pressed his lips together, trying not to frown. His father wasn't healing as fast as he should either and much as Jamie wished otherwise, a long journey by land and sea, now, or even in the spring, would surely be too much for him.

"Sorry, lass." Jamie turned back to his bride. "A spring journey to Eilean Creag is one pleasure I canna give you."

He smoothed his knuckles down her cheek. "Leastways no' this year."

"But you will keep your word and take me to St.

Maelrubha's this afternoon?" She kept her sapphire gaze fixed on him. "I thought we'd take some heather to your mother."

Jamie frowned after all.

And promptly recalled another bit of masterful manly wisdom the great Black Stag of Kintail had once shared. Namely that females have an astonishing ability to take the slightest slip-of-tongue and embroider it to suit them. Most often to an unsuspecting male's distinct disadvantage.

Jamie blew out a breath and shoved back his hair. Truth was, he'd said a very vague something about wishing to pay a call on old Hughie Mac. Close as Hughie's cottage was to the Garbh Uisge, Jamie thought to question him.

After all, Hughie, too, claimed to have seen the ghosts of Jamie's brothers.

That alone made a visit worthwhile.

But a return to the Macpherson kirkyard and the dark and dank-smelling little chapel had not been mentioned. Nor was going there how Jamie preferred to spend the day with his lady.

Especially if such a visit involved taking a clutch of heather to his mother's tomb. Jamie stiffened. That kind of folly was something he hadn't allowed himself since he was a wee lad. Munro had caught him, chasing him from the chapel in fury, ranting that he'd had no right to lay blooms on the grave of a mother he'd killed.

But before he could tell Aveline he had no desire to go there, Gelis ran over to them, all ringing laughter, glowing cheeks, and bright, wind-tangled hair.

"'I' faith! Have you e'er seen such frowners?" she cried, tossing a glance at her father's guardsmen, nary a scowling man amongst them. "They are complaining that I've brought too much baggage! But"—she flung an arm around Aveline and smiled— "Arabella and I were forewarned. 'Tis said that the farther north one travels, the less likely it is to expect even a lumpy pallet to sleep on, much less a palatable meal!"

"No one told us any such thing," Arabella amended, joining them.

She reached to smooth Gelis's hair, her own braid sleek and black as a raven's wing and nary a strand out of place. "You know we are going to visit Lady Mariota's father in Assynt. Archibald Macnicol is as proud a chieftain as our own da. His holding, Dunach Castle, will surely have no less comforts than Eilean Creag."

Gelis swatted at her sister's hand. "Loch Assynt is also known for its dread water horse—lest you've forgotten!" she exclaimed, pulling a face. "And if we do venture on to Lady Juliana's Mackay kin in Strathnaver, 'tis said the land thereabouts is riddled with the faery mounds of the *Sithe* and that the ghosts of fearless and bloodthirsty Norsemen sleep in the high dunes of every strand!"

Arabella sniffed. "Sleeping Norsemen you'd no doubt waken with all your twitter and babbling."

Jamie choked and hid a smile behind his hand.

"Go ahead and laugh," Arabella said, looking at him. "You know it's the truth."

Unfazed, Gelis fluffed her skirts. "Vikings were braw men. Tall blond giants with hot blue eyes and huge, wicked swords they gave names like Wolf Tooth or Leg Biter. They—"

"They were heathen sea-raiders," Arabella corrected.

Flipping her neat black braid over her shoulder, she sent a meaningful glance across the bailey to where Beardie was helping the MacKenzie guardsmen load the long line of pannier horses. As always, he wore his huge Norseman's ax thrust proudly beneath his belt, though he'd forgone his rusty winged helmet. Catching the girls' stares, he lifted a hand in greeting but his most-times good-natured smile appeared a tiny bit forced.

Looking back at her sister, Arabella shook her head. "I daresay you've already broken one *Viking* heart and you can be certain Lady Juliana and I will be watching you closely when we get to Dunach."

Gelis rolled her eyes. "I truly do fear we'll get naught to eat in the far north but dry oatcakes and salt fish," she fussed, hot-eyed Vikings and their swords apparently forgotten. "For truth, I'd rather stay here."

She paused to look at Jamie. "Mother sent us here for a reason. And—"

"We've seen her concerns addressed," Lady Juliana finished for her, "and your father's men are waiting on us. They are ready to ride."

She placed a hand on both girls' shoulders, offering an apologetic look to Jamie and Aveline. "You will have a care?" she asked, speaking to them both though her words were clearly meant for Jamie.

He nodded, wishing the sun hadn't chosen that moment to slip behind a cloud, its abrupt disappearance casting the bailey in shadow and drawing attention to the chill, knifing wind.

"All will be well." Aveline gave the older woman a quick, impulsive hug. "God go with you, and let us know when you've safely returned to Kintail."

When she stepped back, Jamie took Lady Juliana's hand, bringing it to his lips for a farewell kiss. "We shall look forward to seeing you in the spring, my lady. Here at Baldreagan, God willing."

I shall ask the Old Ones to watch o'er you, Jamie thought he heard her say as he released her hand. But already she'd turned and was striding briskly toward the waiting MacKenzie guardsmen and, he saw, his father's own men who were scrambling to open the gates.

"Till the spring!" Gelis cried, throwing her arms around both Jamie and Aveline, hugging them tight. "I shall dance the whole night of your wedding!"

"If you do not run off with a hot-eyed Viking before we return home!" Arabella quipped, waiting for her own chance to embrace her hosts.

When it came, she blinked furiously and dashed at the tears suddenly wetting her cheeks. "Do not do anything foolhardy, James Macpherson," she warned. "My da has a formidable temper as you well know—you willna want him grieved with you for not heeding Mother's message."

Then she whirled on her heels and was gone, Gelis flying after her. A flurry of skirts, a few frantic hand waves and cries, and the whole loud, racket-making party of MacKenzies were through the gates and vanished.

Gone, from one instant to the next, the creeping

autumn mists closing around them, muffling the sounds
of their departure and blocking them from view.

At once, deep silence settled over Baldreagan's bailey . . . until Munro noisily blew his nose.

Jamie glanced him, even started toward him, but
Munro scowled and waved him away. "Do you not have
anything better to do than gawk at an auld done man?" he
snapped, his voice at least two shades thicker than it
should have been.

His jaw thrusting forward, he fixed Jamie with his
fiercest glare. "Patrolling the battlements mayhap? Or
sharpening your sword?"

"Lucifer's knees," Jamie swore beneath his breath.
"He'd try the patience of St. Columba. Does he not ken
that I—"

"Leave be," Aveline urged, placing a hand on Jamie's
arm and squeezing. "He is only sad to see the
MacKenzies leave. Come nightfall, he will be in better
fettle."

"Ach, to be sure," Jamie agreed, watching Morag help
his da back inside the hall. "So soon as he is hungry and
kens no one will serve him so much as a dried bannock
unless he wipes the frown off his face."

Not that Munro was alone in his grimness.

If truth be told, everyone still lurking about the bailey
was frowning.

Or at least looking dispirited.

Glum.

Even the sun's feeble autumn warmth had fled and the
afternoon's chill was increasing with the lengthening
shadows, a faint smirr of cold thin rain even beginning to

splatter the cobbles. The wind was picking up, too, its random gusts sending wispy curtains of damp, gray mist scuttling over the walls and across the bailey. But no one complained, even if something somewhere had set the castle dogs barking and snarling.

The gloom matched the moods of those slowly returning to the keep, the usual goings-on of the castle's daily business.

Only one soul smiled.

A tall and hooded figure standing unnoticed in the deep shadows of one of the wooden byres stretching along the curtain wall.

The departure of the MacKenzie she-bitches and their pack of swell-headed, muscle-packed watchdogs would prove the turning of the tide for Clan Macpherson.

It'd been tedious to move in and out of the keep with so many souls in residence.

So many sets of curious, probing eyes and too many extra sword arms.

The nuisance of unexpected interference.

The figure allowed one slight tightening of the lips. Had it not been for the ill-timed appearance of a drink-taken MacKenzie guardsman careening out of the shadows near the postern gate, a half-clothed kitchen wench still clinging to him, all giggly and smitten, a certain crossbow shot would have fired true.

Blessedly, they'd both been too ale-headed to notice anything amiss.

Indeed, the MacKenzies' visit had been an annoyance, but they'd left now.

The figure's smile returned.

Any other difficulties and disturbances could be easily dealt with. Proving it, the figure wagged a finger at the handful of bristly-backed, snarling castle dogs, then began scrounging inside a worn leather pouch kept for just such purposes.

A fine and large meat bone soon appeared and sailed through the air, landing on the rain-dampened cobbles with a satisfying *kerplunk*.

As was to be anticipated, the offensive yapping and growling ceased at once. The figure forgotten, the mangy curs pounced on the bone, their greedy hunger outweighing the danger of a mere two-legged trespasser.

The figure watched them with pleasure, sure in the knowledge that it mattered not a whit how many dogs prowled Baldreagan's bailey or how often the addle-witted laird changed his sleeping quarters.

Nor would it avail any of them that one son yet lived. For the nonce.

A grievous betrayal would soon be righted, fullest vengeance achieved at last.

And this time nothing would go wrong.

Do not do anything foolhardy.

Arabella MacKenzie's warning rang louder in Jamie's ears the longer he stood in the cold, dank shadows at the back of St. Maelrubha's chapel, an armful of late-blooming heather clutched against his chest and his feet seemingly frozen to the stone-flagged floor. Damnable feet, for each one refused to move, stubbornly ignoring his best efforts and not letting him take the last few steps toward his mother's tomb.

His bride, bless her, showed no such infirmity.

Looking wholly at ease, she moved about the nave placing new candles on wrought-iron prickets, her shining pale-haired presence and fresh violet scent a breath of welcome life in the damp and musty little chapel.

Scores of tiny votive lights were already lit and burning when they'd entered and to Jamie's mind, the pinpoints of twinkling light only strengthened the image of her as a *Sithe* princess in a gold-lit, enchanted glade.

He frowned.

In truth, it was a dark rain-chilled eve with thick mist shrouding the churchyard. Eerie, drifting swaths of gloom, each swirling curtain of gray demonstrated how easily a gullible soul might mistake the like for a bogle gliding across the burial ground.

Jamie put back his shoulders, willing his heart to stop knocking so crazily.

He was anything but gullible.

But if coming here wasn't foolhardy, he didn't know what was.

He swallowed, then immediately wished he hadn't. Doing so only let him know how dry his throat had gone. How discomfited he was. At least this time none of his knightly ancestors were draped in wet plaid, though someone had replenished the rowan clusters.

New sprigs of the bright, red-ribboned charms were tucked in niches throughout the chapel and the Na Clachan Breugach stone just outside the door arch also appeared to have been redressed with a fresh rowan garland.

Red ribbon and all.

Whoe'er had seen to the rowan, and Jamie suspected that someone was Hughie Mac, was looking after the chapel as well, for a trace of recently burned incense overlaid the smell of old smoke and damp stone, and a fine, clean-looking cloth graced the altar.

Even so, the air of oppression almost choked him. He looked about, seeking escape yet knowing he'd ne'er take it.

Not with Aveline already standing at his mother's tomb, her head reverently bowed. She'd clasped her hands solemnly before her and her softly spoken prayers proved a heart-gripping contrast to the chapel's cold stone vaulting, its wicked bone-biting chill.

Glancing aside, Jamie noticed that the door of the aumbry in the chapel's east wall stood cracked, the little cupboard appearing filled with candles. Going there now, he set down his clutch of heather long enough to use his steel and flint to light a taper, then touched its flame to several others, hoping the additional light would help dispel a bit more of the chapel's gloom.

And once lit, the long wax candles did throw warm golden light onto the weathered stone walls. Unfortunately, the light also fell across the carved and silent faces of Jamie's slumbering forebears.

A shudder slid down his spine. He breathed deep, trying not to see the rows of knightly effigies. He also did his best not to imagine the nine new ones that would soon join them.

Above all, he sought to ignore the finest tomb of all, the lovely marble one looming just ahead of him, behind the high altar and the dark oaken rood screen.

There, where his feet refused to go.

Determined to have done with the visit and be gone, he tried to move forward again, and couldn't.

He started then, for the air suddenly felt different. A slight shifting perhaps, almost as if the ancient stone walls had begun to breathe. Shivering openly now, he rubbed his arms and looked around.

The wind must've blown away some of the night's lowering clouds for moonlight was beginning to stream in through the arched doorway and the thin slit windows, each bright and slanting moonbeam an illumination he could have done without.

Jamie, come close . . . I would see you.

He froze, his heart slamming against his ribs.

A beautiful woman, tall and well made, stood beside his mother's tomb, her lush curves limned silver by the moon, the streaming mass of her tumbled, unbound hair the same burnished copper as his own.

She smiled at him and reached a milky white hand in his direction, the peace and love pouring off her making it impossible not to go to her.

But as soon as he took the first step, the moonlight shifted and the illusion faded. The woman standing before him was still beautiful, but her hair was shimmering flaxen, not the gleaming fire of a thousand Highland sunsets.

And though sweet and dear and perfect as he'd e'er wish, her womanly curves were lithe and delicate, not bold, lush and welling.

Nor was she tall.

"Jamie, come close," she said, smiling at him, offering him her hand. "I want you to see how beautiful she is."

But Jamie already knew.

Just as he'd heard his bride's words a moment before she'd spoken them.

If indeed they'd been her words.

He *did* know that now, finally, he'd be welcomed when, after so many years, he looked again on his mother's ornamental grave slab. The hauntingly exquisite effigy so lovely he'd blocked the image from his boyhood mind, unable to bear the guilt of being responsible for her death.

"Jamie, the heather." Aveline touched his arm, giving him a slight shake. "You've dropped it."

And he had, without even realizing.

The whole great bundle of tiny purple and white blooms lay strewn across the floor.

Kneeling, he began to gather them, his annoyance at having dropped the heather turning to dismay when he saw the poor state of the chapel floor beneath his mother's tomb.

Cracked and uneven, the stone flagging looked in dire need of repair. Some of the stones were even broken away, leaving dark holes in the floor's surface.

A dangerous and unacceptable circumstance, especially when he recalled how Aveline had slipped on the slick chapel flooring during their previous visit.

"Nay, stay there." He waved her away when she made to drop down beside him. "I have the blooms," he added, snatching up the last bit of the fallen heather and getting to his feet. "We'll lay them and be gone."

He narrowed his eyes on her, his voice brooking no refusal. "And I'll not have you returning here until the floor
is renewed."

"Then come," she acquiesced, reaching for his hand
again and pulling him to the tomb. "She is beautiful, is
she not?"

"Aye, she is," Jamie agreed, looking down at his
mother's serene marble face but seeing the woman he'd
glimpsed in the moonlight.

Remembering her smile.

And knowing it would always warm him.

"You are beautiful, too." He glanced at his bride as he
placed the heather atop his mother's folded hands. "And
I am certain my mother would bless our union," he added,
half-believing that she just had.

Aveline looked so fetching in the flickering golden
light that other, bolder thoughts flashed through his mind.
Especially when her lips curved in a slow smile and she
lowered her lashes, glancing through them at the chapel's
narrow, deep-set windows.

"The moon rises ever higher," she said, her word
choice giving a certain part of him a most inappropriate
twitch. "And the rain looks to have stopped as well.
Perhaps if we leave now, there will still be time to refresh
ourselves at St. Bride's Well before we return?"

Jamie drew a swift breath, the thought of her bathing
naked in the moonlight beside that very well sending
pulsing, molten heat pouring into his loins.

He stepped closer to her, reaching to touch her cheek.
"A quick stop at Hughie Mac's and then, I promise you,

we shall visit the well," he said, sliding his thumb over the fullness of her lower lip.

But he let his hand fall away almost at once, the temptation to seize her against him and kiss her almost too powerful to resist, yet too unseemly to indulge with his mother and all his reposing ancestors looking on.

"Aye, we will stop at Bride's Well," he said again, grabbing her hand and leading her from the chapel. "But be warned," he added as they stepped out into the cold moonlit night, "the Old Ones who held such ground sacred were not as pious as Maelrubha and his fellow saints. It may be that visiting the well might inspire me."

"That is my wish," Aveline owned, smiling as he lifted her into her saddle.

But her smile and his own faltered, turning to bewilderment, when a short while later they drew up before Hughie Mac's door. The rain had stopped indeed and a handful of glittering stars could be seen through thin, wispy clouds. But mist still curled across the grass and bracken; along the dark edge of the pine wood crowding Hughie's cottage.

A small white-washed cottage, thick-walled and neatly thatched, Hughie's humble dwelling should have welcomed with its usual air of homely pleasantness. Instead, it appeared surprisingly deserted.

Even though a thin blue drift of peat smoke rose from the chimney and, Jamie would have sworn, they'd both seen the beckoning flicker of soft yellow light winking through trees as they'd ridden near.

Candlelight hastily extinguished—or purposely hidden behind quickly latched shutters.

The back of Jamie's neck began to prickle as he swung down onto the damp grass. He was certain he'd seen lights in Hughie's windows and a sidelong glance at his bride assured him she'd seen them, too.

"Could it be he doesn't want visitors?" she asked, proving it.

"Hughie?" Jamie cocked a brow, motioning for her to stay where she was. "That one's door e'er stands open," he said, puzzled, glancing around at the dripping trees and shadows, ill ease licking up and down his spine.

Something was sorely amiss.

Hughie Mac would ne'er turn away a guest. Such just wasn't the Highland way and Hughie was more Highland than most. The old man *wore* these hills, swearing he lived and breathed for love of his home glen. The wee bit of rock and heather he hadn't left since his birth and ne'er cared to.

Jamie frowned. Something was indeed badly wrong.

His pulse quickening, he stared at the darkened cottage, well aware that the erstwhile herd boy even kept the shutters of his windows flung wide just so he'd note a visitor's approach. Hughie liked to know when to toss another peat brick onto his fire and set out his special self-made oatcakes and cheese, a fresh ewer of ale. And, the old man's great pride, his somewhat battered pewter drinking cup, a treasure he saved for guests.

Yet now the shutters were tightly closed.

And Jamie knew without trying that he'd find the cottage door soundly barred.

But he meant to test it all the same.

"Hughie!" he called, hammering his fist on the bolted door. "'Tis Jamie, come to see to you!"

Only silence answered him.

Yawning emptiness, the sighing of the night wind, and from somewhere behind the cottage, the disgruntled bleating of Hughie's sheep.

Jamie's skin began to crawl. He would've sworn he felt eyes watching him. *Hidden eyes*. And with surety, not Hughie Mac's.

Nor any sheep's.

His heart racing, he stared at the cottage, indecision sweeping him. He considered drawing back his foot and kicking in the door, a difficult feat to be sure, but not impossible.

Not for a man of his size and strength.

But Hughie Mac was anything but a fool and if he didn't wish to be disturbed this e'en, he'd have his reasons.

Even so, Jamie couldn't help from lifting his foot and swinging it backward—until his bride's voice stayed him, her small hand lighting on his arm.

"He could be entertaining a woman."

Jamie's eyes rounded and he lowered his foot at once. He wheeled about, turning so quickly, he near tripped over a tree root.

Aveline stood calmly in the moonlight, her placid expression assuring him that she'd meant what she'd said.

"Hughie is older than my da," Jamie blurted, staring back at her. "He—"

"He has e'er kept his dalliances," she informed him, glancing past him to the cottage. "Even in recent years.

Such things canna be kept secret. Not in these hills and glens where ears are e'er peeled and interesting tidings spread like birch seed on the wind."

Still, Jamie couldn't believe it.

He rubbed a hand over his jaw, frowning at the dark night closing in on them. He could feel his brow furrowing despite Aveline's certainty.

"I have heard skirling female laughter coming from those very shuttered windows," she insisted, her smile dimpling. "And I know of two laundresses from Fairmaiden and an unmarried lass in the next glen who openly admit to having succumbed to Hughie's charm."

She came closer, leaning up on her toes to kiss him. "More than once, I was told, and gladly."

"Ah, well . . ." Jamie let his voice trail away, trying to believe her.

"Come," she teased then, sliding a quick hand over a place she knew would stir him, "you can check on Hughie on the morrow if you are still worried. Let us be away to Bride's Well before the night grows colder."

The invitation made, she whirled and strode back to their horses, the pert swaying of her hips leaving no doubt about just why she wished to stop at the sacred pagan well.

But when Jamie started after her, he tripped over the tree root again, his arms flailing as he righted himself before flying facedown into the night-blackened grass.

Slick, wet deer grass, knee-high and tussocky where not clipped short by Hughie's grazing sheep. Scattered patches of autumn-red bracken, dead, soaking, and slippery.

Looking round, he realized the impossibility of his stumbling, leastways over a tree root.

The nearest trees were the tall Caledonian pines edging the steeply sloping braeside to the left of Hughie's cottage and the little birch and alder wood rimming a burn channel a good ways to the right.

There were no other trees in sight.

His ill ease rushing back, Jamie peered down at the *root* he'd tripped over, the mystery quickly solved when he recognized Hughie's walking stick laying half-buried in the grass.

But that posed a question, too, for the old man could scarce move about without the aid of his crummock.

Frowning yet again, Jamie reached down to retrieve the thing, his relief great upon seeing the crummock wasn't the one Hughie favored, but newly whittled.

A fine hazel walking stick, clearly carved by Hughie's hand and, it would seem, dropped unnoticed as the old man shuffled about.

Not quite certain that would have been the way of it, but not knowing what else to think, Jamie carried the crummock back to the cottage and leaned it against the door.

And it wasn't until a short while later when he and Aveline rode into Bride's moonlit glade that he realized why the crummock had bothered him.

It wasn't the crummock at all.

Not truly.

The thing had been a fine walking stick, perfectly made and smooth and pleasing beneath the fingers.

And everyone knew Hughie carved himself a new one

whene'er the need arose. But this crummock could not have been made for Hughie.

Not bent and gnarled as he was, his slight frame barely coming to Jamie's shoulder.

The fine hazel walking stick Jamie had propped against the cottage door had been carved for a much larger man.

One nigh as tall as Jamie.

Chapter Fourteen

❧

Jamie forgot all about Hughie's newly whittled crummock as soon as he and Aveline rode out of the sheltering wood and emerged into the secluded, moonlit clearing of St. Bride's holy well.

They dismounted a few paces from the venerable Celtic site, an innocent-seeming tumble of smooth, lichen-flecked boulders and an ancient altar slab, cracked now but delicately incised with serpent-like creatures and intricate scrollwork. These framed a small stone basin into which the spring's clear, gurgling waters flowed and gathered before disappearing again into the hidden depths of the glade's sacred earth.

Dark, pungent earth filled with long forgotten memories.

Distant hurts that rushed Jamie, called forth just from breathing in the mysterious scent of the holy place. A wild place, it stirred the soul with its blend of wet stone, rich black peat, clean water, and lush, rain-spangled grass.

Inhaling deeply, he could almost feel the years spiraling backward, making him young again.

A wide-eyed and vulnerable lad, ready to believe anything.

But he was a man grown now, so he stood tall and adjusted his plaid against the chill night wind. Not that such measures did much good. Certain powers couldn't be denied. Especially those older than time. Besides, the well's endless array of votive offerings had already caught his eye, beckoning.

The objects, mostly metal, glinted in the moonlight, each one bespeaking some hopeful soul's deepest wish or need. A mad jumble of pins, elaborately carved wire, coins, and even colorful threads and small polished stones, the offerings winked from every imaginable crevice or narrow ledge of the outcropping.

Other votos, coins especially, had been thrust into the living trunk of a nearby holly tree.

Including an ancient Roman coin he'd put there himself.

Jamie ran a hand through his hair, remembering the day as if it were but an hour ago. One of his father's friends had given him the coin when he'd been a lad. The very next morning he'd slipped away from Morag's watchful eye and run all the way to the clearing to kneel at the well and ask St. Bride for his da's favor.

Then he'd pressed the precious coin deep into the wild holly tree that grew up out of the boulders, certain his father would look on him with affection from that moment forward.

But, of course, he hadn't.

Not long thereafter, Munro had turned him out, claiming he should return to the heather that had given him his name.

And so Jamie had gone.

Leaving kith, kin, and the only hearth he'd ever known, he'd set out, making his way south and eventually calling at Eilean Creag Castle where, thankfully, he soon found himself squire to Duncan MacKenzie, the Black Stag of Kintail.

He blew out a breath and frowned, the venerableness of the place clearly getting to him.

"I have not been here for years," he finally said, the winking votives and old memories vanishing when his bride began unbraiding her hair.

An auspicious sign and enough to make his blood quicken with desire.

He took a step closer, his fingers itching to help her. But watching her pleased him, too. Especially when she finished and the pale shimmering strands spilled down past her hips, silky and gleaming.

"You know when I was last here." She looked at him through her lashes, her dimple flashing—"I saw you there, through the trees," she added, gesturing across the clearing to where he'd sat his garron, staring at her.

Slack-jawed and smitten, quite convinced he was seeing a Sithe princess riding moonbeams through the glade.

She angled her head, her sapphire gaze flicking over

him. "I thought I'd ne'er seen a more splendid-looking man."

"And now?"

"Now I know you are."

"Splendid?" Jamie didn't think so at all, but the thought warmed him.

"More than splendid." Her lovely gold-tipped lashes dipped again and she settled her gaze just there where it caused the most havoc. "You are magnificent," she said, the look coming into her eyes heating him.

Stealing his ability to form a single coherent word.

She tilted her head, her bright hair reflecting the moonlight, rippling and tempting him. "Aye, full magnificent—everywhere."

Jamie's breath stopped, his *everywhere* suddenly rock-hard and aching.

Hot all over, despite the cold wind and the night's misty damp.

Even the wet grass beneath the soles of his booted feet felt warm.

Almost alive.

Pulsating with the same hot thrumming warmth coursing all through him.

He closed his eyes and drew a deep breath, almost dizzy from the sweeping force of his need. The fierceness of his passion and the odd sensation that the earth and air around them was altering, that the very ground, grass and trees, even the stars, were beginning to vibrate in rhythm with the wild rushing of his blood.

His mounting desire for Aveline.

He opened his mouth to tell her that he was on fire for

her. That he burned to strip the clothes from her and from himself and then, full-bared and mother-naked, love her until the world stopped spinning or the stars went out, whiche'er came first.

Or perhaps something more romantic like his brother Hamish might have said. That she was the light of his life, his heart's desire, or maybe that he'd love her all their days, even use his last breath to call out her name.

But the words froze on his tongue, held fast by the strange way the air crackled and shimmered. The low, muted humming he'd swear pulsed somewhere deep beneath the glade.

She didn't seem to notice.

Or perhaps she did and just didn't care because she only smiled, then flipped her hair over her shoulder as she turned aside, rummaging in her saddlebags until she withdrew a folded plaid.

"Aye, you are a bonnie man," she declared, flicking out the plaid. "But bonnie or no, you've scarce eaten all day. I heard your stomach growling in the chapel and at Hughie Mac's."

Making for a particularly lovely patch of moon-washed grass not far from the well, she sent him a decidedly bold glance. Cheeky and flirtatious. "'Tis time we do something about your hunger."

Jamie almost choked.

She certainly had the rights of it. He hadn't yet eaten, but it wasn't bread and ale he craved.

O-o-oh, nay.

He ached to pull her against him, lowering his head to nip at the tender flesh beneath her ear, then nibble his way down the smooth arch of her neck, his teeth just grazing her lightly, his tongue lingering.

Lingering and tasting. Savoring and relishing every sweet inch of her, then moving ever lower to explore and claim each dip and curve, worshiping her gleaming moon-silvered flesh until he lost himself in her darker, shadowy places.

Aye, he was especially interested in those dark and shadowy places. Biting back a groan, he reached down to adjust the fall of his plaid.

Seemingly unaware of his discomfort, she was beaming at him again, her eyes alight with promising mischief.

"See, I've brought refreshment," she announced, spreading the plaid on the ground with a flourish. "A feast to strengthen and sustain you for the long hard ride back to Baldreagan."

Jamie's brows shot upward, another rush of hot need tearing through him. He clenched his hands at his sides, wondering at the sudden savageness of his lust. Saints, he could scarce breathe for the near overpowering urge to grab her, lift her high into the air, her skirts flying, then lower her to his mouth, devouring those *shadowy parts* until he was so sated he collapsed to his knees, trembling, his great hunger for her assuaged.

He looked at her, his entire body so hot and tight, he didn't trust himself to move. Her words were making him crazy.

A long hard ride, indeed.

He narrowed his eyes on her, already tasting her, imagining her hot, wet sleekness on his tongue. How her

musky female scent would drench his senses until his
every indrawn breath delighted and intoxicated him.

The thought nearly made him spill.

Steeling himself lest he join the ranks of those lesser
men unable to control their urges, he studied her in the
moonlight, admiring its silvery gleam on her hair, his
blood heating to think what such soft, luminous light
would do to her naked body, all warm, and pliant beneath
him.

Or on top of him.

He smiled.

A wolfish smile, he knew, but he didn't care. Ever since
swinging down off his garron, he *felt* wolfish. Consumed
with a hot, blazing passion he wasn't sure he'd e'er be
able to quench. And maybe he didn't even want to.

He only knew that he had to have her, and badly. Here
in the glade, beside St. Bride's Well and beneath the
streaming moon.

And back at Baldreagan, in Kendrick's large, fur-
covered bed. Truth be told, if the mood so took him, he
might even ravish her in the stair tower on the way up to
Kendrick's room. Not even on a landing, but right on the
tight, winding stairs with a brisk chill wind blowing in
through the slit windows to cool their heated bodies, their
only witness a hissing, smoking wall torch.

Och, aye, he needed her.

Just now, though, she'd gone back to the horses and
was busying herself unfastening the wicker basket she'd
secured to the back of her saddle.

A basket he'd thought only contained the extra candles
and flint she'd taken to St. Maelrubha's.

"Our feast," she declared, coming back to kneel on the plaid. Smiling at him, she opened the basket's lid, revealing the treasures inside.

Wondering if he guessed that, to her, *he* was the greatest treasure.

A prize she'd ne'er dreamed would be hers.

"A flagon of your da's finest Gascon wine," she informed him, hoping to please. "To toast our first meeting," she added, her gaze going again to the other side of the little glade.

There, where he claimed he'd lost his heart.

Aveline swallowed, the notion melting her.

"I shall ne'er be able to pass that spot or this clearing again without remembering," she went on, pulling savories from the basket. A round of cheese, two cold meat pasties, a spiced capon, several freshly baked bannocks, a small jar of butter and another of bilberry jam, sugared almonds, and honey cakes.

After arranging them on the plaid, she looked at him, certain her deepest feelings must be writ all over her.

She gestured to the victuals. "A feast—did I not tell you?"

"O-o-oh, aye, and fit for a king's palate," he agreed, dropping down beside her, then reaching to place one treat after another back into the wicker basket.

Aveline blinked, not missing how his smile turned more wicked, nay, more *devilish,* with every item of food he cleared from the plaid.

So devilish he almost looked capable of teaching Kendrick a thing or two about rogueing.

"What are you doing?" she asked, but a suspicion was already beginning to curl through her.

A deliciously stirring one.

He had to be famished. And she'd taken care to wheedle all his best-loved foods from Baldreagan's cook.

She looked at him, her suspicion strengthening when he returned the honey cakes without even a flicker of an eyelash.

The cook had sworn he loved honey cakes above all else.

The sugared almonds disappeared as quickly and then he sprang to his feet. He began jerking on his sword belt, the look in his eyes warming her and making the special place between her legs tingle.

Not that she minded the tingles.

Or even the long liquid pulls working such wondrous magic deep in her belly. A beautiful, fiery heat pooling low by her thighs and so exquisite her breath was already hitching with fine kindling passion.

Och, nay, she didn't mind.

Seducing him in the glade was her plan, after all.

The whole reason she'd bedeviled him into stopping at the well.

But she'd envisioned a slow and leisurely seduction. A candlelit supper on a plaid beneath the moon, the exchange of long hot-burning gazes and love words as they sipped wine and served each other bits of honey cake.

A tender wooing.

She knew, after all, that he had skilled and tender hands.

Gentle hands.

But there was nothing gentle in the way those hands were now tugging at the latch of his sword belt.

"Are you not hungry?" She glanced at the wicker basket. "Do you not want to eat?"

He whipped off his belt and tossed it aside. "Och, aye, I am fair starving," he said, his boots following the belt and sword. "And you can be sure I intend to dine."

Aveline moistened her lips, everything her sister Maili had e'er told her about her husband ravishing her, flashing in bold and bawdy detail through her mind.

Bold and exciting detail.

But she still had difficulty imagining such a thing. Even though she'd seen the act painted quite unmistakably on Kendrick's window shutters.

Her heart began to thump. The very idea thrilled her. Already her breasts were tightening in anticipation and it was all she could do not to lift her arms and pull him down to her, beg him to fulfill the erotic wish that had been burning inside her ever since he'd first kissed her and she'd wondered what it would be like to have his lips touch her *there*.

And if Maili had spoken true, maybe even his tongue.

She shivered at the deliciousness of that possibility, but before she could encourage him, he stopped flashing his wicked-eyed smile and frowned.

"You are cold," he said, clearly misinterpreting her shiver.

"Nay, I am fine." She lifted her chin, trying to appear as *un*-cold as possible.

Looking unconvinced, he dropped down beside her and slid an arm around her, drawing her close against him. "I won't have you uncomfortable," he said, stroking her hair. "We can ride on to Baldreagan now, going straight to Kendrick's chamber when we return. Though . . ."

He let the words tail off and glanced over at the well and its tumbled outcropping, the stones gleaming white against the black pine wood rising so darkly behind them.

Even the ancient pagan altar stone, cracked, slanting, and half-covered with moss, shimmered bright in the moon glow.

"Though?" She followed his gaze, for one fleeting moment looking as if she, too, were not seeing just the stones and the well, but peering into a distant past.

A long ago time when the old Celtic gods would have called this glade their own.

At the thought, gooseflesh rose on Jamie's arms and the tiny hairs on his nape lifted. His senses alert, he raised a hand to rub the back of his neck, his gaze scanning the dark edge of the encircling trees.

Trees he could well imagine dressed in Druid mist— or bearing silent witness to the mysterious rites of the ancients.

Truth was, he almost believed they still held sway here.

That they'd only slipped away for a few hours and would soon return, their fair voices in the music of the wind, their cautious, watching presence hidden in the soft blue haze that e'er cloaked the hills.

"Though you would rather stay here?" Aveline persisted, watching him closely, almost as if she felt it, too.

"To be sure, I meant to stay here . . . a while," Jamie

admitted, reaching to touch her hair again. "But I'll no' risk you catching a chill. See you, I—" He broke off again, shaking his head to clear it of nonsense.

But even after a few good head shakes and manly denial, the damp grass beneath the plaid still felt warmer than it possibly could and he'd wager all his meals for a year if he honestly couldn't detect a distinct humming deep in the ground beneath them.

He frowned.

His faery was smiling.

"Ach, lass," he blurted, rushing the words, "there is something strange here. A warmth and shimmering in the ground that canna be, but is. I'd hope whate'er it is would warm you as well, that it would keep us from noticing the night's cold if we—" He paused and blew out a frustrated breath. "But I saw you shiver—"

"I shivered because I want those things, too," she said, leaning into him, lighting kisses along his jaw, down his neck. "And I do feel the warmth. As a Highlander, 'tis only natural that you noticed it, too."

She pulled back then, looking over at the well. "'Tis Bride's blessing, see you. Hers and the sun's."

"The sun's?" Jamie's brows arched.

She nodded and a vague memory stirred. Some fireside tale he'd heard as a lad, sung by Hughie Mac or maybe even Morag, he couldn't recall.

"You've heard the tradition but have forgotten," she said, glancing at him. "Shall I retell it for you?"

Jamie shrugged, interested indeed but not wishing to appear overeager to hear what he was sure could only be blether and nonsense.

Clearly thinking otherwise, she nodded solemnly and began. "Far back in time, some might even say farther back than forever, the Old Ones believed the sun disappeared beneath the waters of a night," she said, her voice softening as she settled against him. "They thought the sun needed its rest, you see. But while the sun slept, the waters absorbed the sun's healing power and strength, its warmth and beneficence."

Jamie angled his head and narrowed one eye at her, skeptical. "Are you saying the sun slipped down into St. Bride's well this e'en and is sleeping in its waters? Even now as we sit here?"

She smiled and kissed his nose. "I am saying that the ancient ones believed it, aye. Were they here, they would tell you that it is the underground sun's power throbbing in the earth beneath us, its warmth taking the chill out of the ground we are sitting upon."

"Because we are sitting so near to the well? The well where the sun is now sleeping?"

She nodded again.

Jamie did his best not to snort.

"And you think we feel this warmth and *earth-shimmying* because Bride is blessing us?"

"To be sure," she said, her eyes lighting with a warmth even a thousand suns couldn't match.

Sleeping or otherwise.

"Bride is pleased by our union and showing us."

Jamie *humphed*. "'Tis you I'd wished to please this night."

She smoothed her hand down his arm, then laced her

fingers with his, squeezing lightly. "Are you still hungry?"

Jamie hardened at once, his entire body tightening.

"Och, aye, I have a ravenous hunger," he admitted, putting Bride and her sleeping sun from his mind. "And I think you know what it is I'm craving."

Her lashes fluttered and a quick flush swept into her cheeks, telling him she knew indeed. The sudden catching of her breath and the flash of excitement in her eyes giving him the permission he needed to indulge.

"Aye, I know—I think," she said, banishing any lingering doubt.

Jamie grinned.

"Sweet lass, you willna be sorry." He grabbed her face between his hands and kissed her deeply, a hard and hot tongue-tangling kiss, slaking and furious, sizzling in its intensity.

She returned the kiss with equal fervor, winding her arms around his neck and pressing close, so close he could feel her tightened nipples rubbing against his chest, a sweet torment that only increased his hunger for her.

Breaking the kiss at last, he pulled back to look at her, his breath coming hard and fast. He was fairly certain the whole of his heart must be standing in his eyes, staring right at her.

Trumpeting how much he wanted and adored her.

How deeply he'd fallen in love with her.

And he had.

Truth was, he'd barter his soul to know her safe, make

her happy and see her rise each morn wearing naught but
a smile and ne'er even a single care.

He drew a deep breath, certain *cares* of his own throbbing too insistently for him to wax romantic. That could
come later, after he'd slaked his need to taste and savor
her woman's wetness. And after he'd done so often
enough to leave her sleeping the whole morn through.
Just the time he figured he needed to return to Hughie's
and also take a good look at the Garbh Uisge.

But first he'd look his fill on her.

"This, sapphire eyes, is what I meant by other ways
for us to pleasure each other," he said, doing just that
as he pushed up her skirt. He slid his hands behind her
knees, caressing the tender flesh there, then exploring
higher, his breath catching when his fingers skimmed
across dampness on the smooth, hot skin of her inner
thighs.

"O-o-oh, that is sweet," she breathed, lying back and
arching her body for him. She even parted her legs, instinctively giving him greater access. "Don't stop touching me."

"Och, lass, I haven't begun to touch you yet—no' the
way I mean to." He looked down at her, deliberately letting a fold of her skirt dip down to shield her nakedness.

And she *was* naked beneath the modesty of that one
wee skirt fold.

Her rich musky arousal drifted up between them and
he could feel the melting heat of her. Even just kneeling
on the plaid, gazing at her.

Och, aye, without doubt Aveline Matheson wore nothing but her own tender flesh and woman's curls beneath

her gown and he wasn't quite ready to look fully on such sweetness.

He'd spill when he did. Leastways he suspected he would. Especially when he touched his mouth to her. So he kept her covered for the now and simply savored the sleek, smooth feel of her naked thighs, relishing how each time he slid his hands up and down them, they fell open just a wee bit more.

He wanted her opened as wide as possible when he settled himself between her legs and licked and nibbled his way from her knees up to the soft, fragrant center of her.

A center suddenly freed completely to his view when a particularly soft and warm-feeling wind swept across the glade. Sweet and fragrant as spring sunshine, but brisk enough to lift a certain skirt fold until the moon shone fully on the silky-curled triangle between her legs.

"O-o-oh, lass." Jamie stared at her, incredible heat surging into his loins. "You leave me breathless!"

Not taking his gaze off of her, he reached to touch her, tracing a wondering finger down the very center of her, finding her sleek, slippery, and moist as sun-warmed honey.

Certain she'd taste as delectable, he urged her to lie back on the plaid, then bent her knees, spreading them until she was even more fully exposed to him. The whole of her female sweetness completely open, hot, wet, and glistening.

Her beauty stilled his heart and for several long-seeming moments, he could only sit and look at her. Everything else in the night lost importance. Nothing existed but the lure of her silver-shimmering female curls and the strange warm wind swirling over and around them. A fey wind, it riffled their hair and tugged at their clothes until, somehow, they were both quite naked and the gently swaying grass and the dark ring of trees sheltering the glade sighed in approval.

"Keep touching me," she pleaded then, arching against him when he withdrew his hand, thinking only to cup and knead her breasts for a moment, perhaps tease a bit at her nipples.

She looked at him, her eyes passion-glazed. *Needy.* "Keep touching me there, where you have been," she urged again. "I can't bear it if you do not."

And so he did, returning his hand to her sweetest heat, stroking, probing, and swirling his fingers, teasing caresses across her wet and eager flesh, rubbing and circling until even his most skilled touches weren't enough and she lifted her hips off the plaid, her body begging in a silent, urgent cry as elemental as the sacred ground beneath them.

But when her writhing and gasps of pleasure began growing frantic, he did lift away his hand, quickly positioning himself there where he'd burned to be all night.

"Ach, dia!" she cried when he opened his mouth over her, sucking gently. Then his large hands slipped beneath her, his fingers splaying across her bottom, cupping and lifting her, drawing her even deeper into his seeking mouth.

White-hot pleasure shot through her, the intensity of it almost too glorious to bear.

Especially when he looked up, locking gazes with her as he began doing just what she'd hoped he'd do.

And so wondrously, his eyes never leaving hers as he dragged his tongue over her, again and again, each sweet, slow lick enflaming her, making her twist and wind on the plaid, certain she would soon splinter into so many bright-sparkling pieces she'd ne'er be able to gather them.

His tongue plunged into her then, and the shattering began. A slow, free-falling glide into blinding bliss as his tongue dipped in and out, mirroring the most intimate of acts, then withdrawing to swirl over her again, each luxurious, sweeping glide of his tongue making the earth beneath her tremble and sigh, the very hills around them quivering, crying out with the darkness of her need.

Until his laving tongue found *that place* and she realized the tremors and cries were her own, each hot, fluttery flick and swirl of his tongue on her most pulsing, sensitive spot, hurtling her deeper into the glittering madness, the silent little glade and the whole of the cold, moon-washed night spinning wildly around her.

And still he ravished her. Now grazing his teeth ever so lightly on that tiny, hot-throbbing place, nipping gently. Then drawing back to blow softly on her trembling flesh, cooling her before he lowered his head again, burying his face deeper into her sweetness, losing himself in the heady, saturating taste of her.

He feasted on her, some lone, still-thinking corner of his mind certain he'd ne'er get enough of her. That she was a *Sithe* maid indeed and had ensorcelled him, making him crave her scent and taste. The intoxication of her hot, wet, and slippery femaleness.

"Lass, I canna stop," he groaned, licking her harder, his hunger for her only intensifying.

He looked up at her again and saw answering passion heating her eyes. Her hair spilled all around her, her rose-bud nipples were thrusting at him through the silvery blond strands. She looked so beautiful that his edge raced closer, a wild, tumultuous release almost breaking when she reached for him, pulling him up on top of her.

Crying out, she arched her hips and clamped her legs around him, rubbing against him in a way he couldn't re-fuse. Already her body trembled, shuddering and tensing, her pleasure seizing her, sweeping over him, too, as he plunged inside her, sliding deep.

So deep into her sleek, drenching heat, it was as if the earth split beneath him, revealing the sleeping sun and he'd slid right into its fire, the licking flames consuming him, the glory of her almost bursting his heart.

His passion *did* burst, the hot seed streaming into her even as the first spasms of her own release rocked through her and she clung to him, thrusting her fingers into his hair and pulling him close for a deep, open-mouthed kiss.

A rough and savage kiss so wild and uninhibited, he jerked inside her, the endless-seeming flood of his release still pouring into her. The hot-blazing sunfire licked at them, its heat turning the cold, silent glade into brightest summer.

And only later, when he collapsed against her, full-sated and his breath ragged, did Jamie begin to notice the night's chill. They hadn't been transported to some long-past pagan fire festival, Beltane, or the even greater Midsummer revels, but still lay hotly entwined on their plaid, St. Bride's enchanted glade quiet now. The earth no longer warm and humming, but cold and damp with the wetness of the grass beginning to seep through the plaid's wool.

The prickles at the back of Jamie's nape returned as well. The unnerving sense that they weren't alone, and that whoe'er or whate'er lurked near, their purpose was not to wish them well.

The glade seemed smaller now. Dark and more shadow-filled. Even the well and its outcropping had slipped from sight, the stones and the hoary altar hidden by the night's encroaching mist.

A Druid's mist some might say.

Deep, gray and impenetrable, its shimmering silence surrounded them as they dressed for the ride back to Baldreagan. A silent ride through thick, swirling mist that blotted the hills and slipped through the trees, its luminous, rippling curtains shielding them as they rode. Guarding them, too, from a certain hooded figure's prying, malevolent eyes.

Eyes that had seen far too much.

Not that the galling images couldn't be wiped from memory.

They soon would be.

Banished and forever erased, the cries and writhings forgotten as if they'd never been when shock and recognition replaced blazing passion and cold, deserved death claimed its own.

And all the saints, holy wells, pagan glades, or Highland mist wouldn't save them.

This insult had been too great.

It was time, the figure decided, for the last of the Macphersons to meet their fate.

Chapter Fifteen

❧

Early the next morning, it scarce mattered whether the sun slept in St. Bride's Well or elsewhere. It certainly hadn't yet bestirred itself when Jamie slipped from Aveline's arms. Kendrick's painted shutters were still tightly fastened against the cold and the thin smirr of rain that had started sometime in the small hours of the night, and the bedchamber was yet in deep shadow. Scant illumination came from the hearth fire for it had burned low, its one-time warmth and bright reddish glow, little more than a memory.

Even the thick night candle had guttered out, but a single wall sconce yet flickered, its feeble light slanting through the parted bed curtains and across his bride's nakedness.

Her slumbering nakedness.

Jamie stood looking at her, branding her beauty on his heart, the sweetness of her in his mind.

The image of her sleeping, her vulnerability, would

strengthen his purpose. Not that he wasn't already more than determined and able to put an end to bogles-that-weren't and other mysterious doings.

Perhaps then he could turn more of his attention to winning a certain *cantankerous* heart. Or at the very least, see the fear leave his father's eyes.

That, too, would be a victory.

Naught would please him more than if the clan's famed Horn of Days remained in its place on the wall above the high table for a good many years to come, Munro once again lairding it in high style. Mayhap with a bouncing grandbairn or two on his knee.

Jamie's heart filled at the image and he reached for his bride, pulling back just before he stroked her lovely hair. This morn, simple looking would have to do.

And she did make a fetching sight, sprawled so wantonly across the great four-poster bed, her sweet thighs opened just enough to make it nigh impossible to leave her. The tumbled masses of her luxuriant hair spilled across the pillows, each gleaming strand looking bright and silky even in the half-dark of this early hour.

A devil-damned hour, good only for mewling bairns, graybeards, and those sorry souls unable to appreciate the benefits of deep and restorative sleep.

He certainly did.

Little good that it did him this particular morn.

Other, more pressing matters took precedence, so he stretched and looked round, searching for his strewn clothes. It wouldn't do to stumble and cause a ruckus.

Or worse, step on poor Cuillin's tail. A distinct possibility given the room's darkness and the old dog's penchant for plopping down in the most inconvenient places.

Jamie scratched his elbow and frowned.

Saints, but he loathed rising before cockcrow.

Even if the strictures of his world often required it. At the thought, he almost snorted and would have, did he wish not to disturb his sleeping bride.

Truth was, he crawled from bed so early almost every morn.

But rising before the unholy hour of prime when he hadn't slept a wink was an unnatural evil.

A very great evil.

Though the reason for his lack of a good night's rest had surely been worth it.

Grinning, he slid another look at the bed.

A lingering look, and focusing immediately on the sweet triangular tangle of curls he'd spent so much of the night enjoying. Still damp and fragrant from hours of vigorous love play, those silky-soft curls beckoned irresistibly.

But he'd drained himself at least eight times in the long endless night and the saints only knew how often she'd found her like satisfaction, minxie and insatiable as she was proving herself as a bedmate, much to Jamie's delight.

But he'd pushed himself for another reason as well, needing to get away before she rose and attempted to accompany him about his morning's business.

Manly business.

Doings he hoped to shield from her.

He also didn't want Cuillin trailing after him. The

dog's heart and spirit far exceeded his strength and abilities, so he, too, had been treated to extra care the previous e'en, receiving a generous and rich meal. As well, an especially well-fleshed meat bone waited near the hearth. A precautionary measure to content and distract the dog if he stirred before Jamie had a chance to exit the room.

Blessedly, that didn't seem likely; both bride and dog slept deeply.

And if the saints were merciful, he'd have time to see everything tended and be back at Baldreagan, breaking his fast with his da in the great hall before Aveline or Cuillin even opened their eyes to the morning.

Willing it so, he finished dressing and latched on his sword belt, tucking his trusty Norseman's ax into place as well, just for good measure.

If aught was truly amiss at Hughie Mac's, he'd be prepared.

Though he hoped Aveline had the rights of it and the old rogue had only been enjoying a tryst with one of his female admirers last night.

Aye, he'd much prefer to arrive at the cottage and find Hughie fit and hale, perhaps seeing to his sheep or tossing seed to the broody hens e'er running in his wake.

However he found him, Jamie would insist on an explanation for the discarded crummock he'd tripped over in the grass in front of Hughie's cottage. The size of the thing nagged at him as did something else . . . something he'd thought about his da recently but couldn't recall just now. Jamie pressed his lips together and scratched his elbow again.

That was another reason he so disliked early mornings; they befuddled his wits.

Wits that came spiraling back a short while later as he rode through the empty woodlands toward Hughie's cottage and, by necessity, passed near the great out-thrusting shoulders of the steep, rock-strewn slopes that formed the deep gorge of the Garbh Uisge.

Jamie shuddered. The roar of the rushing water filled his ears, even a safe distance from that dread, lonely place.

But louder than the boiling white waters of the cataracts, his own words slammed into him—words he'd thought when he'd made farewell courtesies to the MacKenzie lasses.

Then when he'd not wanted his da to hear his reason for denying Aveline a springtime visit to Eilean Creag, fearing the travails of the journey and, especially, the rigors of the anticipated sailing adventure on one of the Black Stag's galleys, would prove too strenuous for Munro.

Och, nay he hadn't wanted his da to hear such concerns. Yet, he'd suspected he might.

Again, Jamie's own words flashed through his mind, just as he'd thought them in Baldreagan's bailey.

Truth be told, he'd often suspected the man could listen through walls.

. . . such a feat might be how he always managed to get the better of his fellow Highland cattle lairds, e'er seeming to know what the men said behind his back or when they believed Munro out of earshot.

Jamie's blood ran cold.

He jerked on the reins, pulling up at once. "Well, then!" he swore, wrenching around his garron and digging in his spurs to thunder down a sloping braeside choked with gorse and broom, making for an innocuous-looking outcrop not unlike the stones that sheltered St. Bride's Well.

Only these boulders hid something far more treacherous.

Something he should've recalled long ago.

The latest when he'd mused about his da's seeming ability to hear through walls.

By all the saints, there'd been a time when Munro Macpherson *had* listened through walls.

Baldreagan was riddled with hidden passageways, squints, and subterranean corridors. In the glory days of his cattle dealing, Jamie's father had used them with glee, taking advantage of being able to leave the dais on some cock-and-bull errand while, in truth, sneaking into a secret passage cut through the walls, circling back, and spying on his guests. Listening raptly, then using his gleaned knowledge against them.

Until Jamie's brother Hamish had one day wandered into the maze of passages and gotten lost.

For three days and nights the entire clan had searched for the lad, finally finding him cowering and half-frozen on the morning of the fourth day, huddled in one of the underground passages that led farthest from the keep.

The very one that exited into the outcrop looming up out of the whin and bracken at the bottom of this braeside.

Another, similar passage opened closer to the Garbh Uisge and he'd investigate that one, too.

If he could find the old opening.

Not an easy task, as his da had ordered every last passage filled and sealed after Hamish's disappearance.

Even his favorite squint in the great hall, a craftily placed laird's lug with a fine view onto the dais, had not been spared.

And, Jamie saw, pulling up in front of the outcrop and swinging down to take a better look, whate'er hidden entry to a subterranean passage may once have been concealed in the tumbled rocks, with surety, was no more.

His father's men had been thorough.

All that remained here were boyhood memories of playing with his brothers near the outcrop, each brother daring the others to venture deeper inside the passage's dank and inky darkness.

Jamie shuddered again and pulled a hand down over his chin.

Such a passage, if a passable one yet existed, might be the answer to his da's *bogle* visits.

"By the Almighty God," he swore, certain of it.

His mood darkening, he remounted, his gaze falling on the plump little sack of honey cakes hanging from the saddle bow and meant for Hughie Mac, should the old man need persuasion to discuss his odd behavior last night—and the newly whittled hazel walking stick. But the honey cakes and his questions for Hughie would have to wait.

Whether it would displease his bride and certain long-nosed, clack-tongued MacKenzie females, he needed to spend some time looking around at the Rough Waters. Even so, he couldn't suppress the chill that swept through him. After years squiring at Eilean Creag, he knew better than most how accurate were Lady Linnet's visitations.

Her warnings of doom—when she felt compelled to make one.

But if he ignored his suspicions and further grief came to those he loved, he'd be dooming himself. He *had* to put an end to the misery someone was so determined to inflict on his family.

No matter the cost to himself.

Thus decided, Jamie dug in his spurs yet again and raced onward, sending his garron plunging back up the steep braeside. But at the hill's crest, he turned away from the tall Caledonian pines sheltering Hughie Mac's cottage and headed elsewhere.

Straight for the Garbh Uisge.

The roar of the falls and crashing, racing water soon became deafening, the sound blotting all else as he neared the soaring birch-clad shoulders of the dread defile. The temperature plummeted, too, and the air grew colder, chilled by the icy, foaming cataracts and because the sun had scuttled behind the dark, low-lying clouds.

Jamie's mount balked. Hill-bred and sure-footed, the shaggy-coated garron tossed its head and sidled when a great plume of frothy spray shot up over the edge of the ravine and the beast's hooves slithered on the slick, slippery ground.

"Dinna fret, my friend," Jamie soothed him, "you needn't go any closer to yon gloomy precipice."

Swinging down, he gave the beast an encouraging

open-palmed *thwack* on his broad rump, then watched as he plunged away into the bracken and whins, seeking the safety of a nearby rocky knowe, his scrabbling, clambering hooves sending a glissade of pebbles over the lip of the gorge and into the swirling, splashing water.

Water Jamie meant to ignore, concentrating only on a nearby birch-clad slope and the mossy, broken-down wall of a long-disused cot house, its ancient stones disguising another entrance to one of Baldreagan's subterranean tunnels.

The only other underground passage that stretched for such a goodly distance, all others ending not far from Baldreagan's stout curtain walls.

His heart pounding, Jamie followed the narrow, twisting deer path that ran along the edge of the gorge, the thick, silver-shadowed birchwood pressing close on one side, the steep drop to the ravine and its cataracts on the other.

Twice, his feet slid on the loose stone and the slick carpet of wet, brown leaves. And once, when throwing out an arm to catch his balance, he plunged his hand right into a patch of stinging nettles growing on a pile of tumbled boulders.

"Damnation!" He scowled, rubbing his palm furiously against his plaid.

This was not promising.

His hand burned worse than if a thousand fire-eaters had spewed flames on him and the dismal, pallid light of the birch wood was seeming to dim the farther along the path he went. Equally disturbing, the back of his neck was beginning to tingle.

Someone was watching him.

He was sure of it.

Especially when a twig cracked somewhere behind him and, with a quick rustling of brittle leaves, another scatter of pebbles went sliding into the leaping, swirling waters of the abyss.

"Hold!" he cried, whirling around, his hand reaching for his sword. But nothing more sinister moved in the birch-clogged, rocky-sided gorge save a family of red foxes.

Jamie blew out a breath and shoved back his hair. The foxes, a fine-looking pair and three older pups sure to soon be on their own, ignored him and continued on their way through the bracken. No doubt heading for a cozy den hidden deep in one of the mist-filled corries gouged into the sides of the gorge.

Only the male fox looked back to stare at him. Oddly familiar though Jamie couldn't say why, the creature's queer golden eyes bored into him in such a disconcerting, penetrating manner that the prickles erupted again on his nape. This time they even spilled down his spine.

The little red fox had strange eyes.

But before Jamie could ponder what else about the creature disturbed him, the fox was gone.

And only then did he realize he'd reached his destination: the tumbledown dry stone wall and the ruined cot house, relics of a long-ago time. And, Jamie saw, little more than a pathetic heap of moss-grown stone. Almost entirely covered by thigh-high bracken, the one-time entrance to the Macphersons' secret tunnel was as much a faded memory as the souls who once called this desolate little patch of earth home.

Jamie frowned.

He'd wasted time and effort. And the palm of his left hand still stung like Hades.

He'd been so sure.

But then, he'd also been certain he'd felt hostile eyes watching him. He would've sworn the rustlings and pebble-scatterings behind him had been of malevolent origin.

Truth was, he could still feel a presence.

And not the ethereal, wispy passing of *bogles* he didn't believe in.

Nor strangely gleaming golden fox eyes, odd as the wee creature had struck him.

Then something *did* strike him.

A great running shove from behind. Hard, breath-stealing, and full to the center of his back. So swift and unexpected he only caught a lightning-quick flash of Macpherson plaid as the tall, powerfully built *bogle* skidded to a lurching halt and Jamie, far from halting, went sailing over the cliff edge.

Horror whipped through him as he fell, the wild rush of the wind, icy flying spray, and the roar of the falls all he knew until the churning cauldron of white rushed ever closer and then, blessedly, went black.

There hadn't even been time to cry out.

Not that he'd have been able to with the wind knocked out of him.

Nor could he scream now with frigid, surging water swirling all around him, rushing into his ears, mouth and nose, choking and blinding him, tossing and rolling his body, hurtling him against the rocks, drenching and drowning him.

Just like his brothers had drowned.

Only Jamie didn't want to die.

Not now.

And not like this.

But he couldn't breathe. Each spluttering, gasping attempt only sent more freezing water shooting into his mouth and nose, filling his lungs until he was sure they'd burst.

And if the water was freezing, his body was on fire. His throat burned and his eyes stung and if the searing pain in his chest meant anything, he'd surely cracked his ribs.

But at least he was alive to realize it!

Determined to stay that way, he thrashed about, trying to keep his head above the rapids and using his arms and legs as best he could to avoid crashing into the worst of the jagged, black-glistening rocks.

A battle he was losing, no matter how fiercely he wished otherwise. Desperately, he grabbed at every crack and fingerhold of each rock he shot past, but the rocks proved too slippery, his fingers too numbed by the cold, his split-second chance at each rock too fleeting.

His teeth were chattering now, too, and the weight of his clothes dragged him down, pulling him under the icy, churning water.

There was nothing he could do.

And what he could have done—namely heed Linnet MacKenzie's warning—he'd ignored.

Then, just when he was certain his lungs truly were on fire and his end must be imminent, he saw the fox again.

That it was the same fox, he was sure. The creature had the same startling eyes.

Alone now, he kept pace with Jamie, running along the rock-strewn edge of the rapids, his golden gaze fixed on Jamie even as he seemed to be looking about for something.

Something he apparently spied, for he suddenly shot ahead, vanishing like a flash of red-gold lightning only to reappear where a fallen tree cluttered the riverbank.

A fallen tree that had split into several pieces, one of which was a fat, good-sized log.

Jamie coughed and spluttered, blinking hard.

He couldn't see well at all.

Not tossing about in the rapids as he was. But he *did* see the little fox stop beside the log and the giddiest sense of hope swept him when the creature began nudging the log forward, rolling it ever closer to the water's edge.

"By the saints," Jamie gasped, not caring that the vow cost him another mouthful of choking, freezing water.

By the holy saints! He cried the words in silence the second time, his throat too tight to voice them when the fox gave the log one last push and it fell into the water.

Just there and then when Jamie hurtled past.

His spirits surging, he lunged for the log, his arms closing around its life-saving girth in the very moment he was sure the last of his strength left him.

Clinging tight, he tossed his head, trying to shake the water from his eyes. But the splashing rapids and cold, tossing spray made it impossible. Renewed hope *did* give him a resurgence of strength, though, and he thrashed his legs with greater fervor, summoning all his will and might to reach the water's rock-torn edge.

Then suddenly the log slammed into solid, pebbly ground and Jamie felt the stony riverbank beneath his weakened, quivering knees.

"Saints o' mercy," he gasped, hot tears blinding him this time.

Too weary to do aught but drop his head onto the log and lay sprawled where he was, he dragged in great gasping gulps of air, too grateful to be alive to care that the icy water still swirled over his lower legs.

His heart thundering, he looked around for the strange-eyed little fox, but the creature was gone, the riverbank empty and quiet.

Silent save for the ever-present din of the Rough Waters and, saints preserve him, the rustling *crash* of someone hurrying toward him through the underbrush.

A large someone, tall and powerfully built judging by their pounding footsteps. They were running now, wild-eyed and shouting, their expression murderous.

And they were wearing a Macpherson plaid, its tell-tale folds flapping in the cold wind as the figure raced near, leaping and vaulting over broken stone and debris in their haste to reach him.

A figure Jamie knew, the shock of recognition stilling his heart. The man's tall frame and awkward, somewhat clumsy gait gave him away.

As did the huge wicked-looking Viking ax clanking at his side.

It was Beardie.

*   *   *

Aveline knew something was wrong the instant she came awake.

Dread sluiced over her like icy water and she didn't need to fling out an arm and feel the cold emptiness on Jamie's side of the great four-poster bed to know he was gone.

Or that something dire was the reason for his absence.

Cuillin knew it, too.

The old dog paced in front of the closed bedchamber door, pausing now and again to paw, sniff, and scratch at the door's heavy oaken planks. Or just sit and whimper.

It was his whimpering that had wakened her.

Dogs didn't fret and whine at doors without good reason. Nor did they ignore large and well-fleshed meat bones.

Just such a bone lay temptingly near the hearth fire, Cuillin's favorite sleeping spot, and that could only mean one thing.

Jamie had sought to keep the dog quiet so he could slip away unnoticed. And the wish to do so bode ill. It meant he was off on some nefarious scheme.

Something dangerous.

And without doubt foolhardy, though it was the *danger* part that had Aveline dashing about the room snatching up her clothes and dressing as quickly as possible.

There were only two places he would have gone.

To Hughie Mac's; she'd seen last night that he hadn't accepted her notion that the old man had been entertaining a lady love.

Or he'd gone to the Garbh Uisge.

Indeed, as soon as the dread name crossed her mind, she knew that was where he'd headed. The certainty of it made the floor dip and weave beneath her and she grabbed the bedpost, holding fast as a great, icy shudder ripped through her.

Her stomach churned and her mouth went dry. Every warning that had passed the MacKenzie women's lips flew back at her, each word taking stabs at her, freezing her heart with such ice-cold fear she couldn't breathe.

"I won't let anything happen to him," she vowed, clutching the bedpost, certain that if she let go the floor would split wide and swallow her, plunging her into a deep dark void so cold and unending she'd never see another glimmer of light for all the rest of her days.

A horror she had no intention of allowing.

She lifted her chin and set her jaw, determining to be strong. But even then, her fingers slid over the smooth cool wood of the bedpost and she remembered caressing Jamie's face just the night before.

Anything but cool and unresponsive, he'd turned his cheek into her palm, pressing against her hand until his warmth flowed sweetly through her fingertips, reaching clear to her heart.

A heart that now squeezed with dread.

Her chest tightening, Aveline jerked away from the bedpost, her pulse leaping. She looked at her hands, half certain the bed frame's satiny, impersonal wood had grown viper heads and bit her. She wanted the warmth and solidness of *Jamie*.

She blinked hard, cursing the sleep that had claimed

her so fully. The dark night and its stillness, the quiet cloak of morning he'd used to slip away.

Away on some knightly hero's mission, she was sure.

Saints preserve her if aught should happen to him.

She wasn't sure when or how it had happened, but she'd fallen crazily in love with him and couldn't imagine her life without his sunny-natured smiles and grins. The way he treated her as if she were infinitely precious, worth everything to him. And not despite her smallness, but because he prized her just as she was.

She began to pace, trying to think what to do.

But most of all, she just wanted him safe, and in her arms.

Och, aye, she loved him.

Desperately.

And for many more reasons than his high looks and gallantry.

It was the warmth that welled inside her each time he looked at her or she even just thought his name. The sense of feeling whole only when he was near, and empty and bereft when he wasn't.

She loved him to the roots of her soul. A truth borne home by the lancing pain inside her now, her surety that something horrible had happened to him.

She *knew* it.

And the knowledge gutted her.

Closing her eyes, she sank down onto the bed and bit her lip. She would not cry. If she did the pain already ripping her would tear her into jagged little pieces.

Clearly sharing her dread, Cuillin trotted over to her,

first nosing under her elbow, then nudging her knee, his troubled gaze alternating between her and the door.

But when he leaned into her, dropping his head on her lap with a groan, her resolve almost broke.

"Nay, nay, nay, Cuillin," she said, pushing the words past the tightness in her throat. "Mooning about will serve naught—I only needed to catch myself and now I have."

She pushed to her feet, reaching down to stroke the old dog's head. "Truth is, he may only have gone down to the hall to break his fast earlier than usual."

A lie if ever one passed her lips.

Hearts didn't lie and she felt in the depths of hers that he was in mortal danger.

Her heart also told her who had to be informed first— even if she knew waking his da with such news would only distress him.

It couldn't be helped.

But as soon as she opened the door and stepped into the dimly lit passage a low, keening wail reached her ears.

Munro's wail.

And coming from the stair tower.

Hitching up her skirts, Aveline ran down the corridor, Cuillin trotting at her heels. She nearly collided with Munro in the gloom for he stood teetering in the shadows at the top of the turnpike stair, one hand pressed to his heart, his stricken gaze on a tall, plaid-draped figure slowly mounting the stairs toward him.

A figure Aveline recognized at once, her shock so great she could only stare in horror.

Cuillin growled.

The figure smiled.

Then she nodded at Aveline, looking so pleased Aveline knew before her sister opened her mouth what she'd have to say.

"Jamie is dead," Sorcha told her, confirming it. "I pushed him into the Garbh Uisge—just as I had done with his nine vainglorious brothers."

Chapter Sixteen

❖

Sorcha!" Aveline stared at her sister, disbelief clamping ice-cold talons around her heart. "What have you done?" she cried, the stairwell tilting crazily, the whole world seeming to spin around her. "You've run mad!"

"O-o-oh, with surety," Sorcha agreed, smiling. "Full mad and with the best of reasons!"

Aveline shook her head, shock laming her.

Her sister *was* mad.

The best of reasons?

Chills swept down Aveline's spine. There could be no reason for what Sorcha claimed she'd done.

Nor for her appearance in the stair tower. Her blood-curdling appearance, dressed as she was in her long-flowing hooded cloak, with a Macpherson great plaid slung around her shoulders.

She stood a little more than halfway up the spiraling, corkscrew steps, not far from a well-burning wall torch. The smoking, hissing flames threw a wash of light across her from above, casting her face in dark and eerie shadow while showing the wild, unnatural glint in her eyes.

Looking at her, Aveline shivered, denial pounding through her. Her heart was splitting, such tight, blinding terror winding around her that she couldn't breathe.

Jamie couldn't be dead, he just couldn't.

And her e'er quiet and unassuming sister couldn't possibly be the crazed woman standing before her, with such scorn and hatred blazing in her eyes, her lips twisted with malice.

But the figure was her sister and what she'd said ripped Aveline's soul, rending to shreds every precious, tenuous bit of joy she'd found and relished in Jamie's arms. A loss that slammed through her, spilling her heart's blood and condemning her to an existence in which every indrawn breath would pain her.

Each exhale reminded her of what could have been.

Yet could ne'er be, save in her dreams.

Her memories.

And all her hopes for a future filled with kith, kin, and happiness.

Aveline pressed a hand against her breast. Panic welled inside her, each sickening wave making her stomach clench and hot bile rise in her throat, its bitterness choking her.

She bit her lip, trying to concentrate, to think what to do, but a cold emptiness was spreading through her and an even colder dread pressed heavily on her shoulders. A weight so great she feared she'd soon crumple to her knees.

Shuddering, she reached for Munro's hand, holding

tight to his shaking fingers, fearing that he, too, might slump to his feet any moment.

Watching her, Sorcha laughed. "Hold on to him all you wish. You canna help that one," she sneered, her lip curling. "The *bogle* has already scared him into his grave. His wits are gone."

"'Tis you who've lost your wits." Aveline's heart raced, her mind reeled. "Munro knew all along you weren't a ghost," she blurted, lying to save the old man's pride if nothing else could be salvaged.

She squeezed his hand, hoped he'd heed her warning.

"You ne'er frightened anyone," she continued, scrambling for words. "Munro only pretended to be afeared so you'd feel secure and expose yourself. And now you have!"

"Hah!" Sorcha snorted. "Pretended did he? Did he tell you he sent to Devorgilla of Doon, asking for powdered toadstone and other fool folderol? Charms against *bogles*?"

She laughed again, the sound echoing in the stair tower. "He wanted the spelling goods because his red-ribboned rowan couldn't keep me away."

"I sent for no such foolery!" Munro denied, his fingers tightening on Aveline's, the angry quiver in his voice letting her know he'd sent to the Hebridean wise woman indeed.

"Ahhh, but you did," Sorcha corrected him, looking amused.

She ascended a step or two as she spoke, coming steadily closer. "Your plea ne'er reached the great Devorgilla. See you, your courier called at Fairmaiden on his way and was e'er so pleased when I told him that one of my father's Pabay men had business on Doon and would deliver your missive with gladness."

Munro spluttered and took a step toward her, his hand going to his sword hilt—until he realized he was wearing naught but his bedrobe. "Murderess!" he roared all the same. "I've ne'er laid a hand to a woman, but . . . you! You—" he broke off, his face contorting and would surely have lunged at her if Aveline didn't seize him.

Livid or no, he was no match for Sorcha.

Not weakened and confused as he was these days. Aveline also caught the flash of steel at her sister's waist, knew how deftly she wielded a dagger. Their father's men of Pabay had taught her, as they'd instructed all the Fairmaiden lasses, claiming a woman ought know how to defend herself.

So Aveline kept a firm grip on Munro.

But she couldn't stop Cuillin.

Barking furiously, he plunged down the steps, making straight for Sorcha but brushing past her at the last moment, bounding down the stairs as fast as his stiff legs would carry him, clearly fleeing what he still viewed as a phantom.

"See?" Sorcha glanced after him, her mouth quirking. "Even he thinks I am a bogle," she mocked, lifting her arms and flapping them.

Tall and large-boned as she was, and costumed so oddly, she did look like a ghost.

Even so, Aveline would have recognized her anywhere.

That she hadn't noticed how disturbed her eldest sister

must be and that her oversight had cost Jamie his life was a horror that would haunt her beyond forever.

"You are mad, is what you are," she said again, tightening her fingers on Munro's uninjured arm and slipping around him, placing herself between him and her sister.

The old laird was standing taller now, and no longer trembling. Leastways not with anything that resembled fear. But he was still injured, his wounded arm not yet healed.

And Sorcha had proved herself dangerous. Ruthless and without conscience.

Worse, she was advancing on them again. Her eyes shone with an even wilder glint, her stare seemingly turning inward, unfocused and chillingly blank even as she looked right at them.

Pausing, she whipped out her dirk and flourished it, glancing down and smiling as she turned the blade to catch the light of a flickering wall torch.

Then her head snapped up with frightening speed and her eyes were perfectly clear again, her face flushed with fury. "I ne'er miss with a dagger," she said, pinning Munro with a hate-filled stare. "The fool MacKenzies distracted me when I fired the crossbow at you, but I'll gut you in one slash with my dirk, ridding the world of you just as easily as I had done with your sons."

"But you loved Neill," Aveline reminded her, trying to remain calm, to say something that would stall Sorcha's menacing approach.

Neither she nor Munro had a weapon. And crying out might cause Sorcha to hurl herself at them, her blade sinking home before the first alerted guardsman could reach them.

Aveline drew a breath, relying on her wits. "I know you loved Neill," she said again. "We could all see it, how you bloomed when you spoke of him."

"*How I bloomed!*" Sorcha scoffed, her voice dripping contempt. "Och, I loved him, aye. Neill the beautiful. Neill the betrayer. The breaker of promises."

She'd spat the words and now she stopped on the curving stairs, her eyes narrowing to furious slits.

"I loved him dearly, aye. And I would have followed him into the deepest pit of hell and back," she said, a tear suddenly trickling down her cheek.

Swiping at it, she raised the dagger again, stabbing the air to emphasize her every word. "I loved him right up to the hour he told me he was calling off our wedding. The day he vowed he didn't care how many of his da's alliances ran afoul, he'd rather pick winkels on the farthest Hebridean shore than turn his back on the woman he loved! Some light-skirted Ulster female he met on a journey to Ireland."

Jabbing the dagger in Munro's direction, she seethed, "*You* sent him there! To Lough Foyle where he said you'd hoped the Irish lords might prove eager cattle buyers. But instead of a taker for your stirks, he found his heart—or so he claimed!"

Aveline stared at her. "So you killed him?"

"All ten o' my sons?" Munro's rage filled the stair tower. "The fiend take you!" he shouted. "On my soul— you'll suffer for this!"

"I had no choice," Sorcha said, her eyes going queer

again. "The shame would've been unbearable with all my other sisters wed and her" —she gestured with the dirk at Aveline—"fair as she is. Anyone would have taken her and I'd be left to wither alone, looking on as Neill flaunted his Irish bride."

She raised her voice above the sudden clamor of barking dogs and cries rising up from the hall. "I ne'er meant to kill them all. Only Neill. 'Twas his wont to cross the footbridge more often than the others. And most times alone. I canna be faulted if they chose to join him that day."

Flicking at the Macpherson plaid she'd donned, she glanced over her shoulder, peering down into the gloom behind her, clearly annoyed by the noise.

"After the deed, I knew why they all went to the Garbh Uisge that morn. 'Twas clear I was meant to have done with all of you," she said, looking at Munro. "Neill for his perfidy, the others for their arrogance and pride, and you because you sent Neill to Lough Foyle! We'd be wed this night were it not for you and your meddling."

"Sorcha, how could you?" Aveline's heart twisted. "We all loved you," she said, throwing a glance at Munro. "Even Laird Macpherson oft spoke of you with affection. He—"

"He caused all this!" Sorcha exploded, her face purpling. "These hills will be better served without him. Once he's gone, our father as nearest neighbor and friend, can take over his lands and cattle. He'll thank me, finally seeing how much more useful I am than you. He—"

Munro hooted. "Your da only wants to sit before his hearth fire and have his men drink his health!" he bellowed, glaring at her. "He'd sooner cut off his arms than burden himself with a second holding! 'Tis mad you are, full mad."

"I am not the one who sees bogles," Sorcha quipped, brandishing her dirk.

She lunged forward then, the tip of her blade catching Munro's plaid—until her eyes flew wide and she flung up her arms, her terrified gaze fixed on something behind them, her dirk slipping from her hand and clattering down the stairs.

"Eeeeeeeee . . ." she cried, her eyes rounding even more as she swayed and staggered, tipping right off the steps into nothingness.

"God's mercy!" Munro crossed himself.

"Dear saints," Aveline gasped, clapping a hand to her cheek as her sister fell, Sorcha's flailing arms and a flash of her long white legs, the last Aveline saw of her, the horrible bumps and *thumpings* as she rolled down the stairs, echoing loudly in the stairwell.

Of a sudden, an eerily silent stairwell.

But not quite as dark as it'd been for the warm golden light of one of the wall torches farther up the steps suddenly flared bright, illuminating the now-empty stairs.

A golden light far too luminous for any smoking pitch-pine torch.

"Iona!" Munro cried, staring up at the landing above them, the wonder in his voice leaving no doubt that he saw his wife standing there.

Or, as Aveline was certain, that she'd come to avert further tragedy.

Munro blinked and pressed a trembling hand to his mouth. "By all the living saints!"

Aveline saw only the shimmering light.

Perhaps, if she squinted and looked hard, the vague outline of a tall, shapely woman. Very feminine and loving in spirit, her tumbling, unbound hair a bright and fiery red-gold and gleaming where the torchlight played upon it.

But then the image was gone.

And with its disappearance, the shadows returned and the stair tower was cold and dark once more. The silence vanished, too, shattered by the chaos in the hall. Crashing, banging, and the sound of running feet, great bursts of shouting and cries, the shrill barking of the castle dogs.

Morag spluttering curses and calling out orders, her sharp voice rising above the din, a sure sign that Sorcha's fall had been observed.

Her body discovered.

"Come!" Her emotions whirling, Aveline peered down into the mirk and saw nothing. She flashed a glance at Munro, then hitched up her skirts and raced down the steps to the hall.

Munro hurried after her, surprisingly quick on his heels for an auld done man with tangled, sleep-mused hair, a bandaged arm, and a furred bed robe flapping about his naked legs.

But when they burst out of the stair tower and into the tumult, it wasn't Sorcha's broken body that caught their eye.

Dead beyond doubt, someone had already tossed a

plaid over her and only her large booted feet and one out-thrust arm peeked from beneath it.

Aveline sucked in a breath, but glanced aside as quickly, scanning the throng for the true source of the ruckus if Sorcha's fall had caused so little a ripple.

Something surely had for the hall bustled with raucous, jostling clansmen and the cacophony was deafening.

Pitch-pine torches blazed everywhere, their sputtering, smoking light casting a flickering reddish glow over the whole of the great cavernous area, while the pleasing, homey smells of wood smoke, ale, and roasting meats gave the deceptive impression that this was a day like any other.

As well it would have been save for the sad plaid-draped form lying just inside the shadows of the stair foot.

A pathetic figure, all but ignored for it was Beardie's huge bear-like form that drew all eyes and attention.

Beardie, the aged, barking dog Cuillin running excited circles around him, and the plaid-hung, auburn-haired giant clutched so protectively in Beardie's arms.

Jamie.

Bruised, disheveled, and dripping, but gloriously, wondrously alive.

Aveline stared, her jaw slipping. Her heart split wide.

"Dear saints," she choked, tears burning her eyes. "He's not dead! God be praised!"

A great sob escaped her and she started running, relief surging through her, giving her the strength to plow her way through the crowded hall, chasing after Beardie as he carried Jamie toward the dais.

"By the Rood! My son lives!" Munro shot past her with remarkable speed, elbowing his way through his kinsmen to arrive at the high table even as Beardie lowered Jamie onto the scarred wood of its cleared surface.

"What did that she-bitch do to you?" Munro demanded, his gruff tone belied by the wetness on his cheeks. His tears flowing, he smoothed back Jamie's damp, tangled hair. "I'd pull her apart with my own hands had she no' fell down the stairs!"

"She pushed him o'er the ledge." Beardie stepped back from the table and shoved his own shock of red hair off his face now that he'd laid down his burden. "I saw it all," he revealed, his great bushy beard jiggling as he looked around, clearly eager to share his tale. "She ran right at him, her arms stretched out before her like a lance and hit him full in the back. He ne'er had a chance, just went flying o'er the edge."

Aveline's heart lurched as she listened, the words making her tremble with shock and anger.

"O-o-oh, Jamie," she cried, grabbing his face and raining kisses on his cheeks and brow, every inch of him that she could reach. "Oh, my heart. Why did you go there?" She blinked hard, dashed the tears from her eyes. "You were warned! Linnet MacKenzie sent word. You knew the danger—"

"I had to go." He opened pain-glazed eyes to peer up at her. "Hughie Mac's . . . the crummock," he added, his thoughts running together in a confused jumble.

But he saw her brow knit and knew he wasn't making

any sense, so he swallowed hard and tried again. "I was on my way to Hughie's and remembered Baldreagan's old underground passages. How some ended near the Garbh Uisge. I thought that might be how the *bogle* gained entry, so I went to have a look and—"

"If you'd just asked me, I'd have told you those passages were made unusable years ago!" Munro barked, folding his arms and looking very lairdly despite his bed robe and bare feet. "Sakes, son, I swear if you were still a wee laddie, I'd take a hazel stick to you!"

"And so would I!" Aveline put in, frowning through her tears and looking anything but ferocious.

Truth was, she was the most beautiful sight Jamie had e'er seen. Even with mussed hair, streaming eyes, and a bright red nose.

Nay, especially with those things.

Looking at her, his own eyes began to burn so he grabbed her quickly, pulling her close for a kiss.

A hard and fast kiss because Munro was glaring at him, his bushy brows snapping together. "Aye, 'tis a good lashing with a hazel stick you need," he vowed. "Giving us such a fright. If it weren't for Beardie, we might have lost you."

"Giving you a fright?" Jamie looked at him. "You mean the *bogle*?"

Munro snorted. "Nay, lad, I meant almost losing you. My only remaining son." His face darkened. "And dinna go asking me to explain myself. I've already said more than your flapping ears deserve to know!"

Jamie blinked, trying to make sense of his da's agitation. Not that he really needed to make the effort. The fierceness of the old man's grip on his shoulder and the tears shimmering in his rheumy blue eyes spoke louder than any explanations his father might have given him.

It meant enough to make Jamie's heart slam against his aching ribs.

The love shining in his bride's eyes as she smothered him with kisses meant even more. He caught her hand and pressed a kiss in her palm. "Have I told you how much I love you?"

She shook her head and a tear dropped onto his cheek. "Nay, you haven't—but I know." Leaning close, she whispered in his ear, "As soon as we're alone again I will show you exactly how much I love you, too."

"Ach, lass." Jamie kissed her fingertips. He would've grinned like a fool, but the words *hazel stick* kept circling back to taunt him, weaving in and out of his mind.

Bedeviling and irritating him.

But his head pounded too fiercely to concentrate on why. Even drawing breath was becoming an agony, each hard-won gasp sending new bursts of pain flashing across his ribs, new spurts of dread flitting across his memory.

Ghastly images he couldn't forget.

The dizzying blur of black cliffs and jagged rocks. Flying spray and the thunder of the falls, the roar of his own blood in his ears. The fiery numbing pain when he'd plunged into the icy surging water.

Water that might well have reclaimed him had Beardie not come along when he had, scooping him into his arms and then heaving him onto his horse. He led the beast all the way back to Baldreagan at a snail's pace—to keep from jarring Jamie's cracked ribs, the big lump had said.

And half the torturous journey, Jamie had expected to be dirked in the back.

Guilt squeezing him, he swiveled his head to look at his cousin, not surprised to see the loon had retrieved his rusty Viking helmet and jammed the fool thing on his head.

Something Beardie did whenever he felt . . . in need.

Jamie frowned and drew as deep a breath as his sore ribs would allow.

"What were you doing there?" he rasped, shamed at having suspected Beardie of being the figure. "Skulking about in the mist at such an ungodly hour?"

Beardie flushed and looked at the floor.

"Does it matter?" Aveline leaned down and kissed him, then reached for one of his hands, rubbing warmth into his still-freezing fingers. "You are here, and alive." She paused, sliding a sidelong glance at Munro. "Hearts have been found and mended. Naught else is of importance."

But she erred.

The hazel walking stick was of dire importance.

Jamie was certain of it.

Every inch of his heart and soul screamed it at him.

". . . a sweet lassie," Beardie was saying, his broad face glowing a brighter red than a harvest moon. "She's a tanner's daughter in the next glen and she even likes my bairns." He looked up again, his chest swelling with pleasure. "I've asked her to marry me and she's agreed."

He reached up to adjust his Viking helmet, using the pause to clear his throat. "The way to her glen runs past the Rough Waters and I was coming from her da's cottage when I saw what happened."

Jamie frowned, his cousin's words only reminding him of another cottage.

Namely Hughie's.

And his need to go there.

A need so urgent, he sat up, doing his best to ignore the fire blazing in his chest, the old and gnarled female hands trying to bind his ribs with a length of suffocatingly tight linen.

Or maybe it wasn't Morag at all, but his faery's arms squeezing him so tightly.

But no, she was leaning into him and smoothing his brow again, touching him as if there'd be no tomorrow and lighting so many soft, sweet kisses across his face that he couldn't well see *who* was crowding around him, stroking, prodding, kissing, and fussing.

Shedding tears and loudly blowing noses.

Crying out names he ne'er expected to hear again.

Jamie's heart froze and he cursed his light-headedness. The dizziness making it difficult to stand, to see as well as he would've wished. But he did see the gaping, open-mouthed stares some of his kinsmen were aiming toward the far side of the hall.

Jamie's pulse began to race.

He started grinning. Even if he was having a bit of trouble keeping on his feet, there was nothing wrong with his ears.

"Holy St. Columba!" his da cried, proving his ears were working as well.

His tears spilling freely now, the old man threw back his head and whooped.

Grabbing Jamie by the shoulders, he hugged him so

fiercely he almost crushed him. "A day o' wonders," he cried, whirling to Aveline and throwing his arms around her in a quick, joyous squeeze before he took off running.

Others ran, too, pounding in the same direction until a great swelling uproar filled the hall. The shouts and calls came from all around, the cries rising to the rafters, shaking the smoke-blackened walls.

The noise was deafening.

Everywhere, men fell over themselves to hasten to the hall's shadowed entry arch, the center of the ruckus.

Men were loosing their swords and waving them in the air, stamping feet and slapping backs. Shouting, jesting, and laughing with glee, wiping streaming tears from grinning, bearded faces.

And then, still making his way across the hall, Jamie saw why.

It was the hazel walking stick.

Hughie Mac's newly whittled *crummock*.

Only it was the tall, broad-shouldered man gripping the *crummock's* bone handle that stole Jamie's breath and sent his heart to thundering. A tall, auburn-haired man who could have been Jamie himself, save that he was a number of years older.

His brother Neill.

Looking as hale and fit as the day Jamie had last seen him, excepting a slight limp and the fine long hazel walking stick clutched tightly in his hand.

"'Tis Neill! I dinna believe it!" Jamie stared, tears choking him, blinding him.

He grabbed his faery, lifting her in the air and twirling her before dragging her tight against him, aching ribs or no. "'Tis Neill," he said again, kissing her soundly. "Neill, and he's no' ghost, sure as we're standing here!"

"And look! There's Kendrick!" She pointed as they ran, knocking into trestle tables and benches in their haste. "He's here, too! With Hughie!"

And he was.

There could be no mistaking him.

Just as Jamie knew him, his roguish, laughing-eyed brother stood in the very midst of the chaos, grinning broadly and looking more rakish than ever with a jaunty bandage wrapped around his head.

Hughie Mac was grinning, too.

He stood a bit apart, his arms folded. "'Tis a long tale," he said, his eyes twinkling when Jamie and Aveline drew up beside him. "Word spreads quickly in these parts and when we heard what happened at the Garbh Uisge, we knew it was time for Neill and Kendrick to come out o' hiding and return home."

Looking pleased with himself, he glanced around. "Truth is, so many folk hereabouts have seen the lads, we wouldn't have been able to keep them secret much longer."

"And just where have they been?" Munro's deep voice boomed beside them. "They were dead—I saw their bodies lowered into the ground. Saw the cairn stones piled on top of them with my own two eyes."

He folded his arms over his bedrobe, his narrow-eyed stare latching onto his two returned sons. "Dinna tell me you were sleeping under those stones all this time, for I know full well you aren't bogles! Ghosts don't wear bandages and walk with limps."

Kendrick and Neill looked at each other.

"Och, we slept beneath them long enough," Neill owned, leaning on the crummock. "Two nights, to be sure."

Kendrick moved to stand beside Hughie, sliding an arm around the little man's shoulders. "Hughie dug us out," he explained, flashing a grin at the old man. "Single-handedly, though he did have some wee assistance."

"'Wee assistance'?" Jamie lifted a hand to the back of his neck, rubbing—before the prickling could start. He glanced at Hughie. "What kind of assistance?"

Hughie lifted his chin. "You wouldn't believe me if I told you," he said, shaking his head. "Sometimes I wonder if I imagined it myself."

"I would believe you," Aveline spoke up, her soft voice encouraging. "I've always believed in Highland magic."

Munro grunted, but his gaze whipped to Jamie. "I'll no be denying it either," he said, his expression softening. "My own father swore there's wonder in these hills."

"That's what it must've been," Hughie agreed, nodding vigorously. "See you," he began, lowering his voice, "not three days after we'd laid the brothers to rest, I couldn't sleep because of a pesky scratching at my door. Yet whene'er I went to open it, no one was there."

"No one?" Jamie reached for Aveline, drawing her close.

Hughie looked down, nudging his boot into the floor rushes. "Och, no one save a wee red fox," he finally admitted, his cheeks coloring. "I ignored the creature, but he kept coming back, always scratching at my door and running away when I opened it. After a while I decided to follow him."

"The fox led Hughie to the cairns," Kendrick finished for him. "Neill and I wakened, finding ourselves beneath the stones, alive, but unable to work our way free. We did call out, but no one heard."

"Except the fox?" Aveline smiled.

A chill slipped down Jamie's spine.

Kendrick shrugged. "Who knows? We only know the creature alerted Hughie to our plight." He looked at his da, shaking his head. "A pity it took longer to rout Sorcha."

"Ahhh, but we knew foulness was afoot," Hughie said, taking his two charges by the arm and leading them deeper into the hall, toward their old places at the high table. "We just didn't know who it was or if there were any accomplices."

"That's why we stayed at Hughie's, watching and waiting," Kendrick explained, reaching down to rub Cuillin's ears when the dog nudged his arm. "For all we knew, there was a traitor within Baldreagan's walls and we didn't want to risk endangering the rest of you if word of our survival enraged the *bogle*."

"Nor did we want to attract attention to Hughie," Neill put in. "Not when we were staying beneath his roof to recover, and us too weak and injured to lift an eating dirk much less swing a brand had trouble come calling at Hughie's door."

"So that's why the place was locked and barred the other night?" Jamie asked, glancing at Aveline.

She blushed and looked aside.

Hughie nodded. "We weren't yet ready, lad," he said. "No one e'er meant to deceive or fash you. Too much was at stake to risk letting out our secret too soon."

But much later, after a restorative meal of beef and marrow fritters, stewed eel, and more honey cakes and spiced wine than was wise, Jamie still had questions.

Setting down his wine cup, he cleared his throat. "If Sorcha was behind all this—how did she get in and out of here so easily? And always unseen?" He slid a glance at his da. "You said the secret passages were made unusable."

"And so they were," Munro insisted. "Unless someone reopened one."

At that, Kendrick stood. "I'll just be visiting the priv—"

"Och, nay." Neill shot out an arm and grabbed him, pulling him back onto the bench. "You'll be staying put and telling everyone what you told Hughie and I not an hour ago."

To Jamie's surprise, Kendrick looked uncomfortable. But he sat back down and took a long sip of wine. "You've been using my bedchamber, I hear?" he asked, glancing at Jamie and Aveline. "Did you e'er see the little hole recessed in the side of one of the window arches?"

Jamie and Aveline exchanged glances.

Jamie nodded, remembering how he'd noticed the hole the night Hughie had regaled everyone with the tradition of the MacKenzie Marriage Stone and its ceremony.

He'd thought the hole was caused by fallen masonry.

"Aye, we noticed it," he admitted, waiting.

Kendrick hesitated, then tossed down the remainder of

his wine. "Ach, see you, there's a wee lever inside that hole in the window arch," he said, the color in his cheeks deepening. "I discovered it by accident a few years ago and quickly found out that it triggers the door to a secret passage Da and everyone else must've overlooked."

Munro half rose from his laird's chair. "And you ne'er told me?" He narrowed his eyes on his son as he sank back into his seat. "Dinna tell me the passage opens into my bedchamber?"

Kendrick shook his head. "Nay, it opens into the little anteroom between your bedchamber and mine." He looked down, running a finger around the rim of his wine cup rather than meet his father's eye. "The other end exits next to Mother's tomb, right inside St. Maelrubha's."

He glanced up, his flush an even brighter red. "I would've mentioned it as soon as we learned of the bogle goings-on, but"—he touched his bandaged head—"I haven't been conscious all the while since . . . since the Garbh Uisge. Once the pains in my head started lessening, I remembered the passage."

Munro arched a brow, looking anything but an auld done man. "And why did you not tell me before the Garbh Uisge?"

Kendrick squirmed on the trestle bench. "I kept it secret for my own purposes."

Neill laughed and clapped him on the back. "Soft, warm, and accommodating purposes," he said, wriggling his brows as he glanced round the table. "The sort Kendrick didn't want attracting Morag's attention when they passed through the hall on their way to his bedchamber!"

"That's enough, you." Kendrick tossed his older

brother a warning look, but Neill only laughed all the more and slapped the table.

"Och, aye, Kendrick used the secret passage to entertain the ladies," he went on, his eyes dancing with mirth. "Accommodating ladies. Including one fair damsel twice his age!"

Kendrick flushed scarlet. "She was five summers older than me," he blurted, his eyes shooting daggers at Neill. "Not a day more."

"Ah, well, whate'er you say." Neill let it go.

Kendrick pressed his lips together. "My business is my own," he finally said, looking relieved when Morag appeared with a platter of fresh honey cakes.

Grabbing the largest one, he plunked it onto Neill's trencher. "Eat and quit telling tales no one wishes to hear."

"But it's a tale that explains how Sorcha managed her way in and out of here," Neill couldn't resist adding as he reached for a honey cake. "She must've seen you sneak in one of your lady loves. Some might say *you* showed her the way."

"And I'll show you the edge of my blade once we're fully mended," Kendrick shot back at him. "Mayhap my fist in your nose as well."

"Pigs will fly that day," Neill returned, and bit into a honey cake.

"I'm wondering how we could have e'er missed such bickering," Morag declared suddenly, though the twinkle in her eyes and the wobble in her voice took quite a bit of the sting out of her words.

"And I'm wondering about *your* lady love," Munro announced, cocking a brow at Neill. "An Ulster lass if we caught the rights of it?"

This time Neill looked discomfited. "I meant to tell you," he said. "The day the footbridge . . . ach, you know what happened. She is Oonagh, daughter of O'Cahan of Derry. I met her at Lough Foyle and—"

"You'll be bringing her here, to wed." Munro pushed to his feet, looking around as if to dare anyone present to contradict him. "Like as not as soon as you're fit enough to cross the Irish Sea?" he added, eyeing the great hazel walking stick propped so noticeably against the trestle bench.

Neill nodded. "That is what I've planned, aye. Kendrick agreed to go with me. Though"—he shot a glance at his brother— "I'm no longer sure I desire his company."

Munro hooted. "You'll both go and be glad of the journeying. And your mission," he declared, starting to grin. "'Tis time our house is put to rights.'

"Put to rights?" Neill stared at him.

Everyone did.

Something in his tone and the glint in his eye caused breaths to catch and hearts to still.

Aware of the stares, Munro glared around the high table. "Dinna gawp at me like a bunch o' dimwitted muckle sumphs! I've walked an ill path these years and now"—he paused to look at Jamie—"now, by God, I mean to set things aright."

Jamie swallowed.

Ne'er had he expected an apology from his da. He'd only hoped for acceptance. And mayhap someday, his love. Sliding an arm around Aveline, he drew her close. "He's overwrought by the day's doings," he said, speaking low. "He—" He broke off, his eyes widening when Munro stepped away from the table and turned to the Horn of Days, the clan's sacred relic, e'er watching o'er the hall from beneath a swath of ancient Macpherson plaid.

An heirloom Munro now lifted off the dais wall.

He held it high, letting all see and admire the elegant curve of the ivory drinking horn, the gleaming jewels embedded in its finely carved sides.

It was truly lovely.

A wonder to behold.

And proof that Jamie had misunderstood. His da hadn't meant to make peace with him at all. Something inside Jamie broke and tightened. A hot, stabbing flash of pain, but one he knew and was well used to squelching. Doing that now, he took Aveline's hand in his, lacing their fingers.

Needing her warmth.

"He is about to laird Neill," he told her, his voice discreetly low. Pleased, too, for Neill deserved the honor.

But no Clan Macpherson lairding vows rang out at the high table.

Indeed, a thick silence fell as all eyes turned on Jamie. Wide, awe-filled eyes boring into him until he, too, noticed that Munro had stopped behind him and not Neill.

Realization sweeping him, Jamie leapt to his feet. "You canna laird me," he objected, shaking his head. "Neill is—"

"Neill is my firstborn, aye," Munro agreed, his voice

catching on the words. "And 'tis Neill who'll be the next Macpherson chieftain—someday. This day I mean to start a new tradition. You—"

" 'A new tradition'?" Jamie stared at his father, glancing, too, at the curving ivory horn still clutched in Munro's hand.

"Call it what you will," Munro ceded. "The Horn of Days is our clan's most prized possession and I want you to have it. I can think of naught else worthy enough to express my joy in having you back with us. With me"—he cut a glance at Neill and Kendrick—"your brothers and everyone else at Baldreagan."

"But, I—" Jamie couldn't speak further. Not when his father thrust the fabled horn into his hands and then hugged him, clutching him tight.

"You keep the horn," Munro said, stepping back at last. "Neill and his Irish bride can start their own traditions at Baldreagan. I just hope I can prove to you how much you were missed, laddie."

And how much I love you, Jamie thought he heard him say.

An ear-splitting tumult had erupted all around them and amidst the confusion, Munro was suddenly gone. Swept away by shoulder-thwacking, grinning kinsmen, their boisterous calls, salutes, and foot-stomping drowning out all but the thundering of Jamie's heart, the Horn of Days, its smooth ivory and gemstones already warming in his hands.

And above all, the glow on his bride's face as she beamed up at him. "I always knew he'd missed you," she said, her voice hitching. "He loves you, too. In time, you will believe it."

Jamie leaned down and kissed her, pleased by her words.

But something troubled him and needed airing.

Namely, his lady's heart.

Setting her from him, he put back his shoulders. Then he cleared his throat. "Lass, I must ask you—do you mind being bride to a third son? You have heard that Neill will be the next laird. And Kendrick will surely wish to have his bedchamber returned. My own old one is not near so fine."

He looked at her, arching a brow. "I will understand if you'd rather—"

Aveline pressed her fingers against his lips. "Do you mind if we move to your old bedchamber?" she returned, knowing his answer already, but wanting to show him how foolish his worries were.

She lifted her chin. "Would you still rather be in line for the lairdship? And not have two of your brothers safely returned to you?"

Jamie shook his head. "Saints, no," he vowed, meaning it. "I'd walk naked to the edge of the world and back if I could be the tenth son again. The saints know, I'd even beggar myself if doing so might bring back my other brothers as well."

Aveline smiled.

She touched her fingers to his plaid, her violet scent drifting up to enchant him.

"I knew you'd say that," she said, unable to keep a note of triumph out of her voice. "Then you'll understand when I say that I would walk past a line of all the future lairdlings in the realm and not even glance at them if I knew you were waiting at the end of that line."

Jamie looked at her, certain his heart was bursting.

Then, heedless of staring, long-nosed kinsmen and a certain teary-eyed old nurse, he pulled his bride against him and kissed her. Long, hard, and deep.

But not near as deep as the feelings welling inside him. Good feelings. The likes of which he'd ne'er dreamt to experience.

"Past so many someday chieftains?" He kissed the tip of her nose, her cheek. "You love me that much?"

"I love you more than that," she answered, sliding her arms around him. "More than you will ever know."

Epilogue

✦

BALDREAGAN CASTLE, THE GREAT HALL
IN THE SPRING

Did I no' tell you she'd be here?" Jamie slid a glance down the high table at a tiny, black-garbed woman. A grizzle-headed, ancient-looking woman whose bright blue eyes sparkled with mirth.

"Aye, you did," Aveline agreed, her heart warming to have the far-famed Devorgilla of Doon present at their wedding feast revelries.

Taking Jamie's hand, she squeezed it. "I'll vow even you are surprised she brought along her special friend," she added, her gaze lighting on the little red fox sitting quite contentedly on the cailleach's lap.

Looking proud.

And happily accepting the accolades and edible treats many of the guests pressed upon him.

Jamie gave a good-natured shrug. "From all we've heard, Somerled earned his place at this high table and many others as well," he said, smiling as Beardie dropped to one knee beside the crone and, after doffing his Viking helm, began feeding the little fox a handful of sugared sweetmeats.

"As for surprises"—he broke off to sling an arm around his wife, drawing her close—"I dinna think aught under the sun will e'er again surprise me."

"Say you? I would not be too sure." Aveline lifted a teasing brow, her mind on a certain lumpy leather pouch hidden beneath the high table.

More specifically, beneath Munro's laird's chair.

But for the moment, she let Jamie hold her and simply savored the day.

And it *was* a day like no other.

Full to bursting, the torch-lit, gaily-festooned hall shook with horn-blowing and trumpet blasts, the whole of Baldreagan teeming with well-wishers. Good Highland folk from near and far, all beaming smiles, lusty humor, and good cheer.

One supposedly lusty guest drew Aveline's especial attention, Gunna of the Glen having arrived quite modestly dressed and proving to be of a pleasing, unassuming demeanor far different than Aveline would have expected.

Surprised by the woman's warmth and friendliness, Aveline watched her now, looking on as she danced and flirted with Kendrick in the middle of the hall. Neill and his soon-to-be Irish bride, Oonagh, appeared to be enjoying themselves as well, the clearly besotted pair not leaving out a single fast and furious whirl across the broad space cleared for dancing.

The MacKenzie girls danced as well, each one full of laughter and delight—even if partnered only by their father.

"I swear he ne'er ages," Jamie said, watching the Black Stag deftly maneuver his girls away from a hopeful new partner—a young MacKenzie guardsman who thought perhaps the day's merrymaking might relax Duncan MacKenzie's hawk-eyed watch o'er his lovely daughters.

The Black Stag's wife, sitting next to Jamie, leaned close. "And I vow I have ne'er been so pleased as I was when I heard you'd survived the Garbh Uisge," she said, touching a hand to his arm. "I ne'er thought to see this day."

"Nor did I," a gruff voice said from behind them and Jamie twisted around to see his father standing there, a bulky looking leather pouch clutched in his hands. "But today seems as good a day as any to put this behind me."

Jamie cocked a brow, something in his father's expression warning him something of great significance was about to transpire.

"Put what behind you?" he asked, his throat already thickening with emotion.

A grumbled *humph* answered him.

But then Munro looked down and fumbled with the pouch's drawstring, opening it wide before he unceremoniously plunked the thing into Jamie's lap.

"Have a look in there," his father said, stepping back and folding his arms. "But once you do, you'll keep the contents between ourselves, I'm a-warning you."

But Jamie's fingers froze on the well-worn leather and much to his horror, heat began pricking the backs of his eyes. This was the surprise Aveline had hinted at earlier.

His father's proof that he loved him.

Jamie knew it so sure as he knew the sun would rise on the morrow.

"Well, go on," Munro grumbled, nudging the pouch. "Or would you have me standing here like a fool gawping until all the long-noses in the hall notice?"

Jamie drew a deep breath.

Then he looked into the pouch.

It was crammed full with yellowed scrolls, the wax seals broken, each binding string untied. Jamie's heart clenched, then began thundering out of control when Aveline gave a little sob beside him.

"You must read them," she said, reaching into the pouch and retrieving one, thrusting the brittle parchment into his hands. "As soon as you do, you'll understand."

But, saints preserve him, he already did.

Leastways, he had a good guess. And the knowledge was making his throat so tight he could scarce breathe.

"God in heaven," he managed, unrolling the first missive and scanning the squiggly, faded lines.

Lines that told all about Jamie's safe arrival at Eilean Creag Castle in Kintail, his acceptance as junior squire to Duncan MacKenzie.

A second scroll detailed the time he'd fallen from a horse, breaking his arm, while a third extolled his skill at the quintain.

"God in heaven," Jamie said again, tightening his fingers around the scrolls.

He threw a glance at his da, not surprised to see tears streaming down the old man's face.

His own cheeks were damp, too.

As were everyone else's at the high table.

"Do you believe me now, son?" Munro placed a hand on Jamie's shoulder, gripping hard. "Can you e'er forget and forgive the past?"

Jamie swallowed, unable to answer in words.

Instead, he set aside the leather pouch and jumped to his feet, throwing his arms around his da and letting the fierceness of his embrace speak for his heart.

Others on the dais discreetly looked aside or cleared their throats, while some busied themselves flicking invisible specks of lint off their clothes or finding a variety of ways to avoid intruding on such a private moment.

Even Morag held her peace, bustling about the dais and replenishing emptied ale cups, a telltale brightness in her carefully averted eyes.

E'er congenial guests, Alan Mor and his contingent of Pabay men chose that moment to stretch their legs and enjoy some welcome fresh air in the bailey.

Aveline gave them privacy, too, turning her attention on the dancing until three of Lady Linnet's words echoed in her mind and she near choked on her wine.

See the day, Lady Linnet had said, the words lifting the fine hairs on Aveline's nape.

Her gaze shot to Hughie Mac, fiddling away with fervor, and then to Neill and Kendrick, dancing so vigorously at the heart of the tumultuous throng.

"Dear Saints," she gasped, clapping a hand to her breast. "I *have* seen this day—at the churchyard, near the Na Clachan Breugach stone!" She leapt to her feet, grabbing Jamie's arm. "You'll remember, I told you I saw Neill and Kendrick dancing there, to Hughie's fiddle music."

Awe washing over her, she shook her head. "I wasn't seeing ghosts or bog mists, but this very day."

"To be sure, you were," a sage voice chimed as Devorgilla of Doon shuffled near. "Had anyone asked me, I could have told them the Na Clachan Breugach stone was indeed one of the ancient Stones of Wisdom, able to foretell the future."

Stepping closer, she tapped a knotty finger to Aveline's chest. "Leastways, for those able to see with their hearts."

Aveline swallowed.

She slid a glance at Jamie and his father, her heart squeezing at how much at ease they looked. As if there'd never been a rift between them.

Turning back to the crone, she lowered her voice, "Tell me, do you think the Na Clachan Breugach stone will show me the future for Jamie and me? Perhaps let me know what awaits us?"

Devorgilla shook her head. "Ach, nay, lass, I truly doubt it," she said, reaching down to pet Somerled when he sidled up beside them. "Such magic only works when there is a need."

" 'When there is a need'?"

"So I have said." The crone dipped into a pouch at her belt, offering the little fox a bit of fine, dried beef. "You have no further reason to see into the future. You—"

"What she means," Jamie cut in, "is that you should already *know* our future, sweetness." Sliding an arm around her, he pulled her close and smiled at the wise woman. "Is that not so, Devorgilla?"

And the crone nodded, clearly agreeing.

"Then what is our future?" Aveline probed, her gaze

flitting back and forth between the two of them. "Is it as bright and filled with love as I imagine?"

"Our future is all that and more," Jamie promised, leaning down to kiss her brow. "And our love will last for time and eternity."

Aveline sighed, melting at his answer.

Devorgilla looked pleased, too.

Dashing a spot of dampness from her cheek, she smiled. "Aye, that is the way of it, my hearts. For time and for eternity."

About the Author

SUE-ELLEN WELFONDER is a dedicated medievalist of Scottish descent who spent fifteen years living abroad, and still makes annual research trips to Great Britain. She is an active member of the Romance Writers of America and her own clan, the MacFie Society of North America. Her first novel, *Devil in a Kilt*, was one of Romantic Times's top picks. It won RT's Reviewers' Choice Award for Best First Historical Romance of 2001. Sue-Ellen Welfonder is married and lives with her husband, Manfred, and their Jack Russell Terrier, Em, in Florida.

**MORE CAPTIVATING
HIGHLAND ROMANCE FROM**

SUE-ELLEN WELFONDER!

Turn the page for a preview from

Bride by Seduction

Available in mass market March 2009.

Chapter One

✦

EILEAN CREAG CASTLE
THE WESTERN HIGHLANDS, AUTUMN 1348

Let us speak plainly, my sister, what you would have us do is pure folly."

Lady Gelis MacKenzie dismissed her elder sister's opinion with an impatient flip of one hand. Scarce able to contain her own excitement, she ignored the other's lack of enthusiasm and stepped closer to the arch-topped windows of their tower bedchamber.

A bedchamber she hoped she wouldn't be sharing with Lady Arabella much longer.

Not that she didn't love her sister.

She did.

Just as she adored their lovely room, appointed as it was with every comfort and luxury their father, the Black Stag of Kintail, chose to lavish on them. Elegant trappings met the eye no matter where one gazed and those trusted enough to gain entry to the room, saw immediately that its sumptuous finery rivaled even the Black Stag's own privy quarters. But Gelis cared little for the splendor of the hooded fireplace and matching pair of carved oaken armchairs. The jewel-toned tapestries and extravagant bed hangings of richest brocade, each costly thread glowing in the light of fine wax candles.

Flicking a speck of lint off her sleeve, she cast a glance at her sister. Even if some stubborn souls refused to admit it, *she* knew that life held greater treasures.

Wax candles and hanging oil lamps might banish shadows and a well-doing log fire surely took the worst bite out of a chill Highland morn, but such things did little to warm a woman's heart.

Enflame her passion and make her breath catch with wonder.

Wonder, and love.

Such were Gelis's dreams.

And all her sister's pursed-lipped protestations weren't going to stop her from chasing them.

Apparently bent on doing just that, Arabella joined her in the window embrasure. "Such nonsense will bring you little joy," she contended. "Only a dim—"

"I am not light-minded." Gelis whipped around to face her. "Even Father wouldn't deny Devorgilla of Doon's wisdom."

Arabella sniffed. "There's a difference between spelling charms and herb-craft and expecting moon-infused water to reveal the face of one's future mate."

"Future *love*," Gelis corrected, unable to prevent a delicious shiver of anticipation. "Love as in a girl's one true heart-mate."

Looking unconvinced, Arabella moved closer to the window arch and peered down into the bailey. "Och, to be sure," she quipped, "we shall hasten below, stare into the bowl you hid in the lee of the curtain wall last night, and then we shall see our true loves' faces there in the water."

"So Devorgilla said."

Arabella lifted a brow with predictable skepticism. "And you believe everything you are told?"

Gelis puffed a curl off her forehead. "I believe everything *Devorgilla* says. She has ne'er been known to err. Or can you prove otherwise?"

"I—" Arabella began, only to close her mouth as quickly. Turning aside, she trailed her fingers along the edge of a small table. "'Tis only that you've so much fancy," she said at last, a slight furrow creasing her brow. "I would not see you disappointed."

"Bah!" Gelis tried not to convulse with laughter. "My only disappointment is when Father refuses a bonny suitor! I do not mind him naysaying the toads, but some have been more than appealing."

"Then why bother to peer into a scrying bowl if you already know Father isn't about to let you wed?" Arabella dropped onto the cushioned seat in the window embrasure, a frown still marring her lovely face.

"Isn't about to let either of us wed," Gelis amended, grabbing her sister's arm and pulling her to her feet. "He shall claim we are both too young even when we are withered and gray! Which is why we must use Devorgilla's magic. If the scrying bowl shows us the faces of our future husbands, we shall have the surety that there will *be* husbands for us. I will go mad without that certainty."

You already are mad, Gelis thought she heard her

sister grumble. But when she shot a glance at her, Arabella wore her usual look of eternal composure.

An expression that could needle Gelis beyond patience.

Choosing to ignore it, she tightened her grip on Arabella's arm and dragged her towards the door. "Come," she urged, triumph already surging through her, "there is no one in the bailey just now. If we hurry, we can test our fortune before anyone notices."

"We will see naught but the bottom of the bowl," Arabella decided as they made their way belowstairs and out into the empty courtyard.

An emptiness so stifling its heavy quiet threatened to dampen Gelis's confidence. Brilliant autumn sunshine slanted across the cobbles and nothing stirred. The whole of the vast enclosure loomed silent, the thick curtain walls seeming to watch them, looking on in stern disapproval of their frivolous pursuit.

Gelis paused and took a deep breath. She also lifted her chin and straightened her shoulders. Better to feign bravura than give Arabella the satisfaction of sensing her unease. So she glanced about as unobtrusively as she could, trying to dispel the day's oddness.

But the morn *was* odd.

And unnaturally still.

No sounds reached them from the nearby stables. No birdsong rose from the rowan trees beside the chapel and not a one of their father's dogs darted underfoot as they were wont to do, eager as they were for scraps of food or simply a quick scratch behind the ears. Even Loch Duich lay silent, with nary a whisper of lapping water coming from the other side of the isle-girt castle's stout walling.

The water in the scrying bowl glimmered, its silvery surface beckoning, restoring Gelis's faith as she knelt to peer into its depths.

"See? There is nothing there," Arabella announced, dropping down beside her. "No future husbands' faces and not even a ripple from the wind," she added, poking a finger into the bowl and stirring the surface.

"No-o-o!" Gelis swatted at her sister's hand. "We mustn't touch the water!" she cried, horror washing over her. "Doing so will spoil the magic."

"There wasn't any magic," Arabella scoffed, drying her fingers on a fold of her skirts. "You saw yourself that the bowl showed nothing."

"It was glowing silver," Gelis insisted, frustration beating through her. " 'Twas the light of the full moon, caught there and waiting for us."

Arabella pushed to her feet. "The only thing waiting for us is the stitchery work Mother wishes us to do this morn."

"The embroidery she wishes *you* to help her with," Gelis snipped, tipping the moon-infused water onto the cobbles. "I ply my needle with clumsier fingers than Mother, as well she knows."

"She will be expecting you all the same."

Gelis clutched the empty scrying bowl to her breast, holding fast as if it still shimmered with magic. The face of her one true love, a man she just knew would be as much a legend as her father.

Bold, hot-eyed, and passionate.

Arrogant and proud.

And above all, he'd be hers and no one else's.

"Let us be gone," Arabella prodded. "We mustn't keep Mother waiting."

Gelis splayed her fingers across the bottom of the bowl. It felt warm to the touch. "You go. She won't miss me. Nor would she want me ruining her pillow coverings," she said, distracted. Faith, she could almost feel her gallant's presence. A need and yearning that matched her own. "I'll help her with some other task. Later."

Arabella narrowed her eyes on the bowl. "If you persist in meddling with such foolery, she will be very annoyed."

"Mother is never annoyed." Gelis pinned the older girl's back with a peeved stare as she left Gelis to stride purposefully across the cobbles, making for the keep and hours of stitching drudgery.

"Nor will I be meddling in anything," she added, blinking against the heat pricking her eyes when the bowl went cold and slipped from her fingers. "The magic is gone."

But the day was still bright, the light of the sun and the sweetness of the air too inviting for her to give in to the constriction in her throat. Across the loch, the wooded folds of Kintail's great hills burned red with bracken, their fiery beauty quickening her pulse and soothing her.

She loved those ancient hills with their immense stands of Caledonian pine, rolling moors, and dark, weathered rocks. Even if she wouldn't venture that far, preferring to remain on Eilean Creag's castle island, she could still slip through the postern gate and walk along the shore.

And if her eyes misted with unshed tears, the wind off the loch would dry them. Not that she'd let any spill to begin with. O-o-oh, no. She was, after all, a MacKenzie, and would be until her last breath. No matter who she married.

And she *would* marry.

Even if the notion put a sour taste in her father's mouth.

Swallowing against the persistent heat in her own throat, she glanced over her shoulder, assuring that no one was watching, then let herself out the gate.

It was colder on the lochside of the curtain walls, the wind stronger than she'd realized. Indeed, she'd gone but a few paces before the gusts tore her hair from its pins and whipped long, curling strands of it across her face. Wild, unruly strands as fiery red as the bracken dressing her beloved hills and every bit as unmanageable as Arabella's sleek midnight tresses ever remained in place.

"*She* would look perfectly coiffed in a snowstorm," Gelis muttered, drawing her cloak tighter as she marched across the shingle.

Marching was good.

She wasn't of a mood to amble. And she certainly didn't feel like gliding along gracefully as was her sister's style. Truth be told, if her frustration didn't soon disappear, she might even do some stomping. Great sloshing steps straight through the shallows of the loch, heedless of sea wrack and rocks, needing only to put her disappointment behind her.

It scarce mattered if she looked a fool.

No one could see her.

Only the lone raven circling high above her.

A magnificent creature, his blue-black wings glistening in the sun as he rode the wind currents, sovereign in his lofty domain, impervious to her woes. Or, she decided, after observing him for a few moments, perhaps not so unaffected after all for unless she was mistaken, he'd spotted her.

She could feel his sharp stare.

Even sense a slight angling of his head as he swooped lower, coming ever closer, keen interest in each powerful wing beat. Challenge and conquest in his deep, throaty cries as, suddenly, he dove straight at her, his great wings folded, his piercing eyes fixed unerringly on hers.

Gelis screamed and ducked, shielding her head with her arms, but to no avail. Flying low and fast, the raven was already upon her. His harsh cry rang in her ears as his wings opened to enfold her, their midnight span blotting the sky and stealing the sun, plunging her into darkness.

"Mercy!" Gelis fell to her knees, the swirling blackness so complete she feared she'd gone blind.

"Ach, dia!" she cried, the bird's calls now a loud roaring in her ears. The icy wetness of the rock-strewn shore seeped into her skirts, damping them, the slippery-smooth stones shifting beneath her.

Nay, the whole world was shifting, tilting and spinning around her as the raven embraced her, holding tight, his silken, feathery warmth a strange intimacy in the madness that had seized her.

Gelis shivered, her entire body trembling, her breath

coming in quick, shallow gasps. Mother of mercy, the raven's wings were squeezing her, his fierce grip and the pressing darkness cutting off her air, making her dizzy.

But then his grasp loosened, his great wings releasing her so swiftly she nearly choked on the first icy gulp of air to rush back into her lungs. She tried to push to her feet, but her legs shook too badly and her chill-numbed fingers slid helplessly across the slick, seaweed-draped stones.

Worse, she still couldn't see!

Impenetrable blackness surrounded her.

That, and the unnatural stillness she'd noted earlier in the bailey.

It crept over her now, icing her skin and raising goose-flesh, silencing everything but the thunder of her own blood in her ears, the wild hammering of her heart.

Her well-loved hills were vanished. Loch Duich but a distant memory, the hard, wet coldness of its narrow shore barely discernible against the all-consuming dark-ness. The raven was gone, too, though his breath-stealing magnificence still gripped her.

She hadn't even seen him speed away.

Couldn't see . . . anything.

Terror pounding through her, she bit her lip, biting down until the metallic taste of blood filled her mouth. Then, her legs still too wobbly to merit the effort, she tried to rise again.

"*Please*," she begged, the nightmare of blindness a white-hot clamp around her heart. "I don't want—"

She broke off, losing her balance as she lurched to her feet, her gaze latching onto a dim lightening of the shadows. A slim band of shimmering silver opening ever so slowly to reveal the towering silhouette of a plaid-draped, sword-hung man, his sleek, blue-black hair just brushing his shoulders, a golden, runic-carved torque about his neck. A powerfully-built stranger with a striking air of familiarity, for even without seeing him clearly, Gelis knew he was watching her with the same intensity as the raven.

An unblinking, penetrating stare that went right through her, lancing all resistance.

Claiming her soul.

"You!" she gasped, her voice a hoarse rasp. Someone else's, not hers. She pressed her hands to her breasts, staring back at him, her eyes widening as she sank once more to the ground. "You are the raven."

The bright silver edging him flared in affirmation and he stepped closer, the gap in the darkness opening just enough to show her his glory. And he *was* glorious, a man of mythic beauty, looking as if he could stride through any number of the legends of the Gael. Dark, pure Celt, and irresistibly seductive, it almost hurt to gaze on him. So great was his effect on her. A Highland warrior ripped straight from her dreams, Gelis knew he'd be terrifying in the rage of battle yet insatiable in the heat of his passion.

She also knew he wanted her.

Or, better said, *needed* her.

And in ways that went far beyond the deep sensual burning she could sense rippling all through his powerful body. His eyes made him vulnerable, dark as the raven's and just as compelling, they'd locked fast with hers, something inside them beseeching her, imploring her to help him.

Letting her see the shadows blackening his soul.

Then, just when he drew so near Gelis thrust out a shaking hand to touch him, he vanished, disappearing as if he'd never been.

Leaving her alone on the surf-washed little strand, the high peaks of Kintail and the shining waters of Loch Duich the only witnesses to all that had transpired.

"Oh-dear-saints," Gelis breathed, lowering herself onto a damp-chilled boulder. Scarce aware of what she was doing, she dashed her tangled hair from her brow and turned her face into the stinging blast of the wind, letting its chill cool her burning cheeks, the hot tears now spilling free.

Tears she wasn't about to check, regardless of her proud name.

The blood-and-iron strength of her indomitable lineage. A heritage that apparently held much more than she'd ever suspected.

More than she or anyone in her family would ever have guessed.

Still trembling, she tipped back her head to stare up at the brilliance of the blue autumn sky. To be sure, the raven was nowhere to be seen and the day, nearing noontide now, stretched all around her as lovely as every other late October day in the heart of Kintail.

But this day had turned into a day like no other.

And she now knew two things she hadn't known upon rising.

Her heart full of wonder, she accepted the truth. She

was a *taibhsear* like her mother, inheriting more than Linnet MacKenzie's flame-colored tresses, but also her *taibhsearachd*.

The gift of second sight.

A talent that had slumbered until this startling morn only to swoop down upon her with a vengeance, making itself known and revealing the face of her beloved.

Her future husband and one true love.

There could be no doubt, she decided, getting slowly to her feet and shaking out her skirts, adjusting her cloak against the still-racing wind.

"I was wrong," she whispered, thinking of the scrying bowl as she turned back toward Eilean Creag and the postern gate. The magic hadn't disappeared.

It'd only gone silent.

Waiting to return in a most wondrous manner.

A totally unexpected manner, Gelis owned, slipping back into the now-bustling bailey. *She* possessed her mother's gift and knowing how accurate such magic was, she need only bide her time until her raven came to claim her.

Then true bliss would be hers.

Of that she was certain.

THE DISH

Where authors give you the inside scoop!

♥ ♥ ♥ ♥ ♥ ♥ ♥ ♥ ♥ ♥ ♥ ♥ ♥ ♥ ♥

From the desk of Sue-Ellen Welfonder

Dear Reader,

Anyone familiar with my books knows I enjoy weaving Highland magic into my stories. Scotland is rich in myth, legend, and lore, and it can be difficult to decide on the ideal tradition to use. Sometimes the choice comes easy, the answer appearing out of nowhere, almost as if by magic.

This is the fairy dust that gives writers those amazing ah-ha moments and makes the process so wondrous. Also called serendipity, this phenomena is something I definitely believe in and have seen happen time and again.

It happened to me most recently in Scotland, during the writing of BRIDE FOR A KNIGHT (available now). This book's hero Jamie Macpherson is a special character, larger-than-life, full of charm, and deserving more than his lot in life. I wanted to help him find happiness.

To do that, I needed something unique—a talisman—that would mean everything to Jamie. Something significant and life changing. But nothing felt right until I visited Crathes Castle and saw the Horn of Leys proudly displayed in the great hall. A medieval drinking horn of ivory and embedded with jewels, this treasure was presented to the Burnett family in 1323 by none other than Robert the Bruce.

When I saw the horn and learned its history, I knew Jamie would be well served if I included a Horn of Days in his story. As for serendipity, I hadn't planned on visiting Crathes. I didn't have a car that day and getting there meant walking six miles each way. So I walked. Something just compelled me to go there. I believe that something was Highland magic.

I hope you will enjoy watching Jamie discover the powerful magic of love and forgiveness. Readers wishing a peek at his world, might enjoy visiting my Web site at www.welfonder.com to see photos of Crathes Castle and even its famed Horn of Leys.

With all good wishes,

Sue-Ellen Welfonder

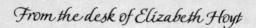

From the desk of Elizabeth Hoyt

Gentle Reader,

Whilst perusing my notes for THE SERPENT PRINCE (available now), I noticed this preliminary interview I made with the hero, Simon Iddesleigh, Viscount Iddesleigh. I present it here in the hope that it may amuse you.

Interview With The Rakehell

Lord Iddesleigh sits at his ease in my study. He wears a pristine white wig, a sapphire velvet coat, and yards of lace at wrist and throat. His right leg is flung over the arm of the chair in which he lounges, and his foot—shod in a large red-heeled shoe—swings idly. His ice-gray eyes are narrowed in faint amusement as he watches me arrange my notes.

Q: My lord, you have been described as a rakehell without any redeeming qualities. How do you answer such an accusation?

Simon: It's always so hard to reply to compliments of this kind. One finds oneself stammering and overcome with pretty blushes.

Q: You do not deny your rakehell tendencies?

Simon: Deny? No, madam, rather I embrace them. The company of beautiful, yet wholly unchaste ladies, the exchange of fortunes at the gambling tables, the late night hours, and even later breakfasts. Tell me, what gentleman would not enjoy such a life?

Q: And the rumors that you've killed two men in separate duels?
Simon: (*stops swinging his foot for a second, then continues, looking me frankly in the eye*) I would not put too much stock in rumors.

Q: But—
Simon: (*admiring the lace at his wrist*) Is that all?

Q: I did want to ask you about love.
Simon: (*sounding uncommonly bored*) Rakehells do not fall in love.

Q: Never?
Simon: Never.

Q: But—
Simon: (*now sounding horribly kind*) Madam, I tell you there is no percentage in it. In order for a rakehell to be foolish enough as to fall in love, he'd have to find a woman so extraordinarily intelligent,

witty, charming, and beautiful that he would for-
sake all other women—and more importantly their
favors—for her. What are the odds, I ask you?

Q: But say a rakehell did fall in love—
Simon: *(heaving an exasperated sigh)* I have told you
it is impossible. But if a rakehell did fall in love . . .

Q: Yes?
Simon: It would make a very interesting story.

Yours Most Sincerely,

Elizabeth Hoyt

www.elizabethhoyt.com